# CLAUDIUS THE GOD

# CLAUDIUS *the* GOD

## *and his wife Messalina*

BY

## ROBERT GRAVES

THE TROUBLESOME REIGN OF TIBERIUS CLAUDIUS
CAESAR, EMPEROR OF THE ROMANS
(BORN 10 B.C., DIED A.D. 54),
AS DESCRIBED BY HIMSELF;
ALSO HIS MURDER AT THE HANDS OF THE
NOTORIOUS AGRIPPINA
(MOTHER OF THE EMPEROR NERO)
AND HIS SUBSEQUENT DEIFICATION,
AS DESCRIBED BY
OTHERS

## VINTAGE BOOKS

*A Division of Random House*
*New York*

# Author's Note

THE "gold piece," here used as the regular monetary standard, is the Latin *aureus,* a coin worth one hundred *sestertii,* or twenty-five silver *denarii* ("silver pieces"): it may be thought of as worth roughly one pound sterling, or five American dollars. The "mile" is the Roman mile, some thirty paces shorter than the English mile. The marginal dates have for convenience been given according to Christian reckoning: the Greek reckoning, used by Claudius, counted the years from the First Olympiad, which took place in 776 B. C. For convenience also, the most familiar geographical names have been used: thus "France," not "Transalpine Gaul," because France covers roughly the same territorial area and it would be inconsistent to call towns like Nîmes and Boulogne and Lyons by their modern names—their classical ones would not be popularly recognized—while placing them in *Gallia Transalpina* or, as the Greeks called it, *Galatia.* (Greek geographical terms are most confusing: Germany was called "the country of the Celts.") Similarly the most familiar forms of proper names have been used—"Livy" for Titus Livius, "Cymbeline" for Cunobelinus, "Mark Antony" for Marcus Antonius. Claudius is writing in Greek, the scholarly language of his day, which accounts for his careful explanation of Latin jokes and for his translation of a passage from Ennius quoted by him in the original.

Some reviewers of *I, Claudius,* the prefatory volume to *Claudius the God,* suggested that in writing it I had merely consulted Tacitus's *Annals* and Suetonius's *Twelve Cæsars,* run them together, and expanded the result with my own

5

"vigorous fancy." This was not so; nor is it the case here. Among the Classical writers who have been borrowed from in the composition of *Claudius the God* are Tacitus, Dio Cassius, Suetonius, Pliny, Varro, Valerius Maximus, Orosius, Frontinus, Strabo, Cæsar, Columella, Plutarch, Josephus, Diodorus Siculus, Photius, Xiphilinus, Zonaras, Seneca, Petronius, Juvenal, Philo, Celsus, the authors of the *Acts of the Apostles* and of the pseudo-gospels of Nicodemus and St. James, and Claudius himself in his surviving letters and speeches. Few incidents here given are wholly unsupported by historical authority of some sort or other and I hope none are historically incredible. No character is invented. The most difficult part to write, because of the meagreness of contemporary references to it, has been Claudius's defeat of Caractacus. For a plausible view of British Druidism, too, I have had to help out the few Classical notices of it with borrowings from archæological works, from ancient Celtic literature and from accounts of modern megalithic culture in the New Hebrides, where the dolmen and menhir are still ceremonially used. I have been particularly careful in my account of early Christianity to invent no new libels; but some old ones are quoted, for Claudius himself was not well-disposed to the Church and derived most of his information about near-Eastern religious matters from his old school-friend Herod Agrippa, the Jewish king who executed St. James and imprisoned St. Peter.

I again thank Miss Laura Riding for her careful reading of the manuscript and her many suggestions on points of literary congruity; and Aircraftman T. E. Shaw for reading the proofs. Miss Jocelyn Toynbee, Lecturer in Classical History at Newnham College, Cambridge, has also given me help for which I am most grateful; and I must acknowledge my indebtedness to Signor Arnaldo Momigliano's monograph on Claudius recently published in translation by the Oxford University Press.

# CLAUDIUS THE GOD
*and his wife*
*Messalina*

# Chapter One

Two years have gone by since I finished writing the long story of how I, Tiberius Claudius Drusus Nero Germanicus, the cripple, the stammerer, the fool of the family, whom none of his ambitious and bloody-minded relatives considered worth the trouble of executing, poisoning, forcing to suicide, banishing to a desert island or starving to death—which was how they one by one got rid of each other—how I survived them all, even my insane nephew Gaius Caligula, and was one day unexpectedly acclaimed Emperor by the corporals and sergeants of the Palace Guard. 41 A. D.

I ended the story at this dramatic point; which was a most injudicious thing for a professional historian like myself to do. A historian has no business to break off at a moment of suspense. I should by rights have carried the story at least one stage farther. I should have told what the rest of the Army thought of the Palace Guards' most unconstitutional act, and what the Senate thought, and how they felt about accepting so unpromising a sovereign as myself, and whether blood-shed ensued, and what were the fates of Cassius Chærea, Aquila, The Tiger—all officers of the Guard—and Vinicius, who was my niece's husband, and Caligula's other assassins. But, no, the last thing I wrote about was the very irrelevant train of thought that passed through my mind as I was being cheered round and round the Palace Court, seated uncomfortably on the shoulders of two Guards' corporals, with Caligula's golden oak-chaplet set crooked on my head.

The reason that I did not take the story any farther was that I wrote it less as ordinary history than as a piece of special pleading—an apology for having ever allowed myself to become the monarch of the Roman world. You may recall, if you have read the story, that both my grandfather and father were convinced Republicans and that I took after them; the reigns of my uncle Tiberius and of my nephew Caligula merely confirming my antimonarchical prejudices. I was fifty years old when I was acclaimed Emperor and at that age one does not lightly change one's political colour. So I wrote, in fact, to show how innocent I was of any desire to reign, and how strong was the immediate necessity for yielding to the caprice of the soldiers: to have refused would have meant not only my own death but that of my wife Messalina, with whom I was deeply in love, and of our unborn child. (I wonder why it is that one feels so strongly about an unborn child?) I particularly did not want to be branded by posterity as a clever opportunist who pretended to be a fool, lying low and biding his time until he got wind of a Palace intrigue against his Emperor, and then came boldly forward as a candidate for the succession. This continuation of my story should serve as an apology for the crooked course that I have taken in my thirteen years of Empire. I hope, that is to say, to justify my seemingly inconsistent acts at different stages of my reign by showing their relation to the professed principles from which I have, I swear, never intentionally departed. If I cannot justify them, then I hope at least to show the extraordinarily difficult position in which I was placed, and leave my readers to decide what alternative course, or courses, remained for me to take.

So to pick up the thread just where I dropped it. First let me repeat that things might have turned out considerably worse for Rome if Herod Agrippa, the Jewish king, had not happened to be here on a visit. He was the only man who really kept his head in the crisis of Caligula's assassination and saved the entire audience of the Palatine Hill theatre from massacre by the German Household Battalion. It is a strange thing, but until almost the last page of my story my readers will not have come across a single direct reference to Herod Agrippa's surprising history, though it intertwined closely with mine at several points. The fact was that to have done justice to his adventures, as worth reading about on their own account, would have meant making him too important a figure in the story I had to tell: its chief centre of emphasis lay elsewhere. As it was, my story was constantly in danger of becoming burdened with matter of doubtful relevance. It was as well that I took this decision, because he does figure most importantly in what follows and I can now, without any fear of digressive irrelevance, tell the story of his life up to the point of Caligula's murder, and then continue it concurrently with my own until I reach his death. In this way there will be no such weakening of dramatic unity as would have occurred if I had spread the story over two books. I do not mean that I am a dramatic historian: as you have seen, I am rather wary of literary formalism. But as a matter of fact one could not possibly write about Herod without presenting the story in somewhat of a theatrical style. For this was how Herod himself lived—like the principal actor in a drama—and his fellow-actors played up to him well throughout. His was not a drama in the purest classical tradition, although his life was finally cut off in classical tragic style by the conventional divine vengeance for the conventional Greek sin of arrogance—no, there were too many un-Greek elements in it. For instance, the God who inflicted the vengeance on him was not one of the urbane Olympian community: he was perhaps the oddest deity that you could find anywhere in my extensive dominions, or out of them, for that matter, a God of whom no image is in existence, whose name his devout worshippers are forbidden to pronounce (though in his honour they clip their foreskins and practise many other curious and barbarous rites) and who is said to live alone, at Jerusalem, in an ancient cedar chest lined with badger-skins dyed blue and to refuse to have anything to do with any other deities in the world or even to acknowledge the existence of such. And then there was too much farce mixed up with the tragedy to have made it a fit subject for any Greek dramatist of the Golden Age to handle. Imagine the impeccable Sophocles faced with the problem of dealing in a serious poetical vein with Herod's debts! But, as I was saying, I must now tell you at some length what I did not tell you before; and the best plan would be to finish off the old history here and now before getting into my stride with the new.

So here finally begins:

## THE STORY OF HEROD AGRIPPA

Herod Agrippa was, you must understand, no blood-relation or connexion by marriage of the great Marcus Vipsanius Agrippa, Augustus's general, who married his only daughter Julia and became by her the grandfather of my nephew Gaius Caligula and my niece Agrippinilla. Nor was he a freedman of Agrippa's: though you might have guessed that too, for in Rome it is the custom of slaves when liberated to assume their former master's surname by way of compliment. No, it was like this: he was named in memory of this same Agrippa, recently dead, by his grandfather, Herod the Great, King of the Jews. For this remarkable and terrible old man owed his throne as much to his interest with Agrippa as to Augustus's patronage of him as a useful ally in the Near East.

The Herod family originally came from Edom, the hilly country lying between Arabia and Southern Judæa: it was not a Jewish family. Herod the Great, whose mother was an

12

Arabian, was given the governorship of Galilee by Julius Cæsar at the same time as his father was given that of Judæa. His age was then only fifteen. He got into trouble almost at once for putting Jewish citizens to death without trial, while repressing banditry in his district, and was brought up before the Sanhedrin, the Jewish supreme court. He showed great arrogance on this occasion, appearing before the judges in a purple gown and surrounded by armed soldiers, but forestalled the verdict by secretly leaving Jerusalem. The Roman Governor of Syria to whom he then went for protection gave him a new appointment in that province, the governorship of a district near Lebanon. To cut a long story short, this Herod the Great, whose father had meanwhile died of poison, was made King of the Jews by the joint order of my grandfather Antony and my granduncle Augustus (or Octavian, as he was then called) and ruled for thirty years, with severity and glory, over dominions that were constantly being enlarged by Augustus's bounty. He married no less than ten wives in succession, among them being two of his own nieces, and finally died, after several ineffectual attempts at suicide, of perhaps the most painful and disgusting disease known to medical science. I never heard that it had any name but *Herod's Evil* or that anyone else had ever suffered from it before him, but the symptoms were a ravenous hunger followed by vomiting, a putrescent stomach, a corpse-like breath, maggots breeding in the privy member and a constant watery flow from the bowels. The disease caused him intolerable anguish and inflamed to madness an already savage nature. The Jews said that it was their God's punishment for Herod's two incestuous marriages. His first wife had been Mariamne, of the famous Maccabee family of Jews, and Herod had been passionately in love with her. But once, when he left Jerusalem to meet my grandfather Antony at Laodicea in Syria he gave his Chamberlain secret orders that if he should fall a victim to the intrigues of his enemies Mariamne should be put to death, to keep her from falling into Antony's hands; and he did the same on a later occasion when he went to meet Augustus at Rhodes. (Both Antony and Augustus had bad reputations as sensualists.) When Mariamne found out about these secret orders she naturally became resentful and said things in the presence of Herod's mother and sister which she would have been wiser to have left unsaid. For they were jealous of Mariamne's power over Herod and repeated her words to him as soon as he returned, at the same time accusing her of having committed adultery in his absence as an act of spite and defiance—they named the Chamberlain as her lover. Herod had them both executed. But afterwards he was overtaken by such extreme grief and remorse that he fell into a fever which nearly killed him; and when he recovered, his temper was so gloomy and ferocious that the slightest suspicion would lead him to execute even his best friends and nearest relatives. Mariamne's eldest son was one of the many victims of Herod's rage: he and his brother were put to death on a charge instigated by a half-brother, whom Herod afterwards also put to death, of plotting against their father's life. Augustus commented wittily on these executions: "I would rather be Herod's pig than Herod's son." For Herod, by religion a Jew, was not permitted to eat pork, and his pigs could therefore be expected to live to a comfortable old age. This unfortunate prince, Mariamne's eldest son, was the father of my friend Herod Agrippa, whom Herod the Great sent to Rome as soon as he had orphaned him, at the age of four, to be brought up at Augustus's court.

Herod Agrippa and I were exact contemporaries and had a good deal to do with each other through my dear friend Postumus, Agrippa's son, to whom Herod Agrippa naturally attached himself. Herod was a very handsome boy and was one of Augustus's favourites when he came to the cloisters of the Boys' College to play at taws and leap-frog and ducking-stones. But what a little rogue he was! Augustus had a favourite dog, one of the big bushy-tailed temple watch-dogs from Adranos near Etna, who would obey nobody in the world but Augustus, unless Augustus definitely told him: "Obey Such-and-Such until I call you again." The brute would then do as he was told but with unhappy yearning looks towards Augustus as he walked away. Somehow little Herod managed to entice this dog when it was thirsty into drinking a basin of very strong wine, and made him as tipsy as any old soldier of the Line on the day of his discharge. Then he hung a goat-bell on his neck, painted his tail saffron-yellow and his legs and muzzle purple-red, tied pig's bladders to his feet and the wings of a goose to his shoulders and set him loose in the Palace Court. When Augustus missed his pet and called "Typhon, Typhon, where are you?" and this extraordinary-looking animal wobbled through the gate towards him, it was one of the most ludicrous moments in the so-called Golden Age of Roman history. But it happened on the All Fools' Festival in honour of the God Saturn, so Augustus had to take it in good part. Then Herod had a tame snake which he taught to catch mice and which he used to keep under his gown in school-hours to amuse his friends when the master's back was turned. He was such a distracting influence that in the end he was sent to study with me under Athenodorus, my old white-bearded tutor from Tarsus. He tried his schoolboy tricks on Athenodorus, of course, but Athenodorus took them in such good part and I sympathized so little with them, because I loved Athenodorus, that he soon stopped. Herod was a brilliant boy with a marvellous memory and a peculiar gift for languages. Athenodorus once told him: "Herod, some day, I foresee, you will be called upon to occupy a position of the highest dignity in your native land. You must live every hour of your youth

15

in preparation for that call. With your talents you may in the end become as powerful a ruler as your grandfather Herod."

Herod replied: "That is all very well, Athenodorus, but I have a large, bad family. You cannot possibly conceive what a cut-throat crew they are, the greatest rogues that you could meet in a year of travel; and since my grandfather died eight years ago they have not improved in the least, I am told. I can't expect to live six months if I am forced to return to my country. (That's what my poor father said when he was being educated here at Rome in the household of Asinius Pollio. And my uncle Alexander who was with him said the same. And they were right.) My uncle the King of Judæa is old Herod reborn, but mean instead of magnificent in his vices; and my uncles Philip and Antipas are a brace of foxes."

"Single virtue is proof against manifold vice, my princeling," said Athenodorus. "Remember that the Jewish nation is more fanatically addicted to virtue than any other nation in the world: if you show yourself virtuous they will be behind you as one man."

Herod answered: "Jewish virtue does not agree any too well with Græco-Roman virtue, such as you teach it, Athenodorus. But many thanks for your prophetic words. You can count on me once I am king to be a really good king; but until I am on the throne I cannot afford to be any more virtuous than the rest of my family."

As for Herod's character, what shall I say? Most men— it is my experience—are neither virtuous nor scoundrels, good-hearted nor bad-hearted. They are a little of one thing and a little of the other and nothing for any length of time: ignoble mediocrities. But a few men remain always true to a single extreme character: these are the men who leave the strongest mark in history, and I should divide them into four classes. First there are the scoundrels with stony hearts,

16

of whom Macro, the Guards Commander under Tiberius and Caligula, was an outstanding example. Next come the virtuous men with equally stony hearts, of whom Cato the Censor, my bugbear, was an outstanding example. The third class are the virtuous men with golden hearts, such as old Athenodorus and my poor murdered brother Germanicus. And last and most rarely found are the scoundrels with golden hearts, and of these Herod Agrippa was the most perfect instance imaginable. It is the scoundrels with the golden hearts, these anti-Catos, who make the most valuable friends in time of need. You expect nothing from them. They are entirely without principle, as they themselves acknowledge, and only consider their own advantage. But go to them when in desperate trouble and say, "For God's sake do so-and-so for me," and they will almost certainly do it—not as a friendly favour but, they will say, because it fits in with their own crooked plans: and you are forbidden to thank them. These anti-Catos are gamblers and spendthrifts; but that is at least better than being misers. They also associate constantly with drunkards, assassins, crooked businessmen and procurers; yet you seldom see them greatly the worse for liquor themselves, and if they arrange an assassination you may be sure that the victim will not be greatly mourned, and they defraud the rich defrauders rather than the innocent and needy, and they consort with no woman against her will. Herod himself always insisted that he was congenitally a rogue. To which I would reply, "No, you are a fundamentally virtuous man wearing the mask of roguery." This would make him angry. A month or two before Caligula's death we had a conversation of this sort. At the end of it he said, "Shall I tell you about yourself?" "There's no need," I answered, "I'm the Official Fool of the Palace." "Well," he said, "there are fools who pretend to be wise men and wise men who pretend to be fools, but you are the first case I have yet encountered of a fool pretending to be a fool. And one day you'll see, my friend, what sort of a virtuous Jew you are dealing with."

When Postumus had been banished Herod attached himself to Castor, my uncle Tiberius's son, and the two became known as the rowdiest young blades in the City. They were always drinking and, if the stories told of them were true, spent the greater part of their nights climbing in and out of windows and having tussles with night-watchmen and jealous husbands and angry fathers of respectable households. Herod had inherited a good deal of money from his grandfather, who died when he was six years old, but ran through it quickly as soon as he had the handling of it. Presently he was forced to borrow. He borrowed first from his noble friends, myself among them, in a casual way that made it difficult for us to press him for repayment. When he had exhausted his credit in this way he borrowed from rich knights who were flattered to give him accommodation because of his intimacy with the Emperor's only son; and when they became anxious about the repayment he made up to Tiberius's freedmen who handled Imperial accounts and bribed them to give him loans from the Treasury. He always had a story ready about his golden prospects —he had been promised this or that Eastern kingdom or was to inherit so many hundred thousands of gold pieces from an old senator now at the point of death. But at last, at the age of thirty-three or so, he began to approach the end of his inventive resources; and then Castor died (poisoned by his wife, my sister Livilla, as we learned some years later) and he was obliged to give his creditors leg-bail. He would have appealed personally to Tiberius for assistance, but Tiberius had made a public statement to the effect that he did not wish ever again to see any of his dead son's friends, "for fear of his grief reviving." That only meant, of course, that he suspected them of participation in the plot against

18

his life which Sejanus, his chief minister, had persuaded him that Castor was contriving.

Herod fled to Edom, the home of his ancestors, and took refuge in a ruined desert fortress there. It was, I think, his first visit to the Near East since his childhood. At this time his uncle Antipas was Governor (or Tetrarch as the title was) of Galilee with Gilead. For the dominions of Herod the Great had been divided up between his three surviving sons: namely, this Antipas; his brother Archelaus, who became King of Judæa with Samaria; and his younger brother Philip who became Tetrarch of Bashan, the country lying east of Galilee across the Jordan. Herod now pressed his devoted wife Cypros, who had joined him in the desert, to appeal on his behalf to Antipas. Antipas was not only Herod's uncle but also his brother-in-law, having married his beautiful sister Herodias, the divorced wife of another of his uncles. Cypros would not consent to this at first, because the letter would have to be addressed to Herodias, who had Antipas completely under her thumb, and she had recently quarrelled with Herodias, during the latter's visit to Rome, and sworn never to speak to her again. Cypros protested that she would far rather stay in the desert among their barbarous but hospitable kinsfolk than humiliate herself before Herodias. Herod threatened to commit suicide by leaping from the battlements of the fortress, and actually persuaded Cypros that he was sincere, though I am sure no man ever lived who was less suicidally inclined than Herod. So she wrote the letter to Herodias after all.

Herodias was much flattered by Cypros's acknowledgment that she had been in the wrong throughout the quarrel and persuaded Antipas to invite Herod and her to Galilee. Herod was made a local magistrate (with a small yearly pension) at Tiberias, the capital town which Antipas had built in honour of the Emperor. But he soon quarrelled with Antipas, an indolent miserly fellow, who made him feel too keenly the obligations under which he was now laid. "Why, nephew, you owe your daily food and drink to me," said Antipas one evening at a banquet to which he had invited Herod and Cypros at Tyre, where they had all gone for a holiday together, "and I wonder that you presume to argue with me." Herod had been contradicting him on a point of Roman Law.

Herod replied, "Uncle Antipas, that is exactly the sort of remark I should have expected you to make."

"What do you mean, Sirrah?" asked Antipas angrily.

"I mean that you're no more than a provincial boor," replied Herod, "as lacking in manners as you are ignorant of the principles of law which govern the Empire, and as ignorant of these principles of law as you are stingy with your money."

"You must be drunk, Agrippa, to talk to me like this," stuttered Antipas, very red in the face.

"Not on the sort of wine that *you* serve out, Uncle Antipas. I have more regard for my kidneys than that. Where in the world do you manage to lay hands on such filthy brew as this? It must take a lot of ingenuity to find it. Perhaps it's salvage from that long-sunken vessel that they were raising in the harbour yesterday? Or do you scald out the lees from empty wine-jars with boiling camel-stale and then run the mixture into that beautiful golden mixing-bowl of yours?"

After that, of course, he and Cypros and the childen had to hurry down to the docks and jump aboard the first outgoing ship. It happened to take them north to Antioch, the capital of Syria, and here Herod presented himself before the Governor of the province, by name Flaccus, who treated him very kindly for my mother Antonia's sake. For you will be surprised to hear that my mother, that virtuous woman, who set her face resolutely against extravagance and disorderliness in her own household, had taken

a great liking to this scapegrace. She felt a perverse admiration for his dashing ways, and he used often to come to her
for advice and with an air of sincere repentance give her
a full account of his follies. She always professed herself
shocked by his revelations but certainly derived a deal of
pleasure from them and was much flattered by his atten-
tiveness. He never asked her for any loans of money, or
not in so many words, but she used voluntarily to lend him
quite large sums from time to time on a promise of future
good behaviour. Some of it he paid back. It was really my
money, and Herod knew it, and used afterwards to come
and thank me profusely as if I were the actual giver. I once
suggested to my mother that she was perhaps a little over-
liberal to Herod; but she flew into a rage and said that
if money had to be wasted she would rather see it wasted
in decent style by Herod than diced away by me in low
pot-houses with my disreputable friends. (I had had to conceal the dispatch of a large sum of money to help my brother Germanicus pacify the mutineers on the Rhine; so I had
pretended that I had lost it by gambling.) I remember once
asking Herod whether he did not sometimes grow impatient
with my mother's long discourses to him about Roman virtue. He said, "I greatly admire your mother, Claudius, and
you must remember that I am still an uncivilized Edomite at
heart, and that it is therefore a great privilege to be instructed by a Roman matron of the highest blood and of such
unblemished character. Besides, she talks the purest Latin
of anyone in Rome. I learn more from your mother, in a
single one of her lectures, about the proper placing of subordinate phrases and the accurate choice of adjectives, than
I would from attending a whole course of expensive lectures
by a professional grammarian."

This Governor of Syria, Flaccus, had served under my
father and so had come to have a great admiration for my
mother, who always accompanied him on his campaigns.

After my father's death he made my mother an offer of marriage, but she refused him, saying that, though she loved him as a very dear friend and would continue to do so, she owed it to her glorious husband's memory never to marry again. Besides, Flaccus was many years her junior and there would have been unpleasant talk if they had married. The two carried on a warm correspondence for a great many years until Flaccus died, four years before my mother. Herod knew about this correspondence and gained Flaccus's goodwill by frequent references to my mother's nobility of soul and beauty and kindliness. Flaccus himself was no moral paragon: he was famous at Rome as the man who once, challenged by Tiberius at a banquet, matched him cup for cup throughout one day and two whole nights of uninterrupted drinking. As a courtesy to his Emperor he let Tiberius drain the last cup at dawn of the second day and so come off victorious; but Tiberius was plainly exhausted and Flaccus, according to witnesses, could have continued at least an hour or two longer. So Flaccus and Herod got on very well together. Unfortunately Herod's younger brother Aristobulus was also in Syria and the two were not friends; Herod had obtained some money from him once, promising to invest it for him in a trading venture to India, and had afterwards told him that the ships had gone to the bottom. But it turned out that not only had the ships not gone to the bottom, but they had never sailed. Aristobulus complained to Flaccus about his swindle, but Flaccus said that he was sure that Aristobulus was mistaken about his brother's dishonesty and that he did not wish to take sides in the matter or even to act as adjudicator. However, Aristobulus kept a close watch on Herod, aware that he needed money badly and suspecting that he would get it by some sort of sleight of hand: he would then blackmail him into paying the trading debt.

A year or so later there was a boundary-dispute between

Sidon and Damascus; and the Damascenes, knowing how much Flaccus had come to depend on Herod for advice in arbitrating on matters of this sort—because of Herod's remarkable command of languages and his capacity, inherited no doubt from his grandfather Herod, for sifting the contradictory evidence given by Orientals—sent a secret deputation to Herod offering him a large sum of money, I forget how much, if he would persuade Flaccus to give a verdict in their favour. Aristobulus found out about this, and when the case was over, settled in favour of Damascus by the persuasive pleading of Herod, he went to Herod and told him what he knew, adding that he now expected payment of the shipping debt. Herod was so angry that Aristobulus was lucky to escape with his life. It was quite clear that he could not be frightened into paying back a single penny, so Aristobulus went to Flaccus and told him about the bags of gold that would shortly be arriving for Herod from Damascus. Flaccus intercepted them at the City gate and then sent for Herod, who, in the circumstance, could not deny that they were sent in payment for services rendered in the matter of the boundary-dispute. But he put a bold face on it and begged Flaccus not to regard the money as a bribe, for he had, while giving evidence in the case, kept strictly to the truth: Damascus had justice on its side. He told Flaccus, too, that the Sidonians had also sent him a deputation whom he had dismissed, telling them that he could do nothing to help them, for they were in the wrong.

"I suppose Sidon didn't offer you so much money as Damascus," sneered Flaccus.

"Please do not insult me," Herod virtuously replied.

"I refuse to have justice in a Roman court bought and sold like merchandise." Flaccus was thoroughly vexed.

"You judged the case yourself, my Lord Flaccus," said Herod.

"And you made a fool of me in my own court," Flaccus

raged. "I have done with you. You can go to Hell for all I care, and by the shortest road."

"I am afraid that it will be the Tænaran road," said Herod, "for if I die now I won't have a farthing in my purse to pay the Ferryman." (Tænarum is the southernmost promontory of the Peloponnese, where there is a short cut to Hell which avoids the River Styx. It was by this way that Hercules dragged the Dog Cerberus to the Upper World. The thrifty natives of Tænarum bury their dead without the customary coin in the mouth, knowing that they will not need it to pay Charon their ferry-fare.) Then Herod said, "But, Flaccus, you must not lose your temper with me. You know how it is. I didn't think that I was doing wrong. It is difficult for an Oriental like myself, even after nearly thirty years of City education, to understand your noble Roman scruples in a case of this sort. I see the matter in this light: the Damascenes were employing me as a sort of lawyer in their defence, and lawyers at Rome are paid enormous fees and never keep nearly so close to the truth, when presenting their cases, as I did. And certainly I did the Damascenes a good service in presenting their case so lucidly to you. So what harm could there have been in taking the money, which they quite voluntarily sent me? It's not as though I publicly advertised myself as having influence with you. They flattered and surprised me by suggesting that it might be so. Besides, as the Lady Antonia, that most extraordinarily wise and beautiful woman, has frequently pointed out to me——"

But it was no use appealing even to Flaccus's regard for my mother. He gave Herod twenty-four hours' law and said that if at the end of that time he was not well on his way out of Syria he would find himself up before the tribunal on a criminal charge.

# Chapter Two

Herod asked Cypros, "Where in the world are we to go now?"

Cypros answered miserably: "So long as you don't ask me to humble myself again by writing begging letters that I would almost rather die than write, I don't care where we go. Is India far enough away from our creditors?"

Herod said, "Cypros, my queen, we'll survive this adventure as we have survived many others and live to a prosperous and wealthy old age together. And I give you my solemn word that you'll have the laugh against my sister Herodias before I have finished with her and her husband."

"That ugly harlot," Cypros cried with truly Jewish indignation. For, as I told you, Herodias had not only committed incest by marrying an uncle but had divorced him in order to marry her richer and more powerful uncle Antipas. The Jews could make certain allowances for the incest, because marriage between uncle and niece was a common practice among Eastern royal families—the Armenian and Parthian royal families especially—and the family of Herod was not of Jewish origin. But divorce was regarded with the greatest disgust by every honest Jew (as, formerly, by every honest Roman) as being shameful both to the husband and to the wife; and nobody who had been under the disagreeable necessity of getting divorced would consider it as the first step towards remarriage. Herodias had, however, lived long enough at Rome to be able to laugh at these scruples. Everyone at Rome who is anyone gets divorced sooner or later. (Nobody, for instance, could call *me* a profligate, and yet I have divorced three wives already and may come to divorcing my fourth.) So Herodias was most unpopular in Galilee.

Aristobulus went to Flaccus and said, "In recognition of my services, Flaccus, would you perhaps be generous enough to give me that confiscated money from Damascus? It would almost cover the debt that Herod owes me—the shipping-fraud that I told you about some months ago."

Flaccus said: "Aristobulus, you have done me no service at all. You have been the cause of a breach between me and my ablest adviser, whom I miss more than I can tell you. As a matter of governmental discipline I had to dismiss him, and as a matter of honour I cannot recall him; but if you had not brought that bribe to light nobody would have been any the wiser and I would still have had Herod to consult on complicated local questions which absolutely baffle a simple-minded Westerner like myself. It's in his blood, you see. I have, in point of fact, lived far longer in the East than he has, but he instinctively knows in cases where I can only clumsily guess."

"What about myself?" asked Aristobulus. "Perhaps I can fill Herod's place?"

"*You,* little man?" Flaccus cried contemptuously. "You haven't the Herod touch. And, what's more, you'll never acquire it. You know that, as well as I do."

"But the money?" asked Aristobulus.

"If it's not for Herod, still less is it for you. But to avoid all ill-feeling between you and me I am going to send it back to Damascus." He actually did this. The Damascenes thought that he must have gone mad.

After a month or so Aristobulus, being out of favour at Antioch, decided to settle in Galilee, where he had an estate. It was only a two-days' journey from here to Jerusalem, a city which he liked to visit on all the important Jewish festivals, being more religiously inclined than the rest of his family. But he did not wish to take all his money with him to Galilee, because if he happened to quarrel with his uncle Antipas he might be forced to go away in a hurry, and Antipas would be just so much the richer. He therefore decided to transfer most of his credit from a banking-firm at Antioch to one at Rome and wrote to me as a trustworthy family-friend, giving me authority to invest it in landed property for him as opportunity should present itself.

Herod could not return to Galilee; and he had also quarrelled with his uncle Philip, the Tetrarch of Bashan, over a question of some property of his father which Philip had misappropriated; and the Governor of Judæa with Samaria —for Herod's eldest uncle, the King, had been removed for misgovernment some years previously and his kingdom proclaimed a Roman province—was Pontius Pilate, one of his creditors. Herod did not wish to retire permanently to Edom —he was no lover of deserts—and his chances of a welcome in Egypt by the great Jewish colony at Alexandria were inconsiderable. The Alexandrian Jews are very strict in their religious observances, almost stricter than their kinsmen at Jerusalem, if that were possible, and Herod from living so long at Rome had fallen into slack habits, especially in the matter of diet. The Jews are forbidden by their ancient law-giver Moses, on hygienic grounds, I understand, to eat a variety of ordinary meat foods: not merely pork—one could make a case against pork, perhaps—but hare and rabbit, and other perfectly wholesome meats; and what they do eat must be killed in a certain way. Wild duck that has been brought down by a sling-stone, or capon that has had its neck wrung, or venison got by bow and arrow, are forbidden them. Every animal that they eat must have had its throat cut and have been allowed to bleed to death. Then, too, they must make every seventh day a day of absolute rest: their very household servants are forbidden to do a stroke of work, even cooking or stoking the furnace. And they have days of national mourning in commemoration of ancient misfortunes, which often clash with Roman festivities. It had been impossible for Herod while he was living at Rome to be at the same time both a strict Jew and a popular member of high society; and so he had preferred the contempt of the Jews to that of the Romans. He decided not to try Alexandria or waste any more of his time in the Near East, where every door seemed closed to him. He would either take refuge in Parthia, where the king would welcome him as a useful agent in his designs against the Roman province of Syria, or he would return to Rome and throw himself upon my mother's protection: it might be just possible to explain away the misunderstanding with Flaccus. He rejected the idea of Parthia, because to go there would mean a complete breach with his old life, and he had greater confidence in the power of Rome than in that of Parthia; and besides it would be rash to try to cross the Euphrates—the boundary between Syria and Parthia—without money to bribe the frontier guards, who were under orders to allow no political refugee to pass. So he finally chose Rome.

And did he get there safely? You shall hear. He had not even enough ready money with him to pay for his sea-passage—he had been living on credit at Antioch and in great style; and though Aristobulus offered to lend him enough to take him as far as Rhodes, he refused to humble himself by accepting it. Besides, he could not risk booking his passage on a vessel sailing down the Orontes, for fear of being arrested at the docks by his creditors. He suddenly thought of someone from whom he could perhaps raise a trifle, namely, a former slave of his mother's whom she had bequeathed in her will to my mother Antonia and whom my mother had liberated and set up as a corn-factor at Acre, a coastal city somewhat south of Tyre: he paid her a percentage of his earnings and was doing quite well. But the territory of the Sidonians lay between and Herod had, as a matter of fact, accepted a gift from the Sidonians as well as from the Damascenes; so he could not afford to fall into their hands. He sent a trustworthy freedman of his to borrow from this man at Acre and himself escaped from Antioch in disguise, travelling east, which was the one direction that nobody expected him to take, and so eluding pursuit. Once in the Syrian desert he made a wide circuit towards the south, on a stolen camel, avoiding Bashan, his uncle Philip's tetrarchy, and Petræa (or, as some call it, Gilead, the fertile Transjordanian territory over which his uncle Antipas ruled as well as over Galilee), and skirting the farther end of the Dead Sea. He came safely to Edom, where he was greeted warmly by his wild kinsmen, and waited in the same desert fortress as before for his freedman to come with the money. The freedman succeeded in borrowing the money—twenty thousand Attic drachmæ: as the Attic drachma is worth rather more than the Roman silver piece, this came to something over nine hundred gold pieces. At least, he had given Herod's note of hand to that amount, in exchange; and would have arrived with the twenty thousand drachmæ complete if the corn-factor at Acre had not deducted twenty-five hundred, of which he accused Herod of having defrauded him some years previously. The honest freedman was afraid that his master would be angry with him for not bringing the whole amount, but Herod only laughed and said: "I counted on that twenty-five hundred to secure me the balance of the twenty thousand. If the stingy fellow had not thought that he was doing a smart trick in making my note of hand cover the old debt he would never have dreamed of lending me any money at all; for he must know by now what straits I am in." So Herod gave a great feast for the tribesmen and then made cautiously for the port of Anthedon, near the Philistine town of Gaza, where the coast begins curving west towards Egypt. Here Cypros and her children were waiting in disguise on board the small trading-vessel in which they had sailed from Antioch and which had been chartered to take them on to Italy by way of Egypt and Sicily. Affectionate greetings between all members of the family thus happily reunited were just being exchanged when a Roman sergeant and three soldiers appeared along-side in a rowing-boat with a warrant for Herod's arrest. The local military governor had signed this warrant, the reason for which was the non-payment to the Privy Purse of a debt of twelve thousand gold pieces.

Herod read the document and remarked to Cypros: "I take this as a very cheerful omen. The Treasurer has scaled down my debts from forty thousand to a mere twelve. We must give him a really splendid banquet when we get back to Rome. Of course, I've done a lot for him since I have been out in the East, but twenty-eight thousand is a generous return."

The sergeant interposed, "Excuse me, Prince, but really you can't think about banquets at Rome until you have seen the Governor here about this debt. He has orders not to let you sail until it's paid in full."

Herod said: "Of course I shall pay it. It had quite escaped my memory. A mere trifle. You go off now in the rowing-boat, and tell His Excellency the Governor that I am entirely at his service, but that his kind reminder of my debt to the Treasury has come a little inconveniently. I have just been joined by my devoted wife, the Princess Cypros, from whom I had been parted for over six weeks. Are you a family man, Sergeant? Then you will understand how earnestly we two desire to be alone together. You can leave your two soldiers on board as a guard if you don't trust us. Come again in the boat in three or four hours' time and we'll be quite ready to disembark. And here's an earnest of my gratitude." He gave the sergeant one hundred drachmæ: upon which the ser-geant, leaving the guard behind, rowed ashore without further demur. An hour or two later it was dusk and Herod cut the cables of the vessel and stood out to sea. He made as if to sail north towards Asia Minor but soon changed his course and turned south-west. He was making for Alexandria, where he thought he might as well try his luck with the Jews.

The two soldiers had been suddenly seized, trussed up and gagged by the crew, who had engaged them in a game of dice; but Herod released them as soon as he was sure that he was not being pursued and said that he would put them safe ashore at Alexandria if they behaved sensibly. He only stipulated that on his arrival there they should pretend to be his military bodyguard for a day or two; and promised in return to pay their passage back to Anthedon. They agreed hastily, terrified of being thrown overboard if they displeased him.

I should have mentioned that Cypros and the children had been helped out of Antioch by a middle-aged Samaritan called Silas, Herod's most faithful friend, He was a gloomy-looking solidly-built fellow with an enormous square-cut black beard, and had once served in the native cavalry as a troop commander. He had been awarded two military decorations for his services against the Parthians. Herod had on several occasions offered to have him made a Roman citizen, but Silas had always refused the honour on the ground that if he became a Roman he would be obliged to shave his chin in Roman fashion, and that he would never consent to do that. Silas was always giving Herod good advice, which he never took, and whenever Herod got into difficulties used to say: "What did I tell you? You should have listened to what I said." He prided himself upon his bluntness of speech, and was sadly wanting in tact. But Herod bore with Silas because he could be trusted to stand by him through thick and thin. Silas had been his only companion during the first flight to Edom, and again but for Silas the family would never have escaped from Tyre the day that Herod insulted Antipas. And at Antioch it had been Silas who had provided Herod with his disguise for escaping from his creditors, besides protecting Cypros and the childen and finding the vessel for them. When things were really bad Silas was at his best and cheerfullest, for then he knew that Herod would need his services and would give him an opportunity for saying, "I am entirely at your disposal, Herod Agrippa, my dear friend, if I may call you so. But if you had taken my advice this would never have occurred." In times of prosperity he always grew more and more gloomy, seeming to look back with a sort of regret to the bad old days of poverty and disgrace; and even encouraging them to return by his warnings to Herod that if he continued in his present course (whatever it might be) he would end as a ruined man. However, things were bad enough now to make Silas the brightest of companions. He cracked jokes with the crew and told the children long complicated stories of his military adventures. Cypros. who usually resented Silas's tediousness, now felt ashamed of her rudeness to this golden-hearted friend.

"I was brought up with a Jewish prejudice against Samaritans," she told Silas, "and you must forgive me if it has taken all these years for me to overcome it."

"I must ask your forgiveness too, Princess," Silas replied, "—forgiveness, I mean, for my bluntness of speech. But such is my nature. I must take the liberty of saying that if your Jewish friends and relatives were in general a little less upright and a little more charitable I would like them better. A cousin of mine was once riding on business from Jerusalem to Jericho. He came upon a poor Jew lying wounded and naked in the hot sun by the roadside. He had been set on by bandits. My cousin cleansed his wounds and bound them up as best he could and then took him on his beast to the nearest inn, where he paid in advance for his room and his food for a few days—the innkeeper insisted on payment in advance—and then visited him on his way back from Jericho and helped him to get home. Well, that was nothing: we Samaritans are made that way. It was all in a day's work for my cousin. But the joke was that three or four well-to-do Jews—a priest among them—whom my cousin had met riding towards him just before he came on the wounded man, must have actually seen him lying by the roadside: but because he was no relation of theirs they had left him there to die and ridden on, though he was groaning and calling out for help most pitifully. The innkeeper was a Jew too. He told my cousin that he quite understood the reluctance of these travellers to attend to the wounded man; if he had died on their hands they would have become ritually unclean from touching a corpse, which would have been a great inconvenience to themselves and their families. The priest, the innkeeper explained, was probably on his way to Jerusalem to worship at the Temple: he, least of all, could risk pollution. Well, thank God, I am a Samaritan, and a man with a blunt tongue. I say what I think. I—"

Herod interrupted, "My dear Cypros, isn't that a most instructive story? And if the poor fellow had been a Samaritan he wouldn't have had enough money to make it worth the bandits' while to rob him."

At Alexandria Herod, accompanied by Cypros, the children and the two soldiers, went to the chief magistrate of the Jewish colony there—or Alabarch, as he was called. The Alabarch was answerable to the Governor of Egypt for the good behaviour of his co-religionists. He had to see that they paid their taxes regularly and refrained from street riots with the Greeks and from other breaches of the peace. Herod greeted the Alabarch suavely and presently asked him for a loan of eight thousand gold pieces, offering in exchange to use his influence at the Imperial Court on behalf of the Alexandrian Jews. He said that the Emperor Tiberius had written asking him to come to Rome immediately to

33

advise him on Eastern affairs and that in consequence he had left Edom, where he was visiting his cousins, in a great hurry and with very little money in his purse for travelling expenses. The Roman bodyguard seemed to the Alabarch to furnish impressive proof of the truth of Herod's story, and he considered that it would indeed be very useful to have an influential friend at Rome. There had been riots lately in which the Jews had been the aggressors and had done serious damage to Greek property. Tiberius might feel inclined to curtail their privileges, which were considerable.

Alexander the Alabarch was an old friend of my family's. He had acted as steward of a large property at Alexandria which had been left to my mother in my grandfather Mark Antony's will and which Augustus, for my grandmother Octavia's sake, had allowed her to inherit, though he cancelled most of the other bequests. My mother brought this property as a dowry to my father when she married him, and it then went to my sister Livilla, who brought it as a dowry to Castor, Tiberius's son, when she married him; but Livilla soon sold it, because she led an extravagant life and needed the money, and the Alabarch lost the management of it. After this, correspondence between him and my family gradually ceased; and though my mother had used her interest with Tiberius to raise him to his present dignity and might be supposed to be well-disposed towards him still, the Alabarch was not sure how far he could count on her support if he became involved in any political trouble. Well, he knew that Herod had once been an intimate friend of the family, and so would have lent him money very readily had he been sure that Herod was still on good terms with us; but he could not be sure. He questioned Herod about my mother; and Herod, who had foreseen the situation very clearly and had been clever enough not to be the first to mention her name, answered that she was in the best of health and spirits when she last wrote. He had brought with him, as if accidentally, a cordial letter from her, written to him just before he left Antioch, in which she included a budget of detailed family news. He handed it to the Alabarch to read and the Alabarch was even more impressed by it than by the bodyguard. But the letter concluded with the hope that Herod was now at last settled down to a useful political life on the staff of her esteemed friend Flaccus, and the Alabarch had just heard from friends at Antioch that Flaccus and Herod had quarreled, and besides he could not be sure that Tiberius had really written the letter of invitation—which Herod had not offered to show him. He could not make up his mind whether to lend the money or not. However, he had just decided to do so, when one of the kidnapped soldiers, who understood a little Hebrew, said, "Give me only eight gold pieces, Alabarch, and I'll save you eight thousand."

"What do you mean, soldier?" asked the Alabarch.

"I mean that this man's a swindler and a fugitive from justice. We are not his bodyguard, but two men whom he has kidnapped. There's an Imperial warrant out for his arrest because of a big debt at Rome."

Cypros saved the situation by falling at the Alabarch's feet and sobbing, "For the sake of your old friendship with my father Phasael have mercy on me and my poor children. Do not condemn us to beggary and utter destruction. My dear husband has committed no fraud. The substance of what he has told you is perfectly true, though perhaps he has slightly coloured the details. We are indeed on our way to Rome, and owing to recent political changes we have the most golden expectations there; and if you lend us just enough money to help us out of our present difficulties, the God of our fathers will reward you a thousand fold. The debt on account of which my dear Herod was so nearly arrested is a legacy of his improvident youth. Once arrived at Rome he will soon find honourable means of repaying it. But to fall into the hands of his enemies in the Syrian Government would be his ruin and the ruin of my children and myself."

The Alabarch turned towards Cypros, whose fidelity to Herod in his misfortunes almost brought tears to his eyes, and asked, kindly but cautiously, "Does your husband observe the Law?"

Herod saw her hesitate a little and spoke for himself: "You must remember, Sir, that I am an Edomite by blood. You cannot reasonably expect as much from an Edomite as from a Jew. Edom and Jewry are blood-brothers through our common ancestor, the patriarch Isaac; but before any Jew congratulates himself on God's peculiar favour to his nation let him remember how Esau, the ancestor of Edom, was tricked of his birthright and of his father's blessing by Jacob, the ancestor of Jewry. Drive no hard bargains with me, Alabarch. Show more compassion to a distressed and improvident Edomite than old Jacob did, or, as the Lord my God lives, the next spoonful of *red lentil porridge* that you put into your mouth will surely choke you. We have lost our birthright to you and with it God's peculiar favour, and in return we demand from you such generosity of heart as we ourselves have never failed to show. Remember Esau's magnanimity when, meeting Jacob by chance at Peniel, he did not kill him."

"But do you observe the Law?" asked the Alabarch, impressed by Herod's vehemence and unable to contradict his historical references.

"I am circumcised, and so are my children, and I and my whole household have always kept the Law revealed to your ancestor Moses as strictly as our difficult position as Roman citizens and our imperfect consciences as Edomites have allowed us."

"There are no two ways of righteousness," said the Alabarch stiffly. "Either the Law is kept, or it is broken."

"Yet I have read that the Lord once permitted Naaman,

the Syrian Proselyte, to worship in the Temple of Rimmon by the side of the King, his master," said Herod. "And Naaman proved a very good friend to the Jews, did he not?"

At last the Alabarch said to Herod: "If I lend you this money will you swear in the name of the Lord—to Whom be Glory Everlasting—to keep His Law as far as in you lies, and cherish His People, and never by sins of commission or omission offend against His Majesty?"

"I swear by His most Holy Name," said Herod, "and let my wife Cypros and my children be my witnesses, that I will henceforth honour Him with all my soul and with all my strength and that I will constantly love and protect His People. If ever willingly I blaspheme, from hardness of heart, may the maggots that fed upon my grandfather Herod's living flesh so feed upon mine and consume me utterly!"

So he got the loan. As he told me afterwards, "I would have sworn anything in the world only to lay my hands on that money, I was so hard pressed."

But the Alabarch made two further conditions. The first was that Herod should now be paid only the equivalent, in silver, of four thousand gold pieces and receive the rest of the money on his arrival in Italy. For he did not yet trust Herod entirely. He might have thoughts of going off to Morocco or Arabia with the money. The second condition was that Cypros should take the children to Jerusalem to be educated as good Jews there under the guardianship of the Alabarch's brother-in-law, the High Priest. To this Herod and Cypros agreed, the more cheerfully as they knew that no good-looking boy or girl in high Roman society was safe from Tiberius's unnatural lusts. (My friend Vitellius, for example, had had one of his sons taken away from him to Capri, under the pretence that he would be given a liberal education there, and put among the filthy Spintrians, so that the boy's whole nature became warped. The name

37

"Spintrian" has stuck to him all his life, and a worse man I do not know.) Well, they decided that Cypros would rejoin him at Rome as soon as she had settled the children safely at Jerusalem.

What had made Herod come to Alexandria to borrow money from the Alabarch was the rumour that his freedman had brought with him from Acre of the fall of Sejanus. At Alexandria it had been fully confirmed. Sejanus had been my uncle Tiberius's most trusted minister but had conspired with my sister Livilla to kill him and usurp the monarchy. It was my mother who discovered the plot and warned Tiberius; and Tiberius, with the help of my nephew Caligula and the stony-hearted villain Macro, soon managed to bring Sejanus to book. It was then discovered that Livilla had poisoned her husband Castor seven years previously and that Castor had, after all, never been the traitor to his father that Sejanus had represented him as being. So naturally Tiberius's strict rule against the reappearance in his presence of any of Castor's former friends must now be considered cancelled; and my mother's patronage was more valuable than ever before. Had it not been for this news Herod would not have wasted his time and dignity by trying to borrow from the Alabarch. Jews are generous but very careful. They lend to their own needy fellow-Jews if they have fallen into misfortune through no fault or sin of their own, and they lend without charging any interest, because that is forbidden in their Law: their only reward is a feeling of virtue. But they will lend nothing to any non-Jew, even if he is dying of starvation, still less to any Jew who has put himself "outside the congregation," as they call it, by following un-Jewish customs in foreign lands—unless they are quite sure that they will get some substantial return for their generosity.

# Chapter Three

M<sup>Y</sup> MOTHER and I were unaware of Herod's return to Italy until one day a hurried note came from him, saying that he was coming to see us and adding darkly that he counted on our help to tide him over a great crisis of his fortunes. "If it's money that he wants," I said to my mother, "the answer is that we have none." And indeed we did not have any money to throw away at this time, as I have explained in my previous book. But my mother said: "It is very base to talk in that strain, Claudius. You were always a boor. If Herod needs money because he is in difficulties we must certainly raise money in some way or other: I owe it to the memory of his dear mother Berenice. In spite of her outlandish religious habits Berenice was one of my best friends. And such a splendid household manager, too!"

My mother had not seen Herod for some seven years and had missed him greatly. But he had been a most dutiful correspondent, writing to her about each of his troubles in turn and in such an amusing way that they seemed the most delightful adventures that you would find anywhere in Greek story-books, instead of genuine troubles. Perhaps the gayest letter of all was the one that he wrote from Edom shortly after leaving Rome, telling how his sweet, dear, silly wife Cypros had discouraged him from his leap from the fortress battlements. "She was quite right," he concluded. "It was an excessively high tower." A recent letter, also written from Edom, was in the same strain; it was while he was waiting for the money from Acre. He told of his shame at having sunk so low morally as to steal a Persian merchant's riding-camel. However, he wrote, shame had soon turned to a feeling of virtue for having done the owner so signal a service: the beast being apparently the permanent home of seven evil spirits, each worse than the last. The merchant must have been incomparably relieved to have awakened one morning and found his possessed possession really gone, saddle, bridle and all. It had been a most terrifying journey through the Syrian desert, the camel doing its best to kill him at every dry watercourse or narrow pass that they came to and even sneaking up at night to trample on his sleeping body. He wrote again from Alexandria to tell us that he had turned the beast loose in Edom, but that it had stalked him with a wicked look in its eye all the way down to the coast. "I swear to you, most noble and learned Lady Antonia, my earliest friend and my most generous benefactress, that it was terror of that horrible camel rather than fear of my creditors that made me give the Governor the slip at Anthedon. It would certainly have insisted on sharing my prison cell with me if I had yielded to arrest." There was a postscript: "My cousins of Edom were extraordinarily hospitable, but I must not allow you to carry away the impression that they were *extravagant*. They carry economy so far that they only put on clean linen on three occasions—when they marry, when they die, and when they raid a caravan which supplies them with clean linen free of charge. There is not a single fuller in the whole of Edom." Herod naturally put the most favourable construction possible on his quarrel, or misunderstanding as he called it, with Flaccus. He blamed himself for his thoughtlessness and praised Flaccus as a man with almost too high a sense of honour, if that were possible —certainly it was much too high for the people whom he governed to appreciate: they regarded him as an eccentric.

Herod now told us the parts of his story that he had omitted from his letters, concealing nothing, or practically nothing, for he knew that this was the best way to behave with my mother; and he especially delighted her—though of course she pretended to be dreadfully shocked—with his story of the kidnapping of the soldiers and his attempt to bluff the Alabarch. He also described his voyage from Alexandria in a dangerous storm when everyone but himself and the captain had, so he said, been prostrated by sea-sickness for five days and nights. The captain had spent all his time weeping and praying, leaving Herod to navigate the vessel single-handed.

Then he went on: "When at last, standing in the forecastle of our gallant ship, which had now stopped its rolling and pitching, and heedless of the thanks and praises of the now convalescent crew, I saw the Bay of Naples stretched shining before me, its shores gleaming with beautiful temples and villas, and mighty Vesuvius towering above, and gently smoking, to my fancy, like a domestic hearth—I confess I wept. I realized that I was coming home to my first and dearest homeland. I thought of all my beloved Roman friends from whom I had been so long parted, and especially of you, most learned and beautiful and noble Antonia—of you too, Claudius, naturally—how happy we would be to greet one another again. But first, it was clear, I had to establish myself decently. It would have been most unsuitable for me to have presented myself at your door like a beggar or poor client, asking for relief. As soon as we had landed and I had cashed the Alabarch's draft, which was on a Naples bank, I wrote at once to the Emperor, at Capri, begging to be allowed the privilege of an audience. He granted it most graciously, saying that he was pleased to hear of my safe return, and we had a most encouraging talk together the next day. I am sorry to say I felt bound to divert him—for he was in a rather morose humour at first—with some Asiatic stories that I certainly would not injure your modesty by repeating here. But you know how it is with the Emperor: he has an ingenious mind and is very catholic in his tastes. Well, when I had told him a particularly characteristic story in that style he said, 'Herod, you're a man after my own heart. I wish you to undertake an appointment of great responsibility—the tutoring of my only grandchild, Tiberius Gemellus, whom I have here with me. As an intimate friend of his dead father you will surely not refuse it, and I trust that the lad will take to you. He is, I am sorry to say, a sullen, melancholy little fellow and needs an open-hearted lively elder companion on whom to model himself.'

"I stopped the night at Capri and by morning the Emperor and I were better friends than ever—he had disregarded his doctors' advice and drunk with me all night. I thought that my fortunes were restored at last, when suddenly the single horse-hair, by which the sword of Damocles had so long been suspended over my unlucky head, contrived to snap. A letter arrived for the Emperor from that idiot of a Governor at Anthedon reporting that he had served a warrant on me for non-payment of a twelve-thousand debt to the Privy Purse and that I had 'eluded arrest by an artifice' and had escaped, kidnapping two of his garrison, who had not yet returned and had probably been murdered. I assured the Emperor that the soldiers were alive and that they had stowed away in my vessel without my knowledge and that no warrant had been served on me. Perhaps they had been sent to serve it, I said, but had decided to go for a holiday to Egypt. At all events we found them hiding in the cargo when we were half-way to Alexandria. I assured the Emperor that at Alexandria I had returned them at once to Anthedon for punishment."

"Herod Agrippa," said my mother severely, "that was a deliberate lie and I am most ashamed of you."

"Not so ashamed as I have been of myself since, dear Lady Antonia," said Herod. "How often have you told me that honesty is the best policy? But in the East everyone tells lies and one naturally discounts nine-tenths of what one hears, and expects one's hearers to do the same. For the moment I had forgotten that I was back in a country where it is considered dishonourable to deviate a hair's breadth from the strict truth."

"Did the Emperor believe you?" I asked.

"I hope so, with all my heart," said Herod. "He asked me, 'But what about the debt?' I told him that it was a loan granted me in proper form and on good security by the Privy Purse and that if a warrant had been issued for my arrest on that account it must have been that traitor Sejanus's doing: I would speak to the Treasurer at once and settle the matter with him. But the Emperor said: 'Herod, unless that debt is paid in full within a week you shall not be tutor to my grandson.' You know how strict he is about debts to the Privy Purse. I said in as casual a tone as I could command, that I would certainly pay it within three days. But my heart was like lead. And so I immediately wrote to you, my dear benefactress, thinking that perhaps . . ."

My mother said again, "It was very, very wrong of you, Herod, to tell the Emperor such lies."

"I know it, I know it," said Herod, feigning deep repentance. "If you had been in my position you would undoubtedly have told the truth: but I lacked the courage. And, as I say, these seven years in the East away from you have greatly blunted my moral sensibilities."

"Claudius," said my mother with sudden resolution, "how can we raise twelve thousand in a hurry? What about the letter you had from Aristobulus this morning?"

By a pretty coincidence I had had a letter from Aristobulus only that morning asking me to invest some money for him in landed property, which was going cheap at that time, because of the scarcity of coin. He had enclosed a banker's draft for ten thousand. My mother told Herod about it.

"Aristobulus!" cried Herod. "How in the world did *he*

rake ten thousand together? The unprincipled fellow must have been making use of his influence with Flaccus to take bribes from the natives."

"I consider, in that case," said my mother, "that he behaved very shabbily towards you in reporting to my old friend Flaccus that the Damascenes were sending you a present for having pleaded their cause so well. I should have thought better of Aristobulus than that. And now perhaps it would be only justice if that ten thousand were used as a temporary—*temporary*, mind you, Herod—loan to help you on your feet again. There will be no difficulty about the remaining two thousand—will there, Claudius?"

"You forget that Herod still has eight thousand from the Alabarch, Mother. Unless he has already spent it. He'll be better off than we are if we entrust Aristobulus's money to him."

Herod was warned that he must repay the debt within three months without fail or I would be guilty of a breach of fiduciary trust. I did not like the business in the least, but I preferred it to mortgaging our house on the Palatine Hill to raise the money, which would have been the only other course. However, everything turned out unexpectedly well. Not only was Herod's appointment as tutor to Gemellus confirmed, as soon as he had paid the Privy Purse the twelve thousand, but he also repaid me the whole amount of the Aristobulus loan two days before it was due and, besides that, a former debt of five thousand which we had never expected to see again. For Herod, as Gemellus's tutor, was thrown a great deal into the company of Caligula, whom Tiberius, now seventy-five years old, had adopted as his son and who was his heir-presumptive. Tiberius kept Caligula very short of money, and Herod, after gaining Caligula's confidence by some fine banquets, handsome presents and the like, became his accredited agent for borrowing large sums, in the greatest secrecy, from rich men who wanted to

stand in well with the new Emperor. For Tiberius was not
expected to live much longer. When Caligula's confidence
in Herod was thus proved and a matter of common knowledge in financial circles, he found it easy to borrow money
in his own name as well as in Caligula's. His unpaid debts
of seven years before had mostly settled themselves by the
death of the creditors: for the ranks of the rich had been
greatly thinned by Tiberius's treason-trials under Sejanus,
and under Macro, Sejanus's successor, the same destructive
process continued. About the rest of his debts Herod was
easy enough in his mind: nobody would dare to sue a man
who stood so high in Court favour as he did. He paid me
back with part of a loan of forty thousand gold pieces which
he had negotiated with a freedman of Tiberius's, a fellow
who, as a slave, had been one of the warders of Caligula's
elder brother Drusus, when he was starved to death in the
Palace cellars. Since his liberation he had become immensely
rich by traffic in high-class slaves—he would buy sick slaves
cheap and doctor them back to health in a hospital which
he managed himself—and was afraid that Caligula when
he became Emperor would take vengeance on him for his
ill-treatment of Drusus; but Herod undertook to soften
Caligula's heart towards him.

So Herod's star grew daily brighter, and he settled
several matters in the East to his entire satisfaction. For
instance, he wrote to friends in Edom and Judæa—and anyone to whom he now wrote as a friend was greatly flattered
—and asked them whether they could provide him with
any detailed evidence of maladministration against the
Governor who had tried to arrest him at Anthedon. He collected quite an imposing amount of evidence in this way and
had it embodied in a letter purporting to come from leading
citizens of Anthedon; which he then sent to Capri. The
Governor lost his appointment. Herod paid back his debt in
Attic drachmæ to the corn-factor at Acre, less twice the

amount which had been unwarrantably deducted from the money sent to him in Edom; explaining that these five thousand drachmae which he was retaining represented a sum which the corn-factor had borrowed from the Princess Cypros some years back and had never returned. As for Flaccus, Herod made no attempt to be revenged on him, for my mother's sake; and Flaccus died shortly afterwards. Aristobulus he decided to forgive magnanimously, knowing that he must be feeling not only ashamed of himself but most vexed at his lack of foresight in antagonizing a brother now grown so powerful. Aristobulus could be made very useful, once he was properly chastened in spirit. Herod also revenged himself on Pontius Pilate, from whom the order for his arrest at Anthedon had originated, by encouraging some friends of his in Samaria to protest to the new Governor of Syria, my friend Vitellius, about Pilate's rough handling of civil disturbances there and to charge him with bribe-taking. Pilate was ordered to Rome to answer these charges before Tiberius.

One fine spring day as Caligula and Herod were out riding together in an open coach in the country near Rome, Herod remarked gaily, "It is high time, surely, for the old warrior to be given his wooden foil." By the old warrior he meant Tiberius, and by the wooden foil he meant the honourable token of discharge that worn-out sword-fighters are given in the arena. He added, "And if you will pardon what may sound suspiciously like flattery, my dear fellow, but is my honest opinion, you will make a far finer showing at the game of games than *he* ever made."

Caligula was delighted, but unfortunately Herod's coachman overheard the remark, understood it and stored it in his memory. The knowledge that he had power to ruin his master encouraged this turnip-witted fellow to attempt a number of impertinences towards him, which for a time, as it happened, passed unnoticed. But at last he took it into his head to steal some very fine embroidered carriage-rugs and sell them to another coachman whose master lived at some distance from Rome. He reported that they had been accidentally ruined by the leakings of a tar-barrel through the planks of the stable-loft, and Herod was content to believe him; but one day, happening to go for a pleasure-drive with the knight to whose coachman they had been sold, he found them tucked about his knees. And so the theft came out. But the knight's coachman gave the thief timely warning and he ran away at once to avoid punishment. His original intention had been to face Herod, if he were found out, with the threat to reveal to the Emperor what he had overheard. But he lost courage when the appropriate moment came, suddenly realizing that Herod was quite capable of killing him if he tried blackmail and of producing witnesses that the blow had been struck in self-defence. The coachman was one of those people whose muddled minds get everyone into trouble, themselves most of all.

Herod knew the fellow's probable haunts in Rome and, not realizing what was at stake, asked the City officers to arrest him. He was found and brought up in court on a charge of theft, but claimed the privilege as a freedman of appealing to the Emperor instead of being summarily sentenced. He added: "I have something to tell the Emperor which concerns his personal security. It is what I once heard when driving a coach on the road to Capua." The magistrate had no alternative but to send him under armed escort to Capri.

From what I have already told you about the character of my uncle Tiberius you will perhaps be able to guess what course he took when he read the magistrate's report. Though he realized that the coachman must have overheard some treasonable remark of Herod's, he did not yet wish to know precisely what it was: Herod obviously was not the sort of man to make any very dangerous statement in a coachman's

47

hearing. So he kept the coachman in prison, unexamined, and instructed young Gemellus, now about ten years old, to keep a sharp watch on his tutor and to report any word or action of his that seemed to have any treasonable significance. Herod meanwhile grew anxious at Tiberius's delay in examining the coachman and talked the matter over with Caligula. They decided that nothing had been said by Herod, on the occasion to which the coachman was apparently referring, that could not be explained away. If Herod himself pressed for an investigation Tiberius would be the more likely to take his word that the "wooden foil" was intended literally. For Herod would say that they had been discussing Yellow Legs, a famous sword-fighter who had since retired, and that he had merely been congratulating Caligula on his fencing abilities.

Herod then noticed that Gemellus was behaving in a most suspicious manner—eavesdropping and turning up at his apartments at curious times. It was clear that Tiberius had set him to work. So he went once more to my mother and explained the whole case, begging her to press for a trial of the coachman, on his behalf. The excuse was to be that he wished to see the man well punished for his theft and for his ingratitude, Herod having voluntarily given him his freedom from slavery only the year before. Nothing was to be said about the man's intended revelations. My mother did as Herod asked. She wrote to Tiberius and, after the usual long delay, back came a letter. It is now in my possession, so that I can quote the very words. For once Tiberius went straight to the point.

"If this coachman means to accuse Herod Agrippa falsely of some treasonable utterance or other in order to cover his own misdoings, he has suffered enough for that folly by his long confinement in my not very hospitable prison cells at Misenum. I was thinking of letting him go with a caution against appealing to me, in future, when about to be sen-

tenced in the lower courts for a trivial offence like theft. I
am too old and too busy to be bothered with such frivolous
appeals. But if you force me to investigate the case and it
turns out that a treasonable utterance was in fact made,
Herod will regret having brought the matter up; for his
desire to see his coachman severely punished will have
brought a very severe punishment upon himself."

This letter made Herod all the more anxious to have the
man tried, and in his own presence. Silas, who had come to
Rome, dissuaded him from this, quoting the proverb: "Don't
tamper with Camarina." (Near Camarina, in Sicily, was a
pestilent marsh which the inhabitants drained for hygienic
reasons. This exposed the city to attack: it was captured and
destroyed.) But Herod would not listen to Silas; the old
fellow had been growing very tiresome after five years of
unbroken prosperity. Soon he heard that Tiberius, who was
at Capri, had given orders for the big villa at Misenum, the
one where he afterwards died, to be made ready to receive
him. He immediately arranged to go down to that neighbourhood himself, with Gemellus, as a guest of Caligula who had
a villa close by at Bauli; and in the company of my mother
who was, you will recall, grandmother both to Caligula and
to Gemellus. Bauli is quite close to Misenum on the north
coast of the Bay of Naples, so nothing was more natural than
for the whole party to go together to pay their respects to Tiberius on his arrival. Tiberius invited them all to dine on the
following day. The prison where the coachman was lan-
guishing lay close by, so Herod persuaded my mother to ask
Tiberius in everyone's presence to settle the case that very
afternoon. I had been invited to Bauli myself, but had declined, for neither my uncle Tiberius nor my mother was
very patient of my company. But I have heard the whole
story from several people who were present. It was a fine
dinner and only spoilt by the great scarcity of wine. Tiberius
was now following his doctor's advice and abstaining al-

together from drink, so as a matter of tact and caution nobody asked for his cup to be refilled after he had emptied it; and the waiters did not offer to do so, either. Going without wine always put Tiberius in a bad humour, but, nevertheless, my mother boldly brought up the subject of the coachman again. Tiberius interrupted her, as if unintentionally, by starting a new topic of conversation, and she made no further attempt until after dinner when the whole party went out for a stroll under the trees surrounding the local race-course. Tiberius did not walk: he was carried in a sedan, and my mother, who had become quite brisk in her old age, walked alongside. She said: "Tiberius, may I speak to you about that coachman? It is high time, surely, that his case was settled, and we would all feel much easier, I think, if you were good enough to settle it to-day, once and for all. The prison is just over there and it could be all got over in a very few minutes."

"Antonia," Tiberius said, "I have already given you the hint to leave well alone, but if you insist I shall do as you ask." Then he called up Herod, who was walking behind with Caligula and Gemellus, and said: "I am now about to examine your coachman, Herod Agrippa, at the insistence of my sister-in-law, the Lady Antonia, but I call the Gods to witness that what I am doing is not done by my own inclination but because I am forced to it."

Herod thanked him profusely for his condescension. Then Tiberius called for Macro, who was also present, and ordered him to bring the coachman up for trial before him immediately.

It seems that Tiberius had enjoyed a few words in private with Gemellus on the previous evening. (Caligula, a year or two afterwards, forced Gemellus to give him an account of this interview.) Tiberius had asked Gemellus whether he had anything to report against his tutor, and Gemellus answered that he had overheard no disloyal words and witnessed no disloyal action; but that he saw very little of Herod these days—he was now always about with Caligula and left Gemellus to study books by himself instead of coaching him personally. Tiberius then questioned the boy about loans, whether Herod and Caligula had ever discussed loans in his presence. Gemellus considered for a while and then answered that on one occasion Caligula had asked Herod about a P. O. T. loan and Herod had answered, "I'll tell you about it afterwards: for little pitchers have long ears." Tiberius immediately guessed what P. O. T. meant. It surely meant a laon negotated by Herod on Caligula's behalf which would be payable *post obitum Tiberii*— that is, after the death of Tiberius. So Tiberius dismissed Gemellus and told him that a P. O. T. loan was a matter of no significance and that he now had the fullest confidence in Herod. But he immediately sent a confidential freedman to the prison, who ordered the coachman, in the Emperor's name, to disclose what remark of Herod's he had overheard. The coachman repeated Herod's exact words and the freedman took them back to Tiberius. Tiberius considered a while and then sent the freedman back to the prison with instructions as to what the coachman must say when brought up for trial. The freedman made him memorize the exact words and repeat them after him to understand that if he spoke them properly he would be set at liberty and given a money reward.

So there on the race-track itself the trial took place. The coachman was asked by Tiberius whether he pleaded guilty to stealing the carriage rugs. He answered that he was not guilty, since Herod had given them to him as a present but afterwards repented of his generosity. At this point Herod tried to interrupt the evidence by exclamations of disgust at his ingratitude and mendacity, but Tiberius begged him to be silent and asked the coachman: "What else have you to say in your defence?"

The coachman replied: "And even if I had stolen those

51

rugs, as I did not, it would have been an excusable act. For my master is a traitor. One afternoon shortly before my arrest I was driving a coach in the direction of Capua with your grandson, the Prince, and my master, Herod Agrippa, seated behind me. My master said: 'If only the day would come when the old warrior finally dies and you find yourself named as his successor in the monarchy! For then young Gemellus won't be any hindrance to you. It will be easy enough to get rid of him, and soon everyone will be happy, myself most of all'."

Herod was so taken aback by this evidence that for the moment he could not think what to say, except that it was perfectly untrue. Tiberius questioned Caligula, and Caligula, who was a great coward, looked anxiously at Herod for guidance, but got none, so said in a great hurry that if Herod had made any such remark he had not heard it. He remembered the ride in the coach and it had been a very windy day. If he had heard any such treasonable words he certainly would not have let them pass but would have reported them immediately to his Emperor. Caligula was most treacherous towards his friends, if his own life was in danger, and always hung on the lightest word of Tiberius: so much so that it was said of him that never was a better slave to a worse master. But Herod spoke up boldly: "If your son, who was sitting next to me, didn't hear the treasons that I am alleged to have uttered—and nobody has quicker ears than he for hearing treasons against you—then surely the coachman could not have heard them, sitting as he was with his back to me."

But Tiberius had already made up his mind. He said shortly to Macro, "Put that man in handcuffs," and then to his sedan-men, "Proceed." They stepped off, leaving Herod, Antonia, Macro, Caligula, Gemellus and the rest staring at each other in doubt and astonishment. Macro could not make out who it was whom he was supposed to handcuff, so when Tiberius, having been carried all the way round the race-track, returned to the scene of the trial, where the whole company was still standing just as he had left them, Macro asked him, "Pardon me, Cæsar, but which of these men am I to arrest?" Tiberius pointed to Herod and said, "That's the man I mean." But Macro, who had great respect for Herod and hoped perhaps to break down Tiberius's resolution by pretending to misunderstand him, once more asked, "You surely cannot mean Herod Agrippa, Cæsar?" "I mean no one else," growled Tiberius. Herod ran forward and all but prostrated himself before Tiberius. He did not dare to do it quite, because he knew Tiberius's dislike of being treated like an Oriental monarch. But he stretched out his arms in a pitiful way and protested himself Tiberius's most loyal servant and absolutely incapable of so much as admitting the least treasonable thought to cross his mind, let alone uttering it. He began to talk eloquently of his friendship with Tiberius's dead son (a victim, like himself, of unfounded charges of treason), whose irreparable loss he had never ceased to mourn, and of the extraordinary honour that Tiberius had done him in appointing him tutor to his grandchild. But Tiberius looked at him in that cold, crooked way of his and sneered, "You can make that speech in your defence, my noble Socrates, when I fix the date of your trial." Then he told Macro, "Take him to the prison yonder. He can use the chain discarded by this honest coachman-fellow."

Herod did not utter another word except to thank my mother for her generous but unavailing efforts on his behalf. He was marched off to the prison, with his wrists handcuffed behind him. It was a place where misguided Roman citizens who had appealed to Tiberius from sentences in lower courts were confined—in cramped and unhealthy quarters, with poor food and no bedding—until Tiberius should have time to settle their cases. Some of them had been there many years.

# Chapter Four

HEROD as he was being led towards the prison gates, saw a Greek slave of Caligula's waiting there. The slave seemed out of breath as if he had been running and held a water pitcher in his hand. Herod hoped that Caligula had sent him there as a sign that he was still a friend, but that he could not openly declare his friendship, for fear of offending Tiberius. He called to the boy, "Thaumastus, for God's sake give me a drink of water." It was very hot weather for September and, as I told you, there had been hardly any wine to drink for dinner. The boy came forward readily, as if he had been warned for this service. Herod, greatly reassured, took the pitcher and drank it nearly dry. For it contained wine, not water. He said to the slave: "You have earned a prisoner's gratitude for this drink and I promise you that when I am free again I shall pay you well for it. I shall see that your master, who certainly is not a man to desert his friends, gives you your liberty as soon as he has secured mine, and I shall then employ you in a position of trust in my own household." Herod was able to keep his promise and Thaumastus eventually became his chief steward. He is still alive at the time I write this, in the service of Herod's son, though Herod himself is dead.

When Herod was led into the prison compound it happened to be the hour for exercise, but there was a strict rule that prisoners should not converse with each other without express permission from the warders. Each group of five prisoners had a warder assigned to it who watched every movement they made. Herod's arrival caused a great commotion among these bored and listless men, for the sight of an Eastern prince wearing a cloak of real Tyrian purple was something that had never been seen there before. He did not greet them, however, but stood gazing at the distant roof of Tiberius's villa, as if he could read on it some message as to what his fate was to be.

Among the prisoners was an elderly German chieftain whose history, it seems, was as follows. He had been an officer of German auxiliaries under Varus when Rome still held the province across the Rhine, and had been given Roman citizenship in recognition of his services in battle. When Varus was treacherously ambushed and his army massacred by the famous Hermann, this chieftain, although he had not (or so he said) served in Hermann's army or given him any assistance in his plans, took no steps to prove his continued loyalty to Rome but became the head-man of his ancestral village. During the wars carried on by my brother Germanicus he left this village with his family and retired inland, only returning when Germanicus was recalled to Rome and the danger seemed past. He was then unlucky enough to be captured by the Romans in one of the cross-river raids that were made from time to time to keep our men in good fighting condition and to remind the Germans that one day the province would be ours again. The Roman general would have had him flogged to death as a deserter, but he protested that he had never shown any disloyalty to Rome, and now exercised his right as a Roman citizen to appeal to the Emperor. (In the interval, however, he had forgotten all his camp-Latin.) This man asked his warder, who understood a little German, to tell him about that melancholy, handsome young man standing under the tree. Who was he? The warder answered that he was a Jew and a man of great importance in his own country. The German begged for permission to speak to Herod, saying that he had never in

55

all his life met a man of the Jewish race, but that he understood the Jews to be by no means inferior in intelligence or courage even to the Germans: one might learn a lot from a Jew. He added that he too was a man of great importance in his own country. "This place is getting to be quite a university," said the warder, grinning. "If you two foreign gentlemen care to swap philosophy, I'll do my best to act as interpreter. But don't expect too much of my German."

Now, while Herod had been standing under the tree, with his head muffled in his cloak because he did not wish the inquisitive prisoners and wardens to see his tears, a curious thing had happened. An owl had perched on the branches above his head and dropped dirt on him. It is very rare for an owl to appear in broad daylight, but only the German had noticed the bird's performance; for everyone else was so busy looking at Herod himself.

The German, speaking through the warder, greeted Herod courteously and began by saying that he had something of importance to tell him. Herod uncovered his face when the warder began speaking and replied with interest that he was all attention. For the moment he expected a message from Caligula, and did not realize that the warder was merely an interpreter for one of the prisoners.

The warder said, "Excuse me, Sir, but this German gentleman wants to know whether you are aware that an owl has just dropped dirt on your cloak? I am acting as this German gentleman's interpreter. He is a Roman citizen but his Latin's got a bit rusty in that damp climate of theirs."

This made Herod smile in spite of his disappointment. He knew that prisoners with nothing to do spend a great deal of their time in playing tricks on each other, and that sometimes the warders, equally bored with their duties, assist them. So he did not look up into the tree or examine his cloak to see whether the man was not perhaps making fun of him. He replied in a bantering tone: "Stranger things than

56

that have happened to me, friend. A flamingo recently flew in at my bedroom window, laid an egg in one of my shoes, and then flew out again. My wife felt quite upset. If it had been a sparrow or a thrush or even an owl she would not have given the incident a second thought. But a flamingo, now . . ."

The German did not know what a flamingo was, so he disregarded this sally, and went on: "Do you know what it signifies when a bird drops dirt on your head or shoulder? In my country it is always taken for a very lucky sign indeed. And that so holy a bird as an owl has done this and has abstained from uttering any ill-omened cries should be a sign to cause you the profoundest joy and hope. We Chaucians know all that is to be known about owls. The owl is our totem and gives our nation its name. If you were a Chaucian I should say that the God Mannus had sent this bird as a sign to you that as a result of this imprisonment, which will only be a short one, you will be promoted to a position of the greatest dignity in your own country. But I am told that you are a Jew. May I ask, Sir, the name of the God of your country?"

Herod, who was still not sure whether the German's earnestness was real or assumed, answered, quite truthfully, "The name of our God is too holy to be pronounced. We Jews are obliged to refer to it by periphrases, and even by periphrases of periphrases."

The German decided that Herod must be making fun of him and said: "Do not think, please, that I am saying this in the hope of any reward from you; but seeing the bird do what it did I felt impelled to congratulate you on the omen. Now I have one more thing to tell you, because I am a well-known augur in my country: when next you see this bird, though it may be in the time of your highest prosperity, and it settles near you and begins to utter cries, then you will know that your days of happiness are over and that the number of those days which still remain for you to live will be no greater than the number of cries that the owl has given. But may that day be long in coming!"

Herod had quite recovered his spirits by this time and said to the German: "I think, old man, that you talk the most charming nonsense that I have heard since my return to Italy. You have my sincere thanks for trying to cheer me and if ever I get out of this place a free man, I shall see what I can do to have you freed too. If you are as good company out of chains as in chains we shall have some enjoyable evenings together, drinking and laughing and telling funny stories."

The German went off in a huff.

Meanwhile Tiberius had given sudden orders to his servants to pack up his things and sailed back to Capri that very afternoon. He was afraid, I suppose, that my mother would try to persuade him to release Herod, and it would be difficult for him to refuse, being so much in her debt over the matter of Sejanus and Livilla. My mother, realizing that she could do nothing for Herod now, except perhaps to arrange that prison life should be made as easy as possible for him, asked Macro to oblige her in this as far as was possible. Macro replied that if he gave Herod more considerate treatment than the other prisoners he would certainly get into trouble with Tiberius. My mother replied, "Short of allowing him any facilities for escape, do all that you can for him, I beg you, and if Tiberius happens to hear of it and to be displeased I promise to bear the full weight of his displeasure myself." She much disliked being in the position of asking favours from Macro, whose father had been one of our family slaves. But she felt great personal concern for Herod and would have done almost anything for him then. Macro was flattered by her pleas and promised to choose a warder for Herod who would show him every consideration, and also to appoint as governor of the prison a captain whom she knew personally. More than this, he arranged that Herod should take his meals with the governor and should be allowed to visit the local baths daily under escort. He said that if Herod's freedmen cared to bring him extra food and warm bedding—for winter was now drawing on—he would see that no difficulties were made, but that the freedmen must tell the porter at the gate that these comforts were for the governor's own use. So Herod's experience of prison was not too painful, though he was chained to the wall by a heavy iron chain whenever his warder was not in actual attendance; but he worried greatly as to what was happening to Cypros and the children, for he was allowed no news from the outside world. Silas, though he had not had the satisfaction of telling Herod that he should have listened to his advice (about not tampering with the marsh of Camarina), saw to it that the freedmen brought the prisoner his food and other necessities punctually and discreetly; and did as much for him as lay in his power to do. In the end he was himself arrested for trying to smuggle a letter into the prison, but was released with a caution.

Early in the following year Tiberius decided to leave Capri for Rome and told Macro to send all the prisoners there, because he intended to settle their cases on his arrival. Herod and the rest were therefore taken from Misenum and marched, by stages, to the detention barracks in the Guards Camp outside the City. You will recall that Tiberius turned back when within sight of the City walls because of an unlucky omen, the death of his pet wingless dragon; he hurried back to Capri but caught a chill and got no farther than Misenum. You will recall too that when he was believed to be dead and Caligula was already strutting about the hall of the villa, flashing his signet ring among a crowd of admiring courtiers, the old man started up from his coma and called loudly for food. But the news of his death and Caligula's succession had already reached Rome by courier. Herod's freedman, the one who brought him the money from Acre, happened to meet the courier on the outskirts of the City, who shouted out the news as he galloped past. The freedman ran to the camp, entered the detention barracks and running excitedly towards Herod cried out in Hebrew, "The Lion is dead." Herod questioned him rapidly in the same language and appeared so extraordinarily pleased that the governor came up and demanded to be told what news the freedman had brought. This was a breach of prison rules, he said, and must not occur again. Herod explained that it was nothing, only the birth of a male heir to one of his relatives in Edom; but the governor made it plain that he insisted on knowing the truth, so Herod finally said, "The Emperor is dead."

The governor, who was on very good terms with Herod by this time, asked the freedmen whether he was sure that the news was true. The freedman replied that he had heard it directly from an Imperial courier. The governor knocked off Herod's chain with his own hands and said, "We must celebrate this, Herod Agrippa, my friend, with the best wine in the camp." They were just eating a most cheerful meal together, Herod being in his best form and telling the governor what a good fellow he was, and how considerately he had behaved, and how happy they would all be now that Caligula was Emperor, when news came that Tiberius was not dead after all. This put the governor into a great state of alarm. He decided that Herod had arranged for this false message to be brought just to get him into trouble. "Back to your chain this instant," he shouted angrily, "and never expect me to trust you again." So Herod had to get up from the table and go gloomily back to his cell. But, as you will again recall, Macro had not allowed Tiberius to enjoy his new lease of life for very long but had gone into the Imperial bed-chamber and smothered him with a pillow. So again the news came that Tiberius was dead, this time really dead.

But the governor kept Herod chained up all night. He was not taking any risks.

Caligula wished to release Herod at once, but curiously enough it was my mother who prevented him from doing so. She was at Baiæ, close to Misenum. She told him that until Tiberius's funeral was over it would be indecent to release anyone who had been imprisoned by him on a charge of treason. It would look much better if Herod, though allowed to return to his house at Rome, were to remain for a time under open arrest. So this was done. Herod went home but still had his warder with him and was expected to wear prison dress. When the official mourning for Tiberius was at an end, Caligula sent Herod a message telling him to shave and put on clean clothes and come to dine with him the next day at the Palace. Herod's troubles seemed over at last.

I do not think that I mentioned the death, three years before this, of Herod's uncle Philip: he left a widow—Salome, Herodias's daughter, reputed the most beautiful woman in the Near East. When the news of Philip's death reached Rome, Herod had immediately spoken to the freedman who was most in Tiberius's confidence where Eastern questions were concerned, and persuaded him to do something for him. The freedman was to remind Tiberius that Philip had left no children, and was to suggest that his tetrarchy of Bashan should be given to no other member of the Herod family but be temporarily attached, for administrative purposes, to the province of Syria. The freedman was on no account to remind Tiberius of the royal revenues of the tetrarchy, which amounted to one hundred and sixty thousand gold pieces a year. Should Tiberius take his advice and instruct him to write a letter informing the Governor of Syria that the tetrarchy would now pass under his jurisdiction, he was to smuggle in a postscript to the effect that the royal revenues must be allowed to accumulate until a successor to

Philip should be appointed. Herod was reserving Bashan and its revenues for his own use. So it happened that when, at the dinner to which he had invited Herod, Caligula gratefully rewarded him for his sufferings by granting him the tetrarchy complete with revenues, with the title of king thrown in too, Herod found himself very well off indeed. Caligula also called for the chain which Herod had worn in prison and gave him an exact replica of it, link for link, in the purest gold. A few days later Herod, who had not forgotten to secure the old German's release and to get the coachman condemned for perjury, deprived of his freedom and whipped nearly to death, sailed joyfully to the East to take over his new kingdom. Cypros went with him, more joyful even than he. During Herod's imprisonment she had been looking thoroughly ill and miserable, for she was the most faithful wife in the world and had even refused to eat or drink anything better than the prison rations that her husband was drawing. She stayed at the house of Herod's younger brother, Herod Pollio.

This happy pair, then, Herod and Cypros, reunited once more, and accompanied as usual by Silas, sailed to Egypt on their way to Bashan. At Alexandria they disembarked, to pay their respects to the Alabarch. Herod intended to enter the city with as little ostentation as possible, not wishing to be the cause of any disturbances between the Jews and Greeks; but the Jews were overjoyed at the visit of a Jewish king, and one so high in the Emperor's favour. They met him at the docks, many thousands strong, in holiday dress, crying "Hosanna, Hosanna!" and singing songs of rejoicing, and so escorted him to their quarter of the city, which is called "The Delta." Herod did his best to calm popular enthusiasm, but Cypros found the contrast between this arrival in Alexandria and their former one so delightful that for her sake he let many extravagances go by. The Alexandrian Greeks were angry and jealous. They dressed up in mock-royal state a well-known idiot of the city, or pretended idiot rather, Baba by name, who used to go begging around the principal squares and raising laughs and coppers by his clowning. They provided this Baba with a grotesque guard of soldiers armed with sausage swords, pork shields and pigs-head helmets and paraded him through "The Delta." The crowd shouted *Marin! Marin!* which means "King! King!" They made a demonstration outside the Alabarch's house and another outside the house of his brother Philo. Herod visited two of the leading Greeks and lodged a protest. He said no more than, "I shall not forget today's performance and I think that one day you'll regret it."

From Alexandria Herod and Cypros continued their voyage to the port of Jaffa. From Jaffa they went to Jerusalem to visit their children there and to stay in the Temple precincts as guests of the High Priest, with whom it was important for Herod to arrive at an understanding. He created an excellent impression by dedicating his iron prison chain to the Jewish God, hanging it up on the wall of the Temple Treasury. Then they passed through Samaria and the borders of Galilee—without, however, sending any complimentary message to Antipas and Herodias—and so came to their new home at Cæsarea Philippi, the lovely city built by Philip as his capital on the southern slopes of Mount Hermon. There they collected the accumulated revenues laid up for them since Philip's death. Salome, Philip's widow, made a set at Herod and tried all her most captivating arts on him, but it was no use. He told her "You are certainly very good-looking and very gracious and very witty; but you must remember the proverb: 'Move into a new house, but take the old hearth with you.' The only possible queen for Bashan is my dear Cypros."

You can imagine that when Herodias heard of Herod's good fortune she was wild with jealousy. Cypros was now a Queen, while she herself was the wife of a mere Tetrarch.

She tried to rouse Antipas into feeling the same as she did; but Antipas, an indolent old man, was perfectly satisfied with his position; though he was only a Tetrarch, he was a very rich one and it was a matter of very little importance to him by what title or titles he was known. Herodias called him a pitiful fellow—how could he expect her to have any further respect for him? "To think," she said, "that my brother, Herod Agrippa, who came here not so long ago as a penniless refugee, dependent on your charity for the very bread that he ate, and then grossly insulted us and fled to Syria, and was hounded out of Syria for corruption, and was nearly arrested at Anthedon for debt, and then went to Rome and was imprisoned for treason to the Emperor—to think that a man with such a record, a spendthrift who has left a trail of unpaid bills behind him wherever he has gone, should now be a king and in a position to insult us! It is unbearable. I insist that you go to Rome at once and force the new Emperor to give you at least equal honours with Herod."

Antipas answered: "My dear Herodias, you are not talking wisely. We are very well off here, you know, and if we tried to improve our position it might bring us bad luck. Rome has never been a safe place to visit since Augustus died."

"I won't speak to you or sleep with you again," said Herodias, "until you give me your word that you will go."

Herod heard of this scene from one of his agents at Antipas's court; and when, shortly after, Antipas started out for Rome he sent a letter to Caligula by a fast vessel, offering the captain a very large reward if he reached Rome before Antipas did. The captain cracked on as much sail as he dared and just managed to win the money. When Antipas presented himself before Caligula, Caligula already had Herod's letter in his hand. It was to the effect that Herod while staying in Jerusalem had heard grave charges against his uncle Herod Antipas, which he had not at first credited.

but which had on investigation proved true. Not only had his uncle been engaged in treasonable correspondence with Sejanus at the time that Sejanus and Livilla were plotting to usurp the monarchy—that was an old story—but he had lately been exchanging letters with the King of Parthia, planning with his help to organize a widespread revolt against Rome in the Near East. The King of Parthia had undertaken to give Samaria, Judæa and Herod's own kingdom of Bashan as a reward for his disloyalty. As a proof of this accusation Herod mentioned that Antipas had seventy thousand complete suits of armour in his palace armoury. What, otherwise, was the meaning of these secret preparations for war? His uncle's standing army numbered only a few hundred men, a mere guard of honour. The armour was certainly not intended for arming *Roman* troops.

Herod was very sly. He knew perfectly well that Antipas had no war-like intentions whatsoever and that it was merely his fondness for display that had led him to stock his armoury in this lavish style. The revenues from Galilee and Gilead were rich, and Antipas, though stingy in his hospitality, liked to spend money on costly objects: he collected suits of armour as rich men at Rome collect statues, pictures and inlaid furniture. But Herod knew that this explanation would not occur to Caligula, whom he had often told about Antipas's miserliness. So when Antipas came to the Palace and saluted Caligula, congratulating him on his accession, Caligula greeted him coldly and asked him at once: "Is it true, Tetrarch, that you have seventy thousand suits of armour in your palace armoury?" Antipas was startled and could not deny it: for Herod had been careful not to exaggerate. He muttered something about the armour being intended for his own personal pleasure.

Caligula said: "This audience is already over. Don't make feeble excuses. I shall consider what to do with you to-morrow." Antipas had to retire, abashed and anxious.

That evening Caligula asked me at dinner: "Where was it that you were born, Uncle Claudius?"

"Lyons," I answered.

"An unhealthy sort of place, isn't it?" asked Caligula, twiddling a gold wine-cup in his fingers.

"Yes," I answered. "It has the reputation of being one of the most unhealthy places in your dominions. I blame the climate of Lyons for having condemned me, while still an infant, to my present useless and inactive life."

"Yes, I thought I had once heard you say that," said Caligula. "We'll send Antipas there. The change of climate may do him good. There's too much sun in Galilee for a man of his fiery character."

Next day Caligula told Antipas that he must consider himself degraded from his rank of Tetrarch, and that a vessel was waiting at Ostia to carry him away to exile at Lyons. Antipas took the matter philosophically—exile was better than death—and I will say this much to his credit, that so far as I know, he never gave Herodias, who had accompanied him from Galilee, a word of reproach. Caligula wrote to Herod thanking him for his timely warning and awarding him Antipas's tetrarchy and revenues in recognition of his loyalty. But knowing that Herodias was Herod's sister, he told her that for her brother's sake he would allow her to keep any property of her own that she might possess and return to Galilee, if she wished, to live under his protection. Herodias was too proud to accept this and told Caligula that Antipas had always treated her very well and that she would not desert him in the hour of his need. She began a long speech intended to soften Caligula's heart, but he cut it short. Herodias and Antipas sailed together for Lyons the next morning. They never returned to Palestine.

Herod replied in terms of the most boundless gratitude for Caligula's gift. Caligula showed me the letter. "But what a man!" Herod had written. "Seventy thousand suits of armour, and all for his own personal pleasure! Two a day for nearly a hundred years! But it seems almost a pity to condemn a man like that to rot away at Lyons. You ought to send him out to invade Germany single-handed. Your father always said that the only way to deal with the Germans was to exterminate them, and here you have the perfect exterminator at your service—such a glutton for combat that he lays in a stock of seventy thousand suits of armour, all made to measure." We had a good laugh over that. Herod ended by saying that he must come back at once to Rome to thank Caligula by word of mouth: pen and paper were not sufficient to express what he felt. He would make his brother Aristobulus temporary regent in Galilee and Gilead, with Silas to keep a careful eye on him, and his youngest brother, Herod Pollio, temporary regent of Bashan.

He came back to Rome, with Cypros, and paid his creditors every penny of his debts: and went about saying that he never intended to borrow again. For the first year of Caligula's reign he had no difficulties worth mentioning. Even when Caligula quarrelled with my mother over his murder of Gemellus—from which you may be sure, Herod had not actively dissuaded him—so that, as I described in my previous story, she was forced to commit suicide, Herod was so sure of Caligula's continued trust in his loyalty that almost alone of her friends he wore mourning for her sake and attended her funeral. He felt her death pretty keenly, I believe, but the way he put it to Caligula was: "I would be a thankless wretch if I failed to pay my respects to the ghost of my benefactress. That you showed your displeasure at her grandmotherly interference in a matter which did not concern her must have affected the Lady Antonia with the profoundest grief and shame. If I felt that I had earned your displeasure by any similar behaviour—but of course the case is absurd—I should certainly do as she has done. My mourning is a tribute to her courage in leaving a mod

67

ern world which has superannuated women of her antique sort."

Caligula took this well enough and said: "No, Herod, you have done rightly. The injury she did was to me, not to you." But when his brain turned altogether as a result of his illness and he declared his divinity and began cutting off the heads of the statues of Gods and substituting his own, Herod began to grow anxious. As ruler of many thousands of Jews he foresaw trouble. The first certain signs of this trouble came from Alexandria, where his enemies, the Greeks, pressed the Governor of Egypt to insist on the erection of the Emperor's statues in Jewish synagogues as well as in Greek temples, and on the use, by Jews as well as by Greeks, of Caligula's divine name in the taking of legal oaths. The Governor of Egypt had been an enemy of Agrippina's and also a partisan of Tiberius Gemellus's, and decided that the best way to prove his loyalty to Caligula was to enforce the Imperial edict which had, as a matter of fact, been intended only for the Greeks of the city. When the Jews refused to swear by Caligula's godhead or admit his statues within the synagogues the Governor published a decree declaring all Jews in the city aliens and intruders. The Alexandrians were jubilant and began a pogrom against the Jews, driving the richer ones from other parts of the city, where they lived in style side by side with Greeks and Romans, into the crowded narrow streets of "The Delta." Over four hundred merchants' houses were sacked, and the owners murdered or maimed. Countless insults were heaped on the survivors. The loss in lives and the danger to property were so heavy that the Greeks decided to justify their action by sending an embassy to Caligula at Rome, explaining that the refusal of the Jews to worship his majesty had so outraged the younger and less disciplined Greek citizens that they had taken vengeance into their own hands. The Jews sent a counter-embassy, led by the Alabarch's brother, this

Philo, a distinguished Jew with a reputation as the best philosopher in Egypt. When Philo reached Rome he naturally called upon Herod, to whom he was now related by marriage; for Herod, after paying back the Alabarch those eight thousand gold pieces, together with interest at ten per cent for two years—greatly to the Alabarch's embarrassment, for as a Jew he could not lawfully accept interest on a loan from a fellow-Jew—had further shown his gratitude by betrothing Berenice, his eldest surviving daughter, to the Alabarch's eldest son. Philo asked Herod to intervene on his behalf with Caligula, but Herod said that he preferred to have nothing to do with the embassy: if events took a serious turn he would do what he could to mitigate the Emperor's displeasure, which he expected to be severe—and that was all that he could say at present.

Caligula listened affably to the Greek embassy, but dismissed the Jews with angry threats, as Herod had foreseen, telling them that he did not wish to hear any more talk about Augustus's promises to them of religious toleration: Augustus, he shouted, had been dead a long time now and his edicts were out of date and absurd. "I am your God, and you shall have no other Gods but me."

Philo turned to the other ambassadors and said in Hebrew: "I am glad that we came; for these words are a deliberate challenge to the Living God and now we can be sure that this fool will perish miserably." Luckily none of the courtiers understood Hebrew.

Caligula sent a letter to the Governor of Egypt informing him that the Greeks had done their duty in forcibly protesting against the Jews' disloyalty, and that if the Jews persisted in their present disobedience he would himself come with an army and exterminate them. Meanwhile, he ordered the Alabarch and all other officials of the Jewish colony to be imprisoned. He explained that but for the Alabarch's kinship with his friend Herod Agrippa he would have put him and his brother Philo to death. The only satisfaction that Herod was at present able to give the Jews in Alexandria was to have the Governor of Egypt removed. He persuaded Caligula to arrest him on the grounds of his former enmity to Agrippina (who was, of course, Caligula's mother) and banish him to one of the smaller Greek islands.

Then Herod told Caligula, who now found himself short of funds: "I must see what I can do in Palestine to raise some money for your Privy Purse. My brother Aristobulus informs me that my fire-eating old uncle Antipas was even richer than we supposed. Now that you are off on your British and German conquests—and, by the way, if you happen to pass through Lyons, please remember me very kindly to Antipas and Herodias—Rome will seem very dismal to us left-behinds. It will be a good opportunity for me to absent myself and visit my kingdom again; but as soon as I hear that you are on the way back I shall hurry home too and I hope that you will be satisfied with my efforts on your behalf." The fact was that most disquieting news had just arrived for Herod from Palestine. He sailed East on the day that Caligula had fixed on for his absurd military expedition; though as a matter of fact it was nearly a year before Caligula set out.

Caligula had given orders for his statue to be placed in the Holy of Holies in the Temple at Jerusalem, a secret inner chamber where the God of the Jews is supposed to dwell in his cedar chest and which is only visited once a year by the High Priest. His further orders were that the statue should be taken out from the Holy of Holies on days of public festival and worshipped in the outer court by the assembled congregation, Jews and non-Jews alike. He either did not know or did not care about the intense religious awe in which the Jews hold their God. When the proclamation was read at Jerusalem by the new Governor of Judæa sent to succeed Pontius Pilate (who by the way had committed suicide on his arrival at Rome) there were such extraordinary scenes of riot that the Governor was forced to take refuge in his camp outside the city, where he sustained something very like a siege. The news reached Caligula at Lyons. He was utterly enraged and sent a letter to the new Governor of Syria who had succeeded my friend Vitellius, ordering him to raise a strong force of Syrian auxiliaries and with these and the two Roman regiments under his command to march into Judæa and enforce the edict at the point of the sword. This Governor's name was Publius Petronius, a Roman soldier of the old school. He lost no time in obeying Caligula's orders, so far as his preparations for the expedition were concerned, and marched down to Acre. Here he wrote a letter to the High Priest and chief notables of the Jews informing them of his instructions and of his readiness to carry them out. Herod meanwhile had taken a hand in the game, though he kept as much in the background as possible. He secretly advised the High Priest as to the best course to follow. At his suggestion the Governor of Judæa and his garrison were sent under safe conduct to Petronius at Acre. They were followed by a delegation of some ten thousand leading Jews who came to appeal against the intended defilement of the Temple. They had come with no warlike intentions, they declared, but nevertheless would rather die than permit this terrible injury to be done to their ancestral land, which would immediately be struck by a curse and never recover. They said that they owed political allegiance to Rome and that there could be no complaints against them for disloyalty or failure to pay their taxes; but that their principal allegiance was to the God of their Fathers, Who had always preserved them in the past (so long as they had obeyed His laws) and had strictly forbidden the worship of any other Gods in His domain.

71

Petronius answered: "I am not qualified to speak on matters of religion. It may be as you say, or it may not be so. My own allegiance to the Emperor is not divided into political and religious halves. It is an unquestioning allegiance. I am his servant and shall obey his orders, come what may."

They replied: "We are the faithful servants of our Lord God and shall obey His orders, come what may."

So there was a deadlock. Petronius then moved down into Galilee. On Herod's advice no hostile act was committed against him, but although it was time for the autumn sowing the fields were left unploughed and everyone went about in mourning dress with ashes sprinkled on his head. Trade and industry were at a standstill. A new delegation met Petronius at Cæsarea (the Samarian Cæsarea), headed by Herod's brother Aristobulus, and he was told again that the Jews had no warlike intentions, but that if he persisted in carrying out the Imperial edict, no God-fearing Jew would have any further interest in life and the land would go to ruin. This put Petronius in a quandary. He wanted to ask Herod for help or advice, but Herod, realizing the insecurity of his own position, had already sailed for Rome. What could a soldier like Petronius do, a man who had always shown himself ready enough to face the fiercest enemy drawn up in line of battle or charging down on him from ambush with shouts, when these venerable old men came forward and stretched out their necks to him saying: "We offer no resistance. We are loyal tributaries to Rome, but our religious duty is to the God of our fathers by Whose laws we have lived from infancy; kill us, if it so please you, for we cannot see our God blasphemed and live"?

He made them a very honest speech. He told them that it was his duty as a Roman to keep the oath of allegiance that he had sworn the Emperor and to obey him in every particular; and they could see that with the armed forces at his disposal he was perfectly capable of fulfilling the orders that he had received. Nevertheless he praised them for their firmness and for their abstention from any act of violence. He confessed that though, in his official capacity as Governor of Syria, he knew where his duty lay, yet as a humane and reasonable man he found it next to impossible to do what he had been charged to do. It was not a Roman act to kill unarmed old men merely because they persisted in worshipping their ancestral God. He said that he would write again to Caligula and present their case in as favourable a light as possible. It was more than likely that Caligula would reward him with death, but if, by sacrificing his own life, he could save the lives of so many thousands of industrious, inoffensive provincials, he was willing to do so. He urged them to pluck up their spirits and hope for the best. The first thing to be done, once he had written the letter, which would be that very morning, was for them to renew the cultivation of their land. If they neglected this, famine would ensue, followed by banditry and pestilence, and matters would become far worse than they already were. It happened that as he was speaking storm-clouds suddenly blew up from the west and a heavy downpour began. The ordinary autumn rains had not fallen that year and it was now almost past the season for them; so this was taken as an omen of extraordinary good fortune, and the crowds of mourning Jews dispersed, singing songs of praise and joy. The rain continued to fall and soon the whole land came alive again.

Petronius kept his word. He wrote to Caligula informing him of the obstinacy of the Jews and asking him to reconsider his decision. He said that the Jews had shown themselves perfectly respectful to their Emperor, but that they insisted that a terrible curse would fall on their land if any statue whatsoever were erected in the Temple—even that of their glorious Emperor. He enlarged on their despairing refusal to cultivate the land and suggested that only two alternatives now presented themselves: the first, to erect the statue and sentence the land to ruin, which would mean an immense loss of revenue; the second, to reverse the Imperial decision and earn the undying gratitude of a noble people. He begged the Emperor at the very least to postpone the dedication of the statue until after the harvest.

But before this letter arrived at Rome Herod Agrippa had already set himself to work on the Jewish God's behalf. Caligula and he greeted each other with great affection after their long absence from each other and Herod brought with him great chests full of gold and jewels and other precious objects. Some came from his own treasury, some from that of Antipas, and the rest had, I believe, been part of an offering made him by the Jews of Alexandria. Herod invited Caligula to the most expensive banquet that had ever been given in the City: unheard-of delicacies were served, including five great pasties entirely filled with the tongues of titlarks, marvellously delicate fish brought in tanks all the way from India, and for the roast an animal like a young elephant, but hairy and of no known species—it had been found embedded in the ice of some frozen lake of the Caucasus, and brought here packed in snow by the way of Armenia, Antioch and Rhodes. Caligula was astonished by the magnificence of the table and admitted that he would never have had sufficient ingenuity to provide such a display even if he had been able to afford it. The drink was as remarkable as the food, and Caligula became so lively as the meal went on that, deprecating his own generosity to Herod in the past as something hardly worth mentioning, he now promised to give him whatever it lay in his power to grant.

"Ask me anything, my dearest Herod," he said, "and it shall be yours." He repeated: "Absolutely anything. I swear by my own Divinity that I will grant it."

Herod protested that he had not provided this banquet in

the hope of winning any favour from Caligula. He said that Caligula had done as much for him already as any prince in the world had done for any subject or ally of his in the whole panorama of history or tradition. He said that he was far more than content: he wanted absolutely nothing at all but to be allowed in some measure to show his gratitude. However, Caligula, continuing to help himself from the crystal wine-decanter, kept on pressing him: wasn't there something very special that he wanted? Some new Eastern kingdom? Chalchis, perhaps, or Iturea? Then it was his for the asking.

Herod said: "Most gracious and magnanimous and divine Cæsar, I repeat that I want nothing for myself at all. All that I can hope for is the privilege of serving you. But you have already read my mind. Nothing escapes your astonishingly quick and searching eyes. There is indeed something that I do really desire to ask, but it is a gift that will directly benefit only yourself. My reward will be an indirect one— the glory of having been your adviser."

Caligula's curiosity was excited. "Don't be afraid to ask, Herod," he said. "Haven't I sworn that I will grant it, and am I not a God of my word?"

"In that case, my one wish," said Herod, "is that you will no longer think of dedicating that statue to yourself in the Temple of Jerusalem."

A very long silence followed. I was present at this historic banquet myself and never remember having felt so uncomfortable or so excited in my life as then, waiting to see the result of Herod's boldness. What in the world would Caligula do? He had sworn by his own Divinity to grant the boon, in the presence of many witnesses; yet how could he go back on his resolution to humble this God of the Jews Who alone of all Gods in the world continued to oppose him?

At last Caligula spoke. He said, mildly, almost beseechingly as though he counted on Herod to help him out of his dilemma: "I don't understand, dearest Herod. How do you suppose the granting of this boon will benefit me?"

Herod had worked the whole thing out in detail before ever he sat down to table. He replied with seeming earnestness: "Because, Cæsar, to place your sacred statue in the Temple at Jerusalem would not redound to your own glory at all. Oh, quite to the contrary! Are you aware of the nature of the statue that is now kept in the innermost shrine of the Temple, and the rites which are performed about it on holy days? No? Then listen and you will at once understand that what you have regarded as wicked obstinacy among my co-religionists is no more than a loyal desire not to injure your Majesty. The God of the Jews, Cæsar, is an extraordinary fellow. He has been described as an anti-God. He has a rooted aversion to statues, particularly to statues of majestic bearing and dignified workmanship like those of the Greek Gods. In order to symbolize His hatred for other divinities He has ordered the erection, in this inner shrine, of a large, crude and ludicrous statue of an ass. It has long ears, huge teeth and enormous genitals, and on every holy day the priests abuse this statue with the vilest incantations and be-spatter it with the most loathsome excrement and offal and then wheel it on a carriage around the Inner Court for the whole congregation to abuse similarly; so that the whole Temple stinks like the Great Sewer. It is a secret ceremony. No non-Jews are admitted to it and the Jews themselves are not allowed to speak about it under penalty of a curse. Besides, they are ashamed. You understand everything, now, don't you? The leading Jews are afraid that if your statue were erected in the Temple it would cause profound mis-understandings; that in their religious fanaticism the common people would subject it to the gravest indignities, while thinking to honour you by their zeal. But, as I say, natural delicacy and the holy silence imposed on them has prevented them from explaining to our friend Petronius why they would rather die than allow him to put your orders into execution. It is lucky that I am here to tell you what they are unable to tell. I am only a Jew on my mother's side, so that perhaps frees me from the curse. In any case I am risking it, for your sake."

Caligula drank all this in with perfect credulity and even I was half-convinced by Herod's gravity. All that Caligula said was: "If the fools had been as frank with me as you have been, my dearest Herod, it would have saved us all a lot of trouble. You don't think that Petronius has yet carried out my orders?"

"I hope for your sake that he has not," Herod replied.

So Caligula wrote Petronius a short letter: "If you have already put my Statue into the temple as I ordered, let it stand; but see that the rites are closely supervised by armed Roman soldiers. If not, disband your army and forget about the matter. On the advice of King Herod Agrippa, I have come to the conclusion that the Temple in question is an extremely unsuitable place for my Sacred Statue to be erected."

This letter crossed with the one Petronius had written. Caligula was furious that Petronius should dare to write as he did, attempting to make him change his mind on mere grounds of humanity. He replied: "Since you appear to value the bribes of the Jews more highly than my Imperial Will, my advice to you is to kill yourself quickly and painlessly before I make such an example of you as will horrify all future ages."

As it happened, Caligula's second letter arrived late—the ship lost its mainmast between Rhodes and Cyprus and lay disabled for several days—so that the news of Caligula's death arrived at Cæsarea first. Petronius almost embraced Judaism, he was so relieved.

This ends the first part of the story of Herod Agrippa, but you shall hear the rest as I continue to tell my own.

# Chapter Five

So HERE we are back again at the point where I was being carried round the great court of the Palace on the shoulders of two corporals of the Guard, with the Household Battalion of Germans crowding about me and dedicating their assegais to my service. Eventually I prevailed on the corporals to put me down and on four Germans to fetch my sedan. They brought it and I climbed into it. I was told that they had decided to take me to the Guards Camp at the other side of the City, where I would be protected from possible attempts at assassination. I was beginning to protest again when I saw a glint of colour at the back of the crowd. A purple-sleeved arm was waving at me in a peculiar circular motion which brought back memories of my schooldays. I said to the soldiers: "I think I see King Herod Agrippa. If he wishes to speak to me, let him come through at once."

When Caligula was murdered Herod had not been far off. He had followed us out of the theatre but had been led aside by one of the conspirators, who pretended that he wished him to speak to Caligula about some favour. So Herod did not witness the actual murder. If I knew him as well as I think I did, he would certainly have saved Caligula's life by some trick or other; and now when he came upon the dead body he showed his gratitude for past favours in no uncertain terms. He embraced it, all bloody as it was, and carried it tenderly in his own arms into the Palace, where he laid it on the Imperial bed. He even sent out for surgeons. as though Caligula was not really dead and had a chance of recovery. He then left the Palace by another door and hurried round to the theatre again, where he prompted Mnester, the actor, to make his famous speech, the one which reassured the excited Germans and prevented them from massacring the audience in vengeance for their master's death. Then back he darted to the Palace. When he heard there what had happened to me he came boldly into the court to see whether he could be of any service. I must admit that the sight of Herod's crooked smile—one corner of the mouth turned up, the other down—heartened me considerably.

His first words were: "Congratulations, Cæsar, on your election: may you long enjoy the great honours that these brave soldiers have bestowed on you, and may I have the glory of being your first ally!" The soldiers cheered lustily. Then, coming close to me and clasping my hand tightly in his, he began talking earnestly in Phœnician, a language with which he knew I was acquainted because of my researches into the history of Carthage, but which none of the soldiers would understand. He gave me no opportunity of interrupting him. "Listen to me, Claudius. I know what you are feeling. I know that you don't really want to be Emperor, but for all our sakes, as well as your own, don't be a fool. Don't let slip what the Gods have given you of their own accord. I can guess what you are thinking. You have some crazy idea of yielding up your power to the Senate as soon as the soldiers let you go. That would be madness; it would be the signal for civil war. The Senate are a flock of sheep, but there are three or four wolves among them who are ready, the moment you lay down your power, to fight for it among themselves. There's Asiaticus for a start, not to mention Vinicius. They were both in the conspiracy, so they are likely to do something desperate for fear of being executed. Vinicius thinks himself a Cæsar already because of his marriage with your niece Lesbia. He'll recall her from banishment and they'll make a very strong combination. If it's not Asiaticus or Vinicius it will be someone else, probably Vinicianus. You are the only obvious Emperor for Rome and you'll have the armies solidly behind you. If you won't take on the responsibility because of some absurd prejudice it will be the ruin of everything. That's all I'll say. Think it over and keep up your spirits!" Then he turned and shouted to the soldiers, "Romans, I congratulate you too. You could not have made a wiser choice. Your new Emperor is courageous, generous, learned and just. You can trust him as completely as you trusted his glorious brother Germanicus. Don't let yourselves be fooled by the Senate or by any of your Colonels. Stick by the Emperor Claudius and he'll stick by you. The safest place for him is in your camp. I have just been advising him to pay you well for your loyalty." With these words he disappeared.

They carried me in my sedan towards their camp, going at a jog trot. As soon as one chairman showed any signs of flagging his place was taken by another. The Germans ran shouting ahead. I sat quite numb; self-possessed but never so blankly miserable in all my life before. With Herod gone the outlook seemed hopeless again. We had just reached the Sacred Way at the foot of the Palatine Hill when messengers came hurrying along it to intercept us and protest against my usurpation of the monarchy. The messengers were two "Protectors of the People." (This office was a survival from the middle days of the Republic, when the Protectors maintained the rights of the common people against the tyrannous encroachments of the nobility: their persons were inviolate and though they claimed no legislative power they had forced from the nobles the right to veto any act of the Senate which displeased them. But Augustus and his two Imperial successors had also adopted the title of "Protector of the People," with its prerogatives; so that the real ones, though they continued to be elected and to perform certain functions under Imperial direction, had lost their original importance.) It seemed clear that the Senate had chosen these messengers not only as an indication that all Rome was behind them in their protest, but also because their inviolateness of person would protect them from any hostility on the part of my men.

These Protectors, who were unknown to me personally, did not behave with conspicuous courage when we stopped to parley with them, or even dare to utter the stern message with which I afterwards learned that they had been entrusted. They called me "Cæsar," a title to which I then had no claim, not being a member of the Julian house; and said very humbly: "You will pardon us, Cæsar, but the Senate would be much obliged by your immediate attendance at the House: they are anxious to learn your intentions."

I was willing enough to go, but the Guards would not allow it. They felt only contempt for the Senate and, now that they had chosen an Emperor of their own, were resolved not to let him out of their sight, and to resist every attempt on the part of the Senate either to restore the Republic or to appoint a rival Emperor. Angry shouts arose, "Clear off, d'ye hear?" "Tell the Senate to mind their own business and we'll mind ours." "We won't allow our new Emperor to be murdered too." I leaned through the window of my sedan and said: "Pray give my respectful compliments to the Senate and inform them that for the present I am unable to comply with their gracious invitation. I have a prior one. I am being carried off by the sergeants, corporals and private soldiers of the Palace Guard to enjoy their hospitality at the Guards Camp. It is as much as my life is worth to insult this devoted soldiery."

So away we went again. "What a wag our new Emperor is!" they roared. When we reached the Camp I was greeted with greater enthusiasm than ever. The Guards Division consisted of some twelve thousand infantrymen besides the attached cavalry. It was not only the corporals and sergeants who now acclaimed me Emperor, but the captains and colonels too. I discouraged them as much as I could while thanking them for their goodwill. I said that I could not consent to become their Emperor until I had been so appointed by the Senate, in whose hands the election rested. I was conveyed to Headquarters, where I was treated with a deference to which I was wholly unaccustomed, but found myself virtually a prisoner.

As for the assassins, as soon as they made sure of Caligula and escaped from the pursuing Germans, and from Caligula's chairmen and yeomen who also came hurrying up with cries of vengeance, they had run down to Vinicius's house, which was not far from the Market Place. Here were waiting the colonels of the three City Battalions, who were the only regular troops stationed in Rome besides the Watchmen and the Imperial Guards. These colonels had not taken any active part in the conspiracy but had promised to put their forces at the disposal of the Senate as soon as Caligula was dead and the Republic restored. Cassius now insisted that someone must go at once and kill Cæsonia and myself: we were too closely related to Caligula to be allowed to survive him. A colonel called Lupus volunteered for the task; he was a brother-in-law of the Guards Commander. He came up to the Palace and, striding sword in hand through many deserted rooms, finally reached the Imperial bedchamber where Caligula's body was lying, bloody and frightful, just as Herod had left it. But Cæsonia was now sitting on the bed with the head on her lap and little Drusilla, Caligula's only child, was at her knees. As Lupus entered Cæsonia was wailing to the corpse, "Husband, husband, you should have listened to my advice." When she saw Lupus's sword she looked up anxiously into his face and knew that she was doomed. She stretched her neck. "Strike clean," she said. "Don't bungle it like the other assassins did." Cæsonia was no coward. He struck and the head fell. He then caught up the little brat who came rushing at him, biting and scratching. He held her by the feet, swung her head against a marble pillar, and so dashed out her brains. It is always unpleasant to hear of the murder of a child: but the reader must take my word for it that if he too had known little Drusilla, her father's pet, he would have longed to do to her precisely what Lupus did.

There has been a great deal of argument since about the meaning of Cæsonia's address to the corpse, which certainly was ambiguous. Some say that what she meant was that Caligula should have listened to some advice that she had given him about killing Cassius, whose intentions she suspected, before he had time to put them in effect. The people who explain it in this way are those who blame Cæsonia for Caligula's madness, saying that it was she who first disordered his wits by giving him the love-philtre which bound him to her so entirely. Others hold, and I must say that I agree with them, that she meant that she had advised Caligula to mitigate what he was pleased to call his "immovable rigour" and behave more like a humane and sensible mortal.

Lupus then came in search of me, to complete his task. But by this time the shouts "Long live the Emperor Claudius" were just beginning. He stood in the doorway of the hall where the meeting was being held, but when he saw how popular I had become he lost courage and stole quietly away.

In the Market Place the excited crowds could not decide whether to cheer themselves hoarse in honour of the assassins or howl themselves hoarse in demands for their blood. A rumour ran about that Caligula had not really been murdered at all, that the whole business was an elaborate hoax stage-managed by himself, and that he was only waiting for them to express joy at his death before beginning a general massacre. That was what he had meant, it was said, by his

83

promise to exhibit an entirely new spectacle that night, to be called *Death, Destruction and the Mysteries of Hell.* Caution prevailed and they had begun to bawl loyally, "Search out the murderers! Avenge our glorious Cæsar's death!" when Asiaticus, an ex-Consul, who was a man of imposing figure and one who had been in Caligula's close confidence, climbed up on the Oration Platform and exclaimed: "You are looking for the assassins? So am I. I want to congratulate them. I only wish I had struck a blow myself. Caligula was a vile creature and they acted nobly in killing him. Don't be idiots, men of Rome! You all hated Caligula, and now that he is dead you will be able to breathe freely again. Go back to your homes and celebrate his death with wine and song!"

Three or four companies of City troops were drawn up close by and Asiaticus said to them: "We are counting on you soldiers to keep the peace. The Senate is supreme once more. Once more we are a Republic. Obey the Senate's orders and I give you my word that every man of you will be considerably richer by the time things have settled down again. There must be no plundering or rioting. Any offence against life or property will be punished by death." So the people changed their tune at once and begun cheering the assassins and the Senate and Asiaticus himself.

From Vinicius's house those of the conspirators who were senators were proceeding to the Senate House, where the Consuls had hastily called a meeting, when Lupus came running down from the Palatine Hill with the news that the Guards had acclaimed me Emperor and were hurrying me off to their camp. So they sent me a threatening message by two Protectors of the People, whom they mounted on cavalry horses and told to overtake me. They were to deliver the message as if from the Senate in session: I have already related how, when it came to the point, the threat lost most of its force. The other conspirators, the Guards officers, headed by Cassius, then seized the Citadel on the Capitoline Hill, manning it with one of the City Battalions.

I should like to have been an eye-witness of that historic meeting of the Senate, to which crowded not only all the senators but a large number of knights and others who had no business to be there. As soon as news came of the successful seizure of the Citadel they all left the Senate House and moved up to the Temple of Jove, near by, thinking it a safer place. But the excuse they gave themselves was that the official designation of the Senate House was "The Julian Building" and that free men should not meet in a place dedicated to the dynasty from whose tyranny they had now at last so happily escaped. When they were comfortably settled in their new quarters everyone began speaking at once. Some senators cried out that the memory of the Cæsars should be utterly abolished, their statues broken and their temples destroyed. But the Consuls rose and pleaded for order. "One thing at a time, my Lords," they said. "One thing at a time." They called on a Senator named Sentius to make a speech—because he always had one ready in his head and was a loud and persuasive orator. They hoped that once somebody began speaking in proper form instead of exchanging random shouts and congratulations and arguments with neighbours, the House would soon settle down to business.

Sentius spoke. "My Lords," he said, "this is wellnigh incredible! Do you realize that we are free at last, no longer slaves to the madness of a tyrant? Oh, I trust that your hearts are all beating as strongly and proudly as mine, though how long this blessed condition will last, who will dare to prophesy? At all events let us enjoy it while we can, and let us be happy. It is nearly a hundred years now since it was possible to announce in this ancient and glorious city, 'We are free', so of course neither you nor I can recall what it felt like in the old days to utter those splendid words, but certainly at the present moment my soul is as buoyant as a cork. How happy are the decrepit old men who at the end of a long life of slavery can breath their last breath to-day with that sweet phrase on their lips—'We are free'! How instructive, too, for the young men, to whom freedom is but a name, to know what it means when they hear the glad universal cry go up: 'We are free'! But, my Lords and gentlemen, we must remember that virtue alone can preserve liberty. The mischief of tyranny is that it discourages virtue. Tyranny teaches flattery and base fear. Under a tyranny we are straws upon the wind of caprice. The first of our tyrants was Julius Cæsar. Since his reign there has been no sort of misery which we have not experienced. For there has been a steady decline since Julius in the quality of the Emperors who have been chosen to rule over us. Each has named as his successor a man a little worse than himself. These Emperors have hated virtue with a malignant hatred. The worst of them all was this Gaius Caligula—may his ghost suffer torment!—the enemy both of men and Gods. Once a tyrant does an injury to a man, that man is suspected of harbouring resentment even if he gives no sign of it. A criminal charge is trumped up against him and he is condemned without hope of reprieve. That happened to my own brother-in-law, a very worthy, honest knight. But now, I repeat, we are free. Now we are only accountable each to the other. Once more this is a House of frank speech and frank discussion. Let us confess it, we are cowards, we have lived like slaves, we have heard of intolerable calamities striking at our neighbours, but so long as they have not struck us we have kept mute. My Lords, let us decree the greatest honours in our power to the tyrannicides, especially to Cassius Chærea who has been prime mover in the whole heroic affair. His name should be made more glorious even than that of Brutus who killed Julius Cæsar, or Cassius's namesake who stood by this Brutus and also struck a blow; for Brutus and Cassius by their action began a civil war which plunged the country into the deepest degradation and misery. Whereas Cassius Chærea's action can lead to no such calamity. He has placed himself like a true Roman at the disposal of the Senate and has made us a gift of the precious freedom that has been so long, ah, so long, denied us."

This puerile speech was applauded vociferously. Somehow nobody considered that Sentius had been one of Caligula's most notorious flatterers and had even earned the nickname of "The Lap-dog." But the senator sitting next to him suddenly noticed that he was wearing on his finger a gold ring with an enormous cameo portrait of Caligula in coloured glass on it. This senator was another former lap-dog of Caligula's, but, anxious to excel in republican virtuousness, he snatched the ring off Sentius's finger and dashed it to the floor. Everyone joined in stamping it to bits. This energetic scene was interrupted by the entry of Cassius Chærea. He was accompanied by Aquila, "The Tiger," two other Guards officers who had been among the assassins, and Lupus. On entering the Senate Cassius did not waste a single glance on the crowded benches of cheering senators and knights, but marched straight up to the two Consuls and saluted. "What is the watchword to-day?" he asked. The jubilant Senate felt this as the greatest moment of their lives. Under the Republic the consuls had been joint commanders-in-chief of the forces, unless there happened to be a dictator appointed who took precedence over them; but it had now been over eighty years since they had given out the watchword of the day. The Senior Consul, another of the lap-dog breed, puffed himself up and replied: "The watchword, Colonel, is *Liberty*."

It was ten minutes before the cheers had died down sufficiently for the voice of the Consul to be heard again. He then rose, in some agitation, to announce that the messengers had returned that had been sent to me in the Senate's name: they reported that I had expressed myself unable to obey their summons, and had explained that I was being forcibly taken away to the Guards Camp. This news caused consternation and confusion among the benches, and a ragged debate followed, the conclusion of which was that my friend Vitellius suggested sending for King Herod Agrippa: Herod, being an outsider, but in close touch with political currents in Rome, and a man of great reputation both in the West and the East, might be able to give them seasonable advice. Someone seconded Vitellius, pointing out that Herod was known to have a strong influence over me, that he was respected by the Imperial Guards and that at the same time he had always been well-disposed towards the Senate, among whom he had numerous personal friends. So a messenger was sent to beg Herod to attend as soon as possible. I believe that Herod had arranged for this invitation, but I cannot be sure. At all events he did not show himself either too ready to go or too slack in going. He sent a servant downstairs from his bedroom to tell the messenger that he would be ready in a few minutes, but that at the moment he must be excused, as he was in a state of dishabille. Presently he came down smelling very strongly of a peculiar Oriental scent called patchouli, which was a standing joke at the Palace: it was supposed to have an irresistible effect on Cypros. Caligula, whenever he smelt it on Herod, used to sniff loudly and say: "Herod, you uxorious old man! How well you advertise your marital secrets!" Herod, you understand, did not wish it to be known that he had spent so long on the Palatine Hill, or they might suspect that he had been taking sides. He had, in fact, left the Palace disguised as a servant, mixed with the crowd in the Market Place and only just reached home when the message came for him. He used the scent as an alibi, and it seems to have been accepted. When he arrived at the Temple the Consuls explained the position to him and he pretended to be surprised to hear that I had been acclaimed Emperor, and made a lengthy protestation as to his absolute neutrality in City politics. He was merely an allied king and the trusted friend of Rome, and so he would remain, by their leave, whatever her government. "Nevertheless," he said, "since you appear to be in need of my advice I am prepared to speak frankly. The republican form of government appears to me in certain circumstances a most estimable thing. I would say the same of a benignant monarchy. Nobody can, in my opinion, make a hard-and-fast pronouncement that one form of government is essentially better than another. The suitability of each form depends on the temper of the people, the capacity of the ruler or rulers, the geographical extent of the State, and so on. Only one general rule can be made, and it is this: No sensible man would give *that*" (here he gave a contemptuous snap with his fingers) "for any government, whether democratic, plutocratic, aristocratic, or autocratic, that cannot count on the loyal support of the armed forces of the State over which it pretends to rule. And so, my Lords, before I begin to offer you any practical advice I must ask you a question. My question is: *Have you the army behind you?*"

It was Vinicius who jumped up to answer him. "King Herod," he cried, "the City Battalions are loyal to a man. You see their three colonels here among us to-night. We have great stores of weapons too and vast supplies of money with which to pay any further forces that we may require to raise. There are many of us here who could enlist a double company of troops from our own household slaves, and would gladly give them their liberty on their undertaking to fight for the Republic."

Herod ostentatiously covered his mouth so that they should see that he was trying not to laugh. "My friend Lord Vinicius," he said, "my advice is, *don't you try it!* What sort of a show do you think your porters and bakers and bath-attendants would make against the Guards, the best troops in the Empire? I mention the Guards because if they had been on your side you would certainly have told me about it. If you think that you can make a slave into a soldier by tying a breastplate on him, putting a spear in his hand, hanging a sword round his middle and saying: 'Now, fight, my boy!'— well, I repeat, *don't you try it!*" Then he addressed the Senate again as a whole. "My Lords," he said, "you tell me that the Guards have acclaimed as Emperor my friend Tiberius Claudius Drusus Nero Germanicus, the ex-Consul, but without first asking your consent. And I gather that the Guards have shown some hesitation in allowing him to obey your summons to attend this House. But I also gather that the message that was sent him did not emanate from you as a body but from an unofficial caucus of some two or three senators; and that only a small party of excited soldiers— no officers among them—were in attendance on Tiberius Claudius when it was delivered. Perhaps if another delegation were now sent to him, with proper authority, the officers at the Guards Camp would advise him to treat it with the respect that it deserves and would check the holiday spirit of the men under their command. I suggest that the same two Protectors of the People should be sent again, and I am ready, if you desire, to go with them and add my voice to theirs—in a quiet disinterested way, of course. I believe that I have sufficient influence with my friend Tiberius Claudius, whom I have known from boyhood—we studied under the same venerable tutor—and sufficient interest with the officers at the Camp—I am a frequent guest at their mess-table—and certainly, let me assure you, my Lords, I have sufficient eagerness for your good opinion, to be able to settle matters to the satisfaction of all parties concerned.

So at about four o'clock that afternoon, as I was eating my long-delayed luncheon in the Colonel's Mess at the Guards Camp, with every movement that I made silently, closely, though respectfully watched by my companions, a captain came in with the news that a delegation had arrived from the Senate and that King Herod Agrippa, who was here too, wished to speak to me privately beforehand.

"Bring King Herod in here," said the Senior Colonel. "He's our friend."

Presently Herod entered. He greeted each of the Colonels by name and slapped one or two of them on the back and then came over to me and made me a most formal obeisance.

"May I speak to you in private, Cæsar?" he asked, grinning.

I was disconcerted at being addressed as Cæsar and asked him to call me by my proper name.

"Well, if *you're* not Cæsar, I don't know who else is," Herod answered, and the whole room laughed with him. He turned round. "My gallant friends," he said, "I thank you. But if you had been present at the meeting of the Senate this afternoon you really would have had something worth laughing at. I have never seen such a mob of infatuated enthusiasts in my life. Do you know what they think? They actually think that they are going to start a civil war and challenge you Guards to a pitched battle, with no one to help them but the City Battalions, and perhaps a Watchman or two, and their own household slaves masquerading as soldiers, under the command of sword-fighters from the amphitheatre! That's rich, eh? As a matter of fact, what I have come to tell the Emperor I can say in front of you all. They have now sent him a delegation of Protectors of the People, because, you see, there is not a single one of their own number who dares come himself: the Emperor is going to be asked to submit himself to the Senate's authority, and if he doesn't, why then they'll make him. What do you think of *that*? I came along with them after promising the Senate that I'd give the Emperor a few words of disinterested advice. I am now going to keep my promise." He turned sharply round again and addressed me. "Cæsar, my advice is, be rough with them! Stamp on the worms and watch them wriggle."

I said stiffly: "My friend King Herod, you seem to forget

that I am a Roman and that the powers even of an Emperor depend constitutionally on the will of the Senate. If the Senate sends me a message which I am able to answer politely and submissively I shall not fail to do so."

"Have it your own way," Herod answered with a shrug, "but they won't treat you any the better for it. Constitutionally, eh? I must bow of course to your superior anthority as an antiquarian, but has the word 'constitution' any practical meaning to-day?"

Then the two Protectors were admitted. They repeated what the Senate had asked them to say, in a mechanical and unpersuasive duet. I was desired to do nothing by violence, but to yield without further hesitation to the power of the Senate. I was reminded of the dangers that they and I had escaped under the late Emperor and begged to commit no act that could be a cause of fresh public disasters.

The sentence about the dangers that they and I had escaped under Caligula was repeated three times in all, because first one of them made a mistake, and then the other went to his rescue, and then the first one said it all over again. I said rather testily: "Yes, that verse occurred once before, I think," and quoted the Homeric tag that is found so often in the *Odyssey*:

"Glad from death's peril to have won scot-free—
Our comrades not so fortunate as we."

Herod was delighted with this. He recited comically: "Our comrades not so fortunate as we," and then whispered to the Colonels: "That's the point. All that they really care about is their own dirty hides."

The Protectors of the People grew flustered and went on gobbling their message like a brace of ducks. If I resigned the supreme power that had been unconstitutionally awarded me, they said, the Senate promised to vote me the greatest honours that a free people could bestow. But, I must place myself unreservedly in their hands. If, on the contrary, I acted foolishly and persisted in my refusal to attend the House, I would have the armed forces of the City sent against me, and once I was captured I need expect no mercy.

The Colonels crowded round the two Protectors with such threatening looks and mutterings that they hastily explained that they were only repeating what had been put into their mouths by the Senate, and that personally they wished to assure me that I was the only proper person, in their opinion, to rule the Empire. They begged us to remember that in their quality both as ambassadors of the Senate and as Protectors of the People their persons were inviolate, and not to do them any indignity. Then they said: "And the Consuls privately gave us a second message that we were to give you in case our first doesn't please you."

I wondered what this second message could be.

"Cæsar," they answered, "we were ordered to tell you that if you *do* want the monarchy you must accept it as the Senate's gift and not as the gift of the Guards."

That made me laugh outright: it was the first time that I had so much as smiled since Caligula's assassination. I asked, "Is that all, or is there a third message in case I don't like the second?"

"No, there is nothing more, Cæsar," they answered humbly.

"Well," I said, still much amused, "tell the Senate that I don't blame them for not wanting another Emperor. The last one somehow lacked the gift of endearing himself to his people. But, on the other hand, the Imperial Guards insist on making me Emperor, and the officers have already sworn their allegiance to me and forced me to accept it—so what can I do? You may carry the Senate my respectful compliments and tell them that I shall do nothing unconstitutional"—here I looked defiantly at Herod—"and that they can trust me not to deceive them. I acknowledge their authority, but at the same time I must remind them that I am in no position to oppose the wishes of my military advisers."

So the Protectors were dismissed, and very glad they were to get away alive. Herod said: "That was all right, but you would have done much better to have spoken firmly, as I suggested. You are only delaying matters."

When Herod had gone the Colonels told me that they expected me to pay every Guardsman one hundred and fifty gold pieces as a bounty on my accession, and five hundred gold pieces each to the Captains. As to what I should pay the Colonels, I could please myself. "Would you be satisfied with ten thousand apiece?" I joked. We agreed on two thousand and then they asked me to appoint one of themselves in the place of Caligula's Commander, who had taken part in the conspiracy and was now apparently attending the meeting of the Senate.

"Choose whomever you like," I said, indifferently.

So they chose the Senior Colonel, who was called Rufrius Pollius. Then I had to go out and make an announcement about the bounty from the tribunal platform and receive the oaths of allegiance from each company of soldiers in turn. I was also asked to announce that the same bounty would be paid to the regiments stationed on the Rhine, in the Balkans, in Syria, in Africa, and in all other parts of the Empire. I was the more willing to do this because I knew that there were arrears of pay owing everywhere, except among the Rhine troops, whom Caligula had paid with the money stolen from the French. The swearing of allegiance took hours, for every man had to repeat the oath and there were twelve thousand of them; and then the City Watchmen came into the camp and insisted on doing the same, and then the sailors of the Imperial Navy came crowding up from Ostia. It seemed endless.

When the Senate received my message they adjourned

until midnight. The motion for adjournment was made by Sentius and seconded by the senator who had pulled the ring off his finger. As soon as it was voted they hurried out and back to their houses, where they packed up a few belongings and drove out of the City to their country estates: they realized the insecurity of their position. Midnight came and the Senate met, but what a thin House it was! Hardly a hundred members were present and even these were in a panic. The officers of the City Battalions were present, however, and as soon as proceedings opened bluntly asked the Senate to give them an Emperor. It was the only hope for the City, they said.

Herod was quite right: the man who first offered himself as Emperor was Vinicius. He seemed to have a few supporters, including his rat-like cousin Vinicianus, but not many, and he was snubbed by the Consuls. They did not even put the motion to the House that the monarchy should be offered to him. As Herod had also foreseen, Asiaticus then came forward as a candidate. But Vinicius rose and asked whether anyone present took the suggestion seriously. A wrangle followed and blows were exchanged. Vinicianus came off with a bloody nose and had to lie down until the flow ceased. The Consuls had difficulty in restoring order. Then news was brought that the Watchmen and Sailors had joined the Guards at the Camp, and the sword-fighters too (I forgot just now to mention the sword-fighters); so Vinicius and Asiaticus both withdrew their candidatures. Nobody else came forward. The meeting broke up into small groups talking anxiously together in whispers. At dawn Cassius Chærea, Aquila, Lupus and The Tiger entered. Cassius attempted to speak. He began by referring to the splendid restoration of the Republic. At this there were angry shouts from the officers of the City Battalions.

"Forget about the Republic, Cassius. We've decided now to have an Emperor, and if the Consuls don't give us one pretty soon, and a good one too, that's the last they'll see of us. We'll go to the Camp and join Claudius."

One of the Consuls said nervously, looking to Cassius for support: "No, we're not quite agreed yet about appointing an Emperor. Our last resolution—carried unanimously—was that the Republic was now restored. Cassius didn't kill Caligula merely for the sake of a change of Emperors—did you, Cassius?—but because he wished to give us back our ancient liberties."

Cassius sprang to his feet, white with passion, and cried: "Romans, I for one refuse to tolerate another Emperor. If another Emperor were appointed I should not hesitate to do to him as I did to Gaius Caligula."

"Don't talk nonsense," the City officers told him. "There's no harm in an Emperor, if he's a good one. We were all very well off under Augustus."

Cassius said, "*I'll* give you a good Emperor, then, if you promise to bring me the watchword from him—I'll give you Eutychus." You may remember that Eutychus was one of Caligula's "Scouts." He was the best charioteer in Rome and drove for the Leek Green faction in the Circus. Cassius was reminding them of the fatigues that Caligula had forced the City troops to do for him, such as building stables for his race-horses and cleaning them out when they were in use, under Eutychus's fussy and arrogant supervision. "I suppose you enjoy going down on your knees and scrubbing the muck from a stable floor at the orders of an Emperor's favourite charioteer?"

One of the Colonels sneered: "You talk very big, Cassius, but you're afraid of Claudius, none the less. Admit it."

"*I* afraid of Claudius?" Cassius shouted. "If the Senate told me to go to the Camp and bring his head back, I'd cheerfully do so. I can't understand you people. It amazes me that after having been ruled for four years by a madman you should be ready to commit the government to an idiot."

But Cassius could not convince the officers. They left the Senate without another word, assembled their men in the Market Place under the company banners and marched out to the Camp to swear allegiance to me. The Senate, or what remained of the Senate, was now left alone and unprotected. Everyone, I am told, began reproaching his neighbours and all pretence of devotion to the failing Republican cause vanished. If a single man of them had shown himself courageous it would have been something: I would have felt less ashamed of my country. I had long suspected the veracity of certain of the heroic legends of ancient Rome related by the historian Livy, and on hearing of this scene in the Senate I even began to have doubts about my favourite passage, the one describing the fortitude of the senators of old after the disaster of the River Allia when the Celts were advancing on the City and all hope of defending the walls was gone. Livy tells how the young men of military age, with their wives and children, withdrew into the Citadel after getting in a store of arms and provisions, resolved to hold out to the last. But the old men, who could be only an encumbrance to the besieged, remained behind and awaited death, wearing senatorial robes and seated in chairs of office in the porticoes of their houses, their ivory rods of office grasped firmly in their hands. When I was a boy, old Athenodorus made me memorize all this and I have never forgotten it:

"The halls of the patricians stood open and the invaders gazed with feelings of true awe upon the seated figures in the porticoes, impressed not only by the super-human magnificence of their apparel and trappings but also by their majestic bearing and the serene expression that their countenances wore: they seemed very Gods. So they stood marvelling, as at so many divine statues, until, as the legend tells, one of them began gently to stroke the beard of a patrician, by name Marcus Papirius—beards in those days were universally worn long—who rose and smote him on the head with his ivory staff. Admiration yielded to passion and Marcus Papirius was the first patrician to meet his death. The rest were butchered still seated in their chairs."

Certainly Livy was a fine writer. He wrote to persuade men to virtue by his inspiring, though unhistorical, tales of Rome's greatness in times past. But no, he had not been particularly successful in his persuasions, I reflected.

Even Cassius, Lupus and The Tiger were quarrelling now. The Tiger swore that he would rather kill himself than consent to salute me as Emperor and see slavery return.

Cassius said, "You don't mean what you say; and it's not yet time to talk like that."

The Tiger shouted angrily: "You too, Cassius Chærea? Are you going to fail us now? You love your life too well, I think. You claim that you planned the whole assassination, but who struck the first blow—you or I?"

"I did," said Cassius promptly, "and I struck him from in front, not from behind. As for loving my life, who but a fool doesn't? I am certainly not going to lay it down unnecessarily. If I had followed Varus's example that day in the Teutoburger forest, more than thirty years ago—if I had killed myself because all hope seemed gone, who would have brought the eighty survivors back and held the Germans in play until Tiberius arrived with his army of relief? No, I loved life that day. And now it is quite possible that Claudius will decide, after all, to resign the monarchy. His answer was quite consistent with such an intention: he's idiot enough for anything, and as nervous as a cat. Until I know definitely that he is not going to do so I shall continue to live."

By this time the Senate had dissolved, and Cassius, Lupus and The Tiger were left arguing in the deserted vestibule. When Cassius looked round and saw that they were alone he burst into a cackle of laughter.

"It's absurd for us, of all people, to quarrel," he said. "Tiger, let's have some breakfast. You too, Lupus! Come on, you Lupus!"

I was having breakfast too, after only an hour or so of uninterrupted sleep, when I was informed that the Consuls and the die-hard Republican senators who had attended the midnight meeting had now arrived in Camp to pay their homage to me and offer their congratulations. The Colonels showed their satisfaction with an ironical "They have come too early: let them wait." Sleeplessness had made me very irritable. I said that, for my part, I was in no mood to receive them: I liked men who clung courageously to their opinions. I tried to dismiss the senators from my mind and went on eating my breakfast. But Herod, who seemed to be everywhere at once throughout those two eventful days, saved their lives. The Germans, who were drunk and quarrelsome, had caught up their assegais and were on the point of killing them, and they were down on their knees yelling for mercy. The Guards made no attempt to interfere; Herod had to use my name to bring the Germans to their senses. He came into the breakfast-room as soon as he had put the rescued senators into a place of safety and said in a bantering voice: "Excuse me, Cæsar, but I didn't expect you to take my advice about stamping on the Senate quite so seriously. You must treat the poor fellows with more gentleness. If any mischief happens to them, where are you going to rake up such a marvellously subservient crew again?"

It was becoming increasingly difficult for me now to sustain my Republican convictions. What a farcical situation— myself, the only true antimonarchist, forced to act as monarch! On Herod's advice I summoned the Senate to meet me at the Palace. The officers made no difficulty about my leaving Camp. The whole Guards Division came with me as escort, nine battalions marching ahead of me and three marching in the rear, followed by the rest of my troops, the Palace guard being in the van. Then a most embarrassing incident occurred. Cassius and The Tiger, having had their breakfast, joined the parade and put themselves at the head of the Palace Guard with Lupus between them. I knew nothing about this myself because the vanguard was far out of sight of my sedan. The Palace Guard, accustomed to obey Cassius and The Tiger, concluded that they were acting under the orders of Rufrius, the new Guards Commander, though as a matter of fact Rufrius had sent these two a message informing them that they were deprived of their command. The spectators were mystified and when they understood that the two were acting in deliberate disobedience of orders they made a scandal of it. One of the Protectors of the People came running down the column to inform me what was happening. I did not in the least know what to say or do. But I could not let this act of bravado pass unnoticed: they were defying Rufrius's orders and my authority too.

When we reached the Palace I asked Herod and Vitellius and Rufrius and Messalina (who greeted me with the greatest delight) to consult with me at once as to what action I should take. The troops were drawn up outside the Palace—Cassius, Lupus and The Tiger still with them, speaking together in loud, confident tones but shunned by all the other officers. I opened the consultation by remarking that although Caligula had been my nephew and although I had promised his father, my dear brother Germanicus, to care for and protect him, I could not find it in me to blame Cassius for the murder. Caligula had invited assassination in a thousand ways. I said, too, that Cassius had a military record unequalled by that of any other officer in the Army, and that if I could be sure that he had struck the blow from such lofty motives as had, for example, animated the second Brutus, I would be very ready to pardon him. But what really had been his motives?

Rufrius spoke first. "Cassius says now that he struck the blow in the name of Liberty, but the fact is that what encouraged him to strike the blow was an injury to his own dignity—Caligula's constant teasing of him by giving him comic and indecent watchwords."

Vitellius said: "And if it had been a sudden strong resentment that overcame him some excuse could be made, but the conspiracy was planned days and even months beforehand. The murder was done in cold blood."

Messalina said: "And are you forgetting that it was not an ordinary murder that he committed, but a breach of his most solemn oath of unquestioning loyalty to his Emperor? For this he has no right to be allowed to live. If he were an honest man he would now already have fallen on his own sword."

Herod said: "And are you forgetting that Cassius sent Lupus to murder you, and the Lady Messalina too? If you let him go free the City will conclude that you are afraid of him."

I sent for Cassius and said to him: "Cassius Chærea, you are a man accustomed to obey orders. I am now your Commander-in-Chief, whether I like it or not; and you must obey my orders, whether you like them or not. My decision is as follows: If you had done as Brutus did, killing a tyrant for the common good although you loved him personally, I should have applauded you; though I should have expected you, since you had broken your solemn oath of fidelity by that act, to die by your own hand. But you planned the murder (and carried it out boldly where others hung back), because of feelings of personal resentment; and such motives cannot earn my praise. Moreover, I understand that on no authority but your own you sent Lupus to murder the Lady Cæsonia and my wife the Lady Messalina and myself too, if he could find me; and for that reason I shall not grant you the privilege of suicide. I shall have you executed like a common criminal. It grieves me to do this, believe me. You have called me an idiot before the Senate and have told your friends that I deserve no mercy from their swords. It may be that you are right. But fool or no fool, I wish now to pay a tribute to your great services to Rome in the past. It was you who saved the Rhine bridges after the defeat of Varus, and my dear brother once commended you to me in a letter as the finest soldier serving under his command. I only wish that this story could have had a happier ending. I have no more to say. Good-bye."

Cassius saluted without a word and was marched out to his death. I also gave orders for Lupus's execution. It was a very cold day and Lupus, who had put off his military cloak so as not to get it blood-stained, began to shiver and complain of the cold. Cassius was ashamed for Lupus and said reprovingly, "A wolf should never complain of the cold." (Lupus is the Latin for wolf.) But Lupus was weeping and seemed not to hear him. Cassius asked the soldier who was to act as executioner whether he had had any previous practice in that trade.

"No," replied the soldier, "but I was a butcher in civil life."

Cassius laughed and said: "That is very well. And now will you do me the favour of using my own sword on me? It is the one with which I killed Caligula."

He was dispatched at a single stroke. Lupus was not so fortunate: when he was ordered to stretch out his neck he did so timorously and then flinched at the blow, which caught him on the forehead. The executioner had to strike several times before he could finish him.

As for The Tiger, Aquila, Vinicius and the rest of the assassins, I took no vengeance on them. They benefited from the amnesty which, on the arrival of the Senate at the Palace, I immediately proclaimed for all words spoken and deeds done on that day and on the day preceding. I undertook to restore Aquila and The Tiger to their commands, provided that they took the oath of allegiance to me, but I gave the former Commander of the Guards another appointment, for Rufrius was too good a man to lose in that capacity. Here I must pay a tribute to The Tiger, as a man of his word. He had sworn to Cassius and Lupus that he would rather die than salute me Emperor, and now that they were executed he felt a debt of honour to their ghosts. He bravely killed himself just before their funeral pyre was lighted, and his body was burned with theirs.

# Chapter Six

THERE were so many things to be done in the process of cleaning up the mess that Caligula had left behind him —nearly four years of misrule—that it makes my head swim even now to think of it. Indeed, the chief argument by which I justified to myself my failure to do what I had intended, namely, to resign the monarchy as soon as the excitement aroused by Caligula's assassination had died down, was that the mess was such a complete mess; I knew of nobody in Rome, besides myself, who would have the patience, even if he had the authority, to undertake the hard and thankless work that the cleaning-up process demanded. I could not with a clear conscience hand the responsibility over to the Consuls. Consuls, even the best of them, are incapable of planning a gradual reconstructive programme to be carried out over a course of five or ten years. They cannot think beyond their single twelve months of office. They always either aim at immediate splendid results, forcing things too quickly, or else do nothing at all. This was a task for a dictator appointed for a term of years. But even if a dictator with the proper qualities could be found, could he be trusted not to consolidate his position by adopting the name of Cæsar and turning despot?

I remembered with dull resentment the beautifully clean start that Caligula had been given: well-filled Treasury and Privy Purse, capable and trustworthy advisers, the goodwill of the entire nation. Well, the best choice of many evils was to remain in power myself, for a time at least, hoping to be relieved as soon as possible. I could trust myself better than

I could trust others. I would concentrate on the work before me and shake things into some sort of order before proving that my Republican principles were real principles and not just talk as they were with Sentius and men of his kind. Meanwhile I would remain as un-Emperor-like as possible. But the problem of what titles I should temporarily allow myself to be voted arose at once. Without titles that carry with them the necessary authority to act, nobody can go very far. I would accept what was necessary. And I would find assistants somewhere, probably more among Greek clerks and enterprising City business men than among members of the Senate. There is a neat Latin proverb, "Olera olla legit," which means "The pot finds its own herbs." I would manage somehow.

The Senate wanted to vote me every title of honour that had ever been held by my predecessors, just to show me how thoroughly they regretted their Republican fervour. I refused as many as I could. I did accept the name of Cæsar, to which I had a right in a way, because I was of the blood of the Cæsars through my grandmother Octavia, Augustus's sister, and no true Cæsars were left. I accepted it because of the prestige that the name carried with foreign peoples like the Armenians, Parthians, Germans and Moroccans. If they had thought that I was a usurper founding a new dynasty they would have been encouraged to make trouble on the frontier. I also accepted the title of Protector of the People, which made my person inviolate and gave me the right to veto decrees of the Senate. This inviolacy of person was important to me because I proposed to annul all laws and edicts imposing penalties for treason against the Emperor, and without it I would not be even reasonably safe from assassination. However, I refused the title of Father of the Country, I refused the title of Augustus, I ridiculed attempts to vote me divine honours, and I even told the Senate that I did not wish to be styled "Emperor." This, I pointed out, had from ancient times been a title of distinction won by successful service in the field: it did not signify merely the supreme command of the armies. Augustus had been acclaimed Emperor on account of his victories at Actium and elsewhere. My uncle Tiberius had been one of the most successful Roman generals in the whole of our history. My predecessor Caligula had allowed himself to be styled Emperor from youthful ambition, but even he had felt it incumbent on him to earn the title in the field; hence his expedition across the Rhine and his attack upon the waters of the English Channel. His military operations, bloodless though they were, were symbolic of his understanding of the responsibilities that the title of Emperor carried with it. "One day, my Lords," I wrote to them, "I may feel it necessary to take the field at the head of my armies, and if the Gods prosper me I shall earn the title, which I shall be very proud to bear, but until that day I must ask you not to address me by it, out of respect for those capable generals of the past who have really earned it."

They were so pleased by this letter of mine that they voted me a golden statue—no, it was three golden statues—but I vetoed the motion on two grounds. One was that I had done nothing to earn this honour; and the other, that it was an extravagance. I did allow them, though, to vote me three statues which were to be put up in prominent places in the City; but the most expensive one was to be of silver, and not solid silver at that, but a hollow statue filled with plaster. The other two were of bronze and marble respectively. I accepted these three statues because Rome was so full of statues that two or three more would not make much difference, and I was interested to sit for my sculptured portrait to a really good sculptor, now that the best sculptors in the world were at my service.

The Senate also decided to dishonour Caligula by every means in their power. They voted that the day of his assassination should be made a festival of national thanksgiving. Again I interposed my veto and, apart from annulling Caligula's edicts about the religious worship that was to be paid to himself and to the Goddess Panthea, which was the name he gave my poor niece Drusilla whom he murdered, I took no further action against his memory. Silence about him was the best policy. Herod reminded me that Caligula had not done any dishonour to the memory of Tiberius, though he had good cause to hate him; he had merely abstained from deifying him and left the arch of honour which had been voted to him uncompleted.

"But what shall I do with all Caligula's statues?" I asked.

"That's simple enough," he said. "Set the City Watchmen to collect them all at two o'clock to-morrow morning when everyone is asleep and bring them here to the Palace. When Rome wakes up it will find the niches and pedestals unoccupied, or perhaps filled again with the statues originally moved to make room for them."

I took Herod's advice. The statues were of two sorts—the statues of foreign Gods whose heads he had removed and replaced with his own; and the ones that he had made of himself, all in precious metals. The first sort I restored as nearly as possible to their original condition, the others I broke up, melted down and minted into my new coinage. The great gold statue that he had placed in his temple melted down into nearly a million gold pieces. I do not think I mentioned about this statue, that every day his priests—of whom I, to my shame, had been one—clothed it with a costume similar to the one he himself was wearing. Not only did we have to dress it in ordinary civil or military costume with his especial badges of Imperial rank, but on days when he happened to believe himself to be Venus or Minerva or Jupiter or the Good Goddess, we had to rig it out appropriately with the different divine insignia.

It pleased my vanity to have my head on the coins, but

this was a pleasure which prominent citizens had enjoyed under the Republic too, so I must not be blamed for that. Portraits on coins, however, are always disappointing because they are executed in profile. Nobody is familiar with his own profile, and it comes as a shock, when one sees it in a portrait, that one really looks like that to people standing beside one. For one's full face, because of the familiarity that mirrors give it, a certain toleration and even affection is felt; but I must say that when I first saw the model of the gold piece that the mint-masters were striking for me I grew angry and asked whether it was intended to be a caricature. My little head with its worried face perched on my long neck, and the Adam's apple standing out almost like a second chin, shocked me. But Messalina said: "No, my dear, that's really what you look like. In fact, it is rather flattering than otherwise."

"Can you really love a man like that?" I asked.

She swore that there was no face so dear to her in the world. So I tried to get accustomed to the coin.

Besides Caligula's statues a good deal of his wasteful expenditure was represented by gold and silver objects in the Palace and elsewhere which could also be removed and converted into bullion. For instance, the golden door-knobs and window-panes and the gold and silver furniture in his temple. I removed it all. I gave the Palace a great clearing-out. In Caligula's bedchamber I found the poison chest which had belonged to Livia and of which Caligula had made good use, sending presents of poisoned sweetmeats to men who had drawn their wills in his favour and sometimes pouring poison into the plates of dinner-guests, after first distracting their attention by some prearranged diversion. (He experienced most pleasure, he confessed, in watching them die from arsenic.) I took the whole chest down to Ostia with me the first calm day of Spring and, rowing down the estuary in one of Caligula's pleasure-barges, dumped it overboard about a mile from the coast. A minute or two later thousands of dead fish came floating up. I had not told the sailors what the chest contained and some of them grabbed at the fish floating near, meaning to take them home to eat; but I stopped that, forbidding them to do so on pain of death.

Under Caligula's pillow I found his two famous books, on one of which was painted a bloody sword and on the other a bloody dagger. Caligula was always followed by a freedman carrying these two books, and if he heard something about a man which happened to displease him he used to say to the freedman, "Protogenes, write that fellow's name down under the dagger" or, "write his name down under the sword." The sword was for those destined to execution, the dagger for those who were to be invited to commit suicide. The last names in the dagger-book were Vinicius, Asiaticus, Cassius Chærea and Tiberius Claudius—myself. These books I burned in a brazier with my own hands. And Protogenes I put to death. It was not only that I loathed the sight of this grim-faced bloody-minded fellow who had always treated me with insufferable impudence, but that I was now given evidence that he had threatened senators and knights to write their names down in the book unless they paid him large sums of money. Caligula's memory was so bad at this time that Protogenes could easily have persuaded him that the entries were his own.

When I tried Protogenes he insisted that he had never uttered any such threats and never put any name down in the book except at Caligula's orders. This raised the question of the authority sufficient for a man's execution. It would be easy for one of my colonels to report to me dishonestly one morning: "So-and-so was executed at dawn in accordance with your instructions of yesterday." If I knew nothing of the matter it would merely be his word against mine that I had issued these instructions; and, as I am always ready to admit, my memory is none of the best. So I re-introduced the practice, started by Augustus and Livia, of immediately committing all decisions and directions to writing. Unless a paper could be produced by my subordinates giving signed orders from me for any strong disciplinary action that they had taken or any important financial commitment or startling innovation in procedure that they had made, such action must not be regarded as authorized by me, and if I disapproved of it they must bear the blame themselves. In the end this practice, which was also adopted by my chief ministers in dealing with their own subordinates, became such a matter of course that one hardly ever heard a word spoken in government offices, during working hours, except for consultations between heads of department or visits from City officials. Every Palace servant carried a wax-tablet about with him in case it should be needed for special orders to be written upon. All casual applicants for posts, grants, favours, indulgences or what-not were warned to present a document on entering the Palace, stating exactly what they wanted, and why; and except in rare instances were not permitted to press their case by pleas and arguments delivered by word of mouth. This saved time but won my ministers an undeserved reputation for arrogance.

I will tell you about my ministers. During the reigns of Tiberius and Caligula the real direction of affairs had fallen more and more into the hands of Imperial freedmen, originally trained in secretarial duties by my grandmother Livia. The Consuls and City magistrates, though independent authorities answerable only to the Senate for carrying out their duties properly, had come to depend on the advice issued to them, in the Emperor's name, by these secretaries, especially in the case of complicated documents connected with legal and financial matters. They were shown where to affix their seals, or sign their names, the documents being already prepared for them, and seldom troubled to acquaint themselves with the contents. Their signature was in most cases a mere formality and they knew nothing at all about administrative detail compared with what the secretaries knew. Besides, the secretaries had developed a new sort of handwriting, full of abbreviations and hieroglyphs and hastily formed letters, that nobody but themselves could read. I knew that it was impossible to expect any sudden change in this relation between the secretariat and the rest of the world, so for the present I strengthened rather than weakened the powers of the secretariat, confirming the appointments of those of Caligula's freedmen who were capable. For instance, I kept Callistus, who had been Secretary both to the Privy Purse and to the Public Treasury, which Caligula treated as a sort of Privy Purse. He had been aware of the plot against Caligula but had taken no active part in it. He told me a long story about having been recently instructed by Caligula to poison my food, but having nobly refused to do so. I did not believe it. In the first place, Caligula would never have given him those orders, but would have administered the poison with his own hands as usual; and in the second place, if he had, Callistus would never have dared to disobey. However, I let that go because he seemed anxious to continue with his Treasury duties and was the only man who really understood the ins and outs of the present financial situation. I encouraged him by saying that I thought he had done remarkably well in keeping Caligula supplied with money so long and that I counted on him henceforth to use his gold-divining powers for the salvation of Rome instead of for its destruction. His responsibilities extended to the direction of judicial inquiries into all public financial questions. I retained Myron as my legal secretary and Posides as my Military Treasurer and put Harpocras in charge of all matters relating to Games and Entertainments; and Amphæus kept the Roll of Citizens. Myron also had the task of accompanying me whenever I went out in public, examining the messages and petitions handed to me, and sorting out the important, immediate ones from the customary shower of irrelevancies and importunities. My other chief ministers were Pallas whom I put in charge of my Privy Purse, his brother Felix whom I made my secretary for Foreign Affairs, Callon whom I made Superintendent of Stores, and his son Narcissus whom I made chief secretary for Home Affairs and private correspondence. Polybius was my religious secretary—for I was High Pontiff—and would also assist me in my historical work if ever I should get time for it. The last-named five were my own freedmen. During my days of bankruptcy I had been forced to dismiss them from my service and they had readily found clerical work to do at the Palace; so they were initiates in the Secretarial Mysteries and had even learned to write illegibly. I gave them all quarters in the New Palace, removing the rabble of swordfighters, charioteers, grooms, actors, jugglers and other hangers-on that Caligula had installed there. I made the Palace above all things a place for governmental work. I lived privately at the Old Palace, and in very modest style too, following the example of Augustus. For important banquets and visits of foreign princes I used Caligula's suite at the New Palace, where Messalina also had a wing for her own use.

When I gave my ministers their appointments I explained that I wanted them to act as much as possible on their own initiative; I could not be expected to direct them all in everything, even if I had been more experienced. I was not in the position of Augustus who, when he assumed control of affairs, was not only young and active but had a corps of capable advisers at his command, men of public distinction—Mæcenas, Agrippa, Pollio, to name only three. I told them that they must do the best they could and that whenever they were faced by any difficulty they should consult *The Roman Transactions of the God Augustus,* the great memorial work published by Livia in the reign of Tiberius, and should keep closely to the forms and precedents that they found in it. If cases occurred where no precedent could be found in this invaluable record, they were, of course, to consult me; but I trusted them to save me as much unnecessary labour as possible. "Be bold," I said, "but not too bold."

I confessed to Messalina, who had helped me with these ministerial appointments, that the sharp edge of my Republican fervour was getting a little blunted: every day I felt more and more sympathy with, and respect for, Augustus. And respect for my grandmother Livia too, in spite of my personal dislike for her. She had surely had a wonderfully methodical mind, and if, before restoring the Republic, I could get the governmental system working again even half as well as it had worked under her and Augustus I would be most satisfied with myself. Messalina smilingly offered to play the part of Livia for the occasion if I undertook that of Augustus. *"Absit omen,"* I exclaimed, spitting in my bosom for luck. She answered that, joking aside, she had something of Livia's gift for summing up people's characters and deciding just what appointments they were fit to hold. If I cared to give her a free hand she would act on my behalf in all social questions, relieving me of all the cares connected with my office as Director of Public Morals. I was deeply in love with Messalina, you must know, and in the matter of choosing my ministers had found her judgment very shrewd, but I hesitated to allow her to take on as much responsibility as this. She begged me to let her give me some stronger proof of her capacity. She suggested that we should together go through the nominal roll of the Senatorial Order: she would tell me which names in her opinion were fit to remain on it. I called for the roll and we began to go through the list. I must confess that I was astonished by her detailed knowledge of the capacities and characters and private and public histories of the first twenty or so senators named in it. Wherever I could check her facts she was so accurate that I readily granted her request. I only consulted my own inclinations in a few doubtful cases, where she did not care very much whether the name was kept on the roll or struck off. After making inquiries through Callistus as to the financial qualifications of certain members, as well as deciding about their mental and moral qualifications, we removed about one-third of the names and filled up the vacancies with the best knights available, and with former senators struck off the roll by Caligula for frivolous reasons. One of my own choices for removal was Sentius. I felt the need of getting rid of him, not merely because of his foolish speech to the Senate and his subsequent cowardice, but because he was one of the two senators who had accompanied me to the Palace at the time of Caligula's assassination and had then deserted me. The other, by the way, was Vitellius, but he now assured me that he had hurried off only to find Messalina and put her into a place of safety, expecting Sentius to stay and look after me; so I quite forgave him. I made Vitellius my understudy in case I should happen to fall ill or anything worse should happen to me. At all events, I got rid of Sentius. The reason that I gave for his degradation was that he had not appeared at the meeting of the Senate that I summoned to the Palace, having fled from Rome to his country estate without informing the Consuls that he would be absent; he had not returned for several days, and thus failed to benefit by the amnesty. Another leading senator that I degraded was Caligula's horse Incitatus who was to have become Consul three years later. I wrote to the Senate that I had no complaints to make against the private morals of this senator or his capacity for the tasks that had hitherto been assigned to him, but that he no longer had the necessary financial qualifications. For I had cut the pension awarded him by Caligula to the daily rations of a cavalry horse, dismissed his grooms and put him into an ordinary stable where the manger was of wood, not ivory, and the walls were whitewashed, not covered with frescoes. I did not, however, separate him from his wife, the mare Penelope: that would have been unjust.

Herod warned me to be constantly on my guard against assassination, saying that our revisions of the Roll of Senators and the further revisions that we had made in the Roll of Knights had won me many enemies. An amnesty was all very well, he said, but the generosity must not be too one-sided. Vinicius and Asiaticus, according to him, were already saying cynically that new brooms sweep clean, that Caligula and Tiberius had also started their reigns with a pretence of benevolence and rectitude, and that I would probably end by becoming as mad a despot as either of them. Herod advised me not to enter the Senate House for some time and even then to take every safeguard against assassination. This alarmed me. It was difficult to decide what safeguards were sufficient, and so I did not enter the Senate House for a whole month. By that time I had decided on the appropriate safeguard: I asked for and was granted permission to enter the House with an armed escort consisting of four Guards Colonels and Rufrius, the Guards Commander. I even put Rufrius on the Roll of Senators, though he did not have the proper financial qualifications; and the Senate at my request gave him permission to speak and vote whenever he entered in my company. On Messalina's advice, too, everyone who came into my presence at the Palace or elsewhere was first searched for concealed weapons; even women and boys. I did not like the notion of women being searched, but Messalina insisted, and I consented on condition that the searching was done by her freedwomen and not by my soldiers. Messalina also insisted on my having armed soldiers in attendance during banquets. In Augustus's day this would have been considered a most despotic practice and I was ashamed to see them lined up along the walls; but I could take no risks.

I worked hard to restore the Senate's self-respect. In choosing new members Messalina and I were as careful in our inquiries about their family histories as we were about their personal capacities. As if at the request of the senior members of the Senatorial Order, though it was really my own idea, I promised not to choose anyone who could not reckon four descents in the male line from a Roman citizen. I kept this promise. The only apparent exception I made was in the case of Felix, my foreign secretary, whom some years later I had occasion to invest with senatorial dignity. He was a younger brother of my freedman Pallas, and born after their father had been given his freedom: so he was never a slave, as Pallas had been. But even here I did not break my promise to the Senate: I asked a member of the Claudian house—not a true Claudian, but a member of a family of Claudian retainers, originally immigrants to the City from Campania, who had been given the citizenship and allowed to take the Claudian name—to adopt Felix as his son. So now Felix, in theory at least, had the necessary four lines of descent. But there were jealous murmurs from the House when I introduced him to them. Someone said: "Cæsar, these things were not done in the days of our ancestors."

I replied angrily: "I do not think, my Lord, that you have any right to talk in this way. Your own family is not so noble as all that: I've heard that they were selling faggots in the streets in my great-great-grandfather's time, and I've heard that they gave short weight, too."

"It's a lie," shouted the Senator. "They were honest inn-keepers."

The House laughed the man down. But I felt obliged to say a little more. "When he was appointed Censor more than three hundred years ago, my ancestor Claudius the Blind, victor of the Etruscans and Samnites and the first Roman author of distinction, admitted the sons of freedmen

116

to the Senate just as I have done. Numerous members of this House owe their presence here to-day to this innovation of my ancestor. Would they care to resign?" The House then welcomed Felix warmly.

There were many rich idlers among the knights—as there had been, indeed, even in Augustus's day. But I did not follow Augustus's example in permitting them to remain idle. I gave out that any man who shirked public office when asked to undertake it would be expelled from the Order. In three or four cases I was as good as my word.

Among the papers that I found at the Palace in Caligula's private safe were those referring to the trials and deaths, under Tiberius, of my nephews Drusus and Nero, and their mother Agrippina. Caligula had pretended to burn the whole lot at the beginning of his reign, as a magnanimous gesture, but had not really done so, and the witnesses against my nephews and sister-in-law and the senators who had voted for their deaths had been in constant terror of his vengeance. I went carefully through the papers and called up before me as many as survived of the men mentioned in them as having been implicated in these judicial murders. The document which concerned each man was read over to him in my presence and then given into his own hands to burn in the fire before him. I may here mention the cipher dossiers of the private lives of prominent citizens which Tiberius had taken from Livia after Augustus's death but had been unable to read. Later I managed to decipher them, but they referred to events by this time so out-of-date that my interest in reading them was more an historical than a political one

The two most important tasks that now presented themselves were the gradual reorganization of State finances and the abolition of the most offensive of Caligula's decrees. Neither could, however, be undertaken in a hurry. I had a long conference with Callistus and Pallas about finances immediately after their appointment. Herod was present too; because he probably knew more than any other man living about the raising of loans and the management of debts. The first question that presented itself was how to get hold of ready money for immediate expenses. We agreed to settle this, as I have already explained, by the melting down of gold statues and gold plate and ornaments in the Palace and the gold furniture in Caligula's temple. Herod suggested that I should add to the money thus realized by borrowing in the name of Capitoline Jove from other Gods whose temple treasuries had become cluttered in the course of the last hundred years or so by useless and showy votive offerings in precious metal. These were mostly the gift of people who wished to call attention to themselves as successful public men, not made in any real spirit of piety. For instance, a merchant, after a successful trading venture to the East, would present the God Mercury with a golden horn of plenty, or a successful soldier would present Mars with a golden shield, or a successful lawyer would present Apollo with a golden tripod. Clearly, Apollo could have no use for two or three hundred gold and silver tripods; and if his father Jove was in need he surely would be only too pleased to lend him a few. So I melted down and minted into coin as many of these votive offerings as I could remove without offending the families of the donors or destroying works of historic or artistic value. For a loan to Jove was the same as a loan to the Treasury. We agreed at this conference that loans must also be raised from the bankers. We would promise them an attractive rate of interest. But Herod said that the most important thing was to restore public confidence and so force back into circulation the money that had been hoarded by nervous business-men. He declared that although a policy of great economy was necessary, economy could be carried too far. It must not be interpreted as meanness. "Whenever I ran short of money," he said, "in my needy days, I always made a point of spending all the money I had left on personal adornment—rings and cloaks and beautiful new shoes. This sent my credit up and enabled me to borrow again. I would advise you to do much the same. A little bit of gold leaf, for example, goes a long way. Suppose you were to send along a couple of goldsmiths to gild the goals in the Circus, it would make everyone feel very prosperous and wouldn't cost you more than fifty or a hundred gold pieces. And another idea occurred to me this morning as I was watching those great slabs of marble from Sicily being carried up the hill for facing the inside of Caligula's temple. You're not going to do any more work on the temple, are you? Well then, why not use them to face the sand-stone barrier of the Circus? It's beautiful marble and ought to cause a tremendous sensation."

Herod was always a man of ideas. I wished that I could keep him always with me, but he told me that he could not possibly stay; he had a kingdom to govern. I told him that if he would stay at Rome for only a few months longer I would make his kingdom as big as his grandfather Herod's had been.

But about this conference. We agreed to raise these Treasury loans and we agreed to abolish, at first, only the most extraordinary of the taxes imposed by Caligula such as taxes on the takings of brothels, on the sales of hawkers and on the contents of the public urinals—the big pots standing at the street corners which the fullers used to carry away, when the liquid reached a certain level, to use for cleaning clothes. In my decree abolishing these taxes I promised that as soon as sufficent money came in I would abolish others too.

# Chapter Seven

I soon found myself popular. Among the edicts of Caligula that I annulled were those concerned with his own religious cult, and his treason edicts, and those removing certain privileges of the Senate and the People. I decreed that the word "treason" was henceforth meaningless. Not only would written treason not be held as a criminal offence, but neither would overt acts; in this I was more liberal even than Augustus. My decree opened the prison gates for hundreds of citizens of all degrees. But on Messalina's advice I kept everybody under open arrest until I had satisfied myself that the charge of treason did not include other crimes of a more felonious nature. For the charge of treason was often only a formality of arrest: the crime might be murder, forgery or any other offence. These cases were not ones that I could leave for settlement to the ordinary magistrates. I felt bound to investigate them myself. I went every day to the Market Place and there, in front of the temple of Hercules, tried cases all morning long with a bench of senator colleagues. No Emperor had admitted colleagues to his tribunal for a number of years—not since Tiberius went to Capri. I also paid surprise visits to other courts and always took my place there on the bench of advisers to the presiding judge. My knowledge of legal precedents was very faulty. I had never taken the ordinary course of honours which every Roman nobleman went through, gradually rising in rank from third-class magistrate to Consul, with intervals of military service abroad; and except for the last three years I had lived out of Rome a great deal and very rarely visited the law courts. So I had to rely on my native wit rather than on legal precedent and to struggle hard the whole time against the tricks of lawyers who, trading on my ignorance, tried to entangle me in their legal webs.

Every day as I came into the Market Place from the Palace I used to pass a stuccoed building across the face of which was tarred in enormous letters:

FORENSIC AND LEGAL INSTITUTE
*Founded and Directed by the most Learned and Eloquent Orator and Jurist Telegonius Macarius of This City and of the City of Athens.*

Underneath this on a huge square tablet appeared the following advertisement:

Telegonius gives instruction and advice to all who have become involved in financial or personal difficulties necessitating their appearance in Civil or Criminal courts; and has a positively encyclopædic knowledge of all Roman edicts, statutes, decrees, proclamations, judicial decisions, etcetera, past and present, operative, dormant, or inoperative. At half an hour's notice the most learned and eloquent Telegonius can supply his clients with precise and legally incontrovertible opinions on any judicial matter under the sun that they care to present to him and his staff of highly trained clerks. Not only Roman Law, but Greek Law, Egyptian Law, Jewish Law, Armenian, Moroccan or Parthian Law—Telegonius has it all at his fingers' ends. The incomparable Telegonius, not content with dispensing the raw

121

material of Law, dispenses also the finished product: namely, beautifully contrived forensic presentations of the same complete with appropriate tones and gestures. Personal appeals to the jury a specialty. Handbook of brilliant rhetorical figures and tropes, suitable for any case, to be had on request. No client of Telegonius has ever been known to suffer an adverse verdict in any court—unless his opponent has by chance also drunk from the same fountain of oratorical wisdom and eloquence. Reasonable fees and courteous attention. A few vacancies for pupils.

*"The tongue is mightier than the blade."*

EURIPIDES.

I gradually came to memorize this tablet by seeing it so often, and now when the counsel for the defence or prosecution used to appeal to me with expressions like, "Surely, Cæsar, you are aware of the fifteenth subsection of the fourth article of Marcus Porcius Cato's Sumptuary Law published in the year that So-and-So and So-and-So were Consuls?" or, "You will agree with me, Cæsar, that in the island of Andros, of which my client is a native, great latitude is shown to forgers if it can be proved that they were influenced by regard for the well-being of their aged parents rather than by hope of personal gain," or similar foolish talk, I would just smile back and reply: "You are mistaken, Sir: I am quite unaware of this. I am not the most learned and eloquent Telegonius, who can supply precise and legally incontrovertible opinions on any judicial matter under the sun. I am merely the Judge of this Court. Proceed, and don't waste my time." If they tried to badger me further I would say: "It's no use. In the first place, if I don't want to answer, I won't answer. You can't make me. I'm a free man, aren't I—in fact one of the freest in Rome?

In the second place, if I do answer now, by Heaven you'll wish that I hadn't."

Telegonius, by the way, seemed to be doing quite a thriving business and I came to resent his activities greatly. I detest forensic oratory. If a man cannot state his case in a brief and lucid way, bringing the necessary witnesses and abstaining from irrelevant talk about the nobility of his ancestry, the number of impoverished relatives dependent on him, the clemency and wisdom of the judge, the harsh tricks that Fate plays, the mutability of human fortune and all that stale silly bag of tricks, he deserves the extreme penalty of the law for his dishonesty, pretension and his waste of public time. I sent Polybius to buy Telegonius's hand-book as advertised; and studied it. A few days later I was visiting a lower court when a defendant launched out on one of the brilliant rhetorical figures recommended by Telegonius. I asked the judge to allow me to intervene. He granted me this, and I said to the orator: "Stop, Sir, this will never do. You have made a mistake in your recitation-lesson. Telegonius's figure was as follows—let me see—'If accused of theft'—yes, here we are." I produced the handbook:

"Hearing of my neighbour's loss, and filled with pity for him, through what woods and vales, over what windy and inhospitable mountains, in what damp and gloomy caverns did I not search for that lost sheep (or lost cow—lost horse —lost mule) until at last, extraordinary to relate, returning home, weary, footsore and disappointed, I found it (*here shade eyes with hand and look startled*): and where but in my own sheepcote (or cowshed—stable—barn) where it had perversely strayed during my absence!"

"Sir," I said, "you put groves where the vales should have been and you left out 'footsore' and the telling adverb 'perversely.' You didn't look startled, either, at the word 'found,'

123

only stupid. The judgment goes against you. Blame youself, not Telegonius."

Because I devoted myself to my judicial duties for so many hours every day, religious holidays not excepted; and even ran the summer and winter law-terms together, so that the dispensation of justice should be continuous and no accused person be forced to spend longer than a few days in prison—because of all this, I expected more considerate treatment from lawyers, court-officials and witnesses than I got. I made it quite plain that the non-appearance or late appearance in court of one of the principal parties in any suit would prejudice me in favour of his opponent. I tried to get through cases as quickly as possible and won (most unfairly) a reputation for sentencing prisoners without giving them a proper opportunity for defence. If a man was accused of a crime and I asked him straight out, "Is this accusation substantially true?" and he shuffled and said: "Let me explain, Cæsar. I am not exactly guilty, but . . . ," I would cut him short. I would pronounce, "Fined a thousand gold pieces" or "Banished to the Island of Sardinia" or just "Death," and then turn to the beadle: "Next case, please." The man and his lawyer were naturally vexed that they had not been able to charm me with their extenuating-circumstance pleas. There was one case in which the defendant claimed to be a Roman citizen and so appeared in a gown, but the plaintiff's lawyer objected and said that he was really a foreigner and should be wearing a cloak. It made no difference to this particular case whether or not he was a Roman citizen, so I silenced the lawyers by ordering the man to wear a cloak during all speeches for the prosecution and a gown during all speeches for the defence. The lawyers did not like me for that and told each other that I was ridiculing justice. Perhaps I was. On the whole they treated me very badly. Some mornings if I had been unable to settle as many cases as I had hoped and it was long past the time for my dinner they would make quite a disturbance when I adjourned proceedings until the next day. They would call to me quite rudely to come back and not keep honest citizens waiting for justice, and would even catch me by the gown or foot as if forcibly to prevent me from leaving the court.

I did not discourage familiarity, provided that it was not offensive, and found that an easy atmosphere in court encouraged witnesses to give proper evidence. If anyone answered me back with spirit when I had expressed an ill-advised opinion I never took it ill. On one occasion the counsel for the defence explained that his client, a man of sixty-five, had recently married. His wife was a witness in the case, and was quite a young woman. I remarked that the marriage was illegal. According to the Poppæan-Papian Law (with which I happened to be familiar) a man over sixty was not allowed to marry a woman under fifty: the legal assumption was that a man over sixty is unfit for parentage. I quoted the Greek epigram:

"The old man weds, for Nature's rule he scorns—
'Father a weakly stock, or else wear horns'."

The lawyer considered for a few moments and then extemporized:

"And that old man, yourself, is a plain fool
To foist on Nature this unnatural rule.
A sturdy old man fathers sturdy sons;
A weakly young man fathers weakly ones."

This was so just a point and so neatly made that I forgave the poet-lawyer for calling me a plain fool, and at the next meeting of the Senate amended the Poppæan-Papian Law accordingly. The severest anger to which I ever remember having given way in court was roused by a court official whose duty it was to summon witnesses and see that they arrived punctually. I had given a fraud case a hearing but had been forced to adjourn it for lack of evidence, the principal witness having fled to Africa to avoid being charged with complicity in the fraud. When the case came on again I called for this witness; but he was not in court. I asked the court-official whether this man had been duly subpœnaed to attend.

"Oh yes, indeed, Cæsar."

"Then why is he not here?"

"He is unfortunately prevented from attending."

"There is *no* excuse for non-attendance, except illness so serious that he cannot be carried into court without danger to his life."

"I quite agree, Cæsar. No, the witness is not ill now. He has been very ill, I understand. But that is all over."

"What was wrong with him?"

"He was mauled by a lion, I am informed, and afterwards gangrene set in."

"It's a wonder he recovered," I said.

"He didn't," sniggered the fellow. "He's dead. I think that death can stand as an excuse for non-attendance." Everyone laughed.

I was so furious that I flung my writing-tablet at him, took away his citizenship and banished him to Africa. "Go and hunt lions," I shouted, "and I hope they maul you properly, and I hope gangrene sets in." However, six months later I pardoned him and reinstated him in his position. He made no more jokes at my expense.

It is only fair at this point to mention the severest anger that was ever directed in court against myself. A young nobleman was charged with unnatural acts against women. The real complainants were the Guild of Prostitutes, an unofficial but well-managed organization which protected its members pretty effectively from abuse by cheats or ruffians. The prostitutes could not very well bring a charge against the nobleman themselves, so they went to a man who had been done a bad turn by him and wanted revenge—prostitutes know everything—and offered to give evidence if he brought the charge: a prostitute was a capable witness in a lawcourt. Before the case came on, I sent a message to my friend Calpurnia, the pretty young prostitute who had lived with me before I married Messalina and had been so tender and faithful to me in my misfortunes: I asked her to interview the women who were to give evidence and privately find out whether the nobleman had really abused them in the manner alleged, or whether they had been bribed by the person who was bringing the charge. Calpurnia sent me word a day or two later that the nobleman had really behaved in a very brutal and disgusting way, and that the women who had complained to the Guild were decent girls, one of whom was a personal friend of hers.

I tried the case, took sworn evidence (overruling the objection of the defending lawyer that prostitutes' oaths were both proverbially and actually worth nothing) and had this put in writing by the court-recorder. When one girl repeated some very filthy and vulgar remark that the accused had made to her, the recorder asked, "Shall I put that down, Cæsar?" and I answered, "Why not?" The young nobleman was so angry that he did just what I had done to the court-official who teased me—he threw his writing-tablet at my head. But whereas I had missed my aim, his aim was true. The sharp edge of the tablet gashed my cheek and drew blood. But all I said was, "I am glad to see, my Lord, that you still have some shame left." I found him guilty and put a black mark against his name in the Roll, which disqualified him from becoming a candidate for public office. But he was a relative by marriage of Asiaticus, who asked me some months later to scratch out the black mark, because his young relative had lately reformed his ways: "I'll scratch it out, to please you," I answered, "but it will still show." Asiaticus later repeated this remark of mine to his friends as a proof of my stupidity. He could not understand, I suppose, that a reputation was, as my mother used to say, like an earthenware plate. "The plate is cracked; the reputation is damaged by a criminal sentence. The plate is then mended with rivets and becomes 'as good as new'; the reputation is mended by an official pardon. A mended plate or a mended reputation is better than a cracked plate or a damaged reputation. But a plate that has never been cracked and a reputation that has never been damaged are better still."

A schoolmaster always appears a very queer fellow to his pupils. He has certain stock-phrases which they come to notice and giggle at whenever he uses them. Everyone in the world has stock-phrases or tricks of speech, but unless he is in a position of authority—as a schoolmaster, or an army captain or a judge—nobody notices them particularly. Nobody noticed them in my case until I became Emperor, but then of course they became world-famous. I had only to remark in court, "No malice or favour whatsoever" or (turning to my legal secretary after summing-up a case), "That's right, isn't it?" or "When once my mind is made up, the thing is fixed with a nail," or quote the old tag:

"As the rascal did he must
Himself be done by. And that's just."

or utter the family oath, "Ten thousand furies and serpents!" —and a great roar of laughter would go up about me as though I had let fall either the most absurd solecism imaginable or the most exquisitely witty epigram.

In the course of my first year in the courts I must have made hundreds of ridiculous mistakes, but I did get the cases settled and sometimes surprised myself by my brilliance.

There was one case, I remember, where one of the witnesses for the defence, a woman, denied any relationship with the accused man, who was alleged by the prosecution to be really her son. When I told her that I would take her word for it and that in my quality as High Pontiff I would immediately join her and him in marriage she was so frightened by the prospect of having incest forced upon her that she pleaded guilty of perjury. She said she had concealed her relationship in order to seem an impartial witness. That gave me a great reputation, which I lost almost at once in a case where the treason charge covered one of forgery. The prisoner was a freedman of one of Caligula's freedmen, and there were no extenuating circumstances to his crime. He had forged his master's will just before his death—whether he was responsible for the death could not be proved—and had left his mistress and her children completely destitute. I grew very angry with this man as I heard his story unfolded and determined to inflict the maximum penalty. The defence was very weak—no denial of the charge, only a stream of Telegonian irrelevancies. It was long past my dinner-time and I had been sitting in judgment solidly for six hours. A delicious whiff of cooking came floating into my nostrils from the dining-chamber of the Priests of Mars near by. They eat better than any other priestly fraternity: Mars never lacks for sacrificial victims. I felt faint with hunger. I said to the senior of the magistrates who were sitting with me, "Please take over this case from me and impose the maximum penalty, unless the defence has any better evidence to offer than has yet been produced."

"Do you really mean the maximum penalty?" he asked.

"Yes, indeed, whatever it may be. The man deserves no mercy."

"Your orders shall be obeyed, Cæsar," he replied.

So my chair was brought and I joined the priests at their dinner. When I returned that afternoon I found that the accused man's hands had been chopped off and hung around his neck. That was a punishment ordained for forgery by Caligula and had not yet been removed from the penal code. Everyone considered that I had acted most cruelly, for the judge had told the Court that it was my sentence, not his own. It was hardly my fault, though.

I recalled all the exiles who had been banished on treason charges; but only after asking the Senate's permission. Among these were my nieces Agrippinilla and Lesbia who had been sent to an island off the coast of Africa. For my own part, though I would certainly not have allowed them to remain there, neither would I have invited them to return to Rome. They had both behaved very insolently to me and had both committed incest with their brother Caligula, whether willingly or unwillingly I do not know, and their other adulteries had been a matter of public scandal. It was Messalina who interceded with me for them. I realize now that it gave her a delightful sense of power to do this. Agrippinilla and Lesbia had always treated her with great haughtiness, and now that they were told that they were being recalled to Rome as a result of her generosity they would feel obliged to humble themselves before her. But at the time I thought it was plain goodness of heart in Messalina. So my nieces returned and I found that exile had by no means broken their spirits, though their delicate skins had become sadly tanned by the African sun. By Caligula's orders they had been forced to earn their living on the island by diving for sponges. However, the only comment that Agrippinilla made on her experiences was that she had not altogether wasted her time. "I have become a first-class swimmer. If anyone ever wants to kill me, he had better not try drowning." They decided to brazen out the disgracefully slave-girlish colour of their faces, necks and arms, by inducing some of their noble friends to adopt sunburn as a fashion. Walnut-juice became a favourite toilet-water. Messalina's intimates, however, kept their natural pink-and-white complexions and referred contemptuously to the sunburn party as "The Sponge Divers." Lesbia's thanks to Messalina were most perfunctory and I was hardly thanked at all. She was positively unpleasant. "You kept us waiting ten days longer than was necessary," she complained, "and the ship that was sent to fetch us was full of rats." Agrippinilla was wiser: she made both of us very graceful speeches of gratitude.

I confirmed Herod's kingship of Bashan, Galilee and Gilead, and added to it Judæa, Samaria and Edom, so that his dominions were now as large as those of his grandfather. I rounded off the northern part with Abilene, which had formed part of Syria. He and I entered upon a solemn league, confirmed by oaths in the open Market Place in the presence of an immense crowd, and by the ritual sacrifice of a pig, an ancient ceremony revived for the occasion. I also conferred on him the honorary dignity of Roman Consul: this had never before been given to a man of his race. It signalized that in the recent crisis the Senate had come for advice to him, not finding a native Roman capable of clear and impartial thought. At Herod's request I also conferred the little kingdom of Chalcis on his younger brother, Herod Pollio: Chalcis lay to the east of the Orontes, near Antioch. He asked nothing for Aristobulus; so Aristobulus got nothing. I also gladly freed Alexander the Alabarch and his brother Philo who were still in prison at Alexandria. While on the subject, I may mention that when the Alabarch's son, to whom Herod had married his daughter Berenice, died, Berenice then married her uncle Herod Pollio. I confirmed Petronius in his governorship of Syria and sent him a personal letter of congratulation on his sensible behaviour in the matter of the statue.

I took Herod's advice about the marble slabs that had been intended for facing the interior of Caligula's temple: they made a fine showing around the Circus. Then I had to decide what to do with the building itself, which was handsome enough even when stripped of its precious ornaments. It occurred to me that it would be only justice to the Twin Gods, Castor and Pollux—a decent apology for the insult that Caligula had offered them by turning their temple into a mere portico of his own—to give it to them as an annex of theirs. Caligula had made a breach in the wall behind their two statues, to form the main entrance to his temple, so that they became as it were his doorkeepers. There was nothing for it but to reconsecrate the premises. I fixed a propitious day for the ceremony and won the Gods' approval of it by augury; for we make this distinction between augury and consecration, that the consecration is effected by the will of man, but first the augury must denote the willing consent of the deity concerned. I had chosen the fifteenth day of July, the day that Roman Knights go out crowned with olive wreaths to honour the Twins in a magnificent horseback procession: from the Temple of Mars they ride through the main streets of the City, circling back to the Temple of the Twins, where they offer sacrifices. The ceremony is a commemoration of the battle of Lake Regillus which was fought on that day over three hundred years ago. Castor and Pollux came riding in person to the help of a Roman army that was making a desperate stand on the lake-shore against a superior force of Latins; and ever since then they have been adopted as the particular patrons of the knights.

I took the auspices in the little tabernacle dedicated to that purpose on the summit of the Capitoline Hill. I invoked the Gods and, after calculation, marked out the appropriate quarter of the Heavens in which to make my observations, namely, the part where the constellation of the Heavenly Twins then lay. I had hardly done so, when I heard a faint creaking sound in the sky and the looked-for sign appeared. It was a pair of swans flying from the direction that I had marked out, the noise of their wings growing stronger and stronger as they approached. I knew that these must be Castor and Pollux themselves in disguise, because, you know, they and their sister Helen were hatched out of the same treble-yolked egg that Leda laid after she had been courted by Jove in the form of a swan. The birds passed directly over their Temple and were soon lost in the distance.

I will get a little ahead of the order of events by describing the festival. It began with a lustration. We priests and our assistants made a solemn procession around the premises, carrying laurel branches which we dipped in pots of consecrated water and waved, sprinkling drops as we went. I had been to the trouble of sending for water from Lake Regillus, where Castor and Pollux, by the way, had another temple: I mentioned the source of the water in the invocation. We also burned sulphur and aromatic herbs to keep off evil spirits, and flute-music was played to drown the sound of any ill-omened word that might be uttered. This lustration made everything holy within the bounds that we had walked, which included the new annex as well as the Temple itself. We walled up the breach: I laid the first stone myself. I then sacrificed. I had chosen the combination of victims that I knew would please the Gods most—for each of them an ox, a sheep and a pig, all unblemished and all twins. Castor and Pollux are not major deities: they are demigods who, because of their mixed parentage, spend alternate days in Heaven and the Underworld. In sacrificing to the ghosts of heroes one draws the head of the victim down, but in sacrificing to Gods one draws it up. So in sacrificing to the Twins I followed an old practice which had lapsed for many years, of alternately drawing one head down and one head up. I have seldom seen more propitious entrails.

The Senate had voted me triumphal dress for the occasion; the excuse was a small campaign that had recently been brought to a conclusion in Morocco, where disturbances had followed Caligula's murder of the King, my cousin Ptolemy.

I had had no responsibility for the Moroccan expedition, and though it was now customary for the Commander-in-Chief to be voted triumphal dress at the close of a campaign, even though he had never left the City, I would not have accepted the honour but for one consideration. I decided that it would look strange for a Commander-in-Chief to dedicate a temple to the only two Greek demigods who had ever fought for Rome, in a dress which was a confession that he had never done any real army-commanding. But I only wore my triumphal wreath and cloak during the ceremony itself: for the rest of the five days' festival I wore an ordinary purple-bordered senator's gown.

The first three days were devoted to theatrical shows in the Theatre of Pompey, which I rededicated for the occasion. The stage and part of the auditorium had been burned down in Tiberius's reign, but rebuilt by him and dedicated to Pompey again. Caligula, however, had disliked seeing Pompey's title, "The Great," in the inscription and had rededicated the Theatre to himself. I now gave it back to Pompey, though I put an inscription on the stage, giving Tiberius credit for its restoration after the fire and myself credit for this rededication to Pompey: it is the only public building on which I have ever let my name appear.

I had never liked the wholly un-Roman practice that had sprung up towards the end of Augustus's reign, of men and women of rank appearing on the stage to show off their histrionic and corybantic talents. I cannot think why Augustus did not discourage them more sternly that he did. I suppose it was because there was no law against the practice, and Augustus was tolerant of Greek innovations. His successor Tiberius disliked the theatre, whoever the actors might be, and called it a great waste of time and an encouragement to vice and folly. But Caligula not only recalled the professional actors whom Tiberius had banished from the City but strongly encouraged noble amateurs to perform and often appeared on the stage himself. The chief impropriety of the innovation lay for me in the sheer incapacity of the noble amateurs. Romans are not born actors. In Greece men and women of rank take their parts in theatrical shows as a matter of course, and never fail to acquit themselves honourably. But I have never seen a Roman amateur who was any good. Rome has only produced one great actor, Roscius, but he won his extraordinary perfection in the art by the extraordinary pains that he took over it. He never once made a single gesture or movement on the stage that he had not carefully rehearsed beforehand, again and again—until it seemed a natural action. No other Roman has ever had the patience to forge himself into a Greek. So on this occasion I sent special messages to all noblemen and noblewomen who had ever appeared on the stage in Caligula's reign, ordering them under pain of my displeasure to act two plays and an interlude which I had chosen for them. They were not to be helped out by any professional actor, I said. At the same time I called on Harpocras, my Games secretary, and told him that I wished him to get together the best cast of professional actors that he could find in Rome and see whether he could not, on the second day of the festival, show what acting really should be. It was to be the same programme; but I kept this a secret. My little object-lesson worked very well. The first day's performances were pitiable to witness. Such wooden gestures and awkward entrances and exits, such mumbling and mangling of parts, such lack of gravity in the tragedies and of humour in the comedies, that the audience soon grew impatient and coughed and shuffled and talked. But next day the professional company acted so brilliantly that since then no man or woman of rank has ever dared to appear upon the public stage.

On the third day the principal performance was the Pyrrhic sword-dance, the native dance of the Greek cities of Asia Minor. It was performed by the sons of the notables of those cities, whom Caligula had sent for on the pretence of wanting them to dance for him; in reality he intended them as hostages for their parents' good behaviour while he visited Asia Minor and raised money by his usual extortionate methods. Hearing of their arrival at the Palace, Caligula had gone to inspect them and was on the point of making them rehearse a song which they had learnt in his honour when Cassius Chærea came up to ask for the watchword; and that was the signal for his assassination. So now the boys danced with the greater joy and skill for knowing what a fate they had escaped; and sang me a very grateful song when they had done. I rewarded them all with the Roman citizenship and sent them home a few days later, loaded with presents.

The fourth and fifth days' performances were in the Circus, which looked very fine with its gilt goals and marble barriers, and in the amphitheatres. We had twelve chariot-races and one camel-race, which was an amusing novelty. We also killed three hundred bears and three hundred lions in the amphitheatres, and had a big sword-fighting display. The bears and the lions had been ordered by Caligula from Africa just before his death and had only just arrived. I frankly told the people, "This is the last big wild-beast show that you will see for some time: I am going to wait until the prices come down before I order any more. The African traders have run them up to an absurd height. If they can't bring them down they can take their wares to another market—but I think that it will puzzle them to find one." This appealed to the crowd's commercial sense and they cheered me gratefully. That was the end of the festival, except for a banquet which I gave afterwards at the Palace to the nobility and their wives, also to certain representatives of the People. More than two thousand were served. There were no far-fetched delicacies, but it was a well-thought-out meal, with good wine and excellent roasts, and I heard no complaints about the absence of tit-lark-tongue pasties or antelope fawns in aspic or ostrich egg omelettes.

# Chapter Eight

I soon came to a decision about sword-fighting and wild-beast hunts. First about the wild beasts. I had heard of a sport practised in Thessaly which had the double advantage of being exciting to watch and cheap to provide. So I introduced it at Rome as an alternative to the usual leopard and lion hunts. It was played with half-grown wild bulls. The Thessalians used to rouse the bull by sticking small darts into its hide as it emerged from the pen where it was imprisoned—not enough to injure it, only enough to vex it. It used to come charging out and then they used to jump nimbly out of its way. They were quite unarmed. Sometimes they used to deceive it by holding coloured cloths before their bodies: when it charged the cloths they moved them away at the last moment without shifting their own ground. The bull would always charge the moving cloth. Or, as it charged, they would leap forward and either clear it in a single bound, or step on its rump for a moment before coming to ground again. The bull would gradually weary, and they would do still more daring tricks. There was one man who could actually stand with his back to the bull, bending down with his head between his legs, and then, as it charged, turn a back-somersault in the air and land standing on the bull's shoulders. It was a common sight to see a man ride around the ring balanced on a bull's back. If a bull would not tire quickly, they would make it gallop around the arena by sitting it as if it were a horse, holding a horn in the left hand and twisting its tail with the right. When it was sufficiently out of breath the chief performer would wrestle with it, holding it by both horns and slowly forcing it to the ground. Sometimes he would catch the bull's ear between his teeth to help him in his task. It was a very interesting sport to watch, and the bull often caught and killed a man who took too great liberties with it. The cheapness of the sport lay in the very reasonable demands for payment made by the Thessalians, who were simple countrymen, and in the survival of the bull for another performance. Clever bulls who learned how to avoid being tricked and dominated soon became great popular favourites. There was one called Rusty who was almost as famous in its way as the horse Incitatus. He killed ten of his tormentors in as many festivals. The crowd came to prefer these bull-baitings to all other shows except sword-fighting.

About the sword-fighters: I decided now to recruit them principally from the slaves who in the reigns of Caligula and Tiberius had testified against their masters at treason-trials and so brought about their deaths. The two crimes that I abominate most are parricide and treachery. For parricide indeed I have reintroduced the ancient penalty: the criminal is whipped until he bleeds and then sewed up in a sack together with a cock, a dog and a viper, representing lust, shamelessness and ingratitude, and finally thrown into the sea. I regard treachery of slaves towards their masters as a sort of parricide too, so I would always make them fight until one combatant was dead or severely wounded; and I never granted any man remission, but made him fight again at the next Games, and so on until he was killed or wholly disabled. Once or twice it happened that one of them pretended to be mortally injured when he had only received a slight cut, and would writhe on the sand as if unable to continue. If I found that he was shamming I always gave orders for his throat to be cut.

I believe the populace enjoyed the entertainments that I

gave them far more than Caligula's, because they saw them much more rarely. Caligula had such a passion for chariot-racing and wild-beast hunts that almost every other day was made the excuse for a holiday. This was a great waste of public time and the audience got bored long before he did. I removed a hundred and fifty of Caligula's new holidays from the calendar. Another decision that I took was to make a regulation about repetitions. It was the custom that if a mistake had been made in the ceremony of a festival, even if it was only a small one on the last day of all, the whole business had to be gone through again. In Caligula's reign repetitions had become quite a farce. The nobles whom he had forced to celebrate games in his honour at their own cost knew that they would never escape with only a single performance: he would be sure to find some flaw in the cere-mony when it was all over and force them to repeat it two, three, four, five and even as many as ten times. So they learnt to appease him as a matter of course by making an obviously intentional mistake on the last day, and so winning the fav-our of only repeating the show once. My edict was that if any festival had to be repeated, the repetition should not occupy more than a single day, and if a mistake were then made, that would be an end of the matter. As a result no mistakes at all were made: it was seen that I did not encour-age them. I also ordered that there should be no official cele-brations of my birthday and no sword-fighting displays given for my preservation. It was wrong, I said, for men's lives to be sacrificed, even the lives of sword-fighters, in an attempt to purchase the favour of the Infernal Gods towards a living man.

Yet, so that I should not be accused of stinting the City's pleasures, I sometimes used to proclaim suddenly one morn-ing that there would be games held that afternoon in the Enclosure in Mars Field. I explained that there was no par-ticular reason for the games, except that it was a good day for them, and that since I had made no particular preparations it would be a case of taking pot-luck. I called them *Sportula* or Pot-luck Games. They lasted only for the single afternoon.

I mentioned just now my hatred of slaves who betrayed their masters. But I realized that unless masters had a properly paternal attitude to their slaves, slaves could not be expected to have a sense of filial duty to their masters. Slaves, after all, are human. I protected them by legislation, of which I may give an example. The rich freedman from whom Herod had once borrowed money to pay back my mother and myself had greatly enlarged his hospital for sick slaves, which was now situated on the Island of Æsculapius, in the Tiber. He advertised himself as ready to buy slaves in any condition with a view to curing them, but promised first option of repurchase to the former owner at a price not to exceed three times the original. His doctors treated the sick slaves exactly like cattle. But he did a very large and profitable business because most masters could not be bothered to have sick slaves in their house, distracting the other slaves from their ordinary duties and, if they were in pain, keeping everyone awake at night by their groans. They preferred to sell them as soon as it was clear that the illness would be a long and tedious one. In this they were, of course, following the base economical precepts of Cato the Censor. But I put a stop to the practice. I made an edict that any sick slave who had been sold to a hospital-keeper should, on recovery, be granted his liberty and not return to his master's service, and that the master should refund the purchase money to the hospital-keeper. If a slave fell sick the master must henceforth either cure him at home or pay for his cure in the hospital. In the latter case he would become free on recovery, like the slaves already sold to the hospital-keeper, and would be expected, like them, to pay a thank-offering to the hospital, to the extent of one-half his money-earnings for the next three years. If any master chose to kill the slave rather than cure him at home or send him to the hospital, he would be guilty of murder. I then personally inspected the island-hospital and gave instructions to the manager for obvious improvements in accommodation, diet and hygiene.

Though, as I say, I removed a hundred and fifty of Caligula's holidays from the calendar, I did, I admit, create three new festivals, each lasting three days. Two were in honour of my parents. I made these fall on their birthdays, postponing to vacant dates two minor festivals which happened to coincide with them. I ordered dirges to be sung in my parents' memories and provided funeral banquets at my own expense. My father's victories in Germany had already been honoured with an Arch on the Appian Way and with the hereditary title Germanicus, which was the surname of which I was proudest; but I felt that his memory deserved to be refreshed in this way as well. My mother had been granted important honours by Caligula, including the title of "Augusta," but when he quarrelled with her and forced her to commit suicide, he meanly took them all away again: he wrote letters to the Senate accusing her of treason to himself, impiety to the other Gods, a life of malice and avarice, and the entertainment in her house of fortune-tellers and astrologers in defiant disobedience to the laws. Before I could decently make my mother "Augusta" once more I had to plead before the Senate that she was entirely guiltless of these charges: that though strong minded she was extremely pious, and though thrifty, extremely generous, and that she never bore malice against anyone and never once consulted a fortune-teller or astrologer in all her life. I introduced the necessary witnesses. Among them was Briseis, my mother's wardrobe-maid, who had been my property as a slave until she was given her freedom in old age. In fulfillment of a promise made a year or two before to Briseis, I presented her to the House as follows: "My Lords, this old woman was once a faithful slave of mine, and for her life of industry and devotion in the service of the Claudian family—as maid first of all to my grandmother Livia, and then to my mother Antonia, whose hair she used to dress—I recently rewarded her with freedom. Some persons, even members of my own household, have suggested that she was really my mother's slave: I take this opportunity of branding any such suggestion as a mischievous lie! She was born as my father's slave when my father was a mere child; on his death my brother inherited her; and then she came to me. She has had no other masters or mistresses. You can place the fullest reliance on her testimony." The senators were astonished at the warmth of my words, but cheered them, hoping to please me; and I was indeed pleased, because to old Briseis this was the most glorious moment of her life and the applause seemed intended as much for herself as for me. She began to weep, and her rambling tributes to my mother's character were hardly audible. She died a few days later in a splendid room in the Palace and I gave her a most luxurious funeral.

My mother's stolen titles were restored to her and in the great Circensian Games her coach was included in the sacred procession, like the coach of my poor sister-in-law Agrippina. The third festival that I created was in honour of my grandfather Mark Antony. He had been one of our most brilliant Roman generals and won many remarkable victories in the East. His sole mistake had been to fall out with Augustus after a long partnership with him and to lose the battle of Actium. I did not see why my grand-uncle Augustus's victory should continue to be celebrated at my grandfather's expense. I did not go as far as to deify my grandfather, whose many failings disqualified him for Olympus, but the festival was a tribute to his qualities as a soldier and gratified the descendants of those Roman soldiers who had been unlucky enough to choose the losing side at Actium.

Nor did I forget my brother Germanicus. I instituted no festival in his honour, for I felt somehow that his ghost would not approve. He was the most modest and self-effacing man of his rank and ability that I have ever known. But I did something that I felt sure would please him. There was a festival held at Naples, which is a Greek colony, and at the competition held there every five years for the best Greek comedy I submitted one that Germanicus had written, which I found among his papers after his death. It was called *The Ambassadors* and was written with considerable grace and wit somewhat in the style of Aristophanes. The plot was that two Greek brothers, one of whom was commander of his city's forces in a war against Persia, and the other a mercenary in the Persian service, happened to arrive at the same time as ambassadors to the court of a neutral kingdom, each asking the king for his military co-operation. I recognized comic reminiscences of the recriminations that had once passed between the two Cheruscan chieftains, Flavius and Hermann, brothers who fought on opposite sides in the German war which followed Augustus's death. The comic ending to the play was that the foolish king was convinced by both brothers. He sent his infantry to help the Persians and his cavalry to help the Greeks. This comedy won the prize, by the unanimous vote of the judges. It may be suggested that a certain favouritism was shown here, not only on account of Germanicus's extraordinary popularity during his lifetime among all who came in contact with him, but because it was known that it was I, the Emperor, who was submitting the entry. But there could be no doubt that it was incomparably the best work that was offered for the prize, and it was much applauded during its performance. Recalling that Germanicus on his visit to Athens, Alexandria and other famous Greek cities had worn Greek dress, I did the same at the Naples festival. I wore a cloak and high boots at the musical and dramatic performances, and a purple mantle and golden crown at the gymnastic contests. Germanicus's prize was a bronze tripod: the judge wanted to vote him a golden one as a peculiar honour; but I refused that on the grounds of extravagance. Bronze was the customary metal for the prize tripod. I dedicated it in his name at the local temple of Apollo.

It only remained for me now to keep the promise I had made to my grandmother Livia. I was bound by my word of honour which I had given her, to use all the influence that I could command to obtain the Senate's consent to her deification. I had not changed my opinion of the ruthlessness and unscrupulousness of the methods that she used for gaining control over the Empire and keeping it in her hands for some sixty-five years; but, as I remarked a little way back, my admiration for her organizing abilities increased every day. There was no opposition in the Senate to my request except from Vinicianus, Vinicius's cousin, who played the same sort of part as Gallus had played twenty-seven years before when Tiberius proposed the deification of Augustus. Vinicianus rose to ask on precisely what grounds I made this unprecedented request and what sign had been given from Heaven to indicate that Livia Augusta would be welcomed by the Immortals as their permanent associate. I was ready with my answer. I told him that not long before her death my grandmother, prompted no doubt by divine inspiration, had called separately first on my nephew Caligula and then on myself and had secretly informed each of us in turn that we would one day become Emperor. In return for this assurance she made us swear that we would do all that lay in our power to deify her when we succeeded to the monarchy; pointing out that she had played as important a part as Augustus in the great work of reform that they had undertaken together after the Civil wars, and that it was most unjust that Augustus should enjoy perpetual bliss in the Heavenly mansions while she went below to the gloomy halls of Hell, to be judged by Æacus and thereafter to be lost for ever among the countless hosts of insignificant and mouth-less shades. Caligula, I told them, was only a lad at the time he made this promise, and had two elder brothers living, so it was remarkable that Livia knew that he and not they would become Emperor; for she extracted no such promise from them. Caligula, at all events, had made this promise, but had broken it when he became Emperor; and if Vini-cianus needed a sure sign of the feelings of the Gods in this matter, he was at liberty to find it in the bloody circumstan-ces of Caligula's death.

I then turned to address the House as a whole. "My Lords," I said, "it is not for me to decide whether my grand-mother Livia Augusta is worthy of national deification by your votes or whether she is not. I can only repeat that I swore to her by my own head that if ever I became Emperor —an event which, I admit, seemed both improbable and ab-surd, though she herself was positive that it would come to pass—I would do my best to persuade you to raise her to Heaven, where she might stand once more at the side of her faithful husband, who is now, next to Capitoline Jove, the most venerated of all our deities. If you refuse my request to-day I shall renew it every year at this same season, until you grant it: so long as my life is spared and so long as I am still privileged to address you from this chair."

That was the end of the little speech that I had prepared but I found myself launched on a further, extempore, appeal, "And I really think, my Lords, that you should consider Augustus's feelings in this matter. For more than fifty years he and Livia worked hand in hand together, all day and every day. There were few things that he did without her knowledge and advice, and if ever he did act on his own ini-tiative, it cannot be said that he always acted wisely or that he met with any great success in these undertakings. Yes, whenever he was faced by a problem which taxed his own powers of judgment, he would always call for Livia. I would not go so far as to say that my grandmother was without the faults that are complementary to the extraordinary qualities with which she was endowed: I am probably more cognizant of them than anybody here. To begin with, she was entirely heartless. Heartlessness is a grave human fault and is unforgivable when combined with profligacy, greed, sloth and disorderliness; but when combined with boundless energy and a rigid sense of order and public decency, heartlessness takes on a different character altogether. It becomes a divine attribute. Many Gods do not indeed possess it in nearly so full a measure as my grandmother did. Then again, she had a will that was positively Olympian in its inflexibility, and though she never spared any member of her own household who failed to show the devotion to duty that she expected of him, or who created a public scandal by his loose living, neither, we must remember, did she spare herself. How she worked! By going at it night and day she enlarged those sixty-five years of rule to one hundred and thirty. She soon came to identify her own will with that of Rome and anyone who withstood it was a traitor in her eyes, even Augustus. And Augustus, with occasional lapses into self-will, saw the justice of this identification; and though, in an official way of speaking, she was merely his unofficial adviser, yet in his private letters to her he made a thousand acknowledgements of his entire dependence on her divine wisdom. Yes, he used the word 'divine,' Vinicianus: I call that conclusive. And you are old enough to remember that whenever he happened to be temporarily parted from her, Augustus was not at all the man that he was in her company; and it may be argued that his present task in Heaven of watching over the fortunes of the Roman people has been made very difficult by the absence of his former helpmeet. Certainly Rome has not flourished since his death nearly so prosperously as during his lifetime, except for the years that my grandmother Livia ruled through her son, the Emperor Tiberius. And has it occurred to you, my Lords, that Augustus is almost the only male deity in Heaven without a consort? When Hercules was raised to Heaven, he was given a bride at once, the Goddess Hebe."

"What about Apollo?" interrupted Vinicianus. "I never heard that Apollo was married. That seems to me a very *lame* argument."

The Consul called Vinicianus to order. It was clear that the word "lame" was intended offensively. But I was accustomed to insults and answered quietly: "I have always understood that the God Apollo remains a bachelor either because he is unable to choose between the Nine Muses, or because he cannot afford to offend eight of them by choosing the other as his bride. And he is immortally young, and so are they, and it is quite safe for him to postpone his choice indefinitely; for they are all in love with him, as the poet what's-his-name says. But perhaps Augustus will eventually persuade him to do his duty by Olympus, by taking one of the Nine in honourable wedlock, and raising a large family—'as quick as boiled asparagus'."

Vinicianus was silenced in the burst of laughter that followed, for "as quick as boiled asparagus" was one of Augustus's favourite expressions. He had several others: "As easily as a dog squats" and "There are more ways than one of killing a cat" and "You mind your own business, I'll mind mine" and "I'll see that it gets done on the Greek Kalends" (which, of course, means never) and "The knee is nearer than the shin" (which means that one's first concern is with matters that affect one personally). And if anyone tried to contradict him on a point of literary scholarship, he used to say: "A radish may know no Greek, but I do." And whenever he was encouraging anyone to bear an unpleasant condition patiently he always used to say: "Let us content ourselves with this Cato." From what I have told you about Cato, that virtuous man, you will easily understand what he meant. I now found myself often using these phrases of Augustus's: I suppose that this was because I had consented to adopt his name and position. The handiest was the one he used when he was making a speech and had lost his way in a sentence—a thing that constantly happens to me, because I am inclined, when I make an extempore speech, and in historical writing too when I am not watching myself, to get involved in long, ambitious sentences—and now I am doing it again, you notice. However, the point is that Augustus, whenever he got into a tangle, used to cut the Gordian knot, like Alexander, saying: "Words fail me, my Lords. Nothing that I might utter could possibly match the depths of my feelings in this matter." And I learned this phrase off by heart and constantly made it my salvation. I used to throw up my hands, shut my eyes and declaim: "Words fail me, my Lords. Nothing that I might utter could possibly match the depths of my feelings in this matter." Then I would pause for a few seconds and recover the thread of my argument.

We deified Livia without further delay and voted her a statue to be placed alongside that of Augustus in his Temple. At the deification ceremony cadets of noble families gave a performance of the sham-fight on horseback which we call the Troy Game. We also voted her a chariot to be drawn by elephants in the procession during the Circensian Games, an honour which she shared only with Augustus. The Vestal Virgins were instructed to offer sacrifices to her in the Temple; and just as in taking legal oaths all Romans now used the name of Augustus, so henceforth all Roman women were to use my grandmother's name. Well, I had kept my promise.

All was fairly quiet in Rome now. Money was coming in plentifully and I was able to abolish more taxes. My secretaries were managing their departments to my satisfaction; Messalina was busy reviewing the roll of Roman citizens. She found that a number of freedmen were describing themselves as Roman citizens and claiming privileges to which they were not entitled. We decided to punish all such pretenders with the greatest rigour, confiscating their property and making them slaves again, to work as City scavengers or road-menders. I trusted Messalina so completely that I allowed her to use a duplicate seal for all letters and decisions made by her on my behalf in these matters. To make Rome still more quiet I disbanded the Clubs. The night-watchmen had been unable to cope with the numerous bands of young rowdies which had recently been formed on the model of Caligula's "Scouts" and which used to keep honest citizens awake at night by their scandalous goings-on. There had, as a matter of fact, been such clubs in Rome for the last hundred years or more—an introduction from Greece. At Athens, Corinth and other Greek cities the club-men had all been young men of family, and it was the same in Rome until Caligula's reign, when he set the fashion of admitting actors, professional sword-fighters, chariot-drivers, musicians and such-like to membership. The result was increased rowdiness and shamelessness, great damage to property—the fellows sometimes even set fire to houses—and many injuries to inoffensive people who happened to be out late at night, perhaps in search of a doctor or midwife, or on some such emergency errand. I published an order disbanding the Clubs, but knowing that this by itself would not be enough to put an end to the nuisance, I took the only effective step possible: I prohibited the use of any building as a club-house, under penalty of a ruinous fine, and made illegal the sale of cooked meat and other ready-dressed food for consumption on the premises where it was prepared. I extended this order to the sale of drink. After sundown no drink must be consumed in the bar-room of any tavern

For it was principally the fact of meeting in a clubroom to eat and drink that encouraged the young fellows, when they began feeling merry, to go out into the cool night-air to sing ribald songs, molest passers-by and challenge the watchmen to tussles and running fights. If they were forced to dine at home this sort of thing would be unlikely to occur.

My prohibition proved effective and pleased the great mass of the people; whenever I went out now I was always greeted enthusiastically. The citizens had never greeted Tiberius so cordially as this, nor Caligula except in the first few months of his reign when he was all generosity and affability. But I did not realize how beloved I was and how seemingly important to Rome the preservation of my life had become until one day a rumour ran through the City that I had been ambushed on my way to Ostia by a party of senators and their slaves and murdered. The whole City began lamenting in the most dismal fashion, wringing their hands and mopping their eyes and sitting groaning on their doorsteps; but those whose indignation prevailed over their grief ran to the Market Place, crying out that the Guards were traitors and the Senate a parcel of parricides. There were loud threats of vengeance and even talk of burning down the Senate House. The rumour had not the faintest foundation except that I was indeed on my way to the Ostia docks that afternoon to inspect the facilities for unloading corn. (I had been informed that in bad weather a great deal of corn was always lost between ship and land, and wanted to see whether this could be avoided. Few great cities were cursed with so awkward a harbour as Rome with Ostia: when the wind blew strongly from the west and heavy tides swept up the estuary the corn-ships had to ride at anchor for weeks on end, unable to discharge their cargoes.) The rumour had been put about, I suspect, by the bankers, though I could get no proof of this: it was a trick to create a sudden demand for cash. It was common talk that if I happened to die civil commotions would immediately ensue, with bloody combats in the streets between the partisans of rival candidates for the monarchy. The bankers, aware of this nervousness, foresaw that property-holders who did not wish to be involved in such disorders would naturally hurry out of Rome a soon as a report of my death was started: and there would be a rush to the banks to offer land and house property in exchange for immediate gold at a price far below its real value. This is what actually happened. But once more Herod saved the situation. He went to Messalina and insisted on her publishing an immediate order in my name for the closing of the banks until further notice. This was done. But the panic was not checked until I had received news at Ostia of what was happening in the City and had sent four or five of my staff—honest men, whose word the citizens would trust—at full speed back to the Market Place, to appear on the Oration Platform as witnesses that the whole story was a fabrication, put about by some enemy of the State for his own crooked ends.

The facilities for discharging corn at Ostia I found most inadequate. Indeed, the whole corn-supply question was a very difficult one. Caligula had left the public granaries as empty as the Public Treasury. It was only by persuading the corn-factors to endanger the vessels that they owned by running cargoes even in bad weather, that I succeeded in tiding over the season. I had, of course, to compensate them heavily for their losses in vessels, crew and corn. I determined to solve the matter once and for all by making Ostia a safe port even in the worst weather and sent for engineers to survey the place and draw up a scheme.

My first real trouble abroad started in Egypt. Caligula had given the Alexandrian Greeks tacit permission to chastise the Alexandrian Jews, as they thought fit, for their refusal to worship his Divine Person. The Greeks were not allowed to bear arms in the streets—that was a Roman prerogative—but they performed countless acts of physical violence nevertheless. The Jews, many of whom were taxfarmers and therefore unpopular with the poorer and more improvident sort of Greek citizens, were exposed to daily humiliations and dangers. Being less numerous than the Greeks they could not offer adequate resistance, and their leaders were in prison. But they sent word to their kinsmen in Palestine, Syria and even Parthia, acquainting them of their plight, and begging them to send secret help in men, money and munitions of war. An armed uprising was their only hope. Help came in abundance and the Jewish revolt was planned for the day of Caligula's arrival in Egypt, when the Greek population would be crowding in holiday dress to greet him at the docks, and the whole Roman garrison would be there as a guard of honour, leaving the city unprotected. The news of Caligula's death had the effect of setting the rebellion off before its proper time in an ineffectual and half-hearted manner. But the Governor of Egypt was alarmed and sent me an immediate appeal for reinforcements: there were few troops in Alexandria itself. However, the next day he received a letter that I had written him a fortnight before in which I announced my elevation to the monarchy and ordered the release of the Alabarch, with the other Jewish elders, as also the suspension of Caligula's religious decrees and his order penalizing the Jews, until such time as I should be able to inform the Governor of their complete abrogation. The Jews were jubilant, and even those who had hitherto taken no part in the rising now felt that they enjoyed my Imperial favour and could get their own back on the Greeks with impunity. They killed quite a large number of the most persistent Jew-baiters. Meanwhile I replied to the Governor of Egypt, ordering him to put an end to the disturbances, by armed force if necessary; but saying that in view of the letter which by now he must have received from me, and the sedative effects that I hoped from it, I did not consider it necessary to send reinforcements. I told him that it was possible that the Jews had acted under great provocation, and hoped that, being men of sense, they would not continue hostilities, now that they knew that their wrongs were in process of being redressed.

This had the effect of ending the disturbances; and a few days later, after consulting the Senate, I definitely cancelled Caligula's decrees and restored to the Jews all the privileges that they had held under Augustus. But many of the younger Jews were still smarting under the sense of injustice and went marching through the streets of Alexandria carrying banners which read: "Now Our Persecutors Must Lose Their Civic Rights," which was absurd, and "Equal Rights For All Jews Throughout The Empire," which was not so absurd. I published an edict which ran as follows:

"Tiberius Claudius Cæsar Augustus Germanicus, High Pontiff, Protector of the People, Consul-Elect for the second time, issues the following decree.

"I hereby very willingly comply with the petitions of King Agrippa and his brother King Herod, personages whom I hold in the highest esteem, that I should grant to the Jews throughout the Roman Empire the same rights and privileges as I have granted, or rather restored, to the Jews of Alexandria. I do these other Jews this favour not only for the gratification of the aforesaid royal petitioners, but because I consider them worthy of these rights and privileges: they have always shown themselves faithful friends of the Roman people. I would not consider it just, however, that any Greek city should (as has been suggested) be deprived of any rights and privilges which were granted it by the Emperor Augustus (now the God Augustus), any more than that the Jewish colony in Alexandria should have been deprived of its rights and privileges by my predecessor. What is justice for Jews is justice for Greeks; and contrariwise. I have therefore decided to permit all Jews throughout my Empire to keep their ancient customs—in so far as these do not conflict with the conduct of Imperial business—without hindrance from anyone. At the same time I charge them not to presume upon the favour that I am hereby granting them, by showing contempt for the religious beliefs or practices of other races: let them content themselves with keeping their own Law. It is my pleasure that this decision of mine shall forthwith be engraved on stone tablets at the instance of the governors of all kingdoms, cities, colonies and municipalities, both in Italy and abroad, whether Roman officials or Allied Potentates, and that these tablets shall be posted for public reading, during a full month, in some prominent public place and at a height from which the words will be plainly legible from the ground."

Talking privately to Herod one night I said: "The fact is that the Greek mind and the Jewish mind work in quite different ways and are bound to come in conflict. The Jews are too serious and proud, the Greeks too vain and laughter-loving; the Jews hold too fast to the old, the Greeks are too restless in always seeking for something new; the Jews are too self-sufficent, the Greeks too accommodating. But though I might claim that we Romans understand the Greeks—we know their limitations and potentialities and can make them very useful servants—I should never claim that we understand the Jews. We have conquered them by our superior military strength but we have never felt ourselves their masters. We recognize that they retain the ancient virtues of their race, which goes back much farther in history than ours, and that we have lost our own ancient virtues; and the result is that we feel rather ashamed before them."

Herod asked: "Do you know the Jewish version of Deucalion's Flood? The Jewish Deucalion was called Noah and he had three married sons who, when the Flood subsided, repeopled the earth. The eldest was Shem, the middle one was Ham and the youngest was Japhet. Ham was punished for laughing at his father when he accidentally got drunk and threw off all his clothes, by being fated to serve the other two who behaved with greater decency. Ham is the ancestor of all the African peoples. Japhet is the ancestor of the Greeks and Italians, and Shem the ancestor of the Jews, Syrians, Phœnicians, Arabians, Edomites, Chaldeans, Assyrians and the like. There is an ancient prophetic saying that if Shem and Japhet ever live under the same roof there will be endless bickering at the fireside, at the table and in the bed-chamber. That has always proved true. Alexandria is a neat example. And if the whole of Palestine were cleared of Greeks, who don't belong there, it would be far easier to govern. The same with Syria."

"Not for a Roman governor," I smiled. "The Romans are not of the family of Shem and they count on Greek support. You'd have to get rid of us Romans too. But I agree with you so far as to wish that Rome had never conquered the East at all. She would have been much wiser if she had limited herself to ruling a federation of the descendants of Japhet. Alexander and Pompey have much to answer for. Both won the title 'The Great' for their Eastern conquests, but I cannot see that either of them conferred a real benefit on his country."

"It will all settle itself one day, Cæsar," said Herod thoughtfully, "if we have patience."

Then I began telling Herod that I was about to betroth my daughter Antonia, who was now nearly old enough to marry, to young Pompey, a descendant of Pompey the Great. Caligula had taken away young Pompey's title, saying that it was too magnificent a one for a boy of his age to bear, and that in any case there was only one "Great" in the world now. I had just restored the title, and all the other titles that Caligula had taken from noble Roman houses, together with such commemorative badges as the Torquatan Torque and the Cincinnatan Lock. Herod did not volunteer any more of his views on the subject. I did not realize that the future political relations of Shem and Japhet was the problem that had recently come to occupy his mind to the exclusion of all others.

# Chapter Nine

WHEN Herod had established me in the monarchy and set me a proper course to follow—this, I am sure, is how he put the situation to himslf—and in return won a number of favours from me, he said that he must take his leave at last unless there was some work of real importance that I wished him to do, such as nobody but himself was capable of undertaking. I could not think of any excuse for detaining him, and I would have felt obliged to pay him with more territory for every extra month he remained, so after a farewell banquet, which was appropriately magnificent, I let him go. We were both rather drunk that evening, I must confess, and I shed tears at the thought of his departure. We recalled our schooldays together and when nobody seemed to be listening I leant across and called him by his old nickname.

"Brigand," I said quietly, "I always expected you to be a king, but if anyone had ever told me that I'd be your Emperor I'd have called him a madman."

"Little Marmoset," he replied in the same low tones. "You're a fool, as I've always told you. But you have fool's luck. And fool's luck holds. You'll be an Olympian God when I'm only a dead hero; yes, don't blush, for that's how it will be, though there's no question which of us two is the better man."

It did me good to hear Herod speak in his old style again. For the last three months he had been addressing me in the most formal and distant way, never failing to call me Cæsar Augustus and to express only the most profound admiration for my opinions, even if he was often regretfully forced to disagree with them. "Little Marmoset" (Cercopithecion) was the playful nickname Athenodorus had given me. I now begged him that when he wrote to me from Palestine he would always enclose with his official letter, signed with all his new titles, an unofficial letter signed "The Brigand" and giving me his private news. He agreed to this on condition that I replied in the same vein signing myself "Cercopithecion." As we shook hands on the bargain he looked me steadily in the eyes and said: "Marmoset, do you want a little more of my excellent knavish advice? I'll give it to you absolutely free this time."

"Please, dear Brigand, let me have it."

"My advice to you, old fellow, is this: *never trust anyone!* Never trust your most grateful freedman, your most intimate friend, your dearest child, the wife of your bosom, or the ally joined to you by the most sacred oath. Trust yourself only. Or at least trust your own fool's luck, if you can't honestly trust yourself."

The earnestness of his tones penetrated the cheerful fumes of wine that were clouding my brain and roused my attention. "Why do you say that, Herod?" I asked sharply. "Don't you trust your wife Cypros? Don't you trust your friend Silas? Don't you trust young Agrippa, your son? Don't you trust Thamastus and your freedman Marsyas, who got you the money at Acre, and brought you food in prison? Don't you trust *me,* your ally? Why did you say that? Against whom are you putting me on my guard?"

Herod laughed stupidly. "Don't pay any attention to me, Marmoset. I'm drunk, hopelessly drunk. I say the most extraordinary things when I'm drunk. The man who made the proverb 'There's truth in wine' must have been pretty well soaked when he made it. Do you know, the other day at a banquet I said to my steward: 'Now, look here, Thaumastus, I never want roasted sucking-pig stuffed with truffles and chestnuts served at my table again. Do you hear? 'Very good, your Majesty,' he replied. Yet if there is one dish in the world which I really love beyond all others it is roasted sucking-pig stuffed with truffles and chestnuts. What was it I told you just now? Never to trust your allies? That was funny, eh? I forgot for the moment that you and I were allies." So I let the remark go, but it came back to me the next day, as I stood at a window watching Herod's coach roll away in the direction of Brindisi: I wondered what he had meant, and felt uncomfortable.

Herod was not the only king at that farewell banquet. His brother Herod Pollio, of Chalcis, was there; and Antiochus to whom I had restored the kingdom of Commagene, on the north-eastern border of Syria, which Caligula had taken away from him; and Mithridates whom I had now made King of the Crimea; and, besides these, the King of Lesser Armenia and the King of Osröene, both of whom had been hanging about Caligula's court, thinking it safer to be at Rome than in their own kingdoms, where Caligula might suspect them of plotting against him. I sent them all back together.

It would be just as well to follow Herod's story a little farther and to bring the account of what happened at Alexandria to a more conclusive point before returning to write of events at Rome and giving an indication of what was happening on the Rhine, in Morocco and on other frontiers. Herod returned to Palestine, with more pomp and glory even than on the last occasion. On arrival at Jerusalem he took down from the Temple Treasury the iron chain which he had hung up there as a thank-offering and put in its place the golden one that Caligula had given him: now that Caligula was dead he could do this without offence. The High Priest greeted him most respectfully, but after the usual compliments had passed took it upon himself to reprove Herod for having given his eldest daughter in marriage to his brother: no good, he said, would come of it.

Herod was not the man to allow himself to be dictated to by any ecclesiastic, however important or holy. He asked the High Priest, whose name was Jonathan, whether or not he considered that he, King Agrippa, had done a good service to the God of the Jews by dissuading Caligula from defiling the Temple and by persuading me to confirm the religious privileges of the Jews at Alexandria, and to grant similar privileges to Jews throughout the world. Jonathan replied that all this was well done. So Herod told him a little parable. A rich man one day saw a beggar by the roadside, who cried out to him for alms and claimed to be a cousin. The rich man said: "I am sorry for you, beggar man, and will do what I can for you, since you are my cousin. To-morrow if you go to my bank you will find ten bags of gold waiting for you there, each containing two thousand gold pieces in coin of the realm." "If you are speaking the truth," the beggar said, "may God reward you!" The beggar went to the bank and, sure enough, the bags of gold were handed to him. How pleased he was and how grateful! But one of the beggar's own brothers, a priest, who had himself done nothing for him when he was in distress, came to call on the rich man the next day. "Do you call this a joke?" he asked indignantly. "You swore to give your poor cousin twenty thousand gold pieces in coin of the realm, and deceived him into thinking that you had actually done so. Well, I came to help him count them, and do you know, in the very first bag I found a Parthian gold-piece masquerading as a real one! Can you pretend to believe that Parthian money passes current here? Is this an honest trick to play on a beggar?"

Jonathan was not abashed by the parable. He told Herod that the rich man had been foolish to spoil his gift by the inclusion of the Parthian coin, if, indeed, he had deliberately done so. And he said too that Herod must not forget that the greatest kings were only instruments in the hands of

God and were rewarded by Him in proportion to their devotion to His service.

"And His High Priests?" asked Herod.

"His High Priests are sufficiently rewarded for their faithfulness to Him, which includes the rebuking of all Jews who fail in their religious duty, by being allowed to put on the sacred vestments and once a year enter that marvellously holy chamber where He dwells apart in immeasurable Power and Glory."

"Very well," said Herod. "If I am an instrument in His hands, as you say, I hereby depose you. Someone else will wear the sacred vestments at the Passover Festival this year. It will be someone who knows the right times and seasons for uttering rebukes."

So Jonathan was deposed and Herod appointed a successor who also after a time offended Herod by protesting that it was not proper for the Master of Horse to be a Samaritan: a Jewish king should have only Jewish officers on his staff. The Samaritans were not of the seed of Father Abraham, but interlopers. This Master of Horse was none other than Silas; and for Silas's sake Herod deposed the High Priest and offered the office to Jonathan again. Jonathan refused it, though with seeming gratitude, saying that he was content to have once put on the sacred vestments and that a second consecration to the High Priesthood could not be so holy a ceremony as the first. If God had empowered Herod to depose him, it must have been a punishment for his pride; and if now God was in a forgiving mood, he rejoiced, but would not risk a second offence. Might he therefore suggest that the High Priesthood be given to his brother Matthias, as holy and God-fearing a man as was to be found in all Jerusalem? Herod consented.

Herod took up his residence in Jerusalem, in the part called Bezetha, or the New City; which surprised me very much, for he now had several fine cities luxuriously built in the Græco-Roman style, any one of which he could have made his capital. He visited all these cities from time to time in ceremonial style and treated the inhabitants with courtesy, but Jerusalem, he said, was the only city for a Jewish king to live and reign in. He made himself extremely popular with the inhabitants of Jerusalem not only by his gifts to the Temple and his beautification of the city but by his abolition of the house-tax, which diminished his revenues by a hundred thousand gold pieces annually. His total income, however, amounted even without this to some half a million gold pieces. What surprised me still more was that he now worshipped daily in the Temple and kept the Law with great strictness: for I remember the contempt that I had often heard him express for "that holy psalm-singer" his devout brother Aristobulus, and in the private letters that he now always enclosed in his official dispatches there was no sign of any moral change of heart.

One letter that he sent me was almost all about Silas. It ran as follows:

"Marmoset, my old friend, I have the saddest and most comical story to tell you: it concerns Silas, the 'faithful Achates' of your brigand friend Herod Agrippa. Most learned Marmoset, from your rich store of out-of-the way historical learning can you inform me whether your ancestor, the pious Æneas, was ever as bored by the faithful Achates as I have lately been by Silas? Have Virgilian commentators anything to tell us on that head? The fact is that I was foolish enough to appoint Silas my Master of Horse, as I think I wrote to you at the time. The High Priest didn't approve of the appointment, because he was a Samaritan—the Samaritans once vexed the Jews at Jerusalem, the ones who had returned there from their Babylonian captivity, by knocking down every night the walls they built by day; and the Jews have never forgiven them this. So I went to the trouble of deposing the High Priest on Silas's account. Silas had already begun to be very self-important and was daily giving fresh proof of his famous frankness and bluntness of speech. My removal of the High Priest encouraged him to put on greater airs than ever. Upon my word, sometimes visitors at Court could not make out which of us was the King and which was only the Master of Horse. Yet if I hinted to Silas that he was presuming on his friendship he used to sulk, and dear Cypros used to reproach me for my unkindness to him, and remind me of all that he had done for us. I had to be pleasant to him again and as good as apologize to him for my ingratitude.

"His worst habit was constantly harping on my former troubles—in mixed company too—and giving most embarrassingly circumstantial details of how he had saved me from this danger and that, and how faithful he had shown himself, and how much excellent advice of his I had neglected, and how he had never looked for any reward but my friendship, in fine weather or rain or tempest—for that was the Samaritan character. Well, he opened his mouth once too often. I was at Tiberias, on the Lake of Galilee, where I was once magistrate under Antipas, and the leading men of Sidon were banqueting with me. You may remember the difference of opinion that I once had with the Sidonians when I was Flaccus's adviser at Antioch? Trust Silas to be on his worst behaviour at a banquet of such unusual political importance. Almost the first thing that he said to Hasdrubal, the harbour-master of Sidon, a man of the greatest influence in Phœnicia, was: 'I know your face, don't I? Isn't your name Hasdrubal? Of course, yes, you were one of the delegation that came to King Herod Agrippa, about nine years ago, asking him to use his influence with Flaccus on behalf of Sidon in that boundary dispute with Damascus. I well remember advising Herod to refuse your presents, pointing out that it was dangerous to take bribes from both parties in a dispute: he would be sure to get into trouble. But he only laughed at me. That's his way.'

"Hasdrubal was a man of delicacy and said that he had no recollection of the incident at all: he was sure that Silas must be mistaken. But you can't stop Silas. 'Surely your memory isn't as bad as that?' he persisted. 'Why, it was because of that case that Herod had to clear out of Antioch in the disguise of a camel-driver—I provided him with it —leaving his wife and children behind—I had to smuggle them aboard a ship to take them away—and make a long detour by way of the Syrian desert to Edom. He went on a stolen camel. No, in case you ask me about that camel, it wasn't I who stole it, but King Herod Agrippa himself.'

"This made me pretty hot, and it was no use denying the main facts of the story. But I did my best to gloze it over with a light-hearted romance of how one day my desert blood stirred in me and I grew weary of Roman life at Antioch and felt an overpowering impulse to ride out into the vast desert spaces and visit my kinsmen in Edom; but knowing that Flaccus would detain me—he was dependent on me for political advice—I was forced to take my leave secretly, and so arranged with Silas for my family to meet me at the port of Anthedon at the conclusion of my adventure. And a very enjoyable holiday it had proved to be. At Anthedon, I said, I had been met by an Imperial courier, who had failed to find me at Antioch, with a letter from the Emperor Tiberius: inviting me to Rome to act as his adviser, because my brains were wasted in the provinces.

"Hasdrubal listened with polite interest, admiring my lies, for he knew the story almost as well as Silas did. He asked, 'May I inquire of your Majesty whether this was your first visit to Edom? I understand that the Edomites are a very noble, hospitable and courageous race, and despise luxury and frivolity with a primitive severity which I find it easier, myself, to admire than to imitate.'

"That fool Silas must needs put his oar in again. 'Oh, no, Hasdrubal, that wasn't his first visit to Edom. I was his only companion—except for the Lady Cypros, as she was then, and the two elder children—on his first visit. That was the year that Tiberius's son was murdered. King Herod had been obliged because of this to escape from his creditors at Rome, and Edom was the only safe place of refuge. He had run up the most enormous debts in spite of my repeated warnings that a day of reckoning would come at last. He loathed Edom, to tell the honest truth, and was contemplating suicide; but the Lady Cypros saved him by swallowing her pride and writing a very humble letter to her sister-in-law Herodias, with whom she had quarrelled. King Herod was invited here to Galilee and King Antipas made him a judge of the Lower Courts in this very town. His annual income was only seven hundred gold pieces.'

"Hasdrubal was opening his mouth to express surprise and incredulity when Cypros suddenly came to my help. She had not minded Silas's telling tales about me, but when he brought up that old memory of the letter to Herodias, it was quite another matter. 'Silas,' she said, 'you talk far too much and most of what you say is inaccurate and nonsensical. You will oblige me by holding your tongue.'

"Silas grew very red and once more addressed Hasdrubal: 'It is my Samaritan nature to tell the truth frankly, however disagreeable. Yes, King Herod passed through many vicissitudes before he won his present kingdom. Of some of these he does not appear to be ashamed—for instance, he has actually hung up in the Temple Treasury at Jerusalem the iron chain with which he was once fettered by order of the Emperor Tiberius. He was put in gaol for treason, you know. I had warned him repeatedly not to have private conversations with Gaius Caligula in the hearing of his coachman, but as usual he disregarded my warning. Afterwards Gaius

Caligula gave him a gold chain, a replica of the iron one, and the other day King Herod hung this gold chain up in the Treasury and took down the iron one, which did not shine brightly enough, I suppose.' I caught Cypros's eye and we exchanged understanding looks. So I told Thaumastus to go to my bedroom where the chain was hanging on the wall facing my bed and bring it down. He did so, and I passed it round the table as a curiosity; the Sidonians examining it with ill-concealed embarrassment. Then I called Silas to me. 'Silas,' I said, 'I am about to do you a signal honour. In recognition of all your services to me and mine, and the fine frankness that you have never failed to show me even in the presence of distinguished guests, I hereby invest you with the Order of the Iron Chain; and may you live long to wear it. You and I are the only two companions of this very select Order and I gladly surrender the regalia to you complete. Thaumastus, chain this man and take him away to prison.'

"Silas was too astonished to say a word and was led away like a lamb to the slaughter. The joke was that if he hadn't been so obstinate at Rome about refusing the citizenship that I had offered to get for him, I would never have been able to play that trick on him. He would have appealed to you and you would no doubt have pardoned him, you soft-hearted fellow. Well, I had to do it, or the Sidonians would never have respected me again. As it was, they seemed gratifyingly impressed and the rest of the banquet proved a great success. That was some months ago, and I kept him there in gaol—unpleaded for by Cypros—to learn his lesson; intending, however, to release him in time to attend my birthday feast, which took place yesterday. I sent Thaumastus to Tiberias to visit Silas in his cell. He was to say: 'I was once a messenger of hope and comfort to our Lord and Master King Herod Agrippa when he was entering the prison gates at Misenum: I am now here, Silas, as a messenger of hope and comfort to you. This pitcher of wine is the token. Our gracious sovereign invites you to banquet with him at Jerusalem in three days' time and will allow you to present yourself, if you prefer it, without the insignia of the Order that he has conferred on you. Here, take this and drink it. And my own advice to you, my friend Silas, is never to remind people of services that you have done them in times past. If they are grateful and honourable men they will not need any reminder, and if they are ungrateful and dishonourable the reminder will be wasted on them.'

"Silas had been brooding over his wrongs all these months and was bursting to tell someone about them—besides his warder. He said to Thaumastus: 'So that is King Herod's message, is it? And I am supposed to be grateful, am I? What new honour does he intend to confer on me? The Order of the Whip, perhaps? When was an honest man ever so badly treated at a friend's hands as I have been at King Herod's? Does he expect that the awful miseries I have suffered here in solitary confinement will have taught me to hold my tongue when I feel impelled to speak the truth and shame his lying counsellors and flattering courtiers? Tell the King that he has not broken my spirit and that if he releases me I shall celebrate the occasion by franker and blunter speech than ever: I shall tell the whole nation through how many dangers and misfortunes he and I passed together and how I always saved the situation in the end after he had nearly ruined us both by his refusal to listen to my warnings in time, and how generously he rewarded me for all this with a heavy chain and a dark dungeon. No, I shall never forget this treatment. My very soul when I die will remember it, and remember too all the glorious deeds I did for his sake.' 'Drink,' said Thaumastus. But Silas would not drink. Thaumastus tried to reason with the madman, but he insisted on sending the message and refusing the wine. So Silas is still in gaol and it is quite impossible for me to release him; as Cypros agrees.

"I was amused by that affair at Doris. You remember what I said to you at that farewell banquet when we were both so drunk and so Samaritanly frank: you'll be a God, my Marmoset, in spite of everything you do to prevent it. You can't stop that sort of thing. And as for what I said then about sucking-pig stuffed with truffles and chestnuts I think I know what I must have meant. I am such a good Jew now that I never, never on any occasion let a morsel of unclean food pass my lips—or at least if I do, nobody but I and my Arabian cook and the watching Moon knows about it. I abstain even when I visit my Phœnician neighbours or dine with my Greek subjects. When you write give me news of cunning old Vitellius and those scheming scoundrels Asiaticus, Vinicius and Vinicianus. I have sent my highflown compliments to your lively Messalina in my official letter. So good-bye for the present and continue to think well (better than he deserves) of your knavish old playmate,

"THE BRIGAND."

I shall explain about the "Doris affair." In spite of my edict some young Greeks at a place in Syria called Doris had got hold of a statue of mine and broken into a Jewish synagogue, where they set it up at the south end, as if for worship. The Jews of Doris at once appealed to Herod, as their natural protector, and Herod went in person to Petronius at Antioch to make a protest. Petronius wrote the magistrates of Doris a very severe letter, ordering them to arrest the guilty persons and send them to him for punishment without delay. Petronius wrote that the offence was a double one—not only to the Jews whose desecrated synogogue could no longer be used for worship, but to myself whose edict on the subject of religious toleration had been shamelessly violated. There was one curious remark in his letter: that the proper place for my statue was not in a Jewish synagogue but in one of my own temples. He thought, I suppose, that by now I

168

must surely have given in to the Senate's entreaties and that therefore it would be polite to anticipate my deification. But I was most firm about refusing to become a God.

You can imagine that the Alexandrian Greeks did their utmost to win my favour now. They sent a deputation to congratulate me on my accession and to offer to build and dedicate a splendid temple to me, at the City's expense; or, if I refused this, at least to build and stock a Library of Italian Studies, and dedicate this to me as the most distinguished living historian. They also asked permission to give special public readings of my *History of Carthage* and my *History of Etruria* every year on my birthday. Each work was to be read out from end to end by relays of highly trained elocutionists, the former in the old library, the latter in the new. They knew that this could not fail to flatter me. In accepting the honour I felt very much as the parents of still-born twins might be expected to feel if, some time after the delivery, the little cold corpses awaiting their funeral in a basket set somewhere in a corner were suddenly to glow with unexpected warmth and sneeze and cry in unison. After all, I had spent more than twenty of the best years of my life on these books and taken infinite trouble to learn the various languages necessary for collecting and checking my facts; and not a single person hitherto had to my knowledge been to the trouble of reading them. When I say "not a single person" I must make two exceptions. Herod had read the *History of Carthage*—he was not interested in the subject of Etruria—and said that he had learned a lot from it about the Phœnician character; but that he did not think that many people would have the same interest in it as he had. "There's too much meat in that sausage," he said, "and not enough spices and garlic." He meant that there was too much information in it and not enough elegant writing. He told me this while I was still a private citizen, so there could be no question of flattery. The only person except my secretaries and research-assistants who had read both books was Calpurnia. She preferred a good book to a bad play, she said, my histories to many quite good plays she had seen, and the Etruscan book to the Carthaginian one because it was about places that she knew. When I became Emperor, I should record here, I bought Calpurnia a charming villa near Ostia and gave her a comfortable annual income and a staff of well-trained slaves. But she never came to visit me at the Palace and I never visited her for fear of making Messalina jealous. She lived with a close friend, Cleopatra, an Alexandrian, who had also been a prostitute; but now that Calpurnia had enough money, and to spare, neither of them continued in the profession. They were quiet girls.

But, as I was saying, I was very proud indeed of the Alexandrian offer, for after all Alexandria is the cultural capital of the world and had I not been addressed by its leading citizens as the most distinguished living historian? I regretted that I could not spare the time for a visit to Alexandria to be present at one of the readings. The day that the embassy came I sent for a professional reader and asked him to read over to me in private a few passages from each of the histories. He did so with so much expression and such beautiful articulation that, forgetting for the moment that I was the author, I began clapping loudly.

# Chapter Ten

M Y IMMEDIATE preoccupation abroad was with the Rhine frontier. Towards the end of Tiberius's reign the Northern Germans had been encouraged by reports of his general inactivity to make raids across the river, into what we call the Lower Province. Small parties used to swim across at unguarded spots by night to attack lonely houses or hamlets, murder the occupants, and loot what gold and jewels they could find; and then swim back at dawn. It would have been difficult to stop them doing this, even if our men had been constantly on the alert—as in the North at least they certainly were not—because the Rhine is an immensely long river and most difficult to patrol. The only effective measure against the raiders would have been retaliation; but Tiberius had refused permission for any large-scale punitive expedition. He wrote: "If hornets plague you, burn their nest; but if it is only mosquitoes, pay no attention." As for the Upper Province, it may be recalled that Caligula during his expedition to France sent for Gætulicus, the commander of the four regiments on the Upper Rhine, and executed him on the unfounded charge of conspiracy; that he crossed the river with an enormous army and advanced a few miles, the Germans offering him no resistance; that he then grew suddenly alarmed and rushed back. The man whom he had appointed as Gætulicus's successor was commander of the French auxiliary forces at Lyons. His name was Galba[1], and he was one of Livia's men. She had marked him out for pre-

[1] Afterwards Emperor (A. D. 69).—R. G.

171

ferment when he was still a youngster and he had amply
justified the trust she had placed in him. He was a courageous soldier and a discerning magistrate, worked hard and
bore an exemplary private character. He had attained his
Consulship six years before this. Livia, when she died, had
left him a special legacy of five hundred thousand gold pieces;
Tiberius, however, as Livia's executor, pronounced that this
must be a mistake. The sum had been written in figures,
not in words, and he ruled that fifty thousand was all the
testatrix had intended. As Tiberius never paid a single one
of Livia's legacies this did not make much difference at the
time, but when Caligula became Emperor and paid Livia's
legacies in full, it was bad luck for Galba that Caligula was
unaware of Tiberius's fraud. Galba did not press for the
whole five hundred thousand, and perhaps it was as well for
him that he did not, for if he had done so Caligula would
have remembered the incident when he ran short of funds
and, so far from giving him this important command on the
Rhine, would propably have accused him of taking part in
Gætulicus's conspiracy.

How Caligula chose Galba makes a curious story. He had
ordered a big parade at Lyons one day, and when it was over
he called before him all the officers who had taken part in it
and gave them a lecture on the necessity for keeping in good
physical condition. "A Roman soldier," he said, "should be
as tough as leather and as hard as iron, and all officers should
set a good example to their men in this. I shall be interested
to see how many of you will survive a simple test which I
am about to set you. Come, friends, let us go for a little run
in the direction of Autun." He was sitting in his chariot with
a couple of fine French cobs in the shafts. His driver cracked
his whip and off they went. The already sweating officers
dashed after him with their heavy weapons and armour.
He kept just far enough ahead of them not to let them drop
behind out of sight, but never let his horses fall into a walk,

for fear that the officers would follow their example. On and on he went. The line strung out. Many of the runners fainted and one dropped dead. At the twentieth milestone he finally pulled up. Only one man had survived the test—Galba. Caligula said: "Would you prefer to run back, General, or would you prefer a seat beside me?" Galba had sufficient breath left to reply that as a soldier he had no preferences: he was accustomed to obey orders. So Caligula let him walk back, but the next day gave him his appointment. Agrippinilla became greatly interested in Galba when she met him at Lyons: she wanted to marry him, though he was married already to a lady of the Lepidan house. Galba was perfectly satisfied with his wife and behaved as coldly towards Agrippinilla as his loyalty to Caligula permitted. Agrippinilla persisted in her attentions and there was a great scandal one day at a reception given by Galba's mother-in-law to which Agrippinilla came without an invitation. Galba's mother-in-law called her out in front of all the noblemen and noblewomen assembled, abused her roundly as a shameless and lascivious hussy and actually struck her in the face with her fists. It would have gone badly for Galba if Caligula had not decided the next day that Agrippinilla was implicated in the plot against his life and banished her as I have described.

When Caligula had fled back to Rome in terror of a reported German raid across the Rhine (a lie humorously put about by the soldiers) his forces were all concentrated at one point. Great stretches of the river were left unguarded. The Germans heard of this at once, and also of Caligula's cowardice. They took the opportunity of crossing the Rhine in force and establishing themselves in our territory, where they did a great deal of damage. Those who crossed were the tribesmen called the Chattians, which means The Mountain Cats. The Cat was their tribal ensign. They had fortresses in the hill country between the Rhine and the Upper Weser. My brother Germanicus always used to give them credit for being the best fighting men in Germany. They kept their ranks in battle, obeyed their leaders almost like Romans and at night used to dig entrenchments and put outposts out—a precaution seldom taken by any other German tribe. It cost Galba several months and considerable losses in men to dislodge them and drive them back across the river.

Galba was a strict disciplinarian. Gætulicus had been a capable soldier but rather too lenient. The day that Galba arrived at Mainz to take over his command the soldiers were watching some games that were being held in Caligula's honour. A huntsman had shown great skill in dispatching a leopard and the men all started clapping. The first words that Galba spoke on entering the General's box were, "Keep your hands under your cloaks, men! I am in command now and I don't permit any slovenliness." He kept this up and for so severe a commander was extremely popular. His enemies called him mean, but that was unjust: he was merely most abstemious, discouraged extravagance in his staff, and exacted a strict account of expenditure from his subordinates. When news came of Caligula's assassination his friends urged him to march on Rome at the head of his corps, saying that he was now the only fit person to take control of the Empire. Galba replied, "March on Rome and leave the Rhine unguarded? What sort of a Roman do you take me to be?" And he continued: "Besides, from all accounts, this Claudius is a hardworking and modest man; and though some of you seem to think him a fool, I would hesitate to call any member of the Imperial family a fool who has successfully survived the reigns of Augustus, Tiberius, and Caligula. I think that in the circumstances the choice is a good one and I shall be pleased to take the oath of allegiance to Claudius. He is not a soldier, you say. So much the better. Campaigning experience is sometimes not altogether a blessing in a Commander-in-Chief. The God Augustus—I speak with all respect—was

174

inclined, as an old man, to hamper his generals by giving them over-detailed instructions and advice: that last Balkan campaign would never have dragged on as it did, if he had not been so anxious to re-fight from far in the rear the battles that he had fought at the head of his troops some forty years previously. Claudius will not, I think, either take the field himself, at his age, or be tempted to override the decisions of his generals in matters of which he is ignorant. But at the same time he is a learned historian and has, I am told, a grasp of general strategical principles that any Commanders-in-Chief with actual fighting experience might envy him."

These remarks of Galba's were later reported to me by one of his staff and I sent him a personal letter of thanks for his good opinion of me. I told him that he could count on me to give my generals a free hand in such campaigns as I ordered or authorized them to undertake. I would merely decide whether the expedition was to be one of conquest or whether it would have merely a punitive character. In the former case vigour was to be tempered with humanity—as little damage as possible was to be done to captured villages and towns and to standing crops, the local Gods were not to be humiliated, and no butchery must be allowed once the enemy was broken in battle. In the case, however, of a punitive expedition no mercy whatsoever need be shown: as much damage as possible must be done to crops, villages, towns and temples, and such of the inhabitants as were not worth taking home as slaves were to be massacred. I would also indicate the maximum number of reserves that could be called upon and the maximum number of Roman casualties that would be permitted. I would decide beforehand, in consultation with the general himself, the precise objectives of attack and ask him to state how many days or months he would need for taking them. I would leave all strategical and tactical dispositions to him, and only exercise my right of taking personal command of the campaign, bringing with me such further reinforcements as I thought necessary, should the objectives not be reached within the agreed time, or should the Roman casualties rise beyond the stipulated figure.

For I had a campaign in mind for Galba to make against the Chattians. It was to be a punitive expedition. I did not propose to enlarge the Empire beyond the natural and obvious frontier of the Rhine, but when the Chattians and the Northern tribesmen, the Istævonians, failed to respect that frontier, a vigorous assertion of Roman dignity had to be made. My brother Germanicus always used to say that the only way to win the respect of Germans was to treat them with brutality; and that they were the only nation in the world of whom he would say this. The Spaniards, for example, could be impressed by the courtesy of a conqueror, the French by his riches, the Greeks by his respect for the arts, the Jews by his moral integrity, the Africans by his calm authoritative bearing. But the German, who is impressed by none of these things, must always be struck to the dust, and struck down again as he rises, and struck again as he lies groaning. "While his wounds still pain him he will respect the hand that dealt them."

At the same time as Galba was advancing, another punitive expedition was to be made against the Istævonian raiders, by Gabinius, the General commanding the four regiments on the Lower Rhine. Gabinius's expedition interested me far more than Galba's, for its object was not merely punitive. Before ordering it I sacrificed in Augustus's Temple and privately informed the God that I was bent on completing a task that my brother Germanicus had been prevented from completing, and which was, I knew, one in which He was Himself much interested: it was the rescue of the third and last of the lost Eagles of Varus, still in German hands after more than thirty years. My brother Germanicus, I reminded Him, had recaptured one Eagle in the year following His Deification and another in the campaigning season after that; but Tiberius had recalled him before he could avenge Varus in a last crushing battle and win back the Eagle that was still missing. I therefore begged the God to favour my arms and restore the honour of Rome. As the smoke of the sacrifice rose, the hands of Augustus's statue seemed to move in a blessing and his head to nod. It may only have been a trick of the smoke, but I took it for a favourable omen.

The fact was, I was now confident that I knew exactly where in Germany the Eagle was hidden, and proud of myself for the way I had discovered this secret. My predecessors could have done what I did if they had only thought of it; but they never did. It was always a pleasure to prove to myself that I was by no means the fool that they had all thought me, and that indeed I could manage some things better than they. It occurred to me that in my Household Battalion, composed of captured tribesmen from almost every district in Germany, there must be a half a dozen men at least who knew where the Eagle was hidden; yet when the question had once been put to them on parade by Caligula, with an offer of freedom and a large sum of money in return for the information, every face had immediately gone blank: it seemed that nobody knew. I tried a very different method of persuasion. I ordered them all out on parade one day and addressed them very kindly. I told them that as a reward for their faithful services I was going to do them an unprecedented kindness; I was going to send back to Germany —the dear, dear Fatherland about which they nightly sang such melancholy and tuneful songs—all members of the battalion who had completed twenty-five years' service with it. I said that I should have liked to send them home with gifts of gold, weapons, horses and the like, but unfortunately I was unable to do this or even to allow them to take back across the Rhine any possessions that they had acquired during their captivity. The obstacle was the still missing Eagle. Until this sacred emblem was returned, Roman honour was still in pawn and it would create a bad impression in the City if I were to reward with anything beyond their bare freedom men who had in their youth taken part in the massacre of Varus's army. However, to true patriots liberty was better than gold and they would, I felt sure, accept the gift in the spirit that it was made in. I did not ask them, I said, to reveal to me the whereabouts of the Eagle, because no doubt this was a secret which they had been bound by oaths to their Gods not to reveal: and I would not ask any man to perjure himself for the sake of a bribe, as my predecessor had done. In two days' time, I promised, all the twenty-five-year veterans would be sent back across the Rhine under safe conduct.

I then dismissed the parade. The sequel was as I had forseen. These veterans were even less anxious to return to Germany than the Romans captured by the Parthians at Carrhæ were to return to Rome when, thirty years later, Marcus Vipsanius Agrippa bargained with the King for their exchange. Those Romans in Parthia had settled down, married, raised families, grown rich and quite forgotten their past. And these Germans at Rome, though technically slaves, lived a most easy and enjoyable life and their regret for home was not at all a sincere emotion, merely an excuse for tears when they were maudlin-drunk. They came to me in a body and begged for permission to remain in my service. Many of them were fathers, and even grandfathers, by slavewomen attached to the Palace, and they were all comfortably off: Caligula had given them handsome presents from time to time. I pretended to be angry, called them ungrateful and base to refuse so priceless a gift as liberty and said that I had no further use for their services. They asked pardon and permission at least to take their families with them. I refused this plea, mentioning the Eagle again. One of them, a Cheruscan, cried out: "It's all the fault of those cursed Chaucians that we have to go like this. Because they have sworn to keep the secret, we other innocent Germans are made to suffer."

This was what I wanted. I dismissed from my presence all but the representatives of the Greater and Lesser Chaucian tribes. (The Chaucians lived on the North German coast between the Dutch Lakes and the Elbe; they had been confederates of Hermann's.) Then I said to these: "I have no intention of asking you Chaucians where the Eagle is, but if any of you have *not* sworn an oath about it, please tell me so at once." The Greater Chaucians, the western half of the nation, all declared that they had not sworn any such oath. I believed them, because the second Eagle that my brother Germanicus won back had been found in a temple of theirs. It was unlikely that one trible would have been awarded two Eagles in the distribution of spoils that followed Hermann's victory.

I then addressed the chief man of the Lesser Chaucians: "I do not ask you to tell me where the Eagle is, or to what God you swore the oath. But perhaps you will tell me in what town or village you took that oath. If you tell me this I shall suspend my order for your repatriation."

"Even to say as much as that would be a violation of my oath, Cæsar."

But I used an old trick on him that I had read about in my historical studies: once, when a certain Phœnician judge visiting a village on his assizes wished to find out where a man had hidden a gold cup that he had stolen, he told the man that he did not believe him capable of theft and would discharge him. "Come, sir, let us go for a friendly walk instead and you will perhaps show me your interesting village." The man guided him down every street but one. The judge found by inquiry that one of the houses in this street was occupied by the man's sweetheart; and the cup was discovered hidden in the thatch of her roof. So in the same way I said:

179

"Very well, I shall not press you further." I then turned to another member of the tribe who also seemed, by his sullen, uncomfortable looks, to be in the secret, and asked conversationally: "Tell me: in what towns or villages in your territory are there temples raised to your German Hercules?" It was probable that the Eagles had been dedicated to this God. He gave me a list of seven names, which I noted down. "Is that all?" I asked.

"I cannot recall any more," he answered.

I appealed to the Greater Chaucians. "Surely there must be more than seven temples in so important a territory as Lesser Chaucia—between the great rivers of Weser and Elbe?"

"Oh yes, Cæsar," they replied. "He has not mentioned the famous temple at Bremen on the eastern bank of the Weser."

That is how I was able to write to Gabinius: "You will, I think, find the Eagle somewhere hidden in the temple of the German Hercules at Bremen on the eastern bank of the Weser. Don't spend too much time at first in punishing the Istævonians: march in close formation straight through their territory and that of the Ansibarians, rescue the Eagle and do the burning, killing and pillaging on your return."

Before I forget it, there is another story that I want to tell about a stolen gold cup, and it may as well go in here as anywhere. Once I invited a number of provincial knights to supper—and would you believe it, one of the rogues, a Marseilles man, went off with the gold wine cup that had been put before him. I didn't say a word to him, but invited him to supper again the next day and this time gave him only a stone cup. This apparently frightened him, for the next morning the gold cup was returned with a fulsomely apologetic note explaining that he had taken the liberty of borrowing the cup for two days in order to get the engravings on it, which he much admired, copied by a goldsmith: he wished to perpetuate the memory of the enormous honour that I had done him, by drinking from a similarly chased gold cup every day for the rest of his life. In answer I sent him the stone cup asking, in exchange, for the reproduction of the gold one as a memento of the charming incident.

I arranged a date in May for both Galba's and Gabinius's expeditions to start, increased their forces by levies in France and Italy to six regiments apiece—leaving two regiments to hold the Upper Rhine, and two to hold the Lower—allowed them each a maximum of two thousand casualties, and gave them until July the First to conclude their operations and be on the way home. Galba's objective was a line of three Chattian towns originally built when the country was under Roman rule—Nuæsium, Gravionarium and Melocavus—which lie parallel with the Rhine about a hundred miles inland from Mainz.

I shall content myself by recording that both campaigns were a complete success. Galba burned one hundred and fifty stockaded villages, destroyed thousands of acres of crops, killed great numbers of Germans, armed and unarmed, and had sacked the three towns indicated by the middle of June. He took about two thousand prisoners of both sexes, including men and women of rank to hold as hostages for the Chattians' good behaviour. He lost twelve hundred men, killed or disabled, of whom four hundred were Romans. Gabinius had the harder task and accomplished it with the loss of only eight hundred men. He took a last-minute suggestion of mine, which was not to make straight for Bremen but to invade the territory of the Angrivarians, who live to the south of the Lesser Chaucians; and from there to send a flying column of cavalry against Bremen, in the hope of capturing the town before the Chaucians thought it worth while to remove the Eagle to some safer repository. It all worked out exactly to plan. Gabinius's cavalry, which he commanded personally, found the Eagle just where I had expected, and he was so pleased with himself that he called up the rest of his forces and drove right through Lesser Chaucia from end to end, burning the timber shrines of the German Hercules one after the other, until none was left standing. His destruction of crops and villages was not so methodical as Galba's, but on the way back he gave the Istævonians plenty to remember him by. He took two thousand prisoners.

The news of the rescue of the Eagle came to Rome simultaneously with that of Galba's successful sacking of the Chattian towns, and the Senate immediately voted me the title of Emperor, which this time I did not refuse. I considered that I had earned it by my location of the Eagle and by suggesting the long-distance cavalry raid, and by the care that I had taken to make both campaigns a surprise. Nobody knew anything about them until I signed the order instructing the French and Italian levies to be under arms and on their way to the Rhine within three days.

Galba and Gabinius were given triumphal ornaments. I would have had them granted triumphs if the campaigns had been more than mere punitive expeditions. But I persuaded the Senate to honour Gabinius with the hereditary surname "Chaucius" in commemoration of his feat. The Eagle was carried in solemn procession to the Temple of Augustus, where I sacrificed and gave thanks for his divine aid: and dedicated to him the wooden gates of the temple where the Eagle had been found—Gabinius had sent them to me as a gift. I could not dedicate the Eagle itself to Augustus, because there was a socket long ago prepared for its reception in the temple of Avenging Mars, alongside the other two rescued Eagles. I took it there later and dedicated it, my heart swelling with pride.

The soldiers composed ballad verses about the rescue of the Eagle. But this time, instead of building them on to their original ballad, "The Three Griefs of Lord Augustus," they made them into a new one called "Claudius and the Eagle." It was by no means flattering to me, but I enjoyed some of the verses. The theme was that I was an abso-

lute fool in some respects and did the most ridiculous things
—I stirred my porridge with my foot, and shaved myself
with a comb, and when I went to the Baths used to drink
the oil handed me to rub myself with and rub myself with
the wine handed me to drink. Yet I had amazing learning, for all that: I knew the names of every one of the stars
in Heaven and could recite all the poems that had ever
been written, and had read all the books in all the libraries
of the world. And the fruit of this wisdom was that I alone
was able to tell the Romans where the Eagle was that had
been lost so many years and had resisted all efforts to recapture it. The first part of the ballad contained a dramatic account of my acclamation as Emperor by the Palace
Guard; and I shall quote three verses to show the sort of
ballad it was:

> Claudius hid behind a curtain,
>   Gratus twitched the thing away,
> "Be our Leader," said bold Gratus.
>   "All your orders we'll obey."

> "Be our Leader," said bold Gratus,
>   "Learned Claudius, courage take!
> There's an Eagle to be rescued
>   For the God Augustus' sake."

> Learned Claudius, feeling thirsty,
>   Drank a mighty pot of ink.
> "*Owl* was it you said, or *Eagle*?
>   I could rescue both, I think."

Early in August, twenty days after I had been voted the
title of Emperor, Messalina bore me her child. It was a boy,
and for the first time I experienced all the pride of father-
hood. For my son Drusillus, whom I had lost some twenty

years before at the age of eleven, I had felt no warm paternal feelings at all, and very few for my daughter Antonia, though she was a good-hearted child. This was because my marriages with Urgulanilla, Drusillus's mother, and with Ælia, Antonia's mother (both of whom I divorced as soon as the political situation enabled me to do so), had been forced on me: I had no love for either of these women. Whereas I was passionately in love with Messalina; and seldom, I suppose, had our Roman Goddess Lucina, who presides over childbirth, been so persistently courted with prayers and sacrifices as she was by me in the last two months of Messalina's pregnancy. He was a fine healthy baby, and being my only son he took all my names, as the custom was. But I gave it out that he was to be known as Drusus Germanicus. I knew that this would have a good effect on the Germans. The first Drusus Germanicus to make that name terrible across the Rhine—more than fifty years before this—had been my father, and the next had been my brother, twenty-five years later; and I was also a Drusus Germanicus and had I not just won back the last of the captured Eagles? In another quarter of a century, no doubt, my little Germanicus would repeat history and slaughter a few score thousands more of them. Germans are like briars on the edge of a field: they grow quickly and have to be constantly checked with steel and fire to prevent them from encroachment. As soon as my boy was a few months old and I could pick him up without risk of injuring him, I used to carry him about with me in my arms in the Palace grounds and show him to the soldiers; they all loved him almost as much as I did. I reminded them that he was the first of the Cæsars since the great Julius who had been born a Cæsar, not merely adopted into the family, as Augustus, Marcellus, Gaius, Lucius, Postumus, Tiberius, Castor, Nero, Drusus, Caligula had each in turn been. But here, as a matter of fact, my pride tempted me

184

into inaccuracy. Caligula, unlike his brothers Nero and Drusus, was born two or three years after his father, my brother Germanicus, had been adopted by Augustus (a Cæsar in virtue of his adoption by Julius) as his son; so he was really born a Cæsar. What misled me was the fact that Caligula was not adopted by Tiberius (a Cæsar in virtue of his adoption by Augustus) as *his* son until he was about twenty-three years old.

Messalina did not keep our little Germanicus at her own breast, as I wished her to do, but found him a foster-mother. She was too busy to nurse a child, she said. But nursing a child is an almost certain insurance against renewed pregnancy, and pregnancy interferes with a woman's health and freedom of action even more than nursing does. So it was bad luck for Messalina when she became pregnant again, so soon afterwards that only eleven months elapsed between Germanicus's birth and that of our daughter Octavia.

There was a poor harvest that summer and so meagre a supply of corn in the public granaries that I grew alarmed and cut down the free ration of corn, which the poor citizens had come to regard as their right, to a very small daily measure. I only maintained it even at that measure by commandeering or buying corn from every possible source. The heart of the populace lies in its belly. In the middle of winter, before supplies began to come through from Egypt and Africa (where, fortunately, the new harvest was a particularly good one), there were frequent disorders in the poorer quarters of the City, and much loose revolutionary talk.

# Chapter Eleven

BY THIS time my engineers had finished the report which I had told them to make on the possibility of converting Ostia into a safe winter harbour. The report was at first sight a most discouraging one. Ten years and ten million gold pieces seemed to be needed. But I reminded myself that the work once carried out would last forever and that the danger of a corn famine would never arise again, or at least not so long as we held Egypt and Africa. It seemed to me an undertaking worthy of the dignity and greatness of Rome. In the first place, a considerable tract of land would have to be excavated and strong retaining walls of concrete built on every side of the excavation, before the sea could be let into it to form the inner harbour. This harbour in turn must be protected by two huge moles built out into deep water, on either side of the harbour entrance, with an island between their extremities to act as a break-water when the wind blew from the west and big seas came rushing up the mouth of the Tiber. On this island it was proposed to build a lighthouse like the famous one at Alexandria, to guide shipping safely in, however dark and stormy the night. The island and the moles would form the outer harbour.

When the engineers brought me their plans they said: "We have done as you told us, Cæsar, but of course the cost will be prohibitive."

I answered rather sharply: "I asked for a plan and an estimate and you have been good enough to provide both, for which many thanks; but I do not employ you as my financial advisers and I shall thank you not to take that upon yourselves."

"But Callistus, your Public Treasurer——" one of them began.

I cut him short: "Yes, of course, Callistus has been speaking to you. He is very careful with public money, and it is right that he should be. But economy can be carried too far. This is a matter of the utmost importance. Besides, I should not be surprised to learn that it is the corn-factors who have persuaded you to send in this discouraging report. The scarcer corn becomes, the richer they grow. They pray for bad weather and thrive on the miseries of the poor."

"Oh, Cæsar," they chorused virtuously, "can you believe that we would take bribes from corn-factors?"

But I could see that my shot had gone home. *"Persuaded,* not *bribed,* was my word. Don't accuse yourselves unnecessarily. Now listen to me. I am determined to carry this plan out whatever it is going to cost; get that into your heads. And I'll tell you another thing: it is not going to take nearly so long a time or cost nearly so much money as you seem to think. Three days from now you and I are going to go into the question thoroughly."

On a hint given me by my secretary Polybius I consulted the Palace archives, and there, sure enough, I found a detailed scheme that had been prepared by Julius Cæsar's engineers some ninety years before for the very same work. The scheme was almost identical with the one that had just been made, but the estimated time and cost were, I was delighted to find, only four years and four millions of gold. Allowing for a slight increase in the cost of materials and labour it should be possible to carry the task out for only half what my own engineers had estimated, and in four years instead of ten. In certain respects the old plan (abandoned as too costly!) was an improvement on the new, though it left out the island. I studied both plans closely, comparing their points of difference; and then visited Ostia myself, in company with Vitellius, who knew a great deal about engineering, to make sure that no important physical changes had occurred on the site of the proposed harbour since Julius's day. When the conference met I was so primed with information that the engineers found it impossible to deceive me—by under-estimating, for instance, the amount of earth that a hundred men could shift from this point to that in a single day, or by suggesting that the excavations would entail the cutting away of many thousands of square feet of living rock. I now knew almost as much about the business as they did. I did not tell them how I came to know: I let it appear that I had taught myself engineering in the course of my historical studies, and that a couple of visits to Ostia had sufficed me for mastering the whole problem and drawing my own conclusions. I profited from the great impression that I thus made on them by saying that if there was any attempt to slow down the work once it started, or any lack of enthusiasm, I would send them all down to the Underworld to build Charon a new jetty on the River Styx. Work on the harbour must begin at once. They should have as many workmen as they needed, up to the number of thirty thousand, and a thousand military foremen, with the necessary material, tools and transport; but begin they must.

Then I called Callistus and told him what I had decided. When he threw up his hands and turned up his eyes in a despairing gesture I told him to stop play-acting.

"But, Cæsar, where's the money to come from?" he bleated like a sheep.

"From the corn-factors, fool," I answered. "Give me the names of principal members of the Corn Ring and I'll see that we get as much as we need."

Within an hour I had the six richest corn-factors in the City before me. I frightened them.

"My engineers report that you gentlemen have been bribing them to send in an unfavourable report on the Ostia scheme. I take a very serious view of the matter. It amounts to conspiracy against the lives of your fellow-citizens. You deserve to be thrown to the wild beasts."

They denied the charge with tears and oaths and begged me to let them know in what way they could prove their loyalty.

That was easy: I wanted an immediate loan of a million gold pieces for the Ostia scheme, which I would pay back as soon as the financial situation justified it.

They pretended that their combined fortunes did not amount to half that sum. I knew better. I gave them a month to raise the money and I warned them that if they did not do so they would all be banished to the Black Sea. Or farther. "And remember," I said, "that when this harbour is built it will be *my* harbour—if you want to use it you will have to come to me for permission. I advise you to keep on the right side of me."

The money was paid over within five days, and the work at Ostia began at once with the erection of shelters for the workmen and the pegging out of tasks. On occasions of this sort it was, I must admit, very pleasurable to be a monarch: to be able to get important things done by smothering stupid opposition with a single authoritative word. But I had to be constantly reminding myself of the danger of exercising my Imperial prerogatives in such a way as to retard the eventual restoration of a Republic. I did my best to encourage free speech and public-spiritedness, and to avoid transforming personal caprices of my own into laws which all Rome must obey. It was very difficult. The joke was that free speech, public-spiritedness and Republican idealism itself seemed to come under the heading of personal caprices of my own. And though at first I made a point of being accessible to everyone, in order to avoid the appearance of monarchical haughtiness, and of speaking in a friendly familiar way with all my fellow-citizens, I soon had to behave more distantly. It was not so much that I had not the time to spare for continuous friendly chat with everyone who came calling at the Palace; it was rather that my fellow-citizens, with few exceptions, shamefully abused my good feelings towards them. They did this either by answering my familiarity with an ironically polite haughtiness, as if to say, "You can't fool us into loyalty," or by a giggling impudence as if to say, "Why don't you behave like a real Emperor?" or by thoroughly false good-comradeship, as if to say, "If it pleases your Majesty to unbend, and to expect us to unbend in conformity with your humour, then look how obligingly we do so! But if you please to frown, down we'll go on our faces at once."

Speaking of the harbour, Vitellius said to me one day: "A republic can never hope to carry through public works on so grand a scale as a monarchy. All the grandest constructions in the world are the work of Kings or Queens. The walls and hanging gardens of Babylon. The Mausoleum at Halicarnassus. The Pyramids. You have never been to Egypt, have you? I was stationed there as a young soldier and, ye Gods, those Pyramids! It is impossible to convey in words the crushing sense of awe with which they overwhelm everyone who sees them. One first hears about them at home, as a child, and asks: 'What are the Pyramids?' and the answer is, 'Huge stone tombs in Egypt, triangular in shape, without any ornaments on them: just faced with white stucco?' That doesn't sound very interesting or impressive. The mind makes 'huge' no huger than some very big building with which one happens to be familiar—say the Temple of Augustus yonder or the Julian Basilica. And then again, visiting Egypt, one sees them at a great distance across the desert, little white marks like tents, and says:

'Why, surely *that's* nothing to make a fuss about! But, Heavens, to stand beneath them a few hours later and look up! Cæsar, I tell you, they are incredibly and impossibly huge. It makes one feel physically sick to think of them as having been built by human hands. One's first sight of the Alps was nothing by comparison. So white, smooth, pitilessly immortal. Such a terrific monument of human aspiration——"

"And stupidity and tyranny and cruelty," I broke in. "King Cheops, who built the Great Pyramid, ruined his rich country, bled it white and left it gasping; and all to gratify his own absurd vanity and perhaps impress the Gods with his superhuman power. And what practical use did this Pyramid serve? Was it intended as a tomb to house Cheops's corpse for all eternity? Yet I have read that this absurdly impressive sepulchre has long been empty. The invading Shepherd Kings discovered the secret entrance, rifled the inner chamber, and made a bonfire of proud Cheops's mummy."

Vitellius smiled. "You haven't seen the Great Pyramid or you wouldn't talk like that. Its emptiness makes it all the more majestic. And as for use, why, it has a most important use. Its pinnacle serves as a mark of orientation for the Egyptian peasants when the yearly Nile flood subsides and they must mark out their fields again in the sea of fertile mud."

"A tall pillar would have served just as well," I said, "and two tall pillars, one on each bank of the Nile, would have been still better; and the cost would have been negligible. Cheops was mad, like Caligula; though apparently he had a more settled madness than Caligula, who always did things by fits and starts. The great city that Caligula planned, to command the Great St. Bernard Pass on the Alps, would never have got very far towards completion, though he had lived to be a centenarian."

Vitellius agreed. "He was a jackdaw. The nearest he ever came to raising a Pyramid was when he built that out-size ship and stole the great red obelisk from Alexandria. A jackdaw and a monkey."

"Yet I seem to remember that you once adored that jackdaw-monkey as a God."

"And I gratefully remember that the advice and example came from you."

"Heaven forgive us both," I said. We were standing talking outside the Temple of Capitoline Jove, which we had just been ritually purifying, because of the recent appearance, on the roof, of a bird of evil omen. (It was an owl of the sort we call "incendiaries" because they foretell the destruction by fire of any building on which they perch.) I pointed across the valley with my finger. "Do you see that? That's part of the greatest monument ever built, and though monarchs like Augustus and Tiberius have added to it and kept it in repair, it was first built by a free people. And I have no doubt that it will last as long as the Pyramids, besides having proved of infinitely more service to mankind."

"I don't see what you mean. You seem to be pointing at the Palace."

"I am pointing at the Appian Way,' I replied solemnly. "It was begun in the Censorship of my great ancestor, Appius Claudius the Blind. The Roman Road is the greatest monument ever raised to human liberty by a noble and generous people. It runs across mountain, marsh and river. It is built broad, straight and firm. It joins city with city and nation with nation. It is tens of thousands of miles long, and always thronged with grateful travellers. And while the Great Pyramid, a few hundred feet high and wide, awes sight-seers to silence—though it is only the rifled tomb of an ignoble corpse and a monument of oppression and misery, so that no doubt in viewing it you may still seem to hear the crack of the taskmaster's whip and the squeals and groans of the poor workmen struggling to set a huge block of stone into position——" But in this unpremeditated gush of eloquence I had forgotten the beginning of my sentence. I broke off, feeling foolish, and Vitellius had to come to the rescue. He threw up his hands, shut his eyes and declaimed: "Words fail me, my Lords. Nothing that I might utter could possibly match the depths of my feelings in this matter." We both laughed uproariously at this. Vitellius was one of the few friends I had who treated me with the right sort of familiarity. I never knew whether it was genuine or artificial; but if artificial, it was so good an imitation of the real thing that I accepted it at its face value. I should never perhaps have called it in question if his former adoration of Caligula had not been so well acted, and if it had not been for the matter of Messalina's slipper. I will tell about this.

Vitellius was going up a staircase at the Palace, one day in summer, with Messalina and myself, when Messalina said: "Stop a moment, please: I've lost my slipper." Vitellius quickly turned and retrieved it for her, handing it back with a deep obeisance. Messalina was charmed. She said, smiling: "Claudius, you won't be jealous, will you, if I confer the Order of the Jewelled Slipper on this brave soldier, our dear friend Vitellius? He really is most gallant and obliging."

"But don't you need the slipper, my dear?"

"No, it's cooler to go barefoot on a day like this. And I have scores of other pretty pairs."

So Vitellius took the slipper and kissed it and put it in the pocket-fold of his robe, where he kept it continually; bringing it out to kiss once more when enlarging, in sentimental private talk with me, on Messalina's beauty, brains, bounty and on my extraordinarily good fortune in being her husband. It always brought a great sense of warmth to my heart and sometimes even tears to my eyes to hear Messalina praised. It was a constant wonder to me that she could care as much for a lame, pedantic, stuttering old fellow like myself as she swore she did; yet nobody, I argued, could pretend that she had married me for mercenary reasons. I was a bankrupt at the time, and as for the possibility of my ever becoming Emperor, it could surely never have occured to her.

The harbour at Ostia was by no means my only great public work. The verse that the Sibyl of Cumæ recited when I visited her once, in disguise, ten years before I became Emperor, prophesied that I should "give Rome water and winter bread." The winter bread was a reference to Ostia, but the water meant the two great aqueducts I built. It is very curious about prophecies. A prophecy is made, perhaps, when one is a boy and one pays great attention to it at the time, but then a mist descends: one forgets about it altogether until suddenly the mist clears and the prophecy is fulfilled. It was not until my aqueducts were completed and consecrated, and the harbour completed too, that I recalled the Sibyl's verse. Yet I suppose that it had been at the back of my mind all the time, as it were the God's whisper to me to undertake these great projects.

My aqueducts were most necessary: the existing water supply was by no means sufficient for the City's needs, though greater than that of any other city in the world. We Romans love fresh water. Rome is a town of baths and fish-pools and fountains. The fact was that, though Rome was now served by no less than seven aqueducts, the rich men had managed to draw away most of the public water for their own use, getting permission to connect private reservoirs with the mains—their swimming-baths had to have fresh water every day, and their great gardens had to be watered—so that many of the poorer citizens were reduced in the summer to drinking and cooking with Tiber water, which was most unhealthy. Cocceius Nerva, that virtuous old man, whom my Uncle Tiberius kept by him as his good genius, and who eventually committed suicide—this

Nerva, then, whom Tiberius had made his Inspector of Aqueducts advised him to show his maganimity by giving the City a water-supply worthy of its greatness; and re-minded him that his ancestor Appius Claudius the Blind had won eternal fame for bringing the Appian Water into Rome, from eight miles away, by the City's first aqueduct. Tiberius undertook to do as Nerva advised, but put the project off, and put it off again and again, as his way was, until Nerva's death. Then he felt remorse and sent his engineers out to discover suitable springs, according to the rules laid down by the famous Vitruvius. Such springs must run strongly all the year round, and run clean and sweet, and not fur the pipes, and must have such an eleva-tion that, allowing for the fall necessary to give the chan-nel of the aqueduct its proper inclination, the water will enter the final reservoir at a height sufficient to allow of its distribution, by pipes, to the highest houses in Rome. The engineers had to go far afield before they came on water that answered their purpose: they found it eventually in the hills to the south-east of the City. Two copious and excellent springs called the Blue Spring and the Curtain Spring broke out near the thirty-eighth milestone on the Sublacentian Road: they could be run together as one. Then there was the New Anio stream which could be drawn upon at the forty-second milestone on the same road, but on the other side: that would have to be carried by a second aqueduct and would pick up another stream, the Herculanean, opposite the Blue Spring. They reported that the water from these sources fulfilled all the necessary conditions, and that there was no nearer supply that did so. Tiberius had plans for two aqueducts drawn out and called for estimates; but de-cided at once that he could not afford the work, and shortly afterwards died.

Caligula, immediately on his accession, to show that he was of a more generous and public-spirited nature than

Tiberius, began work on Tiberius's plans, which were very detailed and good ones. He started well, but as his Treasury grew empty he could not keep it up and, taking his workmen from the most difficult parts (the great arched bridges, arch over arch in tiers, which carried the water across valleys and low ground), he put them to work on the easier levels where the channel ran round the slopes of hills or directly across the plain. He still could boast of rapid progress in terms of miles, and the expense was negligible. Some of the arches which he thus shirked building needed to be over a hundred feet high. The first aqueduct, afterwards called the Claudian Water, was to be over forty-six miles long, of which ten miles were to run on arches. The second, called the New Anio, was to be nearly fifty-nine miles long, and fifteen miles or so were to run on arches. When Caligula quarrelled with the people of Rome, the time they made the disturbance in the amphitheatre and sent him running in fright out of the City, he made his quarrel an excuse for abandoning all work on the aqueducts. He took the workmen away and put them on other tasks, such as building his temple and clearing sites at Antium (his birthplace) for the erection of a new capital city there.

So it fell to me to take up the work, which seemed to me one of first importance, where Caligula had abandoned it, though it meant having to concentrate on the more difficult stretches. If you wonder why the New Anio, though picking up the Herculanean stream close to the beginning of the Claudian Water, had to make a great circuit, instead of being run along the same arches, the answer is that the New Anio started at a much higher level and would have had too swift a flow if it had been brought down immediately to the Claudian Water. Vitruvius recommends an inclination of half a foot in a hundred yards and the height of the New Anio did not allow it to join the Claudian

Water, even on a higher tier of arches, until quite near the City, having travelled thirteen miles farther. In order to keep the water clean, there was a covered top to the channel with vent-holes at intervals to prevent bursts. There were also frequent large reservoirs through which the water passed, leaving its sediment behind. These reservoirs were also useful for purposes of irrigation, and amply paid for themselves by making it possible for the neighbouring landowners to put land under cultivation which otherwise would have been waste.

The work took nine years to complete, but there were no set-backs; and when it was finished it was among the chief wonders of Rome. The two waters entered the City by the Prænestine Gate, the New Anio above, the Claudian below, where a huge double arch had to be built to cross two main roads. The terminus was a great tower from which the water was distributed to ninety-two smaller towers. There were already some one hundred and sixty of these small water-towers in existence at Rome, but my two aqueducts doubled the actual supply of water. My Inspector of Aqueducts now calculated the flow of water into Rome as equal to a stream thirty feet broad and six feet deep, flowing at the rate of twenty miles an hour. Experts and ordinary people agreed that mine was the best quality of water of any, except that brought by the Marcian Water, the most important of the existing aqueducts, which accounted for fifty-four of the towers and had been in existence for about a hundred and seventy years.

I was very strict about the thieving of water by irresponsible persons. The chief thieving in the old days before Agrippa undertook the work of overhauling the whole water-system—he built two new aqueducts himself, one chiefly underground on the left bank of the Tiber—was done by deliberately punching holes in the main, or bribing the persons in charge of the aqueducts to do so, and making the damage look accidental; for there was a law giving people the right to casual water from leaks. This practice had lately started again. I reorganized the corps of aqueduct-workers and gave orders that all leakages were to be immediately repaired. But there was another kind of thieving going on too. There were pipes leading from the main to private water-towers built by the common subscriptions of wealthy families or clans. These pipes were made of lead and of a regulation size, so that no more water should be taken from the main than could flow through the pipe in its normal horizontal position; but by enlarging the pipe by pushing a stake through, lead being a very ductile metal, and furthermore inclining it from the horizontal, a much greater flow of water was obtained. Sometimes more impudent or powerful families substituted pipes of their own. I was determined to stop this. I had the pipes cast of bronze and officially stamped and so fixed to the main that they could not be declined without breaking them, and ordered my inspectors to visit the water-towers regularly to see that nothing was tampered with.

I might as well mention here the last of my three great engineering undertakings, the draining of the Fucine Lake. This lake, which lies some sixty miles due east of Rome under the Alban Hills, surrounded by marshes, is about twenty miles long and ten wide, though of no great depth. The project for draining it had long been discussed. The inhabitants of that part of the country, who are called Marsians, once petitioned Augustus about it, but, after due consideration, he turned down their request on the ground that the task was too laborious and that the possible results could not justify it. Now the question was raised again and a group of rich land-owners came to me and volunteered to pay two-thirds of the expense of the drainage if I undertook to carry it out. They asked in return grants of the land that would be reclaimed from the marshes and from the lake itself when the water was drained off. I refused their offer, because it occurred to me that if they were willing to pay so much for the reclaimed land it was probably worth far more. The problem seemed a simple one. One had only to cut a channel three miles long through a hill at the south-west extremity of the lake, thus allowing the water to escape into the River Liris which ran on the opposite side of the hill. I decided to start at once.

The work began in the first year of my monarchy, but it was soon evident that Augustus had been right in not attempting it. The labour and expense of cutting through that hill was infinitely greater than my engineers had reckoned it would be. They came on huge masses of solid rock that had to be hacked away piece by piece, and the debris dragged off along the channel; and there were troubles with springs in the hill which kept bursting out and interfering with the work. In order to finish it at all I soon had to set thirty thousand men working constantly at it. But I refused to be beaten: I hate throwing up a task. The channel was completed only the other day, after thirteen years' labour. Soon I shall give the signal for opening the sluice-gates and letting out the lake-water.

# Chapter Twelve

O NE day, just before Herod left Rome, he suggested that I should see a really good Greek doctor about my health; pointing out how important it was for Rome that I should take myself in hand physically. I had been showing signs of great fatigue lately, he said, as a result of the extraordinary long hours that I worked. If I did not either shorten these hours or put myself into a condition which would enable me to stand the strain better I could not expect to live much longer. I grew vexed and said that no Greek doctor had been able to cure me as a young man, though I had consulted many; and assured him that it was not only too late to do anything about my infirmities but that I had grown quite attached to them as an integral part of myself, and that I had no use for Greek doctors in any case.

Herod grinned. "This is the first time in my life that I have heard you agree with old Cato. I remember that *Commentary on Medicine* which he wrote for his son, forbidding him ever to consult a Greek doctor. Instead he recommended prayers, common sense and cabbage leaves. They were good enough for every common physical ailment, he said. Well, there are enough prayers going up for your health in Rome to-day to make you a positive athlete, if prayers were enough. And common sense is the birthright of every Roman. Perhaps, Cæsar, you have forgotten the cabbage leaves?"

I stirred irritably on my couch. "Well, what doctor do you recommend? I'll see just one, to please you, but no more.

What about Largus? He's the Palace Physician now. Messalina says that he's quite clever."

"If Largus had known of a cure for your ailments he would have volunteered it quick enough. No use going to him. If you will only consent to consult a single one, consult Xenophon of Cos."

"What, my father's old field-surgeon?"

"No, his son. He was with your brother Germanicus on his last campaign, you may remember; then he went to practice at Antioch. He was extraordinarily successful there and recently he's come to Rome. He uses the motto of the great Asclepiades, *Cure quickly, safely, pleasantly*. No violent purges and emetics. Diet, exercise, massage and a few simple botanical remedies. He cured me of a violent fever with a distillation of the leaves of a little yellow flower called aconite and then set me right generally with advice about diet, and so forth: told me not to drink so much, and what spices to avoid. A marvellous surgeon too, when it comes to that. He knows exactly where every nerve, bone, muscle and sinew in the body lies. He told me that he learned his anatomy from your brother."

"Germanicus wasn't an anatomist."

"No, but he was a German-killer. Xenophon picked up his knowledge on the battle-field: Germanicus provided the subjects. No surgeon can learn anatomy in Italy or Greece. He has either to go to Alexandria, where they don't mind cutting up corpses, or follow in the wake of a conquering army."

"I suppose he'll come if I send for him?"

"What doctor wouldn't? Do you forget who you are? But of course, if he cures you you'll have to pay him handsomely. He likes money. What Greek doesn't?"

"*If* he cures me."

I sent for Xenophon. I took an immediate liking to him because his professional interest in me as a case made

201

him forget that I was Emperor and had the power of life and death over him. He was a man of about fifty. After his first formal obeisances and compliments he talked curtly and drily and kept strictly to the point.

"Your pulse. Thanks. Your tongue. Thanks. Excuse me" (he turned up my eyelids). "Eyes somewhat inflamed. Can cure that. I'll give you a lotion to bathe them with. Slight retraction of eyelids. Stand up, please. Yes, infantile paralysis. Can't cure that, naturally. Too late. Could have done so before you stopped growing."

"You were only a child yourself at the time, Xenophon," I smiled.

He appeared not to hear me. "Were you a premature birth? Yes? I suspected it. Malaria too?"

"Malaria, measles, colitis, scrofula, erysipelas. The whole battalion answers 'present,' Xenophon, except epilepsy, venereal disease and megalomania."

He consented to smile briefly. "Strip!" he said. I stripped. "You eat too much and drink too much. You must stop that. Make it a rule never to rise from the table without an unsatisfied longing for just one little thing more. Yes, left leg much shrunk. No good prescribing exercise. Massage will have to do instead. You may dress again." He asked me a few more intimate questions, and always in a way that showed he knew the answer and was merely confirming it from my mouth as a matter of routine. "You dribble on your pillow at night, of course?" I owned with shame that this was so. "Fits of sudden anger? Involuntary twitching of the facial muscles? Stuttering when in a state of embarrassment? Occasional weakness of bladder? Fits of aphasia? Rigidity of muscles, so that you often wake up cold and stiff even on warm nights?" He even told me the sort of things I dreamed about.

I asked, astonished: "Can you interpret them, too, Xenophon? That ought to be easy."

"Yes," he answered in a matter-of-fact way, "but there's a law against it. Now Cæsar, I'll tell you about yourself. You have a good many more years to live if you care to live them. You work too hard, but I cannot prevent you from doing that, I suppose. I recommend reading as little as possible. The fatigue of which you complain is largely due to eye-strain. Make your secretaries read everything possible out to you. Do as little writing as you can. Rest for an hour after your principal meal: don't rush off to the law-courts as soon as you have gobbled your dessert. You must find time for twenty minutes' massage twice a day. You will need a properly trained masseur. The only properly trained masseurs in Rome are slaves of mine. The best is Charmes: I will give him special instructions in your case. If you break my rules you must not expect a complete cure, though the medicine that I shall prescribe will do you appreciable good. For instance, the violent cramp in the stomach of which you complain, the cardiac passion as we call it: if you neglect your massage and eat a heavy meal in a hurry, when in a state of nervous excitement about something or other, that cramp will come on you again, as sure as fate, in spite of my medicine. But follow my directions and you'll be a sound man."

"What's the medicine? Is it difficult to come by? Will I have to send to Egypt or India for it?"

Xenophon permitted himself a little creaking laugh. "No, nor any farther than the nearest bit of waste land. I belong to the Cos school of medicine: I am a native of Cos, in fact, a descendant of Æsculapius himself. At Cos we classify diseases by their remedies, which are for the most part the herbs that if eaten in great quantities produce the very symptoms that when eaten in moderate quantities they cure. Thus if a child wets his bed after the age of three or four and shows certain other cretinous symptoms associated with bed-wetting we say: 'That child has the

Dandelion disease.' Dandelion eaten in large quantities produces these symptoms, and a decoction of dandelion cures them. When I first came into the room and noticed the twitch of your head and the tremor of your hand and the slight stutter of your greeting, together with the rather harsh quality of your voice, I summed you up at once. 'A typical bryony case,' I said to myself. 'Bryony, massage, diet.' "

"What, Common Bryony?"

"The same. I'll write out a prescription for its preparation."

"And the prayers?"

"What prayers?"

"'Don't you prescribe special prayers to be used when taking the medicine? All the other doctors who have tried to cure me have always given me special prayers to repeat while mixing and taking the medicine."

He answered, rather stiffly: "I suggest, Cæsar, that as High Pontiff and the author of a history of religious origins at Rome, you are better equipped than myself for undertaking the theurgical side of the cure."

I could see that he was an unbeliever, like so many Greeks, so I did not press the matter, and that ended the interview: he begged to be excused because he had patients waiting in his consulting-room.

Well, bryony cured me. For the first time in my life I knew what it was to be perfectly well. I followed Xenophon's advice to the letter and have hardly had a day's illness since. Of course, I remain lame and occasionally I stammer and twitch my head from old habit if I get excited. But my aphasia has disappeared, my hand hardly trembles at all, and I can still at the age of sixty-four do a good fourteen hours' work a day, if necessary, and not feel utterly exhausted at the end of it. The cardiac passion has recurred occasionally, but only in the circumstances against which Xenophon warned me.

You may be sure that I paid Xenophon well for my bryony. I persuaded him to come and live at the Palace as Largus's colleague; Largus was a good physician in his way and had written several books on medical subjects. Xenophon would not come at first. He had built up a large private practice during the few months he had been at Rome: he assessed it as now worth three thousand gold pieces a year. I offered him six thousand—Largus's salary was only three thousand—and when he hesitated even then I said: "Xenophon, you must come: I insist. And when you have kept me alive and well for fifteen years, the Governors of Cos will be sent an official letter informing them that the island where you learned medicine will henceforth be excused from furnishing its military contingent and from paying tribute to the Imperial Government."

So he consented. If you wish to know to whom my freedman addressed prayers when mixing my medicine and to whom I addressed mine when taking it, it was the Goddess Carna, an old Sabine Goddess whom we Claudians have always cultivated since the time of Appius Claudius, of Regillus. Medicine mixed and taken without prayers would have seemed to me as unlucky and useless as a wedding celebrated without guests, sacrifice or music.

Before I forget it, I must record two valuable health hints that I learned from Xenophon. He used to say: "The man is a fool who puts good manners before health. If you are troubled with wind, never hold it in. It does great injury to the stomach. I knew a man who once nearly killed himself by holding in his wind. If for some reason or other you cannot conveniently leave the room—say, you are sacrificing or addressing the Senate—don't be afraid to belch or break wind downwards where you stand. Better that the company should suffer some slight inconvenience than that you should permanently injure yourself. And again, when you suffer from a cold, don't constantly blow your nose. That only increases the flow of rheum and inflames the delicate membranes of your nose. Let it run. Wipe, don't blow." I have always taken Xenophon's advice, at least about nose-blowing: my colds don't last nearly so long now as they did. Of course, caricaturists and satirists soon made fun of me as having a permanently dripping nose, but what did I care for that? Messalina told me that she thought I was extremely sensible to take such care of myself: if I were suddenly to die or fall seriously ill, what would become of the City and Empire, not to mention herself and our little boy?

Messalina said to me one day: "I am beginning to repent of my kind heart."

"Do you mean that my niece Lesbia should after all have been left in exile?"

She nodded. "How did you guess that I meant that? Now tell me, my dear, why does Lesbia go to your rooms in the Palace so often when I'm not about? What does she talk of? And why don't you let me know when she comes? You see, it's no good trying to keep secrets from me."

I smiled reassuringly but felt a little awkward. "There's nothing secret about it, nothing at all. You remember that about a month ago I gave her back the remainder of the estates which Caligula had taken from her? The Calabrian ones that you and I decided not to give back until we saw how she and Vinicius would behave? Well, as I told you, when I gave them back she burst into tears and said how ungrateful she had been and swore that she was now going to change her way of living altogether and conquer her stupid pride."

"Very touching, I am sure. But this is the first word I have heard of any such dramatic scene."

"But I distinctly remember telling you the whole story, one morning at breakfast."

"You must have dreamed it. Well, what *was* the whole story? Better late than never. When you gave her back the estates I certainly thought it rather queer that you should reward her insolence to me. But I said nothing. It was your business, not mine."

"I cannot understand this. I could have sworn I told you. My memory has the most extraordinary lapses sometimes. I am very sorry indeed, my dearest. Well, I gave her back the estates, simply because she said that she had just gone to you and made a whole-hearted apology and that you had said: 'I forgive you freely, Lesbia. Go and tell Claudius that I forgive you.'"

"Oh, what a bare-faced lie! She never came to me at all. Are you sure she said that? Or is your memory at fault again?"

"No, I'm positive about it. Otherwise I would never have given her back the estates."

"You know the legal formula about evidence? 'False in one thing, false in all'. That fits Lesbia. But you haven't yet told me why she visits you. What is she trying to get out of you?"

"Nothing, so far as I know. She just comes occasionally for a friendly visit to repeat how grateful she is and to ask whether she can be of any use to me. She never stays long enough to be a nuisance and always asks how you are. When I say that you're working she says that she wouldn't dream of disturbing you and apologizes for disturbing me. Yesterday she said that she thought you were still a little suspicious of her. I said that I thought not. She chatters a little about things in general for a few minutes, kisses me like a good niece, and off she goes. I quite enjoy her visits. But I was convinced that I'd mentioned them to you?"

"Never. That woman's a snake. I think I know her

plan. She'll worm her way into your confidence, like a good niece, of course, and then begin slandering me. In a quiet, hinting sort of way at first and then more directly as she gets bolder. She'll probably make up a wonderful story about the double life I lead. She'll say that behind your back I live a regular life of debauchery—sword-fighters and actors and young gallants and the rest. And you'll believe her, of course, like a good uncle. O God, what cats women are! I believe she's begun already. Has she?"

"Certainly not. I wouldn't let her. I wouldn't believe anyone who told me that you were unfaithful to me in deed or word. I wouldn't believe it even if you told me so yourself with your own lips. There, does that satisfy you?"

"Forgive me, dear, for being so jealous. It's my nature. I hate you to have friendships with other women behind my back, even relations. I don't trust any woman alone with you. You're so simple-minded. And I'm going to make it my business to find what poisonous trick Lesbia has at the back of her mind. But I don't want her to know that I suspect her. Promise me that you won't let her know that you have caught her out in a falsehood, until I have some more serious charge against her."

I promised. I told Messalina that I didn't believe in Lesbia's change of heart now and that I would report all conversational remarks that she made to me. This satisfied Messalina, who said that now she could continue her work with an easier mind.

I faithfully repeated to Messalina all Lesbia's remarks. They seemed to me of little importance, but Messalina found significance in many of them and caught especially at one—to me—perfectly inoffensive remark that Lesbia had made about a senator called Seneca. Seneca was a magistrate of the second rank, and had once incurred the jealous dislike of Caligula by the eloquence with which he had conducted a case in the Senate. He would certainly

have lost his head then but for me. I had done him the
service of depreciating his oratorical abilities, saying to
Caligula: "Eloquent? Seneca's not eloquent. He's just very
well educated and has a prodigious memory. His father
compiled those *Controversies* and *Persuasories,* school-exercises in oratory on imaginary cases. Childish stuff. He
wrote a lot more which have remained unpublished.
Seneca seems to have got the whole lot off by heart. He
has a rhetorical key now to fit any lock. It's not eloquence.
There's nothing behind it, not even strong personal character. I'll tell you what it is—it's like sand without lime.
You can't build up a reputation for true eloquence out of
that." Caligula repeated my words as his own judgment
on Seneca. "School-exercises only. Puerile declamations,
borrowings from his father's unpublished papers. Sand
without lime." So Seneca was permitted to live.

Now Messalina asked me: "You are sure that she went
out of her way to commend Seneca as an honest and un-
ambitious man? You didn't bring up his name yourself
first?"

"No."

"Then you may depend on it, Seneca's her lover. I have
known for some time that she was keeping a secret lover,
but she hides her tracks so well that I couldn't be sure
whether it was Seneca or her husband's cousin Vinicianus,
or that fellow Asinius Gallus, Pollio's grandson. They all
live in the same street."

Ten days later she told me that she now had complete
proof of adultery between Lesbia and Seneca during the
recent absence from Rome of Vinicius, Lesbia's husband.
She brought witnesses who swore that they had seen Seneca
leave his house late at night, in disguise; had followed him
to Lesbia's house, which he had entered by a side-door; had
seen a light suddenly appear at Lesbia's bedroom window
and presently go out again; and three or four hours later

had seen Seneca emerge and return home, still in disguise.

It was clear that Lesbia could not be allowed to stay at Rome any longer. She was my niece and therefore an important public figure. She had already been banished once on a charge of adultery and recalled by me only on an understanding that she would behave more discreetly in future. I expected all members of my family to set a high moral standard for the City. Seneca would have to be banished too. He was a married man and a senator, and though Lesbia was a beautiful woman I suspected that with a man of Seneca's character ambition was a stronger motive for the adultery than sexual passion. She was a direct descendant of Augustus, of Livia and of Mark Antony, a daughter of Germanicus, a sister of the late Emperor, a niece of the present one: while he was merely the son of a well-to-do provincial grammarian and had been born in Spain.

Somehow I did not wish to interview Lesbia myself, so I asked Messalina to do so. I felt that Messalina had more cause for resentment in the matter than I had, and wished to stand well with her again and show how sorry I was that I had given her occasion for the slightest twinge of jealousy. She gladly undertook the task of lecturing Lesbia for her ingratitude and acquainting her with her sentence; which was banishment to Reggio in the South of Italy, the town where her grandmother Julia had died in banishment for the same offence. Messalina afterwards reported that Lesbia had spoken most insolently, but had finally admitted adultery with Seneca, saying that her body was her own to do with as she liked. On being informed that she would be banished, she had flown into a passion and threatened us both: she said: "One morning the Palace servants will enter the Imperial bedchamber and find you both lying with your throats cut," and "How do you think my husband and his family will take this insult?"

"Only words, my dear," I said. "I don't take them seriously, though perhaps we had better keep a careful watch on Vinicius and his party."

On the very night that Lesbia started out for Reggio, towards dawn, Messalina and I were awakened by a sudden cry and scuffle in the corridor outside our door, some violent sneezing and shouts of, "Seize him! Murder! Assassins! Seize him!" I jumped out of bed, my heart pounding because of the sudden shock, and snatched up a stool as a weapon of defence, shouting to Messalina to get behind me. But my courage was not called in question. It was only one man and he had already been disarmed.

I ordered the guards to stand to arms for the rest of the night and went back to bed, though it took me some time to fall asleep again. Messalina needed a deal of comforting. She seemed scared almost out of her wits, laughing and crying in turns. "It's Lesbia's doing," she sobbed, "I'm sure it is."

When morning came I had the would-be assassin brought before me. He confessed to being a freedman of Lesbia's. But he had come disguised in Palace livery. He was a Syrian Greek and his story was a grotesque one. He said that he had not intended to murder me. It was all his own fault for repeating the wrong words at the close of the Mystery. "What Mystery?" I asked.

"I am forbidden to tell, Cæsar. I'll only reveal as much as I dare. It is the most sacred of all sacred Mysteries. I was initiated into it last night. It happened underground. A certain bird was sacrificed and I drank its blood. Two tall spirits appeared, with shining faces, and gave me a dagger and a pepper-pot, explaining what these instruments symbolized. They blindfolded me, dressed me in a new dress and told me to keep perfect silence. They repeated magic words and told me to follow them to Hell. They led me here and there, up steps and down steps, along streets and through gardens, describing many strange sights as we

211

went. We entered a boat and paid the ferryman. It was Charon himself. We were then put ashore in Hell. They showed me the whole of Hell. The ghosts of my ancestors talked to me. I heard Cerberus bark. Finally they took off the bandage from my eyes and whispered to me: 'You are now in the Halls of the God of Death. Hide this dagger in your gown. Follow this corridor round to the right, mount the stairs at the end, and then turn to the left down a second corridor. If any sentry challenges you, give him the pass-word. The pass-word is "Fate." The God of Death and his Goddess lie asleep in the end room. At their door two more sentries are on watch. They are not like the other sentries. We do not know their pass-word. But creep up close to them in the shadows and suddenly throw this holy pepper-powder in their eyes. Then boldly burst open the door and slay the God and Goddess. If you succeed in this enterprise you shall live for ever in regions of perpetual bliss and be accounted greater than Hercules, greater than Prometheus, greater than Jove himself. There will be no more Death. But, as you go, you must say over and over to yourself the words of the same charm that we have used to bring you so far in safety. If you do not do so, all our guidance will have been wasted. The spell will break and you will find yourself in quite a different place.' I was frightened. I suppose that I must have made a mistake in the spell, because as I drew back my hand to fling the pepper I suddenly found myself back here in Rome, in your Imperial Palace, struggling with the guards at your bedroom-door. I had failed. Death still reigns. Some other bolder, more collected soul than I must one day strike that blow."

"Lesbia's confederates are very clever," Messalina whispered. "What a perfect plot!"

"Who initiated you?" I asked the man. He would not answer, even under torture, and I could not get much information from the Guard at the main gate, who happened to be newly-joined men. They said that they had admitted him because he was wearing Palace livery and had the correct pass-word. I could not blame them. He had arrived at the Gate in the company of two other men in Palace livery, who had said good-night to him and strolled off.

I was inclined to believe the man's story; but he persisted in his refusal to say who it was who had sponsored his initiation into these so-called mysteries. When I assured him in quite a pleasant way that they could not have been real mysteries but an elaborate hoax and that therefore his oath was not binding he flared up and spoke to me most rudely. So he had to be executed. And after long debate with myself I agreed with Messalina that for the sake of public safety it was now necessary to have Lesbia, too, executed. I sent a detachment of Guards Cavalry after her, and on the following day they brought me back her head in token of her death. It was very painful for me to have had to execute a daughter of my dear brother Germanicus after swearing at his death to love and protect all his children as if they were my own. But I comforted myself by the thought that he would have acted as I had done if he had been in my place. He always put public duty before private feeling.

As for Seneca, I told the Senate that unless they knew some good reason to the contrary I desired them to vote for his banishment to Corsica. So they banished him, allowing him thirty hours in which to leave Rome and thirty days in which to leave Italy. Seneca was not popular with the House. While in Corsica he had plenty of opportunity for practising the philosophy of the Stoics—to which he announced himself converted by a chance word of mine once spoken in their commendation. The flattery of which that fellow was capable was really nauseating. When a year or two later my secretary Polybius lost a brother, of whom he was fond, Seneca, who knew Polybius only slightly and his brother not at all, sent him, from Corsica, a long carefully-phrased letter, which at the same time he arranged to have published in the City under the title *Consolation for Polybius*. The consolation took the form of gently reproving Polybius for giving way to private grief for his brother while I, Cæsar, lived and enjoyed good health, and continued to show him my princely favour. "While Cæsar needs Polybius," Seneca wrote, "Polybius has no more right to give way than has the giant Atlas, who is said to carry the world on his shoulders in obedience to the will of the Gods.

"To Cæsar himself, to whom all is permitted, many things are for that very reason denied. His vigilance defends every home; his labours establish general leisure; his industry procures civic happiness; his hard work spells a public holiday. From the very moment that Cæsar first dedicated himself to humanity he robbed himself of himself, and, like the stars which perpetually run their tireless courses, he has never since allowed himself to rest or attend to any business of his own. And in some way, Polybius, your fate is linked with his august fate, and you too cannot now attend to your own personal interests, pursue your own private studies. While Cæsar owns the world you cannot honourably partake of pleasure, of grief, or of any other human emotion. You are wholly Cæsar's. And is it not always on your lips that Cæsar is dearer to you than your life? How, then, is it right for you to complain of this stroke of fortune while Cæsar still lives and thrives?" There was a lot more about my wonderful loving-kindness and mercy and a passage putting into my mouth the most extravagant sentiments about the noblest way of bearing the loss of a brother. I was supposed to cite my grandfather Mark Antony's grief for his brother Gaius, my uncle Tiberius's grief for my father, Gaius Cæsar's grief for young Lucius, my own grief for my brother Germanicus, and then relate how valiantly we had each in turn borne these calamities. The only effect that this slime and honey had on me was to make me quite satisfied in my mind that I had not wronged anyone by his banishment—except perhaps the island of Corsica.

# Chapter Thirteen

THE Alexandrian Greeks sent instructions to their envoys, who were still in Rome, to congratulate me on my victories in Germany, to complain of the insolent behaviour of the Jews towards them (there had been a recrudescence of trouble in the city), to ask my permission for the re-establishment of the Alexandrian Senate, and once more to offer me temples endowed and furnished with priests. They intended several other lesser honours for me besides this supreme one, among them being two golden statues, one representing the "Peace of Claudius Augustus," the other "Germanicus the Victor." The latter statue I accepted because it was principally an honour to my father and brother, whose victories had been far more important than mine, and personally won, and because the statue's features were theirs, not mine. (My brother had been the living image of my father, everyone agreed.) As usual, the Jews sent a counter-embassy, congratulating me on my victories, thanking me for my generosity to them in the matter of the circular letter I had written about religious toleration for all Jews, and accusing the Alexandrians of having provoked these new disturbances by interrupting their religious worship with ribald songs and dances outside the synagogues on holy days. I shall here attach my exact answer to the Alexandrians, to show how I now handled questions of this sort:

"Tiberius Claudius Cæsar Augustus Germanicus, Emperor, High Pontiff, Protector of the People, Consul Elect, to the City of Alexandria, greetings.

"Tiberius Claudius Barbillus, Apollonius son of Artemidorus, Chæreman son of Leonides, Marcus Julius Asclepiades, Gaius Julius Dionysius, Tiberius Claudius Phanias, Pasion son of Potamon, Dionysius son of Sabbion, Tiberius Claudius Apollonius son of Ariston, Gaius Julius Apollonius, and Hermaiscus son of Apollonius, your envoys, have delivered me your decree and spoken to me at length about the City of Alexandria, recalling the goodwill which for many years past, as you know, I have always felt towards you; for you are naturally loyal to the House of Augustus, as many things go to prove. Especially there has been an exchange of amity between your city and my immediate family: I need only mention in this context my brother Germanicus Cæsar whose goodwill toward you was shown more plainly than by any of us: he came to Alexandria and addressed you with his own lips. For this reason I gladly accepted the recent honours you offered me, though I am usually not partial to honours.

"In the first place I permit you to keep my birthday as a 'Day of Augustus' in the way mentioned in your own proclamation. Next, I agree to your erecting, in the places stated, the statues to myself and other members of my family, for I see that you have been zealous to establish memorials of your loyalty to my House on all sides. Of the two golden statues, that representing the Peace of Claudius Augustus, made at the suggestion and plea of my friend Barbillus, I have refused as appearing somewhat offensive to my fellow-men, and it is now to be dedicated to the Goddess Roma; the other shall be carried in your processions in whatever way you think best, on the appropriate birthdays; and you may provide it with a throne too, suitably decorated. It would perhaps be foolish, while accepting these great honours at your hands, to refuse to introduce a Claudian tribe and sanction sacred precincts for each Egyptian district; so I permit you to do both these things and, if you wish, to set up, too, the equestrian statue of my Governor, Vitrasius Pollio. Also, I give my consent to the erection of the four-horse chariots which you wish to establish in my honour at the frontiers: one at Taposiris in Libya, one at the Pharos in Alexandria, the third at Pelusium in Lower Egypt. But I must ask you not to appoint a High Priest for my worship or to build temples in my honour, for I do not wish to be offensive to my fellow-men and it is quite clear to my mind that shrines and temples have, throughout history, been built in honour of the Gods, as their peculiar due.

"As for the requests which you are so anxious for me to grant, these are my decisions:—all Alexandrians who had officially come of age before I entered on the monarchy I confirm in their citizenship with all the privileges and amenities that this carries with it; the only exceptions being such pretenders, born of slave mothers, as may have contrived to intrude themselves among the free-born. And it is also my pleasure that all these favours which were granted you by my predecessors shall be confirmed, and those favours too which were granted by your former kings and City Prefects and confirmed by the God Augustus. It is my pleasure that the ministers of the Temple of the God Augustus of Alexandria shall be chosen by lot, like the ministers of his Temple at Canopus. I commend your plan for making the municipal magistracies triennial as a very sensible one; for the magistrates will behave with the greater prudence during their term of office for knowing that when it ends they will be called upon to account for any maladministration of which they may have been guilty. As for the question about re-establishing the Senate, I am unable to say offhand what your custom was under the Ptolemies, but you know as well as I do that you have not had a Senate under any one of my predecessors of the House of Augustus. So since this is an entirely novel proposal and I am not sure whether it will prove either to your advantage or mine to adopt it,

I have written to your City Prefect, Æmilius Rectus, to hold an inquiry and report whether a Senatorial Order should be formed, and, if so, in what way it should be formed.

"As for the question as to who must bear responsibility for the recent riot and the feud or—to speak frankly—the war that has been waged between you and the Jews, I have been unwilling to commit myself to a decision on this matter, though your envoys, especially Dionysius, son of Theon, pleaded your cause with great spirit in the presence of their Jewish opponents. But I must reserve for myself a stern indignation against whichever party it was that started this new disturbance; and I wish you to understand that if both parties do not desist from this destructive and obstinate hostility I shall be compelled to show you what a benevolent ruler can do when roused to righteous anger. I therefore once more beg you Alexandrians to show a friendly tolerance to the Jews who have been your neighbours in Alexandria for so many years, and offer no outrage to their feelings whilst they are engaged in worshipping their God according to their ancestral rites. Let them practice all their national customs as in the days of the God Augustus, for I have confirmed their right to do so after an impartial hearing of both sides in the dispute. On the other hand, I desire the Jews to press for no privileges in excess of those that they already hold, and never again to send me a separate embassy as if you and they lived in different cities—a quite unheard of procedure!—nor to enter competitors for athletic and other contests at Public Games. They must content themselves with what they have, enjoying the abundance supplied by a great city of which they are *not* the original inhabitants; and they must not introduce any more Jews from Syria or from other parts of Egypt into the city, or they will fall more deeply under my suspicion than at present. If they fail to take this warning I shall certainly

take vengeance on them as deliberately fomenting a world
wide plague. So long therefore as both sides abstain from
this antagonism and live in mutual forbearance and goodwill, I undertake to show the same friendly solicitude for
the interests of Alexandria as my family has always shown
in the past.

"I must testify here to the constant zeal for your interests which my friend Barbillus has now once again shown
in his exertions on your behalf and also to a similar zeal on
the part of my friend Tiberius Claudius Archibus.

"Farewell."

This Barbillus was an astrologer of Ephesus, in whose
powers Messalina had complete faith, and I must admit that
he was a very clever fellow, second only in the accuracy
of his prognostications to the great Thrasyllus. He had
studied in India and among the Chaldees. His zeal for Alexandria was due to the hospitality he had been shown by
the principal men of the city when forced, many years before, to leave Rome because Tiberius had banished from
Italy all astrologers and soothsayers except his favourite
Thrasyllus.

I received a letter from Herod a month or two later formally congratulating me on my victories, on the birth of
my son, and on having won the title of Emperor by my
victories in Germany. He enclosed his usual private letter:

"What a great warrior you are, Marmoset, to be sure!
You just have to put pen to paper and order a campaign,
and presto! banners wave, swords fly from their scabbards,
heads roll on the grass, towns and temples go up in flames!
What fearful destruction you would cause if one day you
were to mount on an elephant and take the field *in person!*
I remember your dear mother once speaking of you, not
very hopefully, as a future conqueror of the Island of

Britain. Why not? For myself, I contemplate no military triumphs. Peace and security are all that I ask. I am busy putting my dominions in a state of defence against a possible Parthian invasion. Cypros and I are very happy and well, and so are the children. They are learning to be good Jews. They learn faster than I do, because they are younger. By the way, I don't like Vibius Marsus, your new Governor of Syria. I am afraid that he and I will fall out one day soon if he doesn't mind his own business. I was sorry when Petronius's term came to an end: a fine fellow. Poor Silas is still in confinement. I have given him the pleasantest possible prison quarters, however, and allowed him writing materials as a vent for his sense of my ingratitude. Not parchment or paper, of course, only a wax-tablet, so that when he comes to the end of one complaint he must scrape it off before starting on another.

"You are extremely popular here with the Jews and the severe phrases in your letter to the Alexandrians were not taken amiss: Jews are quick at reading between the lines. I have heard from my old friend Alexander the Alabarch that copies were circulated to the various city wards of Alexandria to be posted up, with the following endorsement by the City Prefect:

### Proclamation by Lucius Æmilius Rectus.

Since the whole populace was unable owing to its numbers to assist at the reading of that most sacred and gracious letter to the City, I have found it necessary to post it up publicly so that individual readers may admire the Majesty of our God Cæsar Augustus and show their gratitude for His goodwill towards the City.

Fourteenth day of August, in the second year of the reign of Tiberius Claudius Cæsar Augustus Germanicus, Emperor.

"They'll make you a God in spite of yourself; but keep your health and spirits, eat well, sleep sound, and trust nobody.

"THE BRIGAND."

Herod's schoolboy taunt about the ease with which I had won my title of Emperor touched me in a sensitive spot. His reminder of my mother's remark influenced me too: it touched me in a superstitious spot. She had once—many years before—declared in a fit of annoyance when I was telling her of my proposal for adding three new letters to the Latin alphabet: "There are three notably impossible things in this world: the first that shops should stretch across the Bay of Naples yonder, the second that you should conquer the island of Britain, the third that a single one of your ridiculous new letters should ever be put into general circulation." Yet the first impossible thing had already come to pass—on the day that Caligula built his famous bridge from Bauli to Puteoli and lined it with shops. The third impossible thing could be accomplished any day that I pleased, merely by asking the Senate's permission—and why not the second?

A letter came from Marsus a few days later marked "urgent and confidential." Marsus was a capable governor, and an upright man though a most uncongenial companion—reserved, cold in his manner, perpetually sarcastic and without either follies or vices. I had given him his appointment in gratitude for the prominent part he had taken more than twenty years before, while commanding a regiment in the East, in bringing Piso to trial for the murder of my brother Germanicus. He wrote: ". . . . My neighbour, your friend King Herod Agrippa, is, I am informed, fortifying Jerusalem. You are probably aware of this, but I write to make it plain to you that the fortifications when completed will make the city impregnable. I wish to make no accusations of disloyalty against your friend King Herod, but as Governor of Syria I view the matter with alarm. Jerusalem commands the route to Egypt, and if it were to fall into irresponsible hands Rome would be in grave danger. Herod is said to fear a Parthian invasion: he has, however, already amply protected himself against this most improbable occurrence by a secret alliance with his royal neighbours on the Parthian frontier. No doubt you approve of his friendly advances to the Phœnicians: he has made enormous gifts to the city of Beirut and is building an amphitheatre there, also porticoes and public baths. It is difficult for me to understand his motives for courting the Phœnicians. However, for the present the chief men of Tyre and Sidon appear to have little trust in him. Perhaps they have good reason: it is not for me to say. At the risk of your displeasure I shall continue to report on political events to the south and east of my command as they come to my attention."

This made most uncomfortable reading, and my first feeling was one of anger against Marsus for disturbing my confidence in Herod; but when I thought things over the feeling changed to one of gratitude. I did not know what to think about Herod. On the one hand, I was confident that he would keep his oath of friendship, publicly sworn in the Market Place, with me; on the other hand, he was obviously engaged in some private scheme of his own which in the case of any other man I would call thoroughly treasonable. I was glad that Marsus was keeping his eyes open. I said nothing about the business to anyone, not even to Messalina, and wrote to Marsus merely: "I have your letter. Be discreet. Report further events." To Herod I wrote a sly letter:

"I shall probably take your kind advice about Britain, my dear Brigand, and if I do invade that unfortunate isle I shall certainly ride on the back of an elephant. It will be the first elephant ever seen in Britain and no doubt cause widespread admiration. I am glad to hear good news of your family; don't worry about that Parthian invasion on their account. If I hear news of trouble in that quarter I shall send at once to Lyons for your Uncle Antipas to go out and quell it in his seventy-thousand-and-first suit of armour; so Cypros can sleep sound at night in that confidence and you can stop work on your fortifications at Jerusalem. We don't want Jerusalem made too strong, do we? Suppose that there was a sudden raid made by your brigand cousins from Edom, and they managed to get into Jerusalem just before you built the final bastion—why, we'd never get them out again, not even with siege-engines and tortoises and rams—and then what about the trade-route to Egypt? I am sorry that you dislike Vibius Marsus. How is your amphitheatre at Beirut progressing? I shall take your advice about trusting absolutely *nobody,* with the possible exceptions of my dear Messalina, Vitellius, Rufrius, and my old schoolfellow the Brigand, in whose self-accusations of roguery I have never and shall never believe, and to whom I shall always affectionately sign myself his

"MARMOSET."

Herod replied in his usual bantering style as if he did not care one way or the other about the fortifications: but he must have known that my playful letter was not as playful as it pretended to be; and he must have known, too, that Marsus had been writing to me about him. Marsus replied shortly to my short note, reporting that work on the fortifications had now been discontinued.

I took on my second Consulship in March, which is the New Year, but resigned the office two months later in favour of the next senator due for it: I was too busy to be bothered with the routine duties it involved.

A. D. 42

This was the year that my daughter Octavia was born, that the Vinicianus-Scribonianus rising took place, and that I added Morocco to the Empire as a province. I will first tell briefly what happened in Morocco. The Moors had risen again under a capable general named Salabus, who had led them in the previous campaign. Paulinus, who was commanding the Roman forces, overran the country as far as the Atlas range, but was unable to come to grips with Salabus himself and suffered heavy losses from ambushes and night attacks. His term of command presently expired and he had to return to Rome. He was succeeded by one Hosidius Geta whom I instructed, before he set out, not on any account to allow Salabus to become another Tacfarinas. (Tacfarinas was the Numidian who, under Tiberius, had earned three Roman generals the laurel-crown by allowing himself to be defeated by them in apparently decisive engagements, but who always reappeared at the head of his reconstituted army as soon as the Roman forces were withdrawn; however, a fourth general ended the business by catching and killing Tacfarinas himself.) I said to Geta: "Don't be satisfied with partial successes. Search out Salabus's main force, crush it and kill or capture Salabus. Chase him all round Africa if necessary. If he runs off inland to the country where they say that men's heads sprout from under their armpits, why, follow him there. You'll easily recognize him by his having his head in a different place." I also said to Geta: "I won't attempt to direct your campaign: but one word of advice—don't be bound by hard-and-fast campaigning rules like Augustus's general Ælius Gallus who marched to the conquest of Arabia as if Arabia were a second Italy, or Germany. He loaded up his men with the usual entrenching tools and heavy armour instead of water-skins and extra corn-rations, and even brought a train of siege-engines. When colic attacked the men and they began boiling the bad water that they found

225

in the wells, to make it safer to drink, Ælius came along and cried: "What! boiling your water! No disciplined Roman soldier boils his water! And using dried dung for fuel? Unheard of! Roman soldiers collect brush-wood or else go without a fire." He lost the greater part of his force. The interior of Morocco is a dangerous quarter too. Suit your tactics and equipment to the country."

Geta took my advice in the most literal way. He chased Salabus from end to end of Morocco, defeating him twice, and on the second occasion only just failing to capture him. Salabus then fled to the Atlas Mountains and crossed them into the unexplored desert beyond, instructing his men to hold the pass while he collected reinforcements from his allies, the desert nomads. Geta left a detachment near the pass and with the hardiest of his men struggled across another, more difficult, pass a few miles away and went in faithful search of Salabus. He had taken as much water with him as his men and mules could possibly carry, cutting down his equipment to the least possible weight. He reckoned on finding some water at least, but followed Salabus's criss-cross track in the desert sands for more than two hundred miles before he saw so much as a thorn-bush growing. The water began to give out and the men to weaken. Geta concealed his anxiety, but realized that even if he retreated at once, and gave up all hope of capturing Salabus, he had not enough water to see him safely back. The Atlas was a hundred miles off, and only a divine miracle could save him.

Now, at Rome when there is a drought we know how to persuade the Gods to send rain. There is a black stone called the Dripping Stone, captured originally from the Etruscans and stored in a temple of Mars outside the City. We go in solemn procession and fetch it within the walls, where we pour water on it, singing incantations and sacrificing. Rain always follows—unless there has been some slight mistake in the ritual, as is frequently the case. But Geta had no Dripping Stone with him, so he was completely at a loss. The nomads were accustomed to going without water for days at a time and knew the country perfectly, besides. They began to close in on the Roman force; they cut off, killed, stripped and mutilated a few stragglers whom the heat had driven out of their wits.

Geta had a black orderly who had been born in this very desert but had been sold as a slave to the Moors. He could not remember where the nearest water was, because he had been sold when only a child. But he said to Geta, "General, why don't you pray to Father Gwa-Gwa!" Geta inquired who this person might be. The man replied that he was the God of the Deserts who gave rain in time of drought. Geta said, "The Emperor told me to suit my tactics to the country. Tell me how to invoke Father Gwa-Gwa and I shall do so at once." The orderly told him to take a little pot, bury it up to the neck in the sand and fill it with beer, saying as he did so: "Father Gwa-Gwa, we offer you beer." Then the men were to fill their drinking vessels with all the water that they had with them in their water-skins except enough to dip their fingers in and sprinkle on the ground. Then everyone must drink and dance and adore Father Gwa-Gwa, sprinkling the water and drinking every drop in the skins. Geta himself must chant: "As this water is sprinkled, so let rain fall! We have drunk our last drop, Father. None remains. What would you have us do? Drink beer, Father Gwa-Gwa, and make water for us, your children, or we die!" For beer is a powerful diuretic and these nomads had the same theological notions as the early Greeks who considered that Jove made water when it rained; so that the same word (with a mere difference in gender) is still used in Greek for Heaven and for chamber-pot. The nomads considered that their God would be encouraged to make water, in the form of rain, by offer-

227

ing him a drink of beer. The sprinkling of water, like our own lustrations, was to remind him how rain fell, in case he had forgotten.

Geta in desperation called his tottering force together and inquired whether anyone happened to have a little beer with him. And by good luck a party of German auxiliaries had a pint or two hoarded in a water-skin; they had brought it with them in preference to water. Geta made them give it up to him. He then equally distributed all the water that was left, but the beer he reserved for Father Gwa-Gwa. The troops danced and drank the water and sprinkled the necessary drops on the sand, while Geta uttered the prescribed formula of invocation. Father Gwa-Gwa (his name apparently means "Water") was so pleased and impressed by the honours paid him by this imposing force of perfect strangers that the sky was immediately darkened with rain-clouds and a down-pour began which lasted for three days and turned every sandy hollow into a brimming pool of water. The army was saved. The nomads, taking the abundant rain as an undeniable token of Father Gwa-Gwa's favour towards the Romans, came humbly forward with offers of alliance. Geta refused this unless they first delivered up Salabus to him. Salabus was presently brought to the camp in bonds. Presents were exchanged between Geta and the nomads and a treaty made; then Geta marched back without further loss to the mountains, where he caught Salabus's men, who were still holding the pass, in the rear, killing or capturing the whole detachment. The other Moorish forces, seeing their leader brought back to Tangiers as a prisoner, surrendered without further fighting. So two or three pints of beer had saved the lives of more than two thousand Romans and gained Rome a new province. I ordered the dedication of a shrine to Father Gwa-Gwa in the desert beyond the mountains, where he ruled; and Morocco, which I now divided up into two provinces—Western Morocco with its capital at Tangiers and Eastern Morocco with its capital at Cæsarea—had to furnish it with a yearly tribute of a hundred goat-skins of the best beer. I awarded Geta triumphal ornaments and would have asked the Senate to confer on him the hereditary title of Maurus ("of Morocco") had he not exceeded his powers by putting Salabus to death at Tangiers without first consulting me. There was no military necessity for this act; he only did it for vainglory.

I mentioned just now the birth of my daughter Octavia. Messalina had come to be much courted by the Senate and People, because it was well known that I had delegated to her most of the duties which fell to me in my capacity as Director of Public Morals. She acted, in theory, only as my adviser, but had, as I have explained, a duplicate seal of mine to ratify documents with; and within certain limits I let her decide what knights or senators to degrade for social offences and whom to appoint to the resulting vacancies. She had now also undertaken the laborious task of deciding on the fitness of all candidates for the Roman citizenship. The Senate wished to vote her the title of Augusta and made the birth of Octavia the pretext. Much as I loved Messalina, I did not think that she had yet earned this honour: it was something for her to look forward to in middle life. She was as yet only seventeen, whereas my grandmother Livia had earned the title only after her death and my mother in extreme old age. So I refused it for her. But the Alexandrians, without asking my permission—and once the thing was done I could not undo it—struck a coin with my head on the obverse and on the reverse a full-length portrait of Messalina in the dress of the Goddess Demeter, holding in the palm of one hand two figurines representing her little boy and girl, and in the other a sheaf of corn representing fertility. This was a flattering play on the name Messalina—the Latin word *messis* meaning the corn-harvest. She was delighted.

She came to me shyly one evening, peeped up at my face without saying anything, and at last asked, plainly embarrassed, and after one or two false starts: "Do you love me, dearest husband?"

I assured her that I loved her beyond anyone else in the world.

"And what did you tell me, the other day, were the Three Main Pillars of the Temple of Love?"

"I said that the Temple of True Love was pillared on kindness, frankness and understanding. Or rather I quoted the philosopher Mnasalcus as having said so."

"Then will you show me the greatest kindness and understanding that your love for me is capable of showing? *My* love will have to provide only the frankness. I'll come straight to the point. If it's not too hard for you, would you—could you possibly—allow me to sleep in a bedroom apart from you for a little while? It isn't that I don't love you every bit as much as you love me, but now that we have had two children in less than two years of marriage, oughtn't we to wait a little before we risk having a third? It is a very disagreeable thing to be pregnant: I have morning-sickness and heartburn and my digestion goes wrong, and I don't feel I could go through that again just yet. And, to be honest, quite apart from this dread, I somehow feel less passionately towards you than I did. I swear that I love you as much as ever but now it's rather as my dearest friend and as the father of my children than as my lover. Having children uses up a lot of a woman's emotions, I suppose. I'm not hiding anything from you. You do believe me, don't you?"

"I believe you, and I love you."

She stroked my face. "And I'm not like any ordinary woman, am I, whose business is merely to have children and children and children until she wears out? I am your wife—the Emperor's wife—and I heip him in his Imperial work, and that should take precedence over everything, shouldn't it? Pregnancy interferes with work terribly."

I said rather ruefully: "Of course, my dearest, if you really feel like that, I am not the sort of husband to insist on forcing anything on you. But is it really necessary for us to sleep apart? Couldn't we at least occupy the same bed, for company's sake?"

"O Claudius," she said, nearly crying, "it has been difficult enough for me to make up my mind to ask you about this, because I love you so much and don't want to hurt you in the least. Don't make it more difficult. And now that I have frankly told you how I feel, wouldn't it be dreadfully difficult for you if you had violently passionate feelings for me while we were sleeping together and I could not honestly return them? If I repulsed you, that would be as destructive of our love as if I yielded against my will; and I am sure you would feel very remorseful afterwards if anything happened to destroy my love for you. No, can't you see now how much better it would be for us to sleep apart until I feel about you again as I used to do? Suppose, just to distance myself from temptation, I were to move across to my suite in the New Palace? It's more convenient for my work to be over there. I can get up in the morning and go straight to my papers. This lying-in has put me greatly behindhand with my Citizens' Roll."

I pleaded: "How long do you think you will want to be away?"

"We'll see how it works out," she said, kissing the back of my neck tenderly. "Oh, how relieved I am that you aren't angry. How long? Oh, I don't know. Does it matter so much? After all, sex is not essential to love if there is any other strong bond between lovers such as common idealistic pursuit of Beauty or Perfection. I do agree with Plato about that. He thought sex positively an obstruction to love."

231

"He was talking of homosexual love," I reminded her, trying not to sound depressed.

"Well, my dear," she said lightly, "I do a man's work, the same as you, and so it comes to much the same thing, doesn't it? And as for a common idealism, we have to be very idealistic indeed to get through all this drudgery in the name of attempted political perfection, don't we? Well, is that really settled? Will you really be a dear, dear Claudius, and not insist on my sharing your bed—in a literal sense, I mean? In all other senses I am still your devoted little Messalina, and do remember that it has been very, very painful for me to ask you this."

I told her that I respected and loved her all the more for her frankness, and of course she must have her way. But that naturally I would be impatient for the time when she felt again for me as she once had done.

"Oh, please don't be impatient," she cried. "It makes it so difficult for me. If you were impatient I would feel that I was being unkind to you, and would probably pretend feelings that I didn't have. I may be an exception, but somehow sex doesn't mean much to me. I suspect, though, that many women get bored with it—without ceasing to love their husbands or to want their husbands to love them. But I'll always continue to be suspicious of other women. If you were to have affairs with other women I think I would go mad with jealousy. It isn't that I mind the thought of your sleeping with someone other than me; it's the fear that you might come to love her better than me, not merely regarding her as a pleasant sexual convenience, and then want to divorce me. I mean, if you were to sleep with a pretty housemaid occasionally, or some nice clean woman too low in rank for me to be jealous of, I should be very glad, really delighted, to think that you were having a nice time with her; and if you and I ever slept together afterwards we wouldn't consider it as anything that had come between us. We'd merely think of it as a measure that you had taken for the sake of your health—like a purge or an emetic. I wouldn't expect you even to tell me the woman's name, in fact I'd prefer you not to, so long as you first promised not to have doings with anyone about whom I would have a right to feel jealous. Wasn't that how Livia is said to have felt about Augustus?"

"Yes, in a way. But she never really loved him. She told me so. That made it easier for her to be attentive to him. She used to pick out young women from the slave-market and bring them secretly into his bedroom at night. Syrians, mostly, I believe."

"Well, you're not asking me to do *that*, are you? I'm human, after all."

This was how Messalina played, very cleverly and very cruelly, on my blind love for her. She moved over to the New Palace that very evening. And for a long time I said nothing further, hoping that she would come back to me. But she said nothing, only indicating by her tender behaviour that a very fine understanding existed between us. As a great concession she did sometimes consent to sleep with me. It was seven years before I heard so much as a whisper of what went on in her suite at the New Palace when the old cuckold-husband was away at his work or safely snoring in his bed at the Old Palace.

And this brings me to the story of the fate of Appius Silanus, an ex-Consul who had been Governor of Spain since Caligula's reign. It may be recalled that it was marriage with this Silanus that Livia had made the bribe for Æmilia's betrayal of Postumus: Æmilia was Augustus's great-granddaughter, whom as a boy I had nearly married. Through Æmilia, Silanus had become the father of three boys and two girls, now all grown up. Except for Agrippinilla and her little son, they were the only surviving descendants of Augustus. Tiberius had regarded Silanus as a danger

233

because of his illustrious connexions and had arranged to have him accused of treason in company with several other senators, including Vinicianus. However, the evidence against them broke down and they escaped with nothing worse than a bad fright. At the age of sixteen Silanus had been the handsomest youth in Rome; at the age of fifty-six he was still remarkably fine-looking, his hair only slightly grizzled, his eyes bright, and his step and carriage like those of a man in the prime of life. He was now a widower, Æmilia having died of a cancer. One of his daughters, Calvina, had married a son of Vitellius's.

One day, shortly before little Octavia's birth, Messalina had said to me: "The man whom we really need at Rome is Appius Silanus. I wish you could recall him and keep him permanently at the Palace as an adviser. He's remarkably intelligent and quite wasted in Spain."

I said: "Yes, that isn't a bad plan: I admire Silanus, and he's a man of great influence in the Senate. But how can we persuade him to come to live with us? We can't very well plant him in the Palace as we might plant a new secretary or accountant. There must be some sort of honourable pretext for his presence."

"I've thought of that, and I've got a brilliant idea. Why not connect him with the family by marrying him to my mother? She'd like to marry again: she's only thirty-three. And she's your mother-in-law, so it would be a great honour for Silanus. Do say that you think it a good idea."

"Well, if you can make it right with your mother. . . ."

"I have already asked her about it. She says that she'd be charmed."

So Silanus came to Rome and I married him to Domitia Lepida, Messalina's mother, and assigned them a suite in the New Palace next to Messalina's. I soon noticed that Silanus was very ill at ease with me. He readily did any services that I asked him to do, such as paying surprise visits to the lower courts on my behalf to see that justice was being properly done, or inspecting and reporting upon housing conditions in the poorer quarters of the City, or attending the public auction of property confiscated by the State, to see that the auctioneers did not play any tricks; but he seemed unable to look me in the face and always avoided any intimacy with me. I was rather offended. But after all I could not have been expected to guess the truth: which was that Messalina had only asked me to send for Silanus from Spain because she had been in love with him as a girl, and that she had married him to her mother merely as a means of having easy access to him, and that ever since his arrival she had been pressing him to sleep with her. To think of it! Her own step-father and a man five years my senior, with a granddaughter not much younger than Messalina herself! Naturally, his manner to me was queer, since Messalina had told him that she had moved over to the New Palace at my orders, and that I had myself suggested that she should become his mistress. She explained that I wanted to keep her amused while I had a silly affair with that Julia, once the wife of my nephew Nero, whom we used to call Helen, to distinguish her from the other Julias, but now called Heluo because she was such a glutton. Apparently Silanus believed this story, but he firmly refused to sleep with his step-daughter, in spite of her beauty, even at the Emperor's suggestion: he said that he was of an amorous but not an impious nature.

"I'll give you ten days to make up your mind about it," Messalina threatened. "If you refuse me at the end of that time I shall tell Claudius. You know how vain he has become since they made him Emperor. He wouldn't like to hear that you'd scorned his wife. He'd certainly kill you, wouldn't he, Mother?"

Domitia Lepida was entirely under Messalina's thumb, and bore her out. Silanus believed them. His experiences under Tiberius and Caligula had made him a secret anti-monarchist, though he was not a man who mixed much in politics. He fully believed that nobody could now find himself at the head of the State without giving way very soon to tyranny, cruelty and lust. By the ninth day he had not yet yielded to Messalina, but had worked himself up into such a state of nervous desperation that he had, it appears, fully resolved to kill me.

My secretary Narcissus was a witness of Silanus's distracted state that evening; he overtook him in a corridor of the Palace muttering unintelligibly to himelf, "Cassius Chærea—Old Cassius. Do so—but not alone." Narcissus was busy at the moment working out something in his head, and heard the words but did not consider them fully. They stuck in his mind and, as often happens in cases of this sort, when he went to bed that night without having thought about them again, they came into his dream and enlarged themselves into a terrifying picture of Cassius Chærea handing Silanus his bloody sword and shouting, "Do so! Strike! Strike again. Old Cassius is with you. Death to the tyrant!" and of Silanus then rushing at me and hacking me to pieces. The dream was so vivid and so violent that Narcissus leaped out of bed and came hurrying to my bedroom to tell me about it.

The shock of being suddenly awakened just before dawn and told in a terrified voice about this nightmare—I was sleeping alone and not sleeping very well either—put me into a cold sweat of horror. I called for lights—hundreds of lights—and sent at once for Messalina. She was terrified too at this hasty summons; afraid that I had found her out, I suppose. It must have been a great relief to her when I merely told her of Narcissus's dream. She shuddered. "No! Did he really dream that? O Heavens! That's the same terrible nightmare that I've been trying to remember every morning for the last seven days! I always wake

236

up screaming, but I can't ever remember what I was scream-ing about. It must be true. Of course it must. It's a divine warning. Send for Silanus at once and make him confess."

She ran from the room to give the message to one of her freedmen. I know now that she told him to say: "The ten days are over. The Emperor now orders you to his presence immediately and asks for an explanation." The freedman did not understand what ten days were meant, but delivered the message, arousing Silanus from his sleep. Silanus cried: "Come? Indeed I will!" He dressed hurriedly, thrusting something into the fold of his robe and rushed stumbling and wild-eyed ahead of the messenger to my rooms. The freedman was alert. He stopped a slave-boy. "Run like lightning to the Council Chamber and tell the guards there to search Appius Silanus when he arrives." The Guards found the hidden dagger and arrested him. I tried him then and there. It was, of course, impossible for him to explain the dagger, but I asked him whether he had any-thing to say in his defence. His only defence was to rage and splutter inarticulately, cursing me for a monster and Messalina for a she-wolf. When I asked him why he had wished to kill me he would only answer: "Give me back my dagger, tyrant. Let me use it on my own breast." I sen-tenced him to execution. He died, poor fellow, because he did not have the sense to speak out.

# Chapter Fourteen

I T was the execution of Silanus that encouraged Vinicianus to make his insurrection. When I reported in the Senate the same day that Silanus had intended to kill me but that my guards had frustrated his designs and that I had already executed him, a groan of astonishment rose, followed by a dismayed whisper, instantly smothered. This was the first execution of a senator since I had assumed the monarchy, and nobody believed Silanus capable of trying to murder me. It was felt that at last I was showing myself in my true colours and that a new reign of terror was about to start. I had recalled Silanus from Spain under the pretext of doing him a great honour but had really intended all the time to murder him. Just like Caligula! Naturally, I was quite unaware of all this feeling and even ventured on a little joke, saying how grateful I was to Narcissus for being so vigilant for my safety even in his sleep. "But for that dream I would not have sent for Silanus and consequently he would not have been frightened into giving himself away: he would have made his attempt on my life in a more considered manner. He had many opportunities for assassinating me, having lately been taken so deeply into my confidence that I spared him the indignity of being searched for weapons." The applause was hollow.

Vinicianus told his friends afterwards: "So the noble Appius Silanus is executed just because the Emperor's Greek freedman has a bad dream. Are we to allow a creature as weak-minded as this pumpkin-headed Claudius to rule over us? What do you say?"

They agreed that a strong, experienced Emperor was needed, not a makeshift like myself, who knew nothing, learned nothing and acted in a perfectly crazy way half the time. They began reminding each other of my most remarkable errors or eccentricities. Apart from those that I have already mentioned, they brought up, for instance, a decision that I had made a few days before when reviewing the jury-lists. It must here be explained that there were about four thousand qualified jurymen at Rome and that these were obliged to attend trials when called upon, under penalty of a heavy fine; jury-service was extremely laborious and extremely unpopular. The jury-lists were first prepared by a first-rank magistate, and this year more than half the men named in them came forward as usual to excuse themselves on one count or another; but in nineteen cases out of twenty their appeals were dismissed. The magistrate handed me the final lists for my scrutiny with a mark against the names of those whose appeal for exemption had been dismissed. I happened to notice that among the men who had *willingly* presented themselves for jury-service was one whom I knew to be the father of seven children. Under a law of Augustus's he was exempt for the rest of his life; yet he had not pleaded for exemption or mentioned the size of his family. I told the magistrate: "Strike this man's name off. He's a father of seven." He protested: "But, Cæsar, he has made no attempt to excuse himself." "Exactly," I said, "he wants to be a juryman. Strike him off." I meant, of course, that the fellow was concealing his immunity from what every honest man considered a very thankless and disagreeable duty and that he therefore was almost certain to have crooked intentions. Crooked jurymen could pick up a lot of money by bribes, for it was a commonplace that one interested juryman could sway the opinions of a whole bunch of uninterested ones; and the majority verdict decided a case. But the magistrate was a fool and simply reported my words, "He wants to be a jury-man; strike him off," as a characteristic example of my fatuity.

Vinicianus and the other malcontents spoke too of my extraordinary decision in insisting that every man who appeared before me in court should give the usual preliminary account of his parentage, connexions, marriage, career, financial condition, present occupation, and so on—with his own mouth, as best he could, instead of calling upon some patron or lawyer to do it for him. My reasons for this decision should have been obvious: one learns more about a man from ten words which he speaks himself on his own behalf than from a ten-hour eulogy by a friend. It does not matter so much what he says in those ten words: what really counts is the way in which he says them. I had found that to have some knowledge before a case starts as to whether a man is slow-witted or glib, boastful or modest, self-possessed or timorous, capable or muddle-headed, is a great help to my understanding of what follows. But to Vinicianus and his friends I seemed to be doing the accused a great injustice by robbing him of the patronage or eloquence on which he counted.

Strangely enough, what shocked them most of all my Imperial misdemeanours was my action in the case of the silver chariot. This is the story. As I happened to pass through the Goldsmiths' Street one day I saw about five hundred citizens gathered around a shop. I wondered what the attraction could be and told my yeomen to move the crowd on, because it was blocking the traffic. They did so, and I found that the shop was exhibiting a chariot entirely plated with silver, except for the rim of the body, which was gold. The axle was silver-plated too, ending in golden dogs-heads with amethyst eyes; the spokes were ebony carved in the form of negroes with silver girdles, and even the lynchpins were of gold. The silver sides of the body were embossed with scenes illustrating a chariot-race in the Circus and the felloes of the wheels were decorated with a golden inlay of vine-leaves. The extremities of the yoke and pole—silver-plated too—were golden cupids' faces with turquoise eyes. This wonderful vehicle was for sale at a hundred thousand gold pieces. Someone whispered to me that it had been commissioned by a rich senator and already paid for, but that he had asked the goldsmiths to expose it for sale for a few days (at a far higher price than he had actually paid) because he wished publicly to advertise its costliness before taking possession of it. This seemed likely: the goldsmiths themselves would not have built so expensive a thing on the mere chance of its finding a millionaire buyer. In my capacity as Director of Public Morals I had a perfect right to do what I then did. I made the goldsmiths, in my presence, strip off the gold and silver with a hammer and chisel and sell it by weight to the competent Treasury official, whom I sent for, to be melted down into coin. There were loud cries of protest, but I silenced them by saying: "A car of this weight will damage the public pavements: we must lighten it a bit." I had a pretty shrewd notion who the owner was: it was Asiaticus, who now felt it safe to make no secret of his immense riches, though he had successfully concealed them from Caligula's greedy eyes by parcelling them out into hundreds of small deposits which he left with scores of different bankers in the names of his freedmen or friends. His present ostentation was a direct incitement to popular disorder. The extraordinary additions he had made to the Gardens of Lucullus, which he had now bought! They had been considered only second in beauty to the Gardens of Sallust; but Asiaticus boasted, "When I have finished with the Gardens of Lucullus, the Gardens of Sallust will seem by contrast to be little better than a few acres of waste land." He put in such fruits, flowers, fountains and fish-pools as Rome had

241

never seen before. It occurred to me that when food was scarce in the City nobody would like to see a jolly senator with a big belly driving about in a silver car with golden axle-ends and lynchpins. A man wouldn't be human if he didn't at least feel a desire to pull out the lynchpins. I still think that I did right in this instance. But the destruction by me of a work of art—the goldsmith was a famous craftsman, the same who had been entrusted by Caligula with the modelling and casting of his golden statue—was regarded as a wanton act of barbarism and caused far more resentment among these friends of Vinicianus than if I had hauled a dozen common citizens out of the crowd and had them knocked to pieces with hammer and chisel and sold as meat to the butchers. Asiaticus himself did not express any irritation, and was indeed careful not to acknowledge ownership of the chariot, but Vinicianus made the most of my crime. He said: "He'll be pulling our gowns off our backs next and unravelling the wool to sell to the weavers again. The man's insane. We must get rid of him."

Vinicius was not in the party of malcontents either. He guessed that he was under my suspicion for having proposed himself as Emperor in opposition to me, and was now very careful not to offend me in the slightest particular. Besides, he must have known that it was no use trying to get rid of me yet. I was still extremely popular with the Guards, and took so many precautions against assassination—a constant escort of soldiers, careful searchings for weapons, a taster against poisons at every meal—and my household was so faithful and alert, besides, that a man would have had to be extremely lucky as well as ingenious to take my life and escape with his own. There had been two unsuccessful attempts by individuals recently, both made by knights whom I had threatened to degrade from the order for sexual offences. One waited at the gate of Pompey's Theatre to murder me as I came out. That was not a bad idea, but one of my soldiers saw him snatch the hollow top off a stick that he was carrying, showing it to be really a short javelin; he rushed at him and struck him on the head just as he was about to hurl the thing at me. The other attempt was made in the Temple of Mars where I was sacrificing. The weapon on this occasion was a hunting-knife, but the man was immediately disarmed by the bystanders.

The only way to get rid of me, in fact, was by force of arms, and where were troops to be found to oppose me? Vinicianus thought that he knew the answer to this question. He would get help from Scribonianus. This Scribonianus was a first cousin of little Camilla, whom my grandmother Livia had poisoned long ago on the day that she and I were to have been betrothed. When I was in Carthage, the year before my brother died, Scribonianus had been very insulting to me because he had just distinguished himself in a battle against Tacfarinas, in which I had been unable to take part; and his father, Furius Camillus, who was Governor of the province of Africa, had thereupon made him beg my pardon in public. He had been forced to obey, because in Rome a father's word is law, but he had never forgiven me and on two or three occasions since then had behaved very unpleasantly to me. Under Caligula he had been foremost among my tormentors at the Palace: nearly all the booby-traps and similar practical jokes that I had been plagued with were of his contrivance. So you may imagine that when Scribonianus, whom Caligula had recently sent to command the Roman forces in Dalmatia, heard of my election as Emperor he was not only jealous and disgusted but alarmed for his own safety. He began to wonder whether, when his term of command expired and he had to return to Rome, I was the sort of man to forgive him his insults; and if so, whether my forgiveness might not be less easy to bear even than my anger. He decided to pay me the usual respects due to a Commander-in-Chief but to do everything possible to win the personal loyalty of the forces under his command: when the time came to recall him he would write to me what Gætulicus had once written to the Emperor Tiberius from the Rhine: "You can count on my loyalty *so long as I retain my command.*"

Vinicianus was a personal friend of Scribonianus's and kept him informed by letter of what was happening at Rome. When Silanus was executed Vinicianus wrote:

"I have bad news for you, my dear Scribonianus. Claudius, after disgracing the dignity of Rome by his stupidity, ignorance and clowning, and by his complete dependence on the advice of a pack of Greek freedmen, a spendthrift rogue of a Jew, Vitellius his fellow-boozer, and Messalina his lustful and ambitious girl-wife, has committed his first important murder. Poor Appius Silanus was recalled from his command in Spain, kept hanging about the Palace in suspense for a month or two and then suddenly hauled out of bed early one morning and summarily executed. Claudius came into the House yesterday and actually joked about it. All the right-minded men in the City agree that Silanus must be avenged, and consider that if a suitable leader appeared the whole nation would welcome him with open arms. Claudius has turned things completely upside-down and one almost wishes Caligula back again. Unfortunately he has the Guards to rely upon at present, and without troops we can do nothing. Assassination has been unsuccessfully tried: he is such a coward that one can't bring so much as a bodkin into the Palace without having it removed by searchers in the vestibule. We look to you to come to our rescue. If you were to march on Rome with the Seventh and Eleventh Regiments and whatever local forces you are able to muster, all our troubles would be over. Promise the Guards a bounty as big as the one that Claudius gave them and they will desert to you at once. They despise him as a meddling civilian and he hasn't given them more than a single gold piece a man, to drink his health with on his birthday, since his original act of enforced generosity. As soon as you land in Italy—the transport difficulty can easily be got over—we will join you with a volunteer force and provide you with all the money you may need. Don't hesitate. Now is the time before matters get any worse. You can reach Rome before Claudius is able to send for reinforcements from the Rhine; and anyhow I don't think that he would get any if he did send for them. The Germans are said to be planning their revenge, and Galba isn't the man to leave his post on the Rhine when the Chattians are on the move. And Gabinius won't go if Galba stays: they always work in partnership. So the revolution promises to be bloodless. I do not wish to appeal to you by warnings as to your own personal safety, for I know that you put the honour of Rome before self-interest. But it is as well for you to know that Claudius a few nights ago told my cousin Vinicius: 'I don't forget old scores. When a certain Governor returns to Rome from his command in the Balkans, mark my words, he's going to pay with his blood for the tricks he once played me.' One thing more. Don't have any compunction about leaving the province undefended. The regiments need not be away long, and why not take a large number of hostages with you to discourage the provincials from rising in your absence? It's not as though Dalmatia were a frontier province, either. Let me know at once if you are with us, and ready to earn as glorious a name as your great ancestor Camillus, becoming the second saviour of Rome."

Scribonianus decided to take the risk. He wrote to Vinicianus that he would need a hundred and fifty transports from Italy besides what vessels he could himself commandeer in Dalmatian ports. He would also need a million gold pieces in bounty-money to persuade the two regular regiments—each five thousand strong—and the twenty thousand Dalmatian levies whom he would call to the colours, to break their allegiance to me. So Vinicianus and his fellow conspirators—six senators and seven knights, and ten knights and six senators whom I had degraded from their Orders—now left Rome unobtrusively under the pretence of visiting their country estates. The first news that I had of the rebellion was a letter which reached me from Scribonianus, addressed in the most insolent terms: calling me an imposter and an imbecile and ordering me to lay down all my offices immediately and retire into civil life. He told me that I had proved my lamentable incapacity for the task that had been entrusted to me by the Senate in a moment of confusion and aberration, and that he, Scribonianus, now repudiated his allegiance and was on the point of sailing to Italy with a force of thirty thousand men to restore order and decent government to Rome and the rest of the world. If I resigned my monarchy, on receipt of this notice, my life would be spared and the same amnesty granted me and mine as I had been wisely persuaded to grant my political opponents on my accession.

The first thing that I did on reading this letter was to burst out laughing. Good heavens, what a delightful experience that would be, to retire into private life again and live quietly and easily under an orderly government with Messalina and my books and my children! Certainly, of course, and by all means, I would resign if Scribonianus thought himself capable of governing better than I. And to be able to loll back in my chair, so to speak, and watch someone else struggling with the impossible task which I had never wished to undertake and which had proved more burdensome, anxious and thankless than I can easily convey in words! It was as though King Agamemnon had leaped forward when Laocöon and his two children were struggling with the two great serpents sent by an angry God to destroy them and had shouted out: "Here, leave those splendid creatures for me to deal with. You aren't worthy to fight with them. Leave them alone, I say, or it will be the worse for you." But could I trust Scribonianus to keep his word about the amnesty and spare my life and that of my family? And would his government be as orderly and decent as he expected it to be? And what would the Guards have to say on the matter? And was Scribonianus as popular at Rome as he seemed to think? Would the serpents, in fact, consent to leave Laocöon and his children and coil, instead, about the body of this Agamemnon?

I hurriedly convened the Senate and addressed them: "My lords, before reading you this letter, I must tell you that I am most ready to agree to the demands contained in it and should welcome the rest and security that it somewhat severely promises me. The only reason, indeed, that would induce me to decline the propositions made by this Furius Camillus Scribonianus would be a strong feeling on your part that the country would be worse rather than better off if I did so. I admit that until last year I was shamefully ignorant of the arts of government and of legal and military procedure; and though I am daily learning, my education is still in arrears. There are no men of my age and rank who could not teach me plenty of technical commonplaces with which I am totally unfamiliar. But that is the fault of my original bad health and the poor opinion that my brilliant —and now in part deified—family had of my wits when I was a boy; it has not been due to any shirking of my duties to our fatherland. And even when I did not expect ever to be raised to responsible office I improved myself by private study with, I think you will grant, commendable application. I take the liberty of suggesting that my family were mistaken: that I never was an imbecile. I won a verbal testimony to that effect from the God Augustus shortly after his visit to Postumus Agrippa on his island, and from the noble Asinius Pollio in the Apollo Library three days before his death—who however advised me to assume a mask of stupidity, like the first Brutus, as a protection against certain persons who might wish to remove me if I showed too great intelligence. My wife Urgulanilla, too, whom I divorced for her sullen temper, unfaithfulness and general brutality, took the trouble to record in her will—I can show it you if you wish—her conviction that I was no fool. The Goddess Livia Augusta's last words to me on her death-bed, or perhaps I should say 'shortly before her Apotheosis,' were: 'To think that I ever called you a fool.' I admit that my sister Livilla, my mother Antonia Augusta, my nephew the late Emperor Gaius, and my uncle Tiberius, his predecessor, never revised their ill opinion of me; and that the two last-named recorded the same in official letters to this House. My uncle Tiberius refused me a seat among you, on the ground that no speech that I could make could be anything but a trial of your patience and a waste of your time. My nephew Gaius Caligula did allow me a seat, because I was his uncle and he wished to seem magnanimous. But he ruled that I should speak last of all in any debate, and said in a speech which, if you do not remember it, you will find recorded in the archives, that if any member wished to ease himself during any session would he please in future have the good manners to contain himself and not distract attention by running out in the middle of an important speech—his own, for example—but wait until the signal for a general lapse of attention was given by the Consul's calling on Tiberius Claudius Drusus Nero Germanicus (as I was then known) to give his opinion on the matter in hand. Well, you took his advice, I remember, not supposing that I had any feelings to wound, or

248

thinking that they had been so often wounded before that I must by now be armoured all over like Tiberius's wingless dragon; or perhaps agreeing with my nephew that I was indeed an imbecile. However, the considered opinions to the contrary of the two Gods, Augustus and Livia—for which, however, you have to take my word because they are nowhere recorded in writing—surely outweigh those of any number of mere mortals? I would be inclined to hold it blasphemous for anyone here to contradict them. Not that blasphemy is a criminal offence nowadays—we have changed that; but it is at least bad manners and perhaps dangerous if the Gods happen to overhear. Besides, my nephew and uncle both met violent deaths and were not mourned, and their speeches and letters are no longer quoted with the respect with which the God Augustus's speeches and letters are quoted, and much of their legislation has lapsed. They were lions in their day, my Lords, but now they are dead and in the words of the Jewish proverb that the God Augustus was fond of quoting—he borrowed it from King Herod the Great of Judea, for whose wit he had as much respect as I have for the wit of King Herod Agrippa, his grandson—*A live dog is worth more than a dead lion.* I am not a lion—you know that. But I consider that I have not made so bad a watch-dog; and to say that I have grossly mismanaged national affairs or that I am an imbecile is, I think, an insult to you rather than to me, because you pressed the monarchy on me and have on many occasions since congratulated me on my successes and rewarded me with many great honours, including that of Father of the Country. If the father is an imbecile, surely his children will have inherited the taint?"

I then read Scribonianus's letter and glanced around inquiringly. Everyone had been looking extremely uncomfortable during my speech, though nobody ventured to do other than applaud, protest, or show surprise at the points where this seemed to be expected. You, my readers, will no doubt be thinking what no doubt they all were thinking: "What a curious speech to make on the eve of a rebellion! Why should Claudius have insisted on raking up a matter which we might be expected to have forgotten about altogether—his supposed imbecility? Why did he find it necessary to remind us that his family once regarded him as mentally incapable, and to read the passages of Scribonianus's letter referring to this, and why did he lower himself by arguing about it?" Yes, it looked very suspicious, as though I really knew that I was an imbecile and was trying to persuade myself that I wasn't. But I knew just what I was doing. I was, in fact, being rather clever. I had in the first place spoken extremely frankly, and unexpected frankness about oneself is never unacceptable. I was reminding the Senate what sort of a man I was—honest and devoted; not clever, but not self-seeking—and what sort of men they themselves were—clever but self-seeking, and neither honest nor devoted nor even courageous. Cassius Chærea had warned them not to hand over the monarchy to an idiot and they had disregarded his advice for fear of the Guards —yet things on the whole had turned out very well, so far. Prosperity was returning to Rome, justice was being evenly dispensed, the people were contented, our armies were victorious abroad, I was not playing the tyrant in any extravagant way; and, as I told them in the discussion that followed, I had perhaps travelled farther, hobbling on my lame leg, than most men would have travelled on a sound pair; because, only too conscious of my disability, I allowed myself no halts or slackening of pace. On the other hand, I wished to show them by my speech that they were perfectly free to dismiss me if they pleased; and my undignified frankness about my own shortcomings should encourage them not to be harsh or revengeful when I was a private citizen once more.

Several loyal speeches were made, all in rather guarded terms, for fear of the vengeance of Scribonianus, should he force me to resign. Only Vinicius spoke out strongly:

"My Lords, I think that many of us must be feeling keenly the reproach that the Father of the Country has been, however gently, heaping on us. I confess that I am heartily ashamed that I misjudged him before his accession and that I thought him unfitted for the offices which he has since so nobly filled. It is incredible to me now that his mental powers were ever underrated by any of us, and the only explanation that I can offer is that he deceived us, first by his great modesty and next by his deliberate self-depreciation in the reign of the late Emperor. You know the proverb "No man cries 'Stinking Fish.'" That proverb was discredited under Caligula, when no wise man with fish in his basket would cry it as anything but stinking, for fear Caligula should become greedy or jealous. Valerius Asiaticus concealed his wealth, Tiberius Claudius concealed his wit; I had nothing to conceal except my disgust of tyranny, but I concealed that until the time came for action. Yes, we all cried 'Stinking fish'. Caligula is dead now, and under Claudius frankness has come into its own. I shall be frank. My cousin Vinicianus spoke violently against Claudius lately in my presence and suggested his deposition. I reproached him angrily but did not report the matter to the House, because there is no treason-law now in force, and after all, he is my cousin. Free speech must be indulged, especially in the case of kinsmen. Vinicianus is not here to-night. He has left the City. I fear that he has gone to join Scribonianus. Six of his intimate friends are also absent, I notice. They must have gone with him. Yet what are seven discontented men—seven against five hundred? A negligible minority. And is theirs a genuine discontent or is it personal ambition?

"I condemn my cousin's action on three counts: the first, that he is ungrateful; the second, that he is disloyal; the third, that he is foolish. His ingratitude: the Father of the Country freely forgave him for supporting me as a candidate for the monarchy and has shown great tolerance since of his impertinent and obstructive speeches in this House. His disloyalty: he engaged himself by an oath to obey Tiberius Claudius Cæsar as the Head of the State. A breach of this oath could only be excused in the unlikely event of Cæsar flagrantly breaking his oath to rule justly, with respect for the common good; Cæsar has not broken his oath. Disloyalty to Cæsar is therefore impiety to the Gods by whom Vinicianus swore, and enmity to the State, which is more content than ever before to be ruled by Cæsar. His folly: though it is possible that Scribonianus may persuade a few thousand of his troops by lies and bribes to invade Italy and may even win a few military successes, does any member of this honourable House really believe that he is destined to be our Emperor? Does anyone believe that the Guards, our chief bulwark, will secede to him? The Guards are not fools: they know when they are well off. The Senate and People are not fools either: they know that under Claudius they are enjoying a liberty and prosperity consistently denied them by his immediate predecessors. Scribonianus cannot impose himself on the City except by promising to redress existing wrongs, and it will puzzle him to find any wrongs to redress. As I see the case, my Lords, this promised revolt is actuated by personal jealousy and personal ambition. We are now asked not merely to exchange an Emperor who has proved himself in every way worthy of our admiration and obedience for one of whose capacities we know little and whose intentions we suspect, but to run the risk of a bloody Civil War. For supposing that Cæsar were persuaded to resign, would the armies necessarily acknowledge Scribonianus as their commander? There are several men of rank far more capable of undertaking the monarchy than Scribonianus. What is there to prevent some other corps-commander with four regular regiments at his back, instead of Scribonianus's two, from setting himself up as a rival Emperor and marching on Rome? And even if Scribonianus's attempt were to succeed, which I regard as most unlikely, what of Vinicianus? Would he be content to bow the knee to the haughty Scribonianus? Has he not perhaps offered his support only on the understanding that the Empire shall be shared between them? And if so, may we not expect another death-duel to be fought, as once between Pompey and the God Julius Cæsar, and again between Mark Antony and the God Augustus? No, my Lords. This is a case where our loyalty, our gratitude and our interest go hand in hand. We must loyally support Tiberius Claudius Cæsar if we wish to earn the thanks of the country, the approval of the Gods, and our own self-congratulations later when Vinicianus and Scribonianus have met the traitors' deaths that they so richly deserve."

Then Rufrius spoke. "I regard it as unfortunate that the possibility of the Guards' disloyalty has been so much as mentioned in this House. As their Commander I repudiate the notion that even a single man will forget his duty to the Emperor. You must recall, my Lords, that it was the Guards who first called upon Tiberius Claudius Cæsar, now the Father of the Country, to undertake the supreme command of the Army, and that this House was for a time unwilling to confirm their choice. It therefore ill befits a senator to suggest that the Guards will be disloyal. No, as they were the first to acclaim Tiberius Claudius Cæsar Emperor, so they will be the last to desert his cause. And if news reaches the Camp that the Senate has decided to offer the supreme command to any other person—in that case, my Lords, I advise you immediately on reaching the decision either to fortify this edifice as best you can with barricades of benches and piles of cobble-stones, or to adjourn *sine die* and scatter in all directions."

So I was given a unanimous vote of confidence and the Senate authorized me to write to Scribonianus, informing him that he was suspended from his command and must return to Rome forthwith to explain himself. But Scribonianus never received my letter. He was already dead.

I will tell you what had happened. Having succeeded, as he thought, in making himself very popular with his troops by relaxation of discipline, plenty of free entertainments and a wine-ration increased at his own expense, he had paraded the Seventh and Eleventh Regiments together in the local amphitheatre and told them that his life was in danger. He read them Vinicianus's letter, or most of it, and asked them whether they would stand by him in his attempt to deliver Rome from a tyranny which seemed to be rapidly becoming as capricious and cruel as that of Caligula. "The Republic must be restored," he shouted. "Only under the Republic has true liberty ever been enjoyed." He sowed with the sack, as the saying is, and some of the seed seemed to sprout at once. The common soldiers smelt money in his tones: they liked money, and it seemed most unjust that so generous a commander should be sacrificed to my anger or jealousy. They cheered him loudly, and also cheered Vinicianus, who had once commanded the Eleventh Regiment; and swore to follow them both, if need be, to the ends of the earth. Scribonianus promised them ten gold pieces each, on the spot, a further forty each on arrival in Italy, and a further hundred each on the day that they marched victoriously into Rome. He paid out the ten gold pieces and sent them back to camp, ordering them to hold themselves in readiness for the coming campaign. The call would come as soon as the transports arrived from Italy and the native levies were under arms. But Scribonianus had made a great mistake in underrating the loyalty and intelligence of his men. True, they could be easily worked up into a state of temporary indignation on his behalf and were not above accepting gifts in coin while in that mood; but an overt breach of their soldiers' oath was a different matter. That wasn't so easily bought. They would follow him to the ends of the earth; but not to Rome, its centre. It would take more than ten gold pieces a man to persuade them to embark for Italy, with a promise of forty more on landing. To leave their province and invade Italy was to make rebellion, and the punishment for unsuccessful rebellion was death—death in battle, or death under the executioner's sword—perhaps even death by flogging or crucifixion if the Emperor felt like making an example of them.

A meeting of officers was called to decide whether to follow Scribonianus or not. Some sympathy was expressed for him, but no great desire to resort to rebellion. In any case nobody wanted the Republic to be restored. Scribonianus had told them that he counted on their support, and hinted that he would give them over to the just fury of the common soldiers if they refused to join him in so glorious a cause as the restoration of ancient Roman liberties. They decided to play for time. They sent him a deputation informing him that they were not yet agreed among themselves, but would let him know of their common decision—if he would forgive them their conscientious hesitations—on the day that the expedition sailed. Scribonianus told them to please themselves—he had plenty of capable men to put in their places—but warned them that if they declined to join him they must be prepared to die for their obstinacy. More important than this meeting of officers, there was also held a secret meeting of standard-bearers, sergeants and corporals, all men of over twelve years' service and most of them married to Dalmatian women, because all their service had been done here: a Roman legion was almost never shifted from one province to another. The Seventh and Eleventh, in fact, looked on Dalmatia as their permanent home and had no interests or ideas beyond making themselves as comfortable as possible there and defending their possessions.

The Eagle-bearer of the Seventh addressed the meeting: "Lads, you don't really intend to follow the General to Italy, do you? It looks like a very foolish adventure to me, quite apart from the matter of regimental honour. We've sworn allegiance to Tiberius Claudius Cæsar, haven't we? He's proved himself a decent man, hasn't he? He may have a down on old Scribonianus, but who knows on which side the right lies? Old Scribonianus can have *his* downs, we've all noticed. Why not leave the two of them to settle their own differences? I'm ready to fight Germans, Moors, Parthians, Jews, Britons, Arabians, Chinese—send me where you like—that's my job as an enlisted man. But I'm not going to do any fighting in Italy against the Guards Division. The Emperor's very popular with them, I'm told, and besides it's ridiculous in my opinion to think of us and them fighting each other. The General ought never to have asked us. Personally, I haven't spent that gift of his, and I don't intend to do so. My vote is that we call the whole business off."

Everyone agreed. But the young soldiers and the hard cases—old soldiers with bad characters—had grown so excited now with the hope of easy money and plenty of loot that the question before the meeting was how to call the rebellion off without putting themselves into a false position. Someone had a sensible idea. A mutiny among these very regiments thirty years before had been quelled suddenly by an ominous sign from Heaven—an eclipse, followed by torrential rain: why not now provide another ominous sign to discourage the rebellion? So they decided on a suitable one.

Five days later the order came from Scribonianus for the regiments to march down to the port, fully armed, rationed and equipped, prepared to embark at once for Italy. The Eagle-bearers of the Seventh and Eleventh simultaneously reported to their commanders that they had been unable that morning to dress the Eagles in the customary way with laurel garlands. The garlands had fallen off as soon as they tied them on, and immediately withered away! Then the standard-bearers also came running in pretended consternation to report another miracle: the standards had refused to be pulled out from the earth into which they had been stuck! The officers were only too pleased to hear of these dreadful omens and reported them to Scribonianus. Scribonianus flew into a rage and came rushing into the camp of the Eleventh. "You say that the standards refuse to be moved, you liars? It's because you're a pack of cowards and haven't the courage of dogs. Look! Who says that this standard can't be moved?" He went up to the nearest standard and heaved at it. He heaved and tugged and strained until the veins stood out on his forehead like cords: but he couldn't so much as budge the thing. As a matter of fact, it had been secretly planted in concrete on the night of the meeting, and so had all the other standards, with earth heaped above. The concrete had set like rock.

Scribonianus saw that all was lost. He shook his fist at Heaven and running down to the port jumped aboard his private yacht and told his crew to cast off and stand out to sea at once. He was making for Italy, intending, I suppose, to warn Vinicianus of his failure. But instead the crew put him ashore at the island of Lissa, near Corfu, suspecting that his plans had gone astray and not wishing to have anything more to do with him. One freedman alone remained with him and was present when he committed suicide. Vinicianus also killed himself when the news reached him a day or two later; so did most of his fellow-rebels. The revolt was over.

I will not pretend that I did not spend an anxious ten days between addressing the Senate and hearing the happy news of Scribonianus's failure. I grew very excitable, and if it had not been for Xenophon's exertions I would probably have had a serious return of my old nervous trouble. But he dosed me with this and that and kept me well massaged and encouraged me, in his dry way, to have no fears for the future; and so steered me through without serious damage to my health. A verse of Homer's stuck in my head and I kept repeating it to everyone I met:

"Do thou resist that man with all thy might
Who, unprovoked, provokes thee to a fight."

I even gave it to Rufrius one day as a watchword. Messalina teased me about it, but I had an answer ready: "It stuck in Homer's mind too. He used it again and again. Once in the *Iliad* and two or three times in the *Odyssey*." Messalina's devotion was a great comfort, and so were the loyal shouts of the citizens and the soldiers whenever I appeared in public, and the confidence that the Senate seemed to feel in me.

I rewarded the Seventh and Eleventh by asking the Senate to rename them "The Loyal Claudian Regiments," and on Messalina's insistence (Vitellius agreed with her that it was no occasion for an amnesty) I put to death the principal rebels who survived. I did not, however, execute them summarily, as I had executed Silanus, but gave them each in turn a formal trial. The procedure that I adopted was to read the charge sitting on a chair of state with the Consuls standing one on either side of me. I would then retire to my ordinary seat and the Consuls would call for their own chairs of state and conduct the trial as judges. I happened to be suffering from a severe cold, which reduced my voice, never very strong, to a whisper; but I had Narcissus, Polybius and the Guards colonels at my side, and if I wished to cross-examine a prisoner or witness I would hand one of them a list of questions to ask on my behalf, or whisper them to him. Narcissus made the best mouthpiece, so I employed him more often than the rest; this caused a misunderstanding. He was later represented by my enemies as having conducted the prosecution on his own initiative—a mere freedman prosecuting noble Romans, what a scandal! Narcissus certainly had a very assured, independent manner and I must admit that I joined in the general laugh against him, when Scribonianus's faithful freedman, whom he was cross-examining, proved his master in repartee.

NARCISSUS: You were a freedman of Furius Camillus Scribonianus's? You were present at his death?

FREEDMAN: I was.

NARCISSUS: You were in his confidence about this intended rebellion? You knew who his confederates were?

FREEDMAN: You wish to suggest that I was unworthy of his confidence? That if he had confederates, as you call them, in this alleged rebellion I would betray them?

NARCISSUS: I suggest nothing. I am asking you a plain question of fact.

FREEDMAN: Then I give you a plain answer. I do not remember.

NARCISSUS: Not remember?

FREEDMAN: His last words to me were: "Whatever I have said to you in this, forget. Let my secrets die with me."

NARCISSUS: Ah, then I may assume that you *were* in his confidence.

FREEDMAN: Assume whatever you like. It does not interest me. My master's dying injunctions were to forget. I have obeyed him implicitly.

NARCISSUS (*striding forward angrily into the middle of the floor, so that he actually obscured my view of the witness*): A very honest freedman, by Hercules. And tell me, fellow, what would you have done if Scribonianus had made himself Emperor?

FREEDMAN (*with sudden warmth*): I would have stood behind him, fellow, and kept my mouth shut.


Fifteen rebel noblemen or ex-noblemen were put to death, but only one of these was a senator, one Juncus, a magistrate of the first rank, and I made him resign his office before I condemned him. The other senators had committed suicide before arrest. Contrary to the usual custom, I did not confiscate the estates of the executed rebels, but let their heirs inherit as if they had decently killed themselves. In three or four cases, indeed, where their estates were found to be greatly encumbered by debt—the reason probably for their participation in the rebellion—I actually made the heirs a present of money. It has been said that Narcissus took bribes to cover up evidence of guilt against certain rebels: this is certainly an invention. I conducted the preliminary inquiries myself with Polybius's help and took down depositions. Narcissus did not have the opportunity of suppressing any evidence. Messalina, however, had access to the papers and may have destroyed some of them; I cannot say whether she did or not. But neither Narcissus nor Polybius handled them except in my presence. It has also been said that freedmen and citizens were put to the torture in an attempt to extract evidence from them. This is also untrue. A few slaves were racked, but not to force them to give evidence against their masters, only to make them give evidence against certain freedmen whom I suspected of perjury. The origin of the report that I tortured freedmen and citizens must probably be found in the case of certain of Vinicianus's slaves to whom he gave their freedom, when he saw that the rebellion had failed, to prevent them giving evidence against him under torture; he pre-dated their freedom, in the deed of manumission, by twelve months. This was an illegal procedure, or at any rate the men were still liable to be examined under torture, by a law passed under Tiberius to prevent this sort of evasion. One so-called citizen was put to torture when it was discovered that he had no claims to be regarded as such. Juncus indeed protested at his trial that he had been grossly maltreated in prison. He appeared swathed in bandages, with severe cuts on his face, but Rufrius testified that it was a downright lie: the injuries were due to his having resisted arrest—leaping naked from a bedroom window at Brindisi and trying to break through a quickset hedge. Two Guards captains confirmed this.

However, Juncus had his revenge on Rufrius. "If I must die, Rufrius," he said, "then I shall take you with me." Then he turned to me: "Cæsar, your trusted Commander of the Guards hates and despises you as much as I do. Pætus and I interviewed him, on Vinicianus's behalf, asking him whether on the arrival of the forces from Dalmatia he would bring over the Guards to our side. He undertook to do so, but only on condition that he, Scribonianus and Vinicianus should share the Empire between them. Deny that, Rufrius, if you dare."

I arrested Rufrius on the spot. As first he tried to laugh off the charge, but Pætus, one of the rebel-knights awaiting trial, supported Juncus's evidence, and finally he broke down and pleaded for mercy. I gave him the mercy of being his own executioner.

A few women were also executed. I did not see why a woman's sex should protect her from punishment if she had been guilty of fomenting rebellion, particularly a woman who had not married a man in the strict form of marriage but had kept her independence and her own property, and so could not plead coercion. They were brought to the scaffold in chains, just like their husbands, and on the whole showed much greater courage in facing death. One woman, Arria, Pætus's wife but a close friend of Messalina's, married in the strict form, could no doubt have won a pardon if she had dared to sue for one. But no, she preferred to die with Pætus. Pætus, as a reward for his evidence in the case of Rufrius, was allowed to commit suicide before any charge was formally brought against him. He was a coward and could not nerve himself to fall on his sword. Arria snatched it from him and drove it home under her own ribs. "Look, Pætus," she said as she died, "it doesn't hurt."

The most distinguished person to die because of complicity in this rebellion was my niece Julia (Helen the Glutton). I was glad to have a good excuse for getting rid of her. It was she who had betrayed her husband, my poor nephew Nero, to Sejanus and had got him banished to the island where he died. Tiberius afterwards showed his contempt for her by giving her in marriage to Blandus, a vulgar knight of no family. Helen was jealous of Messalina's beauty as well as of her power: she had lost her own great beauty because of her passion for food and her indolence, and become excessively stout; however, Vinicianus was one of those little rat-like men who have the same love for women of abundant charms as rats have for large pumpkins; and if he had become Emperor, as he intended, knowing himself more than a match for Rufrius and Scribonianus combined, Helen the Glutton would have become his Empress. It was Vinicianus who betrayed her to Messalina, as a token of his loyalty to us.

# Chapter Fifteen

So I was still Emperor and my hopes of a safe and speedy return to private life were dashed. I began to tell myself that Augustus had been sincere in the speeches which he made from time to time about soon restoring the Republic, and that even my uncle Tiberius had not been so false as I suspected when he talked of resignation. Yes, it was easy enough for a private citizen to be a staunch Republican and grumble: "Why, what could there be simpler than to choose a moment of general tranquillity, resign and hand the government over to the Senate?" The difficulty could only be understood if that private citizen were to become Emperor himself. It lay in the phrase "moment of tranquillity": there were no moments of tranquillity. There were always disturbing factors in the situation. One said, sincerely enough, "Perhaps in six months' time, perhaps in a year's time." But the six months passed and the year passed; and even if some disturbing factors in the situation had been successfully disposed of, new ones were sure to have sprung up to take their places. I was determined to hand the government over as soon as the confusion left behind by Tiberius and Caligula had been cleared up and I had encouraged the Senate to recover its self-respect—one cannot have liberty without self-respect—by treating it as a responsible legislative body. Yet I could not be more respectful to the Senatorial Order than it deserved. I put the best available men into it, but the tradition of subservience to the Imperial pleasure was hard to break down. They suspected my good-nature, and whispered ill-manneredly to each other behind their

263

hands if I behaved with natural affability towards them; and then if I suddenly lost my temper with them, as sometimes happened, they would suddenly fall silent and tremble like a lot of naughty schoolboys who have trespassed on the forbearance of an easy-going master. No, I could not give up yet. I was thoroughly ashamed of myself, in theory, as having been forced to put to death the leaders of an abortive anti-monarchical revolt; but in practice what else could I have done?

I brooded over the problem. Wasn't it Plato who wrote that the only sound excuse that anyone can offer for ruling is that by doing so he avoids being ruled by people inferior in talents to himself? There's something in that. But I was afraid, on the contrary, that, if I resigned, my place would be taken by someone superior in talents (though, I flattered myself, not in industry)—for example, Galba or Gabinius, from the Rhine—so that the monarchy would become stronger than ever and the Republic never be restored. In any case, the moment of tranquillity had not come. I must get to work again.

The rebellion and its aftermath had interrupted public business and put me back a couple of months in my schedule. To gain time I abolished several more unnecessary public holidays. When the New Year came I took on my third consulship, with Vitellius as my colleague, but resigned after two months in favour of Asiaticus. This was one of the most important years in my life— the year of my expedition to Britain. But before I come to that I must write about a few domestic matters. It was time now for my daughter Antonia to marry young Pompey, a capable young man and apparently well-disposed to me. I did not, however, allow the ceremony to be made the subject of any great public rejoicing—I celebrated it quietly at home. I did not wish it to be thought that I regarded my son-in-law as a member of the Imperial House. In fact, I

A. D. 43

did not care to think of my family as the Imperial House: we were not an Eastern dynasty—we were Julio-Claudians and no better or worse than the Cornelians, Camillans, Servians, Junians, or any other leading family. Nor did I wish my little son to be honoured above all other children of noble birth. The Senate asked permission to celebrate his birthday with Games at the public expense, but I refused this. However, the first-rank magistrates on their own initiative did observe his first birthday with a magnificent spectacle and banquet for which they paid themselves: and this practice was followed by their successors. It would have been discourteous not to have thanked them for their good-will towards me, and the Games pleased Messalina greatly. All that I did for young Pompey was to allow him to stand for his first magistracy five years before the usual time and to make him City Warden during the Latin holidays. Pompey was descended from Pompey the Great through his maternal grandmother, the Pompey heiress: through her he inherited the family masks and statues and was able to adopt the name. I was proud to be able to link the name of Cæsar with that of Pompey after so many generations. My grandmother Octavia had been offered in marriage by Julius Cæsar to Pompey the Great nearly a hundred years before this, but he had refused her and quarrelled with Julius. Later she married Mark Antony and became the great-grandmother of my daughter Antonia, whom I was now marrying to a great-great-grandson of Pompey.

The State finances were still in rather a difficult way, in spite of retrenchment. The world harvests continued to be poor and I had to devote a great deal of money to buying corn at high prices in distant markets. Among other econo-mies I asked for the return of public revenues which had been granted by Caligula to certain of his favourites—charioteers, actors, and so on—as permanent pensions. I had been unaware that these were still being paid, for Callistus never mentioned them to me. He was probably bribed by the pensioners to keep quiet about them.

I arrived at one important decision. Since the time of Augustus the charge of the Public Treasury had been taken from the usual Treasury officials, who formed the lowest of magistrates, and given to the first-rank magistrates. In practice, however, these first-rank magistrates, though acting as paymasters and receivers of revenue, did not do much more than take in or pay out the sums indicated to them by the Emperor, whose freedmen kept all Treasury accounts. I decided to return the charge of the Treasury to the original Treasury officials, who were now employed in other ways— the government of Lombardy, the collection of harbour-dues at Ostia, and so on—and give them a chance to understand State finances thoroughly; so that when the change-over came from monarchical to republican government there would be no confusion. At present the Treasury accounts, which were never audited except by myself, were wholly managed by Callistus and his clerks. But I did not wish any of these officials to take advantage of their position to rob the Treasury—it was, unfortunately, easier to trust freedmen than men of rank. So I only made those men eligible for the post who would undertake to present Public Games at their own expense during their term of office: rich men, I argued, are less likely to rob the State than poor ones. The young men I chose were obliged, for one whole year before their appointment, to attend every day at the New Palace and study Treasury routine. Each, on appointment, was then given a Treasury department under myself—still, of course, represented by Callistus—with a freedman, the head-clerk of the department, as his adviser and secretary. The plan worked well. Freedmen and officials kept check on each other. I instructed Callistus that the cipher-like communications between departments must cease and correct Latin or Greek longhand be substituted: the new officials must be allowed to understand what was going on.

In the same spirit I did my best to inculcate a high sense of duty in all magistrates and governors. For instance, I insisted that senators who had been chosen by lot in the New Year to administer provinces (the home provinces I mean, as opposed to frontier provinces whose military governors I nominated myself in my capacity as Commander-in-Chief) should not hang about in Rome, as they usually did, until June or July when the weather made sailing pleasant, but be on their way by the middle of April.

Messalina and I were making a thorough revision of the Roll of Citizens, into which a great number of quite unworthy persons had inserted themselves. I left most of this business to her and thousands of names were removed and tens of thousands added. I had no objection to the enlargement of the Roll. The Roman citizenship gave all who held it an immense advantage over freedmen, provincials and foreigners, and so long as it was not made either too inclusive or too exclusive a guild, but kept at the right proportion to the great mass of the population in the Roman dominion—say, about one citizen to every six or seven others—it was a great steadying factor in world politics. I only insisted that the new citizens should be men of substance, honest parentage and good reputation, that they should be able to speak Latin, that they should have a sufficient education in Roman law, religion and ethics and that they should dress and comport themselves in a manner worthy of the honour. Any applicant with the necessary qualifications who was sponsored by a senator of good standing I put on the list. I expected him, however, to make a gift proportionate to his means to the Public Treasury, from which he would now benefit in a variety of ways. Persons who could find no sponsor applied to me indirectly through my secretaries, and Messalina then inquired into their antecedents. Those whom she recommended I put on

267

the list without further question. I did not realize at the time that she was charging applicants a heavy fee for her interest with me and that the freedmen, notably Amphæus, and Polybius whom I had temporarily transferred to this duty, were making enormous sums of money too. Many senators who sponsored candidates for citizenship got wind of this and began to take money under the table (as the saying is) and some even advertised in a cautious way through their agents that they made a more reasonable charge for their patronage than any other senator in the business. I knew nothing about this at the time, though. I suppose that they thought I was getting money from the business myself, using Messalina as my agent, and so would wink at their own practices.

I was aware, I own, that many of my secretaries received money-presents from suitors. I discussed this point with them one day. I said: "I permit you to take presents but I forbid you to solicit them. I shall not wrong you by suggesting that you could be bribed to commit any falsification or other irregularity, and I don't see why you should not be rewarded for doing favours for people which take your time and energy, and for, *ceteris paribus,* giving priority to their business. If a hundred applications for the same favour are sent in simultaneously and there is nothing to choose between the candidates, yet only  ten can have their applications granted—well, I would think you foolish not to choose the ten who are capable of showing the most gratitude. My loyal friend and ally, King Herod Agrippa, is fond of quoting a Jewish proverb—or rather a Jewish law which has won proverbial force—'Thou shalt not muzzle the ox that treadeth out the corn.' That is appropriate and just. But I don't want any indecent haggling or auctioning of favours and priorities; and if I find that any of my oxen devote more of their attention to snatching mouthfuls of corn than to treading it out, I shall take them straight from the threshing-floor to the slaughter-house."

My new Commander of the Guards was called Justus; I had called up the other Guards colonels to suggest one of their number for the appointment, and though I would have preferred someone other than Justus I accepted their choice. Justus took too meddling an interest in politics for a mere soldier: for instance, he came to me one day and informed me that some of the new citizens I had created were not adopting my name, as they should do in loyalty, or altering their wills in my favour, as they should do in gratitude. He had a list already prepared of these ungrateful and disloyal men and asked whether I wished to have charges framed against them; I silenced him by asking him whether his recruits made a practice of adopting his name and altering their wills in his favour. Justus took the trouble to tell me this, but neither he nor anyone else let me know that not only was Messalina selling the citizenship and encouraging others to sell it; but, more shameful still, was being paid huge sums of money in return for her influence with me in the choice of magistrates, governors and military commanders. In some cases she not only exacted the money but—I might as well tell you at once—insisted on the man sleeping with her as a seal to the bargain. The most shameful thing of all was that she brought me into it without my knowledge: telling them that I had cast her off in scorn of her beauty, but allowed her to choose what bedfellows she liked on condition that she persuaded them to pay a good price for the appointments which I gave her to sell on my behalf! However, I knew nothing about any of this at the time, and flattered myself that I was doing well enough and acting in an upright way that should command the affection and gratitude of the whole nation.

In my self-confident ignorance I did one particularly stupid thing: I listened to Messalina's advice on the subject of monopolies. You must remember how clever she was and how slow-witted I was, and how much I relied on her: she could persuade me to almost anything. She said to me one day: "Claudius, I have been thinking about something; and that is, that the nation would be much more prosperous if competition between rival merchants were to be suppressed by law."

"What do you mean, my dear?" I asked.

"Let me explain by an analogy. Suppose that in our governmental system we had no departments. Suppose that every secretary in this place were free to move from job to job just as he thought fit. Suppose that Callistus were to come rushing into your study one morning and say: 'I got here first and I want to do Narcissus's secretarial work this morning', and then Narcissus, arriving a moment later and finding his stool occupied by Callistus, were to dash into Felix's room, just in time to anticipate Felix, and begin work on some foreign-affairs document that Felix had not quite finished drawing up the night before. That would be ridiculous, wouldn't it?"

"Very ridiculous. But I don't see what this has to do with merchants."

"I'll show you. The trouble with merchants is that they won't stick to a single task or let their rivals stick to one. None of them is interested in serving the community, but merely in finding the easiest way of making money. A merchant may start with an inherited business as a wine-importer, and manage that soberly for a while, and then suddenly break into the oil-business, underselling some old-established firm in his neighbourhood; perhaps he will force this firm out of business or buy it up, and then perhaps dabble in the fig-trade or slave-trade and either crush competitors or get crushed himself. Trade is constant fighting, and the mass of the population suffers from it, just like non-combatants in a war."

"Do you really think so? Often they get things surprisingly cheap when one merchant is underselling another merchant or when he goes bankrupt."

"You might as well say that sometimes non-combatants can get quite good pickings from a battle-field—scrap-metal, the hides and shoes of dead horses, enough sound parts of broken chariots to build one good one with. Those windfalls aren't to be reckoned against the burning of their farms and the trampling down of their crops."

"Are merchants as bad as all that? They never struck me as being anything but useful servants of the State."

"They could be and ought to be useful. But they do great harm by their lack of co-operation and their insane jealous competition. The word goes round, for example, that there's to be a demand for coloured marble from Phrygia, or Syrian silk, or ivory from Africa or Indian pepper; and for fear of missing a chance they scramble for the market like mad dogs. Instead of persisting with their ordinary lines of commerce, they rush their ships to the new centre of excitement, with orders to their captains to bring as much marble, pepper, silk or ivory as possible at whatever cost, and then of course the foreigners raise the prices. Two hundred shiploads of pepper or silk are brought home at great expense when there is really only a demand for twenty, and the hundred and eighty ships could have been far better employed in importing other things for which there would have been a demand and for which a fair price could have been got. Obviously trade ought to be centrally controlled in the same way as armies and law-courts and religion and everything else is controlled."

I asked her how she would control trade if I gave her the chance. "Why, that's simple enough," she answered. "I would grant monopolies."

"Caligula granted monopolies," I said, "and sent prices up with a rush."

"He *sold* monopolies to the highest bidder, and of course

271

prices went up. I wouldn't do that. And my monopolies wouldn't be so huge as Caligula's. He sold one man the world's trading-rights in figs! I'd simply calculate a normal year's demand for any given commodity and then freely allocate that trade for the next two years to one firm or more of traders. I would, for instance, grant the sole right to import and sell Cyprian wines to such-and-such a firm, and the sole right to import and sell Egyptian glass to such-and-such a firm; and Baltic amber and Tyrian purple and British enamel would go to other firms. Control trade like this and there is no competition, so the foreign manufacturer or dealer in raw materials can't put up the price; 'take it or leave it,' says the trader, as he fixes the price himself. The traders who have not sufficient standing to be granted monopolies must either come to terms with monopoly-holders, if the latter think that they have more trade than they can manage themselves, or must discover new industries or trades. If I had my way everything would be thoroughly orderly, and we should be well supplied, and the State would get bigger harbour-dues than ever."

I agreed that it sounded a very sensible plan; and one good effect would be to release a large number of ships and merchants for the corn trade. I immediately empowered her to grant a large number of monopolies, never suspecting that the clever woman had talked me over to her scheme merely with an eye to the enormous bribes that she would get from the merchants. Six months later the removal of competition in the monopoly trades, which included necessaries as well as luxuries, had sent prices up to a most ridiculous height—the merchants were recovering from the consumers what they had paid in bribes to Messalina—and the City became more restless than at any time since the famine-winter. I was continually shouted at in the streets by the crowd, and there was nothing for me to do but to set up a big platform on Mars Field from which, with the help of a big-voiced Guards captain, I fixed the prices, for the ensuing twelve months, of the commodities affected. I based the prices on those of the previous twelve months, as far as I was able to get accurate figures; and then of course all the monopolists came to the Palace afterwards to beg me to modify my decision in their own particular cases, because they were poor men and beggary was facing their starving families, and nonsense of that sort. I told them that if they could not make their monopolies pay at the prices now fixed they could retire in favour of other traders with better business methods; and then warned them to go away at once before I charged them with "waging war against the State" and threw them from the Capitoline cliff. They made no further protests but tried to beat me by withdrawing their goods from the market altogether. However, as soon as any complaints reached me that a certain class of goods—say pickled fish from Macedonia or medicinal drugs from Crete—was not reaching the City in sufficient quantities I added another firm to those already sharing the monopoly.

I was always most attentive to the City food-supply. I instructed the steward of my Italian estates to devote as much land as possible in the neighborhood of the City to the growing of vegetables for the City Market, especially cabbage, onion, lettuce, endive, leek, skirret and other winter vegetables. My physician Xenophon told me that the frequent outbreaks of disease in the poorer quarters of Rome in the winter months were largely due to the scarcity of green vegetables. I wanted an abundant supply raised, brought in every day before dawn and sold at the lowest possible prices. I also encouraged pig, poultry and cattle-breeding; and a year or two later won special privileges from the Senate for City butchers and wine-sellers. There was some opposition in the Senate to these grants. The Senators themselves were supplied from their own country estates and were not interested in the people's food. Asiaticus said: "Cold water, bread, beans, pulse-porridge and cabbage are good enough for working-men. Why pamper them with wine and butcher's meat?" I protested against Asiaticus's inhumanity and asked him whether he preferred cold water to Chian wine, or cabbage to roast venison. He answered that he had been brought up on a rich diet and would find it quite impossible to change to the simpler sort, but that no doubt he would be a hardier man if he could, and that it was wrong to encourage poor men to a diet above their station.

"I appeal to you, my Lords," I protested, trembling with vexation, "what man is able to live a self-respecting life without a little bit of meat now and then?" The House seemed to think this funny. I didn't. And the same thing happened at the end of the same debate when I was on the subject of the wine-sellers. "They want encouragement," I said. "There has been a great falling-off in the number of wine-shops even in the last five years: I mean honest jug-and-bottle houses, not those dirty places that I have had shut up now where they sold cooked meat as well as wine—and what wine too! Awful stuff, for the most part, doctored with salts of lead—and a brothel full of diseased women attached, with pornographic pictures smudged on the wall. Why, five years ago, within a quarter of a mile of my house on the Palatine, there were at least fifteen—no, what am I saying? at least twenty-five jug-and-bottle houses, and now there aren't more than three or four. And they served good wine too. There was 'The Flask,' and 'The Bacchus,' and 'The Veteran,' and 'The Two Brothers,' and 'The Glory of Agrippa,' and 'The Swan' (The Swan's still in business, but the others are gone—the best wine came from 'The Two Brothers'), and the 'Baucis and Philemon'—that's disappeared too, a very pleasant place. And so has 'The Yew Tree'—I liked the old 'Yew Tree.' . . ."

How they laughed at me! They were all men who kept

their own cellars and had probably never been into a wine-shop to buy drink in their life. I silenced them with an angry look. I said: "You may recall that five years ago, owing to the caprices of my nephew, the late Emperor, I went bankrupt and was forced to live on the charity of my friends—not a man of you among them, by the way—real friends, such as a few grateful freedmen, a girl prostitute and an old slave or two. I visited those taverns to buy wine because my cellar was up for public auction along with my house, of which I could only afford to occupy a few rooms. So I know what I'm talking about. And I hope that if any of you happen to fall a victim to the caprices of an Emperor and find yourself in poverty you will remember this debate, and regret that you have not voted for the maintenance of a proper supply of butcher's meat in the City and for the preservation of such honest wine-shops as the old 'Swan', 'The Coronet', and 'The Black Dog,' which are still in business but won't survive long if you don't do something for them. To Hell with cold water and pulse-porridge! And if I see so much as a smile cross your faces, my Lords, before I have finished this speech—or after—I shall take it as a personal affront."

I was really angry, shaking with anger, and I saw the fear of death gradually stealing over them. They passed my motion without a single contrary vote.

My success gave me momentary pleasure, but afterwards I felt deeply ashamed and made things worse by apologizing to them for my ill-temper. They thought that I was showing weakness and timidity by doing so. Now, I wish to make it quite clear that I had not been using my Imperial power, contrary to all my most cherished principles of equality and justice and human self-respect, to bully and browbeat the Senate. I had just felt outraged by Asiaticus and the rest of those rich heartless men who treated their fellow-citizens like dirt. I was not threatening, I was merely expostulating.

275

But these words of mine were used against me afterwards by my enemies, in spite of my apology for them and in spite of the following letter that I composed and circulated in the City:

"Tiberius Claudius Cæsar Augustus Germanicus, Emperor, High Pontiff, Protector of the People, Consul for the third time, to the Senate and People of Rome, greetings.

"I am aware of a certain failing in myself, which distresses me perhaps more than it distresses you, because one grieves more for a trouble of one's own making than for trouble that comes upon one from another source, particularly from some powerful source over which one has little or no control, such as lightning, disease, hail or the severity of a judge: I refer to the sudden bursts of anger to which I have been increasingly subject since I first assumed the burden of government that, against my inclinations, you laid on me. For example, the other day I sent word to the citizens of Ostia that I was coming to view the progress of the excavations at their new port, sailing down the Tiber, and that they might expect me about noon, and that if they had any complaints to make about the behaviour of my army of workmen there or any petitions to offer I should be pleased to attend to them; but when I reached Ostia no boat put out to meet me and no group of city officials was waiting at the quay. I was incensed and sent for the leading men of the city, including the chief magistrate and the harbour-master, and addressed them in the most violent terms, asking why it was that I had become so contemptible and worthless in their eyes that there was not even a sailor there ready to tie my yacht up to the quay when I landed, and I supposed that they would charge me a fee for entering their port at all, and what sort of ingrates were the men of Ostia to growl and snap at the hand that fed them, or at the best, to turn away from it with indifference? However, a simple explanation was offered: my message had never reached them. They apologized, and I apologized, and we became the best of friends again, no ill-will remaining on either side. But I suffered more from any anger than they did, because they were not conscious of any wrong-doing when I shouted at them, whereas I was most ashamed, afterwards, to have insulted them.

"So let me confess that I am subject to these fits of anger but beg you to bear with me in them. They never last long and are quite harmless: my physician Xenophon says that they are due to over-work, like my insomnia. Recently I have been unable to sleep after midnight; the distant rumble of country wagons coming into the City with market-stuff keeps me awake until dawn, when I sometimes am lucky enough to snatch on hour's sleep. That's why I am often so sleepy at the law-courts after luncheon.

"Another fault to which I must confess is my tendency to bear malice: I cannot lay the blame for this on over-work or ill-health, but I can and do say that any malice to which I may from time to time give way is never wholly unjustified or due to an irrational dislike of a man's features or bearing or to jealousy of his property or parts. It is always based on some unprovoked personal injury once done to me for which apology has never been offered or other satisfaction made. For example, on my first visit to the law-courts —shortly after my accession—to settle the cases of men charged with treason I noticed the same audacious court-official who had once done his best to curry favour with my nephew, the late Emperor, at my expense, on the occasion that I was unjustly charged with forgery. He had then exclaimed, pointing at me: 'One can read guilt written all over his face. Why prolong proceedings? Condemn him at once, Cæsar.' Was it not natural for me to remember this? I cried to the fellow as he cringed towards me at my entry: 'I can read guilt in your face. Leave this court and never appear in any court of law in Rome again!'

"You all know the old patrician saying: *Aquila non captat muscas.* The eagle is the noble soul and he does not hawk for flies, which means that he does not pursue petty ends, or go out of his way to revenge himself on mean little men who have provoked him. But let me quote an enlargement made many years ago by my noble brother, Germanicus Cæsar:

'Captat non muscas aquila; at quæque advolat ultro
    Faucibus augustis, musca proterva perit.'

Bear all this in mind and we shall have no misunderstandings but remain bound in the mutual affection which we have so often protested to each other.

"Farewell."

(The couplet, translated, means: "The eagle does not hawk for flies, but if any impudent fly comes buzzing of its own free will into his august throat, that's the end of the creature.")

My execution of Appius Silanus had been the pretext for the revolt; so to show that I entertained no enmity against his family I arranged for his eldest son, Marcus Silanus, Augustus's great-great-grandson and born in the year that he died, to be Consul in four years' time: and I also promised Appius's youngest son, Lucius Silanus, who had come with his father from Spain to live with us at the Palace, to betroth my daughter Octavia to him as soon as she was able to understand the betrothal ceremony.

# Chapter Sixteen

Bᴿɪᴛᴀɪɴ lies in a northerly position, but the climate, though very damp, is not nearly so cold as one would expect; if properly drained the country could be made extremely fruitful. The aboriginal inhabitants, a small, dark-haired people, were dispossessed, about the time that Rome was founded, by an invasion of Celts from the south-east. Some still maintain themselves independently in small settlements in inaccessible mountains or marshes; the rest became serfs and mixed their blood with that of their conquerors. I use the word "Celts" in the most general sense to cover the many nations which have appeared in Europe in the course of the last few centuries, travelling westward from some remote region lying to the north of the Indian mountains. They have, some authorities hold, been driven from this region, not by any love of wandering or by the pressure of stronger tribes on their borders, but by a slow natural catastrophe on an enormous scale, the gradual drying-up of immense tracts of fertile land which hitherto maintained them. Among these Celts, if the word is to have any true significance, I would reckon not only most of the inhabitants of France—but the Aquitanians are Iberian aborigines—and the many nations of Germany and the Balkans, but even the Achæan Greeks, who had established themselves for some time in the Upper Danube valley before pushing southward into Greece. Yes, the Greeks are comparatively new-comers to Greece. They displaced the native Pelasgians who derived their culture from Crete, and brought new Gods with them, the chief of these being

Apollo. This happened not long before the Trojan War; the Dorian Greeks came still later—eighty years after the Trojan War. Other Celts of the same race invaded France and Italy at about the same time, and the Latin language is derived from their speech. It was then, too, that the first Celtic invasion of Britain took place. These Celts, whose language is akin to primitive Latin, were called Goidels—a tall, sandy-haired, big-limbed, boastful, excitable but noble race, gifted in all the arts, including fine weaving and metal-work, music and poetry; they still survive, in Northern Britain, in the same state of civilization as has been immortalized for the Greeks, now so greatly changed, in the verses of Homer.

Four or five hundred years later another Celtic nation appeared in Northern Europe, namely, those tribes that we call Galates. They invaded Macedonia, after the death of Alexander, and crossed into Asia Minor, occupying the region which is now called Galatia, after them. They also entered Northern Italy, where they broke the power of the Etruscans, penetrating as far as Rome, where they defeated us at the Allia and burned our City. This same nation occupied most of France, though their predecessors remained in the centre, the north-west and the south-east. These Galates are also a gifted people; though inferior to the earlier Celts in arts, they are more united in spirit and finer fighting men. They are of middle stature with brown or black hair, round chins and straight noses. About the time of the Allia disaster some tribes of this nation invaded Britain by way of Kent, the south-eastern district of the island, and compelled the Goidels to spread out fan-wise before them, so that these are now only found, except as serfs, in the North of Britain and in the neighbouring island of Ireland. The Galates who went to Britain became known as the Brythons, or painted men, because they used caste-masks of blue dye on their faces and bodies, and have given their names to the whole island. However, two hundred years later still, came a third race of Celts moving up the Rhine from Central Europe. These were the people whom we call the Belgians, the same that are now settled along the Channel Coast and are known as the best fighting men in France. They are a mixed race, akin to the Galates but with German blood in them; they have light hair, big chins and aquiline noses. They invaded Britain by way of Kent and established themselves in the whole southern part of the island with the exception of the south-west corner, which was still occupied by the Brythons and their Goidel serfs. These Belgians kept in close touch with their kinsmen across the Channel (one of their kings ruled on both sides of the water), trading with them constantly and even sending armed help to them in their wars with Julius Cæsar; as in the south-west Brythons traded with and sent help to their kinsmen, the Galates of the Loire.

So much for the races of Britain; now for the story of their contact with the power of Rome. The first invasion of Britain was made a hundred and eight years ago by Julius Cæsar. He had found numerous Britons fighting in the ranks of his enemies, the Belgians and the Galates of the Loire, and he thought that the island should now be taught to respect the power of Rome. He could not hope to keep France pacified so long as Britain remained a safe place of refuge for the more stubborn of his enemies and a starting-point for new attempts to recover the independence of their country. Next he wished, for political reasons, to gain some remarkable military glory to balance his colleague Pompey's victories. His victories in Spain and France had been an answer to Pompey's in Syria and Palestine, and a campaign in distant Britain could be set off against Pompey's feats among the remote nations of the Caucasus. Lastly, he needed money. The Loire traders and the Channel traders seemed to do very well out of Britain, and Julius wanted to have the market for himself, first exacting a heavy tribute from the islanders. He knew that there was gold in Britain, for gold pieces from there were circulating freely in France. (It was, by the way, an interesting coinage: the original model was the gold stater of Philip of Macedon, which had come to Britain by way of the Danube and Rhine, but the design had become so debased in course of time that of the two horses of the chariot only one remained, the charioteer and chariot having become a mere pattern; of Apollo's laurelled head only the laurel was left.) Britain is not, as a matter of fact, particularly rich in gold, and though the tin mines of the south-west were once of importance—the Carthaginians traded there—and are still worked, the chief supply of tin for Rome now comes from the tin islands off the coast of Galicia. There is some silver in Britain, and copper and lead, and there are important iron-workings on the south-east coast, and fresh-water pearls of a good quality, though small and not to be compared with the Oriental variety. There is no amber, except for tide-washed pieces—it comes from the Baltic—but very fine jet, and other valuable exports, including slaves, skins, wool, flax, domestic animals, enamelled bronze, blue dye, wickerwork baskets and corn. Julius was most interested in gold and slaves; although he knew that the slaves that he would get from the island would not be of a particularly high quality—the women are by no means seductive and have fierce tempers, and the men, except those of the upper classes who make excellent coachmen, only fitted for the roughest sort of farmlabour. He could not expect to find among them cooks, goldsmiths, musicians, barbers, secretaries or accomplished courtesans. The average price they would fetch at Rome would not exceed forty gold pieces.

He twice invaded Britain by way of the south-east, as the Goidels, Brythons and Belgians had all done in their turn. On the first occasion the Britons hotly disputed his landing and gave a good account of themselves: so that apart from some hostages which he took from the men of Kent he accomplished little, only advancing ten miles inland. On the second occasion, however, profiting from his experiences, he landed with a strong force—twenty thousand men; before, only ten thousand. He marched from Sandwich, a point close to the French coast, along the southern bank of the Thames estuary, forcing first the passage of the River Stour and then that of the Thames near London. He was making for the territory of the Catuvellaunians, a Belgic tribe whose king had become the overlord of several petty kings in the south and east of the island: his capital city was Wheathampstead, some twenty-five miles north-east of London. By "city" I do not of course mean a city in the Græco-Roman sense, but a big settlement of wattle-and-daub huts and a few huts of undressed stone. It was this king, Cassivellaunus, who organized the resistance against Julius; but he found that while his cavalry and chariotry were superior to the French cavalry that Julius had brought with him, his infantry could not compete with the Roman infantry. He decided that his best tactics were to dispense with infantry altogether and with his cavalry and chariots prevent the Roman army from deploying. Julius found that he could not safely send foraging parties out except in compact bodies with cavalry supports; the British chariot-fighters had perfected the technique of surprising and cutting off stragglers and small groups. So long as the Roman army remained in column of march the damage that it could inflict by the burning of cornfields and hamlets was of no great importance; and the Britons always had plenty of time to get their women and children and cattle to a safe place. Once across the Thames, however, Julius had the support of some tribesmen who had recently been defeated by their enemies, the Catuvellaunians. These were the Trinovants who lived northwest of

London, with Colchester as their capital. An exiled prince of the Trinovants, whose father had been killed by Cassivellaunus, had fled to Julius in France just before the expedition started and undertaken, if Julius invaded the territory of the Catuvellaunians, to raise the whole east coast in his support. He fulfilled his undertaking, and Julius now had a secure base in Trinovant country. After revictualling there he resumed his march on Wheathampstead.

Cassivellaunus knew that he had little hope of victory now, unless Julius could be forced by some diversion to retrace his steps. He sent an urgent message to his subject allies, the men of Kent, begging them to rise in force and attack Julius's base-camp. Julius had already once been checked, shortly after landing, by the news that a storm had wrecked some of his transports, which he had neglected to draw up on the beach and had left riding at anchor. He had been forced to return all the way from the Stour and it had taken him ten days to repair the damage; which gave the Britons the opportunity of reoccupying and strengthening the positions that he had already with some difficulty captured. If the men of Kent consented to attack the base-camp, which was manned by only two thousand men and three hundred cavalry, and contrived to capture it and to seize the fleet, then Julius would be trapped and the whole island would rise against the Romans—even the Trinovants would desert their new allies. The men of Kent did make a mass attack on the base-camp but were repulsed with heavy loss. On hearing the news of this defeat all the allies of Cassivellaunus who had not already done so sent peace embassies to Julius. But he was now marching on Wheathampstead, which he stormed by a simultaneous attack on two of its fronts. This fortress was a great earth-work ring protected by woods and deep ditches and stockades and was considered impregnable. It served as a place of refuge for all members of the tribe who were too old or too young to fight. In it were captured immense quantities of cattle and hundreds of prisoners. Cassivellaunus, though his army had not yet been beaten, was forced to sue for peace. Julius gave him easy terms, because not much of the summer remained and he was anxious to get back to France; a rebellion threatened there. The Catuvellaunians were merely asked to hand over certain principal men and women as hostages, to pay an annual tribute in gold to the Roman people and to promise not to molest the Trinovants. So Cassivellaunus paid Julius an instalment of tribute and handed over his hostages, as did the kings of all the other tribes except the Trinovants and their east-coast allies, who had voluntarily offered Julius assistance. Julius went back to France with his prisoners and as many of the cattle as he had not sold cheap to the Trinovants to save himself the trouble of getting them safely across the Channel.

The rebellion broke out in France two years later and Julius was so busy crushing it that he could not spare men for a third expedition to Britain; though Cassivellaunus had stopped paying tribute as soon as the news of the rebellion reached him and had sent help to the insurgents in France. Soon after this the Civil Wars started and though, when these had ended, the question of an invasion of Britain was from time to time raised, there was always a good reason for postponing it, usually trouble on the Rhine frontier. Sufficient troops could never he spared. Augustus eventually decided against extending the bounds of the Empire beyond the Channel. He concentrated instead on civilizing France and the Rhine provinces and those parts of Germany across the Rhine captured by my father. When he lost Germany after Hermann's revolt he was still less prepared to add Britain to his anxieties. He had recorded his opinion in a letter to my grandmother Livia, dated the year of my birth, that not until the French were ripe for the Roman citizenship and could be trusted not to rebel in the absence of part of the Roman army of defence, could an invasion of Britain be politically justified:

"But it is none the less my opinion, my dearest Livia, that Britain must eventually be converted into a frontier province. It is unsafe to allow an island, so near to France and manned by so fierce and so numerous a population, to remain independent. Looking into the future, I can see Britain becoming as civilized as southern France is now; and I think that the islanders, who are racially akin to us, will become far better Romans than we shall ever succeed in making of the Germans, who in spite of their apparent docility and willingness to learn our arts, I find more alien-minded even than the Moors or the Jews. I cannot explain my feeling except by saying they have been much too quick in learning: you know the proverb, 'Quick to learn, quick to forget.' You may think me rather foolish in writing of the British as if they were already Romans, but it is interesting to speculate on the future. I don't mean twenty years hence, or even fifty years hence, but allowing the French fifty years to be ready for the citizenship and allowing twenty years or so for the complete subjugation of Britain, perhaps in a hundred years from now Italy will be knit closely with the whole British archipelago and (do not smile) British noblemen may well take their seats in the Roman Senate. Meanwhile we must continue our policy of commercial penetration. This King Cymbeline, who has now made himself overlord of the greater part of the island, gives a generous welcome to Roman-French traders and even to Greek doctors, especially oculists, for the British seem to suffer pretty severely from ophthalmia, owing to the marshiness of the country; and his Roman moneyers strike him a beautiful silver coinage—the gold coins remain barbarous—and he is in friendly touch with our governors in France. British trade has increased greatly in the past few years. I am told that at Cymbeline's court at Colchester as much Latin as British is spoken."

In this context I might quote the historian Strabo who, writing early in the reign of Tiberius, remarks:

"In our own days certain of the princes of Britain have secured the friendship of Cæsar Augustus by their embassies and attentive courtesies: they have even sent votive-offerings to the temple of Capitoline Jove and made the whole island almost, as it were, native soil to the Romans. They pay very moderate customs-dues both on their exports to France and on their imports, the latter being for the most part ivory bracelets, necklaces, amber, glassware and the like." Strabo then lists the exports as gold, silver, iron, skins, slaves, hunting-dogs, corn and cattle. His conclusions—inspired, I think, by Livia herself—are these: "So the Romans have no need to garrison the island. It would take at least one infantry regiment, supported by cavalry, to force them to pay tribute; but the cost of keeping the garrison there would be at least as much as the tribute received, and the imposition of the tribute would necessitate the lowering of the customs-dues, and besides this there would be considerable military risks attendant on the policy of forcible subjection."

This estimate "at least one infantry regiment" was far too modest. "At least four regiments" would have been nearer to the mark. Augustus never raised the question of the interrupted repayment of tribute as a Catuvellaunian breach of faith nor protested against Cymbeline's subjugation of the Trinovants. This Cymbeline was a grandson of Cassivellaunus and reigned for forty years; the later years being clouded, as seems to be the fate of elderly rulers, by family troubles. His eldest son tried to seize the throne and was expelled from the kingdom, but fled to Caligula in France and asked for his help in an invasion of Britain, undertaking if he were put on his father's throne to acknow-

287

ledge the suzerainty of Rome. Caligula sent off dispatches at once to the Senate, informing them of the surrender of the island and then marched to Boulogne at the head of a huge army as if to begin the invasion without a moment's delay. However, he was a nervous man and was afraid of being drowned in the Channel, where the tides run high, or of being killed in battle, or captured and burned in a wicker votive-image; so he announced that since Britain had yielded in the person of this prince the expedition was superfluous. Instead, he launched his attack on Neptune, ordering his troops to shoot arrows and hurl javelins and sling stones into the water, as I have described, and to gather seashells for spoils. He brought the prince back to Rome in chains and, after celebrating his triple triumph over Neptune, Britain and Germany, put him to death as a punishment for the unpaid tribute and for his father's cowardly attack on the Trinovants and for the help sent by certain British tribes to the Autun rebels in the eighth year of Tiberius's reign.

Cymbeline's death occurred in the same month as that of Caligula and was followed by civil war. The eldest surviving prince, by name Bericus, was proclaimed king, but he was a man for whom neither his own tribesmen nor his subject allies had any respect. His two younger brothers Caractacus and Togodumnus rebelled against him a year later and forced him to fly across the Channel. He came to me at Rome and asked for my help in the same way as his brother had asked help from Caligula. I made no promises, but allowed him to live in Rome with his family and a few noblemen who had come with him.

Togodumnus, who now reigned jointly with Caractacus, had been told by merchants that I was no soldier but a cowardly old fool who wrote books. He sent me an insolent letter demanding the instant return of Bericus and the other exiles, together with the sacred regalia—thirteen magical objects—a crown, a cup, a sword and so on—which Bericus had brought to Rome with him. If Togodumnus had written in a courteous tone I should certainly have replied courteously and at least returned the regalia, which it appears were necessary for the proper crowning of a Catuvellaunian king. As it was, I answered shortly that I was not accustomed to being addressed in this disrespectful manner, and did not, in consequence, feel obliged to do him any service. He replied, still more insolently, that I was not telling the truth; for until quite recently everyone, including my own family, had treated me with disrespect; and that since I had refused to obey him he had detained all the Roman-owned trading ships in his ports and would hold these as hostages until I gave him what he had demanded. There was nothing for it but to make war. The French would have lost all respect for me if I had hesitated. I took my decision quite independently of Herod, though his teasing letter happened to coincide with it.

I had other reasons for making war, too. One was that the time had come which Augustus had foreseen: I was about to extend the Roman citizenship to large numbers of our more civilized French allies, but the one element in Northern France that was checking the orderly progress of civilization there was the Druidical cult, a magical religion which was still kept alive, in spite of all that we could do to discourage or suppress it, by Druidical training-colleges in Britain from where it had originally been imported. Young Frenchmen went to Britain for their magical education as naturally as young Spaniards go to Rome to study law, or young Romans to Athens to study philosophy, or young Greeks to Alexandria to study surgery. Druidism could not readily be reconciled with Greek or Roman religious worship, involving as it did human sacrifices and necromancy, and the Druids therefore, though they were not warriors themselves but only priests, were

289

always fomenting rebellion against us. Another reason for war was that the golden reign of Cymbeline was over. Togodumnus and Caractacus were, I learned, about to be involved in a struggle with their north-eastern neighbours, the Icenians, and with two subject tribes on the south coast; so that regular trade with Britain would be interrupted for some time if I did not intervene. I could now count on the help of the Icenians and the other tribes, not to mention the cross-Channel merchants, so the opportunity seemed too good to miss.

It would be as well to give here in brief an account of the main features of Druidism, a religion which seems to be a fusion of Celtic and aboriginal beliefs. I cannot guarantee that the details are true, for reports are conflicting. No Druidical lore is allowed to be consigned to writing and a terrible fate is threatened to those who reveal even the less important mysteries. My account is based on the statements of prominent apostates from the religion, but these include no Druidical priests. No consecrated Druid has ever been persuaded to reveal the inner mysteries even under torture. The word "Druid" means "Oak-man," because that is their sacred tree. Their sacred year begins with the budding of the oak and ends with the falling of its leaves. There is a god called Tanarus whose symbol is the oak. It is he who with a flash of lightning generates the mistletoe on the oak-tree branch, which is the sovereign remedy against witchcraft and all diseases. There is also a sun-god called Mabon whose symbol is a white bull. And then there is Lug, a god of medicine, poetry and the arts, whose symbol is the snake. These are all, however, the same person, a God of Life-in-Death, worshipped in different aspects, like Osiris in Egypt. As Osiris is yearly drowned by a god of waste waters, so this triple deity is yearly killed by the God of Darkness and Water, his uncle Nodons, and restored to life by the power of his sister Sulis, the Goddess of Healing who corresponds to Isis. Nodons manifests himself by a monstrous wave of water, twelve feet high, that at regular intervals comes running up the mouth of the Severn, chief of the western rivers, causing great destruction to crops and huts as far as thirty miles inland. The Druidical religion is not practised by the tribes as such, for they are fighting units commanded by kings and noblemen, but by thirteen secret societies, named after various sacred animals, the members of any one of which belong to a variety of tribes; because it is the month in which one is born—they have a thirteen-month year—which decides the society to which one is to belong. There are the Beavers, and the Mice, and the Wolves, and the Rabbits, and the Wild Cats, and the Owls and so on, and each society has a particular lore of its own and is presided over by a Druid. The Arch-Druid rules over the whole cult. The Druids take no part in fighting, and members of the same society who meet in tribal battles on opposite sides are pledged to run to each other's rescue.

The mysteries of the Druidical religion are concerned with a belief in the immortality of the human soul, in support of which many natural analogies are offered. One of these is the daily death and daily rebirth of the sun, another is the yearly death and yearly rebirth of the leaves of the oak, another is the yearly cutting of the corn and the yearly springing up of the seed. They say that man when he dies goes westward, like the setting sun, to live in certain sacred islands in the Atlantic ocean, until the time shall come for him to be born again. All over the island there are sacred altars known as "dolmens," one flat stone laid on two or more uprights. These are used in the initiation ceremonies of the societies. The initiation is at once a death and a rebirth. The candidate lies on the lintel stone and a mock-sacrifice is then performed. By some magical means the Druid who performs it seems to cut off the man's head, which is exhibited bleeding to the crowd. The head is then joined to the trunk again and the supposed corpse is placed underneath the dolmen, as in a grave, with mistletoe between its lips; from which, after many prayers and charms, the new man comes forth as if he were a child emerging from the womb and is instructed in his new life by godparents. Besides these dolmens there are upright stone altars, devoted to phallic rites; for the Celtic Osiris resembles the Egyptian one in this respect too.

Rank in the societies is decided by the number of sacrifices a man makes to the Gods, standing on the lintel stone of his ancestral dolmen, by the number of enemies he kills in battle and by the honours he wins in the annual religious games as charioteer, juggler, wrestler, poet or harper. Rank is shown by the masks and head-dresses which are worn during the ceremonies and by the blue designs executed in woad (a marsh plant) with which their whole bodies are painted. The Druid priesthood is recruited from young men who have attained high rank in their secret societies and to whom certain marks of divine favour have been given. But twenty years of hard study at the Druidical college are first called for and it is by no means every candidate who succeeds in passing through the necessary thirty-two degrees. The first twelve years are spent in being initiated in turn into all the other secret societies, in learning by heart enormous sagas of mythological poetry and in the study of law, music and astronomy. The next three years are spent in the study of medicine. The next three are spent in the study of omens and magic. The tests put upon candidates for the priesthood are immensely severe. For example, there is a test of poetical composition. The candidate must lie naked all night in a coffin-like box, only his nostrils protruding above the icy water with which it is filled, and with heavy stones laid on his chest. In this position he must compose a poem of considerable length in the most difficult of the many difficult bardic metres, on a subject which is given him as he is placed in the box. On his emergence next morning he must be able to chant this poem to a melody which he has been simultaneously composing, and accompany himself on the harp. Another test is to stand before the whole body of Druids and be asked verse-questions in riddling form which must be answered in further riddles, also in verse. These riddles all refer to obscure incidents in the sacred poems with which the candidate is supposed to be familiar. Besides all this he must be able to raise magic mists and winds and perform all sorts of conjuring tricks.

I will tell you here of my only experience of Druidical magic. I once asked a Druid to show me his skill. He called for three dried peas and put them in a row across the palm of my outstretched hand. He said: "Without moving your arm, can you blow away the middle pea and not blow away the outer ones?" I tried, but of course I could not: my breath blew all three peas away. He picked them up and laid them in a row across his own palm. Then he held down the outer ones with the forefinger and little finger of the same hand and blew the centre one away easily. I was angry at being fooled. "Anyone could do that," I said. "That's not magic."

He handed me the peas again. "Try it," he ordered.

I began to do what he had done, but to my chagrin I found that not only could I not command enough breath to blow away the pea—my lungs seemed suddenly tightened—but that when I wanted to straighten out my bent fingers again I could not. They were tightly cramped against my palm and the nails were gradually driving into my flesh so that it was with difficulty that I refrained from crying out. The sweat was pouring down my face.

He asked, "Is it so easy to do?"

I answered ruefully: "Not when a Druid is present." He

touched my wrist and my fingers recovered from their cramp.

The candidate's last test but one is to spend the longest night of the year seated on a rocking-stone called the "Perilous Seat" which is balanced over a deep chasm in a mountain somewhere in the west of the island. Evil spirits come and talk to him all night and try by various means to make him lose his balance. He must not answer a word, but address prayers and hymns of praise to the Gods. If he escapes from this ordeal he is permitted to take the final test, which is to drink a poisoned cup and go into a death trance, and visit the Island of the Dead, and bring back from there such proofs of his visit as will convince the examining Druids that he has been accepted by the God of Life-in-Death as his priest.

There are three ranks of Druid priests. There are those who have passed all the tests, the true Druids; then come the Bards, those who have passed in the bardic tests but have not yet satisfied the examiners in soothsaying, medicine and magic; then come those who have satisfied the examiners in these latter tests, but have not yet taken their bardic degree—they are known as the Ovates or Listeners. It needs a bold heart to enter for the final tests, which result in the death of three candidates out of every five, I am informed, so most men are content enough with the degree of Bard or Ovate.

The Druids, then, are the law-givers and judges and the controllers of public and private religion, and the greatest punishment that they can inflict is to interdict men from the holy rites. Since this excommunication is equivalent to sentencing men to perpetual extinction—for only by taking part in these rites can they hope to be reborn when they come to die—the Druids are all-powerful, and it is only a fool who will dare to oppose them. Every five years there is a great religious cleansing—like our five-yearly census—

and in expiation of national sins human victims are burned alive in great wicker cages built to resemble men. The victims are bandits, criminals, men who have revealed religious secrets or have been guilty of any similar crime, and men whom the Druids accuse of having unlawfully practised magic to suit their private ends and of having blighted crops or caused a pestilence by doing so. The Druids at that time outlawed any man who had embraced the Roman religion or allied himself by marriage with a family that had done so. That, I suppose, they were entitled to do; but when it came to burning such people alive, then they had to be taught a lesson.

They have two peculiarly holy places. The first is the island of Anglesey on the west coast, where their winter quarters are, among great groves of sacred oaks, and the sacred oak-log fire is kept burning. This fire, kindled originally by lightning, is distributed for the cremation of corpses, to ensure their reincarnation. The other sacred place is a great stone temple in the middle of Britain, consisting of concentric rings of enormous trilithic and monolithic altars. It is dedicated to the God of Life-in-Death, and from the New Year, which they reckon from the spring equinox, until midsummer, they hold their annual religious Games there. A red-haired young man is chosen to represent the God and is dressed in marvellous robes. While the Games last he is free to do exactly as he pleases. Everything is at his disposal, and if he takes a fancy to any jewel or weapon, the owner counts himself honoured and gives it up gladly. All the most beautiful girls are his playmates, and the competing athletes and musicians do everything they can to win his favour. Shortly before midsummer, however, he goes with the Arch-Druid, who is the representative of the God of Death, to an oak on which mistletoe grows. The Arch-Druid climbs the oak and cuts the mistletoe with a golden sickle, taking care that it does not touch the ground.

This mistletoe is the soul of the oak, which then mysteriously withers away. A white bull is sacrificed. The young man is wrapped in leafy oak branches and taken to the Temple, which is so oriented that at dawn on Midsummer Day the sun strikes down an avenue of stones and lights up the principal altar where the young man is laid, fast bound, and where the Arch-Druid sacrifices him with the sharpened stem of the mistletoe. I cannot discover what eventually happens to the body, which for the present remains laid out on the stone of sacrifice, showing no sign of decay. But the priestess of Sulis, from a western town called the "Waters of Sulis," where there are medicinal springs, comes to claim it at the autumn festival of farewell and the Goddess is then supposed to restore it to life. The God is said to go by boat to the western island where Nodons lives and to conquer him after a fierce fight. The winter storms are the noise of that fight. He reappears next year in the person of the new victim. The withered oak tree provides new logs for the sacred fire. At the autumn festival of farewell each society sacrifices its tribal animal, burning a wicker cage full of them, and all ritual masks and head-dresses are burned too. It is at this stone temple that the complicated initiation ceremony for new Druids takes place. It is said to involve the sacrifice of newly-born children. The temple stands in the centre of a great necropolis, for all Druids and men of high religious rank are buried here with ceremonies that ensure reincarnation.

There are British battle-gods and goddesses too, but they have little connexion with the Druid religion and sufficiently resemble our own Mars and Bellona to make no description necessary.

In France the centre of Druidism was at Dreux, a town lying to the west of Paris, some eighty miles from the Channel coast. Human sacrifices continued to be performed there just as if Roman civilization did not exist. Imagine, the Druids used to cut open the bodies of victims whom they had sacrificed to the God Tanarus and examine their entrails for auspices with as little compunction as you or I would feel in the case of a ram or sacred chicken! Augustus had not attempted to put down Druidism; he had merely forbidden Roman citizens to belong to secret societies or to attend Druidical sacrifices. Tiberius had ventured to publish an edict dissolving the Druidical order in France; but this edict was not intended to be literally obeyed, only to withhold Roman official sanction from any decisions arrived at or penalties imposed by a Druidical council.

The Druids continued to cause us trouble in France, though many tribes now abandoned the cult altogether, and adopted our Roman religion. I was determined, as soon as I had conquered Britain, to strike a bargain with the Arch-Druid: in return for permission to conduct his religion in Britain in the customary way (though abstaining from any unfriendly preaching against Rome) he must refuse to admit French candidates for initiation into the Druidical order and must allow no British Druids to cross the Channel. Without priests the religion would soon die out in France, where I would make illegal any Druidical ceremony or festival involving human sacrifice, and charge with murder all who were found to have taken part in one. Eventually, of course, Druidism would have to be stamped out in Britain too; but that need not be thought about yet.

# Chapter Seventeen

MY STUDY of Julius Cæsar's commentaries on his two British campaigns made it clear to me that unless conditions had changed considerably since his day it was possible to beat the Britons in any engagement by only a slight modification of our fighting tactics. Considerable forces, however, would have to be employed. It is a great mistake to start a campaign with only a couple of regiments, get. them badly knocked about in attempting the work of four, and then send home for reinforcements, thereby giving the enemy a breathing space. It is best to start with as imposing a force as can be commanded and to strike as hard as possible.

The British infantry are armed with broadswords and small leather bucklers. Man for man, they are the equals and even the superiors of the Romans, but their fighting value decreases with their numbers, as ours increases. In the clash of a battle a company of British warriors has no chance against an equal force of disciplined Romans. The Roman javelin, short stabbing sword, and long shield with its flanges for interlocking with neighbour shields, make an ideal equipment at close-quarters. British arms are designed for single combat, but need plenty of space for manœuvre. If the press of battle is too close to allow one to swing the broadsword handily and if the locking of enemy shields prevents one from dealing lateral strokes with it, it is of little use; and the small buckler is insufficient protection against javelin-thrusts.

British noblemen fight from chariots like the Greek

heroes at Troy, and like the early Latin chieftains. The chariot has now, of course, disappeared from civilized warfare and only remains as an emblem of high military rank or of victory. This is because cavalry has taken the place of chariotry, the breed of horses having greatly improved. In Britain there are few horses suitable for mounting cavalry. British chariots are drawn by small strong ponies, highly trained. They can be pulled up sharp even when travelling downhill at a good speed and turned right-about in a flash. Each chariot is a fighting unit in itself. The driver and commander is the nobleman, who has two fighters with him in the chariot, and two or more runners, armed with knives, who keep up with the ponies. The fighters often run along the pole and stand balanced on the crosspiece. The runners try to hamstring the ponies of opposing chariots. A column of chariots driven at full speed will usually break an infantry line by dashing straight at it. But if the line seems disposed to stand its ground the chariot column will wheel right past it, the fighting men raining down spears as they go by, and then turn in behind and launch another volley from the rear. When this manœuvre has been repeated several times the charioteers withdraw to a safe place, and the fighting men, dismounting and now joined by infantry supports, lead these to a final attack. Should this attack fail, the chariots are once more manned and are ready to fight a rearguard action. The British chariot combines indeed, as Julius remarked, the celerity of cavalry with the stability of infantry. Naturally, enveloping tactics are much favoured by chariot squadrons. Naturally too, the British suffer from the common fault of undisciplined fighting men—they will always go for plunder before destroying the main body of the enemy. I had to evolve some new tactical plan for dealing with the British chariotry: Julius's French cavalry had been unable to hold them in check—perhaps he should have borrowed an idea from the enemy and used them in conjunction with light-armed infantry. But I could count on winning every infantry engagement.

I decided that the largest force that the Empire could spare for the expedition would be four regular infantry regiments and four regiments of auxiliaries, together with a thousand cavalry. After consultation with my army commanders I withdrew three regiments from the Rhine, namely, the Second, Twentieth and Fourteenth, and one from the Danube, the Ninth. I entrusted the command of the expedition to Galba, with Geta as his Master of Horse, and planned it for the middle of April. But there was considerable delay in getting the transports built, and when these were ready Galba fell ill and I decided to wait for his recovery; by the middle of June he was still very feeble and I had regretfully to decide against waiting any longer. I gave his command to a veteran who had the reputation of being the cleverest tactician and one of the bravest men in the army, Aulus Plautius, a distant connexion of my first wife, Urgulanilla. He was a man in the late fifties and had been Consul fourteen years previously: old soldiers remembered him as a popular commander of the Fourteenth under my brother. He went to Mainz to take command of the regiments detailed for the expedition. The delay caused by Galba's illness was the more unwelcome because news of the coming invasion, which had been kept a close secret until April, had now been carried over the Channel, and Caractacus and Togodumnus were busily preparing defensive positions. The Ninth Regiment had reached Lyons from the Danube some time before and two regiments of French auxiliaries and one of Swiss had long been under arms there too. I sent Aulus the order to march the Rhine regiments up to Boulogne, picking up a regiment of Batavian auxiliaries on his way—the Batavians are a German tribe living on an island at the mouth of the Rhine—and cross the Channel in the transports which he would find waiting there. The Lyons forces would arrive at Boulogne simultaneously. An unexpected difficulty arose. The Rhine regiments could not be persuaded to start. They said quite openly that they were very well off where they were and regarded the expedition to Britain as a dangerous and useless undertaking. They said that the Rhine defences would be seriously weakened by their removal—though I had brought the garrison there up to strength by brigading large forces of French auxiliaries with the remaining regiments, and by forming an entirely new regiment, the Twenty-second—and that the invasion of Britain was against the wishes of the God Augustus, who had permanently fixed the strategic boundaries of the Empire at the Rhine and Channel.

I was at Lyons myself by this time—the middle of July —and would have gone to the Rhine in person to persuade the men to do their duty, but signs of unrest were showing themselves in the Ninth regiment too, and among the French, so I sent Narcissus, who was with me, there as my representative. It was really a foolish thing to do, but my fool's luck gave it a happy ending. I had not quite realized how unpopular Narcissus was. It was commonly believed that I took his advice on every point and that he led me by the nose. Narcissus on his arrival at the Mainz camp greeted Aulus in rather an offhand way and asked him to parade the men before the Tribunal platform. When this was done he mounted it, puffed out his chest and began the following speech: "In the name of our Emperor, Tiberius Claudius Cæsar Augustus Germanicus. Men, you have been ordered to march to Boulogne, there to embark for an invasion of Britain. You have grumbled and made difficulties. This is very wrong. It is a breach of your oath to the Emperor. If the Emperor orders an expedition you are expected to obey and not to argue. I have come here to recall you to your senses. . . ."

Narcissus was not speaking like a messenger but as though he were Emperor himself. Naturally this had an irritating effect on the men. There were shouts of "Get down from that Tribunal, you Greek valet," and "We don't want to hear what *you* have to say."

But Narcissus had a very good opinion of himself and embarked upon floods of reproachful oratory. "Yes," he said, "I am only a Greek, and only a freedman, but it seems that I know my duty better than you Roman citizens."

Suddenly someone shouted out, *"Io Saturnalia"* and all the irritation vanished in a great roar of laughter. *"Io Saturnalia"* is the cry that goes up on our All Fools' Festival, which is celebrated annually in honour of the God Saturn. During the festival everything is topsy-turvy. Everyone has license to say and do just as he likes. Slaves wear their masters' clothes and order them about as though they were slaves. The noble is abased and the base is ennobled. Everyone now took up the cry *"Io Saturnalia, Io Saturnalia! The Freedman is Emperor to-day."* Ranks were broken and an absurd riot of jokes and horseplay started, in which first the captains, then one or two senior officers and finally Aulus Plautius himself strategically joined. Aulus dressed up as a woman of the camp and bustled round with a kitchen cleaver. Four or five sergeants climbed up on the Tribunal and pretended to be rivals for Narcissus's love. Narcissus was bewildered and burst into tears. Aulus rushed to his rescue, swinging his cleaver. "You vile men," he screamed in falsetto, "leave my poor husband alone! He's a worthy, respectable man!" He drove them off the platform and embraced Narcissus, whispering in his ear as he did so: "Leave this to me, Narcissus. They're like a lot of children. Humour them now and afterwards you can do anything you like with them!" He dragged Narcissus forward by the hand and said: "My poor husband isn't quite himself, you see—he's not accustomed to Camp wine and your rough ways. But he'll be all right after a night in bed with me, won't you, my poppet?" He took Narcissus by the ear. "Now listen to me, husband! This Mainz is a tough place. It's where mice nibble iron, and cocks blow the reveillez with little silver trumpets, and wasps carry javelins slung round their waists."

Narcissus pretended to be frightened—and he was frightened. But they soon forgot all about him. There were other games to play. When the fun was beginning to slacken, Aulus resumed his general's cloak and called for a trumpeter and told him to blow The Attention. In a minute or two order was restored and he held up his hand for silence and made a speech:

"Men, we've had our All Fool's Day fun and we've enjoyed it, and now the trumpet has ended it. So let's get back to work and discipline again. To-morrow I shall take the auspices and if they are favourable you must be prepared to strike camp. We have to go to Boulogne, whether we like it or not. It's our duty. And from Boulogne we have to go to Britain, whether we like it or not. It's our duty. And when we get there we are going to fight a big battle, whether we like it or not. It's our duty. And the Britons are going to get the worst beating of their lives, whether they like it or not. It's their bad luck. Long live the Emperor!" That speech saved the situation and there was no further trouble. Narcissus was able to leave the camp without further loss of dignity.

Ten days later, on August the first, my birthday, the expeditionary force sailed. Aulus had agreed with me that it would be best to send over the troops in three divisions, at intervals of two or three hours, because the landing of one division would concentrate all the British forces at that point and the others could sail up the coast to some undefended spot and land unopposed. But as it happened not even the first division met with any resistance on landing, because the news had reached Britain that the Rhine troops had refused to march, and besides it was thought to be too late in the season now for us to attempt anything that year. The only event worthy of note in the crossing was the sudden wind that sprang up and drove the first division back on to the second; but a lucky portent then occurred, a flash of light travelling from the east across to the west, which was the direction in which they were sailing; so everyone who was not incapacitated by sea-sickness took heart again, and the landing was made in a victorious mood. Aulus's task was to occupy the whole southern part of the island, drawing his strategical frontier from the River Severn on the west to the great bay, the Wash, on the east: thus including the whole of the former dominions of Cymbeline in a new Roman province. He was, however, to permit any tribes who voluntarily offered their submission to Rome the usual privileges of subject allies. Since it was a war of conquest and not a mere punitive expedition the greatest magnanimity must be shown the conquered—consistent only with their not mistaking it for weakness. Property must not be needlessly destroyed, nor women ravished, nor children and old people killed. He was to tell his men: "The Emperor wants prisoners, not corpses. And since you are to be permanently stationed in this country his advice is to do as little damage to it in the process as possible. Wise birds do not foul their own nests; not even nests captured from other birds."

His main objective was Colchester, the Catuvellaunian capital city. When it was captured, the Icenians of the east coast would no doubt come to him there to offer him their alliance and he could build a strong base for the conquest of the centre and south-west of the island. I told him that should his losses amount to more than a couple of thousand killed or disabled before the enemy's main resistance was crushed, or should there appear to be any doubt as to the issue of the campaign before winter set in, he was to send me a message at once and I would come to his help with my reserves. The message would be relayed across France and Italy by bonfire signal, and if the bonfire-men kept their eyes open I ought to receive the news at Rome a few hours after the message left Boulogne. The reserves that I would bring up would include eight battalions of Guards, the entire Guards cavalry, four companies of Nubian spearmen and three companies of Balearic slingers. They would be quartered at Lyons in readiness.

I had intended to remain at Lyons with these reserves, but was forced to return to Rome. Vitellius, who was acting as my understudy, wrote that he found the work incredibly difficult, that he was already two months behindhand in his judicial work, and that he had reason to suspect that my legal secretary, Myron, was not as honest as we had both supposed. There was another most unwelcome letter that reached me from Marsus at the same time and made me feel that I ought not to be away from Rome a day longer than I could help. Marsus's letter ran as follows:

"The governor of Syria, Vibius Marsus, has the honour to greet the Emperor on the occasion of his approaching birthday and report that the province is prosperous, contented, orderly and loyal. At the same time he confesses himself somewhat disquieted by a recent incident at the town of Tiberias, on the Lake of Galilee, and begs the Emperor to approve the measures that he had taken in dealing with it.

"An unofficial report reached headquarters at Antioch that King Herod Agrippa had invited to a secret meeting the following neighbouring potentates—Antiochus, King of Commagene, Sampsigeramus, King of Osroëne, Cotys, King of Lesser Armenia, Polemo, King of Pontus and

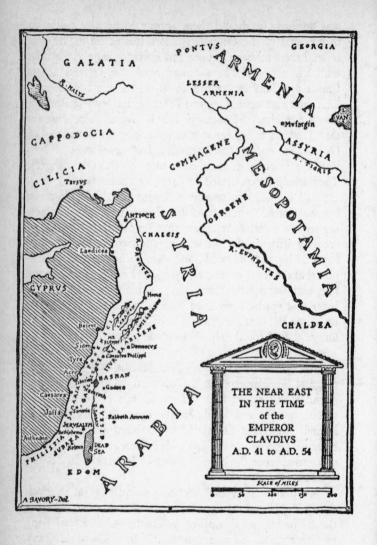

THE NEAR EAST
IN THE TIME
of the
EMPEROR
CLAVDIVS
A.D. 41 to A.D. 54

SCALE of MILES

Cilicia, Sohemus, King of Iturea, Herod Pollio, King of Chalcis. If the news of this meeting leaked out, the explanation was to be that it was a commemoration of King Herod Agrippa's marriage to his Queen Cypros exactly twenty years before. No invitation to any such banquet was sent me as your representative, though the decencies clearly required it: let me repeat that the only information that reached me about this extraordinary assemblage of potentates came from unofficial, not to say underground, sources. Sohemus of Iturea was ill, but sent his chamberlain to represent him. The other kings all obeyed King Herod's summons. Those whose route would naturally have led them by way of Antioch (namely, all those mentioned above except King Herod Pollio and King Sohemus) and who, on a visit to Galilee, should certainly have turned aside to pay their compliments to me as your representative, chose to follow a roundabout route, travelling incognito and for the most part at night. It was only through the vigilance of certain of my agents in the Syrian desert east of Chalcis that I learned that they were already on their way.

"I immediately proceeded to Tiberias myself, at all speed, accompanied by my two daughters and my chief staff-officers, hoping to take the gathering by surprise. King Herod Agrippa, however, must have been informed of my approach. He came driving out from Tiberias in his royal carriage to welcome me. We met at a point seven furlongs from the city. He had not come alone but was escorted by his five royal visitors, the last of whom, the King of Pontus, had only that moment arrived. King Herod did not appear in the least abashed, but climbed out of his coach and came hurrying to greet me in the warmest manner imaginable. He exclaimed how delighted he was that I had managed to come after all, after making no reply to his two letters of invitation, and remarked that this was indeed an extraordinary event—seven Eastern rulers meet-

307

ing at the seventh furlong-stone. He would have the stone replaced by a marble pillar of commemoration with our names and titles engraved on it in letters of gold. I was bound to reply politely and accept his story that he had sent me two invitations, and even swear that as soon as I discovered the enemy who had intercepted the letters—which had not reached me—I would punish him with the utmost rigour of the law. The other kings had also dismounted, and an exchange of civilities began between us. The King of Commagene, whom I used to know at Rome, suggested that perhaps King Herod's invitation had been, somewhat officiously, withheld from me by one of my servants out of consideration for my feelings. I asked him what he meant and he replied that the recent death of my wife might be too fresh in my memory to make an invitation to someone else's wedding anniversary altogether a pleasing one. I replied that my wife had been dead these four years, and he said, sighing: 'As long ago as all that? It seems like yesterday that I saw her. A very lovely woman.' I then asked the King of Pontus point-blank why he had not stopped at Antioch to greet me. He told me without a blush that he had counted on seeing me at the banquet and that he had taken a more easterly route because of the advice of a soothsayer.

"It was impossible to shake the self-possession of any of the six of them, so we all drove into Tiberias together through a cheering mob. The wedding banquet, the most lavish that I have ever attended, was served a few hours later. Meanwhile I sent one of my staff-officers to each of the kings to tell him privately that if he wished to keep the friendship of Rome he would be advised to return to his own country as soon as politeness to our host permitted, and meanwhile not to take part in any secret conference with his royal neighbours. To be brief, the banquet ended at a late hour and the guests made their excuses and left on the following day: no conference took place. I was the last to leave, and the King and I parted with the usual compliments. However, on my return to Antioch I found an unsigned letter awaiting me. It ran: 'You have insulted my guests and you must accept the consequences: I am now your enemy.' I assume it to be a message from King Herod Agrippa.

"My compliments to the most virtuous and beautiful Lady Valeria Messalina, your wife."

The more I studied this report, the less I liked it. It looked as though Herod, taking advantage of my preoccupation with Britain, and the presence there of so large an army—which might easily need further reinforcements—was planning a general rising in the East, for which his fortification of Jerusalem had been the prelude. I grew extremely anxious, but there was nothing that I could do except pray for a speedy victory in Britain and let Herod know that Marsus was keeping me in touch with Near Eastern affairs. I wrote to him at once, giving exaggeratedly cheerful news of the British expedition—for at the time of writing Aulus had not yet been able to get into touch with any considerable force of the enemy, who were adopting the same tactics that their forefathers had employed against Julius in his march through Kent—and saying, quite untruly, that since the expedition was only intended as a punitive one I expected the regiments back across the Channel in a couple of months.

This was the first lie that I had ever told Herod, and since I merely committed it to paper without the embarrassment of telling it verbally, I managed to make him believe it. I wrote:

".... And are you able to tell me anything definite, Brigand, about this prophesied Eastern Ruler who is destined after his death to become the greatest God that has ever appeared on earth? I am continually coming across references to him. There was one in court the other day. A Jew was accused of creating a disturbance in the City. He was alleged to have shaken his fist at a priest of Mars and exclaimed: 'When the Ruler manifests himself, that will be the end of men like you. Your temples will be razed to the ground and you'll be buried in the ruins, you dog! And the time is not far off now.' Under cross-examination he denied having said anything of the sort, and as the evidence was conflicting I did no more than banish him—if you can call it banishment to send a Jew back to Judæa. Well, Caligula believed himself to be this prophesied Ruler and in certain respects the prophecy, as it was reported to me, did indeed seem to point to him. My grandmother Livia had also been misled, by something that the astrologer Thrasyllus said about the year of her death corresponding with that of this prophesied person, into believing that it was she who was meant. She did not realize that it was a God and not a Goddess who was prophesied, nor that his first manifestation should be at Jerusalem—Caligula was there as a child—though later he should reign at Rome. Is there anything written about him in the Jewish sacred writings? If so, precisely what? I understand that your learned relative Philo is an expert in such matters. I was talking the matter over with Messalina the other day and she asked me whether anyone had inherited this peculiar obsession from my now deified grandmother Livia Augusta and from my crazy nephew Caligula. I told her, 'I haven't, I swear, in spite of the divinity that Herod Agrippa is always trying to curse me with.' But what about yourself, my old Brigand? Perhaps you are really the person meant? No, on second thought you certainly are not, in spite of your connexion with Jerusalem. The prophesied Ruler is specified as a man of extreme holiness. Besides, Thrasyllus was quite positive as to the year of his death, the fifteenth year of Tiberius's reign, which was the year Livia was to die—and did actually die. Thrasyllus never to my knowledge made a mistake in dates. So you have lost your chance. But on the other hand, if Thrasyllus was right, why have we not yet heard about this dead King? Caligula knew a part of the prophecy, which was that this King was to die forsaken by his friends and that afterwards they would drink his blood. Curiously enough, that was fulfilled in his case: Bubo, one of the assassins, you remember, had sworn to kill him and drink his blood in revenge, and did dabble his fingers in the wound he had made and then lick them dry, the madman. But Caligula died nine years too late to agree with the prophecy. I should be very grateful if you would tell me what you know about all this. Perhaps there are two or three prophecies that have got mixed up together? Or perhaps Caligula was misinformed as to the particulars? He was told of the prophecy by the poisoner Martina, the one who was concerned in my poor brother Germanicus's murder at Antioch. But I hear that it has long been current in Egypt, as a pronouncement of the oracle of Jupiter Ammon."

Why I wrote in this way was that I now knew that Herod did really fancy himself to be this prophesied Ruler. I had been told all about it by Herodias and Antipas whom I had visited in their place of banishment during my stay in France. I could not allow them to return to Judæa though I knew now that they had not been guilty of plotting against Caligula, but I allowed them to leave Lyons and gave them a fair-sized estate at Cadiz in Spain, where the climate was more like the one to which they were accustomed. They showed me an indiscreet letter from Herodias's daughter Salome, now married to her first-cousin, Herod Pollio's son.

"Herod Agrippa is growing more and more religious

every day. He tells his old friends that he is only playing at being a strict Jew for political reasons, and that he still secretly worships the Roman Gods. But I know now that this is only pretence. He is extraordinarily conscientious in his observances. The Alabarch's son, Tiberius Alexander, who has abandoned the Jewish faith, much to the shame and grief of his excellent family, tells me that while he was staying at Jerusalem the other day he took Herod aside and whispered: 'I hear you have an Arabian cook who really understands how to stuff and roast a midnight suck-ing-pig. Would you be good enough to invite me in some night? It is impossible to get really eatable food in Jerusa-lem.' Herod went scarlet and stammered that his cook was ill! The truth is that he dismissed this cook long ago. Tiber-ius Alexander has another queer story about Herod. You have heard of that farcical occasion when he visited Alex-andria with a bodyguard of two soldiers whom he had kidnapped to prevent them from serving a warrant on him, and borrowed money from the Alabarch? It appears that the Alabarch afterwards went to Philo, that learned brother of his who tries to reconcile Greek philosophy with Jewish scripture, and said, 'I have probably been a fool, brother Philo, but I have lent Herod Agrippa a large sum of money on rather doubtful security. In return he has prom-ised to protect our interests at Rome, and has sworn be-fore Almighty God to cherish and protect His people, so far as in him lies, and to obey His Law.' Philo asked: 'From where did this Herod Agrippa suddenly appear? I thought that he was at Antioch.' The Alabarch said: 'From Edom: wearing a purple cloak—Bozrah purple—and stepping like a king. I cannot help believing that in spite of his former follies and vicissitudes he is destined to play a great part in our national history. He is a man of outstanding talent. And now that he has definitely pledged himself . . .' Philo suddenly grew very serious and began to quote the prophet

Isaiah: 'Who is this that cometh from Edom, with dyed garments from Bozrah? This that is glorious in his apparel, travelling in the greatness of his strength? . . . I have trodden the wine-press alone; and of the people there was none with me. But the day of vengeance is in mine heart, and the year of my Redeemed is come.' Philo has long been convinced that the Messiah is at hand. He has written several volumes on that head. He builds his argument on the text in *Numbers* about the Star out of Jacob, and reconciles it with a number of others in the Prophets. He's quite crazy, poor man. And now that Herod has become so powerful and has kept his promise about observing the Law so faithfully and done the Alexandrian Jews so many services, Philo is really convinced that Herod is the Messiah. What finally decided him was the discovery that Herod's family, though an Edomite one, is descended from a son of Zedekiah, the last king of Judah before the Captivity. (This Zedekiah managed to smuggle his newly-born son out of the city and get him safe to friends in Edom before Nebuchadnezzar captured the place.) Herod seems to have been persuaded by Philo that he really is the Messiah and that he is destined not only to redeem the Jews from the yoke of the foreigner but to combine all the Children of Shem together in a great spiritual Empire under the rule of the Lord of Hosts: this is the only possible explanation for his recent political activities which, I must confess, make me feel extremely nervous for the future. Indeed, there seems to be altogether too much religion in the air. It's a bad sign. It reminds me of what you said when we had that mystical idiot John the Baptist beheaded—'Religious fanaticism is the most dangerous form of insanity'.

"I have said too much, I think, but I can trust you, my dear mother, not to let the story go any farther. Burn this when you have read it."

There was no more news from Marsus and I did not get an answer from Herod himself before I sailed for Britain—for, a fortnight after landing, Aulus was indeed obliged to send for me. But I reckoned that Herod would read between the lines of my letter that I suspected him, though I was careful not to mention Marsus in it, or the wedding celebrations at Tiberias; and that he would be very careful about his next step. I also strengthened the garrison at Alexandria and told Marsus to call up all Greek levies in Syria and give them an intensive drilling: letting the rumour go about that a Parthian invasion was expected. He was to do this as if on his own initiative, and not to tell anyone that the orders came from me.

# Chapter Eighteen

Aulus, as I have already related, landed in Britain without meeting any opposition. He built a strong base camp at Richborough, which he garrisoned with veterans from each regiment, pulled up his transports on the shore, well out of the reach of storms, and began a cautious advance through Kent, taking the route followed by Julius on his second expedition—the route indeed that all invaders of the island have naturally taken. At first he met with less resistance than Julius, because the passage of the Stour did not need to be forced. The King of East Kent, a vassal of Caractacus and Togodumnus, decided not to man the prepared positions there. His overlords had withdrawn their main army to Colchester when they heard that our invasion could not possibly take place that year, and his own forces were insufficient to defend the river successfully. He came to meet Aulus with tokens of peace and after an exchange of presents swore alliance and friendship with Rome. The King of East Sussex, which lies to the west of Kent, came into camp on the same errand a few days later. Between the Stour and the River Medway, the next natural barrier, Aulus encountered little serious resistance. But small parties of chariot-fighters disputed the frequent barriers of felled trees and thorn bushes that had been thrown across the track. Aulus's advance-guard commander was now instructed not to force these barriers, but as soon as they were sighted to envelop them with cavalry detachments and capture the defenders. This slowed down progress, but no lives were wasted. Most of the Kentish men seemed to have retired into the Weald—thick forest-land from which it would be most difficult to dislodge them. But increasingly large forces of chariotry began to appear on the flanks of the advancing column, charging down on foraging parties and forcing them to fall back on the main body. Aulus was aware that the mood in which the Kentish men would finally emerge from the Weald, whether meekly to offer their submission or valiantly to cut off his retreat, depended on his success against the Catuvellaunians. However, his base camp was well defended.

When he came to the tidal reaches of the Medway, which Julius, in his second campaign, had forded without loss, he found the enemy assembled in great force behind positions that had been prepared some months before. Caractacus and Togodumnus were both present with all their tributary princes and an army of some sixty thousand men. Aulus had no more than thirty-five thousand effectives with him. The narrow ford across the river had been made practically impassable by a succession of deep wide channels cut across it parallel with the banks. The Britons were bivouacked in a careless fashion on the other side. The nearest ford upstream was a day's march away and was reported by prisoners to be similarly fortified. Downstream there was no ford: the river after debouching into the Thames estuary not far from this spot spread out across impassable mud-flats. Aulus set his men to work at making the ford passable, filling in the channels with basketfuls of rubble. But it was clear that at this rate two or three days would pass before he could attempt to cross. The enemy bank was defended by two strong stockades, and the Britons, who now harassed the workers with arrows and insults, were building a third one behind that. Twice a day a huge tide welled up into the river-mouth—a commonplace in this part of the world though never seen in the Mediterranean except during storms—and hindered Aulus's work greatly. But he was counting on the tide as his ally. At high tide, just before dawn in the third day, he sent the Batavian auxiliaries swimming across the motionless water. All Germans swim well, and the Batavians better than any. They swam across, three thousand strong, with their weapons tied on their backs, and caught the Britons completely by surprise. However, instead of attacking the startled men at their camp-fires, they rushed to the horse-lines and began disabling the chariot-ponies, putting two or three thousand of these out of action before their owners realized what was happening. They then established themselves at the enemy end of the ford behind the middle barricade, which had been designed to face the other way, and held it against strong British attacks while two battalions of the Ninth Regiment struggled across the river to their assistance, on blown-up wine-skins and improvised rafts and in captured British coracles. The struggle was a fierce one and the British detachments posted higher up the stream, to prevent our men from crossing at any point there, came charging down to take part in the fight. Aulus saw what was happening and detailed the Second under a certain Vespasian[1] to go upstream under cover of a forest and cross over at some now unguarded bend. Vespasian found the right place four or five miles upstream where the river narrowed somewhat and sent a man swimming over with a line. The line served to pull a rope across, which was made fast to a tree on either bank and then tautened. The Second were trained to this manœuvre and were all across the river in an hour or two. Numerous ropes had to be used, because the distance was so great that to keep any one rope taut enough to hold the weight of more than twenty or thirty heavily armed men at a time was to risk its snapping. Once over, they hurried down-stream, meeting none of the enemy as they went, and an hour later suddenly appeared on the enemy's unpro-

[1]Afterwards Emperor (A. D. 69-79).—R. G.

tected right flank. They locked shields, shouted and burst right through to the stockade, killing hundreds of British tribesmen in a single charge. The Batavians and the men of the Ninth joined forces with the Second; and although greatly outnumbered, the combined forces drove the confused and disordered but still courageous enemy slowly backwards until they broke in undeniable rout. The river bank was clear of the British, and Aulus spent the rest of the day in hastily constructing a narrow brushwood causeway across the ford: at low tide this was anchored down firmly and the channels filled in. It was late that night, however, before the work was finished, and the whole army was not safely over—the rising tide interrupted their crossing—until next morning.

The Britons had rallied on the rising ground behind and in the afternoon a pitched battle took place. The French infantry, who had taken no part in the previous day's fighting, led the attack; but the defence was stubborn and a great column of chariotry suddenly broke across the centre from the left flank, cutting in just behind the leading French regiment, which was advancing in line and causing it heavy casualties with a quick volley of spears. When this column, which was led by Caractacus in person, reached the right flank it daringly wheeled round and cut in behind the second French regiment, which was moving up in support, and played the same game with them, driving away without loss. The French were unable to take the ridge, and Aulus, seeing that the British chariotry and cavalry were concentrated on his right flank, about to make a strong attack on the now disordered French, galloped a third of his own cavalry up to the threatened position with instructions to hold it at all costs. Off went the cavalry and Aulus threw the whole of his regular infantry after them, with the exception of the Second Regiment. Leaving the Second to support the French, should the British make a counterattack, and moving Geta with some Batavian infantry and the remainder of the cavalry forward to the left flank, Aulus pushed home the attack on the right. The British chariotry could not check this advance, though our cavalry lost heavily before the leading regiment, the Fourteenth, came up to relieve them. Caractacus then wheeled his column round behind the ridge for an attack on our left flank.

Geta was the hero of the battle. He and his seven hundred cavalrymen stood up against a desperate charge of nearly two thousand chariots; five hundred of the same Batavians who had maimed the ponies during the dawn raid were mixed in with the cavalry and used their knives to good purpose again. But for them Geta would have been overwhelmed. Geta himself was unhorsed and nearly captured, but Caractacus finally withdrew, leaving a hundred wrecked chariots behind him. By this time the pressure of the regular infantry on the right flank was being felt by the British. The French too were more than holding their own, and suddenly the cry went up that Togodumnus had been carried off the field, mortally wounded. The British were disheartened. Their line wavered and broke, streaming towards our left flank, where they ran unexpectedly into Geta's men advancing through a little wood. Geta charged, and when the battle was over fifteen hundred British corpses were found on that part of the field alone. The total British casualties in killed amounted to four thousand. Ours amounted to nine hundred, of whom seven hundred were French; with about the same amount of seriously wounded. Among those who died of wounds was Bericus, the cause of the war, who had been fighting by Geta's side and saved his life when he was unhorsed.

Aulus's next important obstacle was the Thames, which Caractacus now held in much the same way as he had held the Medway. The defeated Britons retired behind it by taking a secret path across the mud-flats at its mouth when the tide was out. Our advance-guard tried to follow them but got bogged and had to retire. The ensuing battle was almost a repetition of the previous one, the conditions being very similar. This time it was Crassus Frugi, the father of young Pompey, my son-in-law, who made the upstream crossing. He forced his way across the bridge at London, which was held by a company of young British noblemen sworn to fight to the last man. The Batavians again swam across the lower reaches of the river at high tide. The British defence was weaker on this occasion and their losses were again heavy. Ours were inconsiderable—three hundred—and two thousand prisoners were taken. London was captured, with rich booty. The victory was spoilt, however, by the loss of nearly a thousand French and Batavians who incautiously pursued the beaten enemy into marshland and were swallowed up in a quaking bog.

Aulus was now across the Thames, but the enemy resistance suddenly stiffened with the arrival of reinforcements from the south, west, and centre of the island. Strong new chariot-contingents appeared. The death of Togodumnus proved a positive advantage to the Britons: the supreme command of the Catuvellaunian army was no longer divided, and Caractacus, who was an able leader and in great favour with the Druids, could make an impassioned plea to his allies and vassals to avenge his noble brother's death. As the Roman losses had exceeded the stipulated maximum and the enemy's resistance could not be claimed to have been broken, Aulus now wisely sent the agreed message back to me. It went to Boulogne by one of the ships which, as arranged, had now reached London from Richborough with a cargo of wine, blankets and military stores. At Boulogne the first beacon was lighted and within a very short time the message had crossed the Alps and was hurrying on to Rome.

It was the day that I had finally found convincing proof

of Myron's fraud and forgeries. I had just had him flogged in the presence of all my other chief secretaries and then executed. I was tired out by a difficult and unpleasant day and had just settled down before supper to a friendly game of dice with Vitellius, when the eunuch Posides, my military secretary, came running in excitedly with the news: "Cæsar, the beacon! You're wanted in Britain."

"Britain?" I exclaimed. I had the dice-cup in my hand, and mechanically shook it once more and threw down the dice before hurrying to the window of the room that faced north. "Show me!" I said. It was a clear evening and in the direction that Posides pointed I could make out, even with my weak eyes, the little red point of light on the summit of Mount Soracte, thirty miles away. I returned to the table, where I found Vitellius beaming at me. "What do you think of that for an omen?" he asked. "Here you have been making the lowest possible scores for the last half-hour and now suddenly you call out 'Britain!' and throw Venus."

Sure enough, the three dice were lying in a neat equilateral triangle and each showed a six! The odds against Venus are two hundred and sixteen to one, so I can be pardoned for feeling great elation. There is nothing like a really good omen for starting a campaign with, and you must understand that Venus was not only the patroness of the dice-cup but was the mother of Æneas, and so my own ancestress through my grandmother Octavia, Augustus's sister, and guardian of the fortunes of the Julian House of which I was now the acknowledged head. I saw significance in the triangle too, for that is the shape of Britain on the maps.

Now that I come to think of it, I wonder whether it was Vitellius, not the Goddess after all, who when my back was turned arranged those dice so nicely for me? I am one of the easiest people in the world to deceive: or at least that is the common verdict against me. If he did, he did well, for Venus sent me off on my conquests in the most exalted mood possible. I offered prayers to her that night (as also to Augustus and Mars) and promised her that if she helped me to victory I would do her whatever service she required of me. "One hand washes the other," I reminded her, "and I really expect you to do your best." It is a custom with us Claudians to address Venus with joking familiarity. She is supposed to enjoy it, as great-grandmothers, especially great-grandmothers with a reputation for having been very gay in their youth, sometimes encourage favourite great-grandchildren to address them with as little courtesy as if they belonged to the same generation.

The next day I sailed from Ostia for Marseilles with my staff and five hundred volunteers for the war. The wind was blowing pleasantly from the south and I preferred sea-travelling to the jolting of a carriage. I would be able to get some well-needed sleep. The whole City came down to the port to see us off and everyone tried to outdo everyone else in his expressions of loyalty and in the warmth of his good wishes. Messalina threw her arms about my neck and wept. Little Germanicus wanted to come too. Vitellius promised the God Augustus to plate his temple doors with gold if I returned victorious.

We were a fleet of five fast-sailing, two-masted, square-rigged men-of-war, each with three banks of oars, and with the hulls well frapped around with strong ropes in case of stormy weather. We raised anchor an hour after dawn and stood out to sea. There was no time to waste, so I told the captain to put on all possible sail, which he did, both sails on each mast, and the sea being calm we were soon driving along at a good ten knots. Late that afternoon we sighted the island of Planasia, near Elba, where my poor friend Postumus had been exiled, and I could make out the now deserted buildings where his guards had been quartered. We had come a hundred and twenty miles, or about a third of the way. The breeze still held. My stomach was unaffected by the pitching of the vessel and I retired to the cabin for a good sleep. That night we rounded Corsica, but the breeze dropped about midnight and we had to rely entirely on oars. I slept well. To shorten the story, the following day we ran into rough weather and made slow progress, the wind veering gradually round to the west-north-west.

The French coast was only sighted at dawn on the third day. The sea was now extraordinarily rough and the oars were often either buried in water up to the row-locks or beating the empty air. Only two of our four sister-vessels were still in sight. We made for the protection of the shore and coasted along it, very slowly. We were now fifty miles west of Fréjus, a station of the fleet, and threading through the Hyères islands. By midday we should have reached Marseilles. As we passed Porquerolles, the largest and most westerly of the islands, separated at one point by only a mile of sea from the peninsula of Giens which puts out to meet it, the wind struck us with terrific force; and though the crew rowed like madmen we could make no headway at all and found ourselves slowly drifting on the rocks. We were within a hundred yards of destruction when the gale momentarily slackened and we managed to pull clear. But a few minutes later we were in trouble again, and this time the danger was greater still. The last headland that we had to struggle past ended in a great black rock which the action of wind and waves had carved into a grinning Satyr-head. The water boiled and hissed at its chin, giving it as it were a white beard. The wind, blowing dead amidships, was rapidly forcing us into this monster's jaws. "If he catches us, he'll crack our bones and mangle our flesh," the captain assured me grimly. "Many a good ship has broken up on that black rock." I offered prayers for succour to every God in the Pantheon. I was told afterwards that the sailors who had overheard me swore that it was the most beautiful praying that they had ever heard in their lives and that it gave them new hope. Especially I prayed to Venus and begged her to persuade her Uncle Neptune to behave with more consideration, for the fate of Rome depended very largely on the survival of this vessel: she must please remind Neptune that I did not associate myself with my predecessor's impious quarrel with him, and that on the contrary I had always held the God in the profoundest respect. The exhausted rowers strained and groaned and the rowing-master ran along the platforms with a rope-end in his hand, cursing and flogging fresh vigour into them. We scraped through somehow—I don't know how—and when a gasp of joy went up that we were out of danger I promised the rowers twenty gold pieces each as soon as we landed.

I was glad that I had kept my head. It was the first time that I had experienced a storm at sea, and I had heard it said that some of the bravest men in the world break down when faced with the prospect of death by drowning. It had even been whispered that the God Augustus was a dreadful coward in a storm, and that only his sense of the dignity of his office kept him from screaming and tearing his hair. He certainly used often to quote the tag about how Impious was the man who first spread sail, And braved the dangers of the frantic deep. He was most unlucky at sea, except in his sea-battles, and—speaking of impiety—once showed his deep resentment at the loss of a fleet in a sudden storm by forbidding the statue of Neptune to be carried as usual in a sacred procession around the Circus. After this he seldom put to sea without raising a storm and was all but shipwrecked on three or four occasions.

Our vessel was the first to reach Marseilles, and fortunately not a single one of the five was lost, though two were forced to turn back and run into Fréjus. The earth felt splendidly firm under my feet at Marseilles: I determined never again to travel by sea when I could possibly travel by land, and have not once departed from this resolution since.

As soon as I had heard that a successful landing had been made in Britain I had moved up my reserves to Boulogne and ordered Posides to have transports assembled there ready, together with whatever extra military stores might suggest themselves as likely to be needed for the campaign. At Marseilles twenty fast gigs were waiting for me and my staff—Posides had arranged this—and carried us, with constant relays of horses, up the Rhône valley from Avignon to Lyons, where we spent the second night, and then on north along the Saône, travelling eighty or ninety miles a day—which was the most that I could manage because of the continuous jolting, which racked my nerves and upset my digestion and gave me violent headaches. The third night, at Chalons, my physician Xenophon insisted on my resting the whole of the next day. I told him that I could not afford to waste a whole day; he answered that if I did not rest I could not expect to be of any use to the army in Britain when I did arrive. I raged at him and tried to override his opinion, but Xenophon insisted on reading this behaviour as a further sign of nervous exhaustion and told me that either he was my doctor or I was my own. In the latter case he would resign and resume his interrupted practice at Rome: in the former, he must ask me to do as he advised me, relax completely and submit to a thorough massage. So I apologized and pleaded that to be suddenly halted in my journey would cause me such nervous anxiety that my physical condition would not be improved by any amount of compensatory massage; and that to say "relax" was no more practical advice in the circumstances than to tell a man whose clothes have caught fire that he must keep cool. In the end we arrived at a compromise: I would not continue my journey in a gig, but neither would I remain in Châlons. I would be carried in a light sedan on the shoulders of six well-trained chairmen and thus knock off at least thirty miles or so of the five hundred that still lay before me. I would submit to as much massage as he pleased both before I started and after the day's journey was over.

From Lyons it took me eight days to reach Boulogne by way of Troyes, Rheims, Soissons and Amiens, for in the stage out of Rheims Xenophon forced me to use a sedan again. All this time I was not exactly idle. I was turning over in my mind my historical memories of great battles of the past—Julius's battles, Hannibal's battles, Alexander's, and especially those of my father and brother in Germany—and wondering whether, when it came to the point, I would be able to apply all this detailed and extensive knowledge to any practical purpose. I congratulated myself that whenever it had been possible to draw a plan of any battle from the accounts handed down by eye-witnesses I had always done so; and had thoroughly mastered the general tactical principles involved in the use of a small force of disciplined fighters against a great army of semi-civilized tribesmen, and also the strategical principles involved in the successful occupation of their country when the battle had been won.

At Amiens, lying sleepless in the early morning, I began picturing the battle-field. The British infantry would probably be occupying a wooded ridge, with their cavalry and chariotry manœuvring in the low ground in front. I would draw up my regular infantry in ordinary battle formation, on a two-regiment front, with the auxiliaries on either flank and the Guards in reserve. The elephants, which would be a complete novelty to the Britons, no such animal having ever been seen on that island—but here a most uncomfortable thought came to me. "Posides," I called, in an anxious voice.

"Yes, Cæsar," Posides answered, springing up from his pallet, half-asleep still.

"The elephants *are* at Boulogne, aren't they?"

"Yes, Cæsar."

"How long ago did I give you the order to move them up there from Lyons?"

"When we heard news of the landing, Cæsar; that would be on the seventh of August."

"And to-day is the twenty-seventh."

"Yes, Cæsar."

"Then how in the world are we going to get those elephants over? We should have had special elephant transports built."

"The ship that brought the obelisk from Alexandria is at Boulogne."

"But I thought that it was still at Ostia."

"No, Cæsar, at Boulogne."

"But if you sent it up there on the seventh it can't possibly have arrived there yet. It can't possibly be any nearer than the Bay of Biscay. It took three weeks to get to Rome from Egypt, you remember, in perfect sailing weather, too."

But Posides was a really able minister. It appears that as soon as I had decided to put elephants among my reinforcements and sent them up to Lyons—in May, I think it was—he had considered the question of transport across the Channel and without saying a word to me had fitted up the obelisk-ship as an elephant-transport—it was the only ship big and strong enough for the purpose—and sent it up to Boulogne, where it had arrived six weeks later. If he had waited for my orders the elephants would have had to be left behind. The obelisk-ship deserves more than a passing mention. It was the largest vessel ever launched. It was no less than two hundred feet long and broad in proportion, and its main timbers were of cedar. Caligula had built it in the first few months of his monarchy to bring from Egypt an eighty-foot red granite obelisk, together with four enormous stones which formed the pediment. The obelisk was originally from Heliopolis, but had been set up in Augustus's temple at Alexandria a few years before. Caligula now wanted it set up in his own honour in the new Circus that he was building on the Vatican Hill. To understand what a monstrous sort of ship it was you must be told that its seventy-foot main mast was a silver fir eight feet in diameter at its base; and that among the ballast used to keep it steady when the obelisk and pediment were secured on deck were one hundred and twenty thousand pecks of Egyptian lentils—a gift for the people of Rome.

When I reached Boulogne I was delighted to find the troops in good spirits, the transports ready and the sea calm. We embarked without delay, and our passage across the Channel was so pleasant and uneventful that on landing at Richborough I sacrificed to Venus and Neptune, thanking the latter for his unexpected favours and the former for her kindly intercession. The elephants gave no trouble. They were Indian elephants, not African. Indian elephants are about three times the size of African, and these were particularly fine ones which Caligula had bought for ceremonial use in his own religion: they had since been employed at the docks at Ostia moving timbers and stones under the direction of their Indian drivers. I found to my surprise that twelve camels had been added to the elephants. That was an idea of Posides's.

# Chapter Nineteen

AT RICHBOROUGH we were anxious to hear the latest news from Aulus, and I found a dispatch from him just arrived. It reported that the Britons had made two attacks, one by day and the other by night, on the camp which he had fortified just north of London, but had been beaten off with some loss. However, new enemy reinforcements seemed to be arriving every day, from as far west as South Wales; and the men of Kent who had retired into the Weald were reported to have sent a message through to Caractacus that as soon as Aulus was forced to retreat they would leave their woods and cut him off from his base. He begged me therefore to join forces with him as soon as possible. I talked to a few seriously wounded men whom Aulus had evacuated to the Base, and they all agreed that the British infantry was nothing to be afraid of, but that their chariotry seemed to be everywhere at once and was now so numerous as to prevent any force of less than two or three hundred regular infantry from leaving the main body.

My column was now preparing for its advance. The elephants carried great bundles of spare javelins and other munitions of war; but certain curious machines slung across the backs of the camels puzzled me.

"An invention of your Imperial Predecessor, Cæsar," Posides explained. "I took the liberty of having a set of six made at Lyons when we were there in July and sent up to Boulogne on camel-back. They're a sort of siege-engine for use against uncivilized tribes."

"I didn't know that the late Emperor had been responsible

for any military inventions."

"I think, Cæsar, that you will find this type of machine extremely effective, especially in conjunction with light rope. I have taken the liberty of bringing up several hundred yards of light rope in coils."

Posides was grinning broadly, and I could see that he had some clever scheme at the back of his mind which he was keeping a secret from me. So I said to him: "Xerxes the Great had a war-minister called Hermotimus, a eunuch like you, and whenever Hermotimus was allowed to solve a tactical problem by himself, such as the reduction of an impregnable town without siege-engines or the crossing of an unfordable river without boats, that problem was always solved. But if Xerxes or anyone else tried to interfere with advice or suggestions Hermotimus used to say that the problem had now become too complicated for him and beg to be excused. You're a second Hermotimus, and for good luck I am going to leave you to your own devices. Your forethought in the matter of the obelisk-ship has earned you my confidence. Understand that I expect great things from your camels and their loads. If you disappoint me I shall be greatly displeased with you and shall probably throw you to the panthers in the amphitheatre on our return."

He answered, still grinning: "And if I help to win the victory for you, what then?"

"Then I'll decorate you with the highest honour that it is in my power to bestow and one not unappropriate to your condition: you shall be awarded the Untipped Spear. Have you any other novelties smuggled away in the baggage? These camels and elephants and black spearmen from Africa already suggest a spectacle on Mars Field rather than a serious expedition."

"No, Cæsar, nothing else much. But I think that the Britons will have an eyeful before we have done, and we can collect the entrance money after the performance is over."

We marched up from Richborough and met with no opposition: the river-crossings were held for us by detachments of the Fourteenth sent back by Aulus for this purpose. When we had passed they fell in behind us. I did not see a single enemy Briton between Richborough and London, where Aulus and I joined forces on the fifth of September. I think that he was as pleased to see me as I was to see him. The first thing I asked him was whether the troops were in good spirits. He answered that they were and that he had only promised them half the force that I had brought, and had not mentioned the elephants, so that our real strength was a surprise to them. I asked him where the enemy were expected to give battle, and he showed me a contour map he had made in clay of the country between London and Colchester. He pointed out a place about twenty miles along the London-Colchester road—not a road in the Roman sense, of course—which Caractacus had been busily fortifying and which would almost certainly be the site of the coming battle. This was a wooded ridge called Brentwood Hill which curved round the road in a great horseshoe, at each tip of which was a great stockaded fort, with another in the centre. The road ran north-east. The enemy's left flank beyond the ridge was protected by marshland, and a deep brook, called the Weald Brook, formed a defendable barrier in front. On the right flank the ridge bent round to the north and continued for three or four miles, but the trees and thorn bushes and brambles grew so densely along it that to try to turn that flank by sending a force of men to hack their way through would, Aulus assured me, be useless. Since the only feasible approach to Colchester was by this road, and since I wished to engage the main forces of the enemy as soon as possible, I studied the tactical problem involved very carefully. Prisoners and deserters volunteered precise information about the defences in the wood and these seemed to be extremely well planned.

I did not welcome the notion of making a frontal attack. If we marched against the central fort without first reducing the other two we would be exposed to heavy attacks from both flanks. But to attack the other two first would not help us much either; for if we succeeded in taking them, at great cost to ourselves, it would mean fighting our way through a series of further stockades inside the wood, each of which would have to be taken in a separate operation.

At a council of war to which Aulus and I summoned all general staff-officers and regimental commanders, everyone agreed that a frontal attack on the central fort was inevitable, and that we must be prepared to suffer heavy losses. It was unfortunate that the forward slopes of the ridge between the wood and the stream were admirably suited to chariot-manœuvre. Aulus recommended a mass-attack in diamond formation. The head of the diamond would consist of a single regiment in two waves, each wave eight men deep. Then would follow two regiments marching abreast, in the same formation as the leading one; then three regiments marching abreast. This would be the broadest part of the diamond and here the elephants would be disposed as a covering for each flank. Then would come two regiments, again, and then one. The cavalry and the rest of the infantry would be kept in reserve. Aulus explained that this diamond afforded a protection against charges from the flank: no attack could be made on the flank of the leading regiment without engaging the javelin-fire of the overlapping second line, nor on the second line without engaging the fire of the overlapping third. The third line was protected by the elephants. If a heavy chariot charge was made from a rear flank the regiments there could be turned about and the same mutual protection given.

My comments on this diamond were that it was a pretty formation and that it had been used successfully in such and such battles—I listed them—in republican times; but that the Britons outnumbered us so greatly that once we had advanced into the centre of the horseshoe they could attack us from all sides at once with forces that we could not drive off without disorganization: the front of the diamond would almost certainly become separated from the rear. I said too, very forcibly, that I was not prepared to suffer one-tenth of the number of casualties that it had been estimated the frontal attack would cost. Vespasian came out with the old proverb about not being able to make an omelette without breaking eggs, and asked somewhat impatiently whether I proposed to cut my losses and return to France immediately, and how long, if so, I expected to keep the respect of the armies.

I countered with: "There are more ways of killing a cat than beating it to death with a horn porridge-spoon; and breaking the spoon into the bargain."

They argued with me in the superior way of old campaigners, trying to impress me with technical military terms, as though I were an entire ignoramus. I burst out angrily: "Gentlemen, as the God Augustus used to say, 'A radish may know no Greek, but I do.' I have been studying tactics for forty years and you can't teach me a thing: I know all the conventional and unconventional moves and openings in the game of human draughts. But you must understand that I am not free to play the game in the way you wish me to play it. As Father of the Country I now owe a duty to my sons: I refuse to throw away three or four thousand of their lives in an attack of this sort. Neither my father Drusus nor my brother Germanicus would ever have dreamed of making a frontal attack against a position as strong as this."

Geta asked, perhaps ironically: "What would your noble relatives have done, Cæsar, in a case of this sort, do you think?"

"They'd have found a way round."

"But there *is* no way round here, Cæsar. That has been established."

"They'd have found a way round, I say."

Crassus Frugi said: "The enemy's left flank is guarded by the Heron King and their right by the Hawthorn Queen. That's their boast, according to prisoners."

"Who's this Heron King?" I asked.

"The Lord of the Marshes. He's a cousin, in their mythology, of the Goddess of Battle. She appears in the disguise of a raven and perches on the spear-heads. Then she drives the conquered into the marshes, and her cousin the Heron King eats them up. The Hawthorn Queen is a virgin who dresses in white in the Spring and helps soldiers in battle by defending their stockades with her thorns: you see, they fell thorn-trees and pile them in a row with the thorns outwards, making the trunks fast together. That's a fearful obstacle to get through. But the Hawthorn Queen holds that right flank of theirs without any artificial felling of trees. Our scouts are positive that the whole wood is in such a fearful tangle that it's no use trying to get through at any point there."

Aulus said: "Yes, Cæsar, I am afraid that we must make up our minds to that frontal attack."

"Posides," I suddenly called, "were you ever a soldier?"

"Never, Cæsar."

"That makes two of us, thank God. Now suppose I undertake to do the impossible and get our cavalry through on the enemy's right flank, past this impenetrable tangle of thorns, can you undertake to get the Guards round on their left though that impassable bog?"

Posides answered: "You have given me the easier flank, Cæsar. There is, as it happens, a track through the marshes. One would have to go along it in single file, but there is a track. I met a man in London yesterday, a travelling Spanish oculist, who goes about the country curing the people of marsh-ophthalmia. He's in the Camp now, and he says he knows that marsh well, and the track—which he always uses to avoid the toll-gate on the hill. Since Cymbeline's death they have been levying no fixed toll, but a traveller must pay according to the amount of money he has in his saddle-bags, and this oculist got tired of being skinned. In the early mornings there's nearly always a mist on the marsh and he takes the path and slips round unobserved. He says that it's easy to follow once you are on it. It comes out half a mile beyond the ridge, at the edge of a pine copse. The Britons are likely to have a guard posted at that end—Caractacus is a careful general—but I think now that I can undertake to dislodge them and get as many men across the marsh as care to follow me."

He explained his ruse, which I approved, though many of the generals raised their eyebrows at it; and then I explained my plan for forcing the other flank, which was really very simple. An important fact had been overlooked in the general concentration of interest on the diamond formation; the fact that Indian elephants are capable of bursting through the densest undergrowth imaginable and are daunted by no briars or thorns. However, in order not to tell the story twice, I shall say no more about the council of war and what was decided at it. I shall proceed to the battle, which took place at Brentwood on the seventh of September, a date that had long been memorable to me as the day on which my brother Germanicus had defeated Hermann at the Weser: if he had lived he would still have been only fifty-eight years old, which was no older than Aulus.

We marched out from London along the Colchester road. Our vanguard was kept busy by British skirmishers, but no serious resistance was offered until we reached Romford, a village about seven miles from Brentwood, where we found the ford across the river Rom strongly defended. The enemy held us up there for a whole morning, at the cost to themselves of two hundred killed and a hundred prisoners. We lost only fifty, but two of these were captains and one was a battalion commander, so in a sense the Britons got the best of the exchange. That afternoon we sighted Brentwood Ridge and encamped for the night this side of the brook, which we used as a defensive barrier.

I took the auspices. Auspices are always taken before battle by giving the sacred chickens lumps of pulse-cake and watching how they eat it. If they have no appetite the battle is already as good as lost. The best possible omen is when the chickens, as soon as the cage-door is opened by the chicken-priest, rush out without any cry or beating of wings and eat so greedily that big bits drop from their mouths. If the sound of these striking the ground can be distinctly heard it prophesies the total defeat of the enemy. And, sure enough, this best possible omen was granted. The chicken-priest did not show himself to the birds, but standing with me behind the cage suddenly slid the door back at the very moment that I threw the cake before them. Out they rushed, without so much as a cackle, and fairly tore at the cake, throwing lumps about in a way which absolutely delighted us all, it was so reckless.

I had prepared what I considered a very suitable speech. It was somewhat reminiscent of Livy, but I felt that the historic importance of the occasion called for something in that style. It ran:

"Romans, let no tongue among you wag and no voice bellow vainly, praising the days of old as days of true gold, and belittling the present age, of whose glories we should be the doughty champions, as a graceless age of gilded plaster. The Greek heroes before Troy, of whom the au-

336

gust Homer sang, bore, if we are to believe his record, this verse perpetually upon their lips:

> We pride ourselves as better men by far
> Than all our forbears who e'er marched to war.

Be not over-modest, Romans. Hold your heads high. Puff out your chests. Ranged in battle before you to-day are men who as closely resemble your ancestors, as eagle, eagle, or wolf, wolf—a fierce, proud, nervous, unrefined race, wielding weapons that are long centuries out of date, driving chariot-ponies of an antique breed, employing pitiable battle tactics only worthy of the pages of epic poets, not organized in regiments but grouped in clans and households —as certain of defeat at your disciplined hands as the wild boar who lowers his head and charges the skilled huntsman armed with hunting-spear and net. To-morrow when the dead are counted and the long ranks of sullen prisoners march beneath the yoke, it will be a matter for laughter to you if you ever for a moment lost faith in the present, if your minds were ever dazzled by the historied glories of a remote past. No, comrades, the bodies of these primitive heroes will be tumbled by your swords upon the field of battle as roughly and indiscriminately as, just now, when I, your general, took the auspices, the holy fowl flung on the soil from their avid bills the fragments of sanctified cake.

"Some of you, I have heard, no doubt slothful rather than fearful or undutiful, hesitated when called upon to set out upon this expedition, alleging as your excuse that the God Augustus had fixed the bounds of the Roman Empire for ever at the waters of the Rhine and the Channel. If this were true, as I undertake to prove to you that it is not, then the God Augustus would be unworthy of our worship. The mission of Rome is to civilize the world—and where in the whole world would you find a race worthier of the benefits

337

which we propose to confer upon it than the British race? The strange and pious task is laid upon us of converting these fierce compeers of our ancestors into dutiful sons of Rome, our illustrious City and Mother. What were the words that the God Augustus wrote to my grandmother, the Goddess Augusta? 'Looking into the future I can see Britain becoming as civilized as Southern France is now. And I think that the islanders, who are racially akin to us, will become far better Romans than we shall ever succeed in making of the Germans. . . . And, one day (do not smile) British noblemen may well take their seats in the Roman Senate.'

"You have already quitted yourselves bravely in this war. Twice you have inflicted a resounding defeat on the enemy. You have slain King Togodumnus, my enemy, and avenged his insults. This third time you cannot fail. Your forces are more powerful than ever, your courage higher, your ranks more united. You, no less than the enemy, are defending your hearths and the sacred temples of your Gods. The Roman soldier, whether his battlefield be the icy rocks of Caucasus, the burning sands of the desert beyond Atlas, the dank forests of Germany, or the grassy fields of Britain, is never unmindful of the lovely City which gives him his name, his valour and his sense of duty."

I had composed several more paragraphs in this same lofty strain, but strangely enough not one word of the speech was delivered. When I mounted the tribunal platform, and the captains shouted in unison: "Greetings, Cæsar Augustus, Father of our Country, our Emperor!" and the soldiers took up the shout with roaring applause, I fairly broke down. My fine speech went altogether out of my head and I could only stretch out my hands to them, my eyes swimming with tears, and blurt out: "It's all right, lads: the chickens say that it's going to be all right, and we

338

have prepared a grand surprise for them, and we're going to give them such a beating as they'll never forget so long as they live—I don't mean the chickens, I mean the British." [Tremendous laughter, in which I thought it best to join, as if the joke had been intentional.]

"Stop laughing at me, lads," I cried. "Don't you remember what happened to the little black boy in the Egyptian story who laughed at his father when he said the evening prayer by mistake for the morning one? The crocodile ate him; so you be careful. Well, I am getting to be an old man now, but this is the proudest moment of my life and I wish my poor brother Germanicus were here to share it with me. Do any of you remember my great brother? Not very many, perhaps, for he died twenty-four years ago. But you've all heard of him as the greatest general Rome has ever had. To-morrow is the anniversary of his magnificent defeat of Hermann, the German chieftain, and I want you to celebrate it suitably. The pass-word to-night is *Germanicus!* and the battle-cry to-morrow will be *Germanicus!* and I think that if you shout his name loud enough he'll hear it down in the Underworld and know that he's remembered by the regiments that he loved and led so well. It will make him forget the wretched fate that overtook him—he died poisoned in bed, as you know. The Twentieth Regiment will have the honour of leading the assault: Germanicus always said that though, in barracks, you Twentieth were the most insubordinate, most drunken and most quarrelsome troops in the entire regular army, you were absolute lions on the field. Second and Fourteenth, Germanicus called you the Backbone of the Army. It will be your duty to-morrow to stiffen the French allies, who will act as the Army's ribs. The Ninth will come up last, because Germanicus always used to say that you Ninth were the slowest regiment in the Army but also the surest. You Guards are detailed for special duty. You have the easiest time and the best pay when you're not on active service, so it's only fair to the rest of the troops to give you the most dangerous and disagreeable task when you are. That's all I have to say now. Be good lads, sleep well, and earn your Father's gratitude to-morrow!"

They cheered me till they were hoarse, and I knew then that Pollio was right and Livy wrong. A good general couldn't possibly deliver a studied oration on the eve of battle, even if he had one already prepared; for his lips would inevitably speak as his heart prompted. One effect of this speech—which, you will agree, reads very poorly by comparison with the other one—was that ever since I made it the Ninth have been familiarly known not as the "Ninth Spanish" (their full title) but as the "Ninth Snails." The Twentieth, too, whose full title is "The Conquering Valerian Twentieth," are known to other regiments as the "Drunken Lions"; and when a man of the Fourteenth meets a man of the Second they are now expected to salute each other as "Comrade Backbone." The French auxiliaries are always known as "The Ribs."

A light mist settled over the camp, but there was a moon soon after midnight, which was of the greatest service; if the weather had been cloudy we would not have been able to manage the marshes. I slept until midnight and then Posides woke me as arranged and handed me a candle and a blazing pine branch from the camp-fire. I lighted the candle with it and prayed to the nymph Egeria. She is a Goddess of Prophecy, and good King Numa in the days of old used to consult her on every occasion. It was the first time that I had performed this family ceremony, but my brother Germanicus and my uncle Tiberius and my father and grandfather and great-grandfather and their ancestors before them had always performed it at midnight on the day before a battle; and if they were to be victorious the same favourable sign was invariably given by the nymph.

It might be the stillest night imaginable, and yet, as soon as the last words of the prayer were uttered, the light would suddenly go out of itself as if snuffed between two fingers.

I had never been sure whether to believe in this mystery or not: I thought that it might perhaps be due to natural causes—a draught, or a bad patch in the wick, or even an involuntary sigh on the part of the watcher. The nymph Egeria could hardly be expected to leave her native grove by Lake Nemi and fly at a moment's notice to the middle of Germany or Northern Spain or the Tyrol—in each of which countries she is said to have obliged at one time or other with the customary sign—at the prayer of a Claudian. So I had set the lighted candle at the farthest end of my tent, screened from any draught that might come in by the flap, and then, walking ten paces away, addressed Egeria in solemn tones. It was a short prayer, in the Sabine dialect. The text had become grossly mutilated by oral tradition, for Sabine, which was the original patrician language, had long fallen into disuse at Rome; but I had studied Sabine in the course of my historical studies and was able to recite the prayer in something like its original form. And sure enough, I had hardly spoken the last word when the candle, as I watched it, suddenly went out. I immediately relighted it, to see whether there was perhaps a fault in the wick, or whether Posides had doctored the wax; but no, it burned brightly again and continued to burn until the wick fell over in a pool of wax no bigger than a farthing. This is one of the very few genuine mystical experiences that have happened to me in a long life. I have no great gift that way. My brother Germanicus, on the other hand, was plagued by visions and apparitions. At one time or another he had met most of the demi-gods, nymphs and monsters celebrated by the poets, and on his visit to Troy, when he was Governor of Asia, was granted a splendid vision of the Goddess Cybele whom our Trojan ancestors worshipped.

# Chapter Twenty

Aulus came hurrying eagerly in. "Our outposts report that the enemy are withdrawing from the Weald Brook, Cæsar. What action shall we take? I suggest putting a regiment over at once. I don't know what the enemy's plan is, but we have to cross the brook to-morrow in any case, and if they have chosen to abandon it to us without fight, that will save us time and men."

"Send the Ninth across, Aulus. Supply them with bridging material. They'll not have as much fighting to do to-morrow as the rest, I hope, so they'll not need so long a sleep. That's splendid news. Scouts must be pushed ahead to get in touch with the enemy and report as soon as they're located."

The Ninth were hurriedly roused and sent across the Weald Brook. A message came back from them that the enemy had withdrawn half-way up the ridge, that twenty plank-bridges were now fixed across the brook and that they were standing by for further orders.

"It's time the Guards were on their way," said Posides.

"Is the oculist trustworthy, do you think?" I asked.

"I'm going ahead with him myself, Cæsar," said Posides. "It's my plan, and, by your leave, if it fails I don't intend to survive."

"Very well. Give them the order to start in five minutes."

So he kissed my hand and I gave him a clap on the back and out he went. A few minutes later I saw the first company of Guards march silently out of the eastern gate of the camp. They were told to break step so that their measured tread should not be heard by the enemy's outposts, and their arms were muffled with rags so that they should not knock together. Each man had his shield slung across his back and a big chalk circle smudged on it. This was to enable them to keep touch in the dark without shouting to each other. The white circles showed up well: Aulus had observed that deer follow each other through dark forests guided by the gleam of the white fur patches on each other's rumps. The oculist led them over three or four miles of rough, boggy country, until they reached the marsh proper. It stank, and the will-o'-the-wisp darted about it, and to reach the beginning of the secret track the Guards had to wade thigh-deep after their guide through a slimy pool full of leeches. But the oculist made no mistakes. He found the track and kept to it.

A British outpost was stationed in the pine copse at the farther end, and as the moon rose these watchful men saw a sight and heard a sound which filled their hearts with the utmost dismay. A great bird with a long shining bill, a huge grey body and legs fifteen feet long suddenly rose through the mist a javelin's throw away and came stalking towards them, stopping every now and then to boom hoarsely, flap his wings, preen his feathers with his dreadful bill and boom again. The Heron King! They crouched in their bivouacs, terrified, hoping that this apparition would disappear, but it came slowly on and on. At last it seemed to notice their camp-fire. It jerked its head angrily and hurried towards them, with outspread wings, booming louder and louder. They sprang up and ran for their lives. The Heron King pursued them through the copse with a fearful chuckling laughter, then turned and slowly promenaded along the edge of the marsh, booming dully at intervals.

In case you imagine that it was indeed the Heron King who had come to frighten them—for if Egeria could appear so strangely, why not a Heron King?—I must explain

343

the ruse. The Heron King was a French soldier from the great marshes which lie to the west of Marseilles, where the shepherds are accustomed to walk on long stilts as a means of striding across soft patches too wide to jump. Posides had rigged this man up in a wicker-work basket constructed in the shape of a bird's body, and stitched over with blanket stuff. Wicker wings covered with cloth were attached to his arms. The head and bill were improvised of stuff-covered laths and fastened to his head: he could move them by moving his neck. The beak was treated with phosphorus. The boom was made by an ingenious water-pipe he carried in his mouth. The soldier knew the habits of herons and imitated the walk with his stilts, which were strapped firmly to his legs. The oculist led him and Posides along the track until the dark outline of the copse could just be made out. The Guards were following two hundred yards behind, and Posides sent back a message halting them. He waited until he saw the bird striding around the copse again and knew that the ruse had been successful. He ran back and told them that the coast was clear. They hurried forward and occupied the copse. Eight thousand men in single file take a long time to pass a given spot, and it was more than five hours before they were all across, by which time dawn had appeared, but the mist had not cleared, so they were not seen from the hill.

An hour before dawn I sacrificed to Mars and then breakfasted with my staff, and we made a few further arrangements about what to do if everything did not go according to plan. But now we knew that most of the Guards must already be in position—for there had evidently been no interruption of their progress across the marsh—and we were confident of victory. Geta was absent: he had taken an odd battalion of the Eighth Regiment (I had forgotten to mention this battalion as part of our reinforcements) with the cavalry, the Batavians and the elephants, to a position about two miles away on our left flank. My son-in-law, young Pompey, was also absent. I had entrusted him with the command of the Nubians and the Balearic slingers, and he had taken them across the Weald Brook. The Balearics carried coils of tent-rope, tent-pegs, and camp mallets; the Nubians, native drums and their long white spears.

It was a fine breakfast and we all drank just the right amount of wine—enough to make us feel very pleased with ourselves and yet not enough to induce recklessness—and in the intervals of serious discussion we did a great deal of joking. They were mostly witticisms about camels, which were much on our minds at the time. My contribution was a quotation from a letter of Herod Agrippa's to my mother: "The camel is one of the seven wonders of nature. He shares this honour with the Rainbow, the Echo, the Cuckoo, the Negro, the Volcano, and the Sirocco. But he is the first and greatest of the seven."

I gave the order for the army to move forward into its positions beyond the Weald Brook. Massed trumpeters blew a call that could be heard miles away. It was answered by a great din of war-horns and shouting from the hill. That gave me a sudden shock. Although, naturally, I had been aware that battles cannot be fought without an enemy, I had been thinking of this battle all night as a diagram on the map, a silent affair of squares and oblongs gently pushing each other this way and that; the Roman squares and oblongs inked in black, the British left white. When the trumpets and horns blew I had to translate the diagram into terms of man, horse, chariot and elephant. I had not slept since midnight, and I suppose my face and gestures betrayed the strain I was under: Xenophon actually suggested that I should rest a few minutes after my breakfast and go forward only when all the regiments were in position. As though it was not essential for me to be waiting at the brook dressed in my Imperial armour and purple cloak to greet each regiment as it arrived and watch it cross over! If Xenophon had so much as whispered the word "massage" I believe I should have killed him.

I rode forward to the brook on a steady old mare, none other than Penelope, the widow of ex-citizen and might-have-been-Consul Incitatus, who had recently broken a leg on the race-track and had to be destroyed. The mist was pretty thick here. One could only see ten or fifteen paces ahead, and what a terrible stink of camel! You have perhaps, at some time or other, passed in the mist through a field where an old he-goat was loose: at ordinary times wind and sun carry off most of the smell, but mist seems to suck it up and hold it, so that you will have been astonished by the rankness of the air. These were he-camels which I had imported for circus-shows—female camels are too expensive—and they smell pretty bad. If there is one thing that horses hate it is the smell of camel, but as all our cavalry were far away on the flank this did not affect us, and Penelope was inured to circus-smells. There was no confusion in the crossing of the brook, and in spite of the mist the regiments formed up beyond in perfect order. A disciplined regiment can perform quite complicated drill movements in the pitch dark: the Guards often practise at night on Mars Field.

Now I want to make you see the battle as it was seen by the Britons, because that way you will be better able to appreciate my plan of attack. The best British infantry are manning the three forts, each of which has a sally-port for sorties and an avenue running back through the wood into the open country behind. The forts are linked together by a strong stockade facing the entire semi-circle of wood, and the wood is so full of Britons that no advantage would be won by attacking the stockade at a point between two forts. Just before dawn the sally-port of the central fort opens and out drives a division of chariotry. It is commanded by Cattigern, Caractacus's brother-in-law, King of the Trinovants. Another division drives out from the fort on the British right flank. It is led by Caractacus himself. The two divisions draw up on either side of the central fort. Caractacus is angry and reproaches Cattigern, because he has just been told that the Trinovantian infantry posted at the Weald Brook have fallen back during the night. Cattigern is angry at being spoken to in this way in front of his whole tribe. He asks Caractacus haughtily whether he accuses the Trinovants of cowardice. Caractacus wishes to know what other excuse they have for deserting their posts. Cattigern explains that they retired for religious reasons. Their commander had been coughing violently because of the mist and suddenly began to cough blood. They regarded this as a most unlucky sign, and respect for the nymph of the brook did not allow them to stay. They therefore offered a propitiatory sacrifice—the chief's two ponies—and withdrew. Caractacus has to accept this explanation, but does not conceal his displeasure. He does not yet know of the retirement of the other outpost from the copse by the marsh, but he has heard alarming rumours of the appearance of the Heron King in person in that quarter: the Heron King has not been seen since legendary times. Our trumpets are then heard and the British reply with horns and shouts. British scouts come rushing up to report that the enemy are crossing the brook in force.

Dawn has broken, and the whole semi-circle of wood stands out clearly, with open ground shelving down towards the brook, but after three or four hundred yards the field of vision is obscured by a sea of mist. Caractacus cannot tell yet in which direction the Roman attack will develop. He sends more scouts forward to report. They hurry back twenty minutes later to report that the enemy are on the move at last. They are coming up the road towards

347

the centre in mass formation. Caractacus wheels his chariot division across to the right flank again and anxiously waits for the first Roman companies to appear through the mist. A Briton comes up to report that before the chariots emerged from the wood a muffled sound of hammering was heard from the mist, as if the Roman soldiers were driving tent-pegs; and that a party sent out to investigate the noise did not return. Caractacus replies, "Tent-pegs can't hurt us."

At last the tramp and clank of our approaching regiments can be clearly heard, and the encouraging shouts of the officers. The leading company of the Twentieth appears dimly through the mist. The Britons roar defiance. Cattigern swings his division across to the left. The Romans suddenly halt. A curious sight is seen. A company of immensely tall long-necked beasts with humps on their backs are being trotted up and down, in and out of the mist, on the flank which Cattigern has been told to attack. The Britons are alarmed at the sight and mutter charms against magic. Cattigern should now be attacking, but he cannot yet be sure whether the Roman advance is only a feint; for only five hundred men are as yet visible. The main attack may be taking place elsewhere. He waits. Caractacus sends a mounted messenger, ordering him to attack without delay. Cattigern signals the advance. And then a strange thing happens. As soon as the column of chariots sweeps down into the mist where the beasts have been seen, the ponies go quite mad. They squeal, buck, snort, baulk and cannot be forced to go a step farther. It is clearly a magic mist. It has a peculiar and frightening odour.

While Cattigern's division is in confusion, the ponies plunging and kicking and the charioteers shouting, cursing and trying to get them under control, trumpets sound and two battalions of the Twentieth, followed by two battalions of the Second, suddenly charge out of the mist at them.

348

"Germanicus! Germanicus!" they shout. Shower after shower of javelins flies from their hands. Caractacus then launches his own attack. His division is unaffected by the spell and sweeps down, three thousand strong, on the flank of the halted Roman mass, which seems unprovided with a flank-guard. But a more powerful charm than a stinking mist protects this flank. The column is going at full speed and is just out of javelin range when suddenly there come six terrific claps of thunder and six simultaneous flashes of lightning. Balls of burning pitch hurtle through the air. The terrified column swings away to the right, and as they go a shower of lead bolts comes whizzing at them from the Balearic slingers posted behind the thunder and lightning. Charioteers fall right and left; as they have the reins tightly wound about their wrists, this involves the wreck of a number of chariots. The column is almost out of control, but Caractacus manages to swing it back again on its course. He is aiming at the Roman rear, which can now be clearly seen, for a light breeze is rolling the mist away to the other flank. But a catastrophe follows. As the column, which has lost its formation and is now pressed together in a disorderly mass, rushes forward, chariot after chariot comes crashing to the ground as if halted by an invisible power. The chariots behind are bunched so close and the impetus of the downhill rush is so great that nobody can pull up or turn without colliding with a neighbour. The mass charges blindly on and the wreckage in front piles higher and higher. Above the crash of splintered chariots, the screams and groans, rises a dreadful noise of drums and up springs a horde of tall, naked black men brandishing white spears. The fling themselves on the wreckage, and their long spears dart here and there among the fallen men. They laugh and crow and shout and no Briton dares defend himself against them, mistaking them for evil spirits. Caractacus escapes from the slaughter. His

349

own car has been among the first to overturn, but he has been thrown clear. He runs off to the right, stumbling as he goes over the tightly-stretched tent-rope pegged knee-high in the long grass. The last section of the column, Belgic chariot-men from the West Country, have realized in time what is happening in front. Five hundred of their chariots manage to avoid disaster by swerving away to the right. There Caractacus hails them and is rescued. The rest of the division is lost, for the Fourteenth has pushed two battalions round in their rear and two battalions of the Ninth rush obliquely forward to assist the Nubians.

Caractacus leads his chariots back up the hill and instructs the Belgic commander to go to Cattigern's aid on the other flank. He himself drives up to the central fort, for he notices that the sally-port is open and wants to know why. He enters and finds the garrison gone. Meanwhile Cattigern is fighting bravely at the head of a force of dismounted chariot-men, supported by infantry-men who have streamed out of the wood to his assistance. He is wounded. His chariotry has disappeared. His brother has headed the flight back to the central fort, down the avenue through the wood, and so away. The garrison of the fort has gone after him. Our Twentieth and Second are gradually forcing Cattigern's men back, keeping unbroken formation as they advance. Caractacus, returning to the sally-port, hears the noise of chariots racing towards him: it is the Belgic section of chariotry, now also in flight. He tries to halt them, but they refuse to listen to him; and realizing that the battle is lost he turns his own chariot and blows two long blasts on his ivory horn as signal for a general retreat. He hopes to overtake the fugitives and rally them a few miles farther along the Colchester road. He hears a sound of Roman trumpets, and as his chariot drives clear of the wood on the other side he sees eight battalions of Roman regulars advancing towards it on his right. It is the Guards.

And away on his left he sees elephants and Roman cavalry emerging from the wood and charging towards him. He shouts to his driver to whip on the horses. He escapes.

With Caractacus gone, the battle was over. The Guards cut off the British retreat from the wood and the infantry remaining in it put up little fight. Cavalry were sent down the avenue to capture the fort on the British right, but half-way along it they came across a party of British spearmen: these had the presence of mind to cut the cords, releasing a sort of portcullis which fell squarely across the avenue, barring progress. The three avenues were all provided with a series of these portcullises, each connected with stockades on either side, but this was the only one of which use had been made. By the time that the cavalry had demolished this obstacle the retreating British party had released another portcullis and hurried on to warn the garrison of the fort that all was lost. The garrison escaped safely in a westerly direction. The other fort surrendered an hour later; by which time Cattigern had been severely wounded and the resistance of his men broken.

We took eight thousand prisoners, and counted four thousand seven hundred corpses on the battle-field. Our own losses were insignificant: three hundred and eighty killed, six hundred wounded, of whom only one hundred and fifty were disabled from further fighting. Our cavalry and elephants were sent ahead in the direction of Colchester, to prevent fugitives from rallying on the road. They overtook Caractacus at Chelmsford, where he was trying to organize the defence of the River Chelmer. The sight of the elephants was enough to send the British scurrying in all directions. Caractacus escaped again. This time he gave up all hope of saving Colchester. With a force of two hundred chariots of his own tribe he turned west and disappeared from the scene. He had gone to throw himself on the protection of his allies, the men of South Wales.

We piled a great trophy on the battle-field, of broken chariots and weapons, and burned it as a thank-offering to Mars. That night we camped on the farther side of the wood. The men had been roaming about in search of plunder. Gold chains and enamelled breastplates and helmets were found in abundance. I had issued strict orders against the violation of captured women—for hundreds of women had been fighting in the wood beside their husbands—and three men of the Fourteenth were duly executed that evening for disobeying me. When night fell I felt the reaction after victory and at supper with my staff was suddenly seized by the most painful attack of stomachic cramp, "the cardiac passion" as they call it, that I have ever experienced. It was like a hundred swords stuck into my vitals at once, and I let out a fearful bellow which made everyone present think that I had been poisoned. Xenophon rushed to my aid and hastily cutting the straps of my corselet with a carving-knife and throwing it aside, he knelt over me and began kneading at my stomach with both hands, while I continued to roar and bellow, unable to stop. He mastered the cramp at last, and had me wrapped in hot blankets and carried away to bed, where I spent one of the wretchedest nights of my life. However, the extraordinary completeness of my victory was the medicine that really cured me. By the time that we reached Colchester, three days later, I was myself again. I travelled on elephant-back like an Indian prince.

Near Colchester the advance-guard of a friendly army met us. It was the Icenians, who had risen in our support on the day that they heard of my arrival at London. Together we invested and stormed the city, which was defended bravely by a few old men and a number of women. I swore honourable alliance there in the name of Rome with the King of the Icenians, the King of East Kent, and the King of East Sussex, in recognition of their assistance in the campaign. The remainder of Caractacus's empire I formally declared a Roman province, under the governorship of Aulus, and presently received the homage of all its petty kings and chiefs, including those Kentish chiefs who had been hiding in the Weald. After this I decided that I had done all that I had come to Britain to do. I said farewell to Aulus and his army and returned to Richborough with the Guards, the elephants and the five hundred volunteers who had sailed with me from Ostia but arrived too late for the battle. We embarked in our transports and crossed without further incident to France. I had been a mere sixteen days in Britain.

My only regret was perhaps rather an ungrateful one. I was with the Ninth throughout the battle and, feeling very courageous at the moment that their two battalions went forward to help the Nubians, I had galloped excitedly ahead of them to join in the fighting. However, I changed my mind: I did not wish to get mixed up with the Nubians, who often in battle mistake friends for foes. I turned Penelope round behind them and pulled up on the flank. There I saw a British chief doubling back between me and the tangle of broken chariots and kicking horses. I drew my sword and spurred after him. I was nearly on him when a big body of chariots swept into view and I had to turn and gallop back. I know now that the chief was Caractacus. To think that I was cheated by a few seconds from a single combat with him! Since I had a horse and a sword and he had neither, I might easily have had the luck to kill him. And if I had done so, what immortal glory I would have won! Only two Roman generals in history have ever killed an enemy commander in single combat, and stripped him of his arms.

# Chapter Twenty-One

A ROMAN general, in order to be granted a full triumph as a reward for victory over his country's enemies, must have fulfilled certain conditions required by ancient custom. In the first place he must have attained consular rank or the rank of first-class magistrate, and be the official Commander-in-Chief of the victorious forces, not an acting-commander or lieutenant: and as Commander-in-Chief he must have personally taken the auspices before battle. Next, he must have been engaged against a foreign enemy, not against rebel citizens; and the war must have been fought not for the recovery of territory that once belonged to Rome, but for the extension of Roman rule over entirely new territory. Next, he must have decisively beaten the enemy in a pitched battle which has ended the campaign; he must have killed at least five thousand of the enemy; and the Roman losses must have been comparatively light. Finally, the victory must have been so complete that he is able to withdraw his victorious troops without prejudice to his conquests and bring them back to Rome to take part in the triumph.

Permission to celebrate a triumph is granted by the Senate, but always after jealous and prolonged deliberation. They usually meet in the Temple of Bellona outside the City to scrutinize the laurel-wreathed dispatch sent in by the general, and if they have reason to suppose that his claims are unfounded or exaggerated they will send for him to substantiate them. If, however, they decide that he has really won a notable victory they proclaim a day of public thanksgiving and ask formal permission from the people of Rome for the victorious army to be led inside the walls for the day of the triumph. The Senate has the discretionary power of relaxing certain of the conditions necessary for a triumph if the victory seems to them of sufficient general merit. That is only just, but I am sorry to record it as my opinion that at least sixty or seventy of the three hundred and fifteen triumphs that have been celebrated since the time of Romulus did not deserve celebration, while, on the other hand, a good many generals have been robbed of well-earned triumphs by the spiteful influence of rivals in the Senate. If, however, a general has been cheated of the honour by enemies or by a mere technicality, he usually celebrates a triumph unofficially on the Alban Mount, outside the City, which the whole City attends, so that it is almost as good as a real triumph; only, it cannot be recorded as such in the City annals nor can his funeral-mask, after his death, be worn with triumphal dress. Perhaps the two most disgraceful triumphs that have been witnessed at Rome were Julius Cæsar's triumph over the sons of Pompey the Great, his relatives, and one celebrated by an ancestor of mine, one Appius Claudius, in spite of the refusal of both the Senate and People to allow him the honour—he induced his sister, a Vestal Virgin, to sit in his triumphal car so that the City officials did not venture to pull him out of it for fear of offending her sanctity.

When I sent in my dispatch and applied for a triumph, it was a foregone conclusion that it would be granted, because nobody would dare oppose my claims, even if they were utterly groundless—as groundless as Caligula's had been when he celebrated his triple triumph over Germany, Britain and Neptune. He had marched a few miles into Germany, met no resistance, fallen a prey to terrors of his imagination and fled in a panic; he had never even crossed the Channel into Britain, nor sent any of his troops there; and as for Neptune, well, the kindest thing to be said about that is that triumphs cannot be awarded for victories, real or supposed, over national Gods. But I was anxious to observe the decencies, and so I stated in my dispatch that the number of Britons killed during my personal conduct of the campaign had been three hundred short of the required figure of five thousand, but that the prisoners were sufficiently numerous, perhaps, to compensate for this shortage, and that the gratifying brevity of our own casualty-list might also weigh with the House, should they consider waiving this condition for once. I undertook, if the triumph were granted, to let six hundred prisoners fight to the death in the Circus, thus bringing the enemy dead up to the five thousand mark. I wrote that I could not return to Rome before March, because Aulus would need the entire expeditionary force with him that winter to accustom the British to our permanent presence in their island; and that even then I could not leave the new province undefended, because hitherto unconquered tribes on the border would probably overrun it. But I could bring back the troops who had been actively engaged in the final battle— namely, the Twentieth Regiment, four battalions of the Fourteenth, two of the Ninth, two of the Second, one of the Eighth and some allied troops—if that was enough to satisfy them. Meanwhile, in accordance with old custom, I would not return to the City (which Vitellius would continue to govern, with their co-operation, as my representative); I would remain in France, with my headquarters at Lyons, hearing appeal cases, settling disputes between tribes or cities, reviewing troops, inspecting defences, auditing departmental accounts and seeing that my order for the total suppression of the Druidical Order was strictly obeyed.

This dispatch was well received and the Senate kindly waived the five-thousand-dead clause and asked the People to vote permission for me to march my army into the City, which the People gladly did. The Senate voted me half a million gold pieces of public money for the celebrations of my triumph, and the date was fixed for New Year's Day, the first of March.

My tour of France was not marked by any event of interest, though I took certain important decisions about the extension of the Roman citizenship. I will not waste time over recording my impressions of the country. Dispatches came from Aulus at regular intervals, reporting the occupation of various Catuvellaunian strong-holds, detailing the distribution of his troops, and sending me for my approval a plan of campaign for the following spring, after the return of the troops from the triumph. I received a great many letters of congratulation from provincial governors, allied kings and cities, and personal friends. Marsus wrote from Antioch that my victory had been most timely. It had caused a great impression in the East, where rumours of the internal decay of Rome and the impending collapse of her empire were being constantly put about by hidden enemies and produced a most disquieting effect on the Syrian provincials. But this was by no means all that Marsus had to tell me. He reported the recent death of the old King of Parthia—the one whom Vitellius had surprised during Caligula's reign, when he was on the point of invading Syria, and forced to give important hostages for future good behaviour—and the accession of his son Gotarzes, an indolent and debauched prince with many enemies among the nobility. He wrote:

"But this Gotarzes has a brother, Bardanes, a most gifted and ambitious prince. I am informed that Bardanes is now on the way to Parthia to dispute the throne with his brother. He has been visiting Alexandria lately, on the pretext of consulting a famous physician there who undertakes to cure deafness—Bardanes is slightly deaf in one ear. But his journey has led him through Jerusalem, and my agents assure me that he went away from King Herod's dominions far richer than he came. With the help of this Jewish gold I expect to see him oust Gotarzes: Parthian nobles can always be bribed. He can count, too, on the unbought assistance of the King of Adiabene—the Assyrian kingdom which, I need hardly remind you, lies across the Tigris River just south of Nineveh—and on the King of Osroëne, in Western Mesopotamia. You will recall that this King of Adiabene recently restored the late King of Parthia to his throne after he had been removed by a conspiracy of nobles, and was rewarded for this service with the Golden Bed and the Upright Tiara. But it will probably be news to you that this important personage is a secret convert to Judaism and that his mother, who was the first of his household to change her religion, is now resident at Jerusalem. She has brought with her five young princes of Adiabene, her grandsons, to be educated in the Jewish language, literature and religion. They have all been circumcised.

"King Herod has now therefore close dealings with the following kings:

"The King of Chalcis,
"The King of Iturea,
"The King of Adiabene,
"The King of Osroëne,
"The King of Lesser Armenia,
"The King of Pontus and Cilicia,
"The King of Commagene and
"The prospective King of Parthia.

"The Crown of Parthia commands, of course, an alliance of a great many other kings of the Middle East—as far as Bactria and the Indian border. King Herod also enjoys the support of Jews throughout the world, not forgetting the

Jews of Alexandria, and of the Edomites and Nabateans, and is now angling for the support of the King of Arabia. The Phœnicians, too, are slowly being won over by his blandishments: only Tyre and Sidon continue cold. He has broken off diplomatic relations with these cities and forbidden his subjects to trade with them under penalty of death. Tyre and Sidon will be forced to come to terms. Their economic prosperity depends on trade with the interior; and, except for the corn which they import from Egypt, and fish, which is often scarce in bad weather, King Herod controls their entire food supply.

"It would be difficult to exaggerate the dangers of the situation and we can all be most thankful that your British victory has been so complete, though I could have wished that the regiments now stationed in Britain were available for hurried transference to the East, where I am pretty sure that they will before long be needed.

"If you are willing to consider, with your usual graciousness and perspicacity, the advice that I have to offer you in these difficult circumstances, it is this: I suggest that you immediately restore tō his throne Mithridates, the ex-King of Armenia, who is at present living at Rome. It was, if I may say so without offence, a lamentable mistake on the part of your uncle, the Emperor Tiberius Cæsar, to allow the late King of Parthia to unite the Armenian crown with his own, and not immediately to avenge with force of arms that most insulting letter the King wrote to him. If, therefore, you send Mithridates to me at Antioch at once, I undertake to put him back on the throne of Armenia while Bardanes and Gotarzes are disputing the throne of Parthia. The present Governor of Armenia can be bribed not to oppose us too strongly and Mithridates is a by no means incapable prince and a great admirer of Roman institutions. His brother, too, is King of Georgia and commands quite a strong army of Caucasian mountaineers. I can get in touch with him and arrange for an invasion of Armenia from the north while we march up from the south-west. If we succeed in restoring Mithridates we can have nothing to fear from the Kings of Pontus and Lesser Armenia, whose kingdoms will be cut off from Parthia by Armenia; nor from the King of Commagene (whose son has now been betrothed to King Herod's daughter Drusilla), because his kingdom lies directly between Armenia and my own command. We will, in fact, hold the north, and when Bardanes has fought his civil war and ousted King Gotarzes (as I think he is bound to do) his next expedition will have to be against Mithridates in Armenia. The recovery of Armenia will be no easy matter if we give Mithridates adequate support, and Bardanes's southern and eastern allies will not easily be persuaded to help him in so distant and hazardous an expedition. And, until he recovers Armenia, Bardanes will be in no position to further any of the imperialistic schemes that I confidently believe King Herod Agrippa to be planning. This is the first definite accusation I have made against the loyalty of your supposed friend and ally, and I know the great danger I am running of incurring your displeasure by making it. But I put the safety of Rome before my own safety and I would consider myself a traitor if I suppressed any of the political information that comes to me, merely because it makes unsavoury reading in an official dispatch. Having said so much, I will further make so bold as to suggest that King Herod's son, Herod Agrippa the Younger, be invited back to Rome to attend your triumph. He can then, if necessary, be detained indefinitely on some pretext, and may prove a useful hostage for his father's good behaviour."

I had two courses before me. The first was to summon Herod to Lyons at once to answer Marsus's charges, in which, in spite of my bias in Herod's favour, I could not help believing. If guilty, he would refuse to come and that would mean an immediate war, for which I was unprepared. The second course was to play for time and give no indication of my mistrust; but the danger of that was that Herod might benefit from the delay more than I would. If I decided on this course I would certainly take Marsus's advice about Armenia; but was Marsus right in reckoning on a friendly Armenia as sufficient protection against the enormously powerful Eastern confederation that Herod seemed to have built up?

Letters came from Herod. In the first he answered my questions about the prophesied king. In the second he congratulated me most warmly on my victories and, curiously enough, asked permission to send his son to Rome to witness my triumph; he hoped that I would not mind the lad enjoying a few months' holiday in Rome before returning to Palestine in the summer to assist him at the great feast in honour of my birthday, which he hoped to celebrate at Cæsarea. The letter about the prophesied king ran as follows:

"Yes, my dear Marmoset, as a child I used to hear plenty of mystical talk about this Anointed One, or Messiah as they call him in our language, and it still goes on in theological circles at Jerusalem; but I never paid much attention to it, until now, when your request for a report on the prophecy has led me to investigate the matter seriously. At your suggestion I consulted our worthy friend Philo, who was in Jerusalem paying some vow or other which he had sworn to our God—he is always either vowing or paying vows. Philo, you know, has made a daring and I should say a most absurd identification of the Deity ideally conceived by Plato and his philosophical crew—Unchanging and Unyielding and Eternal and Uncompounded Intellectual Perfection, exalted above all predicates—with our passionate

361

tribal God at Jerusalem. I suppose that he found the Platonic Deity too cold and abstract, and wanted to infuse some life into him, at the same time glorifying his own God by extending his rule over the universe. At all events, I asked Philo what the sacred Scriptures had to say about this enigmatic Person. Philo grew very serious at once and assured me that the whole hope of our race is centred on the coming of the Messiah. He gave me the following particulars:

"This Messiah is a king who shall come to redeem Israel from its sins, and as the human representative of our Jewish God. He is not necessarily a great conqueror, though he must release the Jews from any foreign yoke which interferes with their freedom of worship. This prophecy was first made, according to Philo, shortly after the Jews had been led out of Egypt by their law-giver Moses in the days of Rameses II. In a book which we call the Book of Numbers, ascribed to Moses, he is spoken of as a 'Star and Sceptre out of Jacob.' In later sacred writings, dating from about the time that Rome was founded, he is spoken of as a man who shall gather the lost sheep of Israel from many quarters and restore them to their native fold in Palestine —for already by that time the Jews had become scattered in colonies all over the Near and Middle East. Some had left Palestine voluntarily as traders and settlers, some had been carried away as captives. Philo says that Jewish theologians have never been able to decide whether this Messiah is a real or a symbolic figure. At the time of the heroic Maccabees (my mother's priestly ancestors) he was regarded as only a symbol. At other times he has not only been regarded as a real person, but has even been popularly identified with non-Jewish deliverers of the race, such as Cyrus the Persian, and even Pompey, who put an end to the Hasmonean oppression. Philo declares that both these views are wrong: the Messiah is yet to come and he must be a Jew, in direct line from our King David whose son Solomon built the Temple at Jerusalem, and must be born in a village called Bethlehem, and must gather Israel together and cleanse it from its sins by a most thorough-going ritual of confession, repentance and placation of the offended Deity. Jerusalem is to be sanctified down to 'the very cooking-pots and the bells on the horses' necks.' Philo even knows the date of the Messiah's birth, namely, five thousand five hundred years from that of the earliest ancestor of the Jewish race: but opinions differ as to when *he* lived, so that is not much help.

"The Scriptures are not entirely consistent in their various foreshadowings of this Messiah. He is sometimes represented as an angry powerful warrior dressed in royal purple and bathed in the blood of his country's foes, and sometimes as a meek, sorrowful outcast, a sort of poor prophet preaching repentance and brotherly love. Philo says, however, that the most trustworthy and clearest statement made about him occurs in a book called *The Psalter of Solomon*. It is in the form of a prayer:

"'Behold, O Lord, and raise up their king, the Son of David, at the time thou hast appointed, to reign over Israel Thy servant; and gird him with strength to crush unjust rulers; to cleanse Jerusalem from the heathen that tread it under foot, to cast out sinners from Thy inheritance; to break the pride of sinners and all their strength as potter's vessels with a rod of iron; to destroy the lawless nations with the words of his mouth; to gather a holy nation and lead them in righteousness. The heathen nations shall serve under his yoke; he shall glorify the Lord before all the earth and cleanse Jerusalem in holiness, as in the beginning. From the ends of the earth all nations shall come to see his glory and bring the weary sons of Zion as gifts; to see the glory of the Lord with which God hath crowned him, for he is over them a righteous King taught of God. In his days there

363

shall be no unrighteousness in their midst; for they are all holy and their king the Anointed of the Lord.'

"This Messiah legend has naturally spread through the East in different fantastic forms, losing its Jewish setting in the process. The version you quote about the King's painful death, deserted by his friends, who afterwards drink his blood, is not Jewish, but I think Syrian. And in the Jewish version he is only a king of the Jews and head of a great religious confederation centred at Jerusalem, not the God himself. He could not usurp godhead, because the Jews are the most obstinate monotheists in the world.

"You ask whether anyone now identifies himself with the Messiah? I have met nobody lately who does so. The last one that I remember was a man called Joshua ben Joseph, a native of Galilee. When I was magistrate of Tiberias (under my uncle Antipas) he had a considerable following among the uneducated and used to preach to large crowds at the lake-side. He was a man of striking appearance and, though his father was only an artisan, claimed descent from David. I have heard that there was a scandal connected with his birth: one Panthera, a Greek soldier in my grandfather's guard, was supposed to have seduced his mother, who was a tapestry worker for the Temple. This Joshua had been an infant prodigy (a common phenomenon among Jews) and knew the Scriptures better than most doctors of divinity. He used to brood about religion and perhaps there was foundation to the story of his Greek parentage, because he found Judaism a very irksome creed (as no true Jew does) and began to criticize it as inadequate for ordinary human needs. He attempted in a naïve manner to do what Philo has since done so elaborately—to reconcile Judaic revelational literature with Greek philosophy. It reminds me of what Horace wrote in his *Art of Poetry* about a painter making a lovely woman end in an ugly fish-tail:

"If there is one thing that I hate more than Orientalized Greek or Roman, it is a Græco-Romanized Oriental, or any attempt at a fusion of cultures. This is written against myself, but I mean it. Your mother never succeeded in making a good Roman of me; she merely spoilt a good Oriental.

"Well, Joshua ben Joseph (or, ben Panthera), had a taste for Greek philosophy. He was handicapped, however, by not being a Greek scholar. And he had to work hard at his trade—he was a joiner—to make his living. However, he made the acquaintance of a man called James, a fisherman with literary tastes who had attended lectures at the Epicurean University at Gadara which lies at the other side of the lake from Tiberias. Gadara was rather a rundown place by then, though in its prime it had produced four great men: Meleager the poet, Mnasalcus the philosopher, Theodorus the rhetorician, under whom your uncle Tiberius studied, and Philo the mathematician who worked out the proportion of the circumference of a circle to its diameter as far as the ten-thousandth decimal place. At any rate, Joshua used James's philosophical gleanings from Gadara and his own knowledge of the Jewish scriptures to compose a synthetic religion of his own. But a religion without authority is nothing, so secretly at first and then publicly he identified himself with the Messiah and spoke (as Moses had once spoken) as if from the mouth of God. He had a most ingenious mind and used to deliver his messages in the form of simple fables with moral endings. He also claimed to perform supernatural cures and miracles. He made himself very troublesome to the Jewish religious authorities, whom he accused of combining strict observance of the Law with rapaciousness and insolence towards the poor. There are many good stories told of him. One of his political opponents tried to catch him out once by asking whether it was right for a conscientious Jew to pay the Roman Imperial tax. If he had answered Yes, he would have lost his hold on the nationalists. If he had answered No, he would have made himself liable for arrest by the civil authorities. So he pretended to be quite innocent about the matter and asked to be shown the amount of money due before he would make any answer. They showed him a silver piece and said: 'Look, every householder has to pay this much.' He asked: 'Whose head is this on the coin? I can't read Latin.' They said: 'It's the head of Tiberius Cæsar, of course.' He said: 'Why, if it's Cæsar's coin, pay it to Cæsar. But don't fail to pay God what is due to God.' They also tried to catch him out on points of Jewish law, but he always had chapter and verse ready to justify his teachings. Eventually, however, he compromised himself as a religious heretic, and the end of the story was that our old friend Pontius Pilate, then Governor of Judæa and Samaria, arrested him for creating popular disorders and handed him over for trial by the supreme Jewish religious court at Jerusalem, where he was condemned to death for blasphemy. When I come to think of it he did die the same year as the Goddess Livia, and his followers did desert him, so that much of the prophecy you quote was fulfilled in him. And there are now people who say that he was God and that they saw his soul ascend to Heaven after his death—just like Augustus's and Drusilla's —and claim that he was born at Bethlehem and that he fulfilled all the other Messianic prophecies in one way or another; but I propose to stop this nonsense once and for all. Only three days ago I arrested and executed James, who seems to be the chief intellect of the movement; I hope to recapture and execute another leading fanatic called Simon, arrested at the same time, who somehow escaped from prison.

"The trouble is that though sensible men may 'laugh to view the sight' of a brightly-painted fish-tailed woman, the mob are just as likely as not to gape at her, see her as a sea-goddess, and worship her."

This apparently ingenuous letter contained one detail which convinced me that Herod really thought himself the Messiah, or at least intended soon to use the tremendous power of that name to further his own ambitions. Once he had revealed himself, the Jews would be his to a man: they would flock back to Palestine at his summons from all over the world, and I foresaw that his prestige would soon be so great that the whole of the Semitic race would embrace the new faith and join with him in removing "the stranger and the infidel" from their midst. The conversion of the King of Adiabene and his entire household was a straw showing which way the wind was blowing, and no small straw either, for this king was known as "The King-maker," and was immensely respected in Parthia. In his next letter Marsus further reported the rumoured conversion to Judaism of the King of Commagene, who had been a favourite of Caligula's. (He was sometimes credited with having first persuaded Caligula to rule with Oriental absoluteness; Caligula certainly always used to appeal to him for approval after having perpetrated some particularly bloody and capricious crime.)

The detail which convinced me that Herod intended to proclaim himself Messiah was that in mentioning Bethlehem he had not mentioned the fact that this was his own birthplace, and not, as was usually supposed, Jerusalem. His mother Berenice once told my mother the story with graphic detail. She had been on her way from her husband's estates in Hebron to Jerusalem for her lying-in, when she had been suddenly overtaken by her pains and had an unforgettably unpleasant experience at a village on the road with an avaricious innkeeper and an unskilled midwife. It was only some hours after Herod had been born that it occurred to Berenice to ask the name of the village, which

367

was a very dirty and dilapidated place; and the midwife answered: "Bethlehem, the birthplace of the patriarch Benjamin, and the birthplace of King David, and the place of which the prophet spoke: 'But thou, Bethlehem Ephratah, though thou be little among the thousands of Judah, yet out of thee shall he come forth unto Me that is to be Ruler in Israel.'" Berenice, infuriated by the treatment she had received, exclaimed in ironical tones: "May God Almighty everlastingly bless Bethlehem!" To which the midwife replied approvingly: "That's what visitors always say!" This story appealed very much to my mother, and for some years after that, when she wished to express her contempt for some very overrated place she used to exclaim in imitation of Berenice's voice: "May God Almighty everlastingly bless Bethlehem!" That was how I remembered the name.

As for this Joshua, or Jesus as his Greek followers call him, he is now also claimed as a native of Bethlehem—I cannot say on what foundation, because Bethlehem is not in Galilee—and his cult has since spread to Rome and seems to flourish here quite strongly in an underground sort of way. The ceremonies include a love-feast which men and women attend in order to eat, symbolically, the flesh of the Anointed One and drink his blood. I am told that this ceremony is often the occasion for disorderly and hysterical scenes, as is only to be expected when most of its initiates are slaves and men and women of the lowest class. Before they are allowed to sit down they must first confess their sins in nauseating detail to the assembled gathering. This provides a deal of entertainment, a sort of competition in self-abasement. The chief priest of the cult (if I may dignify him with the title) is a Galilean fisherman, that Simon of whom Herod wrote, whose chief claim to the position seems to rest on the fact that he deserted this Joshua, or Jesus, on the day of his arrest, and repudiated his beliefs, but has since sincerely repented. For according to the ethics of this sorry sect the greater the original crime, the greater the forgiveness!

Not being a recognized religion (the better sort of Jews repudiate it strongly), the cult falls under the regulations against drinking clubs and sodalities; and is of the dangerous sort that grows the stronger by prohibition. The chief article in the faith is the absolute equality of man with man in the sight of the Jewish God—with whom this Joshua is now practically identified—and of this God's granting everlasting bliss to sinners on the single condition of their repentance and ackowledgement of his supremacy over all other Gods. Anyone can be enrolled in the cult, irrespective of class, race or character, so people join who cannot hope for admittance to the legitimate mysteries of Isis, Cybele, Apollo and the rest, either because they have never had the necessary social standing, or because they have lost it by some disgrace or crime. At first an initiate had to submit to circumcision, but even this ritual preliminary has now been waived because the sect has broken away so completely from orthodox Judaism that a mere sprinkling of water and the naming of the Messiah is the only initiatory ceremony. The cult has occasionally been known to exercise a perverse fascination on quite well-educated persons. Among the converts is an ex-Governor of Cyprus, one Sergius Paullus; whose delight in the society of street-cleaners, slaves and old-clothes hawkers shows the degrading effect of the cult on civilized manners. He wrote to me resigning his governorship on the ground that he could no longer conscientiously take an oath by the God Augustus, because his allegiance to this new God forbade it. I let him resign, but struck him off the roll. Later, when I questioned him about this new faith, he assured me that it was entirely non-political, that Jesus had been a man of deep wisdom and the most exemplary character, and loyal to Roman rule. He denied that Jesus's teaching was a confused medley of

Greek and Jewish religious commonplaces. He said that it derived from and transcended a disciplined body of moderate Jewish opinion called Rabbinical, which contrasted strongly with the superstitious formalism of the party of scribes (on whose support Herod relied) by laying more emphasis on brotherly love, in the name of God, than on the divine vengeance which awaited those who disobeyed the Law; on the spirit rather than on the letter of the Law.

I paid my vow to Venus as soon as I returned to Italy. In answer to a dream in which she appeared to me and said smilingly, "Claudius, my roof leaks: repair it, please," I rebuilt, on a grand scale too, her famous temple at Mount Eryx in Sicily, which had fallen into disrepair: I provided it with priests of ancient Sicilian family and endowed it with a large yearly income from the Treasury. I also built a handsome shrine to the nymph Egeria in her grove at Aricia, and dedicated in it a golden votive offering—a beautiful female hand snuffing a candle, with the following sentence inscribed on the candle-stick in the Sabine dialect:

*To the swift-flying herald of victory, Egeria, from lame Claudius, in gratitude. Grant that his candle may burn to the socket, giving a clear light, and that the flame of his enemies' candles may suddenly fail and go out.*

# Chapter Twenty-Two

I DULY celebrated my triumph at the New Year. The Senate had been good enough to vote me five further honours. First they had voted me a Civic Crown. This was a golden oak-leaf chaplet, originally only awarded to a soldier who, in battle, went to the rescue of a comrade who had been disarmed and was at the mercy of an opponent, killed the opponent and maintained the ground. The honour was more rarely won than you would suppose; because a necessary witness was the man who had been rescued and whose duty it would be to present the crown to his saviour. It was very difficult to make a Roman soldier confess that he had been at the mercy of an enemy champion and only owed his life to the superior strength and courage of a comrade; he was more likely to complain that his foot had slipped and that he was just about to leap up again and finish off his opponent when this ambitious fellow had officiously broken in and robbed him of his victory. Later the honour was also granted to regimental or army commanders who by their heroism or good generalship saved the lives of troops under their command. I was given the Crown in this sense, and really I think that I deserved it for not listening to the advice given me by my staff. It was inscribed *For saving the Lives of Fellow-Citizens*. You will remember that when I was first proclaimed Emperor the Palace Guard had forced me to wear a similar chaplet, the one with which Caligula had been pleased to honour himself for his German victories. I had no right to it then and was much ashamed of wearing it (though real-

A. D. 44

ly Caligula had had no right to it either), so it was a great pleasure to me now to wear one that was rightfully mine. The second honour was a Naval Crown. This crown, decorated with the beaks of ships, was awarded for gallantry at sea—for example, to a sailor for being the first to board an enemy ship or to an admiral for destroying an enemy fleet. It was voted me because I had risked my life by putting to sea in dangerous weather with the object of reaching Britain as soon as possible. I afterwards hung both these Crowns on the pinnacle over the main entrance to the Palace.

The third honour the Senate gave me was the hereditary title of Britannicus. My little son was now known as Drusus Britannicus, or merely as Britannicus, and I shall henceforward always refer to him by that name. The fourth honour was the erection of two triumphal arches in commemoration of my victory: one at Boulogne, because that had been my base for the expedition, the other at Rome itself on the Flaminian way. They were faced with marble, decorated on both sides with trophies and bas-reliefs illustrative of my victory and surmounted with triumphal chariots in bronze. The fifth honour was a decree making the day of my triumph an annual festival for all time. Besides these five honours there were two complimentary ones awarded Messalina, namely, the right to sit in a front seat in the Theatre with the Vestal Virgins, next to the Consuls, magistrates and foreign ambassadors, and the right to use a covered carriage of state. Messalina had now been voted every one of the honours awarded my grandmother Livia in her lifetime, but I still opposed the granting to her of the title Augusta.

The sun consented to shine brightly for the day of triumph, after several days of unsettled weather, and the ward-masters and other officials had seen to it that Rome was looking as fresh and gay as so venerable and dignified a city could possibly look. The fronts of all the temples and houses had been scoured, the streets were swept as clean as the floor of the Senate House, flowers and bright objects decorated every window, and tables heaped with food were set outside every door. The temples were all thrown open, the shrines and statues were garlanded, incense burnt on every altar. The whole population, too, was dressed in its best clothes.

I had not yet entered the City, having spent the night at the Guards Camp. At dawn I ordered a general parade there of the troops who were to take part in the triumph and distributed the bounty-money that I calculated was due to them from the sale of the spoil we had taken at London and Colchester and elsewhere, and from the sale of prisoners. This money amounted to thirty gold pieces for every private soldier and proportionately more for the higher ranks. I had already sent bounty-money on the same scale to the soldiers in Britain who could not be spared to return for the triumph. At the same time I awarded decorations: neck-chains for distinguished conduct on the field, to the number of one thousand; four hundred frontlets (gold medallions in the shape of the forehead-amulets of horses) reserved for gallant cavalry-men or for infantry soldiers who had succeeded in killing an enemy cavalry-man or charioteer; forty massive gold bracelets given in recompense for outstanding valour—when awarding these I read out an account of each of the feats which had earned them; six olive garlands conferred on men who had contributed to the victory, though not actually present at it (the commander of the base camp and the admiral commanding the fleet were among those who won this honour); three Rampart Crowns, for being the first man over the stockade into an enemy's camp; and one Untipped Spear—Posides's—which was granted, like the Civic Crown, for saving life, and which he had earned ten times over.

The Senate, on my recommendation, had voted triumphal ornaments to all men of senatorial rank who had taken part in the campaign—that is to say, to all regimental commanders and senior staff-officers. It was a pity that Aulus could not be spared, or Vespasian, but all the others had come. Hosidius Geta and his brother Lusius Geta, who had commanded the eight Guards Battalions in Britain, were both honoured: I think that this was the first time in Roman history that two brothers have worn triumphal dress on the same day. Lusius Geta became my new Guards Commander, or rather he held the appointment jointly with a man named Crispinus whom Vitellius had appointed temporarily in my absence. For Justus, the former commander, was dead. Messalina had sent an urgent message which reached me on the eve of the battle of Brentwood to tell me that Justus had been sounding various Guards officers as to their willingness to stand by him in an armed revolt. Trusting Messalina completely and not daring to take any risks, I sent an immediate order for his execution. It was years before I learned the true facts: that Justus had got wind of what was going on in Messalina's wing at the Palace in my absence and asked one of his colonels what he had better do about it—whether he ought to write to me at once, or wait for my return. The colonel was one of Messalina's confidants, so he advised Justus to wait, for fear that the bad news might distract me from my military duties; and then went straight to Messalina. Justus's death, the cause of which was soon known throughout the City, was a general warning not to let me into a secret which finally everyone but myself knew—even my enemies in Britain and Parthia, if you can believe it! Messalina had been going from bad to worse. But I shall not record her behaviour in detail here because I was, so far, wholly ignorant of it. She had come to Genoa to meet me on my return from France and the warmth of her greeting was one of the things that was now making me feel so happy.

In six months, too, little Britannicus and his baby sister had grown out of all recognition and were such beautiful children.

You must realize how much this day meant for me. There is nothing in this world, I suppose, so glorious as a Roman triumph. It is not like a triumph celebrated by some barbarous monarch over a rival king whom he has subdued: it is an honour conferred by a free people on one of their own number for a great service he has rendered them. I knew that I had earned it fairly and that I had finally disproved the ill opinion that my family had always had of me as a useless person, born under the wrath of Heaven, an imbecile, a weakling, a disgrace to my glorious ancestors. Asleep in the Guards Camp that night I had dreamed that my brother Germanicus came up to me and embraced me and said in that grave voice of his: "Dear brother, you have done excellently well, better, I confess, than I ever thought you would do. You have restored the honour of Roman arms." When I woke in the early morning I decided to abrogate the law that Augustus had made limiting triumphs to the Emperor himself and his sons or grandchildren. If Aulus continued the campaign in Britain and succeeded in the task I had given him of permanently subduing the whole southern part of the island I should persuade the Senate to give him a triumph of his own. In my opinion, it seemed that to be the only man who could legally be awarded a triumph rather detracted from the glory than added to it. Augustus's enactment had been designed to keep his generals from inciting border tribes to warfare in the hope of winning a triumph over them; but surely, I argued, there were other ways of restraining generals than making the triumph, which had once been open to everyone, a mere family rite of the Cæsars.

The decoration-ceremony over, I gave three audiences: the first to all governors of provinces, for whose temporary attendance at Rome I had asked the Senate's permission, the next to the ambassadors sent me from allied kings, and the last to the exiles. For I had won the Senate's permission for the return from their places of banishment of all exiles, but only for the duration of the triumphal festivities. This last audience was rather a sad one for me, because many of them looked very feeble and ill and they all begged piteously to have their sentences revised. I told them not to despair, for I would personally review every case and if I decided that it was to the public interest for the sentence to be cancelled or mitigated I would intercede with the Senate on their behalf. This I afterwards did, and many of those whose recall I could not recommend were at least allowed a change of their place of banishment—in every case a change for the better. I offered Seneca a change, but he refused it, replying that while he lay under Cæsar's displeasure he could not desire any amelioration of his lot; the perennial frost that (according to the fables of travellers) bound the land of the brutish Finns, the perpetual heat that scorched the sands of the deserts beyond Atlas (where Cæsar's victorious armies had penetrated in defiance of Nature and in expansion of the map of the known world), the fever-ridden marshy estuaries of Britain now subjugated, no less than the fertile plains and valleys of that distant and famous island, by Cæsar's outstanding military genius, nay, even the pestiferous climate of Corsica where the unfortunate Seneca, author of this memorial, had now languished for two years—or was it two centuries?— this frost, this fire, this damp, this Corsican three-in-one medley of damp, fire and frost, would pass as evils scarcely noticed by the exile, Stoic-minded, whose one thought was to bear in patience the crushing weight of the disgrace under which he laboured, and make himself worthy of Cæsar's pardon, should this supreme gift ever, beyond expectation, be bestowed upon him. I was quite ready to send him to his native Spain, as his friend my secretary Polybius pleaded for him, but if he himself insisted on Corsica, why, Corsica it must be. Narcissus learned from the harbour officials at Ostia that among the mementoes of his visit to Rome this brave Stoic took back in his luggage gem-studded golden drinking-cups, down pillows, Indian spices, costly unguents, tables and couches of the fragrant sandarach-wood from Africa, inlaid with ivory, pictures of a sort that would have delighted Tiberius, quantities of vintage Falernian and (though this falls into a somewhat different category from the rest) a complete set of my published works.

At ten o'clock it was time to be on our way. The procession entered the City from the north-east by the Triumphal Gate and passed along the Sacred Way. Its order was as follows. First came the Senate, on foot, in its best robes, headed by the magistrates. Next, a picked body of trumpeters trained to blow triumphant marching tunes like one man. The trumpets were to call attention to the spoils, which then followed on a train of decorated wagons drawn by mules and escorted by the Germans of the Household Battalion dressed in the Imperial livery. These spoils were heaps of gold and silver coin, weapons, armour, horse-furniture, jewels and gold ornaments, ingots of tin and lead, rich drinking-vessels, decorated bronze buckets and other furniture from Cymbeline's palace at Colchester, numerous examples of exquisite North-British enamel work, carved and painted wooden totem-poles, necklaces of jet and amber and pearl, feather head-dresses, embroidered Druidical robes, carved coracle paddles and countless other beautiful, valuable or strange objects. Behind these wagons came twelve captured British chariots, the finest we could choose, drawn by well-matched ponies. To each of these was fixed a placard, on poles above the head of the driver, giving the name of one of the twelve conquered British

377

tribes. Next came more wagons, drawn by horses, containing models in painted wood or clay of the towns and forts we had captured, and groups of living statuary representing the yielding of various river gods to our troops, each group being backed by a huge canvas-picture of the engagement. Last of this series was a model of the famous stone-temple of the Sun God of which I have already spoken.

After these came a body of flute-players playing soft music. They introduced the white bulls that came along behind, under charge of the priests of Jove, roaring angrily and causing a lot of trouble. Their horns were gilded and they wore red fillets and garlands to show that they were destined for sacrifice. The priests carried pole-axes and knives. The acolytes of Jove followed, with golden dishes and other holy instruments. Next came an interesting exhibit—a live walrus. This bull-like seal with great ivory tusks was captured asleep on a beach by the guard of our base camp. The walrus was followed by British wild cattle and deer, the skeleton of a stranded whale, and a transparent-sided tank full of beavers. After this, the arms and insignia of the captured chiefs, and then the chiefs themselves, with all members of their families that had fallen into our hands, followed by all the inferior captives marching in fetters. I was sorry not to have Caractacus in the procession, but Cattigern was there and his wife, and the wife and children of Togodumnus, and an infant son of Caractacus, and thirty chiefs of importance.

After these came a company of public slaves, marching two and two, carrying on cushions the complimentary golden crowns which had been sent me by allied kings and states in token of grateful respect. Next came twenty-four yeomen, dressed in purple, each with an axe tied in a bundle of rods, the axes crowned with laurel. Then came a four-horse chariot which had been built at the order of

378

the Senate, of silver and ebony: except for its traditionally peculiar shape and for the embossed scenes on its sides, which represented two battles and a storm at sea, it was not unlike the chariot which I had broken up in the Goldsmiths' Street as being too luxurious. It was drawn by four white horses and in it rode the author of this history—not "Clau-Clau-Claudius," or "Claudius the Idiot" or "That Claudius" or "Claudius the Stammerer" or even "Poor Uncle Claudius" but the victorious and triumphant Tiberius Claudius Drusus Nero Cæsar Augustus Germanicus Britannicus, Emperor, Father of the Country, High Pontiff, Protector of the People for the fourth year in succession, three times Consul, who had been awarded the Civic and Naval Crowns, triumphal ornaments on three previous occasions and other lesser honours, civil and military, too numerous to mention. This exalted and happy personage was attired in a gold-embroidered robe and flowered tunic and bore in his right hand, which was trembling a little, a laurel bough, and in his left an ivory sceptre surmounted with a golden bird. A garland of Delphic laurel shaded his brows and, in revival of an ancient custom, his face, arms, neck and legs (as much of his body as showed) were painted bright red. In the Victor's chariot rode his little son Britannicus, shouting and clapping his hands, his friend Vitellius, wearing the Olive Crown, who had ruled the State in the Victor's absence, his infant daughter Octavia, held in the arms of young Silanus, who had been chosen as her future husband and who in company with young Pompey, married to the Victor's daughter Antonia, had brought the Senate the laurel-wreathed dispatch. Silanus had been voted triumphal dress and so had young Pompey, who also rode in this chariot and held Britannicus on his knee. Beside the chariot rode young Pompey's father, Crassus Frugi, who had now worn triumphal dress twice, the first time having been after Galba's defeat of the Chattians. And we must not forget the public slave who stood in the chariot holding over the Victor's head a golden Etruscan crown ornamented with jewels, the gift of the Roman people. It was his duty to whisper in the Victor's ear every now and then the ancient formula, "Look behind thee: remember thyself mortal!"—a warning that the Gods would be jealous of the Victor if he bore himself too divinely, and would not fail to humble him. And to avert the evil eye of spectators a phallic charm, a little bell, and a scourge were fastened to the dash-board of the chariot.

Next came Messalina, the Victor's wife, in her carriage of state. Next, walking on foot, the commanders who had been awarded triumphal dress. Then the winners of the Olive Crown. Then the colonels, captains, sergeants and other ranks who had been decorated for valour. Then the elephants. Then the camels, yoked two and two and drawing carriages on which were mounted the six thunder-and-lightning machines of Caligula's invention, which had been put to such apt use by Posides. Then came the Heron King on his stilts, a golden bracelet twisted about his neck. I am told that, after myself, the Heron King earned more cheers than anyone. After him walked Posides with his Untipped Spear, and the Spanish oculist, wearing a gown, for he had been rewarded with the Roman citizenship. Then came the Roman cavalry, and then the infantry in marching order, their weapons adorned with laurel. The younger soldiers were shouting "Io Triumphe!" and singing hymns of victory, but the veterans exercised the right of free speech which was theirs for the day, indulging in sarcastic ribaldry at the Victor's expense. The veterans of the Twentieth had composed a fine song for the occasion:

Claudius was a famous scholar,
Claudius shed less blood than ink.

When he came to fight the Britons
  From the fray he did not shrink,
But the weapons of his choice were
  Rope and stilts and camel stink.

                    O, O, Oh!


Rope and stilts and stink of camel
  Made the British army shake.
Off they ran with yells of horror
  And their cries the dead would wake—
Cries as loud as Claudius utters
  When he's got the stomach-ache.

                    O, O, Oh!


I am told that at the tail of this column there were bawdy
songs sung about Messalina, but I did not hear them where
I was; indeed, if they had been sung by the yeomen walking just ahead of me I should not have heard them, the
crowd was raising such a tremendous din. After the infantry came detachments of auxiliaries, headed by the Balearics and Nubians.

That ended the procession proper, but it was followed
by a laughing and cheering rabble giving a mock triumph
to Baba, the clown of Alexandria, who had come to Rome
to improve his fortunes. He rode in a public dung-cart, to
which had been yoked in a row a goat, a sheep, a pig and
a fox. He was painted blue, with British woad, and dressed
in a fantastic parody of triumphal dress. His cloak was a
patchwork quilt and his tunic an old sack trimmed with
dirty coloured ribbons. His sceptre was a cabbage-stick with
a dead bat tied to the end of it with a string, and his laurel
branch was a thistle. Our most famous native-born clown,
Augurinus, had recently consented to share the government
of the Society of Vagabonds with Baba. Baba was held to resemble me closely and therefore always played the part of

381

Cæsar in the theatricals that the two of them were constantly giving in the back streets of the City. Augurinus played the part of Vitellius, or a Consul of the year, or a Colonel of the Guards, or one of my ministers, according to circumstances. He had a very lively gift for parody. On this particular occasion he represented the slave who held the crown over Baba (an inverted chamber-pot into which, every now and then, Baba's head disappeared) and kept tickling him with a cock's feather. Baba's sack-tunic was torn behind and disclosed Baba's rump, painted blue with bold red markings to make it look like a grinning human face. Baba's hands trembled madly the whole time and he jerked his head about in caricature of my nervous tic, rolling his eyes, and whenever Augurinus molested him struck back with the thistle or the dead bat. In another dung-cart behind, under a tattered hood, reclined an enormous naked negress with a brass ring in her nose, nursing a little pink pig. The spoils of this rival triumph were displayed on handcarts wheeled by ragged hawkers—kitchen refuse, broken bedsteads, filthy mattresses, rusty iron, cracked cooking-pots, and all sorts of mouldy lumber—and the prisoners were dwarfs, fat men, thin men, albinos, cripples, blind men, hydrocephalitics and men suffering from dreadful diseases or chosen for their surprising ugliness. The rest of the procession was in keeping: I am told that the models and pictures illustrating Baba's victories were the funniest things, in a dirty way, ever seen at Rome.

When we came to the Capitoline Hill, I dismounted and went through a performance which custom demanded but which I found a great physical strain: I ascended the steps of the Temple of Jove humbly kneeling on my knees. Young Pompey and Silanus supported me on either side. At this point it was the custom to lead aside the captured enemy chiefs and execute them in the prison adjoining the temple. This custom was the survival of an ancient rite of human sacrifice in thanksgiving for victory. I dispensed with it on grounds of public policy: I decided to keep these chiefs alive at Rome in order to give others in Britain who were still holding out against us a demonstration of clemency. The Britons themselves sacrificed war prisoners, but it would be absurd to commemorate our intention of civilizing their island with an act of primitive barbarism. I would grant these chiefs and their families small pensions from the public funds and encourage them to become Romanized, so that later when regiments of British auxiliaries were formed there would be officers to command them capable of acting in friendly co-operation with our own forces.

Though I failed to sacrifice the chiefs to Jove I did not at any rate fail to sacrifice the white bulls, or to give the God an offering from the spoils (the pick of the golden ornaments from Cymbeline's palace), or to place in the lap of his sacred image the laurel-crown from my brow. Then I and my companions in triumph, and Messalina, were entertained by the college of the Priests of Jove to a public banquet while the troops dispersed and were entertained by the City. A house whose table was not honoured by the presence of at least one triumphant hero was an unlucky house indeed. I had heard unofficially, the night before, that the Twentieth were planning another drunken orgy like the one in which they had taken part during Caligula's triumph: they intended to launch an assault on the Goldsmiths' Street and if they found the doors of the shops barred they would use fire or battering-rams. I thought at first of defending the street with a corps of Watchmen, but that would only have meant bloodshed, so I had the better idea of filling the flasks of all the troops with a free wine-ration with which to drink my health. The flasks were filled just before the procession started and my orders were not to drink until the trumpets gave them the signal that the sacrifice had been duly made. It was all good wine, but what I gave the Twentieth was heavily doctored with poppy-seed. So they drank my health and that put them so soundly to sleep that by the time they woke up the triumph was over: one man, I regret to say, never woke up. But at least there was no serious disturbance of the peace that day.

In the evening I was guided home to the Palace by a long torchlight procession and the corps of flute-players, and followed by enormous crowds of cheering and singing citizens. I was tired out and after washing off my red paint went straight to bed, but the festivities continued all night and would not let me sleep. At midnight I rose and with only Narcissus and Pallas as my companions went out into the streets. I was disguised as an ordinary citizen in a plain white gown. I wanted to hear what people really thought of me. We mixed with the crowd. The steps of the Temple of Castor and Pollux were dotted with groups of people resting and talking, and here we found seats. Everyone addressed everyone else without ceremony. I was glad that free speech had returned to Rome at last, after its long suppression by Tiberius and Caligula, even though some of the things I heard did not altogether please me. The general opinion seemed to be that it had been a very fine triumph but that it would have been still finer if I had distributed money to the citizens as well as to the soldiers, and increased the corn-ration. (Corn had been scarce that winter again, through no fault of mine.) I was anxious to hear what a battle-scarred captain of the Fourteenth sitting near us had to say: he was with a brother whom he had apparently not seen for sixteen years. At first he would not talk about the battle, though his brother pressed him to do so, and would only discuss Britain as a military station: he thought that with luck he could count on very pretty pickings. Soon he would be able to retire, he hoped, with the rank of knight: he had made quite a packet of money in the last ten years by selling exemptions from duty to the men of his company, and "on the Rhine one doesn't get a chance of spending much money—it's not like at Rome." But in the end he said: "Frankly speaking, we officers of the Fourteenth didn't think much of the Brentwood fighting. The Emperor made it too easy for us. Wonderfully clever man, the Emperor. One of these strategists. Gets it all out of books. That trip-rope, now, that was a typical stratagem. And that great bird, flapping its wings and making weird sounds. And getting the camels forward on the flank to scare the enemy's ponies with their stink. A first-class strategist. But strategy isn't what I call soldiering. Old Aulus Plautius was going straight at that central stockade, and be damned to the consequences. Old Aulus is a soldier. He'd have given us a better bloody battle if it had been left to him. We officers of the Fourteenth like a good bloody battle better than a clever bit of strategy. It's what we live for, a bloody battle is, and if we lose heavily, why, that's a soldier's luck and it means promotion for the survivors. No promotion at all in the Fourteenth this time. A couple of corporals killed, that's all. No, he made it too easy. I had a better time than most, of course: I got in among the chariots with my leading platoon and killed a good few British, and I won this chain here, so I can't complain. But speaking for the Regiment as a whole, that battle wasn't up to the standard of the two others we fought before the Emperor came: the Medway fight was a good one, now, nobody will deny that."

An old woman piped up: "Well, Captain, you're very gallant and we're all very grateful and proud of you, I'm sure, but for my part I've two boys serving in the Second, and though I'm disappointed that they didn't get home-leave for to-day, I'm thankful they're alive. Perhaps if your General Aulus had had his way, they'd be lying there on Brentwood Hill for the crows to pick at." An old Frenchman agreed: "For my part, Captain, I wouldn't care how a battle was won, so long as it was well won. I heard two other officers like yourself discussing the battle to-night. And one of them said: 'Yes, a clever bit of strategy, but too clever: smells of the lamp.' What *I* say is, did the Emperor win a splendid victory or did he not? He did. Then long live the Emperor."

But the Captain said: *"Smells of the lamp,* they said, did they? That was very well put. A strategical victory, but it smelled of the lamp. The Emperor's altogether too clever to rank as a good soldier. For my part, I thank the Gods that I never read a book in my life."

I said shyly to Narcissus as we went home: "You didn't agree with that captain, did you, Narcissus?"

"No, Cæsar," said Narcissus, "did you? But I thought he spoke like a brave and honest man and as he's only a captain, perhaps you ought to be rather pleased than otherwise. You don't want captains in the army who know too much or think too much. And he certainly gave you full credit for the victory, didn't he?"

But I grumbled: "Either I'm an utter imbecile or else I'm altogether too clever."

The triumph lasted for three days. On the second day we had spectacles in the Circus and in the amphitheatre simultaneously. At the first we had chariot-races, ten in all, and athletic contests, and fights between British captives and bears; and boys from Asia Minor performed the national sword-dance. At the other a pageant of the storming and sacking of Colchester and the yielding of the enemy chiefs was re-enacted, and we had a battle between three hundred Catuvellaunians and three hundred Trinovants, chariots as well as infantry. The Catuvellaunians won. On the morning of the third day we had more horse-racing and a battle between Catuvellaunian broad-swordsmen and a company of Numidian spearmen, captured by Geta the year before. The Catuvellaunians won easily. The last performance took place in the Theatre—plays, interludes and acrobatic dancing. Mnester was splendid that day; and the audience made him perform his dance of triumph in *Orestes and Pylades*—he was Pylades—three times over. He refused to take a fourth call. He put his head around the curtain and called archly: "I can't come, my Lords. Orestes and I are in bed together."

Messalina said to me afterwards: "I want you to talk to Mnester very sternly, my dearest husband. He's much too independent for a man of his profession and origin, though he *is* a marvellous actor. During your absence he was most rude to me on two or three occasions. When I asked him to make his company rehearse a favourite ballet of mine for a festival—you know that I have been supervising all the Games and Shows because Vitellius found it too much for him, and then I found that Harpocras, the secretary, had been behaving dishonestly, and we had to have him executed, and Pheronactus whom I chose in his place has been rather slow in learning his business—well, anyhow, it was all very difficult for me, and Mnester instead of making things easier was most dreadfully obstinate. Oh no, he said, he couldn't put on *Ulysses and Circe* because he hadn't anyone capable of playing Circe to his Ulysses, and when I suggested *The Minotaur* he said that Theseus was a part he greatly disliked playing but that on the other hand it would be below his dignity to dance in the less important part of King Minos. That's the sort of obstruction he made all the time. He simply refused to grasp that I was your representative and that he simply *must* do what I told him: but I didn't punish him because I thought you might not wish it. I waited until now."

I called Mnester. "Listen, little Greek," I said. "This is my wife, the Lady Valeria Messalina. The Senate of Rome thinks as highly of her as I do: they have paid her exalted honours. In my absence she has been taking over some of my duties for me and performing them to my entire satisfaction. She now complains that you have been both unco-operative and insolent. Understand this: if the Lady Messa-lina tells you to do anything, however much obedience in the matter may happen to hurt your professional vanity, you must obey her. *Anything,* mark you, little Greek, and no arguments either. Anything and everything."

"I obey, Cæsar," Mnester answered, sinking to the floor with exaggerated docility, "and I beg forgiveness for my stupidity. I did not understand that I was to obey the Lady Messalina in *everything,* only in certain things."

"Well, you understand now."

So that was the end of my triumph. The troops returned to duty in Britain, and I returned to civil dress and duty at Rome. It is probable that it will never happen to anyone again in this world, as it is certain that it had never happened to anyone before, to fight his first battle at the age of fifty-three, never having performed military service of any sort in his youth, win a crushing victory, and never take the field again for the rest of his life.

# Chapter Twenty-Three

I CONTINUED my reforms at Rome, especially doing all I could to create a sense of public responsibility in my subordinates. I appointed the Treasury officials whom I had been training and made their appointments run for three years. I dismissed from the Senatorial Order the Governor of Southern Spain because he could not clear himself of the charges brought against him by the troops serving in Morocco that he had cheated them of half their corn-rations. Other charges of fraud were brought against him too, and he had to pay a hundred thousand gold pieces. He went round to his friends trying to gain their sympathy by telling them that the charges were framed by Posides and Pallas whom he had offended by remembering their slavish birth. But he got little sympathy. One early morning this governor brought all his house-furniture, which made about three hundred wagon-loads of exceptionally valuable pieces, to the public auction-place. This caused a lot of excitement because he had an unrivalled collection of Corinthian vessels. All the dealers and connoisseurs came crowding up, licking their lips and searching round for bargains. "Poor Umbonius is finished," they said. "Now's our chance to pick up cheap the stuff which he refused to part with when we made him really handsome offers for it." But they were disappointed. When the spear was stuck upright in the ground, to show that a public auction was in progress, all that Umbonius sold was his senator's gown. Then he had the spear pulled out again to show that the auction was over, and that night at midnight, when wagons were allowed in the streets again, he took all his stuff back home. He was merely showing everyone that he had plenty of money still and could live very comfortably as a private citizen. However, I was not going to let the insult pass. I put a heavy tax on Corinthian vessels that year, which he could not evade because he had publicly displayed his collection and even listed them on the auction board.

This was the time that I began going closely into the question of new religions and cults. Some new foreign god came to Rome every year to serve the needs of immigrants and in general I had no objection to this. For example, a colony of four hundred Arabian merchants and their families from Yemen, which had settled at Ostia, built a temple there to their tribal gods: it was orderly worship, involving no human sacrifices or other scandals. But what I objected to was disorderly competition between religious cults, their priests and missioners going from house to house in search of converts and modelling their persuasive vocabulary on that of the auctioneer or the brothel-pimp or the vagabond Greek astrologer. The discovery that religion is a marketable commodity like oil, figs or slaves was first made at Rome in late Republican times, and steps had been taken to check such marketing, but without great success. There had been a notable breakdown in religious belief after our conquest of Greece, when Greek philosophy spread to Rome. The philosophers, while not denying the divine, made such a remote abstraction of it that a practical people like the Romans began to argue: "Very well, the Gods are infinitely powerful and wise but also infinitely remote. They deserve our respect and we will honour them most devotedly with temples and sacrifices, but it is clear that we were mistaken in thinking that they were immediate presences and that they would bother to strike individual sinners dead or punish the whole city for one man's crime, or appear in mortal disguise. We have been mistaking poetical fiction for prose reality. We must revise our views."

This decision made an uncomfortable void, for the ordinary common citizen, between himself and those remote ideals of (for example) Power, Intelligence, Beauty and Chastity into which the philosophers had converted Jove, Mercury, Venus and Diana. Some intermediary beings were needed. Into the void came crowding new divine or semidivine characters. These were mostly foreign gods with very definite personalities, who could not easily be philosophized about. They could be summoned by incantation and take on visible human shape. They could appear in the middle of a circle of devotees and talk familiarly to each member of the cult. Occasionally they even had sexual intercourse with women-worshippers. There was one famous scandal in the reign of my uncle Tiberius. A rich knight was in love with a respectable married noblewoman. He tried to bribe her to sleep with him and offered her as much as two thousand five hundred gold pieces for a single tryst. She refused indignantly and thereafter would not even acknowledge his greetings when they met in the street. He knew that she was a devotee of Isis, who had a temple at Rome, and bribed the priests of the Goddess, for five hundred gold pieces, to tell her that the God Anubis was in love with her and wished her to visit him. She was greatly flattered by the message and went to the Temple on the night ordained by Anubis and there in the holiest part, on the very couch of the God, the knight, disguised as the God, enjoyed her until morning. The silly woman could not contain herself for felicity. She told her husband and friends of the signal honour that she had been shown. Most of them believed her. Three days later she met the knight in the street and as usual tried to pass by without answering his greeting. He barred her way and taking her familiarly by the arm said: "My dear, you have saved me two thousand gold pieces. A thrifty woman like you ought to be ashamed to throw good money away. Personally, I care nothing for names. You happen to dislike mine and adore Anubis's, and so the other night I had to be Anubis. But the pleasure was just as great as if I had used my own name. Now, goodbye. I've had what I wanted and I'm satisfied." Never was a woman so thunderstruck and horrified. She ran home to her husband and told him how she had been deceived and abused, and swore that if she was not immediately avenged she would kill herself for shame. The husband, a senator, went to Tiberius; and Tiberius, who thought highly of him, had the Temple of Isis destroyed, her priests crucified and her image thrown into the Tiber. But the knight himself boldly told Tiberius: "You know the power of love. Nothing can withstand it. And what I have done should be a warning to all respectable women not to embrace fancy religions but to stick to the good old Roman Gods." So he was only banished for a few years. Then the husband, having had his married happiness ruined by this affair, began a campaign against all religious charlatans. He brought charges against four Jewish missionaries, who had converted a noblewoman of the Fulvian family to their faith, that they had persuaded her to send votive offerings of gold and purple cloth to the Temple at Jerusalem, but had sold these gifts for their own profit. Tiberius found the men guilty and crucified them. As a warning against similar practices he banished all the Jews in Rome to Sardinia: there were four thousand of them and half that number died of fever within a few months after arriving there. Caligula allowed the Jews to come back again.

Tiberius, you will recall, also expelled all the fortune-tellers and pretended astrologers from Italy. He was a curious compound of atheism and superstition, credulity and scepticism. He once said at a dinner that he regarded the worship of the Gods as useless in view of the certainty of the stars: he believed in predestination. His expulsion of the astrologers was due perhaps to his wishing to enjoy the monopoly of prediction; for Thrasyllus remained with him always. What he did not realize was that though the stars may tell no lies, astrologers, even the best of them, cannot be counted upon either to read their messages with perfect correctness or to report with perfect frankness what they have read. I am neither a sceptic nor particularly superstitious. I love ancient forms and ceremonies and have an inherited belief in the old Roman Gods which I refuse to subject to any philosophical analysis. I think that every nation ought to worship its own gods in its own way (so long as it is a civilized way) and not idly adopt exotic deities. As high priest of Augustus I have had to accept him as a god; and after all the demi-god Romulus was only a poor Roman shepherd to begin with, and probably far less gifted and industrious than Augustus. If I had been a contemporary of Romulus I would probably have laughed at the notion of his ever being paid semi-divine rites. But godhead is, after all, a matter of fact, not a matter of opinion: if a man is generally worshipped as a god then he is a god. And if a god ceases to be worshipped he is nothing. While Caligula was worshipped and believed in as a god he was indeed a supernatural being. Cassius Chærea found it almost impossible to kill him, because there was a certain divine awe about him, the result of the worship offered him from simple hearts, and the conspirators felt it themselves and hung back. Perhaps he would never have succeeded if Caligula had not cursed himself with a divine premonition of assassination.

Augustus is worshipped now with genuine devotion by millions. I myself pray to him with almost as much confidence as I pray to Mars or Venus. But I make a clear distinction between the historical Augustus, of whose weaknesses and misfortunes I am well informed, and the God Augustus, the object of public worship, who has attained power as a deity. What I mean to say is that I cannot deprecate too strongly the wilful assumption by a mortal of divine power; but if he can indeed persuade men to worship him and they worship him genuinely, and there are no portents or other signs of heavenly displeasure at his deification—well, then he is a god, and he must be accepted as such. But the worship of Augustus as a major deity at Rome would never have been possible if it had not been for this gulf which the philosophers had opened between the ordinary man and the traditional gods. For the ordinary Roman citizen, Augustus filled the gap well. He was remembered as a noble and gracious ruler who had given perhaps stronger proofs of his loving care for the City and Empire than the Olympian Gods themselves.

The Augustan cult, however, rather provided a political convenience than satisfied the emotional needs of religiously-minded persons, who preferred to go to Isis or Serapis or Imouthes for an assurance, in the mysteries of these gods, that "God" was more than either a remote ideal of perfection, or the commemorated glory of a deceased hero. To offer an alternative to these Egyptian cults—they did not in my opinion play a wholesome part in our Græco-Roman civilization—I prevailed on our standing commission on foreign religions at Rome, the Board of Fifteen, to allow me to popularize mysteries of a more suitable nature. For example, the cult of Cybele, the Goddess worshipped by our Trojan ancestors and therefore well-suited to serve our own religious needs, had been introduced into Rome some two hundred and fifty years before, in obedience to an oracle; but her mysteries were carried on in private by eunuch priests from Phrygia, for no Roman citizen was allowed to castrate himself in the Goddess's honour. I changed all this: the High Priest of Cybele was now to be a Roman knight, though no eunuch, and citizens of good standing might join in her worship. I also attempted to introduce the Eleusian mysteries to Rome from Greece: the conduct of this famous Attic festival in honour of the Goddess Demeter and her daughter Persephone I need hardly describe, for while Greek survives as a language everyone will know about it. But the nature of the mysteries themselves, of which the festival is only the outer pomp, is by no means a matter of common knowledge and I should much like to tell about them; but because of an oath that I once swore I unfortunately cannot do so. I shall content myself by saying that they are concerned with a revelation of life in the world to come, where happiness will be earned by a virtuous life lived as a mortal. In introducing them at Rome, where I would limit participation in them to senators, knights and substantial citizens, I hoped to supplement the formal worship of the ordinary gods with an obligation to virtue felt from within, not enforced by laws or edicts. Unfortunately my attempt failed. Unfavourable oracles were uttered at all the principal Greek shrines, including Apollo's at Delphi, warning me of the terrible consequences of my "transplanting Eleusis to Rome." Would it be impious to suggest that the Greek Gods were combining to protect the pilgrim-trade, which was now a chief source of their country's income?

I published an edict forbidding the attendance of Roman citizens at Jewish synagogues and expelled from the City a number of the most energetic Jewish missioners. I wrote to tell Herod of my action. He replied that I had done very wisely, and that he would apply the same principle, or, rather, its converse, in his own dominions: he would forbid Greek teachers of philosophy to hold classes in Jewish cities and debar all Jews who attended them elsewhere from worship in the Temple. Neither Herod nor I made any comment, in our letters to each other, on events in Armenia or Parthia, but this is what happened. I had sent King Mithridates to Antioch, where Marsus greeted him with honour and sent him to Armenia with two regular battalions, a siege-train and six battalions of Syrian Greek auxiliaries. He arrived there in March. The Parthian Governor marched out against him and was defeated. This did not mean that Mithridates was immediately left in undisputed possession of his kingdom. Cotys, King of Lesser Armenia, sent armed help to the Parthian Governor and, though his expedition was defeated in its turn, the Parthian garrisons of a number of fortresses refused to surrender and the Roman siege-train had to reduce them one by one. However, Mithridates's brother, the King of Georgia, made his promised invasion from the north and by July the two had joined forces on the River Aras and captured Mufarghin, Ardesh and Erzeroum, the three chief towns of Armenia.

In Parthia Bardanes had soon raised an important army, to which the Kings of Osroëne and Adiabene contributed contingents, and marched against his brother Gotarzes, whose court was then at the city of Ecbatana in the country of the Medes. In a sudden surprise raid at the head of a corps of dromedaries—he covered nearly three hundred miles in two days—Bardanes drove the panic-stricken Gotarzes from the throne and presently received the homage of all the subject kingdoms and cities of the Parthian Empire. The only exception was the city of Seleucia, on the River Tigris, which, revolting some seven years before, had obstinately maintained its independence ever since. It was extremely fortunate for us that Seleucia refused to acknowledge Bardanes's suzerainty, because Bardanes made it a matter of pride to besiege and capture it before turning his attention to more important matters, and Seleucia with its huge walls was no easy place to capture. Though Bardanes held Ctesiphon, the city on the opposite bank of the Tigris, he did not command the river itself, and the strong Seleucian fleet could introduce supplies into the city, bought from friendly Arabian tribes on the western shore of the Persian gulf. So he wasted precious time on the Tigris, and Gotarzes, who had escaped to Bokhara, raised a new army there. The siege of Seleucia continued from December until April, when Bardanes, hearing of Gotarzes's new enterprises, raised it and marched north-east for a thousand miles, through Parthia proper, to the province of Bactria where he eventually encountered Gotarzes. Bardanes's forces were somewhat larger and better equipped than his brother's but the issue of the impending battle was doubtful, and Bardanes saw that even if he were the victor it was likely to be a Pyrrhic victory—he would lose more men than he could afford. So when Gotarzes offered at the last moment to bargain with him, he consented. As a result of their conference Gotarzes made a formal cession of his rights to the throne and in return Bardanes granted him his life, estates on the southern shores of the Caspian Sea and a yearly pension worthy of his rank. Meanwhile pressure was put on Seleucia by the King of Adiabene and other neighbouring rulers to surrender on terms; and by the middle of July Marsus at Antioch knew that Bardanes was now the undisputed sovereign of Parthia and was on his way west with an enormous army. He reported this to me at once, and another uncomfortable piece of news, too, namely, that on the pretence of having been insulted and threatened by the Greek regiments stationed at Cæsarea, Herod had disarmed them and put them to work on road-building and the repairing of the city defences. And this was not all—there had been secret drilling in the desert of large bodies of Jewish volunteers, under the command of members of Herod's bodyguard. Marsus wrote: "In three months the fate of the Roman Empire in the East will be decided one way or the other."

I did all that I could do in the circumstances. I dispatched an immediate order to Eastern governors mobilizing all available forces. I also sent one division of the fleet to

Egypt, to smother the Jewish rising that I expected in Alexandria, and another to Marsus at Antioch. I mobilized forces in Italy and the Tyrol. But nobody but Marsus and myself and my foreign minister Felix, in whom I was forced to confide because he wrote my letters for me, knew what tremendous storm-clouds were blowing up from the East. And we were the only three who ever knew, because, by an extraordinary fate, the storm never burst at all.

I have no dramatic gift, like my brother Germanicus: I am merely a historian and no doubt most people would call me, in general, dull and prosy, but I have come to a point in my story where the record of bare facts unimproved by oratorical beauties should stir the wonder of my readers as greatly as they stirred me at the time. Let me first tell in what an exalted mood King Herod Agrippa came up from Jerusalem to Cæsarea to the festival that had been prepared there in honour of my birthday. He was nursing a secret pride so great that it almost choked him. The foundations of the great edifice that he had so long dreamed of raising, the Empire of the East, were grandly and firmly laid at last. He now had only to speak the word and the walls would (these are the very words he used to his Queen Cypros) "shoot up white and splendid into the dark blue sky, the crystal roof would close over it, and lovely gardens and cool colonnades and lily-ponds would surround it, spreading out as far as the enraptured eye could reach." Inside all would be beryl and opal and sapphire and sardonyx and pure gold and in the mighty Hall of Judgment would blaze a diamond throne, the throne of the Messiah, whom men had hitherto known as Herod Agrippa.

He had already revealed himself, in secret, to the High Priest and the Sanhedrin, and they had all with one accord bowed themselves to the ground and glorified God and acknowledged him as the prophesied Messiah. He could now publicly reveal himself to the Jewish nation, and to the whole world. His word would go out: "The Day of Deliverance is at hand, saith the Anointed of the Lord. Let us break the yoke of the Ungodly." The Jews would rise as one man and cleanse the borders of Israel of the stranger and the infidel. There were now two hundred thousand Jews trained in the use of weapons in Herod's dominions alone, and thousands more in Egypt, Syria and the East; and the Jew fighting in the name of his God, as the history of the Maccabees had shown, is heroic to the point of madness. Never was there a better disciplined race. Nor were arms and armour wanting: Herod had added to the seventy thousand suits of armour that he had found in Antipas's treasury two hundred thousand more, besides those that he had taken from the Greeks. The fortifications of Jerusalem were not complete, but in less than six months the city could be made impregnable. Even after my order to cease work Herod had secretly continued hollowing out great store-chambers under the Temple and driving long tunnels under the walls to points more than a mile outside, so that if ever it came to a siege the garrison could make surprise sorties and attack an investing army from the rear.

He had concluded a secret alliance against Rome with all the neighbouring kingdoms and cities for hundreds of miles around. Only Phœnician Tyre and Sidon had rejected his advances, and that had troubled him because the Phœnicians were a seafaring people and their fleet was needed to protect his coasts; but now they too had joined him. A joint deputation from both cities had approached his chamberlain Blastus and humbly told him that, faced with the necessity of having either Rome or the Jewish nation as their enemies, they had chosen the lesser evil and were now here to sue for his royal master's friendship and forgiveness. Blastus had informed them of Herod's terms, which eventually they accepted. To-day their formal submission would be made. Herod's terms were that they should forswear Ashtaroth and their other deities, accept circumcision and swear perpetual obedience to the God of Israel, and to Herod the Anointed, his representative here on earth.

With that symbolic act would Herod initiate his reign of glory? He would mount on his throne, the rams' horns would blow, and he would command his soldiers to bring before him that statue of the God Augustus which had been set up in the market-place of the town, and my own statue which stood next to it (wearing a fresh garland to-day in honour of my birthday), and he would call out to the multitude: "Thus saith the Anointed of the Lord, hew Me in pieces all graven images that are found in My coasts, grind them to powder; for I am a Jealous God." Then with a hammer he would batter at Augustus's statue and mine, would strike off our heads and lop off our limbs. The people would utter a great shout of joy and he would cry again: "Thus saith the Anointed of the Lord, O my children, the children of Shem, first-born of my servant Noah, cleanse ye this land of the stranger and the infidel, and let the habitations of Japhet be a prey unto you, for the hour of your deliverance is at hand." The news would sweep the country like a fire: "The Anointed has manifested himself and has hewn the images of the Cæsars asunder. Be joyful in the Lord. Let us defile the temples of the heathen, and lead our enemies captive." The Jews would hear of it in Alexandria. They would rise three hundred thousand strong, and seize the city, massacring our small garrison there. Bardanes would hear of it at Nineveh and march on Antioch; and the kings of Commagene, Lesser Armenia and Pontus would join forces with him on the Armenian border. Marsus with his three regular battalions and his two regiments of Syrian Greeks would be overwhelmed. Moreover, Bardanes had pledged himself by an oath sworn in the Temple before the High Priest that if by Herod's aid he won the throne from his brother (as he had now done)

400

he would make a public acknowledgement of his debt to Herod by sending him back all the Jews that could be found in the whole Parthian Empire, together with their families, flocks and possessions, and by swearing eternal friendship with the Jewish people. The scattered sheep of Israel would return at last to the fold. They would be as many in number as the sand on the seashore. They would occupy the cities from which they had expelled the stranger and the infidel, and they would be a united holy people as in the days of Moses, but ruled by a greater one than Moses, a more glorious one than Solomon, namely, by Herod, the Beloved, the Anointed of the Lord.

The festival in pretended honour of my birthday was to take place in the amphitheatre at Cæsarea: and wild beasts and sword-fighters and racing chariots were all ready for the performance that Herod never really intended to take place. The audience was composed partly of Syrian-Greeks, and partly of Jews. They occupied different parts of the amphitheatre. Herod's throne was among his own subjects, and next to it were the seats reserved for distinguished visitors. There were no Romans present: they were all at Antioch celebrating my birthday under the presidency of Marsus. But ambassadors from Arabia were there, and the King of Iturea, and the delegation from Tyre and Sidon, and the mother and sons of the King of Adiabene, and Herod Pollio with his family. The spectators were protected against the fierce August sun by great awnings of white canvas, but over Herod's throne, which was made of silver studded with turquoise, the awnings were purple silk.

The audience flocked in and took their seats, waiting for Herod's entrance. Trumpets sounded and presently he appeared at the southern entrance with all his train and made a stately progress across the arena. The whole audience rose. He had on a royal robe of silver tissue worked over with polished silver roundels that flashed in the sun so brightly that it tried the eyes to look at him. On his head was a golden diadem twinkling with diamonds and in his hand a flashing silver sword. Beside him Cypros walked in royal purple, and behind her came his lovely little daughters dressed in white silk embroidered with arabesques and edged with purple and gold. Herod held his head high as he walked and smiled a kingly greeting to his subjects. He reached his throne and mounted on it. King Herod Pollio, the ambassadors from Arabia, and the King of Iturea left their seats and came to the steps of the throne to greet him. They spoke in Hebrew: "O King, live for ever!" But to the men of Tyre and Sidon this was not enough: they felt constrained to make amends for their discourteous treatment of him in the past. They grovelled before him.

The leader of the Tyrians pleaded in tones of the profoundest humility: "Be merciful to us, Great King, we repent of our ingratitude."

And the leader of the Sidonians: "Hitherto we have reverenced you as a man, but we must now acknowledge that you are superior to mortal nature."

Herod answered: "You are forgiven, Sidon."

The Tyrian exclaimed: "It is the voice of a God, not of a man."

Herod answered: "Tyre, you are forgiven."

He raised his hand to give the signal for the rams' horns to blow, but suddenly let it drop again. For a bird had flown in from the gate by which he had himself entered and was fluttering here and there about the arena. The people watched it and shouts of surprise arose: "Look, an owl! An owl blinded by daylight."

The owl perched on a guy-rope above Herod's left shoulder. He turned and gazed up at it. And not until then did he remember the oath he had sworn at Alexandria thirteen years before in the presence of Alexander the Alabarch and Cypros and his children, the oath to honour the living God and keep His laws so far as in him lay, and the curse that he had called upon himself if he ever wittingly blasphemed from hardness of heart. The first and greatest commandment of God, as spoken through Moses, was: "THOU SHALT HAVE NONE OTHER GODS BUT ME," but when the Tyrian had called him a God, had Herod torn his clothes and fallen on his face to avert Heaven's jealous anger? No, he had smiled at the blasphemer and said, "Tyre, you are forgiven," and the people standing about him had taken up the cry, "A God, not a man." The owl was gazing down in his face. Herod turned pale. The owl hooted five times, then flapped its wings, flew up over the tiers of seats and disappeared beyond.

Herod said to Cypros: "The owl that visited me in the prison yard at Misenum—the same owl," and then a fearful groan burst from his lips and he cried weakly to Helcias, his Master of Horse, successor to Silas: "Carry me out. I am ill. Let my brother the King of Chalcis take over from me the Presidency of the Games."

Cypros clasped Herod to her: "Herod, my king and sweetheart, why do you groan? What ails you?"

Herod replied in a dreadful whisper: "The maggots are already in my flesh."

He was carried out. The rams' horns never blew. The statues were not brought in to be broken. The Jewish soldiers posted outside the theatre, prepared to enter at Herod's signal and begin the massacre of the Greeks, remained at their posts. The Games ended before they had begun. The Jewish multitude raised a great wailing and lamentation, tearing their clothes and throwing dust on their heads. The rumour went round that Herod was dying. He was in frightful pain, but he called his brother Herod, and Helcias, and Thaumastus, and the son of the High Priest, to his bedside at the Palace and said to them: "My friends, all is over now. In five days I shall be dead. I am luckier in this than my grandfather Herod: he lived eighteen months after the pain first fastened on him. I have no complaints to make. It has been a good life. I blame only myself for what has come upon me. For six days I was saluted by the elders of Israel as the Lord's Anointed and on the seventh I foolishly allowed His name to be blasphemed without reproof. Though it was my will to enlarge His Kingdom to the ends of the world, and purify it and bring back the lost tribes, and worship Him all the days of my life, yet because of this one sin I am rejected as my ancestor David was rejected for his sin against Uriah the Hittite. Now Jewry must wait another age until a holier Redeemer comes to accomplish what I have been proved unworthy to accomplish. Tell the confederate kings that the key-stone has fallen from the arch, and that no help can come to them now from the Jewish nation. Tell them that I, Herod, am dying and that I charge them not to make war against Rome without me, because without me they are a rudderless boat, a headless spear, a broken arch. Helcias, see that no violence is done the Greeks. Call in the arms that have been distributed secretly to the Jews and lay them up in the Armoury at Cæsarea Philippi, putting a strong guard over them. Give the Greeks back their arms and recall them to their ordinary duties. My servant Thaumastus, see that my debts are paid in full. My brother Herod, see that my dear wife Cypros and my daughters Drusilla and Mariamne come to no harm, and above all dissuade the nation from any folly. Greet the Jews of Alexandria in my name, and ask them to pardon me for having offered them such high hopes and then utterly disappointed them. Go now, and God be with you. I can speak no more."

The Jews put on sackcloth and lay in their tens of thousands prostrate on the ground about the Palace, even in that terrible heat. Agrippa saw them from the window of the upper room where his bed was laid and began to weep for them. "Poor Jews," he said. "You have waited a thousand years, and must now wait a thousand more, perhaps two thousand, before your day of glory breaks. This has been a false dawn. I deceived myself and I deceived you." He called for pen and paper and wrote me a letter while he still had strength to hold the pen. I have the letter here before me with the others he wrote me and it is pitiful to compare the handwritings—the others boldly and decisively written, line under line as regular as a flight of steps, and this scrawled crookedly, each letter jagged and broken with pain, like confessions written by criminals after they have been put on the rack or flogged with the cat-o'-nine-tails. It is short:

"My last letter: I am dying. My body is full of maggots. Forgive your old friend, the Brigand, who loved you dearly, yet secretly plotted to take the East away from you. Why did I do this? Because Japhet and Shem can live as brothers, but each must rule in his own house. The West would have remained yours from Rhodes to Britain. You would have been able to rid Rome of all the Gods and customs of the East: then and only then could the ancient liberty that you prize so much have returned to you. I have failed. I played too dangerous a game. Marmoset, you are a fool, but I envy you your folly: it is a sane folly. Now I charge you with my dying breath not to revenge yourself on my family. My son Agrippa is innocent: he knows nothing of my ambitions, and neither do my daughters. Cypros did all that she could to dissuade me. The best course for you now is to appear to know nothing. Treat all your Eastern allies as faithful allies still. With Herod gone what are they? Adders, but their fangs are drawn. They trusted me, but they have no trust in the Parthian. As for my dominions, make them a Roman province again, as in the time of Tiberius. Do not injure my honour by returning them to my uncle Antipas. To appoint my son Agrippa as my successor would be dangerous, but honour him in some way or other for my sake. Do not put my dominions under the rule of Syria, under my enemy Marsus. Rule them yourself, Marmoset. Make Felix your governor. Felix is a nobody and will do nothing either wise or foolish. I can write little more. My fingers fail me. I am in torment. Do not weep for me: I have had a glorious life and regret nothing but my one single folly—that I underrated the pride and power and jealousy of the ever-living God of Israel, that I bore myself towards Him like any foolish philosophizing Gadarene Greek. Now farewell for the last time, Tiberius Claudius, my friend whom I love more truly than you ever supposed. Farewell, little Marmoset, my schoolfellow, and trust nobody, for nobody about you is worthy of your trust.

"Your dying friend Herod Agrippa, surnamed

"THE BRIGAND."

Before he died Herod called Helcias and Thaumastus and his brother Herod Pollio to him again and said to them: "One last charge I lay upon you. Go to Silas in prison and tell him that I am dying. Say that *Herod's Evil* is on me. Remind him of the oath that I rashly swore at Alexandria in the house of Alexander the Alabarch. Tell him of the agony in which you see me writhing. Ask him to forgive me, if I have wronged him. Tell him that he may visit me and clasp my hand in friendship once more. Then deal with him as you think best, according to his answer."

They went to the prison, where they found Silas in his cell with his writing-tablet on his knee. At sight of them he flung it face downwards on the floor. Thaumastus said: "Silas, if that tablet is filled with reproaches against your King and master, Herod Agrippa, you do well to throw it down. When we tell you of the condition in which the King is lying you will surely weep. You will wish that you had never spoken a word of reproach against him, or put him to public shame by your unmannerly tongue. He is dying in agony. His disease is *Herod's Evil*, with which in a rash moment he once cursed himself at Alexandria, should he ever offend the Majesty of the Most High."

"I know," said Silas. "I was present when he swore that, and afterwards I warned him . . ."

"Silence for the King's message. The King says: 'Tell Silas of the agony in which you see me writhing, and ask him to forgive me if ever I have wronged him. He is at liberty now to leave his cell and come with you to the Palace. I should be pleased to clasp his hand in friendship once more before I die'."

Silas said sullenly: "You are Jews and I am only a despised Samaritan, so I suppose that I ought to feel honoured by your visit. But I'll tell you this about us Samaritans: we prize free speech and honest dealing above all the opinions, good or bad, that our Jewish neighbours may care to entertain about us. As for my former friend and master King Herod, if he is in torment, then he has only himself to blame for not listening to my advice——"

Helcias turned to King Herod Pollio: "He dies?"

"He dies."

Silas continued calmly: "Three times I as good as saved his life, but this time I can do nothing for him. His fate is in God's hands. And as for friendship, what sort of a friend do you call . . .?"

Helcias seized a javelin from the hand of the soldier who was standing guard at the door and ran Silas through the belly. He made no movement to avoid the thrust.

Silas died at the very moment that, worn out by five days of incessant pain, King Herod Agrippa himself died, in Cypros's arms, to the indescribable grief and horror of the Jewish nation.

By now the whole story was known. Herod's curse seemed to rest on all Jews alike: they were utterly unmanned. The Greeks were elated beyond measure. The regiments re-armed by Helcias at Herod's orders behaved in the most shameless and revolting way. They attacked the Palace and seized Cypros and her daughters, intending to lead them in mockery through the streets of Cæsarea. Cypros snatched a sword from a soldier and killed herself, but her daughters were forced to put on their embroidered dresses and accompany their captors, and even to join in the hymns of thanksgiving sung for their father's death. When the procession ended they were taken to the regimental brothels and subjected there, on the roof-tops, to the grossest outrages and indecencies. And not only in Cæsarea but in the Greek city of Samaria too, public banquets were spread in the squares and the Greeks, with garlands on their heads, and sweet-smelling ointments, ate and drank to their hearts' content, toasting each other and pouring libations to the Ferryman. The Jews did not raise a hand or voice in protest. "Whom God has cursed, is it lawful to succour?" For God's curse was held to descend to a man's children. These princesses were aged only six and ten years when they were so mistreated.

# Chapter Twenty-Four

HEROD's death took place ten years ago to-day and I shall tell as briefly as possible what has happened in the East since then: though the East will now have little interest for my readers, I feel conscientiously bound to leave no loose threads in this story. Marsus, as soon as he heard of Herod's death, came down to Cæsarea and restored order there and in Samaria. He appointed an emergency governor of Herod's dominions: this was Fadus, a Roman knight who had big mercantile interests in Palestine and was married to a Jewish woman. I confirmed this appointment and Fadus acted with the necessary firmness. The arms that had been distributed to the Jews had not all been returned to Helcias: the men of Gilead kept theirs for use against eastern neighbours, the Arabs of Rabboth Ammon. There were also a great many arms not returned by Judæans and Galileans, and robber bands were formed which did the country a great deal of damage. However, Fadus, with the help of Helcias and King Herod Pollio, who were anxious to show their loyalty, arrested the leading Gileadites, disarmed their followers, and then hunted down the robber bands one by one.

The confederate Kings of Pontus, Commagene, Lesser Armenia and Iturea took the advice Herod had sent them by his brother and resumed their allegiance to Rome, excusing themselves to Bardanes for not marching to meet him on the borders of Armenia. Bardanes nevertheless continued his westward progress: he was determined to recover Armenia. Marsus sent him a stern warning from Antioch that war against Armenia would spell war with Rome. The King of Adiabene thereupon told Bardanes that he would not join in the expedition, because his children were at Jerusalem and would be seized as hostages by the Romans. Bardanes declared war on him and was about to invade his territory when he heard that Gotarzes had raised another army and had resumed his pretensions to the Empire. Back he marched again and this time the battle between the brothers was fought out stubbornly on the banks of the River Charinda, near the southern shore of the Caspian Sea. Gotarzes was beaten and fled away to the land of the Dahians, which lies four hundred miles away to the east. Bardanes pursued him; but, after defeating the Dahians, he could persuade his victorious army to march no farther, for he had passed the bounds of the Parthian Empire. He returned in the following year and was on the point of invading Adiabene when he was assassinated by his nobles; they decoyed him into an ambush when he was out hunting. I was relieved when he was out of the way, for he was a man of great gifts and unusual energy.

Meanwhile Marsus's term of office had come to an end and I was glad to have him back at Rome to advise me. I sent out Cassius Longinus to take his place. He was a celebrated jurist, whom I had often consulted on difficult legal points, and a former brother-in-law of my niece Drusilla. When the news of Bardanes's death reached Rome Marsus was not surprised: it seems that he had had a finger in the plot. He now advised me to send out, as a claimant to the Parthian throne, Meherdates, the son of a former King of Parthia, who had been kept as a hostage at Rome for many years now. He said that he could undertake that the nobles who had killed Bardanes would favour Meherdates. However, Gotarzes reappeared with a Dahian army and the assassins of Bardanes were forced to pay him homage, so Meherdates had to remain at Rome until a favourable opportunity presented itself for us to send him east. Marsus thought that this would be soon: Gotarzes was cruel, capricious and cowardly and could not keep the loyalty of his nobles for long. Marsus was right. A secret embassy came two years later from various notables of the Parthian Empire, including the King of Adiabene, asking me to send them Meherdates. I agreed to do so, giving Meherdates a good character. In the presence of the ambassadors I admonished him not to play the tyrant but to regard himself merely in the light of a chief magistrate and his people as his fellow-citizens: justice and clemency had never yet been practised by a Parthian king. I sent him to Antioch, and Cassius Longinus escorted him as far as the River Euphrates and there told him to push on to Parthia at once because the throne was his if he acted with speed and courage. However, the King of Osroëne, a pretended ally who secretly favoured Gotarzes, purposely detained Meherdates at his court with luxurious entertainments and hunting and then advised him to go round by way of Armenia instead of risking a march direct through Mesopotamia. Meherdates took this bad advice, which gave Gotarzes time to make preparations, and lost several months in taking his army through the snow-covered Armenian highlands. On emerging from Armenia he marched down the Tigris and captured Nineveh and other important towns. The King of Adiabene welcomed him on his arrival at the frontier, but immediately summed him up as a weakling and decided to abandon his cause at the first opportunity. So when the armies of Gotarzes and Meherdates met in battle, Meherdates was suddenly deserted by the Kings of Osroëne and Adiabene. He fought bravely and nearly won, for Gotarzes was such a cowardly commander that his generals had to chain him to a tree to stop him from running away. In the end, Meherdates was captured and the gallant Gotarzes sent him back to Cassius in mockery with his ears sliced off. Shortly afterwards Gotarzes died. More recent events in Parthia will certainly not interest my readers more than they have interested me, which is very little indeed.

Mithridates kept his Armenian throne for some years but was finally killed by his nephew, the son of his brother the King of Georgia. That was a curious story. The King of Georgia had been ruling for forty years and his eldest son was tired of waiting for him to die and leave him the kingdom. Knowing his son's character and fearing for his own life, the King advised him to seize the throne of Armenia which was a bigger and richer kingdom than Georgia. The son agreed. The King then made a pretence of quarrelling with him, and he fled to Armenia, to Mithridates's protection, and was kindly received by him and given his daughter in marriage. He immediately busied himself with intrigues against his benefactor. He returned to Georgia, pretending to be reconciled to his father, who then picked a quarrel with Mithridates and gave command of an invading army to his son. The Roman colonel who acted as Mithridates's political adviser proposed a conference between Mithridates and his son-in-law, and Mithridates agreed to attend it: but he was treacherously seized by Georgian troops as a blood-covenant was on the point of being sealed, and smothered with blankets. The Governor of Syria, when he heard of this horrid act called a council of his staff to decide whether Mithridates should be avenged by a punitive expedition against his murderer, who now reigned in his stead; but the general opinion seemed to be that the more treacherous and bloody the behaviour of Eastern kings on our frontier, the better for us—the security of the Roman Empire resting on the mutual mistrust of our neighbours—and that nothing should be done. However, the Governor, to show that he did not countenance the murder, sent a formal letter to the King of Georgia ordering him to withdraw his forces and recall his son. When the Parthians heard of this letter they thought it a good opportunity for winning back Armenia. And so they invaded Armenia, and the new king fled, and then they had to abandon the expedition because it was a very severe winter and they lost a lot of men from frost-bite and sickness, so the king returned—but why continue the story? All Eastern stories are the same purposeless on-and-on to-and-fro story, unless very seldom, so seldom as almost to be never, a leader arises to give purpose and direction to the flux. Herod Agrippa was such a one, but he died before he could give full proof of his genius.

As for the Jewish hope of the Messiah, it was kindled again by one Theudas, a magician of Gilead, who gathered a great following during Fadus's governorship and told them to follow him to the River Jordan, for he would part it as the prophet Elisha had once done and lead them dryshod across to take possession of Jerusalem. Fadus sent a troop of cavalry across, charged the fanatical crowd, captured Theudas and cut off his head. (There have been no subsequent pretenders to the title, though indeed the sect about which Herod wrote to me, the followers of Joshua ben Joseph, or Jesus, seems to have made considerable headway recently, even at Rome. Aulus Plautius's wife was accused before me of having attended one of their love-feasts; but Aulus was in Britain and I hushed the affair up for his sake.) Fadus's task was made difficult by a failure of the Palestinian harvest: Herod's treasury was found to be nearly empty (and no wonder, the way he spent his money), so there was no means of relieving the distress by buying corn from Egypt. However, he organized a relief committee among the Jews and money was found to get them through the winter; but then the harvest failed again, and if it had not been for the Queen-Mother of Adiabene, who gave her entire wealth to the purchase of corn from Egypt, hundreds of thousands of Jews must have died. The Jews viewed the famine as God's vengeance on the whole nation for Herod's sin. The second failure of the harvest was indeed not so much the fault of the weather as the fault of the Jewish farmers: they were so low-spirited that instead of sowing the seed-corn with which they had been supplied by Fadus's successor (the son of Alexander the Alabarch, who had abandoned Judaism) they ate it or even left it to sprout in the sack. The Jews are an extraordinary race. Under the governorship of one Cumanus, who came next, there were great disturbances. Cumanus was not a good choice, I am afraid, and his term of office began with a great disaster. Following Roman precedent, he had stationed a battalion of regulars in the Temple cloisters to keep order at the great Jewish Passover feast, and one of the soldiers who had a grudge against the Jews let down his breeches during the holiest part of the festival and exposed his privy members derisively to the worshippers, calling out: "Here, Jews, look this way! Here's something worth seeing." That started a riot, and Cumanus was accused by the Jews of having ordered the soldier to make this provocative and very foolish display. He was naturally annoyed. He shouted to the crowd to be quiet and continue their festival in an orderly manner: but they grew more and more threatening. It seemed to Cumanus that a single battalion was not enough in the circumstances. To overawe the crowd he sent for the entire garrison: which in my opinion was a grave error of judgment. The streets of Jerusalem are very narrow and tortuous and were crowded with vast numbers of Jews who had come as usual from all over the world to celebrate the festival. The cry went up: "The soldiers are coming. Run for your lives!" Everyone ran for his life. If anyone stumbled and fell he was trampled underfoot, and at street corners where two streams of fugitives met the pressure was so great from behind that thousands were crushed to death. The soldiers did not even draw their swords, but no less than twenty thousand Jews were killed in the panic. The disaster was so overwhelming that the final day of the festival was not celebrated. Then as the crowd dispersed to its homes a party of Galileans happened to overtake one of my own Egyptian stewards, who was travelling from Alexandria to Acre to collect some money due to me. He was doing some business of his own on the side and the Galileans robbed him of a very valuable casket of jewels. When Cumanus heard of this he took reprisals on the villages nearest the scene of the robbery (on the borders of Samaria and Judæa), disregarding the fact that the robbers were plainly Galileans, by their accents, and only passing through. He sent a party of soldiers to plunder the villages and arrest the leading citizens. They did so and one of the soldiers in plundering the houses came across a copy of the Laws of Moses. He waved it over his head and then began reading out an obscene parody of the sacred writings. The Jews screamed in horror at the blasphemy and rushed to take the parchment from him. But he ran away laughing, tearing the thing in pieces as he went and scattering them behind him. Feeling ran so high that when Cumanus heard the facts he was forced to execute the soldier as a warning to his comrades and as a sign of goodwill to the Jews.

A month or two later Galileans came up to Jerusalem to another festival and the inhabitants of a Samaritan village refused to let them pass, because of the previous trouble. The Galileans insisted on passing and in the ensuing fight several were killed. The survivors went to Cumanus for satisfaction, but he gave them none, telling them that the Samaritans had a perfect right to forbid their passage through the village: Why couldn't they have gone round by the fields? The foolish Galileans called a famous bandit to their aid and revenged themselves on the Samaritans by plundering their villages with his aid. Cumanus armed the Samaritans and with four battalions of the Samaria garrison made a drive against the Galilean raiders and killed and captured a great number of them. Later, a delegation of Samaritans went to the Governor of Syria and asked satisfaction from him against another party of Galileans whom they accused of setting fire to their villages. He came down to Samaria determined to end this business once and for all. He had the captured Galileans crucified and then went carefully into the origin of the disturbances. He found that the Galileans had a right of way through Samaria and that Cumanus should have punished the Samaritans for the disturbances instead of supporting them, and that his action in taking reprisals on Judæan and Samaritan villages for a robbery committed by Galileans was unjustified; and further, that the original breach of the peace, the indecent self-exposure of the soldier during the Passover Festival, had been countenanced by the colonel of the battalion, who had laughed loudly and said that if the Jews did not like the sight they were not compelled to look at it. By a careful sifting of evidence he also decided that the villages had been burned by the Samaritans themselves and that the compensation which they asked was many times more than the value of the property destroyed. Before the fire had been started all objects of value had been carefully removed from the houses. So he sent Cumanus, the colonel, the Samaritan plaintiffs and a number of Jewish witnesses to me at Rome, where I tried them. The evidence was conflicting, but I eventually came to the same conclusion as the Governor. I exiled Cumanus to the Black Sea; ordered the Samaritan plaintiffs to be executed as liars and incendiaries; and had the colonel who laughed taken back to Jerusalem to be led through the streets of the city for public execration and then executed on the scene of his crime—for I regard it as a crime when an officer whose

duty it is to keep order at a religious festival deliberately
inflames popular feeling and causes the death of twenty
thousand innocent people.

After Cumanus's removal I remembered Herod's advice
and sent Felix out as governor: that was three years ago
and he is still there having a difficult time, because the
country is in a most disturbed state and overrun with bandits. He has married the youngest of Herod's daughters;
she was previously married to the King of Homs, but left
him. The other daughter married the son of Helcias. Herod
Pollio is dead, and young Agrippa who governed Chalcis
for four years after his uncle's death I have now made King
of Bashan.

At Alexandria there were fresh disturbances three years
ago and a number of deaths. I inquired into the case at
Rome and found that the Greeks had provoked the Jews
once more by interrupting their religious ceremonies. I punished them accordingly.

So much, then, for the East and perhaps it would now
be as well to wind up my account of events in other parts
of the Empire, so as to be able to concentrate on my main
story, which centres now in Rome.

At about the same time as the Parthians sent to Rome
for a king, so did the great German confederation over
which Hermann had ruled, the Cheruscans. Hermann had
been assassinated by members of his own family for trying
to reign over a free people in a despotic manner, and a
feud had then started between the two principal assassins,
his nephews, which led to a prolonged civil war and finally
to the extinction of the whole Cheruscan royal house, with
one single exception. This was Italicus, the son of Flavius,
Hermann's brother. Flavius remained loyal to Rome at the
time that Hermann treacherously ambushed and massacred
Varus's three regiments, but had been killed by Hermann
in battle some years after while serving under my brother

Germanicus. Italicus was born at Rome and was enrolled in the Noble Order of Knights, as his father had been. He was a handsome and gifted young man and had been given a good Roman education, but foreseeing that he might one day occupy the Cheruscan throne I had insisted on his learning the use of German weapons as well as Roman ones, and on studying his native language and laws with close attention: members of my bodyguard were his tutors. They also taught him to drink beer: a German prince who cannot drink pot for pot with his thegns is considered a weakling.

A Cheruscan delegation then came to Rome to ask for Italicus as their new king. They created a great stir in the Theatre on the first afternoon of their arrival. None of them had ever been in Rome before. They called on me at the Palace and were told that I was at the Theatre, so they followed me there. A comedy of Plautus's, *The Truculent Man*, was being played, and everyone was listening with the greatest attention. They were shown into the public seats, and not very good ones either, high up, almost out of earshot of the stage. As soon as they had settled down they looked about them and began asking in loud tones: "Are these honourable seats?"

The ushers whisperingly tried to assure them that they were.

"Where's Cæsar sitting? Where are his chief thegns?" they asked.

The ushers pointed down to the orchestra. "There's Cæsar. But he only sits down there because he's slightly deaf. The seats you are in are really the most honourable seats. The higher, the more honourable, you know."

"Who are those dark-skinned men with jewelled caps, sitting quite close to Cæsar?"

"Those are Parthian ambassadors."

"What's Parthia?"

418

"A great Empire in the East."

"Why are they sitting down there? Aren't they honourable? Is it because of their colour?"

"Oh, no, they are very honourable," the ushers said. "But please don't talk so loud."

"Then why are they sitting in such humble seats?" the Germans persisted.

("Hush, hush!" "Quiet there, Barbarians, we can't hear!" and similar protests from the crowd.)

"Out of compliment to Cæsar," the ushers lied. "They swear that if Cæsar's deafness forces him to occupy such a lowly seat, they won't presume to sit any higher."

"And do you expect us to be outdone in courtesy by a miserable parcel of blackamoors," the Germans shouted indignantly. "Come on, brothers, down we go!" The play was held up for five minutes as they forced their way down through the packed seats and fetched up triumphantly among the Vestal Virgins. Well, they meant no harm, and I greeted them honourably as they deserved, and at dinner that night consented to let them have the king they wanted; I was, of course, very glad to be able to do so.

I sent Italicus across the Rhine with an admonition that contrasted strangely with the one I had given Meherdates before I sent him across the Euphrates; for the Parthians and the Cheruscans are the two most dissimilar races, I suppose, that you could find anywhere in the world. My words to Italicus were these: "Italicus, remember that you have been called upon to rule over a free nation. You have been educated as a Roman and accustomed to Roman discipline. Be careful not to expect as much from your fellow-tribesmen as a Roman magistrate or general would expect from his subordinates. Germans can be persuaded but not forced. If a Roman commander says to a military subordinate: 'Colonel, take so many men to such-and-such a place and there raise an earthwork so-and-so many paces long, thick and high,' he replies, 'Very good, General'; off he goes without argument and the earthwork is raised within twenty-four hours. You can't speak to a Cheruscan in that style. He'll want to know precisely why you want the earthwork raised and against whom, and wouldn't it be better to send someone else of less importance to perform this dishonourable task—earthworks are a sign of cowardice, he'll argue—and what gifts will you bestow on him if he consents, of his own free will, to carry out your suggestion? The art of ruling your compatriots, my friend Italicus, is never to give them a downright order, but to express your wishes clearly, disguising them as mere advice of State policy. Let your thegns think that they are doing you a favour, and thus honouring themselves, by carrying out these wishes of their own free will. If there is an unpleasant or thankless task to be done, make it a matter of rivalry between your thegns who shall have the honour of undertaking it, and never fail to reward with gold bracelets and weapons services which at Rome would be regarded as routine duties. Above all, be patient and never lose your temper."

So he went off in high hopes, as Meherdates had gone off, and was welcomed by a majority of the thegns, the ones who knew that they had no chance of succeeding to the vacant throne themselves, but were jealous of all native-born claimants. Italicus did not know the ins-and-outs of Cheruscan domestic politics and could be counted on to behave with reasonable impartiality. But there was a minority of men who thought themselves worthy of the throne themselves and these temporarily sank their differences to unite against Italicus. They expected that Italicus would soon make a mess of the government from ignorance, but he disappointed them by ruling remarkably well. They therefore went secretly round to the chiefs of allied tribes raising feeling against him as a Roman interloper. "The ancient liberty of Germany has departed," they lamented, "and the power of Rome is triumphant. Is there no native Cheruscan worthy of the throne, that the son of Flavius, the spy and traitor, should be permitted to usurp it?" They raised a large patriotic army, by this appeal. Italicus's supporters, however, declared that Italicus had not usurped the throne, but had been offered it with the consent of a majority of the tribe; and that he was the only royal prince left and though born in Italy had studiously acquainted himself with the German language, customs and weapons, and was ruling very justly; and that his father Flavius, far from being a traitor, had on the contrary sworn an oath of friendship with the Romans approved by the whole nation, including his brother Hermann, and unlike Hermann had not violated it. As for the ancient liberty of the Germans, that was hypocritical talk: the men who used it would think nothing of destroying the nation by renewed civil wars.

In a great battle fought between Italicus and his rivals, Italicus came off victorious, and his victory was so complete that he soon forgot my advice and grew impatient of humouring German independence and vanity: he began ordering his thegns about. They drove him out at once. Afterwards he was restored by the armed assistance of a neighbouring tribe, and then ousted again. I made no attempt to intervene: in the West as in the East the security of the Roman Empire rests largely on the civil dissensions of our neighbours. At the time of writing Italicus is king once more but much hated although he has just fought a successful war against the Chattians.

There was trouble farther north about this time. The Governor of the Lower Rhine province died suddenly and the enemy began their cross-river raids again. They had a capable leader of the same type as the Numidian Tacfarinas who had given us so much trouble under Tiberius: like

Tacfarinas he was a deserter from one of our auxiliary regiments and had picked up a considerable knowledge of tactics. Gannascus was his name, a Frisian, and he carried on his operations on an extensive scale. He captured a number of light river transports from us and turned pirate on the coasts of Flanders and Brabant. The new Governor I appointed was called Corbulo, a man for whom I had no great personal liking but whose talents I gratefully employed. Tiberius had once made Corbulo his Commissioner of Highways and he had soon sent in a severe report on the fraud of contractors and the negligence of provincial magistrates whose task it was to see that the roads were kept in good repair. Tiberius, acting on the report, had fined the accused men heavily; and out of all proportion to their culpability, because the roads had been allowed to get into a bad condition by previous magistrates and these particular contractors had only been employed to patch up the worst places. When Caligula succeeded Tiberius and began to feel the need of money, amongst his other tricks and shifts he brought out the Corbulo report and fined all previous provincial magistrates and contractors on the same scale as the ones who had been fined by Tiberius; he gave Corbulo the task of collecting the money. When I succeeded Caligula I paid back these fines, only retaining as much as was needed to repair the roads—about one-fifth of the total amount. Caligula had not, of course, used any of the money for road-repairs, and neither had Tiberius, and the roads were in a worse condition than ever. I really did repair them and introduced special traffic-regulations limiting the use of heavy private coaches on country roads. These coaches did far more damage than country wagons bringing merchandise to Rome. I did not think it right that the provinces should pay for the luxury and pleasure of wealthy idlers. If rich Roman knights wished to visit their country estates, let them use sedan-chairs, or ride horseback.

But I was speaking of Corbulo. I knew him for a man of great severity and precision, and the garrison of the Lower Province needed a martinet to restore discipline there: the Governor who had died was much too easygoing. Corbulo's arrival at his headquarters at Cologne recalled Galba's at Mainz. (Galba was now my Governor of Africa.) He ordered a soldier to be flogged whom he found improperly dressed on sentry-duty at the camp gate. The man was unshaved, his hair had not been cut for at least a month, and his military cloak was a fancy yellow colour instead of the regulation brownish-red. Not long after this Corbulo executed two soldiers for "abandoning their arms in the face of the enemy": they were digging a trench and had left their swords behind in their tents. This scared the troops into efficiency, and when Corbulo took the field against Gannascus and showed that he was a capable general as well as a strict disciplinarian they did all that he could have expected of them. Soldiers, or at least old soldiers, always prefer a reliable general, however severe, to an incompetent one, however humane.

Corbulo fitted out war-vessels, chased and sank Gannascus's pirate fleet, and then marched up the coast and compelled the Frisians to give hostages and swear allegiance to Rome. He wrote out a constitution for them on the Roman model and built and garrisoned a fortress in their territory. This was all very well, but instead of stopping here Corbulo pushed on into the land of the Greater Chaucians, who had taken no part in the raids. He heard that Gannascus had taken refuge in a Chaucian shrine and sent a troop of cavalry to hunt him down and kill him there. This was an insult to the Chaucian Gods, and after Gannascus's assassination the same troop rode on to the Ems and there at Emsbuhren presented the Chaucian tribal council with Corbulo's demands for their instant submission with payment of a heavy yearly tribute.

Corbulo reported his actions to me and I was furiously angry with him: he had done well enough in getting rid of Gannascus, but to pick a quarrel with the Chaucians was another matter. We had not sufficient troops to spare for a war: if the Greater Chaucians called in the Lesser Chaucians to their assistance and the Frisians revolted again I would have to find strong reinforcements from somewhere, and they were not to be had, because of our commitments in Britain. I wrote ordering him to recross the Rhine at once.

Corbulo received my orders before the Chaucians had had time to reply to his ultimatum. He was angry with me, thinking that I was jealous of any general who dared to rival my military feats. He reminded his staff that Geta had not been awarded proper honours for his fine conquest of Morocco and the capture of Salabus; and said that, though I had now made it legal for generals who were not members of the Imperial Family to celebrate a triumph, in practice, it seemed, no one but myself would be allowed to conduct a campaign for which a triumph could legally be awarded. My anti-despotic pretensions were mere affectation: I was just as much of a tyrant as Caligula, but I concealed it better. He said too that I was lowering Roman prestige by going back on the threats that he had made in my name; and that our allies would laugh at him, and so would his own troops. But this was only an angry talk to his staff.

All that he told the troops when he sounded the signal for a general retirement was: "Men, Cæsar Augustus orders us back across the Rhine. We do not yet know why he has reached this decision, and we cannot question it, though I honestly confess that I, for one, am greatly disappointed. How fortunate were the Roman generals who led our armies in the days of old!" However, he was awarded triumphal ornaments and I also wrote him a private letter exculpating myself from the angry charges which, I told him, I had heard that he had made against me. I wrote that if he had been angry, why, so had I, on hearing of his provocation of the Chaucians; and that though he should have thought better of me than to accuse me of jealous motives, I blamed myself for sending him so curt a dispatch instead of explaining at length my reasons for ordering him to withdraw. I then explained these reasons. He wrote back in handsome apology, withdrawing the charge of despotism and jealousy, and I think now that we understood each other. To keep his troops occupied and allow them no leisure for laughing at him, he put them to work on a canal twenty-three miles long between the Meuse and the Rhine to carry off occasional inundations of the sea in this flat region.

Since that time there have been no other events of importance to record in Germany except, four years ago, another raid by the Chattians. They crossed the Rhine in great force one night a few miles north of Mainz. The Commander of the Upper Province was Secundus, the Consul who had behaved with such indecision when I became Emperor. He was also supposed to be the best living Roman poet. Personally, I think very little of the moderns, or indeed of the Augustans: their poetry does not ring true to me. To my mind Catullus was the last of the true poets. It may be that poetry and liberty go together: that under a monarchy true poetry dies and the best that one can hope for then is gorgeous rhetoric and remarkable metrical artifice. For my part I would exchange all twelve books of Virgil's *Æneid* for a single book of Ennius's *Annals*. Ennius, who lived in Rome's grandest Republican days and counted the great Scipio as his personal friend, was what I would call a true poet: Virgil was merely a remarkable verse-craftsman. Compare the two of them when they are both writing about a battle: Ennius writes like the soldier he was (he rose from the ranks to a captaincy), Virgil like a cultured spectator from a distant hill. Virgil borrowed much from Ennius. Some say he overshadowed Ennius's rude genius by his cultured felicity of phrase and rhythm. But that is nonsense. It is like Æsop's fable of the wren and the eagle. The birds all competed as to which could fly the highest. The eagle won, but when he tired and could go no higher, the wren, who had been nestling on his back, mounted up a few score feet and claimed the prize. Virgil was a mere wren by comparison with Ennius the eagle. And even if you concentrate on single beauties, where in Virgil will you find a passage to equal in simple grandeur such lines of Ennius's as these?—

"Fraxinu' frangitur atque abies consternitur alta.
Pinus prōcēras pervortunt: omne sonabat
Arbustum fremitu silväi frondosäi."

"The ash was hewn, the high white fir laid low,
Down toppled they the princely pines, and all
That grove of countless leaves rang with the timber's fall."

But they are untranslatable, and in any case I am not writing a treatise on poetry. And though Secundus's poetry was, in my opinion, as disingenuous and unpraiseworthy as his behaviour in the Senate House that day, he was at least capable of dealing decisively with the Chattians on their return in two divisions from the plunder of our French allies. Victory disorganizes the Germans, especially if their plunder includes wine, which they swill as if it were beer, disregarding its greater potency. Secundus's forces surrounded and defeated both enemy divisions, killing ten thousand men and capturing as many prisoners. He was given triumphal ornaments, but the regulations controlling the award of triumphs did not permit me to grant him one.

I had recently granted a similar honour to Secundus's predecessor, one Curtius Rufus, who, though only the son of a sword-fighter, had risen under Tiberius to the dignity of first-rank magistrate. (Tiberius had won him this appointment, in spite of the competition of several men of birth and distinction, by remarking: "Yes, but Curtius Rufus is his own illustrious ancestor.") Rufus had become ambitious for triumphal ornaments but was aware that I would not approve of his picking a quarrel with the enemy. He knew of a vein of silver that had been discovered a few miles across the river, in the reign of Augustus, just before Varus's defeat, and sent a regiment across to work it. He got a good deal of silver out before the vein ran too far underground to be manageable—sufficient silver indeed to pay the whole Rhine army for two years. This was naturally worth triumphal ornaments. The troops found the mining very arduous and wrote me an amusing letter, in the name of the entire army:

"The loyal troops of Claudius Cæsar send him their best wishes and sincerely hope that he and his family will continue to enjoy long life and perfect health. They also beg that, in future, he will award his generals triumphant ornaments *before* he sends them out to command armies, because then they will not feel obliged to earn them by making Cæsar's loyal troops sweat and drudge at silver-mining, canal-digging and such-like tasks which would be more suitably done by German prisoners. If Cæsar would only permit his loyal troops to cross the Rhine and capture a few thousand Chattians, they would be very pleased to do so, to the best of their ability."

427

# Chapter Twenty-Five

THE year after Herod died I celebrated the first annual festival in honour of my British triumph; and, remembering the complaints that I had overheard that night on A.D. 45 the steps of the Temple of Castor and Pollux, I made a distribution of money to the needy populace—three gold pieces a head with half a gold piece extra for every child in the family who had not yet come of age. In one case I had to pay as much as twelve and a half gold pieces, but that was because there were several sets of twins to subsidize. Young Silanus and young Pompey assisted me in the distribution. When I record that I had now removed all Caligula's extraordinary taxes and paid back the men he had robbed, and that work continued on the Ostia harbour scheme and the aqueducts and the Fucine Lake drainage scheme, and that, without defrauding anyone, I was able to pay out this bounty and still keep a substantial balance in the Public Treasury, you will admit, I think, that I had done extremely well in these four years.

The astronomer Barbillus (to whom I referred in my letter to the Alexandrians) made some abstruse mathematical calculations and informed me that there was to be an eclipse of the sun on my birthday. This caused me some alarm, because an eclipse is one of the most unlucky omens that can happen at any time, and happening on my birthday, which was also a national festival in honour of Mars, it would greatly disturb people and give anyone who wished to assassinate me every confidence of success. But I thought that if I warned the people beforehand that the eclipse was to take place they would feel very differently about it: not despondent but actually pleased that they knew what was coming and understood the mechanics of the phenomenon.

I published a proclamation:

"Tiberius Claudius Drusus Nero Cæsar Augustus Germanicus Britannicus, Emperor, Father of the Country, High Pontiff, Protector of the People for the fifth year in succession, three times Consul, to the Senate, People and Allies of Rome, greetings.

"My good friend Tiberius Claudius Barbillus of the City of Ephesus made certain astronomical calculations last year, since confirmed by a body of his fellow-astronomers in the City of Alexandria, where that science flourishes, and found that an eclipse of the sun, total in some parts of Italy, partial in others, will take place on the first day of August next. Now, I do not wish you to feel any alarm on this account, though superstitious terrors have always in the past been awakened by this natural phenomenon. In the old days it was a sudden and inexplicable event and considered as a warning by the Gods themselves that happiness was to be blotted out on earth for awhile, just as the sun's life-giving rays were blotted out. But now we so well understand eclipses that we can actually prophesy, 'On such and such a day an eclipse will take place.' And I think everyone should feel both proud and relieved that the old terrors are laid at last by the force of intelligent human reasoning.

"The following, then, is the explanation that my learned friends give. The Moon, which revolves in its orbit below the sun, either immediately below it or perhaps with the planets Mercury and Venus intervening—this is a disputed point and does not affect the present argument—has a longitudinal motion, like the Sun, and a vertical motion, as the Sun probably has too; but it has also a latitudinal motion which the Sun never has in any circumstances. So

429

when, because of this latitudinal motion, the moon gets in a direct line with the Sun over our heads and passes invisibly under its blazing disk—invisibly, because the Sun is so bright that by day, as you know, the Moon becomes a mere nothing—then the rays which normally dart from the Sun to the earth are obscured by the Moon's intervention. For some of the earth's inhabitants this obscuration lasts for a longer time than for others, according to their geographical position, and some are not affected by it at all. The fact is that the Sun never really loses its light, as the ignorant suppose, and consequently it appears in its full splendour to all people between itself and whom the Moon does not pass.

"This is the simple explanation, then, of an eclipse of the Sun—as simple a matter as if anyone of you were to shade the flame of an oil-lamp or candle with your hand and plunge a whole room into temporary darkness. (An eclipse of the Moon, by the way, is caused by the Moon running into the cone-shaped shadow thrown by the Earth when the Sun is underneath it; it only happens when the Moon passes through the mean point in its latitudinal motion.) But in the districts most affected by the eclipse, which are indicated on the adjoining map, I desire all magistrates and other responsible authorities to take every precaution against popular panic, or robbery under cover of darkness, and to discourage people from staring at the sun during its eclipse, unless through pieces of horn or glass darkened with candle smoke, because for those with weak eyes there is a danger of blindness."

I think that I must have been the first ruler since the Creation of the World to issue a proclamation of this sort; and it had a very good effect, though of course the country people did not understand words like "longitudinal" and "latitudinal." The eclipse occurred exactly as foretold, and the festival took place as usual, though special sacrifices were offered to Diana as Goddess of the Moon, and Apollo as God of the Sun.

I enjoyed perfect health throughout the following year, and nobody tried to assassinate me, and the one revolution that was attempted ended in a most ignominious way for its prime mover. This was Asinius Gallus, grandson of Asinius Pollio and son of Tiberius's first wife, Vipsania, by Gallus whom she afterwards married and whom Tiberius hated so and finally killed by slow starvation. It is curious how appropriate some people's names are. *Gallus* means cock, and *Asinus* means donkey, and Asinius Gallus was the most utter little donkey-cock for his boastfulness and stupidity that one could find in a month's tour of Italy. Imagine, he had not got any troops ready or collected any funds for his revolution, but believed that the strength of his personality supported by the nobility of his birth would win him immediate adherents!

He appeared one day on the Oration Platform in the Market Place and began to hold forth to a crowd which soon assembled, on the evils of tyranny, dwelling on my uncle Tiberius's murder of his father, and saying how necessary it was to root out the Cæsar family from Rome and give the monarchy to someone really worthy of it. From his mysterious hints the crowd gathered that he meant himself and began to laugh and cheer. He was a wretched orator and the ugliest man in the Senate, not more than four foot six in height, with bottle-shoulders, a great long face, reddish hair and a tiny little bright red nose (he suffered from indigestion); yet he thought himself Hercules and Adonis rolled into one. There was not, I believe, a single person in the Market Place who took him seriously, and all sorts of jokes went flying about such as: *"Asinus in tegulis"* and *"Asinus ad lyram"* and *"Ex Gallo lac et ova."* (A donkey on the roof-tiles is a proverbial expression for any sudden grotesque apparition, and a donkey playing on a lyre stands

431

for any absurdly incompetent performance, and cock's milk and cock's eggs stand for nonsensical hopes.) However, they went on cheering every sentence to see what absurdity would come next: and sure enough, when his speech ended he tried to lead the whole mob up to the Palace to depose me. They followed him in a long column, eight abreast, up to about twenty paces from the outer Palace Gate and then suddenly halted and let him go on by himself, which he did. The sentries at the gate let him through without question, because he was a senator, and he went marching on into the Palace grounds for some distance, shouting threats against me, before he realized that he was alone. (Crowds can be very witty and very cruel sometimes, as well as very stupid and very cowardly.) He was soon arrested, and although the whole affair was so ridiculous I could hardly overlook it: I banished him, but no farther than Sicily, where he had family estates. "Go away and crow on your own dung-hill or bray in your own thistle-field, whichever you prefer, but don't let me hear you," I told the ugly, excitable little man.

The harbour at Ostia was not nearly completed yet and had already cost six million gold pieces. The greatest technical difficulty now lay in forming the island between the extremities of the two great moles; and you may not credit it, but I solved it myself. You remember Caligula's great obelisk-ship which had taken the elephants and camels to Britain, and brought them safely back too? She was at Ostia again and had been used twice since for voyages to Egypt to fetch coloured marble for Venus's temple in Sicily. But the captain told me that she was becoming unseaworthy and he would not care to risk another voyage in her. So one night, as I lay awake, it occurred to me that it would be a good idea to fill her with stones and sink her as a foundation for the island. But I rejected that, because we could only be able to fill her about a quarter full of stones before the water rose over the gunwale, and when she rotted they would just fall out in a loose heap. So I thought, "If we only had a Gorgon's head handy to turn her into a big solid rock!" And that foolish fancy, the sort that often flies into my mind when I am over-tired, gave birth to a really brilliant idea: why not fill her as full as possible with cement powder, which is comparatively light, and then batten down her hatches, sink her, and let the cement set under the water?

It was about two o'clock in the morning when this idea came to me and I clapped my hands for a freedman and sent him off at once to bring my chief engineer to me. About an hour later the engineer turned up from the other side of the City in a great hurry and trembling violently; expecting to be executed, perhaps, for some negligence or other. I asked him excitedly whether my idea was practicable, and was greatly disappointed to hear that cement would not set satisfactorily in sea-water. However, I gave him ten days to find some means of making it set. "Ten days," I repeated solemnly, "or else . . ."

He thought that "or else" was a threat, but if he had failed I would have explained my little joke which was simply "or else we shall have to abandon the idea." Fear improved his wits, and after eight days' frantic experimenting he invented a cement powder that set like a rock when it came into contact with sea-water. It was a mixture of ordinary cement powder from the cement works at Cumæ with a peculiar sort of dust from the hills in the neighbourhood of Puteoli, and the shape of that obelisk-ship is now eternized in the hardest stone imaginable at the mouth of Ostia harbour. We have built an island over it, using large stones and more of the same cement; and there is a tall lighthouse on the island, with a beacon fire fed with turpentine shining every night from its summit. There are polished steel reflectors in the beacon chamber which double the light of the fire and send it out in a steady stream down the estuary. The harbour took ten years to complete and cost twelve millions in gold; and there are still men at work improving the channel. But it is a great gift to the City and so long as we command the seas we can never starve.

Everything seemed to be going very well for me and Rome. The country was contented and prosperous and our armies were victorious everywhere—Aulus was consolidating my conquest of Britain by a series of brilliant victories over the yet unsubdued Belgic tribes of the south and southwest; religious observances were being regularly and punctually performed; there was no distress even in the poorest quarters of the City. I had managed to get even with my law-court business and find means of keeping down the number of cases. My health was good. Messalina was lovelier in my eyes than ever. My children were growing up strong and healthy and little Britannicus was showing the extraordinary precocity which (though, I own, it missed me out) has always run in the Claudian family. The only thing that grieved me now was an invisible barrier between myself and the Senate that I could not break down. All that I could do in the way of paying respect to the Senatorial Order, especially to the Consuls in office and to the first-class magistrates, I did, but I was always met with a mixture of obsequiousness and suspicion that I found it difficult to account for and impossible to deal with. I decided to revive the ancient office of Censor which had been swallowed up in the Imperial Directorship of Morals, and in that popular capacity reform the Senate once more and get rid of all useless and obstruction-making members. I posted a notice in the House requesting every member to consider his own circumstances and decide whether he was still qualified to serve Rome well as a senator: if he decided he was not so qualified, either because he could not afford it, or because he felt himself not sufficiently gifted, he should resign. I hinted that those who failed to resign would be dishonourably expelled. And I hurried things along by sending round private notifications to those whom I proposed to expel if they didn't resign. I thus lightened the Order of about a hundred names, and those who remained I then rewarded by conferring patrician rank on their families. This enlargement of the patrician circle had the advantage of providing more candidates for the higher orders of priesthood and of giving a wider choice of brides and bridegrooms to members of the surviving patrician families; for the four successive patrician creations of Romulus, Lucius Brutus, Julius Cæsar and Augustus had each in turn become practically extinct. One would have thought that the richer and more powerful the family, the more rapidly and vigorously it would breed, but this has never been the case at Rome.

However, even this cleansing of the Senate did not have any appreciable effect. Debates were a mere farce. Once, during my fourth Consulship, when I was introducing a measure about certain judicial reforms, the House was so listless that I was obliged to speak very plainly:

"If you honestly approve of these proposals, my Lords, do me the kindness of saying so at once and quite simply. Or, if you do not approve of them, then suggest amendments, but do so here and now. Or if you need time to think the matter over, take time, but don't forget that you must have your opinions ready to be delivered on the day fixed for the debate. It is not at all proper to the dignity of the Senate that the Consul-Elect should repeat the exact phrases of the Consuls as his own opinion, and that everyone else when his turn comes to speak should merely say, 'I agree to that' and nothing else, and that then, when the House has adjourned, the minutes should read 'A debate took place . . .' "

Among other remarks of respect to the Senate, I restored Greece and Macedonia to the list of Senatorial provinces: my uncle Tiberius had made Imperial provinces of them. And I gave the Senate back the right of minting copper coinage for circulation in the provinces, as in the time of Augustus. There is nothing that commands such respect for sovereignty as coins: the gold and silver currency had my head on it, because after all I was the Emperor and the man actually responsible for the greater part of the government; but the Senate's familiar "S.C." appeared again on the copper, and copper is at once the most ancient, the most useful, and quantitatively the most important coinage.

The immediate cause of my decision to purge the Senate was the alarming case of Asiaticus. One day Messalina came to me and said: "Do you remember wondering last year whether there wasn't something else at A. D. 46 the bottom of Asiaticus's resignation of the Consulship besides the reason he gave—that people were jealous and suspicious of him, because it was his second time as Consul?"

"Yes, it didn't look like the whole reason."

"Well, I'll tell you something which I should have told you about long ago. Asiaticus has been violently in love for some time with Cornelius Scipio's wife; what do you think of that?"

"Oh yes, Poppæa—very good-looking girl, with a straight nose and a bold way of staring at men? And what does she think of it? Asiaticus isn't a good-looking young fellow like Scipio: he's bald and rather fat, but of course the richest man in Rome, and what marvellous gardens he has too!"

"Poppæa, I'm afraid, has thoroughly compromised herself with Asiaticus. Well, I'll tell you. It's best to be frank. Poppæa came to me some time ago—you know what good friends we are, or rather, we used to be—and said, 'Messalina, dearest, I want to ask you a great, great favour. You

436

promise not to tell anyone that I've asked you?' Naturally I promised. She said: 'I'm in love with Valerius Asiaticus and I don't know what to do about it. My husband is fearfully jealous and if he knew I think he'd kill me. And the nuisance is that I'm married to him in the strict form and you know how difficult it is to get a divorce from a strict form of marriage if the husband chooses to be nasty. It means you lose your children, for a start. Do you think that you could possibly do something to help me? Could you ask the Emperor to speak to my husband and arrange a divorce, so that Asiaticus and I can marry?' "

"I hope you didn't say that there was any chance of my consenting. Really, these women . . ."

"Oh, no, dearest, on the contrary. I said that if she never mentioned the subject to me again I would try, for friendship's sake, to forget what I'd heard, but that if so much as a whisper came to me of anything improper still going on between her and Asiaticus I'd come straight to you."

"Good. I'm glad you said that."

"It was soon afterwards that Asiaticus resigned, and do you remember, then, that he asked the Senate's permission to visit his estates in France?"

"Yes, and he was away a long time. Trying to forget Poppæa, I suppose. There are a lot of pretty women in the South of France."

"Don't you believe it. I have been finding out things about Asiaticus. The first thing is that lately he's been giving large money presents to the Guards captains and sergeants and standard-bearers. He does it, he says, because of his gratitude to them for their loyalty to you. Does that sound right?"

"Well, he has more money than he knows what to do with."

"Don't be ridiculous. Nobody has more money than they know what to do with. Then the second thing is that he and Poppæa still meet regularly, whenever poor Scipio's out of town, and spend the night together."

"Where do they meet?"

"At the house of the Petra brothers. They're cousins of hers. The third thing is that Sosibius told me the other day, quite on his own, that he thought it most unwise of you to have allowed Asiaticus to pay so long a visit to his estates in France. When I asked him what he meant, he showed me a letter from a friend of his in Vienne: the friend wrote that Asiaticus had actually spent very little time on his estates. He had gone round visiting the most influential people in the province and had even been for a tour along the Rhine, where he showed great generosity to the officers of the garrison. Then, of course, you must remember that Asiaticus was born at Vienne; and Sosibius says——"

"Call Sosibius at once." Sosibius was the man I had chosen as Britannicus's tutor, so you can imagine that I had the greatest confidence in his judgment. He was an Alexandrian Greek but had long interested himself in the study of early Latin authors and was the leading authority on the texts of Ennius; he was so much at home in the Republican period, which he knew far better than any Roman historian, including myself, that I considered that he would be a constant inspiration to my little boy. Sosibius came, and when I questioned him answered very frankly. Yes, he believed Asiaticus to be ambitious and capable of planning a revolution. Hadn't he once offered himself as a candidate for the monarchy in opposition to me?

"You forget, Sosibius," I said, "that those two days have been wiped off the City records by an amnesty."

"But Asiaticus was in the plot against your nephew, the late Emperor, and even boasted about it in the Market Place. When a man like that resigns his Consulship for no valid reason and goes off to France, where he already has great influence, and there tries to enlarge that influence by scattering money about, and no doubt saying that he was forced to resign his Consulship because of your jealousy, or because he stood up against you for the rights of his fellow-Frenchmen. . . . ."

Messalina said: "It's perfectly plain. He has promised Poppæa to marry her, and the only way that he can do that is by getting rid of you and me. He'll get leave to go to France again, and start his revolt there with the native regiments, and then bring the Rhine regiments into it too. And the Guards will be as ready to acclaim him Emperor as they were ready to acclaim you: it will mean another two hundred gold pieces a man for them."

"Who else do you think is in the plot?"

"Let's find out all about the Petra brothers. That lawyer Suilius has just been asked to undertake a case for them: and he is one of my best secret agents. If there's anything against them besides their having accommodated Poppæa and Asiaticus with a bedroom, Suilius will find it out, you can rely on that."

"I don't like spying. I don't like Suilius, either."

"We have got to defend ourselves, and Suilius is the handiest weapon we have."

So Suilius was sent for, and a week later he made his report, which confirmed Messalina's suspicions. The Petra brothers were certainly in the plot. The elder of them had privately circulated an account of a vision which had appeared to him one early morning between sleeping and waking and which the astrologers had interpreted in an alarming fashion. The vision was of my head severed at the neck and crowned with a wreath of white vine-leaves: the interpretation was that I should die violently at the close of the autumn. The younger brother had been acting as Asiaticus's go-between with the Guards, of which he was a colonel. Apparently associated with Asiaticus and the Petra brothers were two old friends of mine, Pedo Pompey,

439

who used often to play dice with me in the evenings, and Assario, maternal uncle of my son-in-law, young Pompey, who also had free access to the Palace. Suilius suggested that these would naturally have been given the task of murdering me over a friendly game of dice. Then there were Assario's two nieces, the Tristonia sisters, who had an adulterous association with the Petra brothers.

There was nothing for it, I decided, but to strike first. I sent my Guards Commander, Crispinus, with a company of Guards whose loyalty seemed beyond question, down to Assario's house at Baiæ; and there Asiaticus was arrested. He was handcuffed and fettered and brought before me at the Palace. I should, properly, have had him impeached before the Senate, but I could not be sure how far the plot extended. There might be a demonstration in his favour, and I did not wish to encourage that. I tried him in my own study, in the presence of Messalina, Vitellius, Crispinus, young Pompey, and my chief secretaries.

Suilius acted as public prosecutor, and I thought, as Asiaticus faced him, that if ever guilt was written on a man's features it was written there. But I must admit that Crispinus had not warned him what were the charges against him—I had not even told Crispinus—and there are few men who if suddenly arrested would be able to face their judges with absolute serenity of conscience. I know how badly I once felt myself when I was arrested by Caligula's orders on the charge of witnessing a forged will. Suilius was indeed a terrible and pitiless accuser: he had a thin, frosty face, white hair, dark eyes and a long forefinger which probed and darted like a sword. He began with a mild rain of compliments and banter which we all recognized as a prelude to a thunder-storm of rage and invective. First he asked Asiaticus in a mock-friendly conversational tone, exactly when he proposed visiting his French estates again—was it before the vintage? and what had he thought of agricultural conditions in the neighbourhood of Vienne and how had they compared with those of the Rhine valley? "But don't trouble to answer my questions," he said. "I don't really wish to know how high the barley grows in Vienne or how loud the cocks crow there, any more than you really wished to know yourself." Then about his presents to the Guards: how loyal Asiaticus had shown himself! but was there not perhaps a danger of the simple-witted military misunderstanding those gifts?

Asiaticus was growing anxious, and breathing heavily. Suilius came a few steps nearer him, like a wild-beast hunter in the arena, some of whose arrows, fired from a distance, have gone home: he comes nearer, because the beast is wounded, and brandishes his hunting-spear. "To think that I ever called you friend, that I ever dined at your board, that I ever allowed myself to be deceived by your affable ways, your noble descent, the favour and confidence that you have falsely won from our gracious Emperor and all honest citizens. Beast that you are, filthy pathic, satyr of the stews! Bland corrupter of the loyal hearts and manly bodies of the very soldiers to whose trust the sacred person of our Cæsar, the safety of the City, the welfare of the world is committed. Where were you on the night of the Emperor's birthday that you could not attend the banquet to which you were invited? Sick, were you? Mighty sick, I have no doubt. I shall soon confront the court with a selection of your fellow-invalids, young soldiers of the Guards, who caught their infection from you, you filth."

There was a great deal more of this. Asiaticus had turned dead white now, and great drops of sweat stood on his brow. The chain clanked as he wiped them away. He was forbidden by the rules of the court to answer a word until the time came for him to make his defence, but at last he burst out in a hoarse voice: "Ask your own sons, Suilius! They will admit that I am a man." He was called to order. Suilius

441

went on to speak of Asiaticus's adultery with Poppæa, but put little emphasis on this, as if it was the weakest point of his case, though really it was the strongest; and so tricked Asiaticus into making a general denial of all the charges against him. If Asiaticus had been wise he would have admitted the adultery and denied the other charges. But he denied everything, so his guilt seemed proved. Suilius called his witnesses, mostly soldiers. The chief witness, a young recruit from South Italy, was asked to identify Asiaticus. I suppose that he had been coached to recognize Asiaticus by his bald head, for he picked on Pallas as the man who had so unnaturally abused him. A great burst of laughter went up: Pallas was known to share with me a real hatred of this sort of vice, and, besides, everyone knew that he had acted as guest-master throughout my birthday banquet.

I nearly dismissed the case then and there, but reflected that the witness might have a bad memory for faces—I have myself—and that the other charges were not disproved by his failure to identify Asiaticus. But it was in a milder voice that I asked Asiaticus to answer Suilius's charges, point by point. He did so, but failed to account satisfactorily for his movements in France, and certainly perjured himself over the Poppæa business. The charge of corrupting the Guards I regarded as unproved. The soldiers testified in a formal, stilted way which suggested that they had learned the testimony off by heart beforehand, and when I questioned them merely repeated the same evidence. But then I have never heard a Guardsman testify in any other tones, they make a drill of everything.

I ordered everyone out of the room but Vitellius, young Pompey, and Pallas—Messalina had burst into tears and hurried off some minutes before—and told them that I would not sentence Asiaticus without first securing their approval. Vitellius said that, frankly, there seemed no reasonable doubt of Asiaticus's guilt, and that he was as shocked

442

and grieved as I was: Asiaticus was a very old friend and had been a favourite of my mother Antonia's, who had used her interest at court to advance them both. Then he had had a most distinguished career and had never hung back where patriotic duty called: he had been one of the volunteers who came to Britain with me, and though he had not arrived in time for the battle, that was the fault of the storm, not due to any cowardice on his part. So if he had now become mad and betrayed his own past it would not be showing too much clemency to allow him to be his own executioner: of course, strictly, he deserved to be hurled from the Tarpeian Rock, and to have his corpse dishonoured by being dragged off by a hook through the mouth and thrown into the Tiber. Vitellius told me, too, that Asiaticus had practically confessed his guilt by sending him a message, as soon as he was arrested, begging him for old friendship's sake to secure his acquittal or, if it came to the worst, permission to commit suicide. Vitellius added: "He knew that you would give him a fair trial: you have never failed to give anyone a fair trial. So how could my intercession be expected to help him? If he was guilty, then he would be pronounced guilty; or if he was innocent, he would be acquitted." Young Pompey protested that no mercy should be shown Asiaticus; but perhaps he was thinking of his own safety. Assario and the Tristonia sisters, his relations, had been mentioned as Asiaticus's accomplices, and he wished to prove his own loyalty.

I sent a message to Asiaticus to inform him that I was adjourning the trial for twenty-four hours, and that, meanwhile, he was released from his fetters. He would surely understand that message. Meanwhile Messalina had hurried to Poppæa to tell her that Asiaticus was on the point of being condemned, and advised her to forestall her own trial and execution by immediate suicide. I knew nothing about this.

Asiaticus died courageously enough. He spent his last day winding up his affairs, eating and drinking as usual and taking a walk in the Gardens of Lucullus (as they were still called), giving instructions to the gardeners about the trees and flowers and fish-pools. When he found that they had built his funeral pyre close to a fine avenue of hornbeams he was most indignant and fined the freedman responsible for choosing the site a quarter's pay. "Didn't you realize, idiot, that the breeze would carry the flames into the foliage of those lovely old trees and spoil the whole appearance of the Gardens?" His last words to his family before the surgeon severed an artery in his leg and let him bleed to death in a warm bath were, "Good-bye, my dear friends. It would have been less ignominious to have died by the dark artifices of Tiberius or the fury of Caligula, than now to fall a sacrifice to the imbecilic credulity of Claudius, betrayed by the woman I loved and by the friend I trusted." For he was now convinced that Poppæa and Vitellius had arranged for the prosecution.

Two days later I asked Scipio to dine with me, and inquired after his wife's health, as a tactful way of indicating that if he still loved Poppæa and was ready to forgive her, I would take no further action in the matter. "She's dead, Cæsar," he answered, and began sobbing with his head in his hands.

Asiaticus's family, the Valerians, to show that they did not wish to associate themselves with his treasonable words, were then obliged to present Messalina with the Gardens of Lucullus as a peace-offering; though naturally I never suspected it at the time, they were the real cause of Asiaticus's death. I tried the Petra brothers and executed them, and the Tristonia sisters then committed suicide. As for Assario, it seems that I signed his death-warrant but I have no recollection of this. When I told Pallas to warn him for trial I was told that he had already been executed, and was shown the warrant, which was certainly not forged. The only explanation that I can offer is that Messalina, or possibly Polybius, who was her tool, smuggled the death-warrant in among a number of other important ones that I had to sign, and that I signed it without reading it. I know now that this sort of trick was constantly played on me: that they took advantage of the strain from which my eyes were again suffering (so much that I had to stop all reading by artificial light) to read out as official reports and letters for my signature improvisations that did not correspond at all with the written documents.

About this time Vinicius died, of poison. I heard, some years later, that he had refused to sleep with Messalina and that the poison was administered by her; certainly he died on the day after he had dined at the Palace. The story is quite likely to be true. So now, Vinicius, Vinicianus and Asiaticus, the three men who had offered themselves as Emperor instead of me, were all dead, and their deaths seemed to lie at my door. Yet I had a clean conscience about them. Vinicianus and Asiaticus were clearly traitors, and Vinicius, I thought, had died as the result of an accident. But the Senate and People knew Messalina better than I did, and hated me because of her. That was the invisible barrier between them and me, and nobody had the courage to break it down.

As the result of a strong speech that I made about Asiaticus, at a session in which Sosibius and Crispinus were voted cash presents for their services, the Senate voluntarily surrendered to me the power of granting its members permission to leave Italy on any pretext.

# Chapter Twenty-Six

My daughter Antonia had been married for some years to young Pompey but they had no children yet. One evening I visited her at her house, in Pompey's absence, and it occurred to me how disconsolate and bored she now always looked. Yes, she agreed, she was bored, and very bored and more than bored. So I suggested that she would feel much happier if she had a child and told her that I thought it was her duty as a healthy young woman with servants and plenty of money to have not only one child but several. With a family of young children she need never complain of boredom. She flared up and said: "Father, only a fool would expect a field of corn to spring up where no seed has been sown. Don't blame the soil, blame the farmer. He sows salt, not seed." And to my astonishment she explained that the marriage had never been properly consummated; and not only that, but that she had been used in the vilest possible way by my son-in-law. I asked her why she had not told me of this before, and she said that she didn't think that I would believe her, because I had never really loved her, not as I loved her half-brother and half-sister; and that young Pompey had boasted to her that he stood so well with me now that he could make me do anything he wanted and believe anything that he told me. So what chance had she? Besides, there would be the shame of having to testify in court to the horrible things he had done to her, and she could not face that.

I grew angry, as any father would, and assured her that I loved her dearly, and that it was chiefly on her account

446

that I treated Pompey with such respect and confidence. I swore on my honour that if only half what she had told me was true I would take immediate vengeance on the scoundrel. And that her modesty would be spared: the matter would never go before the court. What was the use of being an Emperor if I couldn't use the privileges of my position to good private purpose occasionally, as a slight counter-balance to the responsibility and labour and pain that went with it? And at what hour was Pompey expected back?

"He'll be home at about midnight," said Antonia, miserably, "and by one o'clock he'll be in his room. He'll have a few drinks first. It's nine chances in ten that he'll take that disgusting Lycidas to bed with him: he bought him at the Asiaticus sale for twenty-thousand gold pieces and he's not had eyes for anyone else since. In a way it's been a great relief to me. So you know how bad things must be when I say that I infinitely prefer him to sleep with Lycidas than with me. Yes, I was in love with Pompey once. Love's a funny thing isn't it?"

"Very well, then, my poor, poor Antonia. When Pompey's in his room and settled down for the night, light a pair of oil lamps and put them on the window-sill of this room for a signal. Then leave the rest to me."

She put the oil lamps on the window-sill an hour before dawn; then she came down and made the janitor open the front door. I was there. I brought Geta and a couple of Guards sergeants into the house with me and sent them upstairs while I waited in the hall below with Antonia. She had sent all the servants away except the janitor, who had been a slave-boy of mine. She was crying a little and we clasped hands as we anxiously listened for the sound of screams and scuffling from the bedroom. Not a sound was heard, but presently Geta came down with the sergeants and reported that my orders had been obeyed. Pompey and the

447

slave Lycidas had been killed with a single javelin thrust.

This was the first time that I had used my power as Emperor to avenge a private wrong; but if I had not been Emperor I should have felt just the same and done whatever lay in my power to destroy Pompey; and though the law dealing with unnatural offences has fallen into abeyance for many years now, because no jury seems willing to convict, Pompey legally deserved to die. My only fault was that I executed him summarily; but that was the cleanest way of dealing with him. When a gardener comes across a filthy insect eating the heart out of one of his best roses he does not bring it to court before a jury of other gardeners: he crushes it then and there between his finger-nails. A few months later I married Antonia to Faustus, a descendant of the dictator Sulla, a modest, capable, and hard-working fellow who has turned out an excellent son-in-law. Two years ago he was Consul. They had a child, a boy, but it was very weakly and died, and Antonia has not been able to have another, because of the injury done her by a careless midwife at the time of her delivery.

Shortly after this I executed Polybius, who was now my Minister of Arts, on Messalina's giving me proof that he was selling citizenships for his own profit. It was a great shock when I found that Polybius had been playing me false. I had trained him up in my service from a child, and had trusted him implicitly. He had just helped me complete the official autobiography that the Senate had requested me to write for the national archives. I had treated him so familiarly, in fact, that one day when he and I were walking in the Palace grounds, discussing some antiquarian point or other, I did not dismiss him when the two Consuls came up to give me their customary morning greeting. This offended their dignity, but if I was not too proud to walk beside Polybius and listen to his opinions, why should they have been? I allowed him the greatest freedom, and I had never known him to abuse it, though once he was rather too free with his tongue in the Theatre. They were playing a comedy of Menander's and an actor had just delivered the line:

"A prosperous whipstock scarce can be endured."

Someone in the wings laughed pointedly at this. It must have been Mnester. At any rate everyone turned and stared at Polybius, who as my Minister of Arts had the task of keeping the actors in order: if an actor showed too much independence Polybius saw to it for me that he was severely whipped.

Polybius shouted back: "Yes, and Menander says in his *Thessaly*:

'Who once were goatherds now have royal power.' "

That was a hit at Mnester, who had started life as a goatherd in Thessaly and was now known to be Messalina's chief infatuation.

I did not know it then, but Messalina had been having sexual relations with Polybius too and he was stupid enough to be jealous of Mnester. So she got rid of him, as I have told you. My other freedmen took Polybius's death as an affront to themselves— they formed a very close guild, always shielded each other loyally and never competed for my favour or showed any jealousy among themselves. Polybius had said nothing in his own defence, not wishing, I suppose, to incriminate his guild-brothers, many of whom must have been implicated in the same discreditable traffic in citizenships.

As for Mnester, it now happened on several occasions that when billed to dance he would fail to put in an appearance. It used to cause an uproar in the theatre. I must have been very stupid; though his absence always coincided with a sick headache of Messalina's, which prevented her attendance too, it never occurred to me to draw the obvious conclusion. I had to apologize several times to the public and undertake that it would not occur again. On one occasion I said, in joke: "My Lords, you can't accuse me of hiding him away at the Palace." This remark caused inordinate laughter. Everyone but myself knew where Mnester was. When I got back to the Palace Messalina used to send for me, and I would find her in bed in a darkened room with a damp cloth over her eyes. She would say in a faint voice: "What, my dear, do you mean to say Mnester didn't dance again? Then I didn't miss anything after all. I was lying here simply seething with envy. I got up once and started to dress, to come after all, but the pain was so frightful that I had to get back to bed. Was the play very dull without him?"

I would say: "We really must insist on his keeping his engagements: the City can't be treated like this, time after time."

Messalina would sigh: "I don't know. He's very highly strung, poor fellow. Just like a woman. Great artists are always like that. He gets sick headaches at the least provocation, he says. And if he felt only one-tenth as ill to-day as I have felt, it would be the greatest cruelty to insist on his dancing. It's not shamming, either. He loves his work and he's greatly distressed when he fails his public. Leave me now, dearest; I want to sleep if I can."

So I would tiptoe out and nothing more would be said about Mnester until the same thing happened again. I never thought as highly of Mnester, though, as most people did. He has been compared to the great actor Roscius who under the Republic attained to such eminence in his profession that he became a byword for artistic excellence. People, rather absurdly, still call a clever architect, or a learned historian, or even a smart boxer "a very Roscius." Mnester was no Roscius except in that very loose sense. I admit that I never saw Roscius act. There is nobody now living who ever did. We must all depend on the verdict of our great-grandparents in discussing him, and they agree that Roscius's chief aim in acting was "to keep in character": and that noble king, or cunning pimp, or boastful soldier, or simple clown—whatever Roscius chose to be, that he was, to the life, without affectation. Whereas Mnester was a mass of mannerisms, very charming and graceful mannerisms, I'm sure, but in the final sense he was not an actor, he was just a pretty fellow with a neat pair of legs and a gift for choreographical improvization.

It was now that Aulus Plautius returned home after four years' command in Britain and I had the pleasure of persuading the Senate to grant him a triumph. It was not, however, a full triumph, as I should have liked, but a lesser triumph, or ovation. If a general's services are too great to be rewarded merely with triumphal ornaments and yet have not, for some technical reason, entitled him to a full triumph, he is given this lesser sort. For example, if the war has not yet been completely finished; or if there has been insufficient bloodshed; or if the enemy is not considered a worthy one—as, long ago, after the defeat of the revolted slaves under Spartacus, though, indeed, Spartacus gave our armies more trouble than many a great foreign nation. In the case of Aulus Plautius, the objection was that his conquests were not yet secure enough to allow him to withdraw his troops. So instead of a chariot with four horses, he rode into the City on horseback, and he wore a myrtle wreath, not one of laurel, and carried no sceptre. The Senate did not head the procession, and there was no corps of trumpeters, and when the procession was done Aulus sacrificed a ram, not a bull. But otherwise the proceedings were the same as in a full triumph, and to show that it was no jealousy of mine that prevented him from winning the same honour as I had done, I came to meet him as he rode down the Sacred Way and offered him my congratulations and let him ride on my right side (the more honourable position) and myself supported him as he went on his knees up the Capitol steps. I also acted as his host at the banquet, and when the banquet was over, again put him on my right side when we brought him home to his house by torchlight.

Aulus was very grateful to me for this, but even more grateful, he told me in private, for having hushed up the scandal of his wife and the Christian love-feast (followers of that Jewish sect were now called Christians) and for having left her to his jurisdiction. He said that when a woman is unavoidably parted from her husband—her health had not allowed her to go to Britain—she is apt to feel lonely and take strange fancies into her head and fall an easy prey to religious charlatans, especially the Jewish and Egyptian sort. But she was a good woman and a good wife and he trusted that she would soon be cured of this nonsense. He was right. Two years later I arrested all the leading Christians in Rome, together with all the orthodox Jewish missionaries, and sent them out of the country, and Aulus's wife was a great help to me in rounding them up.

The chief emotional appeal of Christianity was that this Joshua, or Jesus, was said to have risen from the dead, as no man had ever done before, except in legends: after being crucified he had visited his friends apparently none the worse for his experience, had eaten and drunk to prove that he was no vision and then gone up to Heaven in a blaze of glory. And there was no proof that these were all lies, because, as it happened, there had been an earthquake just after the crucifixion, which had dislodged a heavy stone from the mouth of the tomb where the corpse had been put. The guard had fled in panic, and when they came back the corpse was gone; evidently it had been stolen. Once a story like this begins to circulate in the East it is difficult to stop it, and it would have been undignified to argue against its absurdity in a public edict; but I did publish a strong order in Galilee, where the Christians were most numerous, making it a capital offence to violate graves. But I must waste no more time over these ridiculous Christians: I must continue with my own story.

I must tell about the three letters which I added to the Roman alphabet, and about the great Sæcular Games I celebrated, and about the census I took of Roman citizens, and about my revival of the ancient religious art of soothsaying which had now fallen into neglect, and about various important edicts of mine and laws which I inspired the Senate to pass. But perhaps it would be better first to finish briefly my account of Britain; now that Aulus Plautius has been brought safely home what happened there subsequently will not interest my readers greatly. I sent out one Ostorius to take Aulus's place and he had a most difficult time. Plautius had completed the conquest of the plain of South Britain, but, as I say, the mountain tribes of Wales and the warlike North-Midlanders persisted in raiding the frontiers of the new province; Caractacus had married the daughter of the King of South Wales and was leading the South Welsh army in person. As soon as he arrived Ostorius announced that he would disarm all British provincials whose loyalty he suspected; he would thus be free to send his main forces against the tribes beyond the frontier, leaving only small garrisons behind. This announcement was generally resented, and it was understood by the Icenians, who were free allies of ours, that the disarmament rule would be extended to them too. They made a sudden rising and Ostorius at Colchester found himself threatened by a large army of north-eastern tribes, with not one regular regiment at hand: they were all away in the center or far west of the island and he had nobody with him but French and Batavians. However, he chose to risk an immediate battle and came off victorious. The Icenian confederacy sued for peace and was granted easy terms, and Ostorius then pushed his regular regiments north, annexing the entire Midlands, and halting on the frontier of the Brigantians. The Brigantians are a savage and powerful federation of tribes who occupy the north of the island as far as its narrowest point; beyond them, the wild mountainous land that spreads out again, unexplored and frightful, for another few hundred miles is inhabited by those red-headed terrors, the Goidels. Ostorius made an expedition to the River Dee in the west and was plundering the valley of that river, which flows north to the Irish Sea, when he heard that the Brigantians were on the move behind him. He turned back and defeated a considerable force of them, capturing several hundred men, including some leading noblemen and a son of the King. The King of the Brigantians pledged himself to ten years of honourable peace if the prisoners were returned; and Ostorius accepted this, but kept the prince and five noblemen as hostages under the title of guests. He was then free to conduct operations in the Welsh hills against Caractacus. He used three out of his four regular regiments, basing one at Cærleon on the Usk, and two at Shrewsbury on the Severn. The remainder of the island was garrisoned only by auxiliaries, except for the Ninth, at Lincoln, and a colony of time-expired veterans at Colchester, where they had been given lands, live stock, and captives to work for them. This colony was the first Roman municipality in Britain, and I sent a letter sanctioning the foundation there of a temple to the God Augustus.

It took Ostorius three years to subdue South and Mid-Wales. Caractacus was a brave enemy and when he was forced up into North Wales with the remnants of his army he managed to fire the tribes there with his own courage.

But Ostorius eventually defeated him in a last battle, in which we too lost heavily, and captured his wife, his daughter, a brother-in-law, and two of his nephews in the British camp. Caractacus himself fought his way north-east in a desperate rear-guard action and appeared a few days later at the court of the Queen of the Brigantians (her father, the King, had died and she was the only member of the royal house surviving, apart from the hostage prince in Ostorius's hands, so they had made her Queen). He urged her to continue the war, but she was no fool. She had him put in chains and sent him to Ostorius as a proof of her loyalty to the oath her father had sworn. Ostorius in return sent her back the noble hostages, one of whom she married. Her brother, the prince, she put to death because he was known to have shown cowardice on the field of battle, unlike her new husband who had only been captured after receiving seven wounds and accounting for five Roman soldiers. This Queen, whose name is Cartimandua, has proved a most loyal ally. She quarreled with her husband because he said that he did not regard himself as bound by the old King's oath to maintain peace with us. He could not persuade the Brigantians to make war on us, so he went down to South Wales and started a fresh revolt there. Our garrison at Cærleon was suddenly attacked in great force. The enemy were beaten off but our losses included a battalion commander and eight captains of the Second. Not long after this two battalions of French auxiliaries, out foraging, were surprised and annihilated. Ostorius, worn out by three years of incessant fighting, took these reverses too much to heart: he fell sick and died, poor fellow, though it must have been some comfort to him that he was awarded triumphal ornaments just before this. That was two years ago. I sent out a general called Didius to take over the command of the province, but while he was on his way the Fourteenth were beaten in a pitched battle and had to retreat to their camp, leaving prisoners in the hands of the enemy.

Cartimandua's husband then left South Wales and made an attack on Cartimandua herself, who had earned his anger by putting to death two of his brothers who were plotting against her. She appealed for help to Didius and he sent her four battalions of the Ninth and two of Batavians. With these and her own forces she defeated her husband, captured him and made him swear vassalage to herself and friendship to the Romans. She then pardoned him and they are reigning together again with apparent friendliness: there have been no border raids reported since. Meanwhile Didius has restored order in South Wales.

So let me now take leave of my province of Britain, which has cost us heavily in men and money and has so far yielded small returns except in glory. But I regard the occupation as a good investment for Rome in the long run, and if we treat the natives with justice and good faith they will become valuable allies and, eventually, valuable citizens. The riches of a country do not only lie in corn, metals and cattle. What the Empire needs most is men, and if she can add to her resources by the annexation of a country where an honest, warlike and industrious race is bred, that is a better acquisition than any spice island of the Indies or gold-bearing territory of Central Asia. The faith that Queen Cartimandua and her nobles have shown, and the courage in adversity of King Caractacus, are the happiest possible auguries of the future.

Caractacus was brought to Rome and I decreed a general holiday to celebrate his arrival. The whole City came out to look at him. The Guards Division was on parade, outside the Camp, and I was sitting on a tribunal platform erected for the occasion at the Camp gate. Trumpeters sounded and in the distance a small procession was moving across the turf towards me. First came a detachment of captured British soldiers; then Caractacus's household thegns; then wagons heaped with trappings and collars and weapons—not only Caractacus's own, but all that he had won in wars with his neighbours, captured in that camp at Cefn Carnedd; then Caractacus's wife, daughter, brother-in-law, and nephews, and lastly Caractacus himself, carrying his head high and looking neither to the right nor the left until he came to my platform. There he made a dignified obeisance, and asked permission to address me. I granted him permission and he spoke in a frank and noble way, in such remarkably fluent Latin, too, that I positively envied him: I am a wretched speaker and always get entangled in my sentences.

"Cæsar, you see me here in chains before you, suing for my life, after having resisted your country's arms for seven long years. I might well have held out for seven years longer if I had not trusted Queen Cartimandua to respect the sacred guest-right of our island. In Britain when a man claims hospitality at any house, and is given salt and bread and wine, the host then holds himself answerable for his guest's life with his own. A man took refuge once at my father Cymbeline's court and, after having eaten his salt, revealed himself as the murderer of my grandfather. But my father said: 'You are my guest. I cannot harm you.' Queen Cartimandua by putting me in these chains and sending me here did more honour to you as her ally than to herself as the Queen of the Brigantians.

"I make a voluntary confession of my own faults. The letter that my brother Togodumnus wrote to you, and that I did not dissuade him from sending, was as foolish as it was discourteous. We were young and proud then and trusting to hearsay we underestimated the strength of your Roman armies, the loyalty of your generals, and your own great qualities as a commander. If I had matched the glory of my lineage and of my own feats with a becoming moderation in prosperity I should no doubt have entered this City as a friend, not as a captive; nor would you then have disdained to welcome me royally, as a son of my father Cymbeline whom your God Augustus honoured as an ally and overlord like him of many a conquered tribe.

"For my prolonged resistance to you, once I found that you were bent on annexing my kingdom and the kingdoms of my allies, I have no apologies to offer. I had men and arms, chariots, horses and treasure: do you wonder that I was unwilling to part with them? You Romans aim at extending your sway over all mankind, but it does not follow that all mankind will immediately accept that sway. You must first prove your right to rule, and prove it with the sword. It has been a long war between us, Cæsar, and your armies have pursued me from tribe to tribe, and from fort to fort, and I have taken heavy toll of them; but now I am caught and the victory is yours at last. If I had surrendered to your lieutenant Aulus Plautius at that first engagement on the Medway I would have been proved an unworthy foe and Aulus Plautius would not have sent for you, and so you would never have celebrated your deserved triumph. Therefore respect your enemy, now that he is humbled, grant him his life, and your noble clemency will never be forgotten either by your own country or by mine. Britain will reverence the clemency of the victor, if Rome approves the courage of the conquered."

I called Aulus to me. "For my part I am willing to let this brave king go free. To restore him to his throne in Britain would be everywhere regarded as weakness, so that I cannot do. But I am inclined to let him stay here in Rome as a guest of the City, with a pension suited to his needs; and also to release his family and household thegns. What do you say?"

Aulus answered: "Cæsar, Caractacus has shown himself a gallant enemy. He has tortured or executed no prisoners, poisoned no wells, fought fair and kept faith. If you release him I shall be proud to take him by the hand and offer him my friendship."

I freed Caractacus. He thanked me gravely: "I wish for every Roman citizen a heart like yours." That night he and his family dined at the Palace. Aulus was there too and we old campaigners fought the battle of Brentwood over again as the wine went round. I told Caractacus how nearly he and I had met in a hand-to-hand conflict. He laughed and said: "If I had only known! But if you are still eager for the fight, I'm your man. To-morrow morning on Mars Field, you on your mare and me on foot? The disparity of our ages will make that fair." Another remark of his has since become famous: "I cannot understand, my Lords, how as rulers of a City as glorious as this is, with its houses like marble cliffs, its shops like royal treasuries, its temples like the dreams that our Druids report when they return from magical visits to the Kingdom of the Dead, you can ever find it in your hearts to covet the possession of our poor island huts."

# Chapter Twenty-Seven

EXPIATORY games, called Tarentine or Sæcular are celebrated at Rome to mark the beginning of each new cycle, or age of men. They take the form of a festival of three days and nights in honour of Pluto and Proserpine, the Gods of the Underworld. Historians agree that these games were first formally established as a public ritual by Publicola, a Valerian, in the two hundred and fiftieth year after the foundation of Rome—which was also the year in which the Claudians came to Rome from Sabine country; but they had been celebrated one hundred and ten years previously as a family ritual of the Valerians, in accordance with an oracle of Delphic Apollo. Publicola made a vow that they should be performed at the beginning of every new cycle thereafter so long as the City stood. Since his time there have been five celebrations, but at irregular intervals because of differences of opinion as to when each new cycle started. Sometimes the cycle has been taken as the natural cycle of one hundred and ten years, which is the ancient Etruscan method of reckoning, and sometimes as the Roman civil cycle of one hundred years, and sometimes the Games have been celebrated as soon as it was clear that nobody survived who had taken part on the previous occasion.

The most recent celebration under the Republic was in the six hundred and seventh year from the foundation of the City, and the only celebration that had taken place since then was Augustus's in the seven hundred and thirty-sixth year. The year of Augustus's celebration could not be justified as marking the hundredth or hundred-and-tenth year from the previous celebration, nor as marking the death of the last man who had taken part in it; nor could it be understood as a date arrived at by calculation from Publicola's time, reckoning in hundred- or hundred-and-ten-year terms. Augustus, or rather the Board of Fifteen, his religious advisers, were reckoning from a supposed first celebration of the Games in the ninety-seventh year from the foundation of the City. I admit that in my history of his religious reforms I had accepted this date as the correct one, but only because to criticize him on this important point would have got me into serious trouble with my grandmother Livia. The fact was (not to go into the matter in detail) that his reckoning was incorrect even if the first celebration had taken place when he said it did, which was not so. I reckoned forward from Publicola's festival in natural cycles of one hundred and ten years (for this clearly was what a cycle meant to Publicola himself) until I reached the six hundred and ninetieth year from the foundation of the City. That was when the last celebra- A.D. 46 tion should have really taken place, and then not again until the eight hundredth year, the date which we have just reached in this story, namely, the seventh year of my own monarchy.

Now, each cycle has a certain fatal character, which is given it by the events of the inaugurating year. The first year of the previous cycle had been marked by the birth of Augustus, the death of Mithridates the Great, Pompey's victory over the Phœnicians and his capture of Jerusalem, Catiline's unsuccessful attempt at a popular revolution, and Cæsar's assumption of the office of High Pontiff. Is it necessary for me to point out the significance of each of these events? That for the next cycle our arms were destined to be successful abroad and the Empire to be greatly extended, popular liberty to be suppressed, and the Cæsars to be the

461

mouthpieces of the Gods? Now it was my intention to expiate the sins and crimes of this old cycle, and inaugurate a new one with solemn sacrifices. For it was in this year that I counted on completing my work of reform. I would then hand the government of a now prosperous and well-organized nation back to the Senate and People, from whom it had so long been withheld.

I had thought the whole plan out in detail. It was clear that government by the Senate under Consuls elected annually had great disadvantages: the single-year term was not long enough. And the Army did not wish to have its Commander-in-Chief constantly changed. My plan, briefly, was to make a free gift to the nation of the Privy Purse, except so much of it as was needed to support me as a private citizen, and the Imperial lands, including Egypt, and to introduce a law providing for a change of government every fifth year. The ex-Consuls of the previous five-year period together with certain representatives of the People and of the Knights would form a cabinet to advise and assist one of their number, chosen by religious lot and known as the Consul-in-Chief, in the government of the country. Each member of the cabinet would be responsible to the Consul-in-Chief for a department corresponding with the departments that I had been building up under my freedmen, or for the government of one of the frontier provinces. The Consuls of the year would act as a link between the Consul-in-Chief and the Senate, and would perform their usual duties as appeal judges; the Protectors of the People would act as a link between the Consul-in-Chief and the People. The Consuls would be elected from the Senatorial order by popular election, and in national emergencies recourse would be had to a plebiscite. I had thought out a number of ingenious safeguards for this constitution and congratulated myself that it was a workable one: my freedmen would remain as permanent officials in charge of the clerical staff, and the new government would benefit by their advice. Thus the redeeming features of monarchical government would be retained without prejudice to republican liberty. And to keep the Army contented I would embody in the new constitution a measure providing for a bounty of money to be paid every five years, proportionate to the success of our arms abroad and to the increase of wealth at home. The governorships of home provinces would be distributed between knights who had risen to high command in the Army, and senators.

For the present I told nobody of my plans, but continued with a light heart at my work. I was convinced that as soon as I proved by a voluntary resignation of the monarchy that my intentions had never been tyrannical and that such summary executions as I had ordered had been forced on me, I would be forgiven all my lesser errors for the sake of the great work of reform that I had accomplished, and all suspicions would be put to rest. I told myself: "Augustus always said that he would resign and restore the Republic: but somehow he never did, because of Livia. And Tiberius always said the same, but somehow he never did, because he was afraid of the hatred that he had earned by his cruelty and tyranny. But I really am going to resign: there's nothing to prevent me. My conscience is clear, and Messalina's no Livia."

These Sæcular Games were celebrated not in the summer, as on previous occasions, but on the twenty-first of A. D. 47 April, the Shepherds' Festival, because that was the very day on which Romulus and his shepherds had founded Rome eight hundred years before. I followed Augustus's example in not making the Gods of the Underworld the only deities addressed; though the Tarentum, a volcanic cleft in Mars Field, which was the traditional place for the celebration and was said to be one entrance to Hell, was converted into a temporary theatre and illuminated

463

with coloured lights and made the centre of the Festival. I had sent heralds out some months before to summon all citizens (in the old formula) "to a spectacle which nobody now living has ever seen before, and which nobody now living shall ever see again." This provoked a few sneers, because Augustus's celebration of sixty-four years previously was remembered by a number of old men and women, some of whom had actually taken part in it. But it was the old formula, and it was justified by Augustus's celebration not having been performed at the proper time.

On the morning of the first day the Board of Fifteen distributed to all free citizens, from the steps of Jove's temple on the Capitoline Hill and Apollo's on the Palatine, torches, sulphur and bitumen, the instruments of purification; also wheat, barley and beans, some to serve as an offering to the Fates and some to be given as pay to the actors taking part in the festival. Early morning sacrifices had been simultaneously offered in all the principal temples of Rome, to Jove, Juno, Neptune, Minerva, Venus, Apollo, Mercury, Ceres, Vulcan, Mars, Diana, Vesta, Hercules, Augustus, Latona, the Fates, and to Pluto and Proserpine. But the chief event of the day was the sacrifice of a white bull to Jove and a white cow to Juno, on the Capitol, and everyone was expected to attend this. Then we went in procession to the Tarentum theatre and sang choruses in honour of Apollo and Diana. The afternoon was taken up by chariot races and wild-beast hunts and sword-fighting in the Circus and amphitheatres and scenic games in honour of Apollo in the theatre of Pompey.

At nine o'clock that night, after a great burning of sulphur and sprinkling of holy water in consecration of the whole of Mars Field, I sacrificed three male lambs to the Fates on three underground altars built by the bank of the Tiber, while a crowd of citizens with me waved their lighted torches, offered their wheat, barley and beans, and sang a hymn of repentance for past errors. The blood of the lambs was sprinkled on the altars and their carcasses burned. At the Tarentum theater more hymns were then sung and the expiatory part of the festival gone through with appropriate solemnity. Then scenes from Roman legend were acted, including a ballet illustrative of the fight between the three brother Horatius and the three brothers Curiatius which was said to have occurred close by on the day of the first celebration of the Games by the Valerian family.

The next day the noblest matrons in Rome, headed by Messalina, assembled on the Capitol and performed supplications to Juno. The games continued as on the previous day: three hundred lions and a hundred bears were killed in the amphitheatre, not to mention bulls and numerous sword-fighters. That night I sacrificed a black hog and a black pig to Mother Earth. On the last day Greek and Latin hymns were sung in chorus in the sanctuary of Apollo by three times nine beautiful boys and maidens, and white oxen were sacrificed to him. Apollo was so honoured because his oracle had originally ordered the institution of the Festival. The hymns were to implore the protection of Apollo, his sister Diana, his mother Latona, and his father Jove, for all cities, towns and magistrates in the whole Empire. One of them was Horace's famous Sæcular Hymn in honour of Apollo and Diana, which did not have to be brought up to date, as you might have supposed: in fact, one verse of the hymn was more appropriate than when it was first composed:

"Moved by the solemn voice of prayer
Both deities shall make great Rome their care,
Benignly turn the direful woes
   Of famine and of weeping war
   From Rome and noble Cæsar far,
And pour them on our British foes."

Horace had written that at a time when Augustus contemplated a war against Britain, but it never came off, so the British were not officially our foes, as they now were.

More sacrifices to all the Gods, more chariot races, sword-fights, wild-beast hunts, athletic contests. That night at the Tarentum I sacrificed a black ram, a black sheep, a black bull, a black cow, a black boar, and a black sow, to Pluto and Proserpine; and the Festival was over for another hundred and ten years. It had gone through without a single error or evil omen of any sort being reported. When I asked Vitellius whether he had enjoyed the Festival, he said: "It was excellent and I wish you many happy returns of the day." I burst out laughing and he apologized for his absent-mindedness. He had unconsciously been identifying Rome's birthday with mine, he explained, but hoped that the phrase might prove an omen of life prolonged for me to a remarkable and vigorous old age. But Vitellius could be very disingenuous: I believe now that he had thought the joke out weeks beforehand.

To me the proudest moment of the whole festival was on the afternoon of the third day, when the Troy Game was performed on Mars Field and my little Britannicus, then only just six years old, took part in the skirmish with boys twice his age and managed his pony and his weapons like a Hector or Caractacus. The people reserved their loudest cheers for him. They commented on his extraordinary likeness to my brother Germanicus, and prophesied splendid triumphs for him as soon as he was old enough to go to the wars. A grand-nephew of mine also took part in the Games, a boy of eleven, the son of my niece Agrippinilla. His name was Lucius Domitius,[1] and I have mentioned him before, but only in passing. The time has now come for a fuller account of him.

He was the son of that Domitius Ahenobarbus (or Brass-

---

[1] Afterwards the Emperor Nero.—R. G.

beard), my maternal cousin, who had the reputation of being the bloodiest-minded man in Rome. Bloody-mindedness ran in the family, like the red beard, and it was said that it was no wonder they had brass beards, to match their iron faces and leaden hearts. When a young man Domitius Ahenobarbus had served on Gaius Cæsar's staff in the East and had killed one of his own freedmen by locking him up in a room with no water to drink and nothing but salt fish and dry bread to eat, because he had refused to get properly drunk at his birthday banquet. When Gaius heard of this he told Domitius that his services were no longer needed and that he no longer counted him among his friends. Domitius returned to Rome and on the way back, in a freak of petulance, suddenly spurred his horse along a village street on the Appian Way and deliberately ran down a child who was playing in the road with its doll. Again, once in the open Market Place, he picked a quarrel with a knight to whom he owed money, and gouged out one of his eyes with his thumb. My uncle Tiberius made a friend of Domitius in the latter years of his reign: for he deliberately cultivated the society of the cruel and base, with the object, it is supposed, of feeling somewhat virtuous by comparison. He married Domitius to his adoptive granddaughter, my niece Agrippinilla, and there was one child of the marriage, this Lucius. Congratulated by his friends on the birth of an heir, Domitius scowled: "Spare your congratulations, blockheads. If you had any real patriotism you'd go to the cradle and strangle the child at once. Don't you realize that Agrippinilla and I between us command all the known vices, human and inhuman, and that he's destined to grow up the most detestable imp that ever plagued our unfortunate country? That's not guesswork, either: have any of you seen his horoscope? It's enough to make you shudder." Domitius was arrested on the double charge of treason and incest with his sister Domitia—of course, that meant nothing in Tiberius's time, it was a mere formality. Tiberius died opportunely and he was liberated by Caligula. Not long afterwards Domitius himself died, of the dropsy. He had named Caligula in his will as young Lucius's co-heir, leaving him two-thirds of the estate. When Agrippinilla was banished to her island Caligula seized the rest of the estate too, so Lucius was now practically an orphan and quite unprovided for. However, his aunt Domitia took care of him. (She must not be confused with her sister, Domitia Lepida, Messalina's mother.) She was a woman who gave herself wholly to pleasure and only bothered about young Lucius because of a prophecy that he would one day become Emperor: she wanted to stand in well with him. It is a comment on Domitia's character that the three tutors to whom she entrusted his education were a Syrian ex-ballet dancer who shared Domitia's favours with a Tyrolese ex-sword-fighter, this same ex-sword-fighter, and her Greek hair-dresser. They gave him a fine popular education.

When two years later Agrippinilla returned she felt so little maternal feeling for her son that she told Domitia that he might as well stay with her for another few years; she would pay well to have the responsibility taken off her hands. I intervened and made Agrippinilla take him home; she took the tutors too, because Lucius was unwilling to come without them, and Domitia had other lovers. Agrippinilla also took Domitia's husband, an ex-Consul, and married him, but they soon quarrelled and separated. The next event in Lucius's life was an attempt to assassinate him while he was taking his afternoon siesta: two men walked in at the front door unchallenged by the porter, who was also taking his siesta, went upstairs, found nobody about in the corridors, wandered along until they saw a slave sleeping in front of a bedroom door which they decided must be the one that they were looking for, went in, found Lucius asleep in his bed, drew their daggers and tiptoed close. A moment later they came rushing out again screaming: "The snake, the snake!" Though the household was alarmed by the noise no effort was made to stop them, and they escaped. What had frightened them was the sight of a cobra's skin on Lucius's pillow. He had been wearing it wound around his leg as a cure for scrofula, from which he suffered greatly as a child, and I suppose had been playing with it before he went to sleep. In the darkened room it looked like a live cobra. I have since supposed that the assassins were sent by Messalina, who hated Agrippinilla but did not, for some reason or other, dare to bring any charge against her. At any rate, the story went round that two cobras stood on guard at Lucius's bed, and Agrippinilla encouraged it. She enclosed the snakeskin in a gold snake-shaped bracelet for him to wear and told her friends that it had indeed been found on the pillow and must have been sloughed there by a cobra. Lucius told his friends that he certainly had a cobra guard, but that it was probably an exaggeration to say that it was a double guard: he had never seen more than a single cobra. It used to drink from his water jug. No more attempts were made to assassinate him.

Lucius, as well as Britannicus, resembled my dear brother Germanicus, who was his grandfather, but in this case it was a hateful resemblance. The features were almost identical, but the frank, noble, generous, modest character that beamed from Germanicus's face was supplanted here by slyness, baseness, meanness, vanity. And yet most people were blinded to this by the degenerate refinement he had made of his grandfather's handsome looks: he had an effeminate beauty that made men warm to him as they would to a woman; and he knew the power of his beauty only too well, and took as long every morning over his toilet, especially over his hair, which he wore quite long, as his mother or his aunt. His hairdresser tutor tended his beauty as jealously as the head gardener in the Gardens of Lucullus tended the fruit on the famous peach wall or the unique white-fleshed cherry-tree which Lucullus had brought from the Black Sea. It was strange to watch Lucius on Mars Field doing military exercises with sword, shield and spear: he handled them correctly enough, as his Tyrolese sword-fighter tutor had taught him, yet it was less a drill than a ballet-dance. When, at the same age, Germanicus was doing his exercises, one could always in imagination hear the clash of battle, trumpets, groans and shouts, and see the gush of German blood; with Lucius one only heard the rippling applause of a theatre audience and saw roses and gold coins showered on the stage.

But enough of Lucius for the moment. A more pleasant topic is my improvement of the Roman alphabet. In my previous book I explained about the three new letters that I had suggested as necessary for modern usage: consonantal *u*, the vowel between *i* and *u* corresponding with Greek *upsilon*, and the consonant which we have hitherto expressed by *bs* or *ps*. I had intended to introduce these after my triumph, but then postponed the matter until the new cycle should start. I announced my project in the Senate on the day following the Sæcular Games, and it was favourably received. But I said that this was an innovation which personally affected everyone in the Empire and that I did not wish to force my own ideas on the Roman people against their will or in a hurry, so I proposed to put the matter to a plebiscite in a year's time.

Meanwhile I published a circular letter explaining and justifying my scheme. I pointed out that though one was brought up to regard the alphabet as a series no less sacred and unalterable than the year of months, or the order of the numerals, or the signs of the Zodiac, this was not really so: everything in this world was subject to change and improvement. Julius Cæsar had reformed the Calendar; the convention for writing numerals had been altered and extended; the names of constellations had been changed: even the stars that composed them were not immortal—since the time of Homer, for example, the seven Pleiades had become six through the disappearance of the star Sterope, or, as she was sometimes called, Electra. So with the Latin alphabet. Not only had the linear forms of the letters changed, but so also had the significance of the letters as denoting certain spoken sounds. The Latin alphabet was borrowed from the Dorian Greeks in the time of the learned King Evander, and the Greeks had originally had it from Cadmus who brought it with him when he arrived with the Phœnician fleet, and the Phœnicians had it from the Egyptians. It was the same alphabet, but only in name. The fact was that Egyptian writing began in the form of pictures of animals and other natural objects, and that these gradually became formalized into hieroglyphic letters, and that the Phœnicians borrowed and altered them, and that the Greeks borrowed and altered these alterations, and finally the Latins borrowed and altered these alterations of alterations. The primitive Greek alphabet contained only sixteen letters, but it was added to until it numbered twenty-four and in some cities twenty-seven. The first Latin alphabet contained only twenty letters, because three Greek aspirated consonants and the letter Z were found unnecessary. However, about five hundred years from the foundation of Rome, G was introduced to supplement C, and more recently still the Z had returned. And still in my opinion the alphabet was not perfect. It would perhaps be a little awkward at first, if the country voted in favour of the change, to remember to use these convenient new forms instead of the old ones, but the awkwardness would soon wear off and a new generation of boys taught to read and write in the new style would not feel it at all. The awkwardness and inconvenience of the change that was made in the Calendar, not quite a hundred years ago, when one year had to be extended to fifteen months, and thereafter the number of days in each month altered, and the name of one of the months changed too—now, that really was something to complain about, but had it not passed off all right? Surely nobody would wish to go back to the old style?

Well, everyone discussed the matter learnedly, but perhaps nobody cared very much about it, one way or the other, at any rate not so much as I did. When eventually the vote was taken it was overwhelmingly in favour of the new letters; but rather as a personal compliment to me, I think, than from any real understanding of the issue. So the Senate voted for their immediate introduction and they appear now in all official documents and in every sort of literature from poems, scientific treatises and legal commentaries, to advertisements of auctions, duns, love-letters, and pornographic scrawls in chalk on the walls of buildings.

And now I shall give a brief account of various public works, reforms, laws and decrees of mine dating from the latter part of my monarchy; I shall thus, so to speak, have the table cleared for writing the painful last chapters of my life. For I have now reached a turning-point in my story, "the discovery" as tragedians call it, after which, though I continued to carry out my duties as Emperor, it was in a very different spirit from hitherto.

I finished building the aqueducts. I also built many hundreds of miles of new roads and put broken ones into good repair. I prohibited money-lenders from making loans to needy young men in expectation of their fathers' deaths: it was a disgusting traffic—the interest was always extortionate and it happened more often than was natural that the father died soon afterwards. This measure was in protection of honest fathers against prodigal sons, but I also provided for honest sons with prodigal fathers: I exempted a son's lawful inheritance from the sequestration of a father's

472

property on account of debt or felony. I also legislated on behalf of women, freeing them from the vexatious tutelage of their paternal relatives, and forbidding dowries to be pledged in surety for a husband's debts.

On Pallas's suggestion I brought a motion before the Senate which was adopted as a law, that any woman of free birth who married a slave without the knowledge and consent of his master became a slave herself; but that if she did so with his knowledge and consent she remained free, and only her children born of the marriage were slaves. There was an amusing sequel to my introduction of this motion. A senator, who happened to be Consul-Elect, had offended Pallas some years before, and foresaw difficulties when he came into office if he could not regain Pallas's goodwill; I do not say that he was justified in expecting Pallas to show rancour, because Pallas is less subject to this fault than I am, but at any rate he had an uneasy conscience. So he proposed that Pallas should be awarded an honorary first-class magistracy and the sum of a hundred and fifty thousand gold pieces, for having performed a great service to the country by originating this law and prevailing on the Senate to pass it. Scipio, Poppæa's widower, sprang up and spoke with an irony reminiscent of Gallus and Haterius in the reign of my uncle Tiberius: "I second that. And I move that public thanks should also be given this extraordinary man. For some of us amateur genealogists have recently discovered that he is directly descended from the Arcadian King Pallas, ancestor of that literary King Evander, recently mentioned by our gracious Emperor, who gave his name to the Palatine Hill. Public thanks, I say, should be given him not only for his services in the drafting of this law but for his modest magnanimity in concealing his royal descent—for putting himself at the disposal of the Senate like a mere nobody and for even deigning to be known as a freedman secretary of the Emperor's."

473

Nobody dared to oppose this motion, so I played the innocent and pretended to take it seriously and did not interpose my veto. It would have been unfair to Pallas if I had. But as soon as the House adjourned I sent for him and told him about the motion. He grew very red, not knowing whether to be angry at the insult or pleased that it was publicly recognized what an important part he played in public affairs. He asked me what he ought to answer, and I said to him: "Do you need the money?"

"No, Cæsar. I'm very well off."

"How well off? Come on, let's hear how much you're worth. Tell me the truth and I won't be angry."

"About three million pieces, when I last went over my accounts."

"What! Silver pieces?"

"No, gold."

"Good God! And all honestly come by?"

"Every farthing. People present petitions or ask favours and I always say, 'I can't promise to do anything for you!' And then they say, 'Oh, no, we never expected it. But please accept this small money-present as an acknowledgement of your kindness in receiving us.' So I put the money in the bank and smile nicely. It's all yours, Cæsar, if you want it. You know that."

"I know it, Pallas. But I had no idea that you were so wealthy."

"I never get time to spend anything, Cæsar."

And that was true. Pallas worked like a galley-slave. So I told him that I would see that the Senate did not have the laugh over him; and advised him to accept the honorary rank but refuse the money. He consented, and I then gravely assured the Senate that Pallas was quite satisfied with the honorary rank that they had kindly awarded him, and would continue to live in his former poverty.

Scipio was not to be beaten. He introduced a motion begging me to plead with Pallas to yield to the Senate's entreaties, and accept the gift. The motion was passed. But Pallas and I held out. On my own advice he refused my entreaties and the Senate's and the farce was completed by still another motion, introduced by Scipio and passed by the House, congratulating Pallas on his primitive parsimony; these congratulations were even officially engraved on a brass tablet. I think you will agree that it was not Pallas and I who were made fools of, but Scipio and the Senate.

I limited barristers' fees to a hundred gold pieces a case. This limitation was directed against men like Suilius, Asiaticus's prosecutor, who could sway a jury to convict or acquit as surely as a farmer drives his pigs to market. Suilius would accept any brief, however desperate, so long as he got his whole fee: which was four thousand a case. And it was the impressiveness of the fee as much as the assurance and eloquence with which he addressed the court that influenced the jury. Occasionally, of course, even Suilius could not hope to pull a case off, because his client's guilt was too clear to be concealed; but so as not to lose his credit with the court, which he would need in future cases where there was at least a fighting chance, he as good as directed the jury to decide against his client. There was a scandal about this; a rich knight accused of robbing the widow of one of his freedmen had paid Suilius his usual fee and had then been betrayed by him in this way. He went to Suilius and asked for a return of his four thousand gold pieces. Suilius said that he had done his best and regretted he could not pay back the money—that would be a dangerous precedent. The knight committed suicide on Suilius's doorstep.

By thus reducing the barristers' fees, which in Republican Rome had been pronounced illegal, I damaged their prestige with the juries, who were thereafter more inclined to give verdicts corresponding with the facts of the case. I waged a sort of war with the barristers. Often when I was about to judge a case I used to warn the court with a smile: "I am an old man, and my patience is easily tried. My verdict will probably go to the side that presents its evidence in the briefest, frankest and most lucid manner, even if it is somewhat incriminating, rather than to the side that spoils a good case by putting up an inappropriately brilliant dramatic performance." And I would quote Homer:

"Yea, when men speak, that man I most detest
Who locks the verity within his breast."

I encouraged the appearance of a new sort of advocate, men without either eloquence or great legal expertness, but with common sense, clear voices and a talent for reducing cases to their simplest elements. The best of these was called Agatho. I always gave him the benefit of the doubt when he pleaded a case before me in his pleasant, quick, precise way, in order to encourage others to emulate him.

The Forensic and Legal Institute of Telegonius, "that most learned and eloquent orator and jurist," was closed down about three years ago. It happened as follows. Telegonius, fat, bustling and crop-haired, appeared one day in the Court of Appeal where I was presiding, and conducted a case of his own. He had been ordered by a magistrate to pay a heavy fine, on the ground that he had incited one of his slaves to kill a valuable slave of Vitellius's in a dispute. It appears that Telegonius's slave, in a barber's shop, had put on insufferable airs as a lawyer and orator. A dispute started between this fellow and Vitellius's slave, who was waiting his turn to be shaved and was known as the best cook (except mine) in all Rome, and worth at the very least ten thousand gold pieces. Telegonius's slave, with offensive eloquence, contrasted the artistic importance of oratory and cookery. Vitellius's cook was not quarrelsome but made a few dispassionate statements of fact, such as that no proper comparison could be drawn between domestic practitioners of splendid arts and splendid practitioners of domestic arts;

that he expected, if not deference, at least politeness from slaves of less importance than himself; and that he was worth at least a hundred times more than his opponent. The orator, enraged by the sympathy the cook got from the other customers, snatched the razor from the barber's hand and cut the cook's throat with it, crying: "I'll teach you to argue with one of Telegonius's men." Telegonius had therefore been fined the full value of the murdered cook, on the ground that his slave's violence was due to an obsession of argumental infallibility, inculcated by the Institute in all its employees. Telegonius now appealed on the ground that the slave had not been incited to murder by violence, for the very motto of the Institute was: *"The tongue is mightier than the blade,"* which constituted a direct injunction to keep to that weapon in any dispute. He also pleaded that it had been a very hot day, that the slave had been subjected to a gross insult by the suggestion that he was not worth more than a miserable hundred gold pieces—the lowest value that could be put upon his services as a trained clerk would be fifty gold pieces annually—and that therefore the only fair view could be that the cook had invited death by provocative behaviour.

Vitellius appeared as a witness. "Cæsar," he said, "I see it this way. This Telegonius's slave has killed my head-cook, a gentle, dignified person, and a perfect artist in his way, as you will yourself agree, having often highly praised his sauces and cakes. It will cost me at least ten thousand gold pieces to replace him and even then, you may be sure, I'll never get anyone half so good. His murderer used phrases, in praise of oratory and in dispraise of cookery, that have been proved to occur, word for word, in Telegonius's own handbooks; and it has been further proved that in the same handbooks, in the sections devoted to 'Liberty,' many violent passages occur which seek to justify a person in resorting to armed force when arguments and reason fail."

Telegonius cross-examined Vitellius, and I must admit that he was scoring heavily when a chance visitor to the court sprang a surprise. It was Alexander the Alabarch, who happened to be in Rome and had strolled into court for amusement. He passed me up a note:

"The person who calls himself Telegonius of Athens and Rome is a runaway slave of mine named Joannes, born at Alexandria in my own household, of a Syrian mother. I lost him twenty-five years ago. You will find the letter A, within a circle, pricked on his left hip, which is my household brand.

"Signed: ALEXANDER, ALABARCH."

I stopped the case while Telegonius was taken outside by my yeomen and identified as indeed the Alabarch's property. Imagine, he had been masquerading as a Roman citizen for nearly twenty years! His entire property should have gone to the State, except for the ten thousand gold pieces which had been awarded to Vitellius, but I let the Alabarch keep half of it. In return the Alabarch made me a present of Telegonius, whom I handed over to Narcissus for disposal: Narcissus set him to work at the useful, if humble, task of keeping court-records.

This, then, was the sort of way I governed. And I widely extended the Roman citizenship, intending that no province whose inhabitants were loyal, orderly and prosperous should long remain inferior in civic status to Rome and the rest of Italy. The first city of Northern France for which I secured the citizenship was Autun.

I then took the census of Roman citizens.

The total number of citizens, including women and children, now stood at 5,984,072, compared with the 4,937,000 given by the census of the year that Augustus died, and again with the 4,233,000 given by the census A.D. 48

taken in the year after my father died. Written briefly on a page these numbers are not impressive, but think of them in human terms. If the whole Roman citizenry were to file past me at a brisk walk, toe to heel, it would be two whole years before the last one came in sight. And these were only the true citizens. If the entire population of the Empire went past, over seventy millions in number, now that Britain, Morocco and Palestine had to be reckoned in, it would take twelve times as long, namely, twenty-four years, for them to pass, and in twenty-four years an entire new generation has time to be born, so that I might sit a lifetime and the stream would still glide on.

"Would glide and slide with still perpetual flow,"

and never the same face appear twice. Numbers are a nightmare. To think that Romulus's first Shepherds' Festival was celebrated by no more than three thousand three hundred souls. Where will it all end?

What I wish to emphasize most of all in this account of my activities as Emperor is that up to this point at least I acted, so far as I knew how, for the public good in the widest possible sense. I was no thoughtless revolutionary and no cruel tyrant and no obstinate reactionary: I tried to combine generosity with common sense wherever possible and nobody can accuse me of not having done my best.

*Two Documents Illustrating Claudius's Legislative Practise, also his Epistolary and Oratorical Style*

Claudius's edict about certain Tyrolese tribes. A.D. 46.

Published at the Residence at Baiæ in the year of the Consulship of Marcus Junius Silanus and of Quintus Sulpicius Camerius, on the fifteenth day of March, by order of Tiberius Claudius Cæsar Augustus Germanicus.

Tiberius Claudius Cæsar Augustus Germanicus, High Pontiff, Protector of the People for the sixth time, Emperor, Father of the Country, Consul-Elect for the fourth time, issues the following official statement:

"As regards certain ancient controversies, the settlement of which had already been left pending for some years when my uncle Tiberius was Emperor: my uncle had sent one Pinarius Apollinaris to inquire into such of these controversies as concerned the Comensians (so far as I recall) and the Bergalians, but no others; and this Pinarius had neglected his commission because of my uncle's obstinate absence from Rome; and then when my nephew Gaius became Emperor and did not call for any report from him either, he offered none—he was no fool in the circumstances—and after that I had a report from Camurius Statutus to the effect that much of the agricultural and forest land in those parts was really under my own jurisdiction—so then, to come down to the present day, I recently sent my good friend Planta Julius there and, when he had called a meeting of my governors, both the local governors and those whose districts lay some distance away, he went thoroughly into all these questions and drew his conclusions. I now approve the wording of the following edict which—first justifying it with a lucid report—he has drawn up for my signature; though it embodies wider decisions than Pinarius was called upon to make:

"'As regards the position of the Anaunians, the Tulliassians and the Sindunians, I understand from authoritative sources that some of these have become incorporated in the government of the Southern Tyrol, though not all. Now although I observe that the claims of men of these tribes to Roman citizenship rest on none too secure a foundation, yet, since they may be said to have come into possession of it by squatter's right and to have mixed so closely with

480

the Southern Tyrolese that they could not be separated from them now without serious injury being done to that distinguished body of citizens, I hereby voluntarily grant them permission to continue in the enjoyment of the rights which they have assumed. I do this all the more readily because a large number of the men whose legal status is affected are reported to be serving in the Guards Division—a few of them have risen to command companies—and some of their compatriots have been enrolled for jury-service at Rome and are carrying out their duties there.

"'This favour carries with it retrospective legal sanction for whatever actions they have performed, and whatever contracts they have entered into under the impression that they were Roman citizens, either among themselves or among the Southern Tyrolese, or in any other circumstances; and such names as they have hitherto borne, as though they were Roman citizens, I hereby permit them to retain.'"

Surviving fragments of Claudius's speech to the Senate, proposing the extension of the Roman citizenship to the French of the Autun district. A.D. 48.

"I must beg you in advance, my Lords, to revise your first shocked impressions, on listening to the proposal I am about to make, that it is a most revolutionary one: such feelings, I foresee, will be the strongest obstacle which I shall encounter to-day. Perhaps the best way for me to negotiate this obstacle is to remind you how many changes have been made in our constitution in the course of Roman history, how extremely plastic, indeed, it has proved from the very beginning.

"At one time Rome was ruled by kings, yet the monarchy never become hereditary. Strangers won the crown, and even foreigners: such as Romulus's successor, King Numa, who was a native of Sabinum (then still a foreign state though lying so close to Rome), and Tarquin the First who succeeded Ancus Martius. Tarquin was of far from distinguished birth—his father was Demarathus, a Corinthian, and his mother was so poor that though she came of the noble Tarquin family she was forced to marry below her—so, being debarred from holding honourable office at Corinth, Tarquin came here and was elected king. He and his son, or perhaps his grandson—historians are unable to agree even on this point—were succeeded by Servius Tullius who, according to Roman accounts, was the son of Ocresia, a captive woman. Etruscan records make him the faithful companion of the Etruscan Cæle Vipinas and sharer in all his misfortunes: they say that when Cæle had been defeated, Servius Tullius left Etruria with the remnants of Cæle's army and seized the Cælian hill yonder, which he named after their former commander. He then changed his Etruscan name—it was Macstrna—to Tullius, and won the Roman crown, and made a very good king too. Later, when Tarquin the Proud and his sons began to be loathed for their tyrannical behaviour, the Roman people, please observe, grew tired of monarchical government and we had Consuls, annually elected magistrates, instead.

"Need I then remind you of the dictatorship, which our ancestors found a stronger form of government even than the consular power in difficult times of war or political discord? Or of the appointment of Protectors of the People to defend the rights of the commons against encroachment? Or of the Board of Ten which for a time took over the government from the Consuls? Or of the sharing of the consular power between several persons? Or of the irregular appointment of army colonels to the Consulship—it happened seven or eight times? Or of the granting to members of the commons not only the highest magistracies but admission to the priesthood too? However, I shall not dilate on the early struggles of our ancestors and what the outcome of it all has been; you might suspect that I was immodestly making this historical survey an excuse for boasting of our recent extension of the Empire beyond the northern seas. . . .

"It was the will of my uncle, the Emperor Tiberius, that all leading colonies and provincial towns in Italy should have representatives sitting in this House; and representatives were indeed found with the necessary qualifications of character and wealth. 'Yes,' you will say, 'but there is a great difference between an Italian senator and a senator from abroad.' Well, when I begin justifying to you this part of my action, as Censor, in extending the full Roman citizenship to the provinces, I shall show you just how I feel about the matter. But let me say briefly that I do not think that we ought to debar provincials from a seat in this House, if they can be a credit to it, merely because they are provincials. The renowned and splendid colony of Vienne, in France, has been sending us senators for a long time now, has it not? My dear friend Lucius Vestinus comes from Vienne: he is one of the most distinguished members of the Noble Order of Knights and I employ him here to assist me in my administrative duties. (I have, by the way, a favour to ask from you for Vestinus's children: I wish to have the highest honours of the priesthood conferred on them—I trust that later they will earn distinctions by their own merits to add to those granted them on their father's account.) There is, however, one Frenchman whose name I shall keep out of this speech, because he was a rascally robber and I hate the very mention of him. He was a sort of wrestling-school prodigy and carried a Consulship back to his colony before the place had even been granted the Roman citizenship. I have an equally low opinion of his brother—such a miserable and unworthy wretch that he could not possibly be of any use to you as a senator.

"But it is now high time, Tiberius Claudius Germanicus, for you to reveal to the House the theme of your speech: you have already reached the frontiers of the South of France. . . .

". . . This House should be no more ashamed of these noble gentlemen, now standing before me, were they raised to the quality of senators, than my distinguished friend Persicus is ashamed when he finds the French name Allobrogicus among the funeral masks of his ancestors. If you agree that all this is as I say, what more do you want of me? Do you want me to prove to you from the map, putting my finger on the very spot, that you are already getting senators from beyond the frontier of Southern France, that no shame, in fact, has been felt about introducing men into our order who were born at *Lyons*?[1] O my Lords, I protest that it is with the greatest timidity that I venture beyond the familiar home-boundaries of Southern France! However, the cause of the rest of that great country must now definitely be pleaded. I grant you that the French fought against Julius Cæsar (now deified) for ten years, but in return you must grant me that for a whole century since then they have preserved a more devoted loyalty to us, in times of disorder too, than we could ever have believed possible. When my father Drusus was engaged in the conquest of Germany the entire land of France remained at peace in his rear; and that, too, at a time when he had been called away from the business of taking a census of property-holders—a new and disquieting experience for the French. Why, even to-day, as I have only too good reason to know by personal experience, this taking of the census is a most arduous task, though it now means no more than a public review of our material resources. . . ."

[1] A joking reference to himself.—R. G.

# Chapter Twenty-Eight

ONE morning in August, the year of the census, Messalina came early into my bedroom and woke me up. It always takes me a long time to collect my wits when I first wake up, especially if I have been unable to sleep between midnight and dawn, as is often the case. She A.D. 48 bent over me and kissed me and stroked my hair and told me in tones of the greatest concern that she had terrible news for me. I asked drowsily and rather crossly what it was.

"Barbillus the astrologer—you know that he never makes a mistake, don't you? Well, I asked him to read my stars yesterday, because he'd not done it for two or three years, and he observed them last night, and do you know what he has just come and told me?"

"Of course I don't know. Out with it and let me go on sleeping. I've had a wretched night."

"Darling, I wouldn't dare to disturb you like this if it wasn't terribly important. What he said was, 'Lady Messalina, a frightful fate is in store for one very near to you. This is Saturn's baleful influence once more. He is in his most malignant aspect. The blow will fall within thirty days, not later than the Ides of September.' I asked him whom he meant, but he wouldn't tell me. He just kept on hinting, and at last I dragged it out of him by threatening to have him flogged. And guess what he said!"

"I hate guessing when I'm half-asleep."

"But I hate telling you directly, it's so frightening. He said: 'Lady Messalina, your husband will die a violent death.'"

485

"He really said that?"

She nodded solemnly.

I sat up, my heart pounding. Yes, Barbillus was always right in his forecasts. And that meant that I would not survive my attempted introduction of the new constitution by more than a few days. I had planned my speech for the seventh of September, the anniversary of my victory at Brentwood: but I had kept the whole business a complete secret from everyone, even Messalina, from whom otherwise I had no secrets. I said: "Is there nothing to be done? Can't we cheat the prophecy somehow?"

"I can't think of anything. You're my husband, aren't you? Unless . . . unless . . . listen, I have an idea! Suppose that just for this next month you aren't my husband."

"But I am. You can't pretend I'm not."

"You can divorce me, can't you, just for a month? And marry me again when Barbillus reports that Saturn has moved away to a safe distance."

"No, that's not possible. If I divorce you we can't legally remarry, unless there has been a marriage in between."

"I didn't think of that. But don't let us be beaten by a mere technicality. Suppose, then, that I do marry someone —anyone—just as a matter of form. A cook or a porter or one of the Palace Guards. Only the ceremonial part of the marriage, of course. We'd go into the nuptial-chamber by one door and then come right out again by another. That's not a bad idea, is it?"

I thought that there was something in it; but obviously she must marry someone of rank and importance or it would create a bad impression. First I suggested Vitellius, and she said smiling that Vitellius already felt so sentimentally about her that it would be cruel to marry him and not allow him to spend the night with her. Besides, what about the prophecy? I didn't want to doom Vitellius to a violent death, did I?

486

So we discussed various husbands for her. The only one that we could agree on was Silius, the Consul-Elect, a son of that Silius, my brother Germanicus's general, whom Tiberius had accused of high treason and forced to suicide. I disliked him because he had led the opposition in the Senate to my measure for the extension of the franchise and had been very insolent to me. After my speech about the franchise, he had been asked to give his opinion. He said that he thought it strange that our ancient allies, the noble and illustrious Greek cities of Lycia, should remain deprived of their freedom (I had annexed Lycia five years previously because of continued political unrest there, and also the neighbouring island of Rhodes, where they had impaled some Roman citizens) while the Celtic barbarians of the north should be admitted to the fullest rights of Roman citizenship. When I came to answer this objection, which was almost the only one raised, I did so in the pleasantest possible way. I began, "It is indeed a long way from famous Lycia, from

'Xanthus' lucid stream,'

where, in the poet Horace's words that we heard sung last year at the Sæcular Games,

'Apollo most delights to bathe his hair,'

to France and the huge dark River Rhône, the huge dark river Rhône . . . of which no mention whatsoever appears in Classical legend, apart from a doubtful visit by Hercules, in the course of his Tenth Labour, on his way to win the oxen of Geryones. But I do not think . . ." I was interrupted by a tittering that soon swelled into a roar of laughter. It appears that when I repeated "the huge dark River Rhône" and hesitated for a moment, in search of a phrase,

Silius had remarked in an audible voice—but he was sitting on my deaf side, so I had not heard the interruption—"Yes, the huge dark River Rhône, where, if historians do not lie,

'Claudius most delights to bathe his hair'."

A reference to the occasion when I was flung over a bridge into that river at Caligula's orders and nearly drowned. You can imagine how angry I was when Narcissus explained what the laughter was about. It is all very well to make little personal jokes at a private supper table or at the baths, or more boisterous ones during Saturn's All Fools' Festival (to which, by the way, I had restored the fifth day removed by Caligula), but for my own part it would never occur to me to make any sort of personal joke in the Senate which could raise an unkind laugh against a fellow-member; and that a Consul-Elect had done so at my expense, and in the presence too of a group of prominent Frenchmen whom I had brought into the House, I took very ill. I shouted out: "My Lords, I invited you to give your opinions on my motion, but from the noise that you are making anyone would mistake this for the cheapest sort of knocking-shop. Please observe the rules of the House. Whatever will these French gentlemen think of us?" The noise stopped instantly. It always did when they saw I was angry.

Messalina said that she would like very much to marry Silius, not only because of his rudeness to me, which certainly merited astral vengeance, but because by the way he looked at her she felt sure that his rudeness was based on jealousy and that he was passionately in love with her. It would be a neat punishment for his presumption if she told him that she was being divorced and would marry him, and then only at the very last minute let him discover that it was to be a marriage in form only.

So we chose Silius, and that very day I signed a document repudiating Messalina as my wife and permitting her to return to her paternal roof. There were a lot of jokes about it between us. Messalina pretended to plead for permission to stay, falling on her knees before me and asking pardon for her errors. She also weepingly embraced the children, who did not know what to make of the business: "Must these poor darlings suffer for a mother's faults, cruel man?"

I replied that her faults were unpardonable: she was too clever, too beautiful and too industrious to stay with me an hour longer. She set an impossible standard for other wives to live up to, and made me the object of universal jealousy.

She whispered in my ear: "If I come into the Palace some night next week and commit adultery with you, will you banish me? I might be tempted, you know."

"Yes, I'll banish you, all right. I'll banish myself too. Where shall we go? I'd like to visit Alexandria. They say it's an ideal place for banishment."

"And take the children too? They'd love it."

"I don't think the climate would suit them. They'd have to stay here with your mother, I'm afraid."

"Mother knows nothing about the proper bringing-up of children: look at the way she brought me up! If you won't bring the children too, I won't come and commit adultery with you."

"Then I'll marry Lollia Paulina, just to spite you."

"Then I'll murder Lollia Paulina. I'll send her poisoned cakes, like the ones Caligula used to send people who had made him their heir."

"Well, here's your divorce document all signed and sealed, you slut. Now you're restored to all the rights and privileges of an unmarried woman."

"Let us kiss, Claudius, before we part."

489

"It reminds me of the famous farewell between Hector and Andromache in the Sixth Book of the *Iliad*:

'His princess parts with a prophetic sigh,
Unwilling parts, and oft reverts her eye
That streamed at every look; then, moving slow
Sought her own palace and indulged her woe.'

Here, don't be in such a hurry to run off stage with your divorce. You ought to take a few private lessons in acting from Mnester."

"I'm my own mistress now. If you're not careful I'll marry Mnester."

Silius was supposed to be the best-looking nobleman in Rome and Messalina had long been fascinated by him. But he was not by any means an easy victim of her passion. In the first place he was a virtuous man, or at least prided himself on his virtue, and then he was married to a noblewoman of the Silanus family, a sister of Caligula's first wife, and finally, though Messalina attracted him physically in the highest degree, he knew of the indiscriminate generosity with which she had been conferring her favours on nobleman, commoner, sword-fighter, actor, guardsman, even on one of the Parthian ambassadors, and did not consider himself particularly honoured by being asked to join their company. So she had to hook and play her fish with great cunning. The first difficulty lay in persuading him to visit her privately. She invited him several times, but he excused himself. She managed it in the end only by an arrangement with the Commander of the Watchmen, a former lover of hers, who invited Silius to supper and then had him shown into a room where she was waiting for him with supper laid for two Once he was there he could not easily escape, and she was very clever: she did not talk love at all at first, she talked revolutionary politics! She reminded him of his murdered father and asked him whether he could bear to see the murderer's nephew, a bloodier tyrant still, clamping the yoke of slavery tighter and tighter on the neck of a once free people. (This was myself, in case you do not recognize me.) Then she told him that she was in danger of her life because she had been constantly reproaching me for not restoring the Republic and for my cruel murders of innocent men and women. She said, too, that I had despised her beauty and preferred housemaids and common prostitutes and that it was only in revenge for my disregard that she had ever been unfaithful to me; her promiscuity had been the result of extreme despair and loneliness. He, Silius, was the only man she knew who was virtuous and bold enough to help her in the task to which she had now dedicated her life—the restoration of the Republic. Would he forgive the innocent trick that she had played in decoying him there?

Frankly I cannot blame Silius for being deceived by her: she deceived me daily for nine years. Remember that she was very beautiful; and you can assume, too, that she had doctored his wine. Naturally he tried to comfort her, and before he realized what was happening, they were lying in each other's arms on the couch mixing the words "love" and "liberty" with kisses and sighs. She said that only now did she know what true love meant, and he swore that with her help he would restore the Republic at the earliest opportunity, and she swore to remain everlastingly faithful to his love if he divorced his wife, who, she knew, was secretly unfaithful to him, and was barren too—Silius ought not to let his family die out—and so on, and so on. She had hooked him, and now she played him for all her worth.

But Silius was cautious as well as virtuous, and did not feel himself strong enough to raise an armed revolt. He divorced his wife but told Messalina, on second thoughts, that it would be best if they waited for me to die before restoring the Republic. Then he would marry her and adopt Britannicus, and this would make the City and Army look to him as their natural leader. Messalina saw that she would have to take action herself. So she worked the Barbillus trick on me as I have described, and Silius (if what he told me afterwards was the truth) knew nothing of the divorce until she went to him with the document, without explaining how she came by it, and told him joyfully that they could now get married and live happily ever afterwards, but that he must tell nobody about it until she gave him permission.

Everyone at Rome was astounded at the news of Messalina's divorce, particularly as it seemed to make no difference to me: I continued to show her as much respect as before, or even more, and she continued her political work at the Palace. But every day she visited Silius at his house, quite openly, with a full retinue of attendants. When I suggested that she was carrying the joke rather too far, she told me that she was finding some difficulty in making him consent to marry her. "I'm afraid that he suspects that there's some catch in it, and he's very polite and reserved, but underneath he's boiling with passion for me, the beast!" After a few days of this she gleefully reported that he had consented and would marry her on the tenth of September. She asked me to officiate as High Pontiff and see the fun. "Won't it be lovely to watch his baffled face when he finds he's been cheated?" By this time I had begun to repent of the whole business, especially of this practical joke on Silius, although he had insulted me in the Senate again with another ill-mannered interruption. I decided that I should not have taken the prophecy seriously and that I had only done so because I was half-awake when Messalina told me of it. And if the prophecy was really true, how could it be evaded by a mock-marriage? It occurred to me that no marriage is recognized as such by law until it has been physically consummated. I tried to persuade Messalina to drop the whole business, but she told me that I was jealous of Silius and that she thought that I was losing my sense of humour and becoming a silly old spoil-sport and pedant. I said no more.

On the morning of the fifth of September I went down to Ostia to dedicate a big new granary there. I had told Messalina that I would not be back until the following morning. Messalina said that she wanted to come too and it was arranged that we would drive down there together; but at the last moment she had one of her famous sick-headaches and had to stay behind. I was disappointed, but it was too late to change my plans, since a civic reception had been arranged for me at Ostia, and I had promised to sacrifice in the Temple of Augustus there: ever since the occasion on which I had lost my temper with the Ostians for not receiving me properly I had been particularly careful not to hurt their feelings.

Early that afternoon as I was going into the Temple to the sacrifice, Euodus, one of my freedmen, handed me a note. It was now Euodus's duty to protect me from inopportune petitions from the general public: all notes were handed to him and if he considered them frivolous or insane or not worth my attention I was not bothered with them. It is surprising what reams of nonsense people write in petitions. Euodus said, "Excuse me, Cæsar, but I can't read this. A woman handed it to me. Perhaps you can be bothered just this once?" To my surprise it was written in Etruscan, an extinct language known to not more than four or five living people, and read: "Great danger to Rome and yourself. Come to my house at once. Don't waste a moment." It startled and puzzled me. Why Etruscan? Whose house? What danger? And it was a minute or two before I understood. It must be from Calpurnia, the girl, you remember,

493

who had lived with me before I married Messalina: it had amused me to teach her Etruscan while I was compiling my history of Etruria. Calpurnia had probably sent me the note in Etruscan not only because it would be unintelligible to anyone but myself, but because I would know that it really came from her. I asked Euodus: "Did you see the woman?" He said that she looked like an Egyptian and had a pockmarked forehead but was otherwise very good-looking. I recognized this as Cleopatra, Calpurnia's friend who shared the house with her.

I was due to go down to the docks immediately after the sacrifice and could not decently postpone the engagement: it would be thought that I was more interested in visiting a couple of prostitutes than in attending to Imperial business. Yet I knew that Calpurnia was not the sort of person to send me an idle message, and while I was sacrificing I decided that I must hear what she had to say at all costs. I would sham sick, perhaps. Fortunately the God Augustus came to my assistance: the entrails of the ram I now sacrificed to him were the most unpropitious ones I had ever seen. It had seemed a fine animal, too, but inside it was as rotten as an old cheese. It was plainly impossible for me to transact any public business on that day, particularly so serious a matter as the dedication of the largest granary in the world, as this was. So I excused myself and everyone agreed that my decision was a proper one. I went to my own villa and gave out that I would rest there for the remainder of the day, but would be glad to attend the banquet to which I had been invited that night, so long as it had no official character. I then sent my sedan-chair round to the back entrance of the villa and was soon being carried in it, with the curtains drawn, to Calpurnia's pretty house on a hill just outside the town.

Calpurnia greeted me with a look of such anxious sorrow that I knew at once that something very serious had happened. "Tell me at once!" I said. "What's the matter?"

She began to cry. I had never seen Calpurnia cry before, except once on the famous occasion when I was sent for at midnight to the Palace by Caligula's orders and she thought that I was going to my execution. She was a self-possessed girl with none of the tricks and manners of the ordinary prostitute and 'as true as a Roman sword', as the saying is. "You promise to listen? But you'll not want to believe me. You'll want to have me tortured and flogged. I don't want to tell you, either. But nobody else dares tell you, so I must. I promised Narcissus and Pallas that I would. They were good friends to me in the old days when we were all poor together. They said that you'd not believe them, or anyone, but I said that I thought you'd believe me, because once I showed myself your true friend when you were in trouble. I gave you all my savings, didn't I? I was never greedy or jealous or dishonest, was I?"

"Calpurnia, in my life I have known only three really good women, and I'll tell you their names. One was Cypros, a Jewish princess; one was old Briseis, my mother's wardrobe-maid, and the third is you. Now tell me what you have to say."

"You've left out Messalina."

"Messalina goes without saying. Very well then, four really good women. And I don't consider that I'm insulting Messalina by linking her with an Oriental princess, a Greek freedwoman, and a prostitute from Padua. The sort of goodness I mean isn't the prerogative——"

"If you put Messalina in the list, leave me out," she said, gasping.

"Modest, Calpurnia? You needn't be. I mean what I say."

"No. Not modest."

"Then I don't understand."

Calpurnia said, very slowly and painfully: "I hate to hurt you, Claudius. But I mean this. I mean that if Cypros

495

had been a typical princess of the Herod family—if she had been bloodthirsty and ambitious and unscrupulous and without any moral restraint; and if Briseis had been a typical wardrobe-maid—if she had been thieving and base-minded and lazy and clever at covering up her tracks; and if your Calpurnia had been a typical prostitute—if I had been vain, lustful, promiscuous and greedy, and used my beauty as a means for dominating and ruining men—and if you were now listing the three worst types of women you knew and happened to pick on us as convenient examples——"

"—Then what? What are you getting at? You talk so slowly."

"—Then, Claudius, you'd be right to add Messalina to us and to tell me, 'Messalina goes without saying.' "

"Am I mad, or are you?"

"Not I."

"Then what do you mean? What's my poor Messalina done to be suddenly attacked in this violent and extraordinary way? I don't think that you and I are going to remain friends much longer, Calpurnia."

"You left town at seven o'clock this morning."

"Yes. And what of it?"

"I left at ten. I had been up there with Cleopatra doing some shopping. I looked in at the wedding. A curious hour of the day for a wedding, wasn't it? They were having a grand time. Everyone drunk. Marvellous show. The whole house decorated with vine-leaves and ivy and enormous bunches of grapes, and wine-vats, and wine-presses. The vintage festival, that was what it was supposed to represent."

"What wedding? Talk sense."

"Messalina's wedding to Silius. Weren't you invited? She was there dancing and waving a thyrsus in the biggest wine-vat she could find, dressed in a short wine-stained white tunic with one breast exposed and her hair flying loose.

She was almost decent, though, compared with the other women. They only wore leopard-skins, because they were Bacchantes. Silius was Bacchus. He was crowned with ivy and wore buskins. He was even drunker than Messalina. He kept tossing his head about in time to the music and grinning like Baba."

"But . . . but . . .," I said stupidly "The wedding isn't until the tenth. I'm to officiate."

"They're managing nicely without you. So I went to Narcissus at the Palace, and when he saw me, he said: 'Thank God you're here, Calpurnia. You're the only one he'll believe.' And Pallas——"

"I don't believe. I refuse to believe."

Calpurnia clapped her hands. "Cleopatra, Narcissus!" They came in and fell at my feet. "It's true about the wedding, isn't it?"

They agreed that it was true.

"But I know all about it," I said feebly. "It's not a real wedding, my friends. It's a sort of joke that Messalina and I planned. She's not going to bed with him at the end of the ceremony. It's all quite innocent."

Narcissus said: "Silius caught at her and pulled up her tunic and began kissing her body in full view of the company, and she screamed and laughed and then he carried her off to the nuptial-chamber, and they stayed there nearly an hour before coming out again to do a little more drinking and dancing. That's not innocent, Cæsar, surely?"

Calpurnia said: "And unless you act at once, Silius will be master of Rome. Everyone I met told me that Messalina and Silius have sworn by their own heads to restore the Republic, and that they have the whole Senate behind them and most of the Guards."

"I must hear more," I said. "I don't know whether to laugh or cry. I don't know whether to pour gold in your laps or flog you until the bones show."

They told me more, but Narcissus would only speak on condition that I forgave him for hiding Messalina's crimes from me so long. He said that when he was first aware of them and I seemed happy in my innocence, he had resolved to spare me the pain of disillusionment so long as Messalina did nothing which endangered my life or the safety of the country. He had hoped that she might mend her ways or else that I would find out about her for myself. But as time went on and her behaviour grew more and more shameless, it became more and more difficult to tell me. In fact, he could not believe that I did not know by now what all Rome, and all the provinces for that matter, and our enemies over the frontier, knew. In the course of nine years it seemed impossible that I should not have heard of her debaucheries, which were astounding in their impudence.

Cleopatra told me the most horrible and ludicrous story. During my absence in Britain Messalina had issued a challenge to the Prostitutes' Guild asking them to provide a champion to contend with her at the Palace, and see which of the two would wear out most gallants in the course of a night. The Guild had sent a famous Sicilian named Scylla, after the whirlpool in the Straits of Messina. When dawn came Scylla had been forced to confess herself beaten at the twenty-fifth gallant but Messalina had continued, out of bravado, until the sun was quite high in the sky. And, what was worse, most of the nobility at Rome had been invited to attend the contest, and many of the men had taken part in it; and three or four of the women had been persuaded by Messalina to compete too.

I sat weeping with my head in my hands, just as Augustus had done some fifty years before, when his grandsons Gaius and Lucius told him the same sort of story about their mother Julia; and in Augustus's very words I said that I had never heard the slightest whisper or entertained the faintest suspicion that Messalina was not the chastest woman in Rome. And like Augustus I had the impulse to shut myself away in a room and see nobody for days. But they would not let me. Two lines out of a musical comedy that Mnester's company had played a few days before—I forget the name—kept hammering absurdly in my brain:

"I know no sound so laughable, so laughable and sad,
As an old man weeping for his wife, a girl gone to the bad."

I said to Narcissus: "At the first Games I ever saw (I was acting as joint-President with my brother Germanicus)—Games in honour of my father, you know—I saw a Spanish sword-fighter have his shield-arm lopped off at the shoulder. He was close to me and I saw his face clearly. Such a stupid look when he saw what had happened. And the whole amphitheatre roared with laughter at him. I thought it was funny too, God forgive me."

# Chapter Twenty-Nine

THEN Xenophon came in and forced a drink between my lips, because I was on the point of collapse, and took me in hand generally. I don't know exactly what decoction he gave me, but it had the effect of making me feel very clear-headed and self-possessed and utterly impersonal about everything. My feet seemed to be treading on clouds like a god. It also affected the focus of my eyes, so that I saw Narcissus and Calpurnia and Pallas as if they were standing twenty paces away instead of quite close.

"Send for Turranius and Lusius Geta." Turranius was my Superintendent of Stores now that Callon was dead, and Geta, as I have told you, was the joint-Commander of the Guards with Crispinus.

I cross-examined them, after first assuring them that I would not punish them if they spoke the truth. They confirmed all that Narcissus and Calpurnia and Cleopatra had told me, and told me a lot more. When I asked Geta to explain frankly why he had failed to report all this to me before, he said: "May I quote a proverb, Cæsar, that is often on your own lips: *The knee is nearer than the shin?* What happened to Justus, my predecessor, when he tried to let you know what was happening in your wife's wing of the Palace?"

Turranius replied to the same question by reminding me that when recently he had summoned the courage to come to me with a complaint of the seizure of public stores at Messalina's orders—basalt blocks imported from Egypt for the repaving of the Ox Market—for use, it turned out, in a new colonnade that she was building in the Gardens of Lucullus, I had grown angry and told him never again to question any act or order of hers, saying that nothing that she did was done except at my particular instance or at least with my full sanction. I had told him that if he ever again had any complaint to make against the Lady Messalina's behaviour he was to make it to the Lady Messalina herself. Turranius was right. I had actually said that.

Calpurnia, who had been fidgeting impatiently in the background while I was questioning Geta and Turranius, now caught my eye pleadingly. I understood that she wanted a word with me alone. I cleared the room at once and then she said gently and earnestly: "My dear, you won't get anywhere by asking the same question over and over again from different people. It's quite plain: they were all afraid to tell you, partly because they knew how much you loved and trusted Messalina, but mostly because you were Emperor. You have been very foolish and very unlucky and now you must do something to retrieve the position. If you don't act at once you will be sentencing us all to death. Every minute counts. You must go at once to the Guards Camp and get the protection of all the loyal troops there. I can't believe that they'll desert you for Messalina's and Silius's sake. There may be one or two colonels or captains who have been bought over, but the rank and file are devoted to you. Send mounted messengers to Rome at once to announce that you are on your way to take vengeance on Silius and your wife. Send warrants for the arrest of everyone present at the wedding. That will probably be enough to smother the revolt. They'll all be too drunk to do anything dangerous. But hurry!"

"Oh yes," I said. "I'll hurry!"

I called in Narcissus again. "Do you trust Geta?"

"To be honest, Cæsar, I don't altogether trust him."

"And the two captains he has with him here?"

"I trust them, but they're stupid."

"Crispinus is away on leave at Baiæ, so whom shall we put in command of the Guards, if we can't trust Geta?"

"If Calpurnia was a man, I'd say Calpurnia. But since she's not, the next best choice is myself. I'm a mere freedman, I know, but the Guards officers know me and like me, and it would only be for a single day."

"Very well, General-of-the-Day Narcissus. Tell Geta that he's confined to bed by doctor's orders until tomorrow. Give me pen and parchment. Wait a moment. What's the date? September the fifth? Here's your commission, then. Show it to the captains and send them on to Rome at once with their men to arrest the whole wedding party. No violence, though, except in self-defence; tell them. Let the Guards know that I'm coming and that I expect them to remain loyal to me, and that their loyalty won't pass unrewarded."

It is about eighteen miles from Ostia to Rome, but the soldiers covered the distance in an hour and a half, using fast gigs. As it happened, the wedding was just breaking up when they arrived. The cause was a knight called Vettius Valens, who had been one of Messalina's lovers before Silius came on the scene, and was still in her favour. The party had come to the stage that parties reach when the first excitement of drink has worn off and everyone begins to feel a little tired and at a loss. Interest now centred on Vettius Valens: he was hugging a fine evergreen oak-tree which grew outside the house, and talking to an imaginary Dryad inside it. The Dryad had apparently fallen in love with him and was inviting him in a whisper, audible only to himself, to a rendezvous at the top of the tree. He finally consented to join her there and made his friends form a human pyramid to enable him to climb up to the first big bough. The pyramid collapsed twice amid shrieks of laughter, but Vettius persevered and at the third try got astride of the bough. From there slowly and dangerously he climbed higher and higher until he disappeared into the thick foliage at the summit. Everyone stood gazing up to watch what would happen next. Expectation ran high because Vettius was a famous comedian. Soon he began imitating the Dryad's affectionate cries and making loud smacking kiss-noises and uttering little squeals of excitement. Then Vettius kept very quiet, until the crowd began calling up to him: "Vettius, Vettius, what are you doing?"

"I'm just viewing the world. This is the best look-out anywhere in Rome. The Dryad's sitting on my lap and pointing out places of interest; so don't interrupt. Yes, that's the Senate House. Silly girl, I knew that! And that's Colchester! But surely you're mistaken? You can't see as far as Colchester from this tree, can you? You must mean the Guards Camp. No, it *is* Colchester, by God. I can see the name written up on a notice board and blue-faced Britons walking about. What's that? What are they doing? No, I don't believe it. What, worshipping Claudius as a God?" And then in an imitation of my voice: " '*Why*, though, I want to know *why*? Nobody else to worship? Have the other Gods refused to cross the Channel? I don't blame them. I was dreadfully sea-sick myself, crossing the Channel.' "

Vettius's audience was entranced. When he was silent again they called out: "Vettius, Vettius! What are you doing now?"

He answered, imitating my voice again: "In the first place, if I don't want to answer, I won't answer. You can't make me. I'm a free man, aren't I? In fact one of the freest men in Rome."

"Oh, do tell us, Vettius."

"Look there! Look there! A thousand Furies and Serpents! Let me go, Dryad, let me go at once. No, no, another time. Can't wait for that sort of thing now. Must

503

get down. Hands off, Dryad!"

"What's happening, Vettius?"

"Run for your lives. I've just seen a fearful sight. No, stop! Trogus, Proculus, help me down first! But everyone else run for your lives!"

"What? What?"

"A terrific storm coming up from Ostia! Run for your lives!"

And the crowd actually did scatter. Laughing and screaming and headed by the bride and bridegroom they rushed out of the garden into the street a few seconds before my soldiers came galloping up. Messalina got safely away, and so did Silius, but the soldiers had no difficulty in arresting about two hundred of the guests, and later picked up about fifty more who were stumbling drunkenly home. Messalina was accompanied by only three companions. There had been twenty r more with her at first, but as soon as the alarm was raised that the Guards were coming they deserted her. She went on foot through the City until she came to the Gardens of Lucullus, by which time she had sobered somewhat. She decided that she must go to Ostia at once and try the effect of her beauty on me again—it had never hitherto failed to cheat me—and bring the children with her too as a reinforcement. She was still barefooted and wearing her vintage costume, which had earned her hisses and jeers as she hurried through the streets. She sent a maid to the Palace to fetch her the children, sandals, some jewellery and a clean gown. The quality of the love between her and Silius was shown by their immediate desertion of each other at the first sign of danger. Messalina prepared to sacrifice him to my rage, and Silius went to the Market Place to resume his judicial work there as if nothing had happened. He was drunk enough to think that he could pretend complete innocence, and when the captains came to arrest him he told them that he was busy, and what did they want? Their answer was to handcuff him and lead him off to the Camp.

Meanwhile I had been joined by Vitellius and Cæcina (my colleague in my second Consulship) who had accompanied me down to Ostia and after the sacrifice had gone off to visit friends on the other side of the town. I told them briefly what had happened and said that I was returning to Rome immediately: I expected them to support me and witness the impartiality with which I would visit judgment on the guilty of whatever rank or station. The Olympian effect of the drug continued. I talked calmly, fluently and, I think, sensibly. Vitellius and Cæcina made no reply at first, expressing astonishment and concern only in their looks. When I asked them what they thought about the whole business, Vitellius would still only utter exclamations of astonishment and horror such as, "They really told you that! Oh, how horrible! What vile treason!" and Cæcina followed his example. The carriage of state was announced and Narcissus, whom I had directed to write out a charge-sheet against Messalina, and who had been busy questioning the staff so as to make the list of her adulteries as full as possible, then showed himself a brave man and a faithful servant. "Cæsar, please inform your noble friends who I am for to-day and give me a seat in this carriage with you. Until my Lords Vitellius and Cæcina come out with an honest opinion, and refrain from making remarks that can be construed either as a condemnation of your wife or as condemnation of her accusers, it is my duty as your Guards Commander to remain by your side."

I am glad that he came with me. As we drove towards the City I began telling Vitellius about Messalina's pretty ways and how much I had loved her and how vilely she had deceived me. He sighed deeply and said: "A man would have to be stone, not to be melted by beauty like hers." I spoke about the children, too, and Cæcina and

505

Vitellius sighed in unison: "The poor, dear children! They must not be allowed to suffer." But the nearest that either of them came to expressing a real opinion was when Vitellius exclaimed: "It is almost impossible for anyone who has felt for Messalina the admiration and tenderness that I have felt, to believe these filthy accusations, though a thousand trustworthy witnesses were to swear that they were true." And when Cæcina agreed, "Oh, what an evil and sorrowful world we live in!" An embarrassment was in store for them. Two vehicles were seen approaching through the dusk. One was another carriage, drawn by white horses, and in it sat Vibidia, the oldest and most honoured of the Vestal Virgins: eighty-five years old and one of my dearest friends. Behind this carriage followed a cart with a big yellow L painted on it, one of the carts belonging to the Gardens of Lucullus and used for carrying soil and rubbish. In it were Messalina and the children. Narcissus took in the situation at a glance: he had better eyes than I have and stopped the carriage. "Here's the Vestal Vibidia come to meet you, Cæsar," he said. "No doubt she'll ask you to forgive Messalina. Vibidia is a dear old soul, and I think the world of her, but for God's sake don't make her any rash promises. Remember how monstrously you've been treated and remember that Messalina and Silius are traitors to Rome. Be polite to Vibidia, by all means, but don't give away anything at all. Here's the charge-sheet. Look at it, now read the names. Look at the eleventh charge—Mnester. Are you going to forgive that? And Cæsoninus, what about Cæsoninus? What can you think of a woman who can play about with a creature like that?"

I took the parchment from him and as he stepped out of the carriage he whispered something in Vitellius's ear. I don't know what it was, but it decided Vitellius to keep his mouth shut in Narcissus's absence. While I was reading the charges by the light of a lantern Narcissus ran along the road and met Vibidia and Messalina, who had also dismounted, coming towards him. Messalina was comparatively sober now: she called out gently to me from the distance: "Hullo, Claudius! I've been such a silly girl! You'd never believe it of me!" For once my deafness was of service to me. I didn't recognize her voice or hear a word. Narcissus greeted Vibidia courteously, but refused to let Messalina come any farther. Messalina cursed and spat in his face and tried to dodge past, but he ordered the two sergeants whom we had with us to escort her to her cart and see that it drove back to the City. Messalina screamed as if she were being murdered or outraged, and I looked up from the parchment to ask what was the matter. Vitellius said: "A woman in the crowd. Overcome by labour-pains, by the sound of it."

Then Vibidia came slowly up to our carriage and Narcissus panted back after her. Narcissus did all the talking for me. He told Vibidia that Messalina's notorious and unexampled whoredoms and treacheries made it ludicrous for a pious and aged Vestal to come and plead with me for her life. "You Vestals surely don't approve of having the Palace turned into a brothel again, as in Caligula's days, do you? You don't approve of ballet-dancers and sword-fighters performing between the sheets of the High Pontiff's bed, do you, with the active co-operation of the High Pontiff's wife?"

That gave Vibidia a shock: Messalina had only confessed to an "indiscreet familiarity" with Silius. She said: "I know nothing about that, but at least I must urge the High Pontiff to do nothing rashly, to shed no innocent blood, to condemn nobody unheard, to consider the honour of his house and his duty to the Gods."

I broke in: "Vibidia, Vibidia, my dear friend, I shall deal justly with Messalina, you can count on that."

Narcissus said: "Yes, indeed. The danger is that the High

Pontiff may show his former wife an undeserved clemency. It is very difficult indeed for him to judge the case as impartially as it will be his official duty to do. I must therefore ask you on his behalf not to make things more painful for him than they already are. May I courteously suggest that you retire, my Lady Vibidia, and attend to the solemnities of the Goddess Vesta, which you understand so well?"

So she retired, and we drove on. As we came into the City, Messalina made another attempt to see me, I am told, but was restrained by the sergeants. She then tried to send Britannicus and little Octavia to plead with me for her, but Narcissus saw them running towards us and waved them back. I was sitting silent, brooding over the list of Messalina's lovers. Narcissus had headed it: "Provisional and incomplete account of Valeria Messalina's notorious adulteries, from the first year of her marriage to Tiberius Claudius Cæsar Augustus Germanicus Britannicus, Father of the Country, High Pontiff, etc., until the present day." It contained forty-four names, later extended to one hundred and fifty-six.

Narcissus sent a message ordering the cart back to the Gardens: the traffic regulations forbade it to be in the streets at this hour. Messalina saw that she was beaten, so allowed herself to carried back to the Gardens. The children had been sent to the Palace, but her mother Domitia Lepida, though lately there had been a coolness between the two, bravely joined her in the cart; otherwise Messalina would have been quite alone but for the carter. Narcissus then told our coachman to drive on to Silius's house. When we reached it I said: "This isn't the place, is it? Surely this is the family mansion of the Asinians?"

Narcissus explained: "Messalina bought it privately when Asinius Gallus was banished, and gave it to Silius as a wedding present. Come inside and see for yourself what has been going on."

I went in and saw the litter of the wedding—the vine-leaf decorations, the wine-vats and presses, tables covered with food and dirty plates, trampled rose-leaves and garlands on the floor, discarded leopard-skins and wine spilt everywhere. The house was deserted except for an old porter and two dead-drunk lovers lying in each other's arms on the bed in the nuptial-chamber. I had them arrested. One was a staff-lieutenant called Montanus, the other was Narcissus's own niece, a young married woman with two children. What shocked and distressed me most was to find the whole house full of Palace furniture, not merely things that Messalina had brought me as part of her dowry when we were married, but ancient heirlooms of the Claudian and Julian families, including the very statues of my ancestors and the family masks, cupboard and all! There could be no plainer proof of her intentions than that. So we climbed into the carriage again and drove on to the Guards Camp. Narcissus was gloomy and subdued now, because he had been very fond of his niece; but Vitellius and Cæcina had made up their minds that it would be safer for them to believe the evidence of their eyes, and simultaneously began urging me to vengeance. We reached the Camp, where I found the whole Division on parade, by Narcissus's orders, in front of the tribunal. It was dark now and the tribunal was lit by flaring torches. I climbed up on the platform and made a short speech. My voice was clear, but sounded very far away:

"Guards, my friend the late King Herod Agrippa, who first recommended me to you as your Emperor and then persuaded the Senate to accept your choice, told me on the last occasion that I saw him alive, and also wrote to me in the last letter that I ever had from him, never to trust anyone, for nobody about me was worthy of my trust. I did not take his words literally. I continued to repose the fullest confidence in my wife Valeria Messalina, whom I now know to have been a whore, a liar, a thief, a murderess and a traitor to Rome. I don't mean, Guards, that I don't trust you. You're the only people I do trust, you know. You're soldiers and do your duty without question. I expect you to stand by me now and crush the plot which my former wife Messalina and her adulterer, the Consul-Elect Gaius Silius, have formed against my life under a pretence of restoring popular liberty to the City again. The Senate is rotten with conspiracy, as rotten as the entrails of the ram that I sacrificed this afternoon to the God Augustus; you never saw such an unholy sight. I am ashamed to talk as I do, but that's right, isn't it? Help me bring my enemies— our enemies—to book and, once Messalina's dead, if I ever marry again I give you free and full leave to chop me to pieces with your swords, and use my head as a football at the Baths, like Sejanus's. Three times married, and three times unlucky. Well, what about it, lads? Tell me what you think. I can't get a straight answer from my other friends."

"Kill them, Cæsar!"—"No mercy!"—"Strangle the bitch!"—"Death to them all!"—"We'll stand by you!"— "You've been too damn generous."—"Wipe them out, Cæsar!" There was no doubt what the Guards thought of the matter.

So I had the arrested men and women brought up before me there and then, and ordered the arrest of a hundred and ten more men now named in the charge-sheet as Messalina's adulterers, and four women of rank who had prostituted themselves, at Messalina's suggestion, in the course of that notorious Palace orgy. I finished the trial in three hours. But this was because all but thirty-four of the three hundred and sixty persons who answered their names pleaded guilty to the charges brought against them. Those whose only crime was their attendance at the wedding I banished. Twenty knights, six senators, and a Guards colonel, who all pleaded guilty to adultery or attempted revolution, or both, demanded to be executed at once. I granted them this favour. Vettius Valens tried to buy his life by offering to reveal the names of the ringleaders of the plot. I told him that I could find them out without his assistance and he was led off to execution. Montanus was mentioned in Narcissus's list, but pleaded that Messalina had forced him to spend the night with her by showing him an order to do so signed and sealed by me: and that after that single night she had tired of him. Messalina must have got my signature to the document by reading it out to me—"just to save your precious eyes, my darling"—as something quite different. However, I pointed out that he had no order from me to attend the wedding or to commit adultery with my friend Narcissus's niece; so he was executed too. There were also fifteen suicides in the City that night by persons who had not been arrested but expected to be. Three intimate friends of mine, all knights, Trogus, Cotta and Fabius, were among these. I suspect that Narcissus knew of their guilt but left them out of the charge-sheet for friendship's sake, contenting himself with sending them a warning.

Mnester would not plead guilty: he reminded me that he was under orders from me to obey my wife in everything, and said that he had obeyed her much against his will. He pulled off his clothes and showed the marks of a lash on his back. "She gave me that because my natural modesty prevented me from carrying out your orders as energetically as she wished, Cæsar." I was sorry for Mnester. He had once saved that theatre-audience from massacre by the Germans. And what can you expect from an actor? But Narcissus said: "Don't spare him, Cæsar. Look carefully at the bruises. The flesh isn't cut open at all. It's clear to anyone with eyes in his head that the lash wasn't meant to hurt; it was just part of their vicious practices." So Mnester made a very graceful bow to the parade, his last bow, and spoke his usual little speech: "If I have ever pleased you, that is my reward. If I have offended you, I ask your forgiveness." They received it in silence, and he was led off to his death.

The only two people whom I spared except the obviously innocent were one Lateranus, who was accused of conspiracy but pleaded not guilty, and Cæsoninus. The evidence against Lateranus was conflicting, and he was a nephew of Aulus Plautius, so I gave him the benefit of the doubt. Cæsoninus I spared because he was so foul a wretch, though of good family, that I did not wish to insult his fellow-adulterers by executing him alongside of them: in Caligula's reign he had prostituted himself as a woman. I don't know what happened to him: he never reappeared in Rome. I also dismissed the charge against Narcissus's niece: I owed him that.

The Bacchantes, still wearing nothing but their leopard-skins, I ordered to be hanged, quoting Ulysses's speech in the *Odyssey*, when he took vengeance on Penelope's wicked maidservants:

> "Then thus the prince: 'To these shall we afford
> A fate so pure as by the martial sword?
> To these, the nightly prostitutes to shame
> And base revilers of our house and name?' "

I strung them all up in Homeric fashion, twelve in a row, on a huge ship's cable tautened between two trees with a winch. Their feet were just off the ground and as they died I quoted once more:

> "They twitched their feet awhile, but not for long."

And Silius? And Messalina? Silius attempted no defence: but when I questioned him he made a plain statement of fact giving an account of his seduction by Messalina. I pressed him: "But *why*, I want to know *why*? Were you really in love with her? Did you really think me a tyrant?

Did you really intend to restore the Republic, or just to become Emperor in my place?" He answered: "I can't explain, Cæsar. Perhaps I was bewitched. She made me see you as a tyrant. My plans were vague. I talked liberty to many of my friends and, you know how it is, when one talks liberty everything seems beautifully simple. One expects all gates to open and all walls to fall flat and all voices to shout for joy."

"Do you wish your life to be spared? Shall I put you into the custody of your family as an irresponsible imbecile?"

"I wish to die."

Messalina had written me a letter from the Gardens. In it she told me that she loved me as much as ever and that she hoped I wouldn't take her prank seriously; she had just been leading Silius on, as she and I had arranged, and if she had rather overdone the joke by getting beastly drunk, I mustn't be stupid and feel cross or jealous; "There is nothing that makes a man so hateful and ugly in a woman's eyes as jealousy." The letter was handed to me on the tribunal, but Narcissus would not let me answer it until the trials were over, except by a formal "Your communication has been received, and will be granted my Imperial attention in due course." He said that until I was satisfied as to the extent of her guilt it was better not to compromise myself in writing: I must not hold out any hope that she would escape death and merely be exiled to some small prison island.

Messalina's reply to my formal acknowledgement of her letter was a long screed, blotted with tears, reproaching me for my cold answer to her loving words. She now made a full confession, as she called it, of her many indiscretions, but did not admit to actual adultery in a single instance; she begged me for the sake of the children to forgive her and grant her a chance of starting again as a faithful and dutiful wife; and she promised to set a perfect example of matronly

513

deportment to Roman noblewomen for all ages to come. She signed herself by her pet name. It reached me during Silius's trial.

Narcissus saw tears in my eyes and said: "Cæsar, don't give way. A born whore can never reform. She's not honest with you even in this letter."

I said: "No, I won't give way. A man can't die twice of the same disease."

I wrote again "Your communication has been received and will be granted my attention in due course."

Messalina's third letter arrived just as the last heads had fallen. It was angry and threatening. She wrote that she had now given me every chance to treat her fairly and decently, and that if I did not immediately beg her pardon for the insolent, heartless and ungrateful behaviour I had shown her, I must take the consequences; for her patience was wearing out. She secretly commanded the loyalty of all my Guards officers, and of all my freedmen with the exception of Narcissus, and of most of the Senate; she had only to speak the word and I would immediately be arrested and surrendered to her vengeance. Narcissus threw back his head and laughed. "Well, at least she acknowledges my loyalty to you, Cæsar. Now, let's go to the Palace. You must be nearly fainting with hunger. You have had nothing since breakfast, have you?"

"But what shall I answer?"

"It deserves no answer."

We returned to the Palace and there was a fine meal waiting for us. Vermouth (recommended by Xenophon as a sedative) and oysters, and roast goose with my favourite mushroom and onion sauce—made according to a recipe given my mother by Berenice, Herod's mother—and stewed veal with horse-radish, and a mixed dish of vegetables, and apple-pie flavoured with honey and cloves, and water-melon from Africa. I ate ravenously and when I had done I began to feel very sleepy. I said to Narcissus: "My mind won't work any more to-night. I'm tired out. I put you in charge of affairs until to-morrow morning. I suppose that I ought to warn that miserable woman to attend here to-morrow morning and defend herself against those charges. I promised Vibidia that I'd give her a fair trial." Narcissus said nothing. I went to sleep on my couch.

Narcissus beckoned to the Colonel of the Guard. "The Emperor's orders. You are to proceed with six men to the pleasure-house in the Gardens of Lucullus and there execute the Lady Valeria Messalina, the Emperor's divorced wife." Then he told Euodus to run ahead of the Guards and warn Messalina that they were coming, thus giving her an opportunity of committing suicide. If she took it, as she could hardly fail to do, I would not need to hear of the unauthorized order for her execution. Eudous found her lying on her face on the floor of the pleasure-house sobbing. Her mother knelt beside her. Messalina said, without looking up: "O beloved Claudius, I'm so miserable and ashamed."

Euodus laughed: "You're mistaken, Madam. The Emperor is asleep at the Palace, with orders not to be disturbed. Before he went off he told the Colonel of the Guard to come here and cut off your pretty head. His very words, Madam. 'Cut off her pretty head and stick it on the end of a spear.' I ran ahead to let you know. If you've as much courage as you have beauty, Madam, my advice is to get it over before they come. I brought this dagger along in case you hadn't one handy."

Domitia Lepida said: "There's no hope, my poor child; you can't escape now. The only honourable thing left for you to do is to take his dagger and kill yourself."

"It's not true," Messalina wept. "Claudius would never dare to get rid of me like this. It's an invention of Narcissus's. I ought to have killed Narcissus long ago. Vile, hateful Narcissus!"

515

The tramp of heavy feet was heard on the pavement outside. "Guard, halt! Order arms!" The door flew open and the Colonel stood with folded arms in the entrance, outlined against the night sky. He did not say a word.

Messalina screamed at the sight of him and snatched the dagger from Euodus. She felt the edge and point timorously. Euodus sneered: "Do you want the Guards to wait there while I fetch a grindstone and sharpen it up for you?"

Domitia Lepida said: "Be brave, child. It won't hurt if you drive it home quick."

The Colonel slowly unfolded his arms: his right hand reached for the pommel of his sword. Messalina put the point of the dagger first to her throat and then to her breast. "Oh, I can't, Mother! I'm afraid!"

The Colonel's sword was out of its sheath. He took three long steps forward and ran her through.

# Chapter Thirty

XENOPHON had given me another dose of the "Olympian mixture" just before I went to sleep, and the exalted feeling, which had been wearing off slightly during supper, revived in me. I woke up with a start—a careless slave had dropped a pile of dishes—yawned loudly and apologized to the company for my bad table-manners. "Granted, Cæsar," they all cried. I thought how frightened they looked. Bad lives and bad consciences.

"Has anyone been poisoning my drink while I was asleep?" I bantered.

"God forbid, Cæsar," they protested.

"Narcissus, what was the sense of that Colchester joke of Vettius Valens's? Something about the Britons worshipping me as a God."

Narcissus said: "It was not altogether a joke, Cæsar. In fact, you may as well know that a temple at Colchester has been dedicated to the God Claudius Augustus. They have been worshipping you there since the early summer. But I've only just heard about it."

"So that's why I feel so queer. I've been turning into a God! But how did it happen? I wrote to Ostorius, I remember, sanctioning the erection and dedication of a temple at Colchester to the God Augustus, in gratitude for the victory he had given Roman arms in the island of Britain."

"Then I suppose, Cæsar, that Ostorius made the natural mistake of understanding 'Augustus' as meaning yourself, particularly as you specified a victory given by Augustus to Roman arms in Britain. The God Augustus fixed the frontier at the Channel and his name means nothing to the British, in comparison with your own. The natives speak of you there, I am informed, with the deepest religious awe. There are poems composed about your thunder and lightning and your magic mists and your black spirits and your humped monsters and your monsters with snakes for noses. Politically speaking, Ostorius was perfectly correct in dedicating the temple to you. But I much regret that it was done without your consent, and, I suppose, against your wishes."

"So I'm a God, now, am I?" I repeated. "Herod Agrippa always said that I'd end as a God, and I told him that he was talking nonsense. I suppose that I can't cancel the mistake, can I, Narcissus, do you think?"

"It would create a very bad effect on the provincials, I should say," Narcissus answered.

"Well, I don't care, the way I feel now," I said. "I don't care about anything. Suppose that I have that miserable woman brought here for trial at once. I feel completely free from petty mortal passions. I might even forgive her."

"She's dead," Narcissus said in a low voice. "Dead, at your own orders."

"Fill my glass," I said. "I don't remember giving the order, but it's all the same to me now. I wonder what sort of God I am. Old Athenodorus used to explain to me the Stoic idea of God: God was a perfectly rounded whole, immune from accident or event. I always pictured God as an enormous pumpkin. Ha, ha, ha! If I eat any more of this goose and drink any more of this wine I'll become pumpkinified too. So Messalina's dead! A beautiful woman, my friends? But bad?"

"Beautiful but bad, Cæsar."

"Carry me up to bed, someone, and let me sleep the blessed sleep of the Gods. I'm a blessed God now, aren't I?"

So they took me up to bed. I stayed in bed until noon the

next day, fast asleep all the time. The Senate met in my absence and passed a motion congratulating me on the suppression of the revolt, and another expunging Messalina's name from the archives and removing it from every public inscription, and destroying all her statues. I rose in the afternoon and resumed my ordinary Imperial work. Everyone whom I met was extremely subdued and polite, and when I visited the Law Courts nobody, for the first time for years, attempted to bustle or browbeat me. I got through my cases in no time.

The next day I began to talk grandly about the conquest of Germany; and Narcissus, realizing that Xenophon's medicine was having too violent an effect—disordering my wits instead of merely tiding me gently over the shock of Messalina's death, as had been intended—told him to give me no more of it. Gradually the Olympian mood faded and I felt pathetically mortal again. The first morning after I was free from the effects of the drug I went down to breakfast, and asked: "Where's my wife? Where's the Lady Messalina?" Messalina always breakfasted with me unless she had a "sick headache."

"She's dead, Cæsar," Euodus answered. "She died some days ago, by your orders."

"I didn't know," I said weakly. "I mean, I had forgotten." Then the shame and grief and horror of the whole business came welling back to my mind, and I broke down. Soon I was babbling foolishly of my dear, precious Messalina and reproaching myself as her murderer, and saying that it was all my fault, and making an almighty fool of myself. I eventually pulled myself together and called for my sedan. "The Gardens of Lucullus," I ordered. They took me there.

Seated on a garden bench under a cedar, looking across a smooth green lawn and down a wide grassy avenue of hornbeams, with nobody about except my German guards posted out of sight in the shrubbery, and with a long strip of paper on my knee and a pen in my hand, I began solemnly working out just where and how I stood. I have this paper by me as I now write and will copy out what I put down exactly as I find it. My statements fell, for some reason or other, into related groups of three, like the "tercets" of the British Druids (their common metrical convention for verse of a moralistic or didactic sort):

I love liberty: I detest tyranny.
I have always been a patriotic Roman.
The Roman genius is Republican.

I am now, paradoxically, an Emperor.
As such I exercise monarchical power.
The Republic has been suspended for three generations.

The Republic was torn by Civil Wars.
Augustus instituted this monarchical power.
It was an emergency measure only.

Augustus found that he could not resign his power.
In my mind I condemned Augustus as hypocritical.
I remained a convinced Republican.

Tiberius became Emperor. Against his inclination?
Afraid of some enemy seizing power?
Probably forced into it by his mother Livia.

In his reign I lived in retirement.
I considered him a blood-thirsty hypocrite.
I remained a convinced Republican.

Caligula suddenly appointed me Consul.
I only desired to be back at my books.
Caligula tried to rule like an Oriental monarch.

I was a patriotic Roman.
I should have attempted to kill Caligula.
Instead I saved my skin by playing the imbecile.

Cassius Chærea was perhaps a patriotic Roman.
He broke his oath, he assassinated Caligula.
He attempted, at least, to restore the Republic.

The Republic was not then restored.
Instead there was a new Emperor appointed.
That Emperor was myself, Tiberius Claudius.

If I had refused I should have been killed.
If I had refused there would have been Civil War.
It was an emergency measure only.

I put Cassius Chærea to death.
I found that I could not yet resign my power.
I became a second Augustus.

I worked hard and long, like Augustus,
I enlarged and strengthened the Empire, like Augustus,
I was an absolute monarch, like Augustus.

I am not a conscious hypocrite.
I flattered myself that I was acting for the best.
I planned to restore the Republic this very year.

Julia's disgrace was Augustus's punishment.
"Would I had never wed, and childless died."
I feel just the same about Messalina.

I should have killed myself rather than rule:
I should never have allowed Herod Agrippa to persuade
     me.
With the best of intentions I have become a tyrant.

I was blind to Messalina's follies and villainies.
In my name she shed the blood of innocent men and
　　women.
Ignorance is no justification for crime.

But am I the only guilty person?
Has not the whole nation equally sinned?
They made me Emperor and courted my favour.

And if I now carry out my honest intentions?
If I restore the Republic, what then?
Do I really suppose that Rome will be grateful?

"You know how it is when one talks of liberty.
Everything seems beautifully simple.
One expects every gate to open and every wall to fall flat."

The world is perfectly content with me as Emperor,
All but the people who want to be Emperor themselves.
Nobody really wants the Republic back.

Asinius Pollio was right:
"It will have to be much worse before it can be any better."
Decided: I shall not, after all, carry out my plan.

The frog-pool wanted a king.
Jove sent them Old King Log.
I have been as deaf and blind and wooden as a log.

The frog-pool wanted a king.
Let Jove now send them Young King Stork.
Caligula's chief fault: his stork-reign was too brief.

My chief fault: I have been far too benevolent.
I repaired the ruin my predecessors spread.
I reconciled Rome and the world to monarchy again.

Rome is fated to bow to another Cæsar.
Let him be mad, bloody, capricious, wasteful, lustful.
King Stork shall prove again the nature of kings

By dulling the blade of tyranny I fell into great error.
By whetting the same blade I might redeem that error.
Violent disorders call for violent remedies.

Yet I am, I must remember, Old King Log.
I shall float inertly in the stagnant pool.
Let all the poisons that lurk in the mud hatch out.

I kept my resolution. I have kept it strictly ever since. I have allowed nothing to come between me and it. It was very painful at first. I had told Narcissus that I felt like the Spanish sword-fighter whose shield-arm was suddenly lopped off in the arena; but the difference was that the Spaniard died of his wound, and I continue to live. You have perhaps heard maimed men complain, in damp cold weather, of sensations of pain in the leg or arm they have lost? It can be a most precise pain too, described as a sharp pain running up the wrist from the thumb, or as a settled pain in the knee. I felt like this often. I used to worry what Messalina would think of some decision I had taken, or about what effect a long boring play in the theatre was having on her; if it thundered I would remember how frightened she was of thunder.

As you may have guessed, the most painful consideration of all was that my little Britannicus and Octavia were perhaps, after all, not my children. Octavia, I was convinced, was not my child. She did not resemble the Claudian side of the family in the slightest. I looked at her a hundred times before I suddenly realized who her father must have been—the Commander of the Germans under Caligula. I remembered now that when a year after the amnesty, he had disgraced himself and lost his position and finally sunk so low that he became a sword-fighter, Messalina had pleaded for his life in the arena (he was disarmed and a net-man was standing over him with his trident raised)—pleaded for the wretch's life against the protests of the entire audience, who were yelling and booing and turning their thumbs down. I let him off, because she said that it would be bad for her health if I refused: this was just before Octavia's birth. However, a few months later he fought the same net-man and was killed at once.

Britannicus was a true Claudian and a noble little fellow, but the horrible thought came into my mind that he resembled my brother Germanicus far too closely. Could it be that Caligula was really his father? He had nothing of Caligula's nature, but heredity often skips a generation. The notion haunted me. I could not rid myself of it for a long time. I kept him out of my sight as much as possible without seeming to disown him. He and Octavia must have suffered much at this time. They had been greatly attached to their mother, so I had given instructions that they should not be told in detail about her crimes; they were merely to know that their mother was dead. But they soon found out that she had been executed by my orders, and naturally they felt a childish resentment to me. But I could not yet bring myself to talk to them about it.

I have explained that my freedmen formed a very close guild and that a man who offended one of them offended all, and that a man who was taken under the protection of one enjoyed the favour of all. In this they set a good example to the Senate, but the Senate did not follow it, being always torn into factions and only united in their common servility to me. And though now, three months after Messalina's death, a rivalry started between my three chief ministers, Narcissus, Pallas and Callistus, it had been agreed beforehand that the successful one would not use the strong position that he would win by pleasing me as a means of humiliating the other two. You would never guess what the rivalry was about. It was about choosing a fourth wife for me! "But," you will exclaim, "I thought you gave the Guards full permission to chop you in pieces with their swords if you ever married again?" I did. But that was before I took my fateful decision, sitting there under the cedar in the Gardens of Lucullus. For now I had made up my mind, and once I do that, the thing is fixed with a nail. I set my freedmen a sort of guessing game as to what my marital intentions were. It was a joke, for I had already chosen the lucky woman. I started them off one night by remarking casually at supper: "I ought to do something better for little Octavia than put her in charge of freedwomen. I hanged all the maids who understood her ways, poor child. And I can't expect my daughter Antonia to look after her: Antonia's been very poorly ever since her own baby died."

Vitellius said: "No, what little Octavia needs is a mother. And so does Britannicus, though it's easier for a boy than a girl to look after himself."

I made no answer, so every one present knew that I was thinking of marrying again, and everyone knew too how easily I had been managed by Messalina, and thought that if he were the man to find me a wife his fortune was made. Narcissus, Pallas and Callistus each offered a candidate in turn, as soon as a favourable moment came for talking to me privately. It was most interesting to me to watch how their minds worked. Callistus remembered that Caligula had forced a governor of Greece to divorce his wife, Lollia Paulina, and then married her himself (as his third wife) because someone had told him at a banquet that she was the most beautiful woman in the Empire: and he remembered further that this someone had been myself. He thought that since Lollia Paulina had not lost any of her looks in the ten years that had passed since, but had rather improved them, he was pretty safe in suggesting her. He did so the very next day. I smiled and promised to give the matter my careful consideration.

Narcissus was next. He asked me first who it was that Callistus had suggested and when I told him "Lollia Paulina," he exclaimed that she would never suit me. She cared for nothing but jewels. "She never goes about with less than thirty thousand gold pieces around her neck in emeralds or rubies or pearls, never the same assortment either, and she's as stupid and obstinate as a miller's mule. Cæsar, the one woman for you really, as we both know, is Calpurnia. But you can hardly marry a prostitute: it wouldn't look well. My suggestion therefore is that you marry some noblewoman just as a matter of form, but live with Calpurnia, as you did before you met Messalina, and enjoy real happiness for the rest of your life."

"Whom do you suggest as my matter-of-form wife?"

"Ælia Pætina. After you divorced her she married again, you remember. Recently she lost her husband, and he left her very badly off. It would be a real charity to marry her."

"But her tongue, Narcissus?"

"She's chastened by misfortune. That legal tongue of hers will never be heard again, I undertake that. I'll warn her about it and explain the conditions of marriage. She'll be paid all the respect due to her as your wife, and as your daughter Antonia's mother, and have a large private income, but she must sign a contract to behave like a deaf-mute in your presence, and not to be jealous of Calpurnia. How's that?"

"I shall give the matter my careful consideration, my dear Narcissus."

But it was Pallas who made the correct guess. It was either extraordinarily stupid of him or extraordinarily clever. How could he suppose that I would do anything so monstrous as to marry my niece, Agrippinilla? In the first place, the marriage would be incestuous; in the second place she was the mother of Lucius Domitius, to whom I had taken the most violent dislike; in the third place, now that Messalina was dead, she could claim the title of the worst woman in Rome. Even in Messalina's lifetime it would have been a very nice question how to decide between these two: they were equally vicious, and if Messalina had been more promiscuous then Agrippinilla, she had at least never committed incest, as Agrippinilla, to my knowledge, had. But Agrippinilla had one lonely virtue—she was very brave, while Messalina, as we have seen, was a coward. Pallas suggested Agrippinilla, with the same proviso that Narcissus had made, namely, that it need only be a marriage of form: I could keep any mistress I pleased. Agrippinilla, he said, was the only woman in Rome capable of taking over Messalina's political work, and would be a real help to me.

I promised to give the matter my careful consideration. I then arranged a regular debate between Callistus, Narcissus and Pallas, after first giving them time to sound the willingness of their candidates to stand for the office of Cæsar's wife. I called in Vitellius as umpire and the debate took place a few day later. Narcissus, in recommending Ælia, argued that by resuming an old connexion I would introduce no innovation into the family, and that she would be a good mother to little Octavia and to Britannicus, to whom she was already related by being the mother of their half-sister Antonia.

Callistus reminded Narcissus that Ælia had long been divorced from me, and suggested that if she were taken back her pride would be inflamed and she would probably revenge herself privately on Messalina's children. Lollia was a much more eligible match: nobody could deny that she was the most beautiful woman in the world, and virtuous too.

Pallas opposed both choices. Ælia was an old shrew, he said, and Lollia a vacant-minded simpleton who went about looking like a jeweller's shop and would expect a whole new set of gew-gaws, at the expense of the Treasury, as regularly as the sun rose. No, the only possible choice was the Lady Agrippina. (It was only I who still called her by the diminutive "Agrippinilla.") She would bring with her the grandson of Germanicus, who was in every way worthy of the Imperial fortune; and it was of great political importance that a woman who had shown herself fruitful and was still young should not marry into another house and transfer to it the splendors of the Cæsars.

I could see Vitellius sweating hard, trying to guess from my looks which of the three it was that I favoured, and wondering whether perhaps it would not be better to suggest a quite different name himself. But he guessed correctly, perhaps from the order in which I had given my freedmen leave to speak. He took a deep breath and said: "Between three such beautiful, wise, well-born and distinguished candidates, I find it as difficult to judge as the Trojan shepherd, Paris, between the three Goddesses Juno, Venus and Minerva. Let me keep this figure, which is a helpful one. Ælia Pætina stands for Juno. She has already been married and had a child by the Emperor; but as Jove was displeased with Juno, though she was the mother of Hebe, for her nagging tongue, so has the Emperor been displeased by Ælia Pætina, and we want no more domestic wars in this terrestrial Heaven of ours. It is claimed for Lollia Paulina that she is a very Venus, and certainly Paris awarded the prize to Venus; but Paris was an impressionable young swain, you will remember, and beauty unallied with intelligence can have no appeal for a mature ruler with great marital as well as governmental experience. Agrippinilla is Minerva, for wisdom, and she yields little, if anything, to Lollia for beauty. The Emperor's wife should have both good looks and outstanding intelligence: my choice is Agrippinilla."

As though I had only just considered the matter I protested: "But, Vitellius, she's my niece. I can't marry my niece, can I?"

"If you wish me to approach the Senate, Cæsar, I can undertake to obtain their consent. It's irregular, of course, but I can take the same line as you took the other day in your speech about the Autun franchise: I can point out that the marriage laws at Rome have become more and more plastic in course of time. A hundred years ago, for instance, it would have been considered monstrous for first-cousins to marry, but now it is regularly done even in the best families. And why shouldn't uncle and niece marry? The Parthians do it, and theirs is a very old civilization. And in the Herod family there have been more marriages between uncle and niece than any other sort."

"That's right," I said. "Herodias married her uncle Philip, and then deserted him and ran off with her uncle Antipas. And Herod Agrippa's daughter Berenice married her uncle Herod Pollio, King of Chalcis, and now she's supposed to be living incestuously with her brother, young Agrippa. Why shouldn't the Cæsars be as free as the Herods?"

Vitellius looked surprised but said quite seriously: "Incest between brother and sister is another matter. I cannot make out a case for that. But it may well be that our very earliest ancestors allowed uncle and niece to marry; because there is nowhere any disgust expressed in ancient classical literature for Pluto's marriage with his niece Proserpine."

"Pluto was a God," I said. "But then, it seems, so am I now. Pallas, what does my niece Agrippinilla herself think about the matter?"

"She will be greatly honoured and altogether overjoyed, Cæsar," said Pallas, hardly able to conceal his elation. "And she is ready to swear that she will faithfully devote herself

529

as long as she lives entirely to you, your children and the Empire."

"Bring her to me."

When Agrippinilla arrived she fell at my feet; I told her to rise and said that I was prepared to marry her, if she wished it. She embraced me passionately, for answer, and said this was the happiest moment of her life. I believed her. Why not? She would now be able to rule the world through me.

Agrippinilla was no Messalina. Messalina had the gift of surrendering herself wholly to sensual pleasure. In this she took after her great-grandfather, Mark Antony. Agrippinilla was not that sort of woman. She took after her great-grandmother, the Goddess Livia: she cared only for power. Sexually, as I have said, she was completely immoral; yet she was by no means prodigal of her favours. She only slept with men who could be useful to her politically. I have, for instance, every reason to suspect that she rewarded Vitellius for his gallant championship of her, and I know for certain (though I have never told her so) that Pallas was then, and is now, her lover. For Pallas controls the Privy Purse.

So Vitellius made his speech in the Senate (having first arranged a big public demonstration outside) and told them that he had suggested the marriage to me and that I had agreed about its political necessity, but had hesitated to make a definite decision until I had first heard what the Senate and People thought of the innovation. Vitellius spoke with old-fashioned eloquence. ". . . And you will not have long to search, my Lords, before you find that among all the ladies of Rome this Agrippina stands pre-eminent for the splendour of her lineage, has given signal proof of her fruitfulness, and comes up to and even surpasses your requirements in virtuous accomplishments: it is indeed a singularly happy circumstance that, through the providence of the Gods, this paragon among women is a widow and may be readily united with a Person who has always hitherto been a model of husbandly virtue."

You can perhaps guess how his speech was received. They voted for his motion without a single dissentient voice—not by any means because they all loved Agrippinilla, but because nobody dared to earn her resentment now that it seemed likely that she would become my wife—and several senators sprang up in emulous zeal and said that if necessary they would compel me to bow to the consentient will of the whole country. I received their greetings and pleadings and congratulations in the Market Place and then proceeded to the Senate, where I demanded the passing of a decree permanently legalizing marriages between uncles and fraternal nieces. They passed it. At the New Year I married Agrippinilla. Only one person took advantage of the new law, a knight who had been a Guards captain. Agrippinilla paid him well for it.

A. D. 49

I made a statement to the Senate about my temple in Britain. I explained that my deification had come about accidentally, and apologized to my fellow-citizens. But perhaps they would forgive me and confirm the incongruity in view of the political danger of cancelling it. "Britain is far away, and it is only a little temple," I pleaded ironically. "A tiny rustic temple with a mud floor and a turf roof, like the ones in which the Gods of Rome lived, back in Republican times, before the God Augustus rehoused them in their present palatial splendour. Surely you won't object to one little temple, so far away, and an old priest or two, and an occasional modest sacrifice? For my part I never intended to be a God. And I give you my word that it will be my only one. . . ." But nobody, it seemed, grudged me the temple.

After closing the census I had not taken on the office of Censor again, but as a prelude to my restoration of the Republic had given the appointment to Vitellius. It was the first time for a century that the control of public morals had been out of the hand of the Cæsars. One of Vitellius's first acts after arranging my marriage with Agrippinilla was to remove from the Senatorial Order one of the first-rank magistrates of the year, none other than my son-in-law young Silanus! The reason he gave was Silanus's incest with his sister Calvina, who had been his own daughter-in-law, but had lately been divorced by her husband, young Vitellius. Vitellius explained that his son had surprised the two in bed together some time before and had told him of it under the bonds of secrecy; but now that he had become Censor he could not conscientiously conceal Silanus's guilt. I examined the case myself. Silanus and Calvina denied the charge, but it seemed proved beyond all dispute, so I dissolved the marriage-contract between Silanus and my daughter Octavia (or rather Messalina's daughter Octavia) and made him resign this magistracy. It had only a single day to run, but to show how strongly I felt I gave someone else the appointment for the last day. Of course Vitellius would never have dared to reveal the incest if it had not been for Agrippinilla. Silanus stood in the way of her ambitions: she wanted her son Lucius to become my son in law. Well, I had been fond of Silanus, and, after all, he was a descendant of the God Augustus; so I told him that I would postpone judgment in his case—meaning that I expected him to commit suicide. He delayed for some time, and eventually chose my wedding-day for the deed; which was not inappropriate. Calvina I banished and advised the College of Pontiffs to offer sacrifices and atonements at the Grove of Diana, in revival of a picturesque institution of Tullus Hostilius, the third King of Rome.

Baba and Augurinus were in great form about this time. They parodied everything I did. Baba introduced three new letters into the alphabet: one to stand for a hawk of phlegm, one for the noisy sucking of teeth, and the third for "the indeterminate vowel half-way between a hiccup and belch."

He divorced the enormous negress who had hitherto acted the part of Messalina, whipped her through the streets and went through a mock ceremony of marriage with a cross-eyed albino woman whom he claimed to be his fraternal niece. He took a census of beggars, thieves and vagabonds and removed from the Society all who had ever done a stroke of honest work in their lives. One of his jokes was resigning his censorship and appointing Augurinus as his successor for the unexpired period of his office—exactly one hour by the water-clock. Augurinus boasted of all the glorious things that he professed to do in the hour. His one complaint was that Baba's water-clock didn't keep good time: he wanted to go off and fetch his own, which had hours that lasted at least three times as long. But Baba, imitating my voice and gestures, quoted a phrase I had recently used in the law-courts, and was rather proud of, "One can expect agreement between philosophers sooner than between clocks," and refused to let him go. Augurinus insisted that fair was fair; if he was going to be Censor, he needed a full hour of regulation size and weight. They carried on the argument hotly until Augurinus's term of office ended suddenly with nothing done. "And I was going to dip you in boiling tar and then fry you within an inch of your life, according to a picturesque institution of King Tullus Hostilius," Augurinus grieved.

I allow Baba and Augurinus perfect freedom to parody and caricature me. They draw great audiences in their performances outside the Temple of Mercury: Mercury is, of course, the patron of thieves and practical jokers. Agrippinilla was highly offended by the insult to her of Baba's marriage to the albino, but I surprised her by telling her firmly: "So long as I live Baba's life is to be spared, understand—and Augurinus's too."

"Exactly so long, to the very hour," Agrippina agreed in her most unpleasant tones.

There was a plague of vipers this year: I published an order informing the public of an infallible remedy against snake-bite, namely, the juice of a yew-tree. Augurinus and Baba republished it with the addition of the phrase "and contrariwise," which, it seems, is recognized as one of my stock expressions.

# Chapter Thirty-One

I AM near the end of my long story. I have now been five years married to Agrippinilla, but they have been comparatively uneventful years, and I shall not write about them in too great detail. I have let Agrippinilla and my freedmen rule me. I have opened and shut my mouth and gestured with my arms like the little jointed marionettes they make in Sicily: but the voice has not been mine, nor the gestures. I must say at once that Agrippinilla has shown herself a remarkably able ruler of the tyrannical sort. When she comes into a room where a number of notables are gathered, and looks coldly around her, everyone quakes and springs to attention and studies how best to please her. She no longer needs to pretend affection for me. I soon made her realize that I had married her purely on political grounds; and, physically, she was repulsive to me. I was quite frank about it. I explained: "The fact is, that I got tired of being Emperor. I wanted someone to do most of the work for me. I married you not for your heart but for your head. It takes a woman to run an empire like this. There's no reason for us to pretend amorous devotion to each other."

"That suits me," she said. "You're not the sort of lover one dreams about."

"And you're not quite what you were twenty-two years ago, my dear, when you were a bride for the first time. Still, you'll last a little longer if you continue with that daily facial massage and those milk baths: Vitellius pretends to find you the most beautiful woman in Rome."

"And perhaps you'll last too, if you don't exasperate the people you depend on."

"Yes, we two have outlasted all the rest of our family," I agreed. "I don't know how we've done it. I think we ought to congratulate each other, instead of quarrelling."

"You always begin it," she said, "by being what you call 'honest'."

Agrippinilla could not understand me. She soon found that it was unnecessary to coax or cheat or bully me if she wanted things done her way. I accepted her suggestions on almost every point. She could hardly believe her luck when I consented to betroth Lucius to Octavia: she knew what I really thought of Lucius. She could not make out why I consented. She was emboldened to go further and suggest that I should adopt him as my son. But that was already my intention. She first let Pallas sound me on the subject. Pallas was tactful. He began speaking fondly of my brother Germanicus and of his adoption by my uncle Tiberius at Augustus's request, though Tiberius had a son of his own, Castor. He enlarged on the remarkable brotherly love that had sprung up between Germanicus and Castor and the generosity that Castor had shown to Germanicus's widow and children. I knew at once what Pallas was driving at, and agreed that two loving sons were better than one. "But remember," I said, "that was not the end of the story. Germanicus and Castor were both murdered; and my Uncle Tiberius in his old age, as it might be myself, named another pair of loving brothers as his joint heirs—Caligula and Gemellus. Caligula had the advantage of being the elder. When the old man died Caligula seized the monarchy and killed Gemellus."

That silenced Pallas for awhile. When he tried a slightly different line, this time telling me what fast friends Lucius and Britannicus had become, I said, as if quite irrelevantly: "Do you know that the Claudian family has kept its descent direct in the male line, without adoptions, ever since the day of the original Appius Claudius, five whole cycles ago? There's no other family in Rome can make the same boast."

"Yes, Cæsar," Pallas said, "the Claudian family tradition is one of the least plastic things in a remarkably plastic world. But, as you wisely point out, 'all things are subject to change'."

"Listen, Pallas. Why do you go on beating about the bush? Tell the Lady Agrippinilla that if she wishes me to adopt her son as my joint-heir with Britannicus I am ready to do so. As for plasticity, I've gone very soft in my old age. You can roll me in your hands like dough and fill me with whatever stuffing you like and bake me into Imperial dumplings."

I adopted Lucius. He is now called Nero. Recently I married him to Octavia, whom I had first, however, to let Vitellius adopt as his daughter, to avoid the technical crime of incest. On the night of their marriage the whole sky seemed on fire. Lucius (or Nero as he was now called) did his best to win Britannicus's friendship. But Britannicus saw through him and haughtily rejected his advances. He refused at first to address him as Nero, continuing to call him Lucius Domitius until Agrippinilla intervened and ordered him to apologize. Britannicus replied: "I shall apologize only if my father orders me to do so." I ordered him to apologize. I still saw very little of Britannicus. I had fought down my morbid suspicions about his being Caligula's bastard—and loved him now as dearly as ever before. But I concealed my true feelings. I was determined to play Old King Log, and nothing must hinder my resolution. Sosibius was his tutor still and gave him an old-fashioned education. Britannicus was accustomed to the plainest foods and lay at night on a plank bed like a soldier. Horsemanship, fencing, military engineering and early Roman history were his chief studies, but he knew the works of Homer and Ennius and Livy as well as or better than I did. In his holidays Sosibius took him down to my Capua estate, and there he learned about bee-keeping, stock-breeding and

A. D. 50

537

farming. I allowed him no training in Greek oratory or philosophy. I told Sosibius: "The ancient Persians taught their children to shoot straight and speak the truth. Teach my son the same."

Narcissus ventured to criticize me. "The sort of education that Britannicus is being given, Cæsar, would have been all very well in the old days when, as you are so fond of quoting,

> 'Under the oak sat Romulus
> Eating boiled turnips with a will,'

or even a few hundred years later when,

> 'Called to fight his country's foemen
> Cincinnatus left the plough.'

But surely in this new ninth cycle of Roman history it is a little out of date?"

"I know what I am doing, Narcissus," I said.

As for Nero, I provided our young King Stork with the most appropriate tutor in the world. I had to send all the way to Corsica for this prodigy. You will guess his name, perhaps: Lucius Annæus Seneca, the Stoic—that flashy orator, that shameless flatterer, that dissolute and perverted amorist. I pleaded before the Senate myself for his forgiveness and recall. I spoke of the uncomplaining patience with which he had borne his eight years of exile, the rigorous discipline to which he had voluntarily subjected himself, and his deep sense of loyalty to my house. Seneca must have been astounded, after the two false moves he had recently made. For shortly after the publication of his *Consolation to Polybius,* Polybius had been executed as a criminal. Seneca had then tried to remedy the mistake by a panegyric on Messalina. A few days after it was published at Rome, Messalina followed Polybius into disgrace and death, and it was hurriedly withdrawn. Agrippinilla was quite ready to welcome Seneca as Nero's teacher. She valued his talents as a teacher of rhetoric and took all the credit for his recall.

Nero is afraid of his mother. He obeys her in everything. She treats him with great severity. She is certain that she will rule through him after my death, just as Livia ruled first through Augustus and then through Tiberius. I can see farther than she can. I remember the sibyl's prophecy:

"The hairy Sixth to enslave the State
Shall give Rome fiddlers and fear and fire.
His hand shall be red with a parent's blood.
No hairy seventh to him succeeds
And blood shall gush from his tomb."

Nero will kill his mother. It was prophesied at his birth. Barbillus himself prophesied it, and Barbillus never makes a mistake. He was even right about the death of Messalina's husband, was he not? Agrippinilla, being a woman, cannot command the Roman armies or address the Senate. She needs a man to do that for her. When I married her I knew I could count on surviving so long as Nero was too young to step into my shoes.

Agrippinilla asked me to persuade the Senate to give her the title of Augusta. She did not expect me to give her what I had refused Messalina, but I did. She has taken upon herself other unheard-of privileges. She sits on the tribunal beside me when I judge cases, and drives up the Capitoline Hill in a chariot. She has appointed a new Guards Commander to supersede Geta and Crispinus. His name is Burrhus and he is Agrippinilla's man body and soul. (He served with the Guards at Brentwood and there lost three fingers of his right hand to a British broadsword.) Rome's new Augusta has no rivals. Ælia Pætina is dead, perhaps poisoned: I do not know. Lollia Paulina was also removed: her champion, Callistus, having died, the other freedmen made no objection to her removal. She was accused of witchcraft and of circulating an astrological report that my marriage to Agrippinilla was fated to be disastrous to the country. I was sorry for Lollia, so in the speech that I made to the Senate I merely recommended her banishment. But Agrippinilla would not be cheated. She sent a Guards colonel to Lollia's house and he made sure that she killed herself. He duly reported her death, but Agrippinilla was not satisfied. "Bring me her head," she ordered. The head was brought to her at the Palace. Agrippinilla took it by the hair and, holding it up to a window, opened the mouth. "Yes, that's Lollia's head, all right," she said complacently to me as I came into the room. "Here are those gold teeth that she had put in by an Alexandrian dentist to fill out her sunken left cheek. What coarse hair she had, like a pony's mane. Slave, take this thing away. And the mat too: have the bloodstains scrubbed out."

Agrippinilla also removed her sister-in-law Domitia Lepida, Messalina's mother. Domitia Lepida was very attentive to Nero now and used to invite him frequently to her house, where she caressed and flattered him, and gave him a good time and reminded him of all that she had done for him when he was a penniless orphan. It was true that she had occasionally taken charge of him when her sister Domitia went out of town and could not be bothered to take the child with her. Agrippinilla, finding that her own maternal authority, which was based on sternness, was being threatened by Domitia Lepida's auntish indulgences, had her accused of publicly cursing my marriage-bed and also of failing to restrain the slaves on her estate in Calabria from dangerous rioting: a magistrate and two of his staff who attempted to restore order there had been set on and beaten, and Domitia Lepida had locked herself up in the house and done nothing. I allowed her to be sentenced to death on these two charges (the first of which was probably a fabrication) because I was now aware of the assistance she had given Messalina in the Appius Silanus affair and other deceptions practised on me.

One act only of Agrippinilla's I found it hard to take philosophically. When I heard of it I confess that tears came into my eyes. But it would have been foolish for old King Log to have gone back on his resolution at this point, and roused himself and taken vengeance. Vengeance cannot recall the dead to life again. It was the murder of my poor Calpurnia and her friend Cleopatra that made me weep. Someone set fire to their house one night and the two were trapped in their beds and burned to death. It was made to look like an accident; but it was clearly murder. Pallas, who told me about it, had the insolence to suggest that it was done by some friend of Messalina's who knew the part that Calpurnia had played in bringing her to justice. I had been most neglectful of Calpurnia. I had not visited her once since that terrible afternoon. At my private order a handsome marble tomb was erected for her on the ruins of the burned villa, and on it I put a Greek epigram. It was the only one that I have ever composed except as a school exercise: but I felt that I had to do something out of the ordinary to express my great grief for her death and my true gratitude for the love and devotion she had always shown me. I wrote:

> " 'A harlot's love, a harlot's lie'—
> Cast that ancient proverb by.
> CALPURNIA's heart was cleaner far,
> Roman matrons, than yours are."

Last year, the year of Nero's marriage, was marked by a world failure of crops[1] that all but exhausted our granaries.

See Acts xi. 28.—R. G.

This year, though the harbour of Ostia was now completed, a strong north-east wind blowing for weeks on end prevented the Egyptian and African corn fleets from making our shores. The Italian harvest promised well, but was not yet ready to cut, and at one time there was only a fortnight's corn supply left in the public granaries, though I had done everything possible to fill them. I was obliged to reduce corn rations to the lowest possible level. Then, as though I was not doing and had not always done everything possible to keep my fellow-citizens well fed (building the harbour, for instance, in the face of general discouragement, and organizing the daily supply of fresh vegetables), I suddenly found myself regarded as a public enemy. I was accused of purposely starving the City. The crowd groaned and howled at me almost whenever I showed myself in public, and once or twice pelted me with stones and mud and mouldy crusts. On one occasion I narrowly escaped serious injury in the Market Place: my yeomen were set upon by a mob of two or three hundred persons and had their rods of office broken over their own backs. I only just managed to get safely into the Palace by a postern gate not far off, from which a small party of armed Guardsmen dashed out to my rescue. In the old days I would have taken this greatly to heart. Now I just smiled to myself. "Frogs," I thought, "you are getting very frisky."

Nero put on his manly-gown, in the year after his adoption by me. I allowed the Senate to vote him the privilege of becoming Consul at the age of twenty, so at sixteen he was Consul-Elect. I awarded him honorary triumphal dress and appointed him Leader of Cadets, as Augustus had appointed his grandsons, Gaius and Lucius. In the Latin holidays, too, when the Consuls and other magistrates were out of the City, I made him City Warden as Augustus had also done with his grandsons, to give them a first taste of magistracy. It was customary to bring no important cases before the City Warden, but to wait for the return of the proper magistrates. Nero, however, managed a whole series of complicated cases which would have tested the judgment of the most experienced legal officers in the City, and gave remarkably shrewd decisions. This gained him popular admiration, but it was perfectly clear to me as soon as I heard about it, that the whole affair had been stage-managed by Seneca. I do not mean that the cases were not genuine, but that Seneca had reviewed them carefully beforehand and arranged with the lawyers as to just what points they should bring out in their speeches, and had then coached Nero in his cross-examination of witnesses and his summing-up and judgment. Britannicus had not yet come of age. I kept him from the society of boys his own age and rank as much as possible: he only met them under the eye of his tutors. I did not wish him to catch the Imperial infection to which I was purposely subjecting Nero. I let it go about that he was an epileptic. Public flattery was all concentrated now on Nero. Agrippinilla was delighted. She thought that I hated Britannicus for his mother's sake.

There was a big riot about the sale of bread. It was a quite unnecessary riot, though, and according to Narcissus, who loathed Agrippinilla (and found to his surprise that I encouraged him in this), it was instigated by her. It happened when I was suffering from a chill, and Agrippinilla came to my room and suggested that I should issue an edict to reassure and quiet the populace. She wanted me to say that I was not seriously ill and that, even if my illness took a serious turn and I died, Nero was now capable of conducting public affairs under her guidance. I laughed in her face. "You are asking me to sign my own death warrant, my dear? Come on, then, give me the pen, I'll sign it. When's the funeral to be?"

"If you don't wish to sign it, don't," she said. "I'm not forcing you."

543

"Very well, then, I won't," I said. "I'll inquire into that bread riot and see who really started it.'

She walked angrily out. I called her back. "I was only joking. Of course I'll sign! By the way, has Seneca taught Nero his funeral oration yet? Or not yet? I'd like to hear it first if none of you mind."

Vitellius died of a paralytic stroke. A senator who was either drunk or crazy, I can't say which, had suddenly accused him before the House of aiming at the monarchy. The charge appears to have been directed at Agrippinilla, but naturally no one dared to support it, much as Agrippinilla was hated, so the accuser was himself outlawed. However, Vitellius took the matter to heart and the stroke followed soon after. I visited him as he lay dying. He was unable to move a finger but talked quite good sense. I asked him the question that I had always meant to ask: "Vitellius, in a better age you would have been one of the most virtuous men alive: how was it, then, that your upright nature acquired a sort of permanent stoop from playing the courtier?"

He said: "It was inevitable under a monarchy, however benevolent the monarch. The old virtues disappear. Independence and frankness are at a discount. Complacent anticipation of the monarch's wishes is then the greatest of all virtues. One must either be a good monarch like yourself, or a good courtier like myself—either an Emperor or an idiot."

I said: "You mean that people who continue virtuous in an old-fashioned way must inevitably suffer in times like these?"

"Phæmon's dog was right." That was the last thing he said before he lapsed into a coma from which he never recovered.

I could not be content until I had hunted down the reference in the library. It appears that Phæmon the philosopher had a little dog whom he had trained to go to the butcher every day and bring back a lump of meat in a basket. This virtuous creature, who would never dare to touch a scrap until Phæmon gave it permission, was one day set upon by a pack of mongrels who snatched the basket from its mouth and began to tear the meat to pieces and bolt it greedily down. Phæmon, watching from an upper window, saw the dog deliberate for a moment just what to do. It was clearly no use trying to rescue the meat from the other dogs: they would kill it for its pains. So it rushed in among them and itself ate as much of the meat as it could get hold of. In fact it ate more than any of the other dogs, because it was both braver and cleverer.

The Senate honoured Vitellius with a public funeral and a statue in the Market Place. The inscription that is carved on it reads:

*Lucius Vitellius, twice Consul,*
*once Censor.*
*He also governed Syria.*
*Unswervingly loyal to his Emperor*


I must tell about the Fucine Lake. I had lost all real interest in it by now, but one day Narcissus, who is in charge of the work, told me that the contractors reported that the channel was dug through the mountain at last: we A.D. 53 had only to raise the sluice-gates and let the water rush out, and the whole lake would become dry land. Thirteen years, and thirty thousand men constantly at work! "We'll celebrate this, Narcissus," I said.

I arranged a sham sea-fight, but on a most magnificent scale. Julius Cæsar had first introduced this sort of spectacle at Rome, exactly a hundred years before. He dug a basin in Mars Field, which he flooded from the Tiber, and arranged for eight ships, called the Tyrian fleet, to engage eight more, called the Egyptian fleet. About two thousand fighting men were used, exclusive of rowers. When I was eight years old Augustus gave a similar show in a permanent basin on the other side of the Tiber, measuring twelve hundred feet by eighteen hundred, with stone seats around it like an amphitheatre. There were twelve ships a side this time, called Athenians and Persians. Three thousand men fought in them. My show on the Fucine Lake was going to dwarf both spectacles. I didn't care about economy now. I was going to have a really magnificent show for once. Julius's and Augustus's fleets had been composed of light craft only, but I gave orders for twenty-four proper war vessels of three banks of oars each to be constructed, and twenty-six smaller vessels; and I cleared the prisons of nineteen hundred able-bodied criminals to fight in them under the command of famous professional sword-fighters. The two fleets, each consisting of twenty-five vessels, were to be known as the Rhodians and the Sicilians. The hills around the lake would make a fine natural amphitheatre; and though it was a very long way from Rome, I was sure that I could draw an audience there of at least two hundred thousand people. I advised them by an official circular to bring their own food with them in baskets. But nineteen hundred armed criminals are a dangerous force to handle. I had to take the whole Guards Division out there and station some of them on shore and the rest on rafts lashed together across the lake. The line of rafts was a semi-circle which made a proper naval basin of the south-western end of the lake, where it tapered to the point at which the channel had been cut. The whole lake would have been too big: it spread over two hundred square miles. The Guards on the rafts had catapults and mangonels ready to sink any vessel that tried to ram the line and escape.

The great occasion finally came; I proclaimed a ten-days' public holiday. The weather was fine and the numbers of spectators were more like half a million than two hundred thousand. They came from all over Italy, and I must say that it was a wonderfully well-behaved and well-dressed gathering. To prevent overcrowding, I divided up the lakeshore into what I called colonies and put each colony under a magistrate; the magistrates had to make arrangements for communal cooking and sanitation and so on. I built a large canvas field-hospital for the wounded survivors of the battle and for accidents on shore. Fifteen babies were born in that hospital and I made them all take the additional name of Fucinus or Fucina.

Everything was in position by ten o'clock on the morning of the fight. The fleets were manned and came rowing up in parallel lines towards the President, namely, myself, who was sitting on a high throne dressed in a suit of golden armour with a purple cloak over it. My throne was at a point where the shore curved out into the lake and gave the widest view. Agrippinilla sat beside me on another throne, wearing a long mantle of cloth of gold. The two flagships came close up to us. The crew shouted: "Greetings, Cæsar. We salute you in Death's shadow."

I was supposed to nod gravely, but I was feeling in a gay humour that morning. I answered: "And the same to you, my friends."

The rascals pretended to understand this as a general pardon. "Long live Cæsar," they shouted joyfully. I did not at the moment realize what they meant. The combined fleets sailed past me cheering and then the Sicilians formed up on the west and the Rhodians on the east. The signal for battle was given by a mechanical silver Triton that suddenly appeared from the lake-bottom, when I pressed a lever, and blew a golden trumpet. That caused huge excitement among the audience. The fleets met, and expectation ran high. And then—what do you think happened then? They simply sailed through each other, cheering me and congratulating each other! I *was* angry. I jumped down from my throne

547

and rushed along the shore shouting and cursing. "What do you think that I got you all here for, you scoundrels, you scum, you rebels, you bastards? To kiss each other and shout loyal shouts? You could have done that just as well in the prison-yard. Why don't you fight? Afraid, eh? Do you want to be given to the wild beasts instead? Listen, if you don't fight now, by God, I'll make the Guards put up a show. I'll make them sink every one of your ships with their siege-engines and kill every man Jack who swims ashore."

As I have told you, my legs have always been weak, and one is shorter than the other, and I am not accustomed to use them much, and I am old and rather stout now, and besides all this I was wearing an extremely heavy corselet, and the ground was uneven, so you can imagine what sort of a figure I cut—stumbling top-heavily along, with frequent falls, shouting at the top of my not very melodious voice, red and stuttering with anger! However, I succeeded in making them fight, and the spectators cheered me with, "Well done, Cæsar! Well run, Cæsar!"

I recovered my good-humour and joined in the laugh against myself. You should have seen the murderous look on Agrippinilla's face. "You boor," she muttered as I climbed back on my throne. "You idiotic boor. Have you no dignity? How do you expect the people to respect you?"

I answered politely: "Why, of course, as your husband, my dear, and as Nero's father in law."

The fleets met. I shall not describe the battle in much detail, but both sides fought splendidly. The Sicilians rammed and sank nine of the big Rhodian vessels, losing three of their own, and then cornered the remainder close to where we were sitting and boarded them one by one. The Rhodians repelled them time and time again, and the decks were slippery with blood, but finally they were beaten and by three o'clock the Sicilian flag was run up on the last vessel. My field-hospital was full. Nearly five thousand wounded were carried ashore. I pardoned the remainder, except the survivors of three big Rhodian vessels who had not put up a proper fight before being rammed, and six of the Sicilian lighter craft who had consistently avoided combat. Three thousand men had been killed or drowned. When I was a lad I couldn't bear the sight of bloodshed. I don't mind it at all now: I get so interested in the fighting.

Before letting the water out of the lake I thought that I had better satisfy myself that the channel was deep enough to carry it off. I sent out someone to take careful soundings in the middle of the lake. He reported that the channel would have to be dug at least a yard deeper if we were not to be left with a lake a quarter of its present size! So the whole spectacle had been wasted. Agrippinilla blamed Narcissus and accused him of fraud. Narcissus blamed the engineers who, he said, must have been bribed by the contractors to send in a false report as to the depth of the lake, and protested that Agrippinilla was being most unjust to him.

I laughed. It didn't matter. We had witnessed a most enjoyable show and the channel could be dug to the proper depth within a few months. Nobody was to blame, I said: probably there had been a natural subsidence of the lake-bottom. So we all went home again and in four months' time back we came. On this occasion I did not have enough criminals available for a big sea-battle, and did not wish to repeat the spectacle on a smaller scale, so I had another idea. I built a long, wide pontoon-bridge across the end of the lake and arranged for two forces of two battalions apiece, called Etruscans and Samnians, appropriately dressed and armed, to fight on it. They marched towards each other along the bridge, to the accompaniment of martial music, and engaged in the centre, where the bridge widened out to a hundred yards or so, and there fought a vigorous battle. The Samnians twice took possession of this battle-field, but Etruscan counter-attacks forced them back and eventually the

Samnians were on the run, losing heavily, some run through by bronze-headed Etruscan lances or chopped down by two-headed Etruscan battle-axes, some thrown off the bridge into the water. My orders were that no combatant must be permitted to swim ashore. If he was thrown into the water he must either drown or climb back on the bridge. The Etruscans were victorious and erected a trophy. I gave all the victors their freedom, and a few of the Samnians, too, who had fought particularly well.

Then at last the moment came for the water to be let out of the lake. A huge wooden dining-hall had been erected close to the sluice-gates and the tables were spread with a magnificent luncheon for me and the Senate, and the families of senators, and a number of leading knights and their families, and all senior Guards officers. We would dine to the pleasant sound of rushing water. "You're sure that the channel is deep enough now?" I asked Narcissus.

"Yes, Cæsar. I've taken the soundings myself."

So I went to the sluice-gates and sacrificed and uttered a prayer or two—they included an apology to the nymph of the lake, whom I now begged to act as guardian deity of the farmers who would till the recovered land—and finally lent a hand to the crank at which a group of my Germans was posted, and gave the orders, "Heave away!"

Up came the gates and the water rolled crashing into the channel. An immense cheer went up. We watched for a minute or two and then I said to Narcissus: "Congratulations, my dear Narcissus. Thirteen years' work and thirty thousand——"

I was interrupted by a roar like thunder, followed by a general shriek of alarm.

"What's that?" I cried.

He caught me by the arm without ceremony and fairly dragged me up the hill. "Hurry!" he screamed. "Faster, faster!" I looked to see what was the matter, and a huge brown-and-white wall of water, I wouldn't like to say how many feet high, on the model of the one that runs yearly up the Severn River in Britain, was roaring up the channel. *Up* the channel, mark you! It was some time before I realized what had happened. The sudden rush of water had overflowed the channel a few hundred yards down, forming a large lake in a fold of the hills. Into this lake, its foundations sapped by the water, slid a whole hillside, hundreds of thousands of tons of rock, completely filling it and expelling the water with awful force.

All but a few of us managed to scramble to safety, though with wet legs—only twenty persons were drowned. But the dining-chamber was torn to pieces and tables and couches and food and garlands carried far out into the lake. Oh, how vexed Agrippinilla was! She blazed up at Narcissus, telling him that he had arranged the whole thing on purpose to conceal the fact that the channel was still not dug deep enough, and accused him of putting millions of public money into his own pocket, and Heaven only knows what else besides.

Narcissus, whose nerves were thoroughly upset now, lost his temper too and asked Agrippinilla who she thought she was—Queen Semiramis? or the Goddess Juno? or the Commander-in-Chief of the Roman Armies? "Keep your paws out of this pie," he screamed at her.

I thought it all a great joke. "Quarrelling won't give us back our dinners," I said.

I was more amused than ever when the engineers reported that it would take two more years to cut a new passage through the obstruction. "I'm afraid that I'll not be spared to exhibit another fight on these waters, my friends," I said gravely. Somehow the whole business seemed beautifully symbolic. Labour in vain, like all the industrious work that I had done in my early years of monarchy as a gift to an undeserving Senate and People. The violence of that wave gave me a feeling of the deepest satisfaction. I liked it better than all the sea-fighting and bridge-fighting.

Agrippinilla was complaining that a precious set of gold dishes from the Palace had been carried away by the wave and only a few pieces recovered: the others were at the lake bottom. "Why, that's nothing to worry about," I teased. "Listen! You take off those beautiful shining clothes of yours—I'll see that Narcissus doesn't steal them—and I'll make the Guards keep the crowd back and you can give a special diving display from the sluice-gate. Everyone will enjoy that tremendously: they like nothing so much as the discovery that their rulers are human after all. . . . But, my dear, why not? Why shouldn't you? Now, don't lose your temper. If you can dive for sponges, you can dive for gold dishes surely? Look, that must be one of your treasures over there, shining through the water, quite easy to get. There, where I'm throwing this pebble!"

# Chapter Thirty-Two

I T IS now September in the fourteenth year of my reign.
Barbillus has lately read my horoscope and fears that I
am destined to die about the middle of next month. Thrasyllus once told me exactly the same thing: for he al-      A. D. 54
lowed me a life of sixty-three years, sixty-three days,
sixty-three watches, and sixty-three hours. That works out to
the thirteenth of next month. Thrasyllus was more explicit
about it than Barbillus: I remember that he congratulated
me on this combination of multiplied sevens and nines: it
was a very remarkable one, he said. Well, I am prepared to
die. In court this morning I begged the lawyers to behave
with a little more consideration for an old man; I said that
next year I wouldn't be among them, and they could treat
my successor as they pleased. I also told the court, in the
case of a noblewoman charged with adultery, that I had
now been married several times, and that each of my wives
in turn had proved bad, and that I had showed them indul-
gence for awhile, but not for long: so far I had divorced
three. Agrippinilla will get to hear of this.

Nero is seventeen. He goes about with the affected modesty of a high-class harlot, shaking his scented hair out of his
eyes every now and then; or with the affected modesty of a
high-class philosopher, pausing to ponder privately, every
now and then, in the middle of a group of admiring noblemen—right foot thrown out, head sunk on breast, left arm
akimbo, right hand raised, with the finger tips pressing
lightly on his forehead as if in the throes of thought. Soon
he comes out with a brilliant epigram or a happy couplet or

553

a profound piece of sententious wisdom; not however his own—Seneca is earning his porridge, as the saying is. I wish Nero's friends joy of him. I wish Rome joy of him. I wish Agrippinilla joy of him, and Seneca too. I heard privately, by way of Seneca's sister (a secret friend of Narcissus's who gives us a lot of useful information about the nation's latest darling), that the night before Seneca received my order for his recall from Corsica he dreamed that he was acting as schoolmaster to Caligula. I take that as a sign.

On New Year's Day this year I called Xenophon to me and thanked him for keeping me alive so long. I then fulfilled my promise to him, though the agreed fifteen years' term is not yet over, and won from the Senate a perpetual exemption from taxes and military service of his native island of Cos. In my speech I gave the House a full account of the lives and deeds of the many famous physicians of Cos, who all claim direct descent from the God Æsculapius, and learnedly discussed their various therapeutic practices; I ended up with Xenophon's father, who was my father's field-surgeon in his German wars, and with Xenophon himself, whom I praised above them all. Some days later Xenophon asked permission to remain with me a few years longer. He did not put his request in terms of loyalty or gratitude or affection, though I have done much for him— what a curiously unemotional man he is!—but on the grounds of the convenience of the Palace as a place for medical research!

The fact was that when I paid Xenophon this honour I was counting on him to help me carry out a plan that called for the utmost secrecy and discretion. It was a debt that I owed to myself and to my ancestors: it was nothing less than the rescue of my Britannicus. Let me now clearly show why I deliberately preferred Nero to him, why I gave him so old-fashioned an education, why I guarded him so carefully from the infection of the court, from contact with vice and flattery. To begin with, I knew that Nero is fated to rule as my successor, carrying on the cursed business of monarchy, fated to plague Rome and earn everlasting hatred, to be the last of the mad Cæsars. Yes, we are all mad, we Emperors. We begin sanely, like Augustus and Tiberius and even Caligula (though he was an evil character, he was sane at first) and monarchy turns our wits. "After Nero's death surely the Republic will be restored," I argued; and it was my intention that Britannicus should be the one to restore it. But how was Britannicus to live through the reign of Nero? Nero would surely put him to death if he remained at Rome, as Caligula had put Gemellus to death. Britannicus must be removed, I decided, to some safe place where he could grow up virtuously and nobly like a Claudian of ancient times, and keep alight in his heart the fire of true liberty.

"But the world is now wholly Roman, with the exception of Germany, the East, the Scythian deserts north of the Black Sea, unexplored Africa, and the farther parts of Britain: so where can my Britannicus be safe from Nero's power?" I asked myself. "Not in Parthia or Arabia: there could be no worse choice. Not in Germany: I have never loved the Germans. For all their barbaric virtues they are our natural enemies. Of Africa and Scythia I know little. There is only one place for a Britannicus, and that is Britain. The northern Britons are racially akin to us. Queen Cartimandua of the Brigantians is my ally. She is a noble and wise ruler and at peace with my province of South Britain. Her chieftains are brave and courteous warriers. Her young stepson, who is her heir, is coming here in May, accompanied by a band of young nobles and noble-women, as my guest at the Palace. I shall make Britannicus his host and secretly bind the two together in blood-brotherhood, according to the British rite. These Brigantians will remain here for the entire summer. When they sail back (and I shall send them back by long sea, from Ostia direct to their port in the Humber) Britannicus will go with them in disguise. He will have his face and body stained blue, and will be dressed in the red smock and tartan trousers of a young Brigantian nobleman, with gold chains around his neck. Nobody will recognize him. I will load the Brigantian prince with gifts and bind him with the holiest possible oaths to keep Britannicus safe, and to hide his identity from everyone but the Queen. He will bind his companions with the same oaths. At Cartimandua's court Britannicus will be presented as a young Greek of illustrious birth, whose parents have died and who has been left penniless and who has come to seek his fortune in Britain. At Rome he will not be missed. I shall give out that he is unwell, and Xenophon and Narcissus will assist me in the fraud. Presently I will announce his death. Xenophon has a written order from me giving him the right to claim the body of any dead slave in the hospital on the island of Æsculapius for use as a subject for dissection. (He is writing a treatise on the muscles of the heart.) He can surely find a suitable corpse to offer as Britannicus's. At Cartimandua's court Britannicus will grow to manhood: he will teach the Brigantians the useful arts that I have been at pains to have him taught. If he bears himself modestly he will never want for friends there. Cartimandua will permit him to worship his own gods. He will avoid the society of Romans. On Nero's death he will reveal himself and return as the saviour of his country."

It was an excellent plan and I did all I could to put it into execution. When the Brigantian prince arrived, Britannicus was his host, and formed a close friendship with him. Each taught the other his own language and the use of his country's weapons. They worked and played together all summer long. They bound themselves by the blood-rite, unprompted by any suggestion of mine, and exchanged gifts. I was pleased that things were going so well. I told Xenophon and Narcissus of my plan. They undertook to help

556

me. They made all arrangements. But see what has happened! All my ingenuity has been wasted.

Three days ago Narcissus brought Britannicus to me, very early in the morning, when all the Palace was asleep. I embraced him with a warmth that I had abstained from showing him for years. I explained to him why it was that I had treated him as I had done. It was not cruelty or neglect, I said, but love. I quoted to him the Greek line that Augustus had quoted to me just before his death: "Who wounded thee, shall make thee whole." I told him of the prophecy and of my desire to save from the wreckage of Rome the person whom I most loved—himself. I reminded him of the fatal history of our family and begged him to fall in with my plan, in which lay his only chance of survival.

He listened attentively and finally burst out: "No, Father, no! Father, I confess that I have hated you ever since my mother's death. I thought the very worst of you. To me you were a pedant, a coward and a fool, and I was ashamed to be known as your son. I see now that I misjudged you and I ask your pardon. But no, I cannot do what you ask me to do. It is not honourable. A Claudian should not paint his face blue and hide away among barbarians. I am not afraid of Nero: Nero is a coward. Let me put on my manly-gown this New Year. I will still be only thirteen, but you can forgive me the extra year: I'm tall and strong for my age. Once I am officially a man I'll be a match for Nero in spite of the start you've given him, and in spite of his mother. Make us your joint-heirs and then we'll see which of us two gets the upper hand. It is my right as your son. And I don't believe in the Republic, anyway. You can't reverse the course of history. My great-grandmother Livia said that, and it's true. I love the days of old, as you do, but I'm not blind. The Republic's dead, except for old-fashioned people like you and Sosibius. Rome is an Empire now and the choice only lies between good Emperors and bad ones.

Make me joint-heir with Nero and I'll defy the prophecies. Keep alive a few years longer, Father, for my sake. Then when you die, I'll step into your shoes and rule Rome properly. The Guards love me and trust me. Geta and Crispinus have told me that when you're dead they'll see that I become Emperor, not Nero. I'll be a good Emperor, just as you were until you married my stepmother. Give me proper tutors. My present ones are no use to me. I want to study public-speaking, I want to understand finance and legal procedure, I want to learn how to be an Emperor!"

He was not to be dissuaded by anything that I could say, nor even by my tears. Now I have abandoned all hope of his rescue: no doctor can save a patient's life against his determined will to die. Instead, I have done all that he asks of me, like an indulgent father. I have dismissed Sosibius and the other tutors and appointed new ones. I have promised to let him come of age this New Year and am altering my will in his favour: in my previous will he was hardly mentioned. To-day I have made the Senate my farewell speech and humbly recommended Nero and Britannicus to them, and given these two a long and earnest exhortation to brotherly love and concord, calling the House to witness that I have done so. But with what irony I spoke! I knew as certainly as that fire is hot and ice cold that my Britannicus was doomed, and that it was I who was giving him over to his death, and cutting off, in him, the last true Claudian of the ancient stock of Appius Claudius. Imbecilic I.

My eyes are weary, and my hand shakes so much that I can hardly form the letters. Strange portents have been seen of late. A great comet like that which foretold the death of Julius Cæsar has long been blazing in the midnight sky. From Egypt a phœnix has been reported. It flew there from Arabia as its custom is, followed by a flock of admiring other birds. I can hardly think that it was a true phœnix, for that appears only once every fourteen hundred and sixty-one years, and only two hundred and fifty years have elapsed since it was last genuinely reported from Heliopolis in the reign of the third Ptolemy; but certainly it was some sort of phœnix. And as if a phœnix and comet were not sufficient marvels, a centaur has been born in Thessaly and brought to me at Rome (by way of Egypt where the Alexandrian doctors first examined it), and I have handled it with my own hands. It only lived a single day, and came to me preserved in honey, but it was an unmistakable centaur, and of the sort which has a horse's body, not the inferior sort which has an ass's body. Phœnix, comet and centaur, a swarm of bees among the standards at the Guards Camp, a pig farrowed with claws like a hawk, and my father's monument struck by lightning! Prodigies enough, soothsayers?

Write no more now, Tiberius Claudius, God of the Britons, write no more.

# THREE ACCOUNTS OF CLAUDIUS'S DEATH

## I

And not long after this he wrote his will and signed it with the seals of all the head-magistrates. Whereupon, before that he could proceed any further, prevented he was and cut short by Agrippina, whom they also who were privy to her and of her counsel, yet nevertheless informers, accused besides all this of many crimes. And verily it is agreed upon generally by all, that killed he was by poison, but where it should be, and who gave it, there is some difference. Some write that as he sat at a feast in the Capitol castle with the priests, it was presented unto him by Halotus, the eunuch, his taster; others report that it was at a meal in his own house by Agrippina herself, who had offered unto him a mushroom empoisoned, knowing that he was most greedy of such meats. Of those accidents also which ensued hereupon the report is variable. Some say that straight upon the receipt of the poison he became speechless, and continuing all night in dolorous torments died a little before day. Others affirm that at first he fell asleep, and afterwards, as the meat flowed and floated aloft, vomited all up, and so was followed again with a rank poison. But whether the same were put into a mess of thick gruel (considering he was of necessity to be refreshed with food being emptied in his stomach), or conveyed up by a clyster, as if being overcharged with fullness and surfeit he might be eased also by this kind of egestion and purgation, it is uncertain.

His death was kept secret until all things were set in order about his successor. And therefore both vows were made for him as if he had lain sick still, and also comic actors were brought in place colourably to solace and delight him, as having a longing desire after such sports. He deceased three days before the ides of October, when Asinius Marcellus and Acilius Aviola were consuls, in the sixty-fourth year of his age and the fourteenth of his empire. His funeral was performed with a solemn pomp and procession of the magistrates, and canonized he was a saint in heaven;[1] which honour, forelet and abolished by Nero, he recovered afterwards by Vespasian.

Especial tokens there were presaging and prognosticating his death: to wit, the rising of a hairy star which they call a comet; also the monument of his father Drusus was blasted with lightning; and for that in the same year most of the magistrates of all sorts were dead. But himself seemeth not either to have been ignorant that his end drew near or to have dissembled so much; which may be gathered by some good arguments and demonstrations. For both in the ordination of Consuls he appointed none of them to continue longer than the month wherein he died, and also in the Senate, the very last time that ever he sat there, after a long and earnest exhortation of his children to concord, he humbly recommended the age of them both to the lords of that honourable house; and in his last judicial session upon the tribunal once or twice he pronounced openly that come he was now to the end of his mortality, notwithstanding that they that heard him grieved to hear such an osse, and prayed the gods to avert the same.

Suetonius *Claudius.*
Tr. Philemon Holland (1606).

## II

In the midst of this vast accumulation of anxieties Claudius was attacked with illness, and for the recovery of his health had recourse to the soft air and salubrious waters of Sinuessa. It was then that Agrippina, long since bent upon the impious deed, and eagerly seizing the present occasion, well furnished too as she was with wicked agents, deliberated upon the nature of the poison she would use whether, "if it were sudden and instantaneous

[1] i. e. officially deified.—R. G.

in its operation, the desperate achievement would not be brought to light: if she chose materials slow and consuming in their operation, whether Claudius, when his end approached, and perhaps having discovered the treachery, would not resume his affection for his son." Something of a subtle nature was therefore resolved upon, "such as would disorder his brain and require time to kill." An experienced artist in such preparations was chosen, her name Locusta; lately condemned for poisoning, and long reserved as one of the instruments of ambition. By this woman's skill the poison was prepared: to administer it was assigned to Halotus, one of the eunuchs, whose office it was to serve up the emperor's repasts, and prove the viands by tasting them.

In fact, all the particulars of this transaction were soon afterwards so thoroughly known, that the writers of those times are able to recount, "how the poison was poured into a dish of mushrooms, of which he was particularly fond; but whether it was that his senses were stupefied or from the wine he had drunk, the effect of the poison was not immediately perceived:" at the same time a relaxation of the intestines seemed to have been of service to him; Agrippina therefore became dismayed; but as her life was at stake, she thought little of the odium of her present proceedings, and called in the aid of Xenophon the physician, whom she had already implicated in her guilty purposes. It is believed that he, as if he purposed to assist Claudius in his efforts to vomit, put down his throat a feather besmeared with deadly poison; not unaware that in desperate villainies the attempt without the deed is perilous, while to ensure the reward they must be done effectually at once.

The senate was in the meantime assembled and the consuls and pontiffs were offering vows for the recovery of the emperor, when, already dead, he was covered with clothes, and warm applications, to hide it till matters were arranged for securing the empire to Nero. First there was Agrippina, who feigning to be overpowered with grief, and anxiously seeking for consolation, clasped Britannicus in her arms, called him "the very model of his father," and by various artifices withheld him from leaving the chamber; she likewise detained Antonia and Octavia, his sisters; and had closely guarded all the approaches to the palace; from time to time too she gave out that the prince was on the mend; that the soldiery might entertain hopes till the auspicious moment, predicted by the calculations of the astrologers, should arrive.

At last, on the thirteenth day of October, at noon, the gates of the palace were suddenly thrown open, and Nero, accompanied by Burrhus, went forth to the cohort which, according to the custom of the army, was keeping watch. There, upon a signal made by the præfect, he was received with shouts of joy, and instantly put into a litter. It was reported that there were some who hesitated, looking back anxiously, and frequently asking, where was Britannicus? but as no one came forward to oppose it, they embraced the choice which was offered them. Thus Nero was borne to the camp, where after a speech suitable to the exigency, and the promise of a largess equal to that of the late emperor his father, he was saluted emperor. The voice of the soldiers was followed by the decrees of the senate; nor was there any hesitation in the several provinces. To Claudius were decreed divine honours, and his funeral obsequies were solemnized with the same pomp as those of the deified Augustus; Agrippina emulating the magnificence of her great-grandmother Livia. His will, however, was not rehearsed, lest the preference of the son of his wife to his own son might excite the minds of the people by its injustice and baseness.

Tacitus, *Annals*
(Oxford translation).

# III

Claudius was angered by Agrippina's actions, of which he was now becoming aware, and sought for his son Britannicus, who had purposely been kept out of his sight by her most of the time (for she was doing everything she could to secure the throne for Nero, inasmuch as he was her own son by her former husband Domitius); and he displayed his affection whenever he met the boy. He would not endure her behaviour, but was preparing to put an end to her power, to cause his son to assume the *toga virilis,* and to declare him heir to the throne. Agrippina, learning of this, became alarmed and made haste to forestall anything of the sort by poisoning Claudius. But since, owing to the great quantity of wine he was forever drinking and his general habits of life, such as all emperors as a rule adopt for their protection, he could not easily be harmed, she sent for a famous dealer in poisons, a woman named Locusta, who had recently been convicted on this very charge; and preparing with her aid a poison whose effect was sure, she put it in one of the vegetables called mushrooms. Then she herself ate of the others, but made her husband eat of the one which contained the poison; for it was the the largest and finest of them. And so the victim of the plot was carried from the banquet apparently quite overcome by strong drink, a thing that had happened many times before; but during the night the poison took effect and he passed away, without having been able to say or hear a word. It was the thirteenth of October, and he had lived sixty-three years, two months and thirteen days, having been emperor thirteen years, eight months and twenty days.

Agrippina was able to do this deed owing to the fact that she had previously sent Narcissus off to Campania, feigning that he needed to take the waters there for his gout. For had he been present, she would never have accomplished it, so carefully did he guard his master. As it was, however, his death followed hard upon that of Claudius. He was slain beside the tomb of Messalina, a circumstance due to mere chance, though it seemed to be in fulfilment of her vengeance.

In such a manner did Claudius meet his end. It seemed as if this event had been indicated by the comet, which was seen for a very long time, by the shower of blood, by the thunderbolt that fell upon the standards of the Prætorians, by the opening of its own accord of the temple of Jupitor Victor, by the swarming of bees in the Camp, and by the fact that one incumbent of each political office died. The emperor received the state burial and all the other honours that had been accorded to Augustus. Agrippina and Nero pretended to grieve for the man whom they had killed,

564

and elevated to heaven him whom they had carried out on a litter from the banquet. On this point Lucius Junius Gallio, the brother of Seneca, was the author of a very witty remark. Seneca himself had composed a work that he called "Pumpkinification" —a word formed on the analogy of "deification;" and his brother is credited with saying a great deal in one short sentence. Inasmuch as the public executioners were accustomed to drag the bodies of those executed in the prison to the Forum with large hooks, and from there hauled them to the river, he remarked that Claudius had been raised to heaven with a hook. Nero, too, has left us a remark not unworthy of record. He declared mushrooms to be the food of the gods, since Claudius by means of the mushroom had become a god.

At the death of Claudius the rule in strict justice belonged to Britannicus, who was a legitimate son of Claudius and in physical development was in advance of his years; yet by law the power fell also to Nero because of his adoption. But no claim is stronger than that of arms; for everyone who possesses superior force always appears to have the greater right on his side, whatever he says or does. And thus Nero, having first destroyed the will of Claudius and having succeeded him as master of the whole empire, put Britannicus and his sisters out of the way. Why, then should one lament the misfortunes of the other victims?

Dio Cassius, Book LXI,
as epitomised by Xiphilinus and Zonaras (tr. Cary).

# THE PUMPKINIFICATION OF CLAUDIUS,

## A SATIRE IN PROSE AND VERSE

### By Lucius Annæus Seneca

I MUST here put on record what took place in Heaven on the thirteenth day of October of this very year, the year that has ushered in so glorious a new age. No malice or favour whatsoever. That's right, isn't it? If anyone asks me how I get my information, well, in the first place if I don't want to answer, I won't answer. Who is going to compel me to do so? I am a free man, aren't I? I was freed on the day that a well-known personage died, the man who made the proverb true, "Either be born an Emperor or an idiot." If I do, however, choose to answer, I shall say the first thing that springs to my lips. Are historians ever compelled to produce witnesses in court to swear that they have told the truth? Still, if it were absolutely necessary for me to call on someone, I would call on the man who saw Drusilla's soul on its way to Heaven; he will swear that he saw Claudius taking the same road, "with halting gait" (as the poet says). That man simply cannot help observing everything that goes on in Heaven: he's the custodian of the Appian Way, which of course is the road that both Augustus and Tiberius took on their way to join the Gods. If you ask him privately he will tell you the whole story, but he will say nothing when a lot of people are about. You see, ever since he swore before the Senate that he saw Drusilla going up to Heaven, and nobody believed the news, which was certainly a little too good to be true, he has solemnly engaged

himself never again to bear witness to anything he has seen—
not even if he sees a man murdered in the middle of the Market
Place. But what he told me I now report, and all good luck to
him.

> Great Phœbus had drawn in his daily course,
> And longer stretched the darksome hours of sleep.
> The conquering Moon enlarged had her domain
> And squalid Winter from rich Autumn now
> Usurped the throne. To Bacchus the command
> Was "Grow thou old!" and the late vintager
> Gathered the few last clusters of the grape.

You will probably understand me better if I say plainly that
the month was October and the day the thirteenth. I cannot,
however, be so precise about the hour—one can expect an agreement between philosophers sooner than between clocks—but it
was between twelve noon and one o'clock in the afternoon.
"You're not much of a poet, Seneca," I can hear my readers say.
"Your fellow-bards, not content with describing dawn and sun-
set, work themselves up about the middle of the day too. Why
do you neglect so poetical an hour?" Very well, then:

> Phœbus had parted the wide heavens in twain
> And somewhat wearily 'gan shake the reins,
> Urging his chariot nightwards: down the slope
> Of day the grand effulgence, waning, slid.

It was then that Claudius began to give up the ghost, but
couldn't bring the matter to a conclusion. So Mercury, who had
always derived great pleasure from Claudius's wit, took one of
the three Fates aside and said: "I consider, Madam, that you
are extremely cruel to allow the poor fellow to suffer so. Is he
never to have any relief from torture? It's sixty-four years now
since he first started gasping to keep alive. Have you some
grudge against him and against Rome? Please let the astrologers
be right for once: ever since he became Emperor they have laid
him out for burial regularly once a month. However, they can't
really be blamed for getting the hour of his death wrong, be-

cause nobody was ever quite sure whether he had really been born or not. Get on with the business, Clotho:

"Slay him, and in's stead let a worthier rule."

Clotho replied: "I did so wish to give him just a little longer, just enough time to make Roman citizens of the few outsiders who still remain: he had set his heart, you know, on seeing the whole world dressed in the white gown—Greece, France, Spain, even Britain. Still, if you think that a few foreigners ought to be kept for breeding purposes, and you really order me to put an end to him, it shall be done." She opened her box and produced three spindles; one was for Augurinus, one for Baba, and the third for Claudius. "These are to die in the same year quite close to each other, because I don't want him to go off unattended: it would be very wrong for him to be suddenly left alone, after always having had so many thousands marching before him and trailing behind him, and crowding up against him from either side. He will be grateful for these two friends of his as travelling companions.'

> She spoke, and round the ugly spindle twined
> The thread of that fool's life, then snapped it close.
> But Lachesis, her tresses neatly prinked
> And on her brow Pierian laurel set,
> Plucks from a fleece new threads as white as snow
> Which, as she draws them through her happy hand,
> Change hue. Her sisters at the marvel gaze.
> Not common wool, this, but rich thread of gold,
> That runs on, century by century,
> Termless.  They pluck the fleeces with good will
> Rejoicing in their task, so dear the wool:
> Nay, the thread spins itself, no task for them,
> And as the spindle turns, drops silken down,
> Passing Tithonus' lengthy count of years
> (Aurora's husband) and old Nestor's count.
> Phœbus attends, and from a hopeful breast
> Chants as they work, and plucks upon his lyre

And otherwhiles himself assists the task.
Thus the Three Sisters hardly know they spin:
Too close intent on the sweet strains they hear,
And rapt with praise of their great brother's song,
They spin more than the fated human span.
Yet Phœbus cries: "My Sisters, be it thus:
Cut no years short from this illustrious life,
For he whose life you spin, my counterpart,
Yields not to me either in face or grace
For beauty, nor for sweetness in his song.
He is it, who'll restore the age of gold
And break the ban has silenced all the laws.
He is sweet Lucifer who puts to flight
The lesser stars; or Hesperus is he
Who swims up clear when back the stars return;
Nay, rather he's the Sun himself, what time
The blushing Goddess of the Dawn leads in
The earliest light of day, dispersed the shades—
The Sun himself with shining countenance
Who pores upon the world, and from the gates
Of his dark prison whirls his chariot out.
A very Sun is NERO and all Rome
Shall look on NERO with bedazzled eyes,
His face a-shine with regal majesty
And lovelocks rippling on his shapely neck."

Apollo had spoken. But Lachesis, who had an eye for a handsome man herself, went on spinning and spinning and bestowed a great many years more on NERO as her own personal gift.
As for Claudius, they tell everyone to

> Be of good cheer, and from these halls
> Speed him with not impious lips.

And he really did bubble up the ghost at last, and that was the end even of the old pretence that he was alive. (He passed away while listening to a performance given by some comedians, so

569

now you know that I have good cause to be wary of the profession.) The last words that he was heard to utter in this world followed immediately upon a tremendous noise from the part of his body with which he always talked most readily. They were: "O good Heavens, I believe I've made a mess of myself!" Whether this was actually so or not, I cannot say: but everyone agrees that he always made a mess of things.

It would be waste of time to relate what afterwards happened on earth. You all know very well what happened. Nobody forgets his own good luck, so there's no fear of your ever forgetting the popular outburst of joy that followed the news of Claudius's death. But let me tell you what happened in Heaven; and if you don't believe me, there's my informant to confirm it all. First, a message came to Jove that someone was at the gate, a tallish man with white hair; he seemed to be uttering some threat or other because he kept on shaking his head; and when he walked he dragged his right foot. He had been asked his nationality and had answered in a confused nervous manner, and his language could not be identified. It was not Greek or Latin or any other known speech. Jove told Hercules, who had once travelled over the whole earth and so might be expected to know all nations in it, to go and find out where the stranger came from. Hercules went, and though he had never been daunted by all the monsters in the world, he really got quite a shock at the sight of this new sort of creature with its curious mode of progression and its raucous inarticulate voice, which was like that of no known terrestrial animal but suggested some strange beast of the sea. Hercules thought that his Thirteenth Labour was upon him. However, he looked more closely and decided that it was some kind of a man. He went up to it and said what a Greek naturally would say:

Most honoured stranger, let me now demand
Thy name, thy lineage, thy paternal land.

Claudius was pleased to find himself among literary men. He hoped to find some niche in Heaven for his historical works.

So he replied with another quotation, also from Homer, which conveyed the fact that he was Claudius Cæsar.

> The winds my vessel bore
> From ravaged Troy to the Ciconian shore.

But the next verse was much truer and just as Homeric:

> And boldly disembarking there and then,
> I sacked a city, murdering all its men.

And he would have made Hercules, who is not particularly bright-witted, take this literally, if there had not been someone in attendance on Claudius—the Goddess Fever. She alone of the Gods and Goddesses of Rome had left her temple and come along with him. And what she said was: "The man's lying. I can tell you everything about him, because I have lived with him for very many years now. He was born at Lyons, a fellow-citizen of Marcus's. Yes, a native Celt, born at the sixteenth milestone from Vienne: so of course he conquered Rome, as any good Celt would. I give you my honest word that he was born at Lyons—you know Lyons, surely? It's the place where Licinus[1] was king for so long. Surely you know Lyons, you who have covered more miles in the course of your travels than any country carrier? And you must know, too, that it's a long way from the Lycian Xanthus to the Rhône."

This stung Claudius, and he registered his anger in the loudest roar he could command. Nobody could make out exactly what he was saying, but as a matter of fact he was ordering the Goddess Fever to be removed from his presence and making the customary sign with his trembling hand (always steady enough for that, though for practically nothing else) for her head to be cut off. But for all the attention that was paid to this order you might have thought that the people present were his own freedmen.

Hercules said: "Now listen to me, you, and stop making a fool of yourself. Do you know what sort of place this is? It's

---

[1] An unpopular governor of Augustus's.—R. G.

where mice nibble holes in iron, that's the sort of place it is. So let's have your story straight, or I'll spill some of that nonsense from a hole in the top of your head." To impress his personality on Claudius still more strongly, he struck a melodramatic attitude and began rolling out the following lines:

> Quick, the whole truth! Where were you born and why?
> Tell me at once, or with this club you die,
> That's cracked the skull of many a dusky king.
> (What's that? Speak up! I can't make out a thing.)
> Where did you get that wiggly-waggly head?
> Is there a town where freaks like you are bred?
> But stay, once in the course of my tenth quest
> (I had to travel out to the far West
> And bring back with me to a town of Greece
> The oxen of three-bodied Geryones),
> I noticed a large hill, which when he rises
> The very first thing that the Sun God spies is.
> I mean the place where headlong-tumbling Rhône
> Is met by shallow, wandering Saône,
> Most vague of streams—the town between these two,
> Tell me, was it responsible for you?

His delivery was most bold and animated, but all the same he had little confidence in himself and feared the "fool's blow," as the saying is. However, Claudius, finding himself face to face with a big hero like Hercules, changed his tone, and began to realize that what he said here did not have anything like the same force as at Rome; that a cock, in fact, is worth most on its own dung-hill. So this is what he said, or at least what he was understood to say: "O Hercules, bravest of all the Gods, I had hoped you would stand by me; and when your fellow-Gods called for someone to vouch for me, you were the person I was going to name. And you know me very well really, don't you? Think for a moment. I'm the man who used to sit judging cases in front of your temple, day after day, even in July. and August, the hottest months of the year. You know what a miserable time I had there, listening to the barristers talking on and on, all day and night. If you had fallen among that lot, though you're the strongest of the strong, I'm sure you'd have much preferred to clean out the Augean stables again. I reckon that I drained away far more sewage than you did. But since I want . . ."

[*Some pages are missing here. A group of Gods all talking together are now addressing Hercules: he has forcibly introduced Claudius, whom he has consented to champion, into the Heavenly Senate.*]

". . . You even burgled Hell once and went off with Cerberus on your back; so it's not surprising that you managed to burst your way into this House. No lock could ever keep you out."

"—But just tell us, what sort of a God do you want this fellow to be made? He can't be a God in the Epicurean style: for Diogenes Lærtius says: 'God is blessed and incorruptible and neither takes trouble *nor causes trouble to anyone.*' As for a Stoic God, that sort, according to Varro, is a perfectly rounded whole—in fact completely globular without either a head or sexual organs. He can't be that sort."

"Or can he? If you ask me, there *is* something of the Stoic God about him: he has no head, and no heart either."

"—Well, I swear that even if he had addressed this petition to Saturn instead of Jove he would never have been granted it—though when he was alive he kept Saturn's All Fools' Festival going all the year round, a truly Saturnalian Emperor."

"—And what sort of a chance do you think he has with Jove, whom he as good as condemned for incest? I mean, he killed his son-in-law Silanus just because Silanus had a sister, the most delightful girl in the world, whom everyone called Queen Venus, but he preferred to call Juno."

Claudius said: "Yes, *why* did he do it? I want to know *why.* Really, now, his own sister!"

"—Look it up in the book, stupid! Don't you know that you may sleep with your half-sister at Athens, and that at Alexandria it can be a whole one?"

"Well, at Rome," said Claudius, "mice are just mice. They lick meal. . . ."

"—Is this drawing-master teaching us to improve our curves? Why, he doesn't even know what goes on in his own bedroom."

"—And now he's 'conning the secret realms of sky' and wanting to be a God."

"—A God, eh? I suppose he isn't satisfied with his temple in Britain where the savages worship him and humbly pray 'Almighty Fool, have mercy upon us!' "

It occurred to Jove that senators were not allowed to debate while strangers were present in the House. "My Lords," he said, "I gave you permission to cross-examine this person, but by the noise you are making anyone would mistake this for the cheapest sort of knocking-shop. Please observe the rules of the House. I don't know who this person is, but whatever will he think of us?"

So Claudius was taken out again and Father Janus was called upon to open the debate. He had been made Consul for the afternoon of July 1st next, and was a brilliant fellow, with a pair of eyes in the back of his head. He had a temple in the Market Place, so naturally he made a splendid speech; but it was too fast for the official recorder to take down, so I will not attempt to report it in full, not wishing to distort anything he said. At any rate, his theme was the Majesty of the Gods and that one ought not to cheapen Godhead by random distribution of the honour. "It was a great thing once to be a God," he said, "but now you've brought it down to the level of jumping-beans. I don't want you to think that I am speaking against the deification of any one particular man; I am speaking quite generally, and to make this clear I move that, from now on, Godhead be conferred on none of those who, in Homer's phrase,

> eat the harvest of the field,

nor yet of those whom, again in a phrase of Homer's,

> nourishes the fruitful soil.

After my motion has been voted on and pronounced law, it

574

should be made a criminal offence for any man to be made, displayed or portrayed as a God, and any offender against the law should, I suggest, be handed over to the Hobgoblins and at the next Public Show be flogged with a birch among the new sword-fighters."

The next to be called upon was Diespiter, the Underground God, son of Vica Pota, the God of Victory. He had been chosen for the Consulship and was a professional money-lender: he also used to sell citizenships in a quiet way. Hercules went up to him with a friendly smirk and whispered something in his ear, so he came out with the following speech: "The God Claudius is related to the God Augustus. The Goddess Augusta, whom he deified himself, is his grandmother; so, as he is by far the most learned man who has ever lived, and since as a matter of public policy someone ought to join the God Romulus in

> eating boiled turnips with a will,

I propose that the God Claudius be regularly enrolled among the Olympians and enjoy the privileges and perquisites of God-head in its fullest traditional sense, and that a note to that effect be inserted in Ovid's *Metamorphoses*."

The House was divided, and it looked as though Claudius would carry a majority of votes; because Hercules saw that he had a good chance now and went rushing about from one bench to another saying: "Now please don't oppose me. I am personally interested in this measure. If you vote my way now, I'll do as much for you some other day. You know the proverb, '*Hand washes hand*.'"

Then the God Augustus arose, for it was now his turn, and spoke with the greatest eloquence. "I call on you, my Lords, to witness that ever since the day of my official deification I have not uttered a single word. I always mind my own business. But now I cannot keep up the pretence of impartiality any longer, or conceal the sorrow which shame makes deeper still. Was it for this that I made peace over land and sea, and put a truce to Civil War, and endowed Rome with a new constitution, and embellished her with stately public buildings, that . . . that . . ,

575

that . . . Words fail me, my Lords. Nothing that I might utter could possibly match the depth of my feelings in this matter. In my indignation I must borrow a phrase from the eloquent Messala Corvinus: he was elected City Warden and resigned after a few days, saying, 'I am ashamed of my authority'. I feel the same: when I see how the authority that I established has been abused I am ashamed of ever having exercised it. This fellow, my Lords, who looks as though he hadn't guts enough to worry a fly, sat in my place and called himself by my name and ordered men off to execution just as easily as a dog squats. But I won't speak of all his victims, fine men though they were: I am so preoccupied with family disasters that really I have no time to waste over public ones. I'll only speak about family disasters, then, because 'a radish[1] may know no Greek, but I do': I at least know one Greek proverb, 'The knee is nearer than the shin.' This impostor, this pseudo-Augustus, has done me the kindness of killing two great-granddaughters of mine, Lesbia with the sword and Helen by starvation. And one great-grandson, Lucius Silanus. (Here I expect you, my Lord Jove, to be fair in a bad cause, which after all is your own.) Now answer me, you God Claudius, why did you condemn so many men and women to death without first calling on them to defend themselves? What sort of justice is that? Is it the sort that is done in Heaven? Why, here's Jove has been Emperor all these centuries and never did more than once break Vulcan's leg:

> Whom seizing by the foot, his anger high,
> He flung over the threshold of the sky,

and once lose his temper with his wife and string her up. Did he ever actually kill a single member of his family? But you, you killed Messalina, your wife, whose grand-uncle I was as much as yours. ('Did I really?' you ask. A thousand plagues on you,

---

[1] The manuscript reading is *sormea*, which is meaningless; and editors suggest *soror mea*. But Augustus, whose style is here reproduced, could certainly not have been credited with the expression, "*My sister* may know no Greek, but I do." His only sister was the learned Octavia. I suggest the better and simpler reading of *surmea*, which is the Egyptian radish, used by the Romans as an emetic. —R. G.

of course you did! That makes it all the more disgraceful: you go about killing people and don't even know it.) Yes, my Lords, and he went on persecuting my great-grandson Gaius Caligula even when he was dead. It's true that Caligula killed his father-in-law, but Claudius, not content with following his example in that, killed a son-in-law too. And whereas Caligula would not allow young Pompey, Crassus Frugi's son, to take the title 'The Great', Claudius gave him his name back, but took off his head. In that one noble family he killed Crassus Frugi, young Pompey, Scribonia, the Tristionias, and Assario: Crassus, I own, was such a fool that he might almost have been made Emperor instead of Claudius. Do you really want this creature made a real God? Look at his body, born under the wrath of Heaven; and when it comes to that, listen to his talk! Why, if he can say as many as three words on end without stuttering over them, he can have me for a slave! Who is going to worship a God of this sort? Will anyone believe in him? If you turn people like him into Gods, you can't expect anyone to believe in *you*. In brief, my Lords, if I have earned your respect, if I have never given any mortal too definite an answer to his prayer, I count on you to avenge my wrongs. So my motion is"—he read it out from his notes—"that insomuch as a certain God Claudius has killed his father-in-law Appius Silanus; his two sons-in-law, Pompey the Great and Lucius Silanus; his daughter's father-in-law Crassus Frugi (a man who resembled him as closely as one egg resembles another); Scribonia, his daughter's mother-in-law; his wife Messalina; with others too numerous to mention—I hereby move that he should be prosecuted with the utmost rigour of the law, that he should be refused bail, that he should be sentenced to immediate banishment, being allowed no more than thirty days to leave Heaven, and thirty hours to leave Olympus."

A division was hurriedly taken and the motion carried. As soon as the result was known Mercury seized Claudius by the throat and dragged him off to Hell,

Whence none, 'tis said, returns to tell the tale.

As they came down along the Sacred Way, Mercury asked what all those crowds of people meant? Surely it wasn't Claudius's funeral? It was certainly a most marvellous procession and no expense had been spared to show that it was a God who was being buried. Flute music, blaring of horns, a great brass band made up of all sorts of instruments, such a terrific noise, in fact, that even Claudius was able to hear it. Every face was wreathed in smiles: the whole Roman populace was walking about like free men again. Only Agatho and a few amateur barristers were in tears, and for once really meant it. The professional lawyers were slowly crawling out of dark corners, pale and gaunt, hardly alive, but reviving with every breath they drew. One of them, when he saw Agatho's group condoling with one another, came up to them and said, "I told you so. This All Fools' Festival had to come to an end some day or other."

When Claudius saw his funeral go by, he understood at last that he was dead. A great choir was chanting his dirge in antiphonal chorus:

Weep, O Roman, beat thy breast,
　　Mournful be thy Market Place.
We bear a wise man to his rest,
　　The bravest, too, of all thy race.

With swift foot he could outrun
　　Any courser in the land:
He could the rebel Parthian stun,
　　No Persian might his darts withstand.

With steady grasp he bent his bow:
　　Away they streamed in headlong packs.
Slight was the wound, yet the Medes show
　　In rout their ornamental backs.

He sailed across an unknown sea
　　And into Britain's island strode:
He battered down the shields, did he,
　　Of the Brigantians, blue with woad.

He chained them with a Roman chain,
    Then with the Roman rods and axe
He disciplined the Ocean main
    And took its terror for a tax.

Mourn for the judge who could provide
    Quick sentences to marvel at:
Who only listened to one side,
    Who could dispense with even that.

Where shall another such be found,
    To sit and judge the whole year through?
Minos the Cretan, underground,
    Must now resign his bench to you.

You barristers, who have your price,
    Weep, and all small poets weep,
And weep, you rattlers of the dice
    Whom cogging does in plenty keep.

Claudius was charmed by this panegyric and wanted to stay to see the show through to the end. But Mercury, the trusted messenger of the Gods, pulled him away, first muffling his head so that nobody should recognize him, and took him across Mars Field and finally down to Hell between the Tiber and the Subway. His freedman Narcissus had gone down ahead by a short cut, ready to receive him on his arrival, and now came smiling forward, fresh from a bath and exclaiming: "Gods! Gods come to visit us mortals! What may I have the honour . . .?"

"Go and tell them that we're here. And hurry up about it."

At this order of Mercury's Narcissus darted off. The road to Hell's gate is all downhill and, as Virgil remarks somewhere, very easy going; so though Narcissus was suffering from gout it only took him a moment to arrive. Before the gate lay Cerberus or, as I think Horace calls him, "the five-score-pated beast." Narcissus was no hero: he was used to a little white lapdog bitch, and when he saw this enormous shaggy black cur, not at all the sort of animal you would like to meet in a dark place like Hell, he was thoroughly scared. He gave his message, "Claudius is here," in a loud yell.

For answer there came a burst of cheering and out marched a troop of ghosts. They were chanting the well-known song:

> He's found, he's found!
> Let joy resound!
> O clap your hands,
> The lost is found!

The choir included Gaius Silius, Consul-Elect, Juncus the exmagistrate, Sextus Traulus, Marcus Helvius, Trogus, Cotta, Vettius Valens, Fabius—Roman knights whom Narcissus had ordered for execution. Mnester the comedian was there, whose appearance Claudius had improved by the removal of his head. Hell was buzzing now with the news of Claudius's arrival and everyone ran for Messalina. His freedmen, Polybius, Myron, Harpocras, Amphæus and Pheronactus were the first. Claudius had sent them all on ahead here, not wanting to be unescorted anywhere. Then came two Guards Commanders, Catonius Justus and Rufrius Pollio. Then his friends Saturninus Lusius, Pedo Pompey and the two Asinius brothers, Lupus and Celer. Finally came Lesbia, his brother's daughter, and Helen, his sister's daughter, and sons-in-law and fathers-in-law and mothers-in-law —the entire family in fact. They formed up and marched off in a body to meet Claudius. Claudius stared at them and exclaimed in surprise, "Why, what a lot of friends! How in the world did *you* all get here?" Pedo answered: "How did we get here indeed, you bloodthirsty villain! How dare you ask us that? Who sent us here but you yourself, the man who kills all his friends? We're going to prosecute you now, so come along. I'll show you the way to the Criminal Courts."

Pedo brought him into Æacus's court; Æacus was the judge who tried murder cases under the Cornelian Law. Pedo requested him to take the prisoner's name and then filled in the charge-sheet:

Senators murdered: 35.

Knights, Roman, murdered: 221.

Other persons: impossible to keep accurate records.

Claudius applied for counsel, but nobody volunteered to act for him. At last out stepped Publius Petronius, an old drinking friend who could talk the Claudian language quite well, and claimed a remand. Æacus refused to grant it, so Pedo Pompey began his speech for the prosecution, shouting at the top of his voice. Counsel for the defence attempted to reply, but Æacus, who is a most conscientious judge, ruled him out of order, and summed up on the case as presented by the prosecution. Then he pronounced:

> As the rascal did, he must
> Himself be done by. And that's just.

An extraordinary silence followed. Everyone was amazed at the decision, which was considered to be entirely without precedent. Claudius himself, of course, could have quoted precedents, but thought it monstrously unjust nevertheless. Then there was a long argument about the sort of punishment he ought to be awarded. Some said that Sisyphus had been rolling his stone up that hill quite long enough now, and some said that Tantalus ought to be relieved before he died of thirst, and some again said that it was time for a drag to be put on the wheel on which Ixion was perpetually being broken. But Æacus decided not to let off any of these old hands for fear Claudius might count on getting a similar respite himself some day. Instead, some new sort of punishment had to be instituted: they must think up some utterly senseless task conveying the general idea of a greedy ambition perpetually disappointed. Æacus finally delivered the sentence, which was that Claudius should rattle dice for ever in a dice-cup with no bottom to it.

So the prisoner began working out his sentence at once, fumbling for the dice as they fell and never getting any further with the game.

> Ay, for so often as he shook that cup
> And ready sat to cast them on the board,

The dice would vanish through the hole beneath.
Then would he gather them again, and seek
To rattle them and cast them as before.
But still they cheated him, and cheated him,
Retiring through the bottom of the cup.
And when once more he stooped to pick them up
They slipped between his fingers and escaped,
And endlessly continued to escape—
As when his rock with labour infinite
Sisyphus rolls unto Hell's mountain-peak
But down it comes, rebounding on his neck.

Suddenly who should come in but Gaius Caligula. "Why, that's a slave of mine," said Caligula. "I claim him!" He produced witnesses who testified that they had often seen him flogging Claudius with whips and birch-rods, and knocking him about with his fists. So the claim was allowed, and Claudius was handed over to his master. However, Caligula made a present of him to Æacus, and Æacus handed him over to his freedman Menander, who set him the task of keeping the court-records.

[Trans. by R. G.]

## SEQUEL

*Seneca was forced to commit suicide in A.D. 65 at Nero's orders. He survived most of the other characters in this story. Britannicus was poisoned in A.D. 55. Pallas, Burrhus, Domitia, the surviving Silanuses, Octavia, Antonia, Faustus Sulla—all met violent deaths. Agrippinilla lost her hold on Nero after the first two years of his reign, but regained it for a while by allowing him to commit incest with her. He then tried to murder her by sending her to sea in a collapsible ship which broke in two at a considerable distance from the coast. She swam safely ashore. Finally he sent soldiers to kill her. She died courageously, ordering them to stab her in the belly which had once housed so monstrous a son. When in A.D. 68 Nero was declared a public enemy by the Senate and killed by a servant at his own request, no member of the Imperial family was left to succeed him. In A.D. 69, a year of anarchy and civil war, there were four successive Emperors; namely, Galba, Otho, Aulus Vitellius and Vespasian. Vespasian ruled benevolently and founded the Flavian dynasty. The Republic was never restored.*

**HEROD THE GREAT**, son of Antipater, Governor of Judæa, and an Arabian Princess (mentioned in St. Matthew ii.)

married
1. Doris
2. MARIAMNE I, granddaughter of King Hyrcanus
3. ⎫
4. ⎬ Two nieces, names unknown
5. Mariamne II, daughter of Simon, the High Priest
6. Malthace, a Samaritan
7. Cleopatra of Jerusalem
8. Pallas
9. Phædra, mother of one Roxana
10. Elpis, mother of one Salome

and had children

| by Doris | by MARIAMNE I | by Mariamne II |
|---|---|---|
| | | HEROD PHILIP married his niece HERODIAS who divorced him (mentioned in St. Mark vi.) |
| Antipater, put to death by his father B.C. 4 | | |

**ARISTOBULUS** married BERENICE, his first cousin. He was put to death by his father B.C. 6

**ALEXANDER**, put to death by his father B.C. 6

Salampsio married her cousin PHASÆL

**HEROD AGRIPPA** married his cousin CYPROS, died A.D. 44 (mentioned in Acts xii. and xxiii.)

**HERODIAS** married her uncle HEROD PHILIP then her uncle HEROD ANTIPAS (mentioned in St. Matthew xiv.)

**SALOME**, married her uncle PHILIP the Tetrarch then Aristobulus her first cousin (mentioned in St. Mark vi.)

**HEROD AGRIPPA** the Younger, King of Chalcis (mentioned in Acts xxv. and xxvi.)

**BERENICE** married Marcus, son of ALEXANDER THE ALABARCH (mentioned in Acts iv.), then her uncle HEROD POLLIO, then POLEMON, KING OF PONTUS and CILICIA, then lived in incest with her brother HEROD AGRIPPA for twenty-five years, finally had an intimacy with the Emperor Titus, who wished to marry her for her beauty (she was then 45 years old) but could not do so because of her reputation at Rome (mentioned in Acts xxv.)

# The Royal Family of the Herods

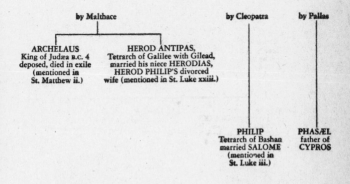

| by Malthace | | by Cleopatra | by Pallas |

**ARCHELAUS**
King of Judæa B.C. 4
deposed, died in exile
(mentioned in
St. Matthew ii.)

**HEROD ANTIPAS,**
Tetrarch of Galilee with Gilead,
married his niece HERODIAS,
HEROD PHILIP'S divorced
wife (mentioned in St. Luke xxiii.)

**PHILIP**
Tetrarch of Bashan
married SALOME
(mentioned in
St. Luke iii.)

**PHASÆL**
father of
CYPROS

**ARISTOBULUS**
married Jotape, a daughter of
SAMPSIGERAMUS, King of
Osroëne

**HEROD POLLIO**
King of Chalcis, died A.D. 48, married his niece BERENICE. He had a
son Aristobulus by a former wife

**MARIAMNE**
married Archelaus, son of Helchias,
Master of Horse, then Demetrius
the Alexandrian Alabarch

**DRUSILLA**
married the King of
Homs, then FELIX,
Governor of Judæa
(mentioned in Acts xxiv.)

**DRUSUS**
died young

ROBERT GRAVES was born in London in 1895. He left school when World War I broke out, and served as a captain with the Royal Welsh Fusiliers in France. First recognized as a "war poet," he won international acclaim in 1929 with the publication of *Goodbye to All That*, an autobiography vividly appraising the effect of the war years on his generation. After the war, Mr. Graves was granted a Classical scholarship at Oxford, and subsequently went to Egypt as the first Professor of English at the newly formed University of Cairo.

Although he is primarily a poet, Robert Graves in over forty years of writing has also made distinguished contributions as a novelist, critic, translator, essayist, scholar, historian, lecturer, and librettist. Among his novels are *I, Claudius,* the companion volume to *Claudius the God,* and *Sergeant Lamb's America* (both are available in Vintage Books).

Since 1932 he has lived with his wife and family in Deya, Majorca, except in time of war.